8·99

ERCHIE
&
JIMMY SWAN

The Collected Erchie and Jimmy Swan Stories

At one time the Glasgow stories of Neil Munro, featuring Erchie MacPherson and Jimmy Swan, were as well known as the same author's tales of the inimitable Para Handy. In their own way, too, the characters were and are as endearing as their puffer skipper counterpart. These stories, written in the first quarter of this century, move from the bustle and gaiety of the Edwardian era, through the Great War, to the ending of the boom years of the roaring twenties.

Erchie, the genial old kirk beadle and part-time Glasgow waiter, is the perfect observer of the changing scene – no whim of fashion nor technological innovation escapes his humorous eye and pawky wit – from Mary Pickford's divorce to tramway traffic jams. There is tremendous affection, too, in the picture of Erchie; with "a flet fit but a warm hert".

In creating Jimmy Swan the kindly, slightly enigmatic commercial traveller, Munro sensed a rich source of story and sentiment in the travelling salesman – a kind of twentieth century knight-errant figure. Before other better-known writers, he realised the literary possibilities of the salesman and gave us Jimmy, this wrily humorous figure "on the road" who travels in haberdashery and more than a touch of poetry.

This edition includes all the stories collected by Munro in his lifetime, together with an astonishing fifty-nine further stories unearthed by the editors from the files of the *Glasgow Evening News*. Notes and references to a wide range of contemporary events and personalities are provided for each story.

ERCHIE
&
JIMMY SWAN

NEIL MUNRO
(HUGH FOULIS)

With fifty-nine previously uncollected stories

Introduced and Annotated
by

BRIAN D. OSBORNE
&
RONALD ARMSTRONG

Birlinn

Birlinn Ltd
13 Roseneath Street, Edinburgh

Typeset in Monotype Plantin by
Koinonia Ltd, Manchester
and printed and bound in Finland by
Werner Söderström OY

A CIP record for this book is available
from The British Library

ISBN 1 874744 05 X

Contents

JIMMY SWAN, THE JOY TRAVELLER

viii

Introduction

The ordinary, the workaday and the distinctly unfashion-
able side of life in Glasgow and the West of Scotland in the
first quarter of the twentieth century may seem, at first
sight, to be an unpromising field in which to find enduring
humorous writing. Life in the city slums has been variously
portrayed in works aimed at stirring the social conscience
and provoking sensation; the activities of the city's mercantile elite, artists and politicians have not gone unre-
corded. Poverty and wealth, bare feet and art noveau, Red
Clydeside and the romanticised camaraderie of the tenements have all had their share of literary attention and
contributed to the library of Glaswegiana.

What distinguishes Neil Munro's three enduring comic
creations of Para Handy, Erchie & Jimmy Swan from
much of the literature of the city is that he sets them in an
entirely credible Glasgow, a Glasgow of "skoosh-cars" and
art tea-rooms, of the Fair Holidays and smoking concerts.
The stories are peopled with figures representative of the
great majority of the city's population; characters who
were as distant from the poverty and violence which was to
be graphically described in "No Mean City" as they were
removed from the artistic coteries of "The Glasgow Boys"
or the wealthy merchants and industrialists of the exclusive
suburbs and coastal mansions. Erchie MacPherson, who
makes ends meet from his two jobs as a waiter and Kirk

Beadle, is undoubtedly a member of the city's working classes while his somewhat more up-market contemporary Jimmy Swan, with his top-hat and pound a day expenses has equally clearly moved into the ranks of the lower middle classes. Jimmy, when on the road with a rose in his buttonhole, speaks in something approaching standard English, though with a strong Scots accent and with the habit of breaking into his native tongue under the stress of emotion. Erchie's speech is at all times broader and has the various characteristics of the richness of Glasgow imprinted in it.

The speech of Glasgow, like the vitality of the city itself, owed much to the influx of migrants. Successive waves of immigrants had come in over the centuries to satisfy the booming city's demand for labour; Highlanders cleared from their glens and islands; Irish escaping from famine and poverty; rural and small-town Scots seeking a better life. To this mixture were added Jewish refugees from the pogroms and poverty of Russia and Eastern Europe; Italians who came to dominate the catering trades. Glasgow drew in to herself all these disparate groups and was enriched both materially, spiritually and linguistically by their presence.

Glasgow itself is at the centre of the two series of stories reprinted in this collection. Both men live in the city and although Jimmy's work as a commercial traveller takes him out on the road through the small towns of Scotland it is for a great Glasgow firm that he works and to their city head office that he returns with the country customers' orders for the latest Autumn lines and fine Shantung fabrics. Erchie, though more geographically confined, has by virtue of his twin roles as waiter and beadle the opportunity to mix with and reflect on a wide cross-section of Glasgow life.

Glasgow, in the period of these stories, could still claim to be the Second City of the Empire. The scores of shipyards on its river were unrivalled for scale, output and for technological innovation. As the first Jimmy Swan stories were appearing great ocean liners such as the majestic

Aquitania were under construction on the Clyde. The locomotives manufactured in the railway suburb of Springburn powered railways from South America to India. Glasgow based shipping lines carried a high proportion of the world's goods on the oceans and rivers of the world. The Scottish engineer, trained in the Clyde's shipyards, was a familiar reality from the Irrawaddy to the Rio Plate and had become a literary convention which has lasted from Kipling's MacAndrew to Star Trek's Scottie.

The confidence, self-esteem and self-image of the city was at a peak. The energy and vision of its citizens and City Council were exemplified in a host of civic projects. The municipal activism of the City ranged from the grandeur of the City Chambers, opened by Queen Victoria in 1888, through tramways, slum clearance & municipal washhouses, to the modern practicalities of the Underground Railway inaugurated in 1896.

There were few more obvious manifestations of this civic pride, municipal enterprise and commitment to the arts and sciences than in the series of three Exhibitions held in the city between 1888 and 1911. The immense impact of these Exhibitions on the citizens of Glasgow runs like a thread through the sequence of Erchie and Jimmy Swan stories. Neil Munro as an experienced journalist was far too skilled a craftsman to overlook the potential of these exuberant occasions as a peg on which to hang a story. Just as wars, strikes, international football matches, Royal visits, the decline of the top-hat and Miss Cranston's tea-rooms all, however improbably, provide settings and subjects for his two heroes, the attraction of the Exhibitions provide rich material. Indeed there is something very fitting in the fact that one of the very last Jimmy Swan stories, published in 1924, is a cry from the heart for another Exhibition and a nostalgic look back at the glorious days of 1888, 1901 and 1911. One of the other stories appearing in book form for the first time in this edition was written in 1911 about a country customer's visit to The Scottish Exhibition of National History, Art and Industry. This piece was not selected by Munro for his 1917 edition of the Jimmy Swan stories, doubtless for the very good reason that the passage of six years is more than enough to make a subject seem dated but not long enough to provoke nostalgia. However it is one of the best of all the Jimmy Swan stories, both for the sense it gives of the flavour of Glasgow at Exhibition time in 1911 and for a classic description of the results of the country customer's unfortunate overindulgence in exotic varieties of strong drink not generally available in his native Galloway.

There are indeed few social and political developments in the period of the stories that do not find some reflection in the thoughts and actions of the waiter and the salesman. These topical references would of course have been apparent to the delighted reader of the *Glasgow Evening News*, a reader who for almost quarter of a century had the pleasure Monday by Monday of finding a new piece of writing by Neil Munro. Such allusions are obviously much less apparent as the stories have been traditionally presented in book form, and in any case with the elapse of time many of them have become obscure. This loss of period context is indeed a main justification for the publication of this annotated edition. In it we hope not only to explain some of the obscurities in the text but to restore the stories to their proper context in time and place, and in so doing enhance the reader's enjoyment.

One might be forgiven for thinking that this topicality on which we set such emphasis, the wealth of local references and concentration on the issues of the day, would have combined to ensure only the most ephemeral of lives for these tales. Nothing could be further from the truth. That Erchie can still entertain readers almost ninety years after the collected edition of stories appeared in 1904 is a remarkable fact. It is also surely a striking tribute to the skill of their author. Although only one collection of the tales of "Erchie, My Droll Friend" appeared, despite Munro later producing enough Erchie stories to fill another volume of the same size, this is no reflection on the quality of the later stories but may owe more to Munro's ambivalent approach to his three comic series. Munro's output of the Jimmy Swan stories was smaller. The 1917 edition included all but seven of his total output of the adventures of the "Joy Traveller", three stories being deliberately excluded. We present them together with four others which were written in a late flurry of interest in the character between 1923 and 1926. Again, as readers will be able to judge, the quality of the unknown stories is excellent.

Munro was a historical novelist of considerable gifts. He was however most anxious to distance his serious work from mere journalism, a trade for which he professed little regard, dismissing it contemptuously as "the jawbox". Munro used the pseudonym of Hugh Foulis for these comic writings and produced the Para, Erchie and Jimmy stories as part of his regular journalistic commitment for the *Glasgow Evening News*. Most of the stories were in fact written when he was no longer working full-time on the paper. He had left the pressures of daily journalism in order to be able to concentrate on his more serious and "literary" writing but maintained his connection with the *News* through the "The Looker-On" column. This appeared almost every Monday and its range reflected Munro's varied interests and concerns while its style and wit betrayed the artist behind the bye-line. Into this wide-ranging column of reportage, comment and criticism Munro inserted at irregular intervals these three comic creations: timeless yet topical; unmistakably Scottish, yet surely representative of universal types. Remarkable pieces, written under the pressures of a deadline for that most transient of platforms, the daily newspaper, but surviving in print and public affection for ninety years.

Why, of all the wealth of humorous writing which appeared in the first quarter of this century, has Munro's trio of Scots comic characters survived? Why, when so many other humorous writers have vanished into obscurity has Munro lasted? Of broadly contemporary humorous writers whose work still has an appeal one can name W.S. Gilbert, Jerome K. Jerome and P.G. Wodehouse. To add Munro's name to this distinguished list is of course to make a very large claim, but the continuing popularity of his creations surely justifies such a claim and such a place. Perhaps it is the very unpretentiousness of Munro's writing, the product of the journalist rather than the self-conscious artist, the craftsman rather than the aesthete, which has ensured that his humorous creations have so successfully survived. Certainly Munro's more elaborate, possibly somewhat mannered, literary style, as exemplified in his excellent historical novels such as *John Splendid* and *The New Road* has not been able to ensure the novels survival in print; an irony which would not have been lost on Munro, however much it might have displeased him.

Munro knew his Glasgow, and his Scotland. He had watched George Geddes dragging bodies from the Clyde and strolled among the bustling warehouses and cranes of the city's docks. He had listened to the talk of the streets, mixed in clubs and coffee-shops with Glasgow's artists and writers and exchanged gossip with prototypes of Erchie, Para and Jimmy. In his 'prentice days as a journalist in Greenock, Falkirk and Glasgow he would have written up Council meetings and Church soirees, flower shows, charity concerts, and Highland Games.

Neil Munro indeed knew his Glasgow, but in the revealing phrase of his bye-line, as a "Looker-On". He was a Highlander in exile in the city, a man happier and more at ease in his native Inveraray but obliged, like so many of his compatriots, to earn his living in the Lowlands. He was at once Neil Munro and Hugh Foulis, the poetic novelist and the journalist, the semi-detached observer watching the world around him with a tolerant though perceptive eye. His young friend and junior colleague on the *News*, the novelist George Blake, hints at this ambivalence and at the two conflicting natures of the man. Blake wrote in the introduction to his posthumous collection of Munro's journalism *The Brave Days*

"Again the paradox confronts us. The fact is that the Neil Munro of real life was the jolliest of men, friendly, simple, infinitely whimsical. Perhaps it was not Neil Munro we knew; perhaps we were allowed intercourse only with Hugh Foulis."

Blake's thought-provoking suggestion of a public and a private face to Munro has interesting echoes in Munro's life. So far as the public face was concerned he was born the son of crofters near Inveraray on 3rd June 1864. In reality he was, as the birth record in General Register House, Edinburgh, shows, the illegitimate son of Ann Munro, an Inveraray kitchen-maid and was born precisely one year earlier than the normally quoted date. In one of the more curious examples of Munro-related ambivalence his tombstone, in Kilmalieu cemetery near Inveraray, bears the false, 1864, date; while the Munro monument in Glen Aray, erected some years after his death and unveiled with great public ceremony, carries the correct birth date of 1863. Despite this very obvious evidence reference books and indeed every book dealing with Munro, until the present editors' edition of the Para Handy stories, continued, and continues to cite the 1864 date.

The absence of an acknowledged father seems not to have held Munro back and indeed local rumour attributed his paternity to the Ducal household of Argyll. On completing his education at Inveraray he was found a place in the office of a leading Inveraray lawyer. This uncongenial position he abandoned, as he wrote himself, "as soon as I arrived at years of discretion and revolt". In 1881 he came south to follow a journalistic and literary career.

Both his journalistic and literary careers were to flourish. In the newspaper world he filled many roles, becoming the *Glasgow Evening News'* assistant editor, art critic, and literary editor. During the First World War he acted for a time as a special correspondent for the *News* on the Western Front and later returned to serve as Editor. Of his role as literary editor the rival *Glasgow Herald* was to write in its obituary:

"No man exercised a more subtle literary influence
on the West of Scotland than Neil Munro. His discriminating praise was sufficient to set aglow the
heart of the young writer..."

This "discriminating praise" had extra value coming
from a novelist who was to be hailed as the obvious successor to Scott and Stevenson; a writer particularly praised for
his handling of Highland subjects:

"... in the matter of Celtic story and character he
excelled Sir Walter because of his more deeply intimate knowledge of that elusive mystery."

Munro's knowledge and love of the Highlands found
expression in his novels and in what is now undoubtedly
his best known work, the Para Handy stories. Only a very
shallow reading of Para Handy would present him as a
stock Highland figure of fun for us to laugh at and ignore
the real affection with which Munro depicts Para. Similarly one cannot doubt the warmth with which Munro
portrays the Glaswegians Erchie and Jimmy. These are
characters to be laughed along with and indeed watched to
be sure that they do not get the last laugh.

For all his literary preoccupation with the Highlands, his
life, from the age of 17 to his death in 1930, was lived out in
and around Glasgow and the Clyde. The links remained
strong however. His last home, at Helensburgh, looking
out across the Clyde to the Argyllshire hills, was named
"Cromalt" after a stream in his native town of Inveraray.

The stories in this collection, though less familiar than
Para Handy, are in many ways the equal of the tales of the
puffer skipper. Surely no one who has read of Erchie, and
his friend the coal-man Duffy, paying a visit to Miss
Craston's Willow Tea-rooms, can forget the scene or the
description of Charles Rennie Mackintosh's decor in the
Room de Luxe (or in Erchie's version the "Room de Looks"):

"... a' roond the place there's a lump o' lookin'-gless
wi' purple leeks pented on it every noo and then."

Similarly the quiet wit, charm and philosophy of Jimmy
Swan, who combines his duties for Campell & McDonald

with acting as a universal provider for the provincial towns of Scotland, because:

"... you can get any mortal thing you like in Glasgow if you have the business experience, and the ready money"

cannot fail to entertain as it recaptures a vanished world of the Caledonian Railway, waggonettes, and Commercial Rooms.

Jimmy Swan first appeared in the columns of the *Glasgow Evening News* in May 1911. However we have an interesting example of the interconnections between Munro's various types of writing in that a piece, "Knights of the Road" which he wrote in February 1910 for his "Looker-On" column featured one John Swan, a draper's traveller, who was clearly to become the inspiration for the comic creation of Jimmy Swan.

"Swan, if you please was Arthur's (or was it Stewart & MacDonald's?); when a draper shook hands with Swan the draper thrilled with pride, for he felt himself in touch with vast affairs, imperial dominions of the soft goods trade, of which the worthy Swan was worthy viceroy."

Many of the themes we will read about in the Jimmy Swan series, the camaraderie of the Commercial Room, the role of the traveller as the carrier of news and jokes from the city to the country towns, the sample cases blocking the pavement, the style and deportment of the traveller on a generous expense allowance, are to be found in embryo in "Knights of the Road". The message of the essay was in fact that the age of "the august and splendid Swan" had gone, to be replaced by a generation of salesmen for "a thousand little mushroom firms" who Munro describes as:

"inexperienced in life, ill-paid, hurried, cadging cheap wares for cheap concerns, with no traditions behind them and no prestige to lend them dignity ..."

It is entirely typical of Munro that he should choose to write a series of stories about a vanished or vanishing world. Just as his novels told of a vanished order in the

Highlands so did his stories of Jimmy and Erchie tell of a
vanishing world in the everyday of lowland Scotland, and
their appeal to contemporaries doubtless owed much to
this nostalgic evocation.

However ambivalently Neil Munro may have felt about
his creations he wrote well over two hundred stories of the
adventures of Jimmy, Erchie and Para over a quarter of a
century. They may have been to him part of the journalistic treadmill, and an unwelcome diversion from his more
serious work but Munro's standards were always of the
highest and he maintained a consistent level of quality.
However hard he tried to distinguish between Hugh Foulis
and Neil Munro, he could not conceal the fact that the two
writers shared a talent, and one of no common order.
Indeed we may assume that he would not have produced
such a quantity of work in this genre unless he had found a
particular satisfaction in pleasing his audiences with the
latest "baur" from the life and travels of Jimmy, or Erchie's
newest reflection on the changing city scene or on the
curious activities of female artists of the Glasgow school:

> "The lady Art penters divna pent windows and
> rhones and hooses; they bash brass, and hack wud,
> and draw pictures."
> "And can they mak' a livin' at that?"
> "Whiles. And whiles their paw helps."

We are privileged to be able to help re-introduce to the
late-twentieth century audiences these two series of stories
which have given pleasure to generations since their first
appearance in the early years of the century. We are particularly glad to be able in this edition to present fifty-nine
stories which have never previously appeared in book
form. This rich harvest from the *Glasgow Evening News*
may give even the most expert student of "Erchie, My
Droll Friend" and "Jimmy Swan, The Joy Traveller" the
unexpected delight of a new story and, indeed, something
of the sense of anticipation that readers of the *News* must
have had when, on so many Mondays, they could turn to
page two and to the delights of that week's "Looker-On".

Erchie, My Droll Friend

1. *Introductory to an Odd Character*

On Sundays he is the beadle[1] of our church; at other times he Waits. In his ecclesiastical character there is a solemn dignity about his deportment that compels most of us to call him Mr MacPherson; in his secular hours, when passing the fruit at a city banquet, or when at the close of the repast he sweeps away the fragments of the dinner-rolls, and whisperingly expresses in your left ear a fervent hope that "ye've enjoyed your dinner," he is simply Erchie.

Once I forgot, deluded a moment into a Sunday train of thought by his reverent way of laying down a bottle of Pommery, and called him Mr MacPherson. He reproved me with a glance of his eye.

"There's nae Mr MacPhersons here," he said afterwards; "at whit ye might call the social board I'm jist Erchie, or whiles Easy-gaun Erchie wi' them that kens me langest. There's sae mony folks in this world don't like to hurt your feelings that if I was kent as Mr MacPherson on this kind o' job I wadna mak' enough to pay for starchin' my shirts."

I suppose Mr MacPherson has been snibbing-in preachers in St Kentigern's Kirk pulpit and then going for twenty minutes' sleep in the vestry since the Disruption;[2] and the more privileged citizens of Glasgow during two or three generations of public dinners have experienced the kindly ministrations of Erchie, whose proud motto is "A flet fit but a warm hert."[3] I think, however, I was the first to discover his long pent-up and precious strain of philosophy.

On Saturday nights, in his office as beadle of St Kentigern's he lights the furnaces that takes the chill off the Sunday devotions. I found him stoking the kirk fires one Saturday, not very much like a beadle in appearance, and much less like a waiter. It was what, in England, they call the festive season.

"There's mair nor guid preachin' wanted to keep a kirk gaun," said he; "if I was puttin' as muckle dross on my fires as the Doctor whiles puts in his sermons, efter a Setturday at the gowf, ye wad see a bonny difference on the plate. But it's nae odds — a beadle gets sma' credit, though it's him that keeps the kirk tosh and warm, and jist at that nice easy-osy temperature whaur even a gey cauldrife[4] member o' the congregation can tak' his nap and no' let his lozenge slip doon his throat for chitterin' wi' the cauld."

There was a remarkably small congregation at St Kentigern's on the following day, and when the worthy beadle had locked the door after dismissal and joined me on the pavement.

"Man," he said, "it was a puir turn-oot yon — hardly worth puttin' on fires for. It's aye the wye; when I mak' the kirk a wee bit fancy, and jalouse[5] there's shair to be twa pound ten in the plate, on comes a blash o' rain, and there's hardly whit wid pay for the starchin' o' the Doctor's bands.

"Christmas! They ca't Christmas, but I could gie anither name for't. I looked it up in the penny almanac, and it said, 'Keen frost; probably snow,' and I declare – to if I hadna nearly to soom frae the hoose.

"The almanacs is no' whit they used to be; the auld chaps that used to mak' them maun be deid.

"They used to could do't wi' the least wee bit touch, and tell ye in January whit kind o' day it wad be at Hallowe'en, besides lettin' ye ken the places whaur the Fair days and the 'ool-markets was, and when they were to tak' place — a' kind o' information that maist o' us that bocht the almanacs couldna sleep at nicht wantin'. I've seen me get up at three on a cauld winter's mornin' and strikin' a licht to turn up Orr's Penny Commercial and see whit day was the Fair at Dunse. I never was at Dunse in a' my days, and hae nae intention o' gaun, but it's a grand thing knowledge, and it's no' ill to cairry. It's like poetry — 'The Star o' Rabbie Burns' and that kind o' thing — ye can aye be givin' it a ca' roond in your mind when ye hae naething better to dae.

"Oh, ay! A puir turn-oot the day for Kentigern's; that's

the drawback o' a genteel congregation like oors — mair nor half o' them's sufferin' frae Christmas turkey and puttin' the blame on the weather.

"The bubblyjock[6] is the symbol o' Scotland's decline and fa'; we maybe bate the English at Bannockburn, but noo they're haein' their revenge and underminin' oor constitution wi' the aid o' a bird that has neither a braw plumage nor a bonny sang, and costs mair nor the price o' three or four ducks. England gave us her bubblyjock and took oor barley-bree.[7]

"But it's a' richt; Ne'erday's comin'; it's begun this year gey early, for I saw Duffy gaun up his close last nicht wi' his nose peeled.

"'Am I gaun hame, or am I comin' frae't, can ye tell me?' says he, and he was carryin' something roondshaped in his pocket-naipkin.

"'Whit's wrang wi' ye, puir cratur?' I says to him.

"'I was struck wi' a sheet o' lichtnin',' says he, and by that I ken't he had been doon drinkin' at the Mull of Kintyre Vaults, and that the season o' peace on earth, guid-will to men was fairly started.

"'MacPherson,' he says, wi' the tear at his e'e, ' I canna help it, but I'm a guid man.'

"'Ye are that, Duffy,' I says, ' when ye're in your bed sleepin'; at ither times ye're like the rest o' us, and that's gey middlin'. Whit hae ye in the naipkin?'

"He gied a dazed look at it, and says, ' I'm no shair, but I think it's a curlin'-stane, and me maybe gaun to a bonspiel[8] at Carsbreck.'

"He opened it oot, and found it was a wee, roond, red cheese.

"'That's me, a' ower,' says he — 'a Christmas for the wife,' and I declare there was as much drink jaupin' in him as wad hae done for a water-shute.

"Scotland's last stand in the way o' national customs is bein' made at the Mull o' Kintyre Vaults, whaur the flet half-mutchkin, wrapped up in magenta tissue paper so that it'll look tidy, is retreatin' doggedly, and fechtin' every fit o'

the way, before the invadin' English Christmas caird. Ten
years ago the like o' you and me couldna prove to a freen'
that we liked him fine unless we took him at this time o' the
year into five or six public-hooses, leaned him up against
the coonter, and grat on his dickie.[9] Whit dae we dae noo?
We send wee Jennie oot for a shilling box o' the year afore
last's patterns in Christmas cairds, and show oor continued affection and esteem at the ha'penny postage rate.

"Instead o' takin' Duffy roon' the toon on Ne'erday,
and hurtin' my heid wi' tryin' to be jolly, I send him a
Christmas caird, wi' the picture o' a hayfield on the ootside
and ' Wishin' you the Old, Old Wish, Dear,' on the inside,
and stay in the hoose till the thing blaws bye.

"The shilling box o' Christmas cairds is the great peace-
maker; a gross or twa should hae been sent oot to Russia
and Japan,[10] and it wad hae stopped the war. Ye may hae
thocht for a twelvemonth the MacTurks were a disgrace to
the tenement, wi' their lassie learnin' the mandolin', and
them haein' their gas cut off at the meter for no' payin' the
last quarter; but let them send a comic caird to your lassie
— 'Wee Wullie to Wee Jennie,' and they would get the len'
o' your wife's best jeely-pan.

"No' but whit there's trouble wi' the Christmas caird.
It's only when ye buy a shillin' box and sit doon wi' the
wife and weans to consider wha ye'll send them to that ye
fin' oot whit an awfu' lot o' freen's ye hae. A score o'
shillin' boxes wadna gae ower half the kizzens I hae, wi' my
grandfaither belangin' to the Hielan's, so Jinnet an' me jist
let's on to some o' them we're no' sendin' ony cairds oot
this year because it's no' the kin' o' society go ony langer.
And ye have aye to keep pairt o' the box till Ne'erday to
send to some o' the mair parteecular anes ye forgot a'
thegither were freen's o' yours till they sent ye a caird.

"Anither fau't I hae to the Christmas cairds is that the
writin' on them's generally fair rideeculous.

"'May Christmas Day be Blythe and Gay, and bring
your household Peace and Joy,' is on the only caird left
ower to send to Mrs Maclure; and when ye're shearin' aff

the selvedges o't to mak' it fit a wee envelope, ye canna but think that it's a droll message for a hoose wi' five weans lyin' ill wi' the whoopin'-cough, and the man cairryin' on the wye Maclure does.

"'Old friends, old favourites, Joy be with you at this Season,' says the caird for the MacTurks, and ye canna but mind that every third week there's a row wi' Mrs MacTurk and your wife aboot the key o' the washin'-hoose[11] and lettin' the boiler rust that bad a' the salts o' sorrel in the Apothecaries 'll no tak' the stains aff your shirts.

"Whit's wanted is a kin' o' slidin' scale o' sentiment on Christmas cairds, so that they'll taper doon frae a herty greetin' ye can truthfully send to a dacent auld freen' and the kind o' cool ' here's to ye!' suited for an acquaintance that borrowed five shillin's frae ye at the Term,[12] and hasna much chance o' ever payin't back again.

"If it wasna for the Christmas cairds a lot o' us wad maybe never jalouse there was onything parteecular merry aboot the season. Every man that ye're owin' an accoont to sends it to ye then, thinkin' your hert's warm and your pouches rattlin'. On Christmas Day itsel' ye're aye expectin' something; ye canna richt tell whit it is, but there's ae thing certain — that it never comes. Jinnet, my wife, made a breenge for the door every time the post knocked on Thursday, and a' she had for't at the end o' the day was an ashet[13] fu' o' whit she ca's valenteens, a' written on so that they'll no even dae for next year.

"I used to wonder whit the banks shut for at Christmas, but I ken noo; they're feart that their customers, cairried awa' wi' their feelin' o' guid-will to men, wad be makin' a rush on them to draw money for presents, and maybe create a panic.

"Sae far as I can judge there's been nae panic at the banks this year.

"Every Ne'erday for the past fifty years I hae made up my mind I was gaun to be a guid man," he went on. "It jist wants a start, they tell me that's tried it, and I'm no' that auld. Naething bates a trial.

"I'm gaun to begin at twelve o'clock on Hogmanay, and mak' a wee note o't in my penny diary, and put a knot in my hankie to keep me in mind. Maist o' us would be as guid's there's ony need for if we had naething else to think o'. It's like a man that's hen-taed — he could walk fine if he hadna a train to catch, or the rent to rin wi' at the last meenute, or somethin' else to bother him. I'm gey faur wrang if I dinna dae the trick this year, though.

"Oh! ay. I'm gaun to be a guid man. No' that awfu' guid that auld freen's 'll rin up a close to hide when they see me comin', but jist dacent — jist guid enough to please mysel', like Duffy's singin'. I'm no' makin' a breenge at the thing and sprainin' my leg ower't. I'm startin' canny till I get into the wye o't. Efter this Erchie MacPherson's gaun to flype[14] his ain socks and no' leave his claes reel-rall aboot the hoose at night for his wife Jinnet to lay oot richt in the mornin'. I've lost money by that up till noo, for there was aye bound to be an odd sixpence droppin' oot and me no' lookin'. I'm gaun to stop skliffin'[15] wi' my feet; it's sair on the boots. I'm gaun to save preens by puttin' my collar stud in a bowl and a flet-iron on the top o't to keep it frae jinkin' under the chevalier[16] and book-case when I'm sleepin'. I'm gaun to wear oot a' my auld waistcoats in the hoose. I'm — "

"My dear Erchie," I interrupted, "these seem very harmless reforms."

"Are they? "said he. "They'll dae to be gaun on wi' the noo, for I'm nae phenomena; I'm jist Nature; jist the Rale Oreeginal."

2. *Erchie's Flitting*

HE CAME down the street in the gloaming on Tuesday night with a bird-cage in one hand and a potato-masher in the other, and I knew at once, by these symptoms, that Erchie was flitting.[1]

"On the long trail, the old trail, the trail that is always

new, Erchie?" said I, as he tried to push the handle of the masher as far up his coat sleeve as possible, and so divert attention from a utensil so ridiculously domestic and undignified.

"Oh, we're no' that bad!" said he. "Six times in the four-and-forty year. We've been thirty years in the hoose we're leavin' the morn, and I'm fair oot o' the wye o' flittin'. I micht as weel start the dancin' again."

"Thirty years! Your household gods plant a very firm foot, Erchie."

"Man, ay! If it wisna for Jinnet and her new fandangles, I wad nae mair think o' flittin' than o' buyin' a balloon to mysel'; but ye ken women! They're aye gaun to be better aff onywhaur else than whaur they are. I ken different, but I havena time to mak' it plain to Jinnet."

On the following day I met Erchie taking the air in the neighbourhood of his new domicile, and smoking a very magnificent meerschaum pipe.

"I was presented wi' this pipe twenty years ago," said he, "by a man that went to California, and I lost it a week or twa efter that. It turned up at the flittin'. That's ane o' the advantages o' flittin's; ye find things ye havena seen for years."

"I hope the great trek came off all right, Erchie?"

"Oh, ay! no' that bad, considerin' we were sae much oot o' practice. It's no' sae serious when ye're only gaun roond the corner to the next street. I cairried a lot o' the mair particular wee things roond mysel' last nicht — the bird-cage and Gledstane's picture and the room vawses[2] and that sort o' thing — but at the hinder-end Jinnet made me tak' the maist o' them back again."

"Back again, Erchie?"

"Ay. She made oot that I had cairried ower sae muckle that the flittin' wad hae nae appearance on Duffy's cairt, and haein' her mind set on the twa rakes,[3] and a' the fancy things lying at the close-mooth o' the new hoose till the plain stuff was taken in, I had just to cairry back a guid part o' whit I took ower last nicht. It's a rale divert the pride o' women! But I'm thinkin' she's vext' for't the day, because yin o' the things I took back was a mirror, and it was broke in Duffy's cairt. It's a gey unlucky thing to break a lookin'gless."

"A mere superstition, Erchie."

"Dod ! I'm no' sae shair o' that. I kent a lookin' gless broke at a flittin' afore this, and the man took to drink a year efter't, and has been that wye since."

"How came you to remove at all?"

"It wad never hae happened if I hadna gane to a sale and seen a coal-scuttle. It's a dangerous thing to introduce a new coal-scuttle into the bosom o' your faimily. This was ane o' thae coal-scuttles wi' a pentin' o' the Falls o' Clyde and Tillitudlem Castle on the lid. I got it for three-and-tuppence; but it cost me a guid dale mair nor I bargained for. The wife was rale ta'en wi't, but efter a week or twa she made oot that it gar'd the auld room grate we had look shabby, and afore ye could say knife she had in a new grate wi' wally[4] sides till't, and an ash-pan I couldna get spittin' on. Then the mantelpiece wanted a bed pawn[5] on't to gie the grate a dacent look, and she pit on a plush yin. Ye wadna hinder her efter that to get plush-covered chairs instead o' the auld hair-cloth we got when we were mairried. Her mither's chist-o'-drawers didna gae very weel wi' the plush chairs, she found oot in a while efter that, and they were swapped wi' twa pound for a chevalier and book-case, though the only books I hae in the hoose is the Family Bible, Buchan's ' Domestic Medicine,' and the ' Tales o' the Borders.' It wad hae been a' richt if things had gane nae further, but when she went to a sale hersel' and bought a Brussels carpet a yaird ower lang for the room, she made oot there was naethin' for't but to flit to a hoose wi' a bigger room. And a' that happened because a pented coal-scuttle took ma e'e."

"It's an old story, Erchie; 'c'est le premier pas que coûte,' as the French say."

"The French is the boys!" says Erchie, who never gives himself away. "Weel, we're flittin' onywye, and a bonny trauchle it is. I'll no' be able to find my razor for a week or twa."

"It's a costly process, and three flittin's are worse than a fire, they say."

"It's worse nor that; it's worse nor twa Irish lodgers.

"'It'll cost jist next to naethin',' says Jinnet. 'Duffy'll tak' ower the furniture in his lorry for freen'ship's sake, an' there's naethin' 'll need to be done to the new hoose.'

"But if ye ever flitted yersel', ye'll ken the funny wyes o' the waxcloth that's never cut the same wye in twa hooses; and I'll need to be gey thrang at my tred for the next month or twa to pay for the odds and ends that Jinnet never thought o'.

"Duffy flitted us for naethin', but ye couldna but gie the men a dram. A flittin' dram's by-ordinar;[6] ye daurna be scrimp wi't, or they'll break your delf for spite, and ye canna be ower free wi't either, or they'll break everything else oot o' fair guid-natur. I tried to dae the thing judeecious, but I forgot to hide the bottle, and Duffy's heid man and his mate found it when I wasna there, and that's the wye the lookin'-gless was broken. Thae cairters divna ken their ain strength.

"It's a humblin' sicht your ain flittin' when ye see't on the tap o' a coal-lorry."

"Quite so, Erchie; chiffoniers[7] are like a good many reputations — they look all right so long as you don't get seeing the back of them."

"And cairters hae nane o' the finer feelin's, I think. In spite o' a' that Jinnet could dae, they left the pots and pans a' efternoon on the pavement, and hurried the plush chairs up the stair at the first gae-aff. A thing like that's disheartenin' to ony weel-daein' woman.

"'Hoots!' says I to her, 'whit's the odds? There's naebody heedin' you nor your flittin'.'

"' Are they no'?' said Jinnet, keekin' up at the front o' the new land. 'A' the venetian blinds is doon, and I'll guarantee there's een behind them.'

"We werena half-an-oor in the new hoose when the

woman on the same stairheid chappet at the door and tellt us it was oor week o' washin' oot the close.[8] It wasna weel meant, but it did Jinnet a lot o' guid, for she was sitting in her braw new hoose greetin'."

"Greetin', Erchie? Why?"

"Ask that! Ye'll maybe ken better nor I dae."

"Well, you have earned your evening pipe at least, Erchie," said I.

He knocked out its ashes on his palm with a sigh.

"I hiv that! Man, it's a gey dauntenin' thing a flittin', efter a'. I've a flet fit, but a warm hert, and efter thirty years o' the auld hoose I was sweart to leave 't. I brocht up a family in't, and I wish Jinnet's carpet had been a fit or twa shorter, or that I had never seen yon coal-scuttle wi' the Falls o' Clyde and Tillitudlem Castle."

3. *Degenerate Days*

"THE TRED'S done," said Erchie.

"What! beadling?" I asked him.

"Oh! there's naethin' wrang wi' beadlin'," said he; "there's nae ups and doons there except to put the books on the pulpit desk, and they canna put ye aff the job if ye're no jist a fair wreck. I'm a' richt for the beadlin' as lang's I keep my health and hae Jinnet to button my collar, and it's generally allo'ed — though maybe I shouldna say't mysel' — that I'm the kind o' don at it roond aboot Gleska. I michtna be, if I wasna gey carefu'. Efter waitin' at a Setturday nicht spree, I aye tak' care to gie the bell an extra fancy ca' or twa on the Sunday mornin' jist to save clash and mak' them ken MacPherson's there himsel', and no' some puir pick-up that never ca'd the handle o' a kirk bell in his life afore.

"There's no' a man gangs to oor kirk wi' better brushed boots than mysel', as Jinnet 'll tell ye, and if I hae ae gift mair nor anither it's discretioncy. A beadle that's a waiter has to gae through life like the puir troot they caught in the

Clyde the other day — wi' his mooth shut, and he's worse aff because he hasna ony gills — at least no' the kind ye pronounce that way.

"Beadlin's an art, jist like pentin' photograph pictures, or playin' the drum, and if it's no' in ye, naethin' 'll put it there. I whiles see wee skinamalink[1] craturs dottin' up the passages in U.F. kirks carryin' the books as if they were M.C.'s at a dancin'-schule ball gaun to tack up the programme in front o' the band; they lack thon rale releegious glide; they havena the feet for't.

"Waitin' is whit I mean; it's fair done!

"When I began the tred forty-five year syne in the auld Saracen Heid Inn,[2] a waiter was looked up to, and was well kent by the best folk in the toon, wha aye ca'd him by his first name when they wanted the pletform box o' cigaurs handed doon instead o' the Non Plus Ultras.

"Nooadays they stick a wally door-knob wi' a number on't in the lapelle o' his coat, and it's ' Hey, No. 9, you wi' the flet feet, dae ye ca' this ham?'

"As if ye hadna been dacently christened and brocht up an honest faimily!

"In the auld days they didna drag a halflin callan'[3] in frae Stra'ven, cut his nails wi' a hatchet, wash his face, put a dickle and a hired suit on him, and gie him the heave into a banquet-room, whaur he disna ken the difference between a finger-bowl and a box o' fuzuvian lichts.[4]

"I was speakin' aboot that the ither nicht to Duffy, the coalman, and he says, 'Whit's the odds, MacPherson? Wha the bleezes couldna sling roon' blue-mange at the richt time if he had the time-table, or the menu, or whitever ye ca't, to keep him richt?'

"'Wha couldna sell coal,' said I, ' if he had the jaw for't? Man, Duffy,' says I, ' I never see ye openin' your mooth to roar coal up a close[5] but I wonder whit wye there should be sae much talk in the Gleska Toon Cooncil aboot the want o' vacant spaces.'

"Duffy's failin'; there's nae doot o't. He has a hump on him wi' carryin' bags o' chape coal and dross up thae new,

genteel, tiled stairs, and he let's on it's jist a knot in his
gallowses, but I ken better. I'm as straucht as a wand
mysel' — faith, I micht weel be, for a' that I get to cairry
hame frae ony o' the dinners nooadays. I've seen the day,
when Blythswood Square[6] and roond aboot it was a' the
go, that it was coonted kind o' scrimp to let a waiter hame
withoot a heel on him like yin o' thae Clyde steamers gaun
oot o' Rothesay quay on a Fair Setturday.

"Noo they'll ripe your very hip pooches for fear ye may
be takin' awa' a daud o' custard, or the toasted crumbs frae
a dish o' pheasant.

"They needna' be sae awfu' feart, some o' them. I ken
their dinners — cauld, clear, bane juice, wi' some strings o'
vermicelli in't; ling-fish hash; a spoonfu' o' red-currant
jeely, wi' a piece o' mutton the size o' a domino in't, if ye
had time to find it, only ye're no' playin' kee-hoi[7]; game
croquette that's jist a flaff o' windy paste; twa cheese
straws; four green grapes, and a wee lend o' a pair o' silver
nut-crackers the wife o' the hoose got at her silver weddin'.

"Man! it's a rale divert! I see big, strong, healthy Bylies[8]
and members o' the Treds' Hoose and the Wine, Speerit,
and Beer Tred risin' frae dinners like that, wi their big,
braw, gold watch-chains hingin' doon to their knees.

"As I tell Jinnet mony a time, it's women that hae fair
ruined dinner-parties in oor generation. They tak' the
measure o' the appetites o' mankind by their ain, which
hae been a'thegether spoiled wi' efternoon tea, and they
think a man can mak' up wi' music in the drawin'-room for
whit he didna get at the dinner-table.

"I'm a temperate man mysel', and hae to be, me bein' a
beadle, but I whiles wish we had back the auld days I hae
read aboot, when a laddie was kept under the table to
lowse the grauvats[9] o' the gentlemen that fell under't, in
case they should choke themsel's. Scotland was Scotland
then!

"If they choked noo, in some places I've been in, it wad
be wi' thirst.

"The last whisk o' the petticoat's no roon' the stair-landin' when the man o' the hoose puts the half o' his cigarette bye for again, and says, ' The ladies will be wonderin' if we've forgotten them,' and troosh a' the puir deluded craturs afore him up the stair into the drawin'-room where his wife Eliza's maskin' tea,[10] and a lady wi' tousy hair's kittlin' the piano till it's sair.

"'Whit's your opinion about Tschaikovski? ' I heard a wumman ask a Bylie at a dinner o' this sort the ither nicht.

"'I never heard o' him,' said the Bylie, wi' a gant,[11] 'but if he's in the proveesion tred, there'll be an awfu' run on his shop the morn's morn'.'

"Anither thing that has helped to spoil oor tred is the smokin' concerts.[12] I tak' a draw o' the pipe mysel' whiles, but I never cared to mak' a meal o't. Noo and then when I'm no' very busy other ways I gie a hand at a smoker, and it mak's me that gled I got ower my growth afore the thing cam' into fashion; but it's gey sair on an auld man to hear 'Queen o' the Earth' five or six nichts in the week, and the man at the piano aye tryin' to guess the richt key, or to get done first, so that the company 'll no' rin awa' when he's no' lookin' withoot paying him his five shillin's.

"I've done the waitin' at a' kinds o' jobs in my time — Easy-gaun Erchie they ca' me sometimes in the tred — a flet fit but a warm hert; I've even handed roond seed-cake and a wee drap o' spirits at a burial, wi' a bereaved and mournfu' mainner that greatly consoled the weedow; but there's nae depths in the business so low as poo'in' corks for a smokin' concert. And the tips get smaller and smaller every ane I gang to. At first we used to get them in a schooner gless; then it cam' doon to a wee tumbler; and the last I was at I got the bawbees in an egg-cup."

4. *The Burial of Big Macphee*

ERCHIE LOOKED pityingly at Big Macphee staggering down the street. "Puir sowl!" said he, "whit's the maitter wi' ye noo?"

Big Macphee looked up, and caught his questioner by the coat collar to steady himself. "Beer," said he; "jist beer. Plain beer, if ye want to ken. It's no' ham and eggs, I'll bate ye. Beer, beer, glorious beer, I'm shair I've perished three gallons this very day. Three gallons hiv I in me, I'll wager."

"Ye wad be far better to cairry it hame in a pail," said Erchie. "Man, I'm rale vexed to see a fine, big, smert chap like you gaun hame like this, takin' the breadth o' the street."

"Hiv I no' a richt to tak' the breadth o' the street if I want it?" said Big Macphee. "Am I no' a ratepayer? I hiv a ludger's vote,[1] and I'm gaun to vote against Joe Chamberlain and the dear loaf."[2]

"Och! ye needna fash aboot the loaf for a' the difference a tax on't 'll mak' to you," said Erchie.

"If ye gang on the wye ye're daein' wi' the beer, it's the Death Duties yer freends 'll be bothered aboot afore lang."

And he led the erring one home.

Big Macphee was the man who for some months back had done the shouting for Duffy's lorry No. 2. He sustained the vibrant penetrating quality of a voice like the Cloch fog-horn on a regimen consisting of beer and the casual hard-boiled egg of the Mull of Kintyre Vaults. He had no relatives except a cousin "oot aboot Fintry," and when he justified Erchie's gloomy prediction about the Death Duties by dying of pneumonia a week afterwards, there was none to lament him, save in a mild, philosophical way, except Erchie's wife, Jinnet.

Jinnet, who could never sleep at night till she heard Macphee go up the stairs to his lodgings, thought the funeral would be scandalously cold and heartless lacking the customary "tousy tea"[3] to finish up with, and as Duffy, that particular day, was not in a position to provide this solace for the mourners on their return from Sighthill Cemetery, she invited them to her house. There were Duffy and a man Macphee owed money to; the cousin from "oot aboot Fintry" and his wife, who was, from the outset, jealous of the genteel way tea was served in Jinnet's parlour, and suspicious of a "stuckupness" that was only in her own imagination.

"It's been a nesty, wat, mochy, melancholy day for a burial," said Duffy at the second helping of Jinnet's cold boiled ham; "Macphee was jist as weel oot o't. He aye hated to hae to change his jaicket afore the last rake, him no' haein' ony richt wumman buddy aboot him to dry't."

"Och, the puir cratur!" said Jinnet. "It's like enough he had a disappointment ance upon a time. He was a cheery chap."

"He was a' that," said Duffy. "See's the haud o' the cream-poorie."

The cousin's wife felt Jinnet's home-baked seed-cake was a deliberate taunt at her own inefficiency in the baking line. She sniffed as she nibbled it with a studied appearance of inappreciation. "It wasna a very cheery burial he had, onyway," was her astounding comment, and at that Erchie winked to himself, realising the whole situation.

"Ye're richt there, Mistress Grant," said he. "Burials are no' whit they used to be. Perhaps — perhaps ye were expectin' a brass band?" and at that the cousin's wife saw this was a different man from her husband, and that there was a kind of back-chat they have in Glasgow quite unknown in Fintry.

"Oh! I wasna sayin' onything aboot brass bands," she retorted, very red-faced, and looking over to her husband for his support. He, however, was too replete with tea and cold boiled ham for any severe intellectual exercise, and was starting to fill his pipe. "I wasna saying onything aboot brass bands; we're no' used to thae kind o' operatics at burials whaur I come frae. But I think oor ain wye o' funerals is better than the Gleska wye."

Erchie (fearful for a moment that something might have been overlooked) glanced at the fragments of the feast, and at the spirit-bottle that had discreetly circulated somewhat earlier. "We're daein' the best we can," said he. "As shair as death your kizzen — peace be wi' him! — 's jist as nicely buried as if ye paid for it yersel' instead o' Duffy and —

and Jinnet; if ye'll no' believe me ye can ask your man. Nae doot Big Macphee deserved as fine a funeral as onybody, wi' a wheen coaches, and a service at the kirk, wi' the organ playin' and a' that, but that wasna the kind o' man your kizzen was when he was livin'. He hated a' kinds o' falderals."[4]

"He was a cheery chap," said Jinnet again, nervously, perceiving some electricity in the air.

"And he micht hae had a nicer burial," said the cousin's wife, with firmness.

"Preserve us! "cried Erchie. "Whit wad ye like? — Flags maybe? Or champagne wine at the liftin'? Or maybe wreaths o' floo'ers? If it was cheeriness ye were wantin' wi' puir Macphee, ye should hae come a month ago and he micht hae ta'en ye himsel' to the Britannia Music-ha'.[5]"

"Haud yer tongue, Erchie," said Jinnet; and the cousin's wife, as fast as she could, took all the pins out of her hair and put them in again. "They think we're that faur back in Fintry," she said with fine irrelevance.

"Not at all," said Erchie, who saw his innocent wife was getting all the cousin's wife's fierce glances. "Not at all, mem. There's naething wrang wi' Fintry; mony a yin I've sent there. I'm rale chawed we didna hae a Fintry kind o' funeral, to please ye. Whit's the patent thing aboot a Fintry funeral?"

"For wan thing," said the cousin's wife, "it's aye a rale hearse we hae at Fintry and no' a box under a machine, like thon. It was jist a disgrace. Little did his mither think it wad come to thon. Ye wad think it was coals."

"And whit's the maitter wi' coals?" cried Duffy, his professional pride aroused. "Coals was his tred. Ye're shairly awfu' toffs in Fintry aboot yer funerals."

The cousin's wife stabbed her head all over again with her hair-pins, and paid no heed to him. Her husband evaded her eyes with great determination. "No' that great toffs either," she retorted, "but we can aye afford a bit crape. There wasna a sowl that left this close behind the corp the day had crape in his hat except my ain man."

Then the man to whom Big Macphee owed money laughed.

"Crape's oot o' date, mistress," Erchie assured her.

"It's no' the go noo at a' in Gleska; ye micht as weel expect to see the auld saulies.⁶"

"Weel, it's the go enough in Fintry," said the cousin's wife. "And there was anither thing; I didna expect to see onybody else but my man in weepers,⁷ him bein' the only freen' puir Macphee had but — "

"I havena seen weepers worn since the year o' the Tay Bridge," said Erchie, "and that was oot at the Mearns."

"Weel, we aye hae them at Fintry," insisted the cousin's wife.

"A cheery chap," said Jinnet again, at her wits'-end to put an end to this restrained wrangling, and the man Big Macphee owed money to laughed again.

"Whit's mair," went on the cousin's wife, "my man was the only wan there wi' a dacent shirt wi' tucks on the breist o't; the rest o' ye had that sma' respect for the deid ye went wi' shirt-breists as flet as a sheet o' paper. It was showin' awfu' sma' respect for puir Macphee," and she broke down with her handkerchief at her eyes.

"Och! to bleezes! Jessie, ye're spilin' a' the fun," her husband remonstrated.

Erchie pushed back his chair and made an explanation. "Tucks is no' the go naither, mistress," said he, "and if ye kent whit the laundries were in Gleska ye wadna wonder at it. A laundry's a place whaur they'll no stand ony o' yer tucks, or ony nonsense o' that kind. Tucks wad spoil the teeth o' the curry-combs they use in the laundry for scourin' the cuffs and collars; they're no' gaun awa' to waste the vitriol they use for bleachin' on a wheen tucks. They couldna dae't at the money; it's only threepence ha'penny a shirt, ye ken, and oot o' that they hae to pay for the machines that tak's the buttons aff, and the button-hole bursters — that's a tred by itsel'. No, mem, tucked breists are oot o' date; ye'll no' see such a thing in Gleska; I'm shair puir Macphee himsel' hadna ane. The man's as

weel buried as if we had a' put on the kilts, and had a piper
in front playin' 'Lochaber no More.' If ye'll no believe us,
Duffy can show ye the receipted accoonts for the undertaker and the lair; can ye no', Duffy?"

"Smert!" said Duffy.

But the cousin's wife was not at all anxious to see
accounts of any kind, so she became more prostrate with
annoyance and grief than ever.

"Oot Fintry way," said Erchie, exasperated, "it's a' richt
to keep up tucked shirt-breists, and crape, and weepers,
and mort-cloths, and the like, for there canna be an awfu'
lot o' gaiety in the place, but we have aye plenty o' ither
things to amuse us in Gleska. There's the Kelvingrove
Museum, and the Waxworks. If ye're no' pleased wi' the
wye Macphee was buried, ye needna gie us the chance
again wi' ony o' yer freen's."

The cousin's wife addressed herself to her husband.
"Whit was yon ye were gaun to ask?" she said to him. He
got very red, and shifted uneasily in his chair.

"Me!" aid he. "I forget."

"No ye dinna; ye mind fine."

"Och, it's a' richt. Are we no' haein' a fine time?"
protested the husband.

"No, nor a' richt, Rubbert Grant." She turned to the
others. "Whit my man was gaun to ask, if he wasna such a
sumph,[8] was whether oor kizzen hadna any money put by
him."

"If ye kent him better, ye wadna need to ask," said
Duffy.

"He was a cheery chap," said Jinnet.

"But was he no' in the Shepherds,[9] or the Oddfellows,
or the Masons, or onything that wye?"

"No, nor in the Good Templars nor the Rechabites,"
said Erchie. "The only thing the puir sowl was ever in was
the Mull o' Kintyre Vaults."

"Did I no' tell ye?" said her husband.

"Good-bye and thenky the noo," said the cousin's wife,
as she went down the stair. "I've spent a rale nice day."

"It's the only thing ye did spend," said Erchie when she was out of hearing. "Funerals are managed gey chape in Fintry."

"Oh ye rascal, ye've the sherp tongue!" said Jinnet.

"Ay, and there's some needs it! A flet fit, too, but a warm hert," said Erchie.

5. *The Prodigal Son*

JINNET, LIKE a wise housewife, aye shops early on Saturday, but she always leaves some errand — some trifle over-looked, as it were — till the evening, for, true daughter of the city, she loves at times the evening throng of the streets. That of itself, perhaps, would not send her out with her door-key in her hand and a peering, eager look like that of one expecting something long of coming: the truth is she cherishes a hope that some Saturday to Erchie and her will come what comes often to her in her dreams, sometimes with terror and tears, sometimes with delight.

"I declare, Erchie, if I havena forgotten some sweeties for the kirk the morn," she says; "put on yer kep and come awa' oot wi' me; ye'll be nane the waur o' a breath o' fresh air."

Erchie puts down his "Weekly Mail," stifling a sigh and pocketing his spectacles. The night may be raw and wet, the streets full of mire, the kitchen more snug and clean and warm than any palace, but he never on such occasion says her nay. "You and your sweeties!" he exclaims, lacing his boots; "I'm shair ye never eat ony, in the kirk or onywhere else."

"And whit dae ye think I wad be buyin' them for if it wasna to keep me frae gantin' in the kirk when the sermon's dreich?"

"Maybe for pappin' at the cats in the back coort,"[1] he retorts. "There's ae thing certain shair, I never see ye eatin' them."

"Indeed, and ye're richt," she confesses. "I havena the teeth for them nooadays."

"There's naething wrang wi' yer teeth, nor onything else aboot ye that I can see," her husband replies.

"Ye auld haver!" Jinnet will then cry, smiling.

"It's you that's lost yer sicht, I'm thinkin'. I'm a done auld buddy, that's whit I am, and that's tellin' ye. But haste ye and come awa' for the sweeties wi' me: whit'll thae wee Wilson weans in the close say the morn if Mrs MacPherson hasna ony sweeties for them?"

They went along New City Road[2] together, Erchie tall, lean, and a little round at the shoulders; his wife a little wee body, not reaching his shoulder, dressed by-ordinar for her station and "ower young for her years," as a few jealous neighbours say.

An unceasing drizzle blurred the street lamps, the pavement was slippery with mud; a night for the hearth-side and slippered feet on the fender; yet the shops were thronged, and men and women crowded the thoroughfare or stood entranced before the windows.

"It's a wonnerfu' place, Gleska," said Erchie. "There's such diversion in't if ye're in the key for't. If ye hae yer health and yer wark, and the weans is weel, ye can be as happy as a lord, and far happier. It's the folk that live in the terraces where the nae stairs is, and sittin' in their paurlours readin' as hard's onything to keep up wi' the times, and naething to see oot the window but a plot o' grass that's no' richt green, that gets tired o' everything. The like o' us, that stay up closes and hae nae servants, and can come oot for a daunder efter turnin' the key in the door, hae the best o't. Lord! there's sae muckle to see — the cheeny-shops and the drapers, and the neighbours gaun for paraffin oil wi' a bottle, and Duffy wi' a new shepherd tartan-grauvit, and Lord Macdonald singin' awa' like a' that at the Normal School,[3] and — "

"Oh, Erchie! dae ye mind when Willie was at the Normal?" said Jinnet.

"Oh, my! here it is already," thought Erchie. "If that

laddie o' oors kent the hertbrek he was to his mither, I wonder wad he bide sae lang awa'."

"Yes, I mind, Jinnet; I mind fine. Whit for need ye be askin'? As I was sayin', it's aye in the common streets that things is happenin' that's worth lookin' at, if ye're game for fun. It's like travellin' on the railway; if ye gang first-class, the way I did yince to Yoker by mistake, ye micht as weel be in a hearse for a' ye see or hear; but gang third and ye'll aye find something to keep ye cheery if it's only fifteen chaps standin' on yer corns gaun to a fitba'-match, or a man in the corner o' the cairriage wi' a mooth-harmonium playin' a' the wye."

"Oh! Erchie, look at the puir wean," said Jinnet, turning to glace after a woman with an infant in her arms. "Whit a shame bringin' oot weans on a nicht like this! Its face is blae wi' the cauld."

"Och! never mind the weans," said her husband; "if we were to mind a' the weans ye see in Gleska, ye wad hae a bonnie job o't."

"But jist think on the puir wee smout, Erchie. Oh, dear me! there's anither yin no' three months auld, I'll wager. It's a black burnin' shame. It should be hame snug and soond in its wee bed. Does 't no' mind ye o' Willie when I took him first to his grannie's?"

Her husband growled to himself, and hurried his step; but that night there seemed to be a procession of women with infants in arms in New City Road, and Jinnet's heart was wrung at every crossing.

"I thocht it was pan-drops[4] ye cam' oot for, or conversation-losengers," he protested at last; "and here ye're greetin' even-on aboot a wheen weans that's no' oor fault."

"Ye're a hard-herted monster, so ye are," said his wife indignantly.

"Of course I am," he confessed blythely. "I'll throw aff a' disguise and admit my rale name's Bluebeard, but don't tell the polis on me. Hard-herted monster — I wad need to be wi' a wife like you, that canna see a wean oot in the street at nicht withoot the drap at yer e'e. The weans is

maybe no' that bad aff: the nicht air's no' waur nor the day
air: maybe when they're oot here they'll no' mind they're
hungry."

"Oh, Erchie! see that puir wee lame yin! God peety him!
— I maun gie him a penny," whispered Jinnet, as a child in
rags stopped before a jeweller's window to look in on a
magic world of silver cruet-stands and diamond rings and
gold watches.

"Ye'll dae naething o' the kind!" said Erchie. "It wad jist
be wastin' yer money; I'll bate ye onything his mither
drinks." He pushed his wife on her way past the boy, and,
unobserved by her, slipped twopence in the latter's hand.

"I've seen the day ye werena sae mean, Erchie
MacPherson," said his wife, vexatiously. "Ye aye brag o'
yer flet fit and yer warm hert."

"It's jist a sayin'; I'm as mooly's[5] onything," said Erchie,
and winked to himself.

It was not the children of the city alone that engaged
Jinnet's attention; they came to a street where now and
then a young man would come from a public-house staggering; she always scanned the young fool's face with
something of expectancy and fear.

"Jist aboot his age, Erchie," she whispered. "Oh, dear! I
wonder if that puir callan' has a mither," and she stopped
to look after the young man in his cups.

Erchie looked too, a little wistfully. "I'll wager ye he
has," said he. "And like enough a guid yin, that's no'
forgettin' him, though he may gang on the ran-dan,[6] but in
her bed at nicht no' sleepin', wonderin' whit's come o'
him, and never mindin' onything that was bad in him, but
jist a kind o' bein' easy-led, but mindin' hoo smert he was
when he was but a laddie, and hoo he won the prize for
composeetion in the school, and hoo prood he was when
he brocht hame the first wage he got on a Setturday. If
God Almichty has the same kind o' memory as a mither,
Jinnet, there'll be a chance at the hinderend for the warst o'
us."

They had gone at least a mile from home; the night grew

wetter and more bitter, the crowds more squalid, Jinnet's interest in errant belated youth more keen. And never a word of the sweets she had made-believe to come out particularly for. They had reached the harbour side; the ships lay black and vacant along the wharfs, noisy seamen and women debauched passed in groups or turned into the public-houses. Far west into the drizzling night the river lamps stretched, showing the drumly[7] water of the highway of the world. Jinnet stopped and looked and listened. "I think we're far enough, Erchie; I think we'll jist gang hame," said she.

"Right!" said Erchie, patiently; and they turned, but not without one sad glance from his wife before they lost sight of the black ships, the noisy wharves, the rolling seamen on the pavement, the lamplights of the watery way that reaches to the world's end.

"Oh! Erchie," she said piteously, "I wonder if he's still on the ships."

"Like enough," said her husband. "I'm shair he's no' in Gleska at onyrate without comin' to see us. I'll bate ye he's a mate or a captain or a purser or something, and that thrang somewhere abroad he hasna time the noo; but we'll hear frae him by-and-by. The wee deevil! I'll gie him't when I see him, to be givin' us such a fricht."

"No' that wee, Erchie," said Jinnet. "He's bigger than yersel'."

"So he is, the rascal! am I no' aye thinkin' o' him jist aboot the age he was when he was at the Sunday school."

"Hoo lang is't since we heard o' him, Erchie?"

"Three or four years, or maybe five," said Erchie, quickly. "Man! the wye time slips bye! It doesna look like mair nor a twelvemonth."

"It looks to me like twenty year," said Jinnet, "and it's naething less than seeven, for it was the year o' Annie's weddin', and her wee Alick's six at Mertinmas. Seeven years! Oh, Erchie, where can he be? Whit can be wrang wi' him? No' to write a scrape o' a pen a' that time! Maybe I'll no' be spared to see him again."

"I'll bate ye whit ye like ye will," said her husband.

"And if he doesna bring ye hame a lot o' nice things — shells and parrots, and bottles of scent, and Riga Balsam for hacked hands, and the rale Cheena cheeny, and ostrich feathers and a' that, I'll — I'll be awfu' wild at him. But the first thing I'll dae 'll be to stand behind the door and catch him when he comes in, and tak' the strap to him for the rideeculous wye he didna write to us."

"Seeven years," said Jinnet. "Oh, that weary sea, a puir trade to be followin' for ony mither's son. It was Australia he wrote frae last; whiles I'm feared the blecks catched him oot there and killed him in the Bush."

"No! nor the Bush! Jist let them try it wi' oor Willie! Dod! he would put the hems on[8] them; he could wrastle a score o' blecks wi' his least wee bit touch."

"Erchie."

"Weel, Jinnet?"

"Ye'll no' be angry wi' me; but wha was it tellt ye they saw him twa years syne carryin' on near the quay, and that he was stayin' at the Sailors' Home?"

"It was Duffy," said Erchie, hurriedly. "I have a guid mind to — to kick him for sayin' onything o' the kind. I wad hae kicked him for't afore this if — if I wasna a beadle in the kirk."

"I'm shair it wasna oor Willie at a'," said Jinnet.

"Oor Willie! Dae ye think the laddie's daft, to be in Gleska and no' come to see his mither?"

"I canna believe he wad dae't," said Jinnet, but always looked intently in the face of every young man who passed them.

"Weel, that's ower for anither Setturday," said Erchie to himself, resuming his slippers and his spectacles.

"I declare, wife," said he, "ye've forgotten something."

"Whit is't?" she asked.

"The sweeties ye went oot for," said Erchie, solemnly.

"Oh, dear me! amn't I the silly yin? Thinkin' on that Willie o' oors put everything oot o' my heid."

Erchie took a paper bag from his pocket and handed it

to her. "There ye are," said he. "I had them in my pooch since dinner-time. I kent ye wad be needin' them."

"And ye never let on, but put on your boots and cam' awa' oot wi' me."

"Of coorse I did; I'm shairly no' that auld but I can be gled on an excuse for a walk oot wi' my lass?"

"Oh, Erchie! Erchie!" she cried, "when will ye be wise? I think I'll put on the kettle and mak' a cup o' tea to ye."

6. *Mrs Duffy Deserts Her Man*

"THEY'RE yatterin' awa' in the papers there like sweetie wives aboot Carlyle and his wife,"[1] said Erchie. "It's no' the thing at a' makin' an exposure. I kent Carlyle fine; he had a wee baker's shop in Balmano Brae,[2] and his wife made potted heid.[3] It was quite clean; there was naething wrang wi't. If they quarrelled it was naebody's business but their ain.

"It's a gey droll hoose whaur there's no' whiles a rippit. Though my fit's flet my hert's warm; but even me and Jinnet hae a cast-oot noo and then. I'm aye the mair angry if I ken I'm wrang, and I've seen me that bleezin' bad-tempered that I couldna light my pipe, and we wadna speak to ane anither for oors and oors.

"It'll come the nicht, and me wi' a job at waitin' to gang to, and my collar that hard to button I nearly break my thoombs.

"For a while Jinnet 'll say naethin', and then she'll cry, ' See's a haud o't, ye auld fuiter!'

"I'll be glowerin' awfu' solemn up at the corner o' the ceilin' when she's workin' at the button, lettin' on I'm fair ferocious yet, and she'll say, 'Whit are ye glowerin' at? Dae ye see ony spiders' webs?'

"' No, nor spiders' webs,' I says, as gruff as onything. 'I never saw a spider's web in this hoose.'

"At that she gets red in the face and tries no' to laugh. "'There ye are laughin'! Ye're bate!' I says.

"'So are you laughin', says she; 'and I saw ye first. Awa', ye're daft! Will I buy onything tasty for your supper?'

"Duffy's different. I'm no' blamin' him, for his wife's different too. When they quarrel it scandalises the close and gies the land a bad name. The wife washes even-on, and greets into her washin'-byne till she mak's the water cauld, and Duffy sits a' nicht wi' his feet on the kitchen-hobs singin' 'Boyne Water,' because her mither was a Bark,[4] called M'Ginty, and cam' frae Connaught. The folk in the flet abin them hae to rap doon[5] at them wi' a poker afore they'll get their nicht's sleep, and the broken delf that gangs oot to the ash-pit in the mornin' wad fill a crate.

"I'm no' sayin', mind ye, that Duffy doesna like her; it's jist his wye, for he hasna ony edication. He was awfu' vexed the time she broke her leg; it pit him aff his wark for three days, and he spent the time lamentin' aboot her doon in the Mull o' Kintyre Vaults.

"The biggest row they ever had that I can mind o', was aboot the time the weemen wore the dolmans.[6] Duffy's wife took the notion o' a dolman, and told him that seein' there was a bawbee up in the bag o' coal that week, she thocht he could very weel afford it.

"'There's a lot o' things we'll hae to get afore the dolman,' says he; I'm needin' a new kep mysel', and I'm in a menoj[7] for a bicycle.'

"' I'm fair affronted wi' my claes,' says she; 'I havena had onything new for a year or twa, and there's Carmichael's wife wi' her sealskin jaicket.'

"' Let her!' says Duffy; 'wi' a face like thon she's no' oot the need o't.'

"They started wi' that and kept it up till the neighbours near brocht doon the ceilin' on them.

"' That's the worst o' leevin' in a close,' said Duffy, 'ye daurna show ye're the maister in yer ain hoose withoot a lot o' nyafs[8] above ye spilin' a' the plaister.'

"Duffy's wife left him the very next day, and went hame to her mither's. She left oot clean sox for him and a bowl o'

mulk on the dresser in case he micht be hungry afore he
could mak' his ain tea.

"When Duffy cam' hame and found whit had happened, he was awfu' vexed for himsel' and begood to greet.

"I heard aboot the thing, and went in to see him, and
found him drinkin' the mulk and eatin' shaves o' breid at
twa bites to the shave the same as if it was for a wager.

"'Isn't this an awfu' thing that's come on me, Mac-
Pherson?' says he; 'I'm nae better nor a weedower except
for the mournin's.'

"' It hasna pit ye aff yer meat onywye,' says I.

"' Oh! ' he says, ' ye may think I'm callous, but I hae
been greetin' for twa oors afore I could tak' a bite, and I'm
gaun to start again as soon as I'm done wi' this mulk.'

"'Ye should gang oot,' I tells him, 'and buy the mistress
a poke o' grapes and gang roond wi't to her mither's and
tell her ye're an eediot and canna help it.'

"But wad he? No fears o' him!

"' Oh! I can dae fine withoot her,' he tells me quite
cocky. 'I could keep a hoose wi' my least wee bit touch.'

"'Ye puir deluded crature,' I tell't him, 'ye micht as well
try to keep a hyena. It looks gey like a collie-dug, but it'll
no' sup saps, and a hoose looks an awfu' simple thing till ye
try't; I ken fine because Jinnet aften tellt me.'

"He begood to soop the floor wi' a whitenin'-brush, and
put the stour under the bed.

"'Go on,' says I, 'ye're daein' fine for a start. A' ye
want's a week or twa at the nicht-schools, where they learn
ye laundry-work and cookin', and when ye're at it ye
should tak' lessons in scientific dressmakin'. I'll look for ye
comin' up the street next week wi' the charts under your
oxter and your lad wi' ye.'

"For a hale week Duffy kept his ain hoose.

"He aye forgot to buy sticks for the fire at nicht, and had
to mak' it in the mornin' wi' a dizzen or twa o' claes-pins.
He didna mak' tea, for he couldna tak' tea withoot cream
till't, and he couldna get cream because he didna ken the
wye to wash a poorie,[9] so he made his breakfast o' cocoa

and his tea o' cocoa till he was gaun aboot wi' a broon taste in his mooth.

"On the Sunday he tried to mak' a dinner, and biled the plates wi' soap and soda to get the creesh aff them when he found it wadna come aff wi' cauld water and a washin'-clout.

"'Hoo are ye gettin' on in yer ain bonny wee hoose noo?' I asks him ae dirty, wet, cauld day, takin' in a bowl o' broth to him frae Jinnet.

"'Fine,' says he, quite brazen; 'it's like haein' a yacht. I could be daein' first-rate if it was the summertime.'

"He wore them long kahootchy[10] boots up to your knees on wet days at his wark, and he couldna get them aff him withoot a hand frae his wife, so he had just to gang to his bed wi' them on. He ordered pipeclay by the hunderwicht and soap by the yard; he blackleaded his boots, and didna gang to the kirk because he couldna get on his ain collar.

"'Duffy,' I says, 'ye'll mak' an awfu' nice auld wife if ye leeve lang enough. I'll hae to get Jinnet started to knit ye a Shetland shawl.'

"Efter a week it begood to tell awfu' bad on Duffy's health. He got that thin, and so wake in the voice he lost orders, for a wheen o' his auldest customers didna ken him when he cried, and gave a' their tred to MacTurk, the coalman, that had a wife and twa sisters-in-law to coother him up wi' beef-tea on wet days and a' his orders.

"Duffy's mind was affected too; he gave the richt wicht,[11] and lost twa chances in ae day o' pittin' a ha'penny on the bag wi' auld blin' weemen that couldna read his board.

"Then he ca'd on a doctor. The doctor tell't him he couldna mak' it oot at a', but thocht it was appen —what d'ye ca't?—the same trouble as the King had,[12] and that Duffy had it in five or six different places. There was naething for him but carefu' dietin' and a voyage to the Cape.

"That very day Duffy, gaun hame frae his wark gey shauchly, wi' a tin o' salmon in his pooch for his tea, saw

his wife comin' doon the street. When she saw him she
turned and ran awa', and him efter her as hard's he could
pelt. She thocht he was that wild he was gaun to gie her a
clourin'; and she was jist fair bate wi' the runnin' when he
caught up on her in a back coort.

"'Tig !' says Duffy, touchin' her; 'you're het !'[13]

"'Oh, Jimmy!' she says, 'are ye in wi' me?'[14]

"' Am I no'?' says Duffy, and they went hame thegither.

"'There was a stranger in my tea this mornin',' says
Duffy: 'I kent fine somebody wad be comin'.'

"His wife tell't Jinnet a while efter that that she was a
great dale the better o' the rest she got the time she went
hame to her mither's; it was jist the very thing she was
needin'; and, forbye, she got the dolman."

7. *Carnegie's Wee Lassie*

ERCHIE SOUGHT me out on Saturday with a copy of that
day's "News" containing a portrait of Carnegie's[1] little
daughter Margaret.

"Man, isn't she the rale wee divert?" said he, glowing.
"That like her faither, and sae weel-put-on! She minds me
terrible o' oor wee Teenie when she was jist her age."

"She has been born into an enviable state, Erchie," I
said

"Oh, I'm no' sae shair aboot that," said Erchie. 'It's a
gey hard thing, whiles, bein' a millionaire's only wean. She
canna hae mony wee lassies like hersel' to play the peever
wi', or lift things oot o' the stanks o' Skibo Castle[2] wi' a bit
o' clye and a string. I'm shair it must be a hard job for the
auld man, her paw, to provide diversions for the puir wee
smout. And she'll hae that mony things that she'll no' can
say whit she wants next. I ken fine the wye it'll be up
yonder at Skibo.

"It'll be, 'Paw, I'm wantin' something.'

"'Whit is't, my dawtie, and ye'll get it to break?' Mr
Carnegie 'll say, and lift her on his knee, and let her play

wi' the works o' his twa thoosand pound repeater watch.

"'I dinna ken,' says the wee lassie, 'but I want it awfu' fast.'

"'Whit wad ye be sayin' to an electric doll wi' a phono-graph inside it to mak' it speak?' asks Mr Carnegie.

"'I'm tired o' dolls,' says the wee yin, 'and, besides, I wad rather dae the speakin' mysel'.'

"'Ye're a rale wee woman there, Maggie,' says her paw.

"'Weel, whit dae ye say to a wee totey motor-car a' for your ain sel', and jewelled in four-and-twenty holes?' says he efter that, takin' the hands o' his watch frae her in case she micht swallow them.

"'Oh! a motor-car,' says the wee lassie. 'No, I'm no carin' for ony mair motor-cars; I canna get takin' them to my bed wi' me.'

"'Ye're weel aff there,' says he. 'I've had the hale o' the Pittsburg[3] works to my bed wi' me,' he says.

"'They were in my heid a' the time when I couldna sleep, and they were on my chest a' the time when I was sleepin'.'

"' Whit wye that, paw?' says the wee lassie.

"'I was feart something wad gae wrang, and I wad lose a' the tred, and be puir again.'

"'But I thocht ye wanted to die puir, paw?' says the wee lassie.

"'Ay, but I never had ony notion o' leevin' puir,' says Mr Carnegie as smert's ye like, 'and that mak's a' the differ-ence. If ye're no' for anither motor carriage, wad ye no' tak' a new watch?'

"'No, paw,' says the wee lassie, 'I'm no' for anither watch. The only thing a watch tells ye is when it's time to gang to bed, and then I'm no' wantin' to gang onywye. Whit I wad like wad be ane o' thae watches that has haunds that dinna move when ye're haein' awfu' fine fun.'

"'Oh, ay!' says her paw at that; 'that's the kind we're a' wantin', but they're no' makin' them, and I'm no' shair that I wad hae muckle use for yin nooadays even if they were. If ye'll no hae a watch, will ye hae a yacht, or a brass band, or a fleein'-machine,[4] or a piebald pony?'

"'I wad raither mak' mud-pies,' says the wee innocent.

"' Mud-pies!' cries her faither in horror, lookin' roond to see that naebody heard her. 'Wheesh! Maggie, it wadna look nice to see the like o' you makin' mud-pies. Ye havena the claes for't. Beside, I'm tellt they're no' the go nooadays at a'.'

"'Weel,' says she at that, 'I think I'll hae a hairy-heided lion.'

"'Hairy-heided lion. Right!' says Mr Carnegie. 'Ye'll get that, my wee lassie,' and cries doon the turret stair to the kitchen for his No. 9 secretary.

"The No. 9 secretary comes up in his shirt sleeves, chewin' blot-sheet and dichting the ink aff his elbows.

"'Whit are ye thrang at the noo?' asks Mr Carnegie as nice as onything to him, though he's only a kind o' a workin' man.

"'Sendin' aff the week's orders for new kirk organs,' says the No. 9 secretary, 'and it'll tak' us till Wednesday.'

"'Where's a' the rest o' my secretaries?' asks Mr Carnegie.

"'Half o' them's makin' oot cheques for new leebraries[5] up and doon the country, and the ither half's oot in the back-coort burning letters frae weedows wi' nineteen weans, nane o' them daein' for themsel's, and frae men that were dacent and steady a' their days, but had awfu' bad luck.'

"'If it gangs on like this we'll hae to put ye on the night-shift,' says Mr Carnegie. 'It's comin' to't when I hae to write ma ain letters. I'll be expected to write my ain books next. But I'll no' dae onything o' the kind. Jist you telegraph to India, or Africa, or Japan, or wherever the hairy-heided lions comes frae, and tell them to send wee Maggie ane o' the very best at 50 per cent. aff for cash.'

"Early ae mornin' some weeks efter that, when the steam-hooter for wakenin' the secretaries starts howlin' at five o'clock, Mr Carnegie comes doon stair and sees the hairy-heided lion in a crate bein' pit aff a lorry. He has it wheeled in to the wee lassie when she's at her breakfast.

"'Let it oot,' she says; 'I want to play wi't.'

"'Ye wee fuiter!' he says, lauchin' like onything, 'ye canna get playin' wi't oot o' the cage, but ye'll can get feedin't wi' sultana-cake.'

"But that disna suit wee Maggie, and she jist tells him to send it awa' to the Bronx Zoo in New York.

"'Bronx Zoo. Right!' says her paw, and cries on his No. 22 secretary to send it aff wi' the parcel post at yince.

"'That minds me,' he says, 'there's a cryin' need for hairy-heided lions all over Europe and the United States. The moral and educative influence o' the common or bald-heided lion is of no account. Noo that maist o' the kirks has twa organs apiece, and there's a leebrary in every clachan in the country, I must think o' some ither wye o' gettin' rid o' this cursed wealth. It was rale 'cute o' you, Maggie, to think o't; I'll pay half the price o' a hairy-heided lion for every toon in the country wi' a population o' over five hundred that can mak' up the ither half by public subscription.'

"And then the wee lassie says she canna tak' her parridge.

"'Whit for no'?' he asks her, anxious-like. ' Are they no guid?'

"'Oh, they're maybe guid enough,' she says, but I wad raither hae toffie.'

"'Toffie. Right!' says her paw, and orders up the chef to mak' toffie in a hurry.

"'Whit's he gaun to mak' it wi'?' asks the wee yin.

"'Oh, jist in the ordinar' wye—wi' butter and sugar,' says her paw.

"'That's jist common toffie,' says the wee lassie; 'I want some ither kind.'

"'As shair's death, Maggie,' he says, 'there's only the ae wye o' makin' toffie.'

"'Then whit's the use o' haein' a millionaire for a paw?' she asks.

"'True for you,' he says, and thinks hard. 'I could mak' the chef put in champed rubies or a di'mond or twa grated doon.'

"'Wad it mak' the toffie taste ony better?' asks the wee cratur'.

"'No' a bit better,' he says. 'It wadna taste sae guid as the ordinary toffie, but it wad be nice and dear.'

"'Then I'll jist hae to hae the plain, chape toffie,' says wee Maggie.

"'That's jist whit I hae to hae mysel' wi' a great mony things,' says her paw. 'Being a millionaire's nice enough some wyes, but there's a wheen things money canna buy, and paupers wi' three or four thoosand paltry pounds a-year is able to get jist as guid toffie and ither things as I can. I canna even dress mysel' different frae ither folks, for it wad look rideeculous to see me gaun aboot wi' gold cloth waistcoats and a hat wi' strings o' pearls on it, so' a' I can dae is to get my nickerbocker suits made wi' an extra big check. I hae the pattern that big noo there's only a check-and-a-half to the suit; but if it wasna for the honour o't I wad just as soon be wearin' Harris tweed.'"

"Upon my word, Erchie," I said, "you make me sorry for our philanthropic friend, and particularly for his little girl."

"Oh, there's no occasion!" protested Erchie. "There's no condeetion in life that hasna its compensations, and even Mr Carnegie's wee lassie has them. I hae nae doot the best fun her and her paw gets is when they're playin' at bein' puir. The auld man 'll nae doot whiles hide his pocket-money in the press, and sit doon readin' his news-paper, wi' his feet on the chimney-piece, and she'll come in and ask for a bawbee.

"'I declare to ye I havena a farden, Maggie,' he'll say; 'but I'll gie ye a penny on Setturday when I get my pay.'

"'I dinna believe ye,' she'll say.

"'Then ye can ripe me,'[6] says her paw, and the wee tot'll feel in a' his pooches, and find half a sovereign in his waistcoat. They'll let on it's jist a bawbee (the wee thing never saw a rale bawbee in her life, I'll warrant), and he'll wonner whit wye he forgot aboot it, and tell her to keep it and buy jujubes[7] wi't, and she'll be awa' like a whitteruck[8]

and come back in a while wi' her face a' sticky for a kiss, jist
like rale.

"Fine I ken the wee smouts; it was that wye wi' oor ain
Teenie.

"Other whiles she'll hae a wee tin bank wi' a beeskep
on't, and she'll hae't fu' o' sovereigns her faither's veesitors
slip't in her haund when they were gaun awa', and she'll
put it on the mantelpiece and gang out. Then her paw'll
get up lauchin' like onything to himsel', and tak' doon the
wee bank and rattle awa' at it, lettin' on he's robbin't for a
schooner o' beer, and at that she'll come rinnin' in and
catch him at it, and they'll hae great fun wi' that game. I
have nae doot her faither and mither get mony a laugh at
her playin' at wee washin's, too, and lettin' on she's fair
trauchled aff the face o' the earth wi' a family o' nine dolls,
an' three o' them doon wi' the hoopin'-cough. Oh! they're
no that bad aff for fine fun even in Skibo Castle."

8. *A Son of the City*

MY OLD friend came daundering down the street with what
might have been a bag of cherries, if cherries were in
season, and what I surmised were really the twopenny pies
with which Jinnet and he sometimes made the Saturday
evenings festive. When we met he displayed a blue hya-
cinth in a flower-pot.

"Saw't in a fruiterer's window," said he, "and took the
notion. Ninepence; dod! I dinna ken hoo they mak' them
for the money. I thocht it wad please the wife, and min' her
o' Dunoon and the Lairgs and a' thae places that's doon
the watter in the summer-time.

"Ye may say whit ye like, I'm shair they shut up a' thae
coast toons when us bonny wee Gleska buddies is no'
comin' doon wi' oor tin boxes,[1] and cheerin' them up wi' a
clog-wallop on the quay.[2]

"It's a fine thing a flooer; no' dear to buy at the start,
and chaper to keep than a canary. It's Nature — the Rale

Oreeginal. Ninepence! And the smell o't! Jist a fair phenomena!"

"A sign of spring, Erchie," I said; "thank heaven! the primrose is in the wood, and the buds bursting on the hedge in the country, though you and I are not there to see it."

"I daursay," said he, "I'll hae to mak' a perusal doon the length o' Yoker on the skoosh car³ when the floods is ower. I'm that used to them noo, as shair's death I canna get my naitural sleep on dry nichts unless Jinnet gangs oot to the back and throws chuckies at the window, lettin' on it's rain and hailstanes. When I hear the gravel on the window I cod mysel' it's the genuine auld Caledonian climate, say my wee 'Noo I lay me,' and gang to sleep as balmy as a nicht polisman.

"There's a great cry the noo aboot folks comin' frae the country and croodin' into the toons and livin' in slums and degenerating the bone and muscle o' Britain wi' eatin' kippered herrin' and ice-cream. Thoosands o' them's gaun aboot Gleska daein' their bit turns the best way they can, and no' kennin', puir craturs! there's a Commission sittin' on them as hard's it can.

"'Whit's wanted,' says the Inspectors o' Poor, 'is to hustle them aboot frae place to place till the soles o' their feet gets red-hot wi' the speed they're gaun at; then gie them a bar o' carbolic soap and a keg o' Keatin's poother,⁴ and put them on the first train for Edinburgh.'

"'Tear doon the rookeries,'⁵ says anither man, 'and pit up rooms and kitchens wi' wally jawboxes⁶ and tiled closes at a rent o' eighteenpence a-week when ye get it.'

"'That's a' very fine,' says the economists, 'but if ye let guid wally jawbox hooses at ten shillin's a-year less than the auld-established and justly-popular slum hoose, will't no' tempt mair puir folk frae the country into Gleska and conjest the Gorbals worse than ever?' The puir economists thinks the folks oot aboot Skye and Kamerhashinjoo's⁷ waitin' for telegrams tellin' them the single apairtment hoose in Lyon Street, Garscube Road, 's doon ten shillin's

a-year, afore they pack their carpet-bags and start on the
Clansman[8] for the Broomielaw. But they're no'. They divna
ken onything aboot the rent o' hooses in Gleska, and
they're no' carin', for maybe they'll no' pay't onywye.
They jist come awa' to Gleska when the wife tells them,
and Hughie's auld enough for a polisman.

"Slums! wha wants to abolish slums? It's no' the like o'
me nor Duffy. If there werena folk leevin' in slums I
couldna buy chape shirts, and the celebrated Stand Fast
Craigroyston serge breeks at 2s. 11¾d. the pair, bespoke,
guaranteed, shrunk, and wan hip-pocket.

"When they're proposin' the toast o' the 'Army, Navy,
and Reserve Forces,' they ought to add the Force that live
in Slums. They're the men and women that's aye ready to
sweat for their country — when their money's done. A
man that wants the chapest kind o' chape labour kens he'll
aye can get it in the slums; if it wasna for that, my Stand
Fast Craigroyston breeks wad maybe cost 7s. 6d., and
some of the elders in the kirk I'm beadle for wad hae to
smoke tuppenny cigars instead o' sixpenny yins.

"The slums 'll no' touch ye if ye don't gang near them.

"Whit a lot o' folk want to dae 's to run the skoosh cars
away oot into the country whaur the clegs and the midges
and the nae gas is, and coup them oot at Deid Slow[9] on the
Clyde, and leave them there wander't. Hoo wad they like it
themsel's? The idea is that Duffy, when he's done wi' his
last rake o' coals, 'll mak' the breenge for Deid Slow, and
tak' his tea and wash his face wi' watter that hard it stots aff
his face like a kahootchy ba', and spend a joyous and
invigoratin' evenin' sheuchin' leeks and prunin' cauli-
flooer-bushes in the front plot o' his cottage home.

"I think I see him! He wad faur sooner pay twelve
pounds rent in Grove Street, and hae the cheery lowe o'
the Mull o' Kintyre Vaults forenent his paurlor window,
than get his boots a' glaur wi' plantin' syboes[10] roond his
cottage home at £6, 10s.

"The country's a' richt for folks that havena their health
and dinna want to wear a collar to their wark, and Deid

Slow and places like that may be fine for gaun to if ye want to get ower the dregs o' the measles, but they're nae places for ony man that loves his fellow-men.

"And still there's mony a phenomena! I ken a man that says he wad stay in the country a' the year roond if he hadna to bide in Gleska and keep his eye on ither men in the same tred's himsel', to see they're no' risin' early in the mornin' and gettin' the better o' him.

"It wadna suit Easy-gaun Erchie. Fine I ken whit the country is; did I no' leeve a hale winter aboot Dalry when I was a halflin'?

"It's maybe a' richt in summer, when you and me gangs oot on an excursion, and cheers them up wi' our melodeon wi' bell accompaniment; but the puir sowls havena much diversion at the time o' year the V-shaped depression's[11] cleckin' on Ben Nevis, and the weather prophets in the evening papers is promisin 'a welcome change o' weather every Setturday. All ye can dae when your wark's done and ye've ta'en your tea 's to put on a pair o' top-boots and a waterproof, and gang oot in the dark.' There's no' even a close to coort in,[12] and if ye want to walk along a country road at nicht thinkin' hoo much money ye hae in the bank, ye must be gey smert no' to fa' into a ditch. Stars? Wha wants to bother glowerin' at stars? There's never ony change in the programme wi' them in the country. If I want stars I gang to the Britannia.[13]

"Na, na, Gleska's the place, and it's nae wonder a' the country-folks is croodin' into't as fast's they can get their cottage homes sublet.

"This is the place for intellect and the big pennyworth of skim-milk.

"I declare I'm that ta'en wi' Gleska I get up sometimes afore the fire's lichted to look oot at the window and see if it's still to the fore.

"Fifteen public-hooses within forty yairds o' the close-mooth; a guttapercha works at the tap o' the street, and twa cab-stances at the foot. My mornin' 'oors are made merry wi' the delightfu' strains o' factory hooters and the sound o' the dust-cart man kickin' his horse like onything whaur it 'll dae maist guid.

"I can get onywhere I want to gang on the skoosh cars for a bawbee or a penny, but the only place I hae to gang to generally is my wark, and I wad jist as soon walk it, for I'm no' in ony hurry.

"When the rain's blashin' doon at nicht on the puir miserable craturs workin' at their front plots in Deid Slow, or trippin' ower hens that 'll no' lay ony eggs, I can be improvin' my mind wi' Duffy at the Mull o' Kintyre Vaults, or daunderin' alang the Coocaddens[14] wi' my hand tight on my watch-pocket, lookin' at the shop windows and jinkin' the members o' the Sons of Toil Social Club (Limited), as they tak' the breadth o' the pavement.

"Gleska! Some day when I'm in the key for't I'll mak' a song aboot her. Here the triumphs o' civilisation meet ye at the stair-fit, and three bawbee mornin' rolls can be had efter six o'clock at nicht for a penny.

"There's libraries scattered a' ower the place; I ken, for I've seen them often, and the brass plate at the door tellin' ye whit they are.

"Art's a' the go in Gleska, too; there's something aboot it every ither nicht in the papers, when Lord Somebody-or-ither's no' divorcin' his wife, and takin' up the space; and I hear there's hunders o' pictures oot in yon place at Kelvingrove.

"Theatres, concerts, balls, swarees, lectures — ony mortal thing ye like that'll keep ye oot o' your bed, ye'll get in Gleska if ye have the money to pay for't."

"It's true, Erchie."

"Whit's true?" said the old man, wrapping the paper more carefully round his flower-pot. "Man, I'm only coddin'. Toon or country, it doesna muckle maitter if, like me, ye stay in yer ain hoose. I don't stay in Gleska; not me! it's only the place I mak' my money in; I stay wi' Jinnet."

9. *Erchie on the King's Cruise*

I DELIBERATELY sought out Erchie one day in order to elicit his views upon the Royal progress¹ through the Western Isles, and found him full of the subject, with the happiest disposition to eloquence thereon.

"Man! I'm that gled I'm to the fore to see this prood day for Scotland," said he. "I'm daein' hardly onything but read the mornin' and evenin' papers, and if the Royal yacht comes up the length o' Yoker I'm gaun doon mysel' to wave a hanky. 'His Majesty in Arran. Great Reception,' says they. 'His Majesty in Glorious Health. Waves his hand to a Wee Lassie, and Nearly Shoots a Deer,' says they. 'His Majesty's Yacht Surrounded by the Natives. Escape round the Mull. Vexation of Campbeltown, and Vote of Censure by the Golfers of Machrihanish,' says they. Then the telegrams frae 'Oor Special Correspondent': 'OBAN, 1 P.M. — It is confidently expected that the Royal yacht will come into the bay this evenin' in time for tea. The esplanade is being washed with eau-de-Cologne, and a' the magistrates is up at Rankine's barber shop gettin' a dry shampoo.' 'OBAN, 1.30 P.M. — A wire frae Colonsay says the Royal yacht is about to set sail for Oban. Tremendous excitement prevails here, and the price o' hotel bedrooms is raised 200 per cent. It is decided to mobilise the local Boys' Brigade, and engage Johnny M'Coll to play the pipes afore the King when he's comin' ashore.' '6 P.M. — The Royal yacht has just passed Kerrera, and it is now certain that Oban will not be visited by the Royal party. All the flags have been taken down, and scathing comments on the extraordinary affair are anticipated from the local Press.'

"Maybe ye wadna think it, but his Majesty's gaun roond the West Coast for the sake o' his health.

"'Ye'll hae to tak' a month o' the rest cure,' the doctors tellt him, 'a drap o' claret wine to dinner, and nae worry aboot business.'

"'Can I afford it?' said his Majesty, that vexed-like, for he was pullin' aff his coat and rollin' up his sleeves to start work for the day.

"'There's nae choice in the maitter,' said the doctors; 'we order it.'

"'But can I afford it?'" again said his Majesty. 'Ye ken yoursel's, doctors, I have had a lot o' expense lately, wi' trouble in the hoose, and wi' the Coronation and aething and another. Could I no' be doin' the noo wi' Setturday-to-Monday trips doon the watter?'

"But no; the doctors said there was naethin' for him but rest. So his Majesty had to buy a new topcoat and a yachtin' bunnet, and start oot on the *Victoria and Albert*[2].

"It's a twa-funnelled boat, but I'm tellt that, bein' Government built, yin o' the funnels has a blaw-doon, and they daurna light the furnace below't if the win's no' in a certain airt.

"The yacht made first for the Isle o' Man, and wasna five meenutes in the place when the great novelist, Hall Corelli or Mary Caine,[3] or whichever it is, was aboard o' her distributin' hand-bills advertisin' the latest novel, and the King took fright, and left the place as soon as he could.

"I'm tellin' ye it's a gey sair trauchle[4] bein' a King. The puir sowl thought the Hielan's wad be a nice quate place where naebody wad bother him, and so he set sail then for Arran.

"'What is that I see afore me?' said he, comin' up past Pladda.

"The captain put his spy-gless to his e'e, and got as white's a cloot.

"'It's your Majesty's joyous and expectant subjects,' says he. 'They've sixty-seven Gleska steamers oot yonder waitin' on us, and every skipper has his hand on the string o' the steam-hooter.'

"'My God!' groaned the puir King, 'I thought I was sent awa' here for the guid o' my health.'

"Before he could say knife, a' the Gleska steamers and ten thoosan' wee rowin'-boats were scrapin' the pent aff the sides o' the *Victoria and Albert,* and half a million

Scottish taxpayers were cheerin' their beloved Sovereign, Edward VII, every mortal yin o' them sayin', 'Yon's him yonder!' and p'intin' at him.

"'Will I hae to shoogle hands wi' a' that crood?' he asked the captain o' the *Victoria and Albert*, and was told it wad dae if he jist took aff his kep noo and then.

"And so, takin' aff his kep noo and then, wi' a' the Gleska steamers and the ten thoosan' wee rowin'-boats hingin' on to the side o' the yacht, and half a million devoted subjects takin' turn aboot at keekin' in through the port-holes to see what he had for dinner, his Majesty sailed into Brodick Bay.

"'The doctors were right,' says he; 'efter a', there's naething like a rest cure; it's a mercy we're a' spared.'

"The following day his Majesty hunted the deer in Arran. I see frae the papers that he was intelligently and actively assisted in this by the well-known ghillies, Dugald M'Fadyen, Donald Campbell, Sandy M'Neill, and Peter M'Phedran.

"They went up the hill and picked oot a nice, quate he-deer, and drove it doon in front o' where his Majesty sat beside a stack o' loaded guns.

"His Majesty was graciously pleased to tak' up yin o' the guns, and let bang at the deer.

"'Weel done! That wass gey near him,' said Dugald M'Fadyen, strikin' the deer wi' his stick to mak' it stop eatin' the gress.

"His Majesty fired a second time, and the deer couldna stand it ony langer, but went aff wi' a breenge.[5]

"'Weel, it's a fine day to be oot on the hull onywye,' says M'Phedran, resigned-like, and the things that the heid ghillie Campbell didna say was terrible.

"The papers a' said the deer was shot, and a bloody business too; but it wasna till lang efter the cauld-clye corpse o't was found on the hill.

"'Here it is!' said M'Fadyen.

"'I daursay it is,' said M'Neill.

"'It'll hae to be it onywye,' said the heid man, and they had it weighed.

"If it was sold in Gleska the day it would fetch ten shillin's a-pound.

"If there's ae thing I've noticed mair nor anither aboot Hielan' ghillies, it's that they'll no' hurt your feelin's if they can help it. I'm Hielan' mysel'; my name's MacPherson; a flet fit but a warm hert, and I ken.

"Meanwhile Campbeltoon washed its face, put a clove in its mooth, and tried to look as spruce as it could for a place that has mair distilleries than kirks.[6] The Royal veesit was generally regairded as providential, because the supremacy o' Speyside whiskies over Campbeltoon whiskies o' recent years wad hae a chance o' being overcome if his Majesty could be prevailed on to gang through a' the distilleries and hae a sample frae each o' them.

"It was to be a gala day, and the bellman went roon the toon orderin' every loyal ceetizen to put oot a flag, cheer like onything when the King was gaun to the distilleries, and bide inside their hooses when he was comin' back frae them. But ye'll no' believe't — THE YACHT PASSED CAMPBELTOON!

"The Provost and Magistrates and the hale community was doon on the quay to cairry the Royal pairty shouther-high if necessary, and when they saw the *Victoria and Albert* they cheered sae lood they could be heard the length o' Larne.

"'Whit's that?' said his Majesty.

"'By the smell o't I wad say Campbeltoon,' said his skipper, 'and that's mair o' your Majesty's subjects, awfu' interested in your recovery.'

"'Oh man!' said the puir King, nearly greetin', 'we divna ken whit health is, ony o' us, till we lose it. Steam as far aff frae the shore as ye can, and it'll maybe no' be sae bad.'

"So the yacht ran bye Campbeltoon.

"The folk couldna believe't at first.

"'They must hae made a mistake,' says they; 'perhaps they didna notice the distillery lums,' and the polis sergeant birled his whustle by order of the Provost, to ca' the King's attention, but it was o' no avail. A rale divert!

"The yacht went on to Colonsay.

"That's the droll thing aboot this trip o' his Majesty's; it's no' ony nice, cheery sort o' places he gangs to at a', but oot-o'-the-wye wee places wi' naethin' aboot them but hills and things — wee trashy places wi' nae nice braw new villas aboot them, and nae minstrels or banjo-singers on the esplanade singin' 'O! Lucky Jim!' and clautin' in the bawbees.[7] I divna suppose they had half a dizzen flags in a' Colonsay, and ye wad fancy the King's een's no' that sair lookin' at flags but whit he wad be pleased to see mair o' them.

"Colonsay! Man, it's fair peetifu'! No' a Provost or a Bylie in't to hear a bit speech frae; nae steamboat trips to gang roond the Royal yacht and keek in the port-holes; but everything as quate as a kirk on a Setturday mornin'.

"A' the rest o' Scotland wanted to wag flags at his Majesty Edward VII, and here he maun put up at Colonsay! The thing was awfu' badly managed.

"If Campbeltoon was chawed at the yacht passin' withoot giein' a cry in, whit's to describe the vexation o' Oban?

"Oban had its hert set on't. It never occurred to the mind o' Oban for wan meenute that the King could pass the 'Charin' Cross o' the Hielans'[8] 'withoot spendin' a week there at the very least, and everything was arranged to mak' the Royal convalescent comfortable.

"The bay was fair jammed wi' yachts, and a' the steam-whustles were oiled. The hotels were packed to the roof wi' English tourists, some o' them sleepin' under the slates, wi' their feet in the cisterns, and gled to pay gey dear for the preevilege o' breathin' the same air as Edward VII.

"Early in the day somebody sent the alarmin' tidin's frae Colonsay that the *Victoria and Albert* micht pass Oban efter a', and to prevent this, herrin'-nets were stretched aff Kerrera to catch her if ony such dastardly move was made.

"But it was nae use; Oban's in sackcloth and ashes.

"'Where are we noo?' asked the Royal voyager, aff Kerrera. 'Is this Shingleton-on-the-Sea?'

"'No, your Majesty,' says the skipper of the Royal yacht, 'it's Oban, the place whaur the German waiters get their education.'

"'Heavens!' cried his Majesty, shudderin'; 'we're terrible close; put a fire under the aft funnel at a' costs and get past as quick as we can.'

"It was pointed oot to his Majesty that the toon was evidently expectin' him, and so, to mak' things pleasant, he ordered the steam pinnace to land the week's washin' at the Charin' Cross o' the Hielan's — while the *Victoria and Albert* went on her way to Ballachulish."

10. *How Jinnet saw the King*

"I SAW him and her on Thursday,"[1] said Erchie, "as nate's ye like, and it didna cost me mair nor havin' my hair cut. They gaed past oor kirk, and the session put up a stand, and chairges ten shillin's a sate.

"'Not for Joe,' says I; 'I'd sooner buy mysel' a new pair o' boots'; and I went to Duffy and says I, 'Duffy, are ye no' gaun to hae oot yer bonny wee lorry at the heid o' Gairbraid Street[2] and ask the wife and Jinnet and me to stand on't?'

"'Right,' says Duffy, 'bring you Jinnet and I'll tak' my wife, and we'll hae a rale pant.'

"So there was the four o' us standin' five mortal 'oors on Duffy's coal-lorry. I was that gled when it was a' bye. But I'll wager there was naebody gledder nor the King himsel', puir sowl! Frae the time he cam' into Gleska at Queen Street Station till the time he left Maryhill, he lifted his hat three million seven hundred and sixty-eight thousand and sixty-three times.

"Talk aboot it bein' a fine job bein' a King! I can tell ye the money's gey hard earned. Afore he starts oot to see his beloved people, he has to practise for a week wi' the dumb-bells, and feed himsel' up on Force, Grape-nuts, Plasmon, Pianolio, and a' thae strengthenin' diets that Sunny Jim eats.[3]

"I thocht first Jinnet maybe wadna gang, her bein' in the Co-operative Store[4] and no' awfu' ta'en up wi' Royalty, but, dod! she jumped at the chance.

"'The Queen's a rale nice buddy,' she says; 'no' that I'm personally acquainted wi' her, but I hear them sayin'. And she used to mak' a' her ain claes afore she mairried the King.'

"So Jinnet and me were oot on Duffy's lorry, sittin' on auld copies o' 'Reynolds' News,'[5] and hurrayin' awa' like a pair o' young yins.

"The first thing Jinnet saw was a woman wi' a wean and its face no' richt washed.

"'Fancy her bringin' oot her wean to see the King wi' a face like that,' says Jinnet, and gies the puir wee smout a sweetie.

"Frae that till it was time for us to gang hame Jinnet saw naething but weans, and her and Duffy's wife talked aboot weans even on. Ye wad think it was a baby-show we were at and no' a King's procession.

"Duffy sat wi' a Tontine face[6] on him maist o' the time, but every noo and then gaun up the street at the back o' us to buy himsel' a bottle o' broon robin,[7] for he couldna get near a pub; and I sat tryin' as hard's I could to think hoo I wad like to be a King, and what kind o' waistcoats I wad wear if I had the job. On every hand the flags were wavin', and the folk were eatin' Abernaithy biscuits.

"At aboot twelve o'clock cannons begood to bang.

"'Oh my! I hope there's nae weans near thae cannons or they micht get hurt,' says Jinnet.

"Little did she think that at that parteecular meenute the King was comin' doon the tunnel frae Cowlairs,[8] and tellin' her Majesty no' to be frichted.

"When the King set foot in the Queen Street Station he gied the wan look roond him, and says he, 'Is this Gleska, can ony o' ye tell me?'

"'It is that, wi' your Majesty's gracious permission,' says the porter; 'sees a haud o' yer bag.'

"'I mind fine o' bein' here yince afore,' says the King, and gangs oot into George Square.

"'Whitna graveyaird's this?'[9] he asks, lookin' at the statues.

"'It's no' a graveyaird; it's a square, and that's the Municeepal Buildin','' somebody tells him. His Majesty then laid a foundation-stone as smert's ye like wi' his least wee bit touch, and then went into the Municeepal Buildin's and had a snack.

"He cam' oot feelin' fine. 'The Second City o' the Empire!'[10] he says. 'I can weel believ't. If it wasna for my business bein' in London I wad hae a hoose here. Whit am I to dae next?'

"They took his Majesty doon Buchanan Street.

"'No bad!' says he.

"Then he cam' to Argyle Street, and gaed west, past the Hielan'man's Cross[11] at the heid o' Jamaica Street. He sees a lot o' chaps there wi' the heather stickin' oot o' their ears, and a tartan brogue that thick it nearly spiled the procession.

"'The Hielan'man's Cross,' says he; 'man, ay! I've heard o't. Kamerhashendoo. If I had thocht o't I wad hae brocht my kilts and my pibroch and a' that.'

"A' the wey doon the Dumbarton Road the folk were fair hingin' oot o' their windows, wavin' onything at a' they could get a haud o', and the Royal carriage was bump-bump-bumpin' like a' that ower the granite setts.[12]

"'Whit's wrang wi' the streets o' Gleska?' says the King, him bein' used to wud streets in London, whaur he works.

"'It's granite, if ye please,' says they.

"'Oh ay!' says the King; 'man, it mak's a fine noise. Will we soon be there? I like this fine, but I wadna like to keep onybody waitin'.'

"At Finnieston the folk cam' up frae the side streets and fair grat wi' patriotic fervour. Forbye, a' the pubs were shut for an 'oor or twa.

"'Whit I want to see's the poor,' says the King. 'I'm tired lookin' at the folk that's weel aff; they're faur ower common.'

"'Them's the poor,' he was tellt; 'it's the best we can dae for your Majesty.'

"'But they're awfu' bien-lookin' and weel put on,' says he.

"'Oh ay! 'they tells him, 'that's their Sunday claes.'

"And so the Royal procession passed on its way, the King being supplied wi' a new hat every ten minutes, to mak' up for the yins he spiled liftin' them to his frantic and patriotic subjects.

"In ten to fifteen minutes he examined the pictures in the Art Galleries — the Dutch, the English, the Italian, and the Gleska schools o' painters;[13] the stuffed birds, and the sugaraully hats[14] the polis used to hae when you and me was jinkin' them.

"'Och, it's fine,' says he; 'there's naething wrang wi' the place. Are we no' near Maryhill noo?'

"Ye see his Majesty had on a bate he could see the hale o' Gleska in five 'oors or less, an' be oot sooner nor ony ither king that ever set a fit in it. They wanted him to mak' a circular tour o't, and come back to the Municeepal Buildin's for his tea.

"'Catch me,' says he. 'I'm gaun back to Dalkeith.[15]

"A' this time we were standin' on Duffy's lorry, flanked on the left by the Boys' Brigade, lookin' awfu' fierce, and the riflemen frae Dunoon on the richt. Every noo an' then a sodger went bye on a horse, or a lassie nearly fainted and had to be led alang the line by a polisman, and him no' awfu' carin' for the job. Duffy was gaun up the street to buy broon robin that aften he was gettin' sunburnt, and my wife Jinnet nearly hurt her een lookin' for weans.

"'Look at thon wee wean, Erchie,' she wad aye be tellin' me, 'does't no' put ye in mind o' Rubbert's wee Hughie? Oh, the cratur!'

"'Wumman,' I tellt her, 'this is no' a kinderspiel[16] ye're at; it's a Royal procession. I wonder to me ye wad be wastin' yer e'esicht lookin' at weans when there's sae mony braw sodgers.'

"'Oh, Erchie!' says she, 'I'm bye wi' the sodgers'; and jist wi' that the procession cam' up the street. First the Lancers wi' their dickies stickin' ootside their waistcoats.

"'Man, them's fine horses,' says Duffy, wi' a professional eye on the beasts. 'Chaps me that broon yin wi' the white feet.'

"Then cam' the King and Queen.

"'Whaur's their croons?' asks Duffy's wife. 'I divna believe that's them at a'.'

"'That's them, I'll bate ony money,' I says. 'Ye can tell by the hurry they're in.'

"'Oh, the craturs!' says Jinnet, and then says she, 'Oh, Erchie! look at the wean hanging ower that window. I'm feart it'll fa' ower.'

"Afore she could get her een aff the wean the King's cairrage was past, and the rest o' the Lancers cam' clatterin' after them.

"'Noo for the brass bands!' says Duffy, lookin' doon the street. But there was nae brass bands. The show was bye.

"'If I had kent that was to be a' that was in't, I wad never hae ta'en oot my lorry,' says Duffy, as angry as onything, and made a breenge for anither bottle o' broon robin.

"'Och, it was fine,' says Jinnet. 'I never saw sae mony weans in a' my days.'

"And the crood began to scale.

"His Majesty reached Maryhill Station exact to the minute, wi' his eye on his watch.

"'Weel, that's bye onywye,' says he, and somebody cries for a speech.

"'People o' Gleska,' he says, 'I have seen your toon. It's fine — there's naething wrang wi't,' and then the gaird blew his whustle, and the train went aff.

"The great event was ower, the rain begood to fa' again; the Gilmorehill student hurried hame to blacken his face and put on his sister's frock.[17] The coloured ping-pong balls strung ower Sauchieha' Street was lighted, the illuminated skoosh cars began to skoosh up and doon the street, the public-hooses did a fine tred.

"'I'm gled it's a' bye,' says Jinnet, when we got hame to oor ain hoose.

"'Indeed, and so am I,' says I. 'There wad be fine fun in this warld a' the time if we werena trying for't.'"

11. *Erchie Returns*

FOR WEEKS I had not seen Erchie. He was not to be met on the accustomed streets, and St Kentigern's Kirk having been closed since July for alterations and repairs, it was useless to go there in search of its beadle. Once I met Duffy, and asked him what had become of the old

"Alloo you[1] Erchie!" was all the information he would vouchsafe; "if he's keepin' oot o' sicht, he'll hae his ain reason for't. Mind, I'm no' sayin' onything against the cratur, though him and me's had mony a row. He's a' richt if ye tak' him the richt wye. But sly! He's that sly, the auld yin, ye can whiles see him winkin' awa' to himsel' ower something he kens that naebody else kens, and that he's no gaun to tell to them. I havena seen the auld fuiter since the Fair week; perhaps he's gotten genteel and bidin' doon at Rothesay till the summer steamboats stop. There's yin thing sure — it's no' a case o' wife-desertion, for Jinnet's wi' him. I can tell by the venetian blinds and the handle o' their door. Sly! Did ye say sly? Man, it's no' the word for't. Erchie MacPherson's fair lost at the waitin'; he should hae been a poet, or a statesman, or something in the fancy line like that."

It was with the joy of a man who has made up his mind he has lost a sovereign and finds it weeks after in the lining of his waistcoat, I unexpectedly met Erchie on Saturday.

"Upon my word, old friend," I said, "I thought you were dead."

"No, nor deid!" retorted Erchie. "Catch me! I'm nane o' the deein' kind. But I micht nearly as weel be deid, for I've been thae twa months in Edinburgh. Yon's the place for a man in a decline; it's that slow he wad hae a chance o' livin' to a grand auld age. There's mair o' a bustle on the road to Sichthill Cemetery ony day in the week than there is in Princes Street on a Setturday nicht. I had a bit job there for the last ten weeks, and the only pleesure I had was gaun doon noo and then to the Waverley Station to see the bonny wee trains frae Gleska. They're a' richt for scenery and the like o' that in Edinburgh, but they're no' smert."

"But it's an old saying, Erchie, that all the wise men in Glasgow come from the East — that's to say, they come from Edinburgh."

"Yes, and the wiser they are the quicker they come," said Erchie. "Man! and it's only an 'oor's journey, and to see the wye some o' them gae on bidin' ower yonder ye wad think they had the Atlantic Ocean to cross. There should be missionaries sent ower to Edinburgh explainin' things to the puir deluded craturs. Ony folk that wad put thon big humplock o' a hill they ca' the Castle in the middle o' the street, spilin' the view, and hing their washin's on hay-rakes[2] stuckoot at their windows, hae muckle to learn."

"Still, I have no doubt Edinburgh's doing its best, Erchie," I said.

"Maybe, but they're no' smert; ye wad hae yer pouch picked half a dizzen times in Gleska in the time an Edinburgh polisman tak's to rub his een to waken himsel' when ye ask him the road to Leith.

"Did ye ever hear tell o' the Edinburgh man that ance ventured to Gleska and saw the hopper dredgers clawtin' up the glaur[3] frae the Clyde at Broomielaw?

"'Whit are ye standin' here for? Come awa' and hae a gless o' milk,' said a freen' to him.

"'No, nor awa',' said he, glowerin' like onything; 'I've coonted 364 o' thae wee buckets comin' oot the watter, and I'll no move a step oot o' here till I see the last o' them!'

"The puir cratur never saw a rale river in his life afore. Och! but Edinburgh's no' that bad; ye can aye be sure o' gettin' yer nicht's sleep in't at ony 'oor o' the day, it's that quate. They're aye braggin' that it's cleaner than Gleska, as if there was onything smert aboot that.

"'There's naething dirtier nor a dirty Gleska man,'" said yin o' them to me ae day.

"'There is,' says I.

"'Whit?' says he.

"'Twa clean Edinburgh yins,' says I.

"Och! but I'm only in fun. Edinburgh's a' richt; there's naething wrang wi' the place ance ye're in it if ye hae a book to read. I hate to hear the wye Duffy and some o' them speak aboot Edinburgh, the same as if it was shut up a' thegither; hoo wad we like it oorsel's? I hae maybe a flet fit, but I hae a warm hert, and I'll aye stick up for Edinburgh. I had an uncle that near got the jyle there for running ower yin o' their tramway caurs. They've no skoosh cars in Edinburgh;[4] they're thon ither kin' that's pu'ed wi' a rope, and whiles the rope breaks; but it doesna maitter, naebody's in ony hurry gaun to ony place in Edinburgh, and the passengers jist sit where they are till it's mended."

"Well, anyhow, Erchie, we're glad to see you back," I said.

"Gled to see me back!" he cried. "I'll wager ye didna ken I was awa', and the only folk that kent we werena in Gleska for the past twa or three months was the dairy and the wee shop we get oor vegetables frae.

"When I was in Edinburgh yonder, skliffin' alang the streets as fast's I could, and nippin' mysel' every noo and then to keep mysel' frae fa'in' asleep, I wad be thinkin' to mysel', 'Hoo are they gettin' on in Gleska wantin' Erchie MacPherson? Noo that they've lost me, they'll ken the worth o' me.' I made shair that, at least, the skoosh cars wad hae to stop runnin' when I was awa', and that the polis band wad come doon to the station to meet me when I cam' hame.

"Dod! ye wad hardly believe it, but ever since I cam' back I meet naebody but folk that never ken't I was awa'. It's a gey hertless place Gleska that way. Noo, in Edinburgh it's different. They're gey sweart to lose ye in Edinburgh ance they get haud o' ye; that's the way they keep up the price o' the railway ticket to Gleska.

"I was tellin' Duffy aboot Edinburgh, and he's gaun through wi' a trip to see't on Monday. It'll be a puir holiday for the cratur, but let him jist tak' it. He'll be better there than wastin' his money in a toon. When Duffy goes onywhere on ony o' the Gleska holidays, it's generally to Airdrie, or Coatbrig, or Clydebank he goes, and walks aboot the streets till the polis put him on the last train hame for Gleska, and him singin' 'Dark Lochnagar' wi' the tears in his een.

"He'll say to me next morning, 'Man! Erchie, thon's a thrivin' place, Coatbrig, but awfu' bad whisky.'

"There's a lot like him aboot a Gleska holiday. They'll be gettin' up to a late breakfast wi' no parridge till't on Monday mornin', and sayin', 'Man! it's a grand day for Dunoon,' and then start druggin' themsel's wi' drams. Ye wad think they were gaun to get twa teeth ta'en oot instead o' gaun on a holiday.

"That's no' my notion o' a holiday, either in the Autumn or the Spring. I'm takin' Jinnet oot on Monday to Milliken Park[5] to see her kizzen that keeps a gairden. We'll hae an awfu' wrastle in the mornin' catchin' the train, and it'll be that crooded we'll hae to stand a' the way. The wife's kizzen 'll be that gled to see us she'll mak' tea for us every half-'oor and send oot each time to the grocer's for mair o' thon biled ham ye aye get at burials. I'll get my feet a' sair walkin' up and doon the gairden coontin' the wife's kizzen's aipples that's no' richt ripe yet, and Jinnet and me 'll hae to cairry hame a big poke o' rhuburb or greens, or some ither stuff we're no wantin', and the train 'll be an 'oor late o' gettin' into Gleska.

"That's a holiday. The only time ye enjoy a holiday is when it's a' bye."

12. *Duffy's First Family*

MORE THAN a year after the King's visit Erchie and I one day passed a piano-organ in the street playing 'Dark Lochnagar.' The air attracted him; he hummed it very much out of tune for some minutes after.

"Do ye hear that?" said he, "'Dark Lochnagar'; I used ance to could nearly play't on the mooth harmonium. I learned it aff Duffy. Him and me was mairried aboot the same time. We lived in the same close up in the Coocaddens — him on the top flet, and Jinnet and me in the flet below. Oor wifes had turn aboot o' the same credle — and it was kept gey throng, I'm tellin' ye. If it wasna Duffy up the stair at nicht, efter his wark was done, rockin' awa' wi' a grudge to the tune o' 'Dark Lochnagar,' it was me below at no' 'Auld Lang Syne,' but yon ither yin ye ken fine. I daresay it was rockin' the credle helped to mak' my feet flet, and it micht hae happened in a far waur cause.

"It was Duffy's first wife; she dee'd, I think, to get rid o' him — the cratur! Duffy's yin o' thae men wi' a great big lump o' a hert that brocht the tear to his ain een when he was singin' 'Bonny Annie Laurie' doon in the Mull o' Kintyre Vaults, but wad see his wife to bleezes afore he wad brush his ain boots for Sunday, and her no' weel. She fair adored him, too. She thocht Duffy was jist the ordinar' kind o' man, and that I was a kind o' eccentric peely-wally sowl, because I sometimes dried the dishes, and didna noo' an then gie Jinnet a beltin'.

"'His looks is the best o' him,' she wad tell Jinnet.

"'Then he's gey hard up!' I wad say to Jinnet when she tellt me this.

"'He's no very strong,' — that was aye her cry, when she was fryin' anither pun' o' ham and a pair o' kippers for his breakfast.

"Duffy's first wean was Wullie John. Ye wad think, to hear Duffy brag aboot him, that it was a new patent kind o' wean, and there wasna anither in Coocaddens, whaur, I'm tellin' ye, weans is that rife ye hae to walk to yer work skliffin' yer feet in case ye tramp on them.

"Duffy's notion was to rear a race o' kind o' gladiators, and he rubbed him a' ower every nicht wi' olive-oil to mak' him soople. Nane o' your fancy foods for weans for Wullie John. It was rale auld Caledonia — parridge and soor dook,[1] that soor the puir wee smout went aboot grewin' wi' its mooth a' slewed to the side, as if it was practising the wye the women haud their hairpins.

"Mony a time I've seen oor Jinnet sneak him into oor hoose to gie him curds and cream; he said he liked them fine, because they were sae slippy.

"'Show your temper, Wullie John,' Duffy wad tell him when onybody was in the hoose; and the wee cratur was trained at that to put on a fearfu' face and haud up his claws.

"'See that! 'Duffy wad say as prood as onything; 'the game's there, I'm tellin' ye.'

"Then Duffy began to harden him. He wad haud him up by the lug to see if he was game, and if he grat that was coonted wan to Duffy, and Wullie John got nae jeely on his piece. He was washed every mornin', winter and summer, in cauld watter in the jaw-box, and rubbed wi' a tooel as coorse as a carrot-grater till the skin was peelin' aff his back.

"'Ye need to bring oot the glow,' Duffy wad say to me.

"'If it gangs on much further,' I tellt him, 'I'll bring oot the polis.'

"Wullie John was fair on the road for bein' an Al gladiator, but he went and dee'd on Duffy, and I never saw a man mair chawed.

"Duffy's next was a laddie too — they ca'd him Alexander. There was gaun to be nane o' their hardenin' dydoes wi' Alexander.

"It was aboot the time Duffy took to politics, and said the thing the Democratic Pairty[2] wanted was educated men wi' brains. He made up his mind that Alexander wad never cairry a coalpoke, but get the best o' learnin' if it cost a pound.

"He wasna very strong, was Alexander, and Duffy fed him maist o' the time on Gregory's mixture,[3] cod-ile, and ony ither stuff he could buy by word o' mooth at the apothecary's withoot a doctor's line. Alexander was getting medicine poored into him that often he was feared to gant in case he wad jar his teeth on a table-spoon when his een was shut. He wore hot-water bottles to his feet in the deid o' summer, and if he had a sair heid in the mornin' afore he started for the school on the geography days he was put to his bed and fed on tapioca. Everything went wrang wi' puir wee Alexander. The hives[4] went in wi' him, and the dregs o' the measles cam' oot. He took every trouble that was gaun aboot except gymnastics; Duffy took him to Professor Coats,[5] the bump-man, and had his heid examined; the Professor said it was as fine a heid o' its kind as ever he saw, and Duffy put a bawbee on the bag o' coals richt aff, and began to put the money bye for Alexander's college fees.

"Alexander's a man noo, and daein' fine. He's in the gas office; the only time he went to college was to read the meter there.

"Ye canna tell whit laddies 'll turn oot, and it's no' ony better wi' lassies. Duffy had a wheen o' lassies; I forget hoo mony there was a'thegither, but when they were coortin' ye wad think ye were gaun doon the middle o' the Hay-makers' country dance when ye cam' up the close at nicht.

"The auldest — she was Annie — was naething particu-lar fancy; she jist nursed the rest, and made their peenies, and washed for them, and trimmed her ain hats, and made Duffy's auld waistcoats into suits for the wee yins, and never got to the dancin', so naebody married her, and she's there yet.

"A' the chaps cam' efter her sisters.

"The sisters never let on aboot the coal-ree and Duffy's lorry, but said their paw was in the coal tred — a kind o' a coal-maister. It was a bonny sicht to see them merchin' oot to their cookery lessons in the efternoons, their hair as curly's onything, and their beds no' made.

"The days they tried new dishes frae the cookery lessons

at hame, Duffy took his meat in the Western Cookin'
Depot, and cam' hame when it was dark. Yin o' them
played the mandoline. The mandoline's a noble instrument; it cheers the workman's hame; a lassie gaun alang
the street wi' a nice print dress, and a case wi' a mandoline,
is jist the sort I wad fancy mysel' if I was a young yin and
there wasna Jinnet.

A fruiterer married the mandoline. The nicht she was
merrit, Duffy sang 'Dark Lochnagar,' and winked at me
like a' that.

"'Learn your dochters the mandoline Erchie,' says he in
my lug, 'and they'll gang aff your haunds like snaw aff a
dyke. That's the advice I wad gie ye if ye had ony dochters
left. I wad hae made it the piano, but we couldna get a
piano up past the bend on the stair.'

"Efter the mandoline went, the boys begood to scramble
for Duffy's dochters as if they were bowl-money,[6] The
close-mooth was never clear o' cabs, and the rice was
always up to your ankles on the stair. Duffy sang 'Dark
Lochnagar' even-on and aye kept winkin' at me.

"'That's the mandoline awa',' says he, 'and the scientific dressmakin', and the shorthand, and the "Curfew
must not Ring To-night," and the revival meetin's, and the
no' very-weel yin that needs a nice quate hame; they're a'
gane, Erchie, and I'm no' gien jeely-dishes awa' wi' them
either. I'm my lee-lane, me and Annie; if ony o' the chaps
cam' efter Annie, I wad chase him doon the stair.'

"'Man ! Duffy,' I says till him, 'ye're selfish enough
workin' aff a' them ornamental dochters on the young men
o' Gleska that did ye nae hairm, and keepin' the best o' the
hale jingbang in the hoose a' the time in case they see her.'

"'Let them tak' it !' says Duffy, 'I'm no' a bit vexed for
them,' and he started to sing 'Dark Lochnagar' as lood as
ever, while Annie was puttin' on his boots.

"That was in Duffy's auld days. He married a second
wife, and it was a fair tak'-in, for he thocht a wee greengro-
cer's shop she had was her ain, and a' the time it was her
brither's.

"'That's the mandoline for you, Duffy,' says I, when he tellt me.

"But that yin died on him too; she died last Mertinmas; Duffy's kind o' oot o' wifes the noo. And the warst o't is that his dochter Annie's gettin' married."

13. *Erchie goes to a Bazaar*

THERE WAS a very self-conscious look on Erchie's face on Saturday when I met him with a hand-painted drainpipe of the most generous proportions under his arm.

"It's aye the way," said he. "Did ye ever hae ony o' yer parteecular freen's meet ye when ye were takin' hame a brace o' grouse? No' a bit o' ye! But if it's a poke o' onything, or a parcel frae the country, whaur they havena ony broon paper, but jist 'The Weekly Mail,' and nae richt twine, ye'll no' can gang the length o' the street without comin' across everybody that gangs to yer kirk."

He put the drain-pipe down on the pavement — it was the evening — and sat on the end of it.

"So you are the latest victim to the art movement,[1] Erchie?" I said. "You will be putting away your haircloth chairs and introducing the sticky plush variety; I was suspicious of that new dado in your parlour the day we had the tousy tea after Big Macphee's burial."

"Catch me!" said Erchie. "Them and their art! I wadna be encouragin' the deevils. If ye want to ken the way I'm gaun hame wi' this wally umbrella-staun', I'll tell ye the rale truth. It's jist this, that Jinnet's doon yonder at the Freemasons' Bazaar wi' red-hot money in her pooch, and canna get awa' till it's done. She's bocht a tea-cosy besides this drain-pipe, and a toaster wi' puce ribbons on't for haudin' letters and papers, and she'll be in luck for yince if she disna win the raffle for the lady's bicycle that she had twa tickets for. Fancy me oot in Grove Street in the early mornin' learnin' Jinnet the bicycle, and her the granny o' seeven!

"Of course, Jinnet's no' needin' ony bicycle ony mair than she's needin' a bassinette,[2] but she has a saft hert and canna say no unless she's awfu' angry, and a young chap, speakin' awfu' Englified, wi' his hair a' Vaseline, got roond her. She's waitin' behin' there to see if she wins the raffle, and to pick up ony bargains just a wee while afore the place shuts up — the rale time for bazaar bargains if ye divna get yer leg broken in the crush. I only went there mysel' to see if I could get her to come hame as lang as she had enough left to pay her fare on the skoosh car, but I micht as weel speak to the wind. She was fair raised ower a bargain in rabbits. It's an awfu' thing when yer wife tak's to bazaars; it's waur nor drink.

"It's a female complaint; ye'll no' find mony men both-ered wi't unless they happen to be ministers. Ye'll no' see Duffy sittin' late at nicht knittin' wee bootees for weans they'll never in this warld fit, nor crochetin' doyleys, to aid the funds o' the Celtic Fitba' Club.[3] Ye micht watch a lang while afore ye wad see me makin' tinsey 'ool ornaments wi' paste-heided preens for hingin' up in the best room o' dacent folk that never did me ony hairm.

"There wad be nae such thing as bazaars if there werena ony weemen. In thoosands o' weel-daein' hames in this Christian toon o' Gleska there's weemen at this very meenute neglectin' their men's suppers to sit doon and think as hard's they can whit they can mak' wi' a cut and a half o' three-ply fingerin' worsted, that'll no' be ony use to ony body, but 'll look worth eighteenpence in a bazaar. If ye miss your lum hat,[4] and canna find it to gang to a funeral, ye may be shair it was cut in scollops a' roond the rim, and covered wi' velvet, and that wee Jeenie pented flooers on't in her ain time to gie't the richt feenish for bein' an Art work-basket at yer wife's stall in some bazaar.

"Maist weemen start it withoot meanin' ony hairm, maybe wi' a table-centre, or a lamp-shade, or a pair o' bedroom slippers. There's no' much wrang wi' that; but it's a beginnin', and the habit grows on them till they're scoorin' the country lookin' for a chance to contribute whit they ca' Work to kirk bazaars and ony ither kinds o' bazaars that's handy. It mak's my hert sair sometimes to see weel-put-on-weemen wi' men o' their ain and dacent faimilies, comin' hame through back-streets staggerin' wi' parcels o' remnants for dressin' dolls or makin' cushions wi'. They'll hide it frae their men as long as they can, and then, when they're found oot, they'll brazen it oot and deny that it's ony great hairm.

"That's wan way the trouble shows itsel'.

"There's ither weemen — maistly younger and no' mairried — that's dyin' for a chance to be assistant stall-keepers, and wear white keps and aiprons, jist like table-maids.

"That's the kind I'm feared for, and I'm nae chicken.

"When they see a man come into the bazaar and nae wife wi' him to tak' care o' him, they come swoopin' doon on him, gie him ony amount o' cleck, jist in fun, and ripe his pooches before he can button his jaicket.

"'I'm no' sayin' they put their hands in his pooches, but jist as bad; they look that nice, and sae fond o' his tie and the way he has o' wearin' his moustache, that he's kittley doon to the soles o' his feet, and wad buy a steam road-roller frae them if he had the money for't. But they're no' sellin' steam road-rollers, the craturs! They're sellin' shillin' dolls at twa-and-six that can open and shut their een, and say 'Maw' and 'Paw.' They're sellin' carpet slippers, or bonny wee bunches o' flooers, or raffle tickets for a rale heliotrope Persian cat. It's the flyest game I ken. When that puir sowl gets oot o' the place wi' naething in his pooches but his hands, and a dazed look in his een, the only thing he can mind is that she said her name was Maud, and that her hair was crimp, and that she didna put a preen in his coat-lapelle when she was puttin' the shillin' rose there, because she said a preen wad cut love. She said that to every customer she had for her flooers that day, wi' a quick look up in their face, and then droppin' her eyes confused like, and her face red, and a' the time, her, as like as no', engaged to a man in India.

"I wonder hoo it wad dae to hae a man's bazaar? They ocht to have made the Freemasons' bazaar a man's yin, seein' the Freemasons 'll no tell the weemen their secrets nor let them into their lodges.

"A man's bazaar wad be a rale divert: naethin' to be sold in't but things for use, like meerschaum pipes, and kahootchy collars, and sox the richt size, and chairs, and tables, and concertinas — everything guaranteed to be made by men and them tryin'.

"The stalls wad be kept by a' the baronets that could be scraped thegither and could be trusted withoot cash registers, and the stall assistants wad be the pick o' the best-lookin' men in the toon — if ye could get them sober enough. If Jinnet wad let me, I wad be willin' to gie a hand mysel'; for though I've a flet fit I've a warm hert, I'm tellin' ye.

"I think I see Duffy walkin' roond the St Andrew's Hall,[5] and it got up to look like the Fall o' Babylon, tryin' to sell bunches o' flooers. Dae ye think he wad sell mony to the young chaps like whit Maud riped? Nae fears! He wad hae to tak' every customer oot and stand him a drink afore he wad get a flooer aff his hands.

"Can ye fancy Duffy gaun roond tryin' to sell tickets for a raffle o' a canary in a cage?

"'Here ye are, chaps and cairters! the chance o' yer lives for a graund whustler, and no' ill to feed!'

"Na, na! a man o' the Duffy stamp wad be nae use for a bazaar, even wi' a dress suit on and his face washed. It wad need young stockbrokers, and chaps wi' the richt kind o' claes, wi' a crease doon the front o' their breeks — Grosvenor Restaurant chaps,[6] wi' the smell o' cigars aff their topcoats, and either ca'd Fred or Vincent. Then ye micht see that the ither sex that hiv a' the best o't wi' bazaars, the wye they're managed noo, wad flock to the man's bazaar and buy like onything. And maybe no'."

Erchie rose off the drain-pipe, and prepared to resume his way home with that ingenious object that proves how the lowliest things of life may be made dignified and beautiful — if fashion says they are so.

"Well, good night, old friend," I said. "I hope Mrs MacPherson will be lucky and get the bicycle."

"Dae ye, indeed?" said he. "Then ye're nae freen' o' mine. We're faur mair in the need o' a mangle."

"Then you can exchange for one."

"I'm no' that shair. Did I ever tell ye I ance won a powney in a raffle? It was at the bazaar oor kirk had in Dr Jardine's time when they got the organ. I was helpin' at the buffet, and I think they micht hae left me alane, me no' bein' there for fun, but at my tred, but wha cam' cravin' me to buy a ticket aff her but the doctor's guid-sister.

"'There's three prizes,' says she; 'a powney wi' broon harness, a marble nock, and a dizzen knifes and forks.'

"'I wad maybe risk it if it wisna for the powney,' I tellt her; 'I havena kep' a coachman for years, and I'm oot o' the way o' drivin' mysel'.'

"'Oh! ye needna be that feared, ye'll maybe no' get the powney,' said she, and I went awa' like a fool and took the ticket.

"The draw took place jist when the bazaar was shuttin' on the Setturday nicht. And I won the powney wi' the broon harness.

"I tore my ticket and threeped[7] it was a mistake, but I couldna get oot o't; they a' kent the powney was mine.

"It was stabled behind the bazaar, and had to be ta'en awa' that nicht. I offered it to onybody that wanted it for naething, but naebody wad tak' it aff my hands because they a' said they had to tak' the car hame, and they wadna be allooed to tak' a powney into a car wi' them. So they left me wi' a bonny-like prize.

"I put its claes on the best way I could, fanklin' a' the straps, and dragged it hame. We lived in the close at the time, and I thocht maybe Jinnet wad let me keep it in the lobby till the Monday mornin' till I could see whit I could dae. But she wadna hear tell o't. She said it wad scrape a' the waxcloth wi' its airn buits,[8] and wad be a bonny-like thing to be nicherrin' a' Sunday, scandalisin' the neebours, forbye there bein' nae gress in the hoose to feed it on. I said

I wad rise early in the mornin' and gaither dentylions[9] for't oot at the Three-Tree Well, but she wadna let me nor the powney inside the door.

"It wasna an awfu' big broad powney, but a wee smout o' a thing they ca' a Shetland-shawl powney, and its harness didna fit it ony place at a'. It looked at the twa o' us, kind o' dazed like.

"'Ye're no' gaun to turn my hoose into a stable, and me jist cleaned it this very day,' said Jinnet.

"'And am I gaun to walk the streets a' nicht wi't?' I asked, near greetin'.

"'Put it oot in the ash-pit, and the scavengers 'll tak' it awa' in the mornin',' she said; and I did that, forgettin' that the mornin' was the Sunday.

"But it didna maitter; the powney wasna there in the mornin', and I took guid care no' to ask for't."

14. *Holidays*

"WELL, ERCHIE; not away on the Fair holidays?" I asked the old man one July day on meeting him as he came out of a little grocer's shop in the New City Road. The dignity of his profession is ever dear to Erchie; he kept his purchase behind his back, but I saw later it was kindling material for the morning fire.

"Not me!" said he. "There's nae Fair holidays for puir auld Erchie, no' even on the Sunday, or I might hae ta'en the skoosh car doon the wye o' Yoker, noo that a hurl on Sunday's no' that awfu' sair looked doon on, or the 'Mornin' Star' 'bus to Paisley. But Jinnet went awa' on Setturday wi' her guid-sister to Dunoon, and I'm my lee-lane in the hoose till the morn's mornin'. It's nae divert, I'm tellin' ye; there's a lot o' things to mind forbye the windin' o' the nock on Setturday and watering the fuchsia. I can wait a municeepal banquet wi' ony man in my tred, but I'm no' great hand at cookin' for mysel'.

"Did I ever tell ye aboot the time the wife was awa' afore

at a Fair, and I took a notion o' a seed-cake Duffy's first wife had to the tea she trated me to on the Sawbath?

"'It's as easy to mak' as boilin' an egg,' says Mrs Duffy, and gied me the receipt for't on condeetion that when I made it I was to bring her a sample. Something went wrang, and I brought her the sample next day in a bottle. It was a gey damp seed-cake thon!

"I havena been awa' at a Fair mysel' since aboot the time Wullie was in the Foondry Boys,[1] and used to gang to the Hielan's. I mind o't fine. Nooadays, in oor hoose, ye wad never jalouse it was the Fair at a' if it wasna for the nae parridge in the mornin's.

"Ye'll hae noticed, maybe, that though we're a' fearfu' fond o' oor parridge[2] in Scotland, and some men mak' a brag o' takin' them every mornin' just as they were a cauld bath, we're gey gled to skip them at a holiday and just be daein' wi' ham and eggs.

"But in thae days, as I was sayin', the Fair was something like the thing. There was Mumford's and Glenroy's shows, and if ye hadna the money to get in, ye could aye pap eggs at the musicianers playing on the ootside, and the thing was as broad as it was lang. Forbye ye didna get the name o' bein' keen on the theatricals if your faither was parteecular.

"I mind ance I hit a skeely-e'ed trombone, or maybe it was an awfuclyde,[3] wi' an egg at Vinegar Hill.[4] The glee pairty[5] — as ye might ca' him if ye were funny — chased me as far doon as the Wee Doo Hill.[6] I could rin in thae days; noo I've ower flet feet, though I've a warm hert too, I'm tellin' ye.

"If ye werena at the Shows in thae days ye went a trip wi' the steamer *Bonnie Doon*,[7] and ye had an awfu' fine time o't on the Setturday if ye could jist mind aboot it on the Sunday mornin'. Duffy's gey coorse, bein' in the retail coal tred and cryin' for himsel'; I'm no' like that at a' mysel'; it widna dae, and me in the poseetion, but I mind aince o' Duffy tellin' me he could never fa' asleep at the Fair Time till his wife gave him the idea o' lyin' on his left side, and coontin' yin by yin a' the drams he had the night afore. He said it worked on him like chloryform.

"I hope ye'll no' mind me speakin' aboot drink; it's awfu' vulgar coonted noo, I hear, to let on ye ever heard that folk tak' it, but in thae days there was an awfu' lot o't partaken o' aboot Gleska. I'm tellt noo it's gaen clean oot o' fashion, and stane ginger's a' the go, and I see in the papers every Monday efter the Fair Setturday that 'there has been a gratifying decrease in the number o' cases at the Central Police Court compared wi' last year.' I'm that gled! I have been seein' that bit o' news in the papers for the last thirty years, and I hae nae doot that in a year or twa drunks and disorderlies 'll be sae scarce in Gleska at the Fair, the polis 'll hae to gang huntin' for them wi' bloodhounds.

"It's a fine thing the Press. It's aye keen to keep oor herts up. Ye'll notice, perhaps, that at every Gleska holiday the papers aye say the croods that left the stations were unprecedented. They were never kent to be ony ither wye.

"I daursay it's true enough. I went doon to the Broomielaw on Setturday to see Jinnet aff, and the croods on the Irish and Hielan' boats was that awfu', the men at the steerage end hadna room to pu' oot their pocket-hankies if they needed them. It's lucky they could dae withoot. When the butter-and-egg boats for Belfast and 'Derry left the quay, the pursers had a' to have on twa watches — at least they had the twa watch-chains, ane on each side, for fear the steamer wad capsize. I says to mysel', 'It's a peety a lot o' thae folk for Clachnacudden and County Doon dinna lose their return tickets and bide awa' when they're at it, for Gleska's a fine toon, but jist a wee bit ower crooded nooadays.'

"I hae nae great notion for doon the watter mysel' at the Fair. Jinnet jist goes and says she'll tell me whit it's like. Whit she likes it for is that ye're never lonely.

"And it's that homely doon aboot Rothesay and Dunoon, wi' the Gleska wifes hangin' ower the windows tryin' as hard as they can to see the scenery, between the whiles they're fryin' herrin' for Wull. And then there's wee Hughie awfu' ill wi' eatin' ower mony hairy grossets.[8]

"But it's fine for the weans, too, to be gaun sclimbin' aboot the braes pu'in' the daisies and the dockens and the dentylions and — and — and a' thae kin' o' flooers ye'll can touch withoot onybody findin' fau't wi' ye. It's better for the puir wee smouts nor moshy[9] in the back-coort, and puttin' bunnets doon the stanks. They'll mind it a' their days — the flooers and the dulse for naething, and the grossets and the Gregory's mixture. It's Nature; it's the Rale Oreeginal.

"It does the wife a lot o' guid to gae doon the watter at the Fair. She's that thrang when she's at hame she hasna had time yet to try a new shooglin'chair we got at the flittin'; but 'it's a rest,' she'll say when she comes back a' moth-eaten wi' the midges. And then she'll say 'I'm that gled it's ower for the year.'

"That's the droll thing aboot the Fair and the New Year; ye're aye in the notion that somethin' awfu' nice is gaun to happen, and naethin' happens at a', unless it's that ye get your hand awfu' sair hashed pu'in' the cork oot o' a bottle o' beer."

"You'll be glad, I'm sure, to have the goodwife back, Erchie?" I said, with an eye on the fire-kindlers. He betrayed some confusion at being discovered, and then laughed.

"Ye see I've been for sticks," said he. "That's a sample o' my hoose-keepin'. I kent there was something parteecular to get on the Setturday night, and thought it was pipeclye. The grocer in there wad be thinkin' I was awa' on the ping-pong if he didna ken I was a beadle. Will ye be puttin' ony o' this bit crack in the papers?"

"Well, I don't know, Erchie; I hope you won't mind if I do."

"Oh! I'm no heedin'; it's a' yin to Erchie, and does nae hairm to my repitation, though I think sometimes your spellin's a wee aff the plumb. Ye can say that I said keepin' a hoose is like ridin' the bicycle; ye think it's awfu' easy till ye try't."

"That's a very old discovery, Erchie; I fail to understand why you should be anxious to have it published now."

Erchie winked. "I ken fine whit I'm aboot," said he. "It'll please the leddies to ken that Erchie said it, and I like fine to be popular. My private opeenion is that a man could keep a hoose as weel as a woman ony day if he could only bring his mind doon to't."

15. *The Student Lodger*

IT WAS with genuine astonishment Erchie one day had his wife come to him with a proposal that she should keep a lodger.

"A ludger!" he cried. "It wad be mair like the thing if ye keepit a servant lassie, for whiles I think ye're fair wrocht aff yer feet."

"Oh, I'm no' sae faur done as a' that," said Jinnet. "I'm shair I'm jist as smert on my feet as ever I was, and I could be daein' wi' a ludger fine. It wad keep me frae wearyin'."

"Wearyin'!" said her husband. "It's comin' to't when my ain wife tells me I'm no' company for her. Whit is't ye're wantin', and I'll see whit I can dae. If it's music ye're for, I'll buy a melodian and play't every nicht efter my tea. If it's improvin' conversation ye feel the want o', I'll ask Duffy up every ither nicht and we'll can argue on Fore Ordination[1] and the chance o' the Celtic Fitba' Club to win the League Championship the time ye're darnin' stockin's. 'Wearyin'' says she! Perhaps ye wad like to jine a dancin' school; weel, I'll no' hinder ye, I'm shair, but I'll no' promise to walk to the hall wi' ye every nicht cairryin' yer slippers. Start a ludger! I'm shair we're no' that hard up!"

"No, we're no' that hard up," Jinnet confessed, "but for a' the use we mak' o' the room we micht hae somebody in it, and it wad jist be found money. I was jist thinkin' it wad be kind o' cheery to have a dacent young chap gaun oot and in. I'm no' for ony weemen ludgers; they're jist a fair bother, aye hingin' aboot the hoose and puttin' their nose into the kitchen, tellin' ye the richt wye to dae this and that, and burnin' coal and gas the time a man ludger wad be oot takin' the air."

"Takin' drink, mair likely," said Erchie, "and comin' hame singin' 'Sodgers o' the Queen,' and scandalisin' the hale stair."[2]

"And I'm no' for a tredsman," Jinnet went on, with the air of one whose plans were all made.

"Of course no'," said her husband, "tredsmen's low. They're no' cless. It's a peety ye mairried yin. Perhaps ye're thinkin' o' takin' in a Chartered Accoontant, or maybe a polisman. Weel I'm jist tellin' ye I wadna hae a polisman in my paurlor; his helmet wadna gang richt wi' the furniture, and the blecknin' for his boots wad cost ye mair than whit he pyed for his room."

"No, nor a polisman!" said Jinnet. "I was thinkin' o' maybe a quate lad in a warehouse, or a nice factor's clerk, or something o' that sort. He wad be nae bother. It's just the ae makin' o' parridge in the mornin'. Ye're no' to thraw wi' me aboot this, Erchie; my mind's made up I'm gaun to keep a ludger."

"If your mind's made up," he replied, "then there's nae use o' me argy-bargyin' wi' ye. I'm only your man. It bates me to ken whit ye're gaun to dae wi' the money if it's no' to buy a motor cairrage. Gie me your word ye're no' gaun in for ony sports o' that kind. I wad hate to see ony wife o' mine gaun skooshin' oot the Great Western Road on a machine like a tar-biler, wi' goggles on her een and a kahootchy trumpet skriechin' 'pip! pip!'"

"Ye're jist an auld haver," said Jinnet, and turned to her sewing, her point gained.

A fortnight after, as a result of a ticket with the legend "Apartments" in the parlour window, Jinnet was able to meet her husband's return to tea one night with the annoucement that she had got a lodger. "A rale gentleman!" she explained. "That weel put-on! wi' twa Gledstone bags, yin o' them carpet, and an alerm clock for waukenin' him in the mornin'. He cam' this efternoon in a cab, and I think he'll be easy put up wi' and tak' jist whit we tak' oorsel's."

"I hope he's no' a theatrical," said Erchie. "Me bein' a beadle in a kirk it wadna be becomin' to hae a theatrical for a ludger. Forbye, they never rise oot o' their beds on the Sunday, but lie there drinkin' porter and readin' whit the papers say aboot their play-actin'."

"No, nor a theatrical!" cried Jinnet. "I wadna mak' a show o' my hoose for ony o' them! it's a rale nice wee fair-heided student."

Erchie threw up his hands in amazement. "Michty me!" said he, "a student. Ye micht as weel hae taen in a brass baun' or the Cairter's Trip[3] when ye were at it. Dae ye ken whit students is, Jinnet? I ken them fine, though I was never at the college mysel', but yince I was engaged to hand roond beer at whit they ca'd a Gaudiamus.[4] Ye have only to tak' the mildest wee laddie that has bad e'e-sicht and subject to sair heids frae the country and mak' a student o' him to rouse the warst passions o' his nature. His mither, far awa' in Clachnacudden, thinks he's hurtin' his health wi' ower muckle study, but the only hairm he's daein' himsel' is to crack his voice cryin' oot impidence to his professors. I'm vexed it's a student, and a fair-heided yin at that: I've noticed that the fair-heided yins were aye the warst."

"Weel, he's there onywye, and we'll jist hae to mak' the best we can wi' him," said Jinnet. "Forbye, I think he's a guid-leevin' lad, Erchie; he tellt me he was comin' oot for a minister."[5]

"Comin' oot for a minister!" said Erchie. "Then that's the last straw! I'm sorry for your chevalier and book-case; he'll be sclimbin' int't some nicht thinkin' it's the concealed bed."

The room door opened, a voice bawled in the lobby, "Mrs MacPherson, hey! Mrs MacPherson," and the student, without waiting his landlady's appearance, walked coolly into the kitchen.

"Hulloo! old chap, how's biz?" he said to Erchie, and seated himself airily on the table, with a pipe in his mouth. He was a lad of twenty, with spectacles.

"I canna complain," said Erchie. "I hope ye're makin' yersel' at hame."

"Allow me for that!" said the student.

"That's nice," said Erchie, blandly. "See and no' be ower blate, and if there's onything ye're wantin' that we havena got, we'll get it for ye. Ye'll no' know whit ye need till ye see whit ye require. It's a prood day for us to hae a diveenity student in oor room. If we had expected it we wad hae had a harmonium."

"Never mind the harmonium," said the student. "For music lean on me, George P. Tod. I sing from morn till dewy eve. When I get up in the morning, jocund day stands on the misty mountain top and I give weight away to the bloomin' lark. Shakespeare, Mr MacPherson. The Swan of Avon. He wrote a fairly good play. What I wanted to know was if by any chance Mrs MacPherson was a weepist?"

"Sir?" said Jinnet.

"Do you, by any chance, let the tear doon fa'?"[6]

"Not me !" said Jinnet, "I'm a cheery wee woman."

"Good!" said Tod. "Then you're lucky to secure a sympathetic and desirable lodger. To be gay is my forte. The last landlady I had was thrice a widow. She shed the tears of unavailing regret into my lacteal nourishment with the aid of a filler, I think, and the milk got thinner and thinner. I was compelled at last to fold my tent like the justly celebrated Arabs of song and silently steal away. 'Why weep ye by the tide, ladye?' I said to her. 'If it were by the pint I should not care so much, but methinks your lachrymal ducts are too much on the hair-trigger.' It was no use, she could not help it, and — in short, here I am."

"I'm shair we'll dae whit we can for ye," said Jinnet. "I never had a ludger before."

"So much the better," said George Tod. "I'm delighted to be the object of experiment — the *corpus vile*, as we say in the classics, Mr MacPherson - and you will learn a good deal with me. I will now proceed to burn the essential midnight oil. Ah, thought, thought! You little know, Mr MacPherson, the weary hours of study —"

"It's no' ile we hae in the room, it's gas," said Erchie. "But if ye wad raither hae ile, say the word and we'll get it for ye."

"Gas will do," said the student; "it is equally conducive to study, and more popular in all great congeries of thought."

"When dae ye rise in the mornin', Mr Tod?" asked Jinnet. "I wad like to ken when I should hae your breakfast ready."

"Rise !" said Tod. "Oh, any time! 'When the morn, with russet mantle clad, walks o'er the dew on yon high eastern hill.'"

"Is't Garnethill or Gilshochill?" said Erchie, anxiously. "I wad rise mysel', early in the mornin', and gang oot to whichever o' them it is to see the first meenute the dew comes, so that ye wadna lose ony time in gettin' up and started wi' your wark."

The lodger for the first time looked at his landlord with a suspicious eye. He had a faint fear that the old man might be chaffing him, but the innocence of Erchie's face restored his perkiness.

"I was only quoting the bard," he explained, as he left the kitchen. "Strictly speaking, the morn with russet mantle clad can go to the deuce for me, for I have an alarm clock. Do not be startled if you hear it in the morning. It goes off with incredible animation."

"Oh, Erchie, isn't he nice?" said Jinnet, when the lodger had withdrawn. "That smert, and aye talks that jovial, wi' a lot o' words I canna mak' heid nor tail o'."

Erchie filled his pipe and thought a little, "Smert's the word, Jinnet," said he. "That's whit students is for."

"I don't think he's very strong," said Jinnet. "If he was in his mither's hoose she wad be giein' him hough soup for his dinner. I think I'll jist mak' some for him to-morrow, and put a hot-water bottle in his bed."

"That's richt," said Erchie; "and if ye hae a haddie or a kippered herrin', or onything else handy, it'll dae for me."

"Ye're jist a haver!" said Jinnet.

For a week George P. Tod was a model lodger.

He came in at early hours of the evening and went to bed timeously, and was no great trouble to his landlady, whose cookery exploits in his interest were a great improvement on anything he had ever experienced in lodgings before.

When he was in his room in the evenings Jinnet insisted on the utmost quietness on the part of her husband. "Mr Tod's at his hame lessons," she would say. "It'll no' dae to disturb him. Oh, that heid wark! that heid wark! It must be an awfu' thing to hae to be thinkin' even-on."

"Heid wark!" said her husband. "I ken the heid wark he's like enough at; he's learnin' the words o' 'Mush, Mush, tu-ral-i-ady 'to sing at the students' procession, or he's busy wi' a dictionary writin' hame to his paw to send him a post-office order for twa pounds to jine the Y.M.C.A. But he's no' thinkin' o' jinin' the Y.M.C.A.; he's mair likely to start takin' lessons at a boxin' cless."

But even Erchie was compelled to admit that the lad was no unsatisfactory lodger.

"I declare, Jinnet," he said, "I think he's yin o' the kind o' students ye read aboot but very seldom see. His faither 'll be a wee fairmer up aboot Clachnacudden, hainin' a' the money he can, and no' giein' his wife her richt meat, that he may see his son through the college and waggin' his heid in a pu'pit. Him and his faither's the stuff they mak' the six shillin' Scotch novells oot o' — the kind ye greet at frae the very start — for ye ken the puir lad, that was aye that smert in the school, and won a' the bursaries, is gaun to dee in the last chapter wi' a decline."

"Puir things," said Jinnet.

"Ye divna see ony signs o' decline aboot Mr Tod, do ye?" asked Erchie, anxiously.

"I didna notice," replied Jinnet, "but he tak's his meat weel enough."

"The meat's the main thing! But watch you if he hasna a hoast and thon hectic flush that aye breaks oot in chapter nine jist aboot the time he wins the gold medal."

"Och, ye're jist an auld haver, Erchie," said the wife. "Ye're no' to be frichtenin' me aboot the puir callant, jist the same age as oor ain Willie."

The time of the Rectorial Election approached, and Tod began to display some erratic habits. It was sometimes the small hours of the morning before he came home, and though he had a latch-key, Jinnet could never go to bed until her lodger was in for the night. Sometimes she went out to the close-mouth to look if he might be coming, and the first night that Erchie, coming home late from working at a civic banquet, found her there, Tod narrowly escaped being told to take his two bags and his alarm clock elsewhere.

"I was needin' a moothfu' o' fresh air onywye," was Jinnet's excuse for being out at such an hour. "But I'm feared that puir lad's workin' himsel' to death."

"Whaur dae ye think he's toilin'?" asked her husband.

"At the nicht-school," said Jinnet. "I'm shair the college through the day's plenty for him."

"The nicht-school! "cried Erchie. "Bonny on the nicht-school! He's mair likely to be roond in Gibson Street[7] batterin' in the doors o' the Conservative committee-rooms, for I ken by his specs and his plush weskit he's a Leeberal. Come awa' in to your bed and never mind him. Ye wad be daein' him a better turn maybe if ye chairged the gazogene[8] to be ready for the mornin', when he'll be badly wantin't, if I'm no' faur mistaken."

Erchie was right — the gazogene would have been welcome next morning. As it was, the lodger was indifferent to breakfast, and expressed an ardent desire for Health Salts.

Erchie took them in to him, and found him groaning with a headache.

"The dew's awfu' late on the high eastern hills this

mornin', Mr Tod," said Erchie. "Losh, ye're as gash as the Laird o' Garscadden![9] I'm feart ye're studyin' far ower hard; it's no' for the young and growin' to be hurtin' their heids wi' nicht-schools and day-schools; ye should whiles tak' a bit rest to yersel'. And no' a bit o' yer breakfast touched! Mrs MacPherson 'll no' be the pleased woman wi' ye this day, I can tell ye!"

Tod looked up with a lack-lustre eye. "Thought, Mr MacPherson, thought!" said he. "Hard, incessant, brain-corroding thought! In the words of the Bard of Avon, 'He who increaseth knowledge increaseth sorrow.'"

"I aye thocht that was 'Ecclesiastes,' Mr Tod," said Erchie, meekly.

"In a way, yes," hastily admitted Tod. "It *was* 'Ecclesiastes,' as you say; but Shakespeare had pretty much the same idea. You will find it in — in — in his plays."

That afternoon began the more serious of Jinnet's experiences of divinity students. Nine young gentlemen with thick walking-sticks visited Tod's apartment *en masse;* the strains of "Mush Mush, tu-ral-i-ady," bellowed inharmoniously by ten voices, and accompanied by the beating of the walking-sticks on the floor, kept a crowd of children round the close-mouth for hours, and somewhat impeded the ordinary traffic of the street.

"There must be a spree on in auld MacPherson's," said the tenement. When Erchie came home he found Jinnet distracted. "Oh, whit a day I've had wi' them students!" she wailed.

"But look at the money ye're makin' aff your room," said her husband. "Wi' whit ye get frae Tod, ye'll soon hae enough for the motor cairrage and a yacht forbye."

"I'm feart to tell ye, Erchie," said Jinnet, "but I havena seen the colour o' his money yet."

"Study! study!" said Erchie. "Ye canna expect the puir lad to be thinkin' even-on aboot his lessons, and learnin' Latin and the rest o't, no' to mention ' Mush Mush,' and still keep mind o' your twa or three paltry bawbees."

"I mentioned it to him on Setturday and he was rale annoyed. He yoked on me[10] and said I was jist as bad as the weedow he lodged wi' afore; that he was shair I was gaun to let the tear doon-fa'. He gied me warnin' that if I let the tear doon-fa' he wad leave."

"If I was you I wad start greetin' at yince," said Erchie. "And he'll leave onywye, this very Setturday."

That afternoon the students were having a torchlight procession, when, as usual, most of them marched in masquerade. It was the day of the Rectorial Election, and the dust of far-flung pease-meal — favourite missile of the student — filled the air all over the classic slopes of Gilmorehill. It had been one of Erchie's idle days; he had been in the house all afternoon, and still was unbedded, though Jinnet for once had retired without waiting the home-coming of her lodger.

There came a riotous singing of students along the street, accompanied by the wheezy strains of a barrel-organ, and for twenty minutes uproar reigned at the entrance to the MacPherson's close.

Then Tod came up and opened the door with his latch-key. He had on part of Erchie's professional habiliments — the waiter's dress-coat and also Erchie's Sunday silk hat, both surreptitiously taken from a press in the lobby. They were foul with pease-meal and the melted rosin from torches. On his shoulders Tod had strapped a barrel-organ, and the noise of it, as it thumped against the door-posts on his entry, brought Erchie out to see what was the matter.

He took in the situation at a glance, though at first he did not recognise his own clothes.

"It's you, Mr Tod!" said he. "I was jist sittin' here thinkin' on ye slavin' awa' at your lessons yonder in the Deveenity Hall. It maun be an awfu' strain on the intelleck. I'm gled I never went to the college mysel', but jist got my education, as it were, by word o' mooth."

Tod breathed heavily. He looked very foolish with his borrowed and begrimed clothes, and the organ on his back, and he realised the fact himself.

"'S all ri', Mr MacPherson," he said. "Music hath charms. Not a word! I found this — this instuimet outside, and just took it home. Thought it might be useful. Music in the house makes cheerful happy homes — see advertisements — so I borrowed this from old friend, what's name — Angina Pectoris, Italian virtuoso, leaving him the monkey. Listen."

He unslung the organ and was starting to play it in the lobby when Erchie caught him by the arm and restrained him.

"Canny, man, canny," said he. "Did I no' think it was a box wi' your bursary. I never kent richt whit a bursary was, but the lad o' pairts in the novells aye comes hame wi' a bursary, and hurts the spine o' his back carryin' his prizes frae the college. I jalouse that's the hectic flush on your face; puir laddie, ye're no' lang for this warld."

Erchie stared more closely at his lodger, and for the first time recognised his own swallow-tail coat.

"My goodness!" said he, "my business coat, and my beadlin' hat. It was rale ill done o' ye, Mr Tod, to tak' them oot withoot my leave. It's the first time ever I was ashamed o' them. Jist a puir auld waiter's coat and hat. I wonder whit they wad say if they kent o't up in Clachnacudden. The auld dominie that was sae prood o' ye wad be black affronted. My business coat! Tak' it aff and gang to your bed like a wise man. Leave the hurdy-gurdy on the stairheid; ye divna ken whit the other monkey micht hae left aboot it, and Jinnet's awfu' parteecular."

Next day Mr Tod got a week's notice to remove, and went reluctantly, for he knew good lodgings when he got them. He paid his bill when he went, too, "like a gentleman," as Jinnet put it. "He was a rale cheery wee chap," she said.

"I've seen faur worse," Erchie admitted. "Foolish a wee, but Nature, the Rale Oreeginal! I was gey throughither[11] mysel' when I was his age. Ye never tellt me yet whit ye wanted wi' the ludging money."

"I was jist thinkin' I wad like to see ye wi' a gold watch

the same as Carmichael's, next door," said Jinnet. "It's a thing a man at your time o' life, and in your poseetion, should hae, and I was ettlin' to gie ye't for your New Year."

"A gold watch!" cried her husband. "Whit nonsense!"

"It's no' nonsense at a'," said Jinnet. "It gies a man a kind o' bien, weel-daein' look, and I thocht I could mak' enough aff ludgers to buy ye yin."

"If it was for that ye wanted the ludger, and no' for a motor cairrage," said Erchie, "I'm gled Tod's awa'. You and your watch! I wad be a bonny like la-di-da wi' a watch at the waitin'; the folks wad be feared to tip me in case I wad be angry wi' them."

And so Erchie has not yet got a gold watch.

16. *Jinnet's Tea-Party*

ERCHIE'S GOODWIFE came to him one day full of thrilling news from the dairy, where she had been for twopence worth of sticks.

"Oh, Erchie, dae ye ken the latest?" said she. "The big fat yin in the dairy's gaun to mairry Duffy!"

"Lord peety Duffy! Somebody should tell the puir sowl she has her e'en on him. I'll bate ye he disna ken onything aboot it," said Erchie.

"Havers!" said Jinnet. "It's him that's wantin' her, and I'm shair it's a guid thing, for his hoose is a' gaun to wreck and ruin since his last wife dee'd. Every time he comes hame to dry his claes on a wet day he's doon in the dairy for anither bawbee's worth o' mulk. The man's fair hoved up[1] wi' drinkin' mulk he's no needin'. I hae catched him there that aften that he's kind o' affronted to see me. 'I'm here again, Mrs MacPherson,' says he to me yesterday when I went doon and found him leanin' ower the coonter wi' a tumbler in his haund. He was that ta'en he nearly dropped the gless."

"It wasna for the want o' practice — I'll wager ye that!"

said Erchie. "He could haud a schooner a hale nicht and him haulf sleepin'."

"'I'm here again,' says he, onywye; 'the doctor tellt me yon time I had the illness I was to keep up my strength. There's a lot o' nourishment in mulk.' And the big yin's face was as red as her short-goon.

"'It's a blessin' the health, Mr Duffy,' says I; 'we divna ken whit a mercy it is till we lose it,' and I never said anither word, but took my bit sticks and cam' awa'."

"And is that a' ye hae to gang on to be blamin' the chap?" said Erchie. "Mony's a man 'll tak' a gless o' mulk and no' go ower faur wi't. But I think mysel' ye're maybe richt aboot the big yin, for I see Duffy's shaved aff his Paisley whiskers, and wears a tie on the Sundays."

Less than a week later the girl in the dairy gave in her notice, and Duffy put up the price of coals another ha'penny. He came up the stair with two bags for Jinnet, who was one of his customers.

"Whit wye are they up a bawbee the day?" says she.

"It's because o' the Americans dumpin'," said Duffy. "They're takin' a' the tred frae us, and there's a kind o' tariff war.²"

"Bless me! is there anither war?" said Jinnet. "Weel, they're gettin' a fine day for't onywye. I hope it'll no put up the price o' the mulk."

Duffy looked at her and laughed uneasily. "I'm kind o' aff the mulk diet the noo," he said, seeing disguise was useless. "Ye're gey gleg,³ you weemen. I needna be tellin' ye me and big Leezie's sort o' chief this while back."

"Man! dae ye tell me?" said Jinnet, innocently. "A rale dacent lassie, and bakes a bonny scone. And she's to be the new mistress, is she? We'll hae to be savin' up for the jeely-pan. I'm shair I aye tellt Erchie a wife was sair wanted in your hoose since Maggie dee'd."

"Jist at the very time I was thrangest," said Duffy, with regret. "I was awfu' chawed at her."

"Ye'll hae to bring yer lass up to see me and Erchie some nicht," said Jinnet. "It's a tryin' time the mairryin'."

"There faur ower mony palavers aboot it," confided the coalman. "I wish it was ower and done wi', and I could get wearin' my grauvit at nicht again. Leezie's awfu' pernicketty aboot me haein' on a collar when we gang for a walk."

"Oh, ye rascal!" said Jinnet, roguishly. "You men! you men! Ah, the coortin' time's the best time."

"Ach! it's richt enough, I daursay; but there's a lot o' nonsense aboot it. Ye get awfu' cauld feet standin' in the close. And it's aye in yer mind. I went to Leezie's close-mooth the ither nicht to whistle on her, and did I no' forget, and cry oot 'Coal!' thinkin' I was on business."

And thus it was that Jinnet's tea-party came about. The tender pair of pigeons were the guests of honour, and Jinnet's niece, and Macrae the night policeman, were likewise invited. Macrae was there because Jinnet thought her niece at thirty-five was old enough to marry. Jinnet did not know that he had drunk milk in Leezie's dairy before Duffy had gone there, and he himself had come quite unsuspicious of whom he should meet. In all innocence Jinnet had brought together the elements of tragedy.

There was something cold in the atmosphere of the party. Erchie noticed it. "Ye wad think it was a Quaker's meetin'," he said to himself, as all his wife's efforts to encourage an airy conversation dismally failed.

"See and mak' yer tea o't, Mr Macrae," she said to the night policeman. "And you, Sarah, I wish ye would tak' yin o' thae penny things, and pass the plate to Mr Duffy. Ye'll excuse there bein' nae scones, Mr Duffy; there hasna been a nice scone baked in the dairy since Leezie left. There's wan thing ye'll can be shair o' haein' when ye're mairret till her, and that's guid bakin'."

Macrae snorted. "What's the maitter wi' dough-feet, I wonder?" thought Erchie, as innocent as his wife was of any complication. "That's the worst o' askin' the polis to yer pairties — they're no' cless; and I'm shair, wi' a' Jinnet's contrivance, Sarah wadna be made up wi' him."

"A wee tete mair tea, Mr Macrae? Leezie, gie me Mr

Macrae's cup if it's oot."

Macrae snorted again. "I'll not pe puttin' her to the bother, Mrs MacPherson," said he, "Murdo Macrae can be passin' his own teacups wisout botherin' anybody."

"Dough-feet's in the dods,"[4] thought Erchie, to whom the whole situation was now, for the first time, revealed like a flash.

"I think, Jinnet," said he, "ye wad hae been nane the waur o' a pun' or twa o' conversation-losengers."

They ate oranges after tea, but still a depression hung upon the company like a cloud, till Erchie asked Macrae if he would sing.

"Onything ye like," said he, "as lang's it's no' yin o' yer tartan chants that has a hunder verses, and that needs ye to tramp time wi' yer feet till't. I've a flet fit mysel', though my hert's warm, and I'm nae use at batin' time."

Macrae looked at Leezie, who had all night studiously evaded his eye, cleared his throat, and started to sing a song with the chorus —

"Fause Maggie Jurdan
She made my life a burden;
I don't want to live,
And I'm gey sweart to dee.
She's left me a' forlorn,
And I wish I'd ne'er been born,
Since fause Maggie Jurdan
Went and jilted me."

Leezie only heard one verse, and then began hysterically to cry.

"Look you here, Mac," broke in Erchie, "could ye no' mak' it the sword dance, or the Hoolichan, or something that wadna harrow oor feelin's this way?"

"Onything that'll gie us a rest," said Duffy, soothing his fiancée. "The nicht air's evidently no' very guid for the voice."

"Coals!" cried the policeman, in a very good imitation of Duffy's business wail; and at that Leezie had to be assisted into the kitchen by the other two women.

Duffy glared at his jealous and defeated rival, thought hard of something withering to hurl at him, and then said "Saps!"

"What iss that you are saying?" asked Macrae.

"Saps! Big Saps! That's jist what ye are," said Duffy. "If I wasna engaged I wad gie ye yin in the ear."

Jinnet's tea-party broke up as quickly as possible after that. When her guests had gone, and she found herself alone in the kitchen with Erchie and the tea dishes he carried in for her, she fell into a chair and wept.

"I'll never hae anither tea-pairty, and that's tellin' ye," she exclaimed between her sobs. "Fancy a' that cairry-on ower a big, fat, cat-witted cratur like thon! Her and her lads!"

"It's a' richt, Jinnet," said Erchie; "you syne oot⁵ the dishes and I'll dry them if ye'll feenish yer greetin'. It's no' the last tea-pairty we'll hae if we hae oor health, but the next yin ye hae see and pick the company better."

17. *The Natives of Clachnacudden*

"You are looking somewhat tired, Erchie," I said to the old man on Saturday. "I suppose you were waiter at some dinner last night?"

"Not me!" said he promptly. "I wasna at my tred at a' last nicht; I was wi' Jinnet at the Clachnacudden conversashion. My! but we're gettin' grand. You should hae seen the twa o' us sittin' as hard as onything in a corner o' the hall watchin' the young yins dancin', and wishin' we were hame. Och, it's a fine thing a conversashion; there's naething wrang wi't; it's better nor standin' aboot the street corners, or haudin' up the coonter at the Mull o' Kintyre Vaults. But I'll tell ye whit, it's no' much o' a game for an auld couple weel ower sixty, though no' compleenin', and haein' their health, and able to read the smallest type withoot specs. I wadna hae been there at a', but Macrae, the nicht polisman that's efter Jinnet's niece, cam' cravin' me to buy tickets.

"'I'm no' a Clachnacudden native,' says I till him. 'If it was a reunion o' the natives o' Gorbals and district, it micht be a' richt, for that's the place I belang to; and if a' the auld natives cam' to a Gorbals swaree I micht get some o' the money some o' them's owin' me. But Clachnacudden! — I never saw the place; I aye thocht it was jist yin o' thae comic names they put on the labels o' the whisky bottles to mak' them look fancy.'

"Ye'll no' believe't, but Macrae, bein' Hielan' and no haein' richt English, was that angry for me sayin' that aboot Clachnacudden, that he was nearly breakin' the engagement wi' Jinnet's niece, and I had to tak' the tickets at the hinder-end jist for peace' sake. Jinnet said it was a bonny-like thing spilin' Sarah's chances for the sake o' a shillin' or twa.

"So that's the wye I was wi' the Clachnacudden chats. Dae ye no' feel the smell o' peat-reek aff me? If it wasna that my feet were flet I could gie ye the Hielan' Fling.

"But thae natives' reunions in Gleska's no' whit they used to be. They're gettin' far ower genteel. It'll soon be comin' to't that ye'll no can gang to ony o' them unless ye have a gold watch and chain, a dress suit, and £10 in the Savin's Bank. It used to be in the auld days when I went to natives gatherin's for fun, and no' to please the nicht polis, that they were ca'd a swaree and ball, and the ticket was four-and-six for yoursel' and your pairtner. If ye didna get the worth o' your money there was something wrang wi' your stomach, or ye werena very smert. Mony a yin I've bin at, either in the wye o' tred, or because some o' Jinnet's Hielan' kizzens cam' up to the hoose in their kilts to sell us tickets. There was nae dress suits nor fal-lals aboot a reunion in thae days' ye jist put on your Sunday claes and some scent on your hanky, wi' a dram in your pocket (if ye werena in the committee), turned up the feet o' your breeks, and walked doon to the hall in the extra-wide welt shoes ye were gaun to dance in. Your lass — or your wife, if it was your wife — sat up the nicht before, washin' her white shawl and sewin' frillin' on the neck o' her guid

frock, and a' the expense ye had wi' her if ye werena
married to her was that ye had to buy her a pair o' white
shammy leather gloves, size seeven.

"A' the auld folk frae Clachnacudden in Gleska were at
thae swarees, as weel as a' the young folk. Ye were packed
in your sates like red herrin' in a barrel, and on every hand
ye heard folk tearin' the tartan[1] and misca'in' somebody at
hame in Clachnacudden. The natives wi' the dress suits
that had got on awfu' weel in Gleska at the speerit tred or
keeping banks, sat as dour as onything on the pletform
lettin' on they couldna speak the tartan. Ithers o' them —
that had the richt kind o' legs for't — wad hae on the kilts,
wi' a white goat-skin sporran the size o' a door-bass[2] hung
doon to their knees fornent them, haudin' in their breaths
in case the minister wad smell drink aff them, and tryin' to
feel like Rob Roy or Roderick Dhu.

"In thae days they started oot wi' giein' ye tea and a
poke o' fancy breid — penny things like London buns and
fruit-cakes; and between the speeches oranges were passed
roond, and wee roond hard sweeties, fine for pappin' at the
folk in front. Ye aye made a guid tea o't, the same as if ye
never saw tea in your life afore, and preferred it weel biled.

"When the tea was bye and the boys were blawin' as
much breath as they had left into the empty pokes, and
bangin' them aff like cannons, the chairman wad stand up
on the pletform and make a speech aboot Clachnacudden.
I used to ken that speech by hert; it was the same yin for
a' the natives' reunions. He said that Clachnacudden
was the bonniest place ever onybody clapped eyes on. That
the Clachnacudden men were notorious a' ower the world
for their honesty and push, and aye got on like onything
if they were tryin', and didna tak' to the drink; and that
the Clachnacudden lassies were that braw, and nice,
and smert, they were lookit up to every place they went.
When he said that the natives o' Clachnacudden kent fine
it was the God's truth he was tellin' them, they got on their
feet and waved their hankies and cheered for ten
meenutes.

"Havin' taken a drink o' watter frae the caraffe at his side — efter makin' a mistake and tryin' to blaw the froth aff the tumbler — the chairman then begood generally to say that Gleska was a gey cauld, sooty, dirty, wicked place for onybody to hae to live in that had been born in the bonny wee glens, and the hulls, and hedges, and things aboot Clachnacudden, but still

' Their herts were true, their herts were Hielan',
And they in dreams beheld the Hebrides.'[3]

At that ye wad see the hale o' the Clachnacudden folk puttin' whit was left o' their pastry in their pouches and haudin' their hankies wi' baith hands to their e'en to kep the tears frae rinnin' on their guid waistcoats or their silk weddin' goons. And the droll thing was that for a' they misca'd Gleska, and grat aboot Clachnacudden, ye couldna get yin o' them to gang back to Clachnacudden if ye pyed the train ticket and guaranteed a pension o' a pound a week.

"Clachnacudden bein' Hielan', they aye started the music efter the chairman's speech wi' a sang frae Harry Linn[4] ca'd ' Jock Macraw, the Fattest Man in the Forty-Twa,' or some ither sang that kind o' codded themsel's. Then the minister made a comic speech wi' jokes in't, and tried to look as game as onything; and the folk frae Clachnacudden leaned forrit on their sates and asked the wifes in front if they had mind wen his mither usd to work in the tawtie field. 'Fancy him a minister!' says they, 'and tryin' to be comic, wi' his mither jist yin o' the MacTaggarts!' A' the time the puir minister was thinkin' he was daein' fine and wonderin' if 'The Oban Times' was takin' doon a' his speech.

"And then a lot o' nyafs in the back sates aye began to heave orange-peelin's at folk that was daein' them nae hairm.

"Efter the swaree was ower, the weemen went into the ladies' room to tak' aff their galoshes, and tak' the preens oot o' their trains, and the men went ower to the Duke o' Wellington Bar, rinnin' like onything, for it was nearly

eleeven o'clock. The folk the hall belanged to started to
tak' oot the sates for the dancin', and sweep the corks aff
the floor; and at eleeven prompt the Grand Merch started.
Whiles they had Adams's or Iff's band, and whiles they jist
had Fitzgerald, the fiddler that used to play on the
Lochgoilhead boat. It didna maitter, for a' the Clachnacudden folk were fine strong dancers, and could dance to
onything. Man! I aye liked the Grand Merch. The man wi'
the reddest kilts aye started it at the Clachnacudden, and
when the Grand Merch got a' fankled, they jist started
'Triumph'; and did the best they could.

"That was in the grand auld days afore they got genteel.
Nooadays, as I'm tellin'; ye, it's a' conversashions, and
they work aff their speeches on ye wi' no tea at a' and no
pokes o' pastry, nor naething. ye're no use unless ye hae
the lend o' a dress suit, and your pairtner has to hae pipe-
clyed shoon, a muslin frock no' richt hooked at the neck,
her hair put up at Bamber's,[5] and a cab to tak' her hame in.
It's naething but the waltzin'. I'm prood to say I never
waltzed in a' my born days, though they say I have the richt
kind o' feet for't, me bein' so lang at the waitin'. And a'
they auld classic dances, like La-va and the Guaracha
Waltz and Circassian Circle's oot o' date; I havena even
seen Petronella for mony a day.

"And the music's a' spiled; it's a' fancy music they hae
noo, wi' nae tune ye can sing to't as ye gang up the back or
doon the middle. Ye'll see them yonder wi' their piano,
three fiddles, and a cornet. If I was gaun to hae a cornet I
wad hae a cornet and no' a brass feenisher.

"Ye'll no' see ony o' the dacent auld Clachnacudden
folk at their modern reunions; the puir sowls has to bide at
hame and gang to ther beds early that they may get up in
time to mak' a cup o' tea for their dochters that was at the
conversashion. No; Jinnet and me's no' keen on
Clachnacudden or onything o' the kind nooadays; we wad
faur sooner stay at hame and read 'The Weekly Mail.'"

18. *Mary Ann*

"I SEE frae 'the News,'" said Erchie, "that Mary Ann's no' gaun to see her kizzen on her nicht oot the noo, but has the kitchen table cleared for action wi' a penny bottle o' Perth ink and a quire o' paper to write letters to the editor, telling him and his readers that the country doesna ken her value.

"If ye're in the habit o' tryin' to keep a general,[1] ye canna be shair but at this very meenute she's doon the stair, wi' her sleeves rowed up and her fingers a' Perth Blue Black, paintin' your wife's photograph as a slave-driver, and givin' your hoose a character that would mak' ye lose your nicht's sleep if ye kent it. Faith, it's comin' to it!

"The servant problem is the only ane that's railly o' ony interest to the country, as far as I can mak' oot frae hearin' things when I'm either beadlin', or waitin' at waddin'-breakfasts. Twa women canna put their heads thegither ower a cup o' tea withoot gaun ower a list o' a' the lassies they've had since last November; and the notion ye get is that they change frae place to place that often they must hae motor cairrages.

"Mary Ann sails in with her kist and a fine character[2] frae her last place on Monday at 8 p.m., and aboot ten minutes efter that she's on the road again. She is the greatest traveller o' the age; it is estimated by them that kens aboot thae things, that the average domestic, if she keeps her health and gets ony chance at a' gangs 15,000 miles every three years shifting her situation.

"It is the age of the lairge-built, agile, country girl; no ither kind can stand the strain o' humpin' kists up and doon area stairs. An aluminium kist that when packed weighs only fifteen pounds has been invented specially for the 'strong and willing general, early riser, no washin', fond o' weans'; but in spite o' that, she canna get ower mair nor 250 to 263 different situations in the year.

"The Hielan's is the peculiar home o' the maist successful domestic servants, though a very gude strain o' them is said to come frae Ayrshire and roon' aboot Slamannan.

"They are catched young, carefully clipped, curry-combed and shod, and shipped to Gleska at the beginnin' o' the winter, wi' fine characters frae the U.F. minister. On the day they start their first situation they're generals, that say 'Whit is't?' quite angry, at the door to folk that come to their mistress's efternoon teas; on the Wednesday they're wanting their wages up; and on the Thursday they start in anither place as experienced hoose- and table-maids. At least, that's whit I gaither frae overhearin' the ladies: we have nae servant in oor hoose — Jinnet does everything hersel'.

"When Mary Ann's no' packin' her kist, or haein' con-fabs wi' the butcher, or trimmin' a frock for the Clachna-cudden natives' swarree and ball, she's lookin' the papers to see the rate o' servants' wages in Kimberley,[3] near whaur the wars were. Some day she's gaun to Kimberley, or Australia, or ony ither foreign pairt, whaur intelligent cooks get the wages o' Cabinet Ministers, and can get mairrit jist as easy's onything.

"In the fine auld times servant lassies used to bide wi' ye till they were that auld and frail ye had to have somebody sittin' up wi' them at nicht.

"Yince they got a fit in yer hoose ye couldna get quat o' them: they fastened their kists to the floor wi' big screwnails, and wad scarcely go oot the length o' the kirk for fear ye wad shut up the hoose and rin awa' and leave them. As for the wages they got, they were that small, folks used to toss up a bawbee to see whether they wad keep a servant or a canary.

"But nooadays a man that's in the habit o' payin' ony heed to the servant lassies that opens the door for him or hands him his letters, thinks it's a magic-lantern show he's at, wi' a new picture every twa seconds.

"He doesna see his wife except on the Sundays, for a' the ither days o' the week she's cyclin' roond the registries wi' five pounds o' change in silver, payin' fees.

"'Hoose-tablemaid, ma'am? Certainly, ma'am; we'll see whit we can dae for ye between noo and the next Gleska

Exhibeetion,' says the registry, rakin' in the half-croons as hard's she can.

"When there's a rumour gets aboot Dowanhill[4] that a servant lass, oot o' a situation, was seen the week afore last, hundreds o' ladies mak' for the registries, and besiege them in the hope o' catchin' her; and of late, I'm tellt they're engagin' trained detectives for trackin' plain cooks.

"Domestic service is the only profession in Europe the day whaur the supply's less than the demand, and if I had twa or three boys ready to gang oot and work for themselves, I wad sooner mak' them into scullerymaids than apprentice them wi' an electrical engineer.

"In the last ten years wha ever heard o' a servant lassie oot o' a situation ony langer than the time she took to rin frae ae hoose to anither, if she had the richt number o' hands and een?

"She disna need to gang onywhere lookin' for a place; the sleuth-hounds o' Dowanhill track her to her lair as soon as she's landed at the Broomielaw or Buchanan Street Station, and mak' a grab at her afore she learns enough o' the language to ask her wye to a registry.

"A new servant in a hoose is like a Field-Marshal back frae the front — she's trated wi' sae muckle deference. Ye daurna mak' a noise through the day for fear it'll spoil her sleep. Ye pit on the fire for her in the mornin', and brush her golfin' buits afore ye start for the office. Ye pay sixpence a day o' car fares for her to go and see ker kizzens in case she's wearyin', puir thing! And if 'Rob Roy's' on at the theatre ye'll be as weel to let her know and gie her tickets for it, or she'll gie notice when she reads the creeticism in the paper and finds oot she missed it. Mair nor a dizzen societies have been started for giving medals and rewards to servant lassies that have been a lang lang while in the ae situation; they're worked on a graduated scale: —

"Hoosemaids, in one situation two months — Bronze medal of the Society and 30s.

"Generals, three months — Silver medal and fountain pen.

"Plain cook, six months — Gold medal, £5, and gramophone.

"Whit the country wants is the municeepilisation[5] o' domestic service. The better hoosin' o' the poor's a thing that there's nae hurry for. Plain cooks and general servants that ken the difference between a cake o' black lead and a scrubbing-brush are a communal needcessity; they can nae mair be done without than gas, water, skoosh cars, or the telephone.

"The Corporations should import and train Mary Anns in bulk, gie them a nate uniform and thirty shillin's a week, and hire them oot 'oorly, daily, weekly, or monthly, as required, reserving for them a' the rights and privileges that belong to them, wi' limitation o' workin' 'oors, strick definition o' duties, stipulated nichts oot, and faceelities for followers. Look at the polis. Ye can depend on gettin' a polisman nine times oot o' ten if ye want him; a lassie to gang oot wi' the pramlater,[6] or a hoose-tablemaid, should be jist as easy got by every ratepayer when wanted, and that's only to be secured by the Corporations takin' the domestic service into their ain haunds."

19. *Duffy's Wedding*

I DID not see Erchie during the New-Year holidays, and so our greetings on Saturday night when I found him firing up the church furnace had quite a festive cheerfulness.

"Where have you been for the past week?" I asked him. "It looks bad for a beadle to be conspicuous by his absence at this season of the year."

"If ye had been whaur ye ocht to hae been, and that was in the kirk, last Sunday, ye wad hae found me at my place," said Erchie. "Here's a bit bride's-cake," he went on, taking a little packet from his pocket. "The rale stuff! Put that below your heid at nicht and ye'll dream aboot the yin that's gaun to mairry ye. It's a sure tip, for I've kent them that tried it, and escaped in time."

I took the wedding-cake. To dream of the one I want to marry is the desire of my days — though, indeed, I don't need any wedding-cake below my pillow for such a purpose. "And who's wedding does this — this deadly comestible — come from, Erchie?" I asked him.

"Wha's wad it be but Duffy's," said Erchie. "'At 5896 Braid Street, on the 31st, by the Rev. J. Macauslane, Elizabeth M'Niven Jardine to James K. Duffy, coal merchant.' Duffy's done for again; ye'll can see him noo hurryin' hame for his tea when his work's bye and feared ony o' the regular customers o' the Mull of Kintyre Vaults 'll stop him on the road and ask him in for something. His wife's takin' him roond wi' a collar on, and showin' him aff among a' her freen's and the ither weemen she wants to vex, and she's him learning to ca' her 'Mrs D.' when they're in company. He wasna twa days at his work efter the thing happened when she made him stop cryin' his ain coals[1] and leave yin o' his men to dae't, though there's no' twa o' them put thegither has the voice o' Duffy. I wadna wonder if his tred fell aff on accoont o't, and it's tellin' on his health. 'She says it's no' genteel for me to be cryin' my ain coals,' he says to me; 'but I think it's jist pride on her part, jist pride. Whit hairm does it dae onybody for me to gie a wee bit roar noo and then if it's gaun to help business?' I heard him tryin' to sing 'Dark Lochnagar' on Friday nicht in his ain hoose, and it wad vex ye to listen, for when he was trampin' time wi' his feet ye could hardly hear his voice, it was that much failed. 'Duffy,' I says till him, takin' him aside, 'never you mind the mistress, but go up a close noo and then and gie a roar to keep your voice in trim withoot lettin' on to her onything aboot it.'

"Yes, Duffy was mairried on Hogmanay Nicht, and we were a' there — Jinnet and me, and her niece Sarah, and Macrae the nicht polis, and a companion o' Macrae's frae Ardentinny, that had his pipes wi' him to play on, but never got them tuned. It was a grand ploy, and the man frae Ardentinny fell among his pipes comin' doon the stair in the mornin'. 'Ye had faur ower much drink,' I tellt him, takin' him oot frae amang the drones and ribbons and things. 'I'm shair ye've drunk a hale bottle.' 'Whit's a bottle o' whusky among wan?' says he. If it wasna for him it wad hae been a rale nice, genteel mairrage.

"Duffy had on a surtoo coat,[2] and looked for a' the warld like Macmillan, the undertaker, on a chape job. He got the lend o' the surtoo frae yin o' the men aboot the Zoo, and he was aye tryin' to put his haunds in the ootside pooches o' them no' there. 'Oh, Erchie,' he says to me, 'I wish I had on my jaicket again, this is no' canny. They'll a' be lookin' at my haunds.' 'No, nor yer feet,' I tellt him; 'they'll be ower busy keepin' their e'e on whit they're gaun to get to eat.' 'If ye only kent it,' says he, 'my feet's a torment to me, for my buits is far ower sma'.' And I could see the puir sowl sweatin' wi' the agony.

"The bride looked fine. Jinnet nearly grat when she saw her comin' in, and said it minded her o' hersel' the day she was mairried. 'Ye're just haverin',' I tellt her, gey snappy. 'She couldna look as nice as you did that day if she was hung wi' jewels.' But I'll no' say Leezie wasna nice enough — a fine, big, sonsy, smert lass, wi' her face as glossy as onything.

"When the operation was by, and the minister had gane awa' hame, us pressin' him like onything to wait a while langer, and almost breakin' his airms wi' jammin' his topcoat on him fast in case he micht change his mind, we a' sat down to a high tea that wad dae credit to F. & F.'s.[3] If there was wan hen yonder there was haulf a dizzen, for the bride had a hale lot o' country freen's, and this is the time o' the year the hens is no' layin'.

"There were thirty-five folk sat doon in Duffy's hoose that nicht, no' coontin' a wheen o' the neighbours that stood in the lobby and took their chance o' whit was passin' frae the kitchen. Duffy hadna richt started carvin' the No. 6 hen when a messenger cam' to the door to ask for the surtoo coat, because the man in the Zoo had his job changed for that nicht and found he needed the coat for his work; so Duffy was quite gled to get rid of it, and put on his

Sunday jaicket. 'Ask him if he wadna like a wee lend o' my
new tight boots,' he says to the messenger frae the Zoo; 'if
he does, come back as fast's ye can for them, and I'll pay
the cab.'

"Efter the high tea was by, the Ardentinny man never
asked onybody's leave, but began to tune his pipes,
stoppin' every twa or three meenutes to bounce aboot the
player he was, and that his name was M'Kay — yin o' the
auld clan M'Kays. Macrae, the nicht polis, was awfu'
chawed that he brocht him there at a'. Ye couldna hear
yersel' speakin' for the tunin' o' the pipes, and they werena
nearly half ready for playin' on when the bride's mither
took the liberty o' stoppin' him for a wee till we wad get a
sang frae somebody.

"'James 'll sing,' says the bride, lookin' as prood's ye like
at her new man. 'Will ye no' obleege the company wi'
"Dark Lochnagar"?'

"'I wad be only too willin',' he tellt her, 'if I had on my
ither boots and hadna ett thon last cookie.' But we got him
to sing 'Dark Lochnagar' a' richt. In the middle o't the
man frae Ardentinny said if Duffy wad haud on a wee he
wad accompany him on the pipes, and he started to tune
them again, but Macrae stopped him by puttin' corks in
his drones.

"Jinnet sang the 'Auld Hoose.' Man! I was prood o' her.
Yon's the smertest wumman in Gleska. The Rale
Oreeginal!"

"Don't you yourself sing, Erchie?"

"Not me! I'm comic enough withoot that. A flet fit and a
warm hert, but timmer in the tune.[4] Forbye, I was too busy
keepin' doon the man frae Ardentinny. He was determined
to hae them pipes o' his tuned if it took him a' nicht. I tried
to get him to gang oot into the back-coort to screw them
up, but he aye said they were nearly ready noo, they wadna
tak' him ten meenutes, and he kept screechin' awa' at
them. It was fair reediculous.

"At last the bride's mither got him put into the kitchen,
and was clearin' the room for a dance. Duffy was very red

in the face, and refused to rise frae the table. 'Whit's the use o' dancin'?' says he; 'are we no' daein' fine the way we are?' And then it was found oot he had slipped his tight boots aff him under the table, and was sittin' there as joco as ye like in his stockin' soles.

"The young yins were dancin' in the room to the playin' o' a whustle, and the rest o' us were smokin' oot on the stairheid, when the man frae Ardentinny cam fleein' oot wi' his bagpipes still gaspin'. He said it was an insult to him to start dancin' to a penny whustle and him there ready to play if he could only get his pipes tuned.

"'Never you heed, Mac,' says I; 'ye'll hae a chance at Macrae's waddin' if ye can get the pipes tuned afore then; he's engaged to oor Sarah.'

"I was that gled when the cat-wutted cratur fell amang his pipes gaun doon the stair in the mornin'; it served him richt."

"And where did Duffy and his bride spend their honeymoon, Erchie?" I asked.

"They took the skoosh car oot to Paisley; that was a' their honeymoon."

20. *On Corporal Punishment*

"ON THIS question of corporal punishment in the schools, Erchie," I said to my old friend, "what are your views? I've no doubt you're dead against any alteration on use and wont."

"Whiles," said Erchie; "whiles! I buy the paper ae day, and when I read the wye brutal and ignorant schoolmaisters abuse their poseetion, I feel that angry I could fling bricks at the windows o' a' the schools I pass on the wye to my wark; but the next day when I read whit perfect wee deevils a' the weans is nooadays, and hoo they'll a' turn oot a disgrace to their faithers and mithers if they divna get a beltin' twice a-day, I'm sair tempted to gae ower to my guid-dochter's in the Calton[1] and tak' a razor-strop to wee Alick afore he gangs to his bed, jist in case he's bein' negleckit. That's the warst o' the newspapers; they're aye giein' ye the differen' sets o't, and ye read sae much on the ae side and then the ither that ye're fair bate to mak' up your mind. My ain puir auld faither — peace be wi' him! — didna seem to be muckle fashed wi' the different sets o't in the newspapers; he made up his mind awfu' fast, and gied ye his fit-rule ower the back o' the fingers afore ye could gie your wee brither a clip on the nose for clypin' on ye. They may abolish corporal punishment in the Gleska schools, but they'll no' pit an end to't in hooses whaur the faither's a plumber and aye has a fit-rule stuck doon the outside seam o' his breeks."

"Ah yes! Erchie, but these paternal ebullitions of ill-temper — "

"Ill-temper or no'," said Erchie, "it's a' in the scheme o' nature, and an angry man's jist as much the weepon o' nature as a thunderbolt is, or a lichted caundle lookin' for an escape o' gas. If ye dinna get your licks in the school for bein' late in the mornin', ye'll get fined an awfu' lot o' times for sleepin' in when ye're auld enough to work in Dubs's;[2] so the thing's as braid as it's wide, as the Hielan'man said."

"Then you seem to think a fit of anger is essential to paternal punishment, Erchie? That's surely contrary to all sober conclusions."

"Sober conclusions hae naethin' to dae wi' skelpin' weans, as I ken fine that brocht up ten o' a family and nearly a' that's spared o' them daein' weel for themsel's. The auld Doctor in oor kirk talks aboot love and chastisement, but in my experience human nature wad be a' to bleezes lang afore this if faithers and mithers didna whiles lose their tempers and gie their weans whit they deserved. If you're the kind o' man that could thresh a puir wee smout[3] o' a laddie in cauld bluid, I'm no', and I canna help it."

"And did you thrash your ten much, Erchie?" I asked, with a doubt as to that essential ill-temper in his case.

"That has naethin' to dae wi't," said he, quickly. "My private disinclination to hae the wee smouts greetin' disna affect the point at a'. If oor yins needed it, I went oot for a daunder and left the job to Jinnet. A woman's aye the best hand at it, as I ken by my aunty Chirsty. When she had the threshin' o' me, she aye gied me tuppence efter it was done if I grat awfu' sair, and I took guid care I never went wantin' money in thae days. I was only vexed she couldna thresh me threepence-worth the time the shows were roond oor wye, and mony's the time I worked for't.

"When the papers mak' me wonder whether corporal punishment's guid for the young or no', I jist tak' a look at mysel' in Jinnet's new wardrobe looking-gless, and, except for the flet feet — me bein' a waiter — I don't see muckle wrang wi' Erchie MacPherson, and the Lord kens there was nae slackness o' corporal punishment in his days, though then it was simply ca'd a leatherin'. My mither threshed me because it wadna gae wrang onywye — if I wasna need'nt the noo I wad be need'nt some ither time; and my faither threshed me because there was a hard knot in the laces o' his boots, and he couldna lowse't. It didnae dae me ony hairm, because I ken't they were fond enough o' me.

"In the school we were weel threshed in the wintertime to keep us warm, and in the summer-time a stirrin'up wi' the tawse a' roond made up for the want o' ventilation. If I never learned much else in the school, I got a fair grup o' naitural history, and yin o' the tips I got was that a horse-hair laid across the loof[4] o' the haund 'll split a cane or cut the fingers aff a tawse,[5] when ye're struck by either the yin or the ither. I made twa or three cairt-horses bald-heided at the tail wi' my experimentin', but somethin' aye went wrang; the maister either let fly ower sudden, or it was the wrang kind o' horse — at onyrate, I never mind o' cuttin' the cane or the tawse.

"Whiles when I'm across at my guid-dochter's, I hear her wee laddie, Alick, greetin' ower his coonts,[6] and fear't the maister 'll cane him because they're no' richt.

"'If a cistern wi' an inlet pipe twa-and-a-half inches in diameter lets in seventy-nine gallons eleeven quarts and seeven pints in twenty-fower and a half 'oors, and an ootlet pipe o' three-quarters o' an inch diameter discharges forty-eight gallons nineteen quarts and five pints in the six 'oors, whit o'clock will the cistern be empty if the ootlet pipe hiz a big leak in't?'

"That's the kind o' staggerer puir wee Alick gets thrashed for if he canna answer't richt. I couldna dae a coont like that mysel', as shair's death, if I was pyed for't, unless I had the cistern aside me, and a len' o' the measures frae the Mull o' Kintyre Vaults, and Jinnet wi' a lump o' chalk keepin' tally. I'm no' shair that it's ony guid to thrash wee Alick for no' can daein' a coont o' that kind, or for no' bein' able to spell 'fuchsia,' or for no' mindin' the exact heights o' a' the principal mountains in Asia and Sooth America.

"Noo wad ye like it yoursel'? Ye canna put mathematics into a callan's heid by thrashin' him ower the fingers, if he's no' made wi' the richt lump in his heid for mathematics; and if Alick's schoolmaister gaes on thinkin' he can, I'll gae oot some day to his school and maybe get the jyle for't."

"Come, come, Erchie," I protested; "you are in quite an inconsistent humour to-day; surely Alick's thrashings are all in the scheme of nature. If he is not punished now for inability to do that interesting proposition in compound proportion, he will be swindled out of part of his just payment when paid for bricklaying by the piece when he has taken to the trade, and the thing — once more as the Highlandman said — is as broad as it's wide."

"Nane o' my guid-dochter's sons is gaun to tak' to treds," said Erchie, coldly; "they're a' gaun to be bankers and electreecians and clerks and genteel things o' that sort. If I'm no' consistent aboot this, it's because o' whit I tellt ye, that I've read ower mony o' thae letters and interviews in the papers, and canna mak' up my mind. I ken fine a' the beltin's I got in the school were for my guid, but — but

— but it's different wi' wee Alick."

"But we have all our wee Alicks, Erchie."

"Then we're a' weel aff," said Erchie, glowing, "for yon's the comicalest wee trate! The Rale Oreeginal."

"But the teachers don't understand him?"

"That's the hale p'int," said Erchie, agreeably; "the teachers never dae. They're no' pyed for understandin' a' the wee Alicks: a' that can be expected for the wages the schoolmaisters get in Gleska is that they'll haul the wee cratur by the scruff o' the neck through a' the standards. The schoolmaister and the mither ought to be mair prized and bigger pyed than ony ither class in the country, but they're no', and that's the reason their jobs are often sae badly filled up.

"If education was a' that folk think it is, there was lang syne hae been nae need for cane nor strap. For mair nor a generation noo, every bairn has had to go to the school — a' the parents o' a' the weans in school the noo have had an education themsel's, so that baith at hame and in the school the young generation of the present day have sae mony advantages ower whit you and I had, they ought to be regular gems o' guid behaviour and intelligence.

"But I canna see that they're ony better than their grandfaithers were at the same age. Except my guid-dochter's boy Alick, I think they're a' worse.

"A' the difference seems to be that they're auld sooner than we were, smoke sooner, and swear sooner, and in a hunner wyes need mair leatherin' than we did. Education o' the heid's no' education o' the hert, and the only thing that comes frae crammin' a callant o' naiturally bad disposeetion with book-learnin' is that he's the better trained for swindlin' his fellow-men when he's auld enough to try his hand at it. I wad be awfu' prood o' every new school that's in Gleska if I didna ken that I had to pye a polis tax for't by-and-bye as well as school tax."

"How glad we ought to be, Erchie, that we were born in a more virtuous age," I said, and Erchie screwed up his face.

"We werena," said he. "It's aye been the same since the start o' things. I've jist been sayin' to ye whit I mind o' hearin' my faither say to mysel'. There'll aye be jist enough rogues in the world to keep guid folk like you and me frae gettin' awfu' sick o' each ither."

21. *The Follies of Fashion*

MY OLD friend has a great repugnance to donning new clothes. His wife Jinnet told me once she had always to let him get into a new suit, as it were, on the instalment system: the first Sunday he reluctantly put on the trousers; the second he ventured the trousers and waistcoat; and on the third he courageously went forth in the garb complete, after looking out at the closemouth first to see that Duffy or any other ribald and critical acquaintance was no tlooking.

I saw a tell-tale crease down the front of the old man's legs yesterday.[1]

"New sartorial splendour, Erchie?" I said, and pinched him for luck.

He got very red.

"You're awfu' gleg in the een," said he; "am I no' daein' my best to let on they're an auld pair cleaned? Blame the wife for't! there's naethin' o' the la-di-da aboot easy-gaun Erchie. But weemen! claes is their hale concern since the day that Adam's wife got the shape o' a sark frae the deevil, and made it wi' a remender o' fig-leafs.

"There's no much wrang wi' Jinnet, but she's far ower pernicketty[2] aboot whit her and me puts on, and if she has naething else to brag aboot she'll brag I hae aye the best-brushed buits in oor kirk. She took an awfu' thraw yince at yin o' the elders, for she thocht he bate me wi' the polish o' his buits, and she could hardly sleep ower the heid o't till I tellt her they were patent.

"'Och!' says she, 'is that a'? Patent's no' in the game.'

"'Onything's in the game,' says I to her, 'that's chaper nor heeling and soling.'

"It's bad enough," he went on, "to be hurtin' yer knees wi' new breeks, and haein' the folk lookin' at ye, but it's a mercy for you and me we're no weemen. You and me buys a hat, and as lang's the rim and the rest o't stick thegither, it's no' that faur oot the fashion we need to hide oorsel's. The only thing I see changes in is collars, and whether it's the lying-doon kind or the double-breisted chats, they hack yer neck like onything. There's changes in ties, but gie me plain black.

"Noo, Jinnet has to hae the shape o' her hat shifted every month as regular's a penny diary. If it's flet in June, it's cockin' up in July; and if the bash is on the left side in August, it has to be on the right side in September.

"Och! but there's no muckle wrang wi' Jinnet for a' that; she wanted to buy me a gold watch-chain last Fair.

"'A gold watch-chain's a nice, snod,[3] bien-lookin' thing aboot a man,' says she, 'and it's gey usefu'.'

"'No, nor usefu',' says I; 'a watch-chain looks fine on a man, but it's his gallowses[4] dae the serious wark.'"

"Still, Erchie," I said, "our sex can't escape criticism for its eccentricities of costume either. Just fancy our pockets, for instance!"

"Ye're right, there," Erchie agreed; "hae I no' fifteen pouches mysel' when I hae my top-coat on? If I put a tramway ticket into yin o' them I wadna be able to fin' oot which o' them it was in for an 'oor or twa.

"Pockets is a rale divert. Ye canna dae without nine or ten in Gleska if ye try yer best. In the country it's different. Doon aboot Yoker, and Gargunnock, and Deid Slow and them places, a' a man needs in the wye o' pouches is twa trooser yins — yin for each haund when he's leanin' against a byre-door wonderin' whit job he'll start the morn.

"There's a lot o' fancy wee pouches that'll no' haud mair nor a pawn-ticket aboot a Gleska man's claes, but in the country they dae wi' less and dig them deep.

"Sae faur as I can see, the pouch is a new-fashioned thing a'thegither.[5] Look at them auld chaps ye see in pictures wi' the galvanised or black-leaded airn suits on; if yin o' them wanted a pouch he wad need to cut it himsel' wi' a sardine-opener, and then he wad peel a' his knuckles feelin' for his hanky or the price o' a pint. I'm gled I wisna gaun aboot when them galvanised airn suits was the go; it must hae been awfu' sair on the nails scratchin' yersel'. Yer claes were made then in a biler-works. When ye went for the fit-on, the cutter bashed in the slack bits at the back wi' a hammer and made it easier for ye under the oxter wi' a cauld chisel.

"'I want it higher at the neck,' says you.

"'Right!' says he, quite game, and bangs in twa or three extra rivets. And your wife, if ye had yin, had to gie your suits a polish up every Friday when she was daein' the kitchen grate.

"It was the same when the Hielan's was the wye ye read aboot in books, and every Hielan'man wore the kilts.

"There was nae pocket in a pair of kilts.

"I daursay that was because the Hielan'man never had onything worth while to put in a pocket if he had yin. He hung his snuff-mull and his knife and fork ootside his claes, and kept his skean-dhu in his stockin'.

"It's a proof that weemen's no' richt ceevilised yet that they can be daein', like the men I'm speaking aboot, withoot ony pooches. Jinnet tells me there's nae pooch in a woman's frock nooadays, because it wad spoil her sate on the bicycle. That's the wye ye see weemen gaun aboot wi' their purses in their haunds, and their bawbees for the skoosh car inside their glove, and their bonny wee watches that never gang because they're never rowed up, hingin' just ony place they'll hook on to ootside their claes.

"I was yince gaun doon to Whiteinch on a Clutha[6] to see a kizzen o' the wife's, and Jinnet was wi' me. Me bein' caury-haunded,[7] I got aff by mistake at Govan on the wrang side o' the river, when Jinnet was crackin' awa' like a pengun wi' some auld wife at the sherp end o' the boat, and she didna see me.

"'Oh! Erchie!' she says when she cam' hame, 'the time I've put in! I thocht ye wis drooned.'

"'And ye hurried hame for the Prudential book,[8] I suppose?' says I.

"'No,' says she, 'but I made up my mind to hae a pooch o' my ain efter this, if I merrit again, to haud my ain Clutha fares, and no' be lippenin'[9] to onybody.'"

22. *Erchie in an Art Tea-Room*

"I saw you and Duffy looking wonderfully smart in Sauchiehall Street on Saturday," I said to Erchie one morning.

"Man, were we no'?" replied the old man, with an amused countenance. "I must tell ye the pant we had. Ye'll no' guess where I had Duffy. Him and me was in thon new tea-room wi' the comic windows.[1] Yin o' his horses dee'd on him, and he was doon the toon liftin' the insurance for't. I met him comin' hame wi' his Sunday claes on, and the three pound ten he got for the horse. He was that prood he was walkin' sae far back on his heels that a waff o' win' wad hae couped him, and whustlin' 'Dark Lochnagar.'

"'Come on in somewhere and hae something,' says he, quite joco.

"'Not me,' says I — 'I'm nane o' the kind; a beadle's a public man, and he disna ken wha may be lookin' at him, but I'll tell ye whit I'll dae wi' ye — I'll tak' ye into a tea-room.' 'A' richt,' says Duffy; 'I'm game for a pie or onything.'

"And I took him like a lamb to the new place.

"When we came fornent it, he glowered, and 'Michty!' says he, 'wha did this?'

"'Miss Cranston,'[2] says I.

"'Was she tryin'?' says Duffy.

"'She took baith hands to't,' I tellt him. 'And a gey smert wumman, too, if ye ask me.'

"He stood five meenutes afore I could get him in, wi' his een glued on the fancy doors.

"'Do ye hae to break yer wey in?' says he.

"'No, nor in, I tells him; look slippy in case some o' yer customers sees ye!'

"'Och! I havena claes for a place o' the kind,' says he, and his face red.

"'Man!' I says, 'ye've henned — that's whit's wrang wi' ye: come in jist for the pant; naebody 'll touch ye, and ye'll can come oot if it's sore'

"In we goes, Duffy wi' his kep aff. He gave the wan look roond him, and put his hand in his pooch to feel his money. 'Mind I have only the three flaffers and a half,[3] Erchie,' says he.

"'It'll cost ye nae mair than the Mull o' Kintyre Vaults,' I tellt him, and we began sclimmin' the stairs. Between every rail there was a piece o' gless like the bottom o' a soda-water bottle, hangin' on a wire; Duffy touched every yin o' them for luck.

"'Whit dae ye think o' that, noo?' I asked him.

"'It's gey fancy,' says Duffy; 'will we be lang?'

"'Ye puir ignorant cratur!' I says, losin' my patience a'thegither, 'ye havena a mind in the dietin' line above a sate on the trams o' a lorry[4] wi' a can o' soup in your hand.'

"I may tell ye I was a wee bit put aboot mysel', though I'm a waiter by tred, and seen mony a dydo in my time. There was naething in the hale place was the way I was accustomed to; the very snecks o' the doors were kind o' contrairy.

"'This way for the threepenny cups and the guid bargains,' says I to Duffy, and I lands him into whit they ca' the Room de Looks.[5] Maybe ye havena seen the Room de Looks; it's the colour o' a goon Jinnet use to hae afore we mairried: there's whit Jinnet ca's insertion on the table-cloths, and wee beeds stitched a' ower the wa's the same as if somebody had done it themsel's. The chairs is no' like ony other chairs ever I clapped eyes on, but ye could easy guess they were chairs; and a' roond the place there's a

lump o' lookin'-gless wi' purple leeks[6] pented on it every
noo and then. The gasalier in the middle was the thing that
stunned me. It's hung a' roond wi' hunners o' big gless
bools,[7] the size o' yer nief — but ye don't get pappin'
onything at them.

"Duffy could only speak in whispers. 'My Jove!' says he,
'ye'll no' get smokin' here, I'll bate.'

"'Smokin'!' says I; 'ye micht as weel talk o' gowfin'.'

"'I never in a' my life saw the like o't afore. This cows
a'!' says he, quite nervous and frichtened lookin'.

"'Och!' says I, 'it's no' your fau't; you didna dae't
onywye. Sit doon.'

"There was a wheen lassies wi' white frocks and tippets
on for waitresses, and every yin o' them wi' a string o' big
red beads roond her neck.

"'Ye'll notice, Duffy,' says I, 'that though ye canna get
ony drink here, ye can tak' a fine bead[8] onywye,' but he
didna see my joke.

"'Chaps me no'!' says he. 'Whit did ye say the name o'
this room was?'

"'The Room de Looks,' I tellt him.

"'It'll likely be the Room de Good Looks,' says he,
lookin' at the waitress that cam' for oor order. 'I'm for a pie
and a bottle o' Broon Robin.'

"'Ye'll get naething o' the kind. Ye'll jist tak' tea, and
stretch yer hand like a Christian for ony pastry ye want,'
said I, and Duffy did it like a lamb. Oh! I had the better o'
him; the puir sowl never saw onything fancy in his life afore
since the time Glenroy's was shut in the New City Road,
where the Zoo[9] is. It was a rale divert. It was the first time
ever he had a knife and fork to eat cookies wi', and he
thocht his teaspoon was a' bashed oot o' its richt shape till
I tellt him that was whit made it Art.

"'Art,' says he, 'whit the mischief's Art?'

"'I can easy tell ye whit Art is,' says I, 'for it cost me
mony a penny. When I got mairried, Duffy, haircloth
chairs was a' the go; the sofas had twa ends to them,
and you had to hae six books wi' different coloured

batters[10] spread oot on the paurlor table, wi' the tap o' yer weddin'-cake under a gless globe in the middle. Wally dugs[11] on the mantelpiece, worsted things on the chair-backs, a picture o' John Knox ower the kist o' drawers, and 'Heaven Help Our Home' under the kitchen clock — that was whit Jinnet and me started wi'. There's mony a man in Gleska the day buyin' hand-done pictures and wearin' tile hats to their work that begun jist like that. When Art broke oot — '

"'I never took it yet,' says Duffy.

"'I ken that,' says I, 'but it's ragin' a' ower the place; ye'll be a lucky man if ye're no' smit wi't cairryin' coals up thae new tenements they ca' mansions, for that's a hotbed o' Art. But as I say, when Art broke oot, Jinnet took it bad, though she didna ken the name o' the trouble, and the haircloth chairs had to go, and leather yins got, and the sofa wi' the twa ends had to be swapped for yin wi' an end cut aff and no' richt back. The wally dugs, and the worsted things, and the picture o' John Knox, were nae langer whit Jinnet ca'd the fashion, and something else had to tak' their place. That was Art: it's a lingerin' disease; she has the dregs o't yet, and whiles buys shillin' things that's nae use for onything except for dustin'.'

"'Oh! is that it?' says Duffy; 'I wish I had a pie.'

"'Ye'll get a pie then,' I tellt him, 'but ye canna expect it here; a pie's no' becomin' enough for the Room de Looks. Them's no' chairs for a coalman to sit on eatin' pies.'

"We went doon the stair then, and I edged him into the solid meat department. There was a lassie sittin' at a desk wi' a wheen o' different coloured bools afore her, and when the waitresses cam' to her for an order for haricot mutton or roast beef or onything like that frae the kitchen, she puts yin o' the bools doon a pipe[12] into the kitchen, and the stuff comes up wi' naething said.

"'Whit dae ye ca' that game?' asks Duffy, lookin' at her pappin' doon the bools; 'it's no' moshy, onywye.'

"'No, nor moshy,' I says to him. 'That's Art. Ye can hae yer pie frae the kitchen withoot them yellin' doon a pipe for't and lettin' a' the ither customers ken whit ye want.'

"When the pie cam' up, it was jist the shape o' an ordinary pie, wi' nae beads nor onything Art aboot it, and Duffy cheered up at that, and said he enjoyed his tea."

"I hope the refining and elevating influence of Miss Cranston's beautiful rooms will have a permanent effect on Duffy's taste," I said.

"Perhaps it will," said Erchie; "but we were nae sooner oot than he was wonderin' where the nearest place wad be for a gless o' beer."

23. *The Hidden Treasure*

"I WISH somebody would leave me some money," said Jinnet, "and the first thing I would dae wi't would be to buy ye a new topcoat. That yin's gettin' gey shabby, and that glazed I can almaist see my face in the back o't."

"Then ye're weel aff," said Erchie, "for there's seldom ye'll see a bonnier yin in a better lookin'-gless."

"Oh, ye auld haver!" cried Jinnet, pushing him. "I wonder ye divna think shame to be talkin' like a laddie to his first lass; and me jist a done auld body! If I could jist get a shape I wad buy a remnant and mak' ye a topcoat mysel'. I could dae't quite easy."

"I ken fine that," said her husband, "but I'll bate ye would put the buttons on the wrang side, the wye ye did wi' yon waistcoat. It's a droll thing aboot weemen's claes that they aye hae their buttons on caurey-handed. It jist lets ye see their contrairiness."

"Oh! it's a peety ye mairried me," said Jinnet; "a contrairy wife must be an awfu' handfu'."

"Weel, so ye are contrairy," said Erchie firmly.

"It tak's twa to be contrairy, jist the same wye as it tak's twa to mak' a quarrel," said Jinnet, picking some fluff off his sleeve. "Whit wye am I contrairy I would like to ken?"

"If ye werena contrairy, ye would be thinkin' o' buyin' something for yersel' instead o' a topcoat for me, and ye're

far mair needn't," said Erchie, and with that a knock came
to the door.

"There's somebody," said Jinnet hastily; "put on the
kettle."

"Come awa' in, Mr Duffy, and you, Mrs Duffy," said
Jinnet; "we're rale gled to see ye, Erchie and me. I was jist
puttin' on the kettle to mak' a drap tea."

Duffy and his wife came into the cosy light and warmth
of the kitchen, and sat down. There was an elation in the
coalman's eye that could not be concealed.

"My jove! I've news for ye the nicht," said he, taking out
his pipe and lighting it.

"If it's that the bag o' coals is up anither bawbee," said
Erchie, "there's nae hurry for't. It's no' awfu' new news
that onywye."

"Ye needna be aye castin' up my tred to me," protested
Duffy. "Whaur would ye be wantin' coals?"

"Mr MacPherson's quite richt," said Mrs Duffy;
"everybody kens it's no' an awfu' genteel thing sellin'
coals, they're that — that black. I'm aye at him, Mrs
MacPherson, to gie up the ree and the lorries and start a
eatin'-house. I could bake and cook for't fine. Noo that
this money's comin' to us, we could dae't quite easy. Look
at the profit aff mulk itsel'!"

"Dear me! hae ye come into a fortune?" cried Jinnet
eagerly. "Isn't that droll? I was jist saying to Erchie that I
wisht somebody would leave me something and I would
buy him a new topcoat."

"That'll be a' richt," said Duffy. "If he'll gie me a haund
wi' this thing I called aboot the nicht, I'll stand him the
finest topcoat in Gleska, if it costs a pound."

"If it's ca'in on lawyers and the like o' that ye want me to
dae," said Erchie, "I'm nae use to ye. I've a fine wye wi' me
for ministers and the like o' that, that's no' aye wantin' to
get the better o' ye, but lawyers is different. I yince went to
a lawyer that was a member in oor kirk to ask him if he

didna think it was time for him to pay his sate-rents.
He said he would think it ower, and a week efter that he sent
me an account for six-and-eightpence for con-sultation.
But I'm prood to hear ye've come in for something, Duffy,
whether I get a topcoat or no'. I never kent ye had ony rich
freen's at a'. Faith, ye're weel aff; look at me, I havena a
rich freen' in the warld except — except Jinnet."

"Oh, I never kent she was that weel aff," cried Mrs Duffy.

"Is it her!" said Erchie. "She has that much money in
the bank that the bank clerks touch their hats to her in the
street if she has on her Sunday claes. But that wasna whit I
was thinkin' o'; there's ither kinds o' riches besides the sort
they keep in banks."

"Never mind him, he's an auld fuiter," said Jinnet,
spreading a table cloth on the table and preparing for the
tea. "I'm shair I'm gled to hear o' your good luck. It
doesna dae to build oorsel's up on money, for money's no
everything, as the pickpocket said when he took the watch
as weel; but we're a' quite ready to thole't. Ye'll be
plannin' whit ye'll dae wi't, Mrs Duffy?"

"First and foremost we're gaun to get rid o' the ree, at
onyrate," said Mrs Duffy emphatically. "Then we're gaun
to get a piano."

"Can ye play?" asked Erchie.

"No," admitted Mrs Duffy, "but there's nae need tae
play sae lang's ye can get a vinolia[1] to play for ye. I think
we'll flit at the term to yin o' yon hooses roond the corner,
wi' the tiled closes,[2] and maybe keep a wee servant lassie.
I'm that nervous at havin' to rise for the mulk in the
mornin'. No' an awfu' big servant wi' keps and aiprons, ye
understaund, but yin I could train into the thing. I'm no'
for nane o' your late dinners: I jist like to tak' something in
my hand for my supper."

"Och ay, ye'll can easy get a wee no' awfu' strong yin frae
the country, chape," said Erchie. "Ye must tak' care o' yer ain
health, Mrs Duffy, and if ye're nervous, risin' in the mornin'
to tak' in the mulk's no' for ye. But my! ye'll no' be for
speakin' to the like o' us when ye come into your fortune."

"It's no' exactly whit ye wad ca' a fortune," Duffy explained, as they drew in their chairs to the table.

"But it's a heap o' money to get a' at yince withoot daein' onything for't."

"Will ye hae to gang into mournin's for the body that left it?" Jinnet asked Mrs Duffy. "I ken a puir weedow wumman that would come to the hoose to sew for ye."

"Ye're aff it a'thegither," said Duffy. "It's naebody that left it to us — it's a medallion. Whit I wanted to ask ye, Erchie, is this — whit's a medallion?"

"Jist a kind o' a medal," said Erchie.

"My jove!" said Duffy, "the wife was richt efter a'. I thocht it was something for playin' on, like a melodian. Weel, it doesna maitter, ye've heard o' the hidden treasure the newspapers's puttin' here and there roond the country? I ken where yin o' them's hidden. At least I ken where there's a medallion."

"Oh, hoo nice!" said Jinnet. "It's awfu' smert o' ye, Mr Duffy. I was jist readin' aboot them, and was jist hopin' some puir body wad get them."

"No' that poor naither!" said Mrs Duffy, with a little warmth.

"Na, na, I wasna sayin' — I didna mean ony hairm," said poor Jinnet. "Streetch yer hand, and tak' a bit cake. That's a rale nice brooch ye hae gotten."

Erchie looked at Duffy dubiously. For a moment he feared the coalman might be trying on some elaborate new kind of joke, but the complacency of his face put it out of the question.

"Then my advice to you, Duffy, if ye ken where the medallion is," said Erchie, "is to gang and howk it up at yince, or somebody 'll be there afore ye. I warrant it'll no' get time to tak' root if it's within a penny ride on the Gleska skoosh cars. There's thoosands o' people oot wi' lanterns at this very meenute scrapin' dirt in the hunt for that medallion. Hoo do ye ken whaur it is if ye havena seen it?"

"It's there richt enough," said Mrs Duffy; "it's in the paper, and we're gaun to gie up the ree; my mind's made

up on that. I hope ye'll come and see us sometime in our
new hoose — house."

"It says in the paper," said Duffy, "that the medallion's
up a street that has a public-hoose at each end o't, and a
wee pawn in the middle, roond the corner o' anither street,
where ye can see twa laundries at yince, and a sign ower yin
o' them that puts ye in mind o' the battle o' Waterloo, then
in a parteecular place twenty yairds to the richt o' a pend-
close wi' a barrow in't."

Erchie laughed. "Wi' a barrow in't?" said he.

"They micht as weel hae said wi' a polisman in't; barrows is like bobbies — if ye think ye'll get them where ye
want them ye're up a close yersel'. And whit's the
parteecular place, Duffy?"

Duffy leaned forward and whispered mysteriously, "MY
COAL-REE."

"But we're gaun to gie't up," explained his wife.

"Oh, ay, we're gaun to give the ree up. Ye hae no idea
whaur — where — I could get a smert wee lassie that
would not eat awfu' much, Mrs MacPherson?"

"I measured it a' aff," Duffy went on. "It's oor street
richt enough; the pubs is there — "

"— I could bate ye they are," said Erchie. "If they
werena there it wad be a miracle."

" — and the laundries is there. 'Colin Campbell' over yin
o' them, him that bate Bonypart, ye ken, and twenty yairds
frae the pend-close is richt under twenty ton o' coal I put in
last week. It's no' M'Callum's wid-yaird; it's my ree."

"My papa was the sole proprietor of a large widyaird,"
irrelevantly remarked Mrs Duffy, who was getting more
and more Englified as the details of the prospective fortune
came out.

"Was he, indeed," said Jinnet. "That was nice!"

"Noo, whit I wanted you to dae for me," Duffy went on,
"was to come awa' doon wi' me the nicht and gie's a hand
to shift thae coals. I daurna ask ony o' my men to come, for
they wad claim halfers."

Erchie toyed with a teaspoon and looked at the coalman, half in pity, half with amusement. "Man, ye're a rale divert," said he at last. "Do ye think the newspapers would be at the bother o' puttin' their medallion under twenty ton o' coal in your coal-ree, or onybody else's? Na, na, they can mak' their money easier nor that. If ye tak' my advice, ye'll put a penny on the bag o' coal and gie short wecht, and ye'll mak' your fortune far shairer than lookin' under't for medallions."

"Then ye're no' game to gie's a hand?" said Duffy, starting another cookie. "See's the sugar."

"Not me!" said Erchie promptly. "I've a flet fit and a warm hert, but I'm no' a'thegither a born idiot to howk coal for medallions that's no' there."

Next day Duffy came up with two bags of coals which Jinnet had ordered.

"Did ye find the medallion?" she asked him.

"I didna need to look for't," he replied. "I heard efter I left here last nicht that a man found it in a back-coort in the Garscube Road. Them sort of dydoes should be put doon by the polis."

"Oh, whit a peety!" said Jinnet. "And hoo's the mistress the day?"

"She's fine," said Duffy. "She's ca'in' me Jimmy again; it was naething but Mr Duffy wi' her as lang's she thocht we were to get rid o' the ree."

24. *The Valenteen*

ON THE night of the last Trades House[1] dinner I walked home with Erchie when his work was done. It was the 13th of February. There are little oil-and-colour shops in New City Road, where at that season the windows become literary and artistic, and display mock valentines. One of these windows caught my old friend's eye, and he stopped to look in.

"My!" he said, "time flies! It was only yesterday we had

the last o' oor Ne'erday currant-bun, and here's the valenteens! That minds me I maun buy — " He stopped and looked at me, a little embarrassed.

I could only look inquiry back at him.

"Ye'll think I'm droll," said he, "but it just cam' in my heid to buy a valenteen. To-morrow's Jinnet's birthday, and it would be a rale divert to send her ladyship yin and tak' a kind o' rise oot o' her. Come and gie's a hand to pick a nice yin."

I went into the oil-and-colour shop, but, alas! for the ancient lover, he found there that the day of sentiment was done so far as the 14th of February was concerned.

"Hae ye ony nice valenteens?" he asked a boy behind the counter.

"It's a comic ye mean?" asked the boy, apparently not much amazed at so strange an application from an elderly gentleman.

"A comic!" said my friend in disdain. "Dae I look like the kind o' chap that sends mock valenteens? If ye gie me ony o' your chat I'll tell yer mither, ye wee — ye wee rascal! Ye'll be asking me next if I want a mooth harmonium. Dae ye think I'm angry wi' the cook in some hoose roond in the terraces because she' chief wi' the letter-carrier? I'll comic ye!"

"Weel, it's only comics we hae," said the youthful shop-keeper; "the only ither kind we hae's Christmas cairds, and I think we're oot o' them."

He was a business-like boy — he flung a pile of the mock valentines on the counter before us.

Erchie turned them over with contemptuous fingers. "It's a gey droll age we live in," said he to me. "We're far ower funny, though ye wadna think it to see us. I have a great respect for valenteens, for if it wasna for a valenteen there maybe wadna hae been ony Jinnet — at least in my hoose. I wad gie a shillin' for a rale auld-fashioned valenteen that gaed oot and in like a concertina, wi' lace roond aboot it, and a smell o' scent aff it, and twa silver herts on't skewered through the middle the same as it was for brandering. Ye havena seen mony o' that kind, laddie?

Na, I daursay no'; they were oot afore your time, though I thocht ye micht hae some in the back-shop. They were the go when we werena nearly sae smert as we are nooadays. I'm gled I havena to start the coortin' again."

He came on one of the garish sheets that was less vulgar than the others, with the picture of a young lady under an umbrella, and a verse of not unkindly doggerel.

"That'll hae to dae," said he, "although it's onything but fancy."

"I hope," said I dubiously, "that Mrs MacPherson will appreciate it."

"She's the very yin that will," he assured me, as he put it in his pocket. "She's like mysel'; she canna play the piano, but she has better gifts — she has the fear o' God and a sense o' humour. You come up the morn's nicht at eight, afore the post comes, and ye'll see the ploy when she gets her valenteen. I'll be slippin' oot and postin't in the forenoon. Though a young lassie canna get her valenteens ower early in the mornin', a mairried wife's 'll dae very weel efter her wark's done for the day."

"It's yersel'?" said Mrs MacPherson when I went to her door. "Come awa' in. I kent there was a stranger comin' — though indeed I wadna be ca'in' you a stranger — for there was a stranger on the ribs o' the grate this mornin', and a knife fell aff the table when we were at oor tea."

"Ay, and who knocked it aff deeliberate?" interposed her husband, rising to welcome me. "Oh, she's the sly yin. She's that fond to see folk come aboot the hoose she whiles knocks a knife aff the table to see if it'll bring them."

"Oh, Erchie MacPherson!" cried his wife.

"I'm no' blamin' ye," he went on; "I ken I'm gey dreich company for onybody. I havena a heid for mindin' ony scandal aboot the folk we ken, and I canna understaund politics noo that Gledstone's no' to the fore, and I canna sing, or play a tune on onything."

"Listen to him!" cried Jinnet. "Isn't he the awfu' man?

Did ye ever hear the like o' him for nonsense?"

The kettle was on the fire: I knew from experience that it had been put there when my knock came to the door, for so the good lady's hospitality always manifested itself, so that her kettle was off and on the fire a score of times a-day, ready to be brought to the boil if it was a visitor who knocked, and not a beggar or a pedlar of pipeclay.

"Tak' a watter biscuit," Jinnet pressed me as we sat at the table; "they're awfu' nice wi' saut butter."

"Hae ye nae syrup to put on them?" asked her husband with a sly glance.

"Nane o' yer nonsense," she exclaimed, and attempted a diversion in the conversation, but Erchie plainly had a joke to retail.

"I'll tell ye a baur aboot watter biscuits and syrup," said he. "When I was coortin' my first lass I wasna mair nor nineteen years o' age, and jist a thin peelywally callant, mair like playin' moshy at the bools than rinnin' efter lassies. The lassie's faither and mither jist made fun o' us, and when I wad be gaun up to her hoose, lettin' on it was her brither I wanted to see, they used to affront me afore their dochter wi' speakin' aboot the Sunday School and the Band o' Hope I belanged to (because the lassie belanged to them tae), and askin' me if I was fond o' sugar to my parridge, and when I was thinkin' o' startin' the shavin'. I didna like it, but I jist had to put up wi't. But the worst blow ever I got frae them was yince when I gaed up wi' a new pair o' lavender breeks, and the lassie's mither, for the fun o' the thing, asked me if I wad hae a piece and jeely. I tellt her I wasna heedin', that I was jist efter haein' my tea; but she went and spread syrup on a watter biscuit and handed it to me the same as if I was a wee lauddie wi' a grauvit on."

Jinnet laughed softly at the picture.

"Oh, ye may lauch," said her husband.

"There was nae lauchin' in my heid, I'm tellin' ye. For there was the syrup comin' dreepin' through the holes in the watter biscuit, so that I had to haud the biscuit up every noo and then and lick in below't so as to keep the syrup frae gaun on my braw lavender breeks. A bonny object for a lass to look at, and it was jist to mak' me look reediculous her mither did it. She thocht I was faur ower young to be comin' efter her dochter."

"So ye were," said Jinnet. "I'm shair ye hadna muckle sense at the time, or it wadna be yon yin ye went coortin'.'"

"Maybe no'; but I never rued it," said Erchie.

"She was as glaikit as yersel'," said Jinnet.

"She was the cleverest lass in the place," protested Erchie. "My! the things she could sew, and crochet, and mak' doon, and bake!"

"Her sister Phemie[2] was faur cleverer than she was," said Jinnet. "She couldna haud a candle to her sister Phemie in tambourin'[3] or in gingerbreid."

"And dancin'! She could dance on a cobweb and no' ut a toe through't."

"Ye'll need a line wi' that yin Erchie," said his wife, who did not seem remakably jealous of this first love.

"Ye should hear her singin' —"

"She wad hae ben far better mendin' her wee brither's stockin's, and no' leavin' her mither to dae't," said Jinnet. "She was a gey licht-heided yin."

Erchie seemed merciless in his remniscence — I really felt sorry for his wife.

"Ye may say whit ye like to run her doon, but ye canna deny her looks."

"Her looks dinna concern me," said Jinnet abruptly.

"Ye're jist an auld haver; think shame o' yersel'!"

"Ye ken ye canna deny't," he went on. "It was alooed all over the place she was the belle. I wasna the only yin that was efter her wi' my lavender breeks. She kept the Band o' Hope for nearly twa years frae burstin' up."

"I'll no' listen to anither word," protested Jinnet, now in obvious vexation; and mercifully there came a rapping at the door.

She returned to the kitchen with an envelope and a little parcel. Erchie winked at me, hugging to himself a great delight.

"I wonder wha in the world can be writin' to me," said she, looking at the addresses.

"It'll likely be an accoont for di'mond tararas[4] or dress-making," said Erchie. "Oh you weemen! Ye're a perfect ruination. But if I was you I wad open them and see."

She opened the envelope first. It was Erchie's valentine, and she knew it, for when she read the verse she shook her head at him laughingly, and a little ashamed. "When will ye be wise?" said she.

Then she opened the little parcel: it contained a trivial birthday gift from an anonymous friend in whose confidence only I, of all the three in the room, happened to be. Vainly they speculated about his identity without suspecting me; but I noticed that it was on her valentine Jinnet set most value. She held it long in her hand, thinking, and was about to put it into a chest of drawers without letting me see it.

"Ye needna be hidin' it," said her husband then. "He saw it already. Faith! he helped me to pick it."

"I'm fair affronted," she exclaimed, reddening at this exposure. "You and your valenteens!"

"There's naething wrang wi' valenteens," said her husband. "If it wasna for a valenteen I wad never hae got ye. I could never say to your face but that I liked ye; but the valenteen had a word that's far mair brazen than 'like,' ye mind."

"Oh, Erchie!" I cried, "you must have been blate in these days. The word was — "

He put up his hand in alarm and stopped me. "Wheesht!" said he. "It's a word that need never be mentioned here where we're a' three Scotch!"

"But what came over the first lass, Erchie?" I asked determined to have the end of that romance.

He looked across at his wife and smiled. "She's there hersel'," said he, "and ye better ask her."

"What! Jinnet? "I cried, amazed at my own obtuseness.

"Jinnet of course," said he. "Wha else wad it be if it wasna Jinnet? She's the Rale Oreeginal."

25. *Among the Pictures*

"WHAUR ARE ye gaun the day?" said Erchie to Duffy on Saturday afternoon when he came on the worthy coalman standing at his own close-mouth, looking up and down the street with the hesitation of a man who deliberates how he is to make the most of his Saturday half-holiday.

"I was just switherin'," said Duffy. "Since I got mairried and stopped gaun to the Mull o' Kintyre Vaults, there's no' much choice for a chap. I micht as weel be leevin' in the country for a' the life I see."

"Man, aye!" said Erchie, "that's the warst o' Gleska; there's nae life in't — naethin' daein'. Ye should try yer hand at takin' oot the wife for a walk, jist for the novelty o' the thing."

"Catch me!" said Duffy. "She wad see ower mony things in the shop windows she was needin'. I was jist wonderin' whether I wad buy a 'Weekly Mail' or gang to the fitba' match at Parkheid."

Erchie looked pityingly at him. "A fitba' match!" said he. " Whit's the use o' gaun to a fitba' match when ye can see a' aboot it in the late edeetion?[1] Forbye, a fitba' match doesna improve the mind; it's only sport. I'll tell ye whit I'll dae wi' ye if ye're game. I'll tak' ye to the Art Institute;[2] the minister gied me twa tickets. Awa' and put on your collar and I'll wait here on ye."

"Do you need a collar for the gallery?" asked Duffy, who thought the Art Institute was a music-hall. On this point Erchie set him right, and ten minutes later, with a collar whose rough edges rasped his neck and made him unhappy, he was on his way to Sauchiehall Street.

The band was playing a waltz tune as they entered the Institute.

"Mind, I'm no' on for ony dancin'," Duffy explained. "I canna be bothered dancin'."

"There's naebody gaun to ask ye to dance," said Erchie. "Do you think there couldna be a baun' playin' withoot dancin'? It's jist here to cod a lot o' folk into the notion that they can be cheery enough in a place o' the kind in spite o' the pictures. And ye can get aifternoon tea here, too."

"I could be daein' wi' a gless o' beer," said Duffy.

"No. They're no' that length yet," Erchie explained. "There's only the tea. The mair determined lovers o' the Fine Arts can dae the hale show in an aifternoon wi' the help o' a cup o' tea, so that they needna come back again. It's a great savin'. They used to hae to gang hame for their tea afore, and whiles they never got back. The Institute wasna popular in thae days; it was that quate and secluded that if a chap had done onything wrang and the detectives were efter him he took a season ticket, and spent a' his days here. Noo, ye can see for yersel' the place is gaun like an inn. That's the effect o' the baun' and the aifternoon tea. If they added a baby incubator to the attractions the same's they hae in the East-End Exhibeetion,[3] they would need the Fire Brigade wi' a hose to keep the croods oot. Ye hae nae idea o' the fascination Art has for the people o' Gleska if they're no' driven to't."

"My jove!" exclaimed Duffy, at the sight of the first gallery. "Whit a lot o' pictures! There'll be a pile o' money in a place o' this kind. Hiv they no water-shoot, or a shootin' jungle, or onything lively like that?"

"Man, ye're awfu' common, whiles, Duffy," said Erchie. "I'm fear't I wasted my ticket on ye. This is no' an ordinary show for haein' fun at; it's for enlargin' the mind, openin' the e'en to the beauties o' nature, and sellin' pictures."

"Are they a' for sale?" asked Duffy, looking with great intentness at a foggy impression by Sidaner,[4] the French artist.

"No' the hale o' them; there's some on lend."

"I could hae lent them a topper," said Duffy — "faur aheid o' onything here. It's a drawin' o' a horse I yince had in my first lorry; it was pented for me by a penter that lodged above us, and had a great name for sign-boards. It cost me nearly a pound wan wye or anither, though I provided the pent mysel'."

"Ay, Art's a costly thing," said Erchie. "Ye'll seldom get a good picture under a pound. It's no' a'thegither the pent, it's the layin' o't on by hand."

"This yin's done by hand onywye," said Duffy, pointing to the foggy impression by Sidaner. "It's awfu' like as if somebody had done it themsel's in their spare time."

"You and me's no' judges o' that sort o' thing," said Erchie. "Maybe it's no' near so bad as it looks."

"Ye see," Erchie went on, "Art pentin's a tred by itsel'. There used to be hardly ony picture-penters in Gleska; it was a' shipbuildin' and calanderin',[5] whitever that is, and chemical works that needed big lums. When a Gleska man did a guid stroke o' business on the Stock Exchange, or had money left him in thae days, and his wife wanted a present, he had his photygraph ta'en big size, ile-coloured by hand. It was gey like him, the photygraph, and so everybody kent it wasna the rale Art. Folk got rich that quick in Gleska, and had sae much money to spend, that the photygraphers couldna keep up wi' the demand, and then the hand-pentin' chaps began to open works in different pairts o' the city. Ye'll hardly gang into a hoose noo whaur ye'll no' see the guidman's picture in ile, and it micht be bilin' ile sometimes, judgin' from the agony on his face."

"My jove!" said Duffy, "is it sore to get done that wye?"

"Sore!" replied Erchie; "no, nor sore. At least, no' that awfu' sore. They wadna need to dae't unless they liked. When maistly a' the weel-aff Gleska folk had got their photygraphs done and then de'ed, the penters had to start the landscape brench o' the business. Them's landscapes a' roon' aboot" — and Erchie gave his arm a comprehensive sweep to suggest all the walls.

"They must be pretty smert chaps that does them," said Duffy. "I wish I had gone in for the pentin' mysel'; it's cleaner nor the coals. Dae ye hae to serve your time?"

"No, nor time; ye can see for yersel' that it's jist a kind o' knack like poetry — or waitin'. And the plant doesna cost much; a' ye need to start wi' 's paper, brushes, pent, and a saft hat."

"A saft hat!"

"Ay; a saft hat's the sure sign o' an artist. I ken hunners o' them; Gleska's fair hotchin' wi' artists. If the Cairters' Trip wasna abolished, ye wad see the artists' tred union walkin' oot wi' the rest o' them."

The two friends went conscientiously round the rooms, Erchie expounding on the dimensions, frames, and literary merits of the pictures, Duffy a patient, humble student, sometimes bewildered at the less obvious transcripts of nature and life pointed out to him.

"Is there much mair o' this to see?" he asked at last, after having gone through the fourth gallery. "I'm gettin' dizzy. Could we no' hae something at the tea bar if we gied them a tip? They micht send oot for't. Or we might get a pass-oot check."[6]

"Mair to see!" exclaimed Erchie. "Ye're awfu' easy made dizzy! The like o' you wad faur raither be oot skreichin' yer heid aff at the fitba' match at Parkheid, instead o' improvin' the mind here. Ye canna get onything at the tea place but jist tea, I'm tellin' ye, and there's nae pass-oot checks. They ken better nor to gie ye pass-oot checks; hauf o' your kind wad never come back again if yince ye escaped.

"My jove!" said Duffy, suddenly, "here's a corker!" and he indicated a rather peculiar drawing with a lady artist's name attached to it.

Erchie himself was staggered. "It's ca'd 'The Sleeper'[7] in the catalogue," said he. "It's a wumman, and her dozin'. The leddy that pented it wasna ower lavish wi' her pent. That's whit they ca' New Art, Duffy; it jist shows ye whit weemen can dae if ye let them."

"And dae ye tell me there's weemen penters?" asked Duffy in astonishment.

"Of course there's weemen penters."

"And hoo dae they get up and doon lethers?"[8] asked Duffy.

"I'm tellin' ye Art pentin's a brench by itsel," said Erchie. "The lady Art penters divna pent windows and rhones and hooses; they bash brass, and hack wud, and draw pictures."

"And can they mak' a living at that?"

"Whiles. And whiles their paw helps."

"My jove!" said Duffy, bewildered.

"We'll gang on to the next room noo," said Erchie.

"I wad raither come back some ither day," said Duffy. "I'm enjoyin' this fine, but I promised the wife I wad be hame early for my tea." And together they hastily made an exit into Sauchiehall Street.

"I wonder wha won the semi-final at Parkheid,"⁹ said Duffy. "We'll awa' doon the toon and see; whit's the use o' hurryin' hame?"

26. *The Probationary Ghost*

ONE DAY I observed Erchie going off the pavement rather than walk under a ladder.

"And are you superstitious too?" I asked him, surprised at this unsuspected trait in a character so generally sensible."

"I don't care whither ye ca't supersteetion or no'," he replied, "but walkin' under lethers is a gey chancy thing; and there's mony a chancy thing, and I'm neither that young nor that weel aff that I can afford to be takin' ony risks."

"Dear me!" I said; "I wouldn't be surprised to learn that you believed in ghosts."

"Do I no'?" he answered. "And guid reason for't! Did I no' yince see yin? It was the time I had the rheumatic fever, when we were stayin' in Garnethill.¹ I was jist gettin' better, and sittin' up a wee while in the evenin' to air the bed, and Jinnet was oot for a message. The nicht was wild and wet, and the win' was daudin' awa' at the window like onything, and I was feelin' gey eerie, and wearyin' for the wife to come back. I was listenin' for her fit on the stair, when the ootside door opens, and in a second there was a chap at the kitchen door.

"'Come in if your feet's clean,' says I, pretty snappy. 'Seein' ye've made sae free wi' the ae door ye needna mak' ony ceremony wi' this ane.' I heard the hinges screechin', but naebody cam' in, and I looks roon' frae where I was sittin' wi' a blanket roond me at the fire, and there was the ghost keekin' in. He was a wee nyaf o' a thing, wi' a Paisley whisker, a face no bigger than a Geneva watch, a nickerbocker suit on, Rab Roy tartan tops to his gowfin' stockings, and potbellied to the bargain. I kent fine he was a ghost at the first gae-aff.

"'It's you,' says I. 'Come in and gies yer crack till Jinnet comes. Losh, it's no' a nicht for stravaigin'.'[2]

"He cam' glidin' in withoot makin' ony soond at a' and sat doon on a chair."

"'Ye're no' feared,' says he, trying to gnash his teeth, and makin' a puir job o't, for they were maistly arteeficial.

"'Feared?' says I. 'No me! I never did onybody ony hairm that wad mak' it worth ony ghost's while to meddle wi' me. A flet fit but a warm hert.'

"'We'll see aboot that,' says he, as cocky as onything. 'I had a fine job findin' oot where ye were. Fancy me gaun awa' doon to Millport on a nicht like this to haunt ye, and findin' that ye had flitted up here last term.' And he begood to gnash his teeth again.

"'Millport!' says I. 'Man! I was never near the place, and I've lived in this hoose for seventeen year, and brocht up a faimily in't.'

"I never seen a ghost mair vexed than he was when I tell't him that. His jaw fell; he was nearly greetin'.

"'Whit's yer name?' he asked.

"'Erchie MacPherson, and I'm no' ashamed o't. It's no' in ony grocers' nor tylers' books that I ken o', and if I ever murdered ony weans or onything o' that sort, it must hae been when I was sleepin'. I doot, my man, ye're up the wrang close.'

"The ghost begood to swear. Oh my! such swearin'. I never listened to the bate o't. There was fancy words in't I never heard in a' my life, and I've kent a wheen o' cairters."

"'That's jist like them,' says he. 'They tellt me Millport; and efter I couldna find the man I was wantin' at Millport, I was tellt it was here, No. 16 Buccleuch Street.[3] Fancy me bungin' awa' through the air on a nicht like this! My nickerbockers is fair stickin' to me knees wi' wet.'

"'Peter,' says I (of course I didna ken his richt name, but I thocht I wad be nice wi' the chap seein' he had made such a mistake), 'Peter,' said I, 'ye're needin' yer specs on. This is no' No. 16, it's No. 18, and I think the man ye maun be lookin' for is Jeckson, that canvasses for the sewin'-machines. He came here last term frae aboot Millport. If he's done ony hairm to onybody in his past life — murdered a wife, and buried her under the hearth-stane, or ony daft-like thing o' that sort — I'm no' wantin' to hear onything aboot it, for he's a guid enough neebour, has twa bonny wee weans, comes hame regular to his tea, and gangs to the kirk wi' his wife. He's been teetotal ever since he came here. Gie the chap a chance!'

"'Jeckson!' said the ghost, and whips oot a wee book. 'That's the very man!' said he. 'Man! is't no' aggravatin'? Here's me skooshin' up and doon the coast wi' my thin flannels on lookin' for him, and him toastin' his taes at a fire in Buccleuch Street! Jist you wait. It shows ye the wye the books in oor place is kept. If the office was richt up-to-date, Jeckson wadna be flitted ten meenutes when his new address wad be marked doon. No wonder the Americans is 'batin' us![4] Weel, it's no' my faut if I'm up the wrang close, and I'm no' gaun to start the job the nicht. I'm far ower cauld.'

"There was an empty gless and a teaspoon on the dresser, for Jinnet had been giein' me a drap toddy afore she gaed oot. The ghost sat doon on a chair and looked at the gless.

"'Could ye save a life?' said he.

"'Whit wad be the use o' giein' it to you, Peter?' I asked him; 'ye havena ony inside, seein' ye're a ghost.'

"'Have I no'?' says he. 'Jist try me.' So I pointed to the press, and he took oot the decanter as smert's ye like and helped himsel'.

"He turned oot a rale nice chap in spite o' his tred, and he gave me a' the oots and ins o't. 'I've nae luck,' he said. 'It's my first job at the hauntin', and I've made a kind o' botch o't, though it's no' my faut. I'm a probationer; jist on my trial, like yin o' thae U.F. ministers. Maybe ye think it's easy gettin' a haunter's job; but I'm tellin' ye it's no' that easy, and when ye get it, it's wark that tak's it oot o' ye. There's mair gangs in for the job there than for the Ceevil Service here, and the jobs go to competition. Ye hae to pass an examination, and ye hae nae chance o' gettin' yin if ye divna mak' mair nor ninety per cent. o' points. Mind ye, there's mair than jist plain ghostwark. It used to be, in the auld days, that a haunter wad be sent to dae onything — to rattle chains, or gie ye the clammy hand, or be a blood-curdler. Nooadays there's half a dizzen different kinds o' haunters. I'm a blood-curdler mysel',' and he gied a skreich that nearly broke a' the delf on the dresser.

"'Nane o' that!' says I, no' very weel pleased, 'Ye'll hae the neebours doon on us. Forbye, there's naething patent aboot that sort o' skreich. Duffy the coalman could dae better himsel'. That's no' the wye a dacent ghost should cairry on in ony hoose whaur he's gettin' a dram.'

"'Excuse me,' he says; 'it's the dram that's ta'en my heid. Ye see, I'm no' used to't. It's mony a day since I had yin.'

"'Are they that strict yonder?' I asked.

"'Strict's no' the word for't! If a blood-curdler on probation was kent to gang to his work wi' the smell o' drink aff him, he wad lose his job': and he helped himsel' to anither dram.

"'Weel, ye're no' blate onywye,' says I.

"'Blate! Catch me,' says he. 'I wadna need to be blate at this tred, I'm tellin' ye. Jist you think o' the kind o' customers we hae to dale wi'! They wad' sooner see a tax-collector comin' into their hooses than yin o' us chaps.

There's some hooses ye hae to gang to work in where it's easy. I ken a ghost that's been fifteen years on the same job, and gettin' fat on't. He has the name o' bein' the best white-sheet ghost in the Depairtmen', and he's stationed in an auld castle up aboot the Hielan's, a job he got because he had the Gaelic. He made it sae hot for the folk, walkin' aboot their bedrooms at a' 'oors o' the nicht, that naebody 'll stay in the place but himsel' and an auld deaf and dumb housekeeper. There's naething for him to dae, so he can lie in his bed a' nicht and no' bother himsel' aboot onything. It's a very different thing wi' anither chap I ken — a chain-clanker in England. He has to drag ten yairds o' heavy chain up and doon stairs every nicht; and it's no easy job, I'm tellin' ye, wi' the folk the hoose belang to pappin' things and shootin' at whaur they think the soond comes frae. Oh ay! there's a great run on the best jobs. My ain ambeetion is to be in the clammy-hand brench o' the business in some quate wee place at the coast. I hae my e'e on a likely thing at Rothesay. Of course the clammy hand's no' a very nice occupation for the winter, but this is a hoose that's shut up in the winter, and I wad only hae to work it in the fine summer nichts.'

"'Hoo dae ye dae the clammy hand, Peter?' I asked him, and he just winked.

"'If I was tellin' ye that,' says he, 'ye wad be as wise as mysel'. Never you mind, MacPherson; ask me nae questions and I'll tell ye nae lees. Weel, as I was sayin', I aye had a notion o' a quate job at the coast. I couldna stand Gleska; there's such a rush aboot it, and sae mony stairs to sclim,[5] and pianos aye playin' next door. And the accent's awfu'! Gie me a nice wee country hoose whaur somebody hanged himsel', wi' roses on the wa', and dandelions in the front plot. But there's plenty o' us lookin' efter jobs o' that sort — far ower mony; and it's generally them wi' influence that gets them at the hinder-end.'

"'That's whit everybody says aboot the situations here, Peter,' says I. 'If they're nae use at their tred they talk a lot aboot influence. I'm thinkin' ye wad soon get a job at the coast if ye were fit for't.'

"He was the shortest-tempered ghost ever I seen. I had nae sooner said that than he gied anither skreich, and disappeared in a blue lowe wi' an awfu' smell o' brimstone.

"'Come oot o' that!' I says to him; 'I can see the taps o' yer gowfin' stockings'; and at that he gied a kind o' shamed lauch and was sittin' in the chair again, helpin' himsel' to anither dram.

"'I'll tell ye whit I'll dae wi' ye,' said he. 'I'll no' mind aboot Jeckson at a', but I'll hing aboot your hoose for a week or a fortnight, and they'll never ken at the office. I canna think to gang into Jeckson's hoose if he's a teetotaler. Teetotalers is aye that — that — that teetotal. I wad never get sittin' doon in Jeckson's to a jovial gless like this.'

"'Ye're far ower jovial for me,' says I. 'See's that decanter,' and I took it frae him. 'I'm awfu' prood to see ye, but ye better be slidin' afore her ladyship the wife comes in, or she'll put the hems on ye. She canna stand ghosts.'

"'Michty!' said he. 'Have ye a wife?'

"'The nicest wee wife in Gleska,' said I. 'And I wish to goodness she was hame, for I'm awfu' tired.'

"'Then I'm no' playin',' said the ghost. 'I'll awa' roon' and gie Jeckson a cry afore he gangs to his bed.'

"He grabbed the decanter and emptied it into the tumbler, gied ae gulp, and anither gnash to his teeth, and went awa' withoot sae much as 'thenk ye.'

"Jinnet's step was on the stair. Fine I kent it! Man, that's the smertest wee wumman!

"'There's nae livin' in this hoose wi' ghosts,' says I to her when she cam' in, and she had some grapes for me.

"'Is there no', Erchie?' she said, lookin' at me. 'My ain puir auld man!'

"'Look at that decanter,' says I; 'the rascal emptied it.'

"'Hoots! the decanter's a' richt,' says she, takin't frae the press; and as shair's onything, there wasna a drap oot o't!

"And she put me to my bed there and then."

27. *Jinnet's Christmas Shopping*

JINNET HAD money in the Savings Bank. Erchie used to chuckle when some neighbour had gone out to whom she had casually mentioned the fact and say, "That's it, Jinnet, you be braggin o' your deposits like that, and they'll be thinking I mairried ye for your fortune." But the truth was that when their savings at first were lodged in Erchie's name, they had an unfortunate way of disappearing without Jinnet's knowledge, and it was to protect himself from himself that the husband finally opened the account in the name of his wife.

The first day she went to the bank with money it was with no little trepidation. "Maybe they'll no' tak' sae much as twenty-wan pounds," she suggested; "it's a guid pickle money to hae the responsibility o'."

"Ay, and gled to get it!" he replied. "That's whit they're there for. If it was twice twenty-wan they wad mak' room for't, even if they had to shift forrit the coonter. Ye hae nae idea o' the dacency o' thae banks!"

"But whit if the bank was to burst?" said Jinnet. "Lots o' folk losses their money wi' banks burstin',[1] and hae to go on the Board[2] a' the rest o' their days."

"Burst!" laughed Erchie. "Man! ye wad think it was a kitchen biler ye were talkin' aboot. It'll no' burst wi' a' we'll put into it, I'll warrant ye."

"Will ye hae to pay them much for takin' care o't?" she asked, still dubious of these immense financial operations.

Erchie laughed till the tears ran into his tea.

"Oh, my!" said he, "but ye're the caution! It's them that pays you. If ye leave the twenty-wan pound in for a twelvemonth, they'll gie ye something like twenty-wan pound ten shillin's when ye gang to lift it."

This troubled Jinnet worse than ever. "It's rale nice o' them," said she, "but I'm no' needin' their ten shillin's; we're no' that faur doon in the warld, and it's like enough they wad jist be takin' it aff some ither puir cratur."

But eventually the money was lodged in Jinnet's name. She used to take out her bank-book and examine it once a week, to make sure, as she said, "the money was still there," a proceeding at which Ernie would wink to himself, and with difficulty restrain his laughter.

On Saturday Jinnet expressed a wish that she had some of her money to make purchases for Christmas and the New Year.

"Weel," said her husband, "whit's to hinder ye gaun to the bank and liftin' a pound or twa?"

Her face turned white at the very thought. "Me!" she cried. "I wadna ask for money at that bank if I was stervin'."

"But, bless my sowl! it's yer ain money; they canna keep ye frae gettin' it if ye want it," said her husband.

"I'm no' carin'," Jinnet protested. "I divna like to ask for't, and them maybe busy. Perhaps the puir craturs havena got it to spare the noo."

"Weel, they can jist send oot for a wee lend o't frae somebody they ken," said Erchie. "It's your money, and if ye want ony o't oot they must gie ye't; that's whit banks is for."

"Will you no' gang for the twa pound ten for me, and I'll mak' something nice and tasty for your tea the nicht?" said Jinnet coaxingly; but Erchie had his own way of teaching Jinnet self-confidence, and refused. "They wadna gie't to me withoot a lot o' palaver," he explained; "ye'll just hae to gang yersel'. Speak nice to them, and they'll no' touch ye. There hasna been a customer murdered in a Gleska bank for years and years." He explained the process she was to follow, and she set out with great misgivings.

"Weel, hoo did ye get on?" Erchie asked her when she returned. "Ye got the money onywye — I can see by the wye yer nief's shut."

"Oh, Erchie!" she cried hysterically, and dropped into a chair. "I wad never mak' a man o' business. My hert's in a palpitation — jist fair stottin'. I peety them that has the bother o' muckle money."

"My jove!" said Erchie in alarm. "Were they no' nice to ye? If they werena nice and ceevil, I'll— I'll tak' oot every penny, and then they'll see whaur they are."

"Oh, they were as nice as they could be," Jinnet hurried to explain. "And I got the money a' richt. But oh! I was that put-aboot. Thon slippy floor aye frichtens me, and the gentlemen inside the coonter in their wee cages like Duffy's goldie — "

"Goldies — ay, that's jist whit they are," said Erchie. "It's a fine bird a goldie if ye get a guid yin; it can whustle better nor a canary."

" — like Duffy's goldie, and that rale weel put-on. Each o' them had as muckle gold and silver aboot him as wad fill a bakie.[3] I nearly fented when yin o' them spoke to me awfu' Englified, and askit whit he could dae for me the day. 'Oh,' says I, 'I see ye're throng;'[4] I'll can come back anither time,' and I was makin' for the door when he cried me back, and said he wasna that throng but that he wad be gled to dae onything he could for me. I thocht he wad gie me the money wi' a grudge when he found I wanted twa pound ten in silver, but he coonted it oot like lichtnin', and bangs it fornent[5] me. A rale obleegin' lad he was, but no' lookin' awfu' strong; I think I'll knit him a pair o' warm socks or a muffler for his New Year."

"Ye're a rale divert, Jinnet!" said Erchie.

"I jist picked up the money withoot coontin' it and turned to gang awa'. 'Hold on, Mistress Macpherson,' he cries; 'ye'll be as weel to coont yer siller afore ye leave the bank in case I'm cheatin' ye,' and my face got as red's the fire. 'I wadna hae the cheek to doot ye efter seein' ye coontin't yersel',' I tellt him, and cam' awa'. But I went up a close farther along the street and coonted it."

"I could bate a pound ye did," said Erchie.

And now, having got out her money, Jinnet had to go shopping. Ordinary shopping had no terrors for her; she loved to drop into Lindsay the grocer's, and discourse upon the prices of simple things to eat, and feel important when he offered to send his boy with the goods; she was quite at home in the little side-street shops where they sell trimming, and bolts of tape, and remnants of print; or the oil-and-colour shops where she was known and could spend a pleasant ten minutes' gossip over the purchase of a gallon of paraffin. But Christmas shopping was no ordinary shopping, and was entered on with almost as much apprehension as her expedition to the bank. It had to be done in big warehouses, where the attendants were utter strangers to her, and had ways frigid and unfamiliar.

"Put on your kep and come awa' doon the toon wi' me," she said to Erchie. "I hate gaun into some o' thae big shops mysel'."

"Then whit wye dae ye no' jist gang into the wee yins ye ken?" he asked her. "If ye're feared they'll eat ye in the big yins I wadna gang to them."

"Oh, that's a' very weel, but the wee yins havena the turnover," she explained. "Ye get things far fresher at this time o' the year doon the toon."

"I'll gang wi' ye, for I ken that if I didna gang they wad tak' a fair lend o' ye," Erchie agreed at last; "but mind, I'm no' gaun to stand lookin' in at baby-linen shop-windows or onything o' that sort. Me bein' a public man in a kind o' wye, it disna dae."

"I'll no' ask ye to dae onything o' the kind, ye pridefu' auld thing ye," she promised, and off they set.

She wanted a pair of gloves for a favourite grand-daughter, an umbrella for a sister of Erchie's, who was a widow and poor, and something as a wedding-present for Duffy's fiancée.[6]

There was scarcely a drapery warehouse in Argyle Street whose window did not attract her. Erchie never looked into any of them, but patiently stood apart on the edge of the pavement or walked slowly ahead.

"Come here and see this at seevenpence threefardens," she entreated him.

"It's fine, a rale bargain; I wad tak' that," he replied, looking towards the window from afar off, and quite ignorant of what she alluded to, but determined not to be caught by any one, who knew him as waiter or beadle, looking into a shop-window full of the most delicate feminine mysteries of attire.

She went into the warehouse, while he walked on to the next shop — a cutler's — and looked intently in at the window of it, as if he were contemplating the purchase of a costly pocket-knife with five blades, a corkscrew, and an appliance popularly supposed to be for taking stones out of a horse's hoof. When he was joined by Jinnet, she had plainly begun to lose her nerve.

"I've got gloves," said she, "and a thing for Duffy's lass, but they're naither o' them whit I was wantin'." "Of course they're no'," said Erchie. "Ye've got a grate consait o' yersel', if ye think a puir auld body like you can get exactly whit ye want in yin o' them warehooses wi' the big turnover ye aye talk aboot. Was it a peerie and a fiddle ye wanted that made ye tak' gloves?"

"Oh! dinna bother me, Erchie; I canna help it; the lassies that serve ye in there's that Englified and that smert that when they havena got whit I'm wantin' I jist aye tak' whit they can gie me."

"I've seen you in a big shop afore noo," said her husband, "and I ken fine the wye ye aye spile yersel' wi' them Englified smert yins. Ye gang forrit to the coonter as if ye were gaun to ask if they had ony windows to clean, or back-stairs to wash oot, and ye get red in the face and tak' yer money oot o' yer pocket to show ye have it, and ye lauch to the lassie as if ye kent her fine, and ye say, 'If you please' to her, or, 'Oh! it's a bother to ye.' That mak's the lassie see at yince ye're no' cless; she gets a' the mair Englified, lettin' on to hersel' she's the Duchess o' Montrose, and can put the like o' you in your place wi' the least wee bit touch. That's no' the wye to dae in a shop o' that kind. Ye should breenge up to the coonter, and cry 'Gloves!' as hard as Duffy cries 'Coals!' then sit doon withoot askin' on a chair, and wi' a gant noo and then watch them puttin' oot gloves by the hunderwicht in front o' ye, and them a' in the shakers in case ye'll no' think they're smert enough.

"Dinna be blate; that's my advice to ye. Talk Englified yersel', and sniff wi' yer nose noo and then as if ye felt a nesty smell in the place, and run doon the goods like dirt. Never let your e'e rest on the folk that serve ye, unless they happen to hae a shabby tie on or a button aff somewhere; glower at that, and it'll mak' them uncomfortable, and — "

"Oh, that's a' richt, Erchie," said Jinnet; "ye'll hae to come into the next shop I gang to, and show me the wye."

"No fears o' me," said Erchie promptly; "I'm tellin' ye whit to dae, but I divna say I could dae't mysel'."

But when it came to the purchase of the umbrella he did go into the shop with her, and she got what she thought was a bargain, as well as the finest affability and courtesy from the gentleman who sold it.

"That's because I was wi' ye," said Erchie, when they came out.

"I daresay," she agreed; "there's aye some use for a man."

28. *A Bet on Burns*

DUFFY CAME round to Erchie's on Saturday night for the loan of a copy of Burns, which he knew the old man had on the shelves of what he called his chevalier and book-case. "I'm wantin' to learn a sang," said he, "for I'm gaun to the Haggis Club in the Mull o' Kintyre Vaults on Monday if I'm spared."

"Are ye, indeed!" said Erchie, drily. "Ye'll be takin' the new wife wi' ye?"

"No fears o' me," said Duffy. "Wha ever heard o' a wife at a Burns meetin'?"

"Oh! I divna ken onything aboot it," said Erchie; "I thocht maybe the weemen were gaun to thae things nooadays, though they didna go when I was young, and I thocht maybe you bein' sae lately mairried ye wanted to gie her a trate. It's a droll thing aboot Burns that though the weemen were sae ta'en up wi' him when he was leevin', they're no' awfu' keen on him noo that he's deid. There'll be thoosands o' men hurrayin' Burns on Monday nicht in a' pairts o' the warld, and eatin' haggis till they're no' weel, but I'll bate ye their wifes is no' there. No; their wifes is at hame mendin' their men's sox, and chairgin' the gazogene for the morn's mornin', when it'll be sair wanted. And ye're gaun to a Haggis Club, are ye? I didna ken ye were such a keen Burns hand."

"Me!" cried Duffy — "I'm jist daft for Burns. Fifty or mair o' the members tak' their coals frae me. Burns! Man, Erchie, I could gie ye Burns by the yaird — 'Dark Lochnagar,' and 'The Flooers o' the Forest,' 'We're a' Noddin',' and 'Rollin' Hame to Bonnie Scotland' —

'Rollin' hame to Bonnie Scotland,

Rollin' hame across the sea.'"

He sang the lines with gusto.

"Stop!" said Erchie, in alarm, "stop! There's nae deafenin' in thae ceilin's, and the folk abin 'll think I'm giein' Jinnet a leatherin'. Man! I didna think ye kent sae mony o' Rabbie's sangs. It's a credit to ye. I'm shair ye divna need ony book to learn affa."

"To tell ye the rale sets o't, Erchie," said Duffy, "it's a bate. There's a chap yonder at the coal hill thrieps doon my throat Burns didna write 'Dark Lochnagar'[1] the wye I sing 't, and I want to show him 't in the book."

"Hoo much is the bate?" asked Erchie.

"Hauf-a-croon," said Duffy.

"Then sell yin o' yer horses and pye the money," said Erchie, "for ye've lost the bate. Burns had nae grudge against his countrymen. They did him nae hairm. He didna write 'Dark Lochnagar' the wye you sing it, for Burns never made his sangs wi' a saw; in fact, he never wrote 'Dark Lochnagar' at a'; it was put oot by anither firm in the same tred, ca'd Byron."

"My jove!" said Duffy," I never kent that afore!"

"There's lots o' things ye never kent," said Erchie. "Seein' ye're gaun to eat haggis on Monday nicht, ye micht tell us whit ye ken, no' aboot Burns's sangs, but aboot Burns himsel'."

"There was naething wrang wi' the chap," said Duffy, "if he just had stuck to his wark. When I'm sellin' coal I'm sellin' coal, and no' pentin' pictures. But there was Burns! — if he happened to come on a moose's nest in the field when he was plewin', or see a flooer in his road when he was oot workin' at the hye, he wad stop the plew, or lay doon his rake, and tak' the efternoon aff to mak' a sang aboot the moose or the daisy."

"A', and jist wi' his least wee bit touch," said Erchie, admiringly. "He was great, that's whit he was."

"Maybe he was, but it spiled the wark; we wadna aloo that in the coal tred," said Duffy. "He didna ken what compeetition was. I've seen things in my ain tred a knacky chap could mak' a fine sang aboot if he was jist lettin' himsel' go."

"Then for mercy's sake aye keep a grip o' yersel'," said Erchie. "Mind ye hae a wife dependin' on ye!"

"And then," said Duffy, "he was a bit o' the la di-da. There's naething o' the la-di-da aboot me."

"There is not!" admitted Erchie, frankly.

"But Burns, although he was a plewman to tred, went aboot wi' a di'mond ring spilin' folks' windows. If he saw a clean pane o' gless he never lost the chance o' writin' a bit verse on't wi' his di'mond ring. It was gey chawin' to the folk the windows belanged to, but Burns never cared sae lang's he let them see he had a rale di'mond ring that wad scratch gless."

"It was the fashion at the time, Duffy," said Erchie. "Nooadays when a poet has an idea for twa lines he keeps it under the bed till it sproots into a hale poem, and then he sends it to a magazine, and buys his wife, or somebody's else's, a di'mond ring wi' whit he gets for't. Writin' on window-panes is no' the go ony langer. It's oot o' date."

"But I'm no' runnin' doon the chap," said Duffy "Only I aye thocht it was him that wrote 'Dark Lochnagar.' Are ye shair it wasna?"

Erchie nodded. "Nor 'Rollin' Hame to Bonnie Scotland' either. He was far ower busy writin' sangs aboot the Marys, and the Jeans, and the Peggys at the time to write aboot ony o' yer 'Dark Lochnagars.'"

"So he was," admitted Duffy. "Yon's a rare yin aboot Mary — 'Kind, kind, and gentle is she —

... kind is my Mary

The tender blossom on the tree

Is half sae sweet as Mary'."

"Calm yersel', Duffy," said Erchie, in dramatic alarm. "I'm no deaf."

"That was written aboot 'Hielan' Mary'," said Duffy. "He met her at Dunoon[2] the Fair Week, and I've seen her monument."

"It's yonder as nate's ye like," said Erchie. "Faith! it's you that's weel up in Burns, Duffy."

"Oh! I'm no' that faur back in my history," said Duffy, quite pleased with himself. "But I could hae sworn it was him that put thegither 'Rollin' Hame to Bonnie Scotland'; it's his style. He micht be rollin' but he aye got hame. He was a gey wild chap, Burns."

"I'm no' denyin't, Duffy," said Erchie. "But he hadna ony o' the blessin's we have in oor time to keep him tame. There was nae Free Leebrary to provide him wi' books to keep him in the hoose at nicht, nae Good Templar Lodges to help him in keepin' clear o' the horrors o' drink; and Poosy Nancy's public-hoose didna shut at ten o'clock, nor even eleeven. If Burns had thae advantages, there's nae sayin' whit he micht hae risen to; perhaps he might hae become an M.P., and dee'd wi' money in the bank."

"Och! there's worse than Burns," said Duffy. "I was gey throughither mysel' when I was a young chap."

"Ah! but ye couldna hae been that awfu' bad, for ye never made ony poetry."

"I never tried," said Duffy; "I was the youngest o' nine, and I was put oot to wark early. So there wasna time for me to try and be fancy in ony wye. But a gey wild chap, Burns!"

"Maybe no' that awfu' wild," said Erchie. "Ye're aye harpin' on the wild. Burns was like a man takin' a daunder oot in a country road on a fine nicht: he kept his een sae much on the stars that sometimes he tripped in the sheuch. If it was the like o' you and me, Duffy, we wad be keepin' oor e'e a' the time on the road at oor feet to see if onybody hadna dropped onything, and there wad be nae fears o' us fa'in in the sheuch. Except for his habit o' makin' sangs when he micht be makin' money, Burns wasna very different frae the rest o' us. There was ae thing aboot him — he aye payed his way, and never forgot his freen's. He had a warm hert."

"Man, ye should be doon at the Mull o' Kintyre Vaults Haggis Club on Monday and propose the toast," said Duffy, admiringly.

"I'm better whaur I am," said Erchie; "the best Burns Club a man can hae 's a weel-thumbed copy o' the poems on his chevalier and book-case, and a wife that can sing 'Ye Banks and Braes' like oor Jinnet."

29. *The Prodigal's Return*

A SAILOR-MAN with a thick black beard, and all his belongings apparently on his back — for the dunnage bag[1] he carried was so poorly stuffed it could have held little more than a pair of sea-boots — went into Erchie's close one afternoon, and slowly climbed the stair. He put the bag at his feet when he came to Erchie's door with "Mac-Pherson" on the name-plate, scratched his head, hitched his waist-belt once or twice, and seemed in a mood to turn and flee rather than to ring or knock. At last he faintly tugged the bell-pull, and leaned against the door-post with the air of one who expected he might have some parley before getting admittance.

There was a step in the lobby, and Erchie himself in his shirt-sleeves came to the door.

"We're no' for onything the day," said he. "We have a

sewin'-machine already, and we're a' in the Prudential Insurance, and the staircase windows were cleaned on Setturday, and — "

"Faither," said the sailor-man, "do ye no' ken me?"

Erchie came clóser and looked at the bearded face, and put his hand tremblingly upon the young man's shoulder.

"Willie!" said he. "Willie!" he repeated. "Man ye're sair needin' shavin'." He shook his son, and "O, Willie," said he, "whit'll yer mither say? I suppose if I was the rale thing mysel', I should kill the fatted calf or start the greetin'; but as shair's death we havena kept a calf in this hoose since ye left it yoursel', and I was never yin o' the greetin' kind. My goodness! Willie!"

He was so bewildered he forgot his visitor stood on the door-mat, until Willie lifted his dunnage-bag, and then he urged him into the kitchen.

"Where's — where's mother?" said the sailor.

"She micht be deid and in her grave for you," said his father; "but she's no'. She's doon at Lindsay the grocer's for a loaf. Oh, ye rogue! ye rogue! Whit 'll she say to ye? Seeven years, come the fifth o' June! Oh, ye're awfu' needin' shavin'. I hope — I hope the health's fine?"

"Fine," said Willie, and sat in a chair uneasily, like a stranger.

"And whaur in a' the warld did ye come frae?" said his father, putting the kettle on the fire. They had not even shaken hands.

"China and roond aboot there," said the son.

"China!" said his father. "And hoo did ye leave them a' in China? They're throng at the war[2] there the noo, I see. I hope ye werena hurted."

"No, nor hurted," said Willie. "I hope ye're fine yersel' — and mother?"

"Me!" said Erchie. "Jist a fair gladiator! Divna ken my ain strength, and can eat onything, jist like a connoshoor. As for yer mother, she's wonderfu'; a wee frail, but aye able to dae her turns. She'll be the gled wumman this — Whit I mean to say is, ye should get a reg'lar leatherin' for your cairry-on. If I hadna my rheumatism in my shoother gey bad, I wad tak' a stick to ye. I'm pretty wild at ye, mind I'm tellin' ye. Whit dae ye think o' yersel', to gang awa' and no' write us for seeven years?"

"No' an awfu' lot," said the son.

"That's hopeful," said his father. "I'm gled ye're no' puttin' the blame on us. And I'm gled ye havena ony brass buttons on your claes."

"Brass buttons?" said Willie.

"Ay! When your mother was wearyin' to hear frae ye, I used to be tellin' her that ye were likely a mate, or a purser, or something o' that sort, and that busy in foreign pairts liftin' the tickets in the fore saloon, where the dram's cheaper and maist o' the passengers go, that ye hadna time to write. Yince I took her doon to the docks and showed her a big ship gaun awa' to Australia, wi' the Captain on the tap flet, ca'in a handle[3] and roarin' 'Let go that gangway!' and 'Nae smokin' abaft the funnel!' and she was as pleased as onything to see't. Ever since then she thinks o' her son Willie as a chap wi' brass buttons ca'in a handle the same as he was a tramway driver, and that busy he hadna time to write. I'm gled ye havena brass buttons," concluded Erchie, looking at his rather shabbily clothed scion. "It's mair to your credit that ye were jist a fool and no' a rascal."

"Man, ye're jist as great a caution as ever," said Willie, with the sincerest admiration.

"Duffy the coal-man tellt me he saw ye yince doon aboot the Broomielaw," said Erchie. "It was three years ago. I daursay ye were ower throng at the time to come up and see your mither and me. It's a guid wye up here frae the Broomielaw; it costs a penny on the skoosh car. Or maybe it was a wet day."

Willie's face got red. "It wasna only yince I was at the Broomielaw," he said. "I've been in Gleska four times since I left it."

"Were ye indeed?" said his father. "Weel, weel, it was rale considerate o' ye no' to bother your auld mither and me. I'll wager ye werena needin' ony money."

"I was needin' money gey bad every time," said the son. "I aye had some when I landed, but it never got past the Broomielaw wi' me. And that's the wye I never cam near ye. I was ashamed, as shair's death. Every time I was in the Clyde I cam up here at nicht, or to the auld hoose afore ye flitted, and looked at the close or went roond to the back coort and looked at the kitchen window."

"It's a good thing I didna see ye there, or I wad maybe hae gien ye a clourin'."[4]

"I wad hae liked it fine if ye had," said the young man. "A clourin' was the very thing I was needin', and I kent it mysel'. I was an awfu' fool, faither."

"That's jist whit ye were," Erchie admitted. "It's a lingerin' disease, and that's the warst o't. I hope ye'll maybe get ower't."

"If I didna think I had got ower't I wadna hae been here the nicht," said the son. "I'll warrant ye'll no' hae to complain o' me again."

Erchie took his hand. "Willie," said he, "gie me your thoomb on that. I ken the MacPhersons, if their mind's made up, and I think ye're auld enough noo to try your hand at sense. It'll no' hurt ye. Willie, Willie, it wasna mysel' I worried aboot thae seeven years, nor you either; for I kent fine the prodigal wad come back, if it was only to see if his faither de'ed and left him onything. The prodigal son! Awfu' needin' a shave! Your mither 'll be the prood wumman this nicht."

Before Jinnet had come back from the grocer's Erchie put his son into the parlour, so that the returned wanderer might not too abruptly confront his mother. She suspected nothing for a little, going about her ordinary offices in the kitchen till something fidgety in her husband's appearance directed her more close attention to him, and there was seen then an elation in his countenance that made her ask him what the matter was.

"Ye're awfu' joco," said she. "Are ye plannin' some baur for Duffy?"

"Not me," said Erchie. "I'm jist wearyin' for my tea. And, by the wye, Jinnet," he added, "ye micht put doon anither cup for a frien' o' mine I'm expectin' frae abroad."

"Frae abroad!" cried Jinnet, turning pale. "Ye havena heard onything o' — o' —"

"Have I no'?" said Erchie. "There's a chap in the room at this meenute that wad be awfu' like Willie if he had a clean shave."

Ten minutes later Erchie joined his wife and Willie in the room. The dunnage-bag was being emptied before Jinnet by a son who was anxious to make the most of his gifts from foreign parts, though painfully conscious of their value.

"Oh, whit braw shells!" cried his mither. "Jist the very thing I was needin' for the mantelpiece. The Carmichaels say wally dugs is no' the go noo at a'. It was rale thochtfu' o' ye to tak' them a' the wye frae abroad for me."

"And here a song folio and a pund o' sweet tobacco for you, faither," said Willie.

Erchie took them in his hand. "Man, that's the very thing," said he. "If 'Dark Lochnagar's' in't, I'll be upside wi' Duffy."

"Whit's this?" asked Jinnet, as the sailor brought forth for her a bottle containing some dark thick fluid.

"Riga balsam — whit the sailors use for sair hands," said Willie.

"Oh, it's the very thing Erchie used to say ye wad bring back when ye cam," cried Jinnet in delight. "It'll be awfu' useful. I'm almost vext I havena onything sair aboot me the day."

"No' even a sair hert,"[5] said Erchie, and the son looked contritely at his mother.

30. *Erchie's Politics*[1]

"THERE'S something faur wrang wi' my eyes," said Jinnet, putting down the newspaper, and cleaning her spectacles with a corner of her apron. "I'll need to get a new pair o' specs, or something. I've looked, and I've better looked a' ower that paper for onything to read, and I canna see a thing but speeches aboot the price o' the loaf in Germany. I'm shair I'm no heedin' whits the price of the loaf in Germany. I was never there. They must be awfu' hard up the noo for news to fill the papers."

Erchie finished his shaving, having used the Election Address[2] of one of the local candidates to clean his razor, and turned to his wife with a pawky smile.

"There's naething wrang wi' your eyes," he assured her; "and the price o' loaf in Germany's maist parteecular; everything depends on't."

"Is it different from ony ither kind o' loaf?" asked Jinnet.

"It's no like oor loaf at a'," said Erchie; "the German kind is made o' Indian corn and gunpoother, and it's black. The Germans eat it even-on, and that's whit mak's them so ferocious. They keep on eatin' it because they canna be shair whit the price'll be for ten minutes; the cost and the weight of the German loaf changes that fast ye would think ye were seein' it in yin o' thae cinematographs. It weighs two pounds at twelve o'clock, and at half-past three in the afternoon, when the evenin' papers comes oot, it's up to four pounds. It's fourpence the loaf if ye buys for your breakfast, sixpence ha'penny if ye want it for your tea, and elevenpence in a' the months that have an "r" in them."

"Isn't that silly!" exclaimed Jinnet; "I'm gled I'm no a German. It would be an awfu' sin if Lloyd George brocht in a loaf like that to this country to bamboozle us. But of course we could a' dae oor ain bakin'."

"Then you're a free Fooder?" said her husband.

"I am" she answered, "and thank the Lord we have aye

had whit would pay for't. I'm no owin' a penny to Mackay the baker."

"But look at it this way," continued Erchie, lighting his pipe; "ye ken whit the Dukes are — livin' in their castles and carryin' on like onything? They want twa shillin's a quarter extra tax on corn because it's a raw product —."

"Well let them!" said Jinnet, firmly; "corn's a thing that never comes inside the hoose. It's the Dukes themsel's that keep the horses."

"I admit that's an argument," said her husband, with the air of a candidate who has to confess that his heckler has cornered him. "But on the ither hand the price o' the half-loaf would go up a ha'penny if foreign corn was taxed. Whit did George Adam Smith,[3] the great Free Trade man say to Mr Gladstone in 1863? He said — well, ye can see for yoursel' in the papers whit he said, and he was a man that studied the subject."

"Was he a Free Trader?" asked Jinnet.

"He was. He invented it. He was a tariff Reformer, too, and the things he wrote aboot tariffs were like the ace o' clubs, nae maitter whit end of them ye look at it, they're aye the same; at least that's whit I gaither from readin' the Letters to the Editors."

"I wouldna be in favour o' a ha'penny on the loaf at a'," said Jinnet, "It's dear enough at threepence ha'penny, and they don't even gie ye a farden Abernethy wi't, the way they used to dae before they started politics."

"Then you're a Protectionist?" said Erchie,

"Indeed I am! If we didna protect oorsel's, what would dae't for us?" said Jinnet.

"It doesna maitter whether there's a ha'penny on the loaf or no if ye havena the money to buy a loaf at ony price, and that's the argyment on the other side," continued Erchie. "If you calculate that the Germans can build three Dreadnoughts[4] a month; that a suit o' claes costs six pound ten in America; and, that £5,604,324 worth o' boot protectors came into this country from abroad in 1893, ye can see for yoursel' that somebody must pay for the extra cost o' country eggs."

"Eggs is dear enough this winter," said Jinnet, sharply; "and wha's to pey the extra?"

"That's the point," said her husband. "I've gone into the thing carefully, and I see quite plain that the exporter, the importer, the shop-keeper, and the hen-farmer are gaun to quarrel among themsel's to get payin' 't. The only body that's jeck-easy about the hale thing is the hen. And that leads us up to anither point — do we pay for imports wi' exports, or do we jist send the money? There's no' the slightest doot that when we imported £2,646,408 worth o' Geneva watches into British ports in 1908, the Geneva watchmakers must have got something in exchange. What did they get? They got Bills o' Exchange. They cashed them pretty smart at the Post Office for gold. That bein' so, they got gold for their watches, and £2,646,408 of good British gold that micht hae paid the wages o' 6,432 British workmen for seventy-nine weeks at £2.10s a-week no' coontin' the Gleska Fair, went to pamper the foreigner."

"It shouldna be allood!" said Jinnet, emphatically. "I'm against puttin' money oot o' the country."

"Exactly!" said Erchie. "You're a Retaliator. But if ye look at it this way, gold's no use —"

"It's gey handy, whiles." said Jinnet; "I wish I seen mair o't'"

— "It's no' use; it's jist a medium o' exchange. Ye canna eat it, nor mak' a topcoat oot o't, nor use it in the kitchen grate. The gold the chaps in Geneva got for their watches was the equivalent o' labour. You tak' a man on a desert island, where there's nae minin' royalties, and say that in three years he imports 654,000 tons o' beet sugar and exports 1,642,000 tons o' whale bone —"

"Tuts! I'm aye startin' to read aboot that chap on the desert island," interrupted Jinnet; "but there's naething worth while reading' aboot ever happens to him. And ye needna try to bamboozle me wi' a' thae figures, for I canna understand them."

"Right!" said Erchie. "Neither can I. But they sound fine and big, and that's politics. When a man starts to be a politician he buys a Ready Reckoner, an almanack for the year afore last, and a book aboot astronomy. He multiplies the day o' the month by 79 and divides by the distance to Jupiter, and havin' got his information that way sends it in a letter to the papers heided "Exports v. Imports: Which?"

"I'm aye feared for thae Germans," said Jinnet, a little irrelevantly. "Dae ye think they're gaun to fight us?[5]

"Them!" said Erchie, contemptuously. "They'll no' fight us as lang's we tip them dacently. I ken hunders o' German waiters here in Gleska, and ye coudna chase them hame — nice enough chaps, tae. They mak' faur mair money aff takin' orders in the restaurants here than they would mak' by fightin' us. Forbye, they havena the time to fight the Germans; they're so busy buildin' men-o-war."

"Whit for?" asked Jinnet:

"For fun," said Erchie. "And the mair they build the better for us, for that mak's us build men-o'-war tae, and brings work to the Clyde. The warst thing that could happen to the Clydebank rivetter would be a Universal Peace."

"But we ha'e to pay for the new boats a' the same," Jinnet pointed out, and her husband twinkled.

"H'm!" said he;' "ye're awfu' ready wi' your argyments; if ye don't tak' care ye'll be a politeecian yoursel' before the election's over. Leave you a' the politics to men;[6] we understand them better."

"I'm no' so shair," said Jinnet. "Are you a Liberal or a Tory?"

"As shair as daith," he replied, "I canna tell. I'm baith o' them time aboot, and I canna mak' up my mind as lang's I read the papers."

31. *A Menagerie Marriage*[1]

ERCHIE CAME home two hours late for his supper.

"Whit in a' the world's come ower ye?" said his wife, with a significant glance at the clock.

"I was at a mairrage," replied her husband, taking off his coat. "Bostock's Jungle.[2] A.1. They played 'The Voice that Breathed O'er Eden' on the drum and cornet, and the bride, hypnotisin' the lions, wi' yin eye', and keepin' her ither on the bridegroom in case he would change his mind, swore to love, honour and obey. It went aff wi' a bang. I've never seen a cheerier weddin'."

"Tuts!" said Jinnet; "ye're haiverin', will ye ha'e an egg?"

"I'll ha'e twa eggs, and I'm no' haiverin'. I've been at a mairrage in the Jungle. The determined and happy couple went into the lions' cage. The bride wore a white silk dress and a bunch o' lily o' the valley, and the bridegroom, in a dark blue corded mornin' coat, took his poseetion next the gate. 'Whit new game is this?' says the lions to themsel's, gantin', and the minister hurried through wi' the thing in case they would mak' a breenge. At a distant part of the arena the monkeys sat disconsolate on their hunkers, wonderin' whit way they were neglected. 'Where's them pea-nuts?' they says to themsel's. 'Are we, or are we not, entitled to some public recognition?' But the fickle public hadna a single peanut or a gingersnap for the monkeys; that's the worst of a mairrage matinee — it distracts attention from the regular hands."

"I suppose ye're talkin' aboot that lassie that mairried the lion-tamer," suggested Jinnet.

"He must be awfu' busy when he had to tak' her into a cage to mairry her. Was the lions no' awfu' angry?"

"It wasna a lion-tamer at a'," said Erchie; "it was jist a common workin' chap. 'Noo's the chance for ye to mak' a reputation for yoursel', they tell't him; 'be mairried in a lions' cage, and ha'e your name in a' the papers.'

"'Could I no' be mairried among the love-birds, or

sittin' on an elephant?' he says.

"'There's naething for't but the lions' cage,' says Mr Bostock, firmly; 'whit we want to prove is the sagacity o' the animal.'

"'But the lions micht mak' a dash at us,' said the chap.

"'Whit's the odds?' says Mr Bostock; 'ye're gettin' mairried onyway! Everything'll be tip-top — a rale minister wi' Geneva bands on, a brides-cake, a cab, and a poke o' confetti. Whit mair could ye ask for?'"

"I'm gled," said Jinnet; "there were nae operatics o' that kind at my weddin'. I would rather no' be mairried at a' than mairried in a cage, like a canary. Whit's the sense o't?"

"It's an American idea," said Erchie. "A kirk's the last place on earth onybody would think o' mairryin' in in America; the ceremony must tak' place in a balloon, or doon a coal-pit or in a warehoose window. The thing's so common there that they ha'e a special breed o' minister that spend most o' their time in balloons, coal-pits or warehoose windows. We have been a little late in taking up the idea in Scotland, but if ye're spared ye'll see mairrages on the stage before the transformation scene in the pantomime; on the roller rinks; in billiard-rooms, and at half-time at the fitba-matches. The common mairrage in a kirk, or up a stair wi' a wheen o' laddies cryin' 'Hard up!' at the fit o' the close'll be oot o' date in nae time; ony pushin' young man that's thinkin' o' enterin' the sacred bonds o' matrimony 'll no' be blessed unless he can hae a brass band, and five or six thoosand folk lookin' on."

"Did the lions growl?" asked Jinnet.

"They did not!" said Erchie, taking off his boots. "They didna want to ha'e anything to dae wi' the thing at a', and the trainer had to egg them on. I was vexed for them lions, they would be faur happier scourin' the desert plains o' Africa than sittin' like a lot o' neds at a mairrage pairty wi' naething to eat. They never got the least chance, for three or four tamers with a pistol in every hand stood between them and the blushin', pair, and—"

"Were they railly blushin'?" interrupted Jinnet,

"They were," said Erchie. "At least the bride was; the bridegroom he had his back to the lions, and every noo and then he gied a glance over his shoother to see if onybody was gaun to heave a cocoanut. The minister kept near the gate, handy for backin' out if there was any need for't; and he had the pair mairried before the lions could mak' up their mind whether they would start wi' the bride or bridegroom."

"'Ha'e ye that ring aboot ye?' says the minister to the bridegroom.

"'It's in my hip p-p-pocket!' says the puir chap trimlin' in his shoes.

"'Oot wi't slippy then, and put it on her finger,' says the minister; 'the big yellow yin's lickin' his lips.'

"The bridegroom slipped on the ring, and then dashed for the door, and ye never saw lions mair chawed."

"Did he no' kiss his wife?" asked Jinnet.

"He hadna time. Forbye, he wouldna like to dae't wi' such a lot o' strangers looking' on."

"I canna understand whit in the world ye went to such a performance for, and you a beadle," said Jinnet. "I'm sure ye've seen plenty o' weddin's."

"Hundreds," agreed her husband. "But this was a bye-ordinar' weddin'. There was aye a chance that the lions micht be hungry, and I've never seen a lion swallow a bridegroom. Duffy was wi' me, and he was awfu' disappointed; 'I wouldna care though the lions let the newly-mairried couple aff, for it's bad enough to be mairried,' he says, 'but the least the silly brutes could ha'e done was to chase the minister. Whit did we pay oor shullin' for? I doot, Macpherson, the management's gaun awa' and fed thae lions up afore the weddin' started. Either that or they should ha'e a fatter minister.'"

"Was he a rale minister?" asked Jinnet, with surprise.

"Of course he was a rale minister; he made a speech to the audience frae the inside o' the cage, and tell't them that he wouldna ha'e been there that nicht at a' if it wasna that he was sure a mairrage in a lions' cage was a moral and spiritual exhibeetion. Some o' the people laughed at that, and later on he expresed his surprise that they didna realise the solemnity of the occasion. It was solemn enough for the puir lions — no' a bite of onything a' the time."

"Was he no' nervous?"

"He must ha'e been, for he forgot to mak' a collection; and he didna dwell on the moral lesson."

"Whit was the moral lesson o' the mairrage in a menagerie?" asked Jinnet.

"I would ha'e to see the Rev. Mr Morris and ask him," said her husband; " I couldna find out mysel'. But I can tell ye I was vexed for them puir lions!"

32. *Erchie and the Earthquake*[1]

ERCHIE, WHO had fallen asleep by the kitchen fire in an effort to discover by the utmost concentration of his intellect upon a newspaper leading article, whether it was the Unionists, the Liberals, the Nationalists, the Irish Americans, or the Socialists who were winning the Election, awoke suddenly with a startled movement which upset the winter-dykes on which Jinnet had been toasting some of his own professional linen.

The tin tea-caddie on the mantel-piece had toppled over on its side, and was trickling a sample of the Finest Tea the World produces at 1s 7d per pound straight from the Plantation, on to the hearth-stone; the Bonnie Lass of Ballochmyle (Wilson the Grocer's Calendar, 1910) was strangely swinging from side to side on the tack suspending her over a pair of cast-iron sheep which Jinnet faithfully black-leaded every time she did the gate. Two highly-polished Britannia-metal dish-covers that had never been used for their legitimate purpose, and were merely ornamental, like the cast-iron sheep, were shaking and tinkling against the wall they hung upon above the coal-bunker, and every plate on the dresser rattled.

"I'll bate ye whit ye like that's McCallum the sailor hame from another voyage," said Erchie, looking up at the ceiling; "I wonder what he brought this time; it sounded awfu' like a chevalier-and-bookcase."

Surprised to get no answer from his wife, he turned about in his chair, and was even more surprised to see her bent below the set-in bed.[2]

"My! what a start I got!" she exclaimed, when she had emerged. "I was shair that Williamson's cat had got in this afternoon when I was washin' doon the stair, and shut himsel' up in the wee tin trunk I had at Rothesay. But there's nae cat there, and I'm a' in a palpitation!"

"Did it soond like a cat?" asked Erchie.

"It wasna exactly a soond, but jist a queer sensation. First I felt the soles o' my feet a' prinklin'; then the caddie coupit, and the delf begood to rattle on the dresser. I could swear the hale o' the land was shakin'."

"It's whit I tell't ye'; it's McCallum hame from sea," said her husband, confidently. "Wait a wee and ye'll hear yin o' his kahootchy top-boots gaun bungin' into the back coort through his kitchen window. Ye canna blame the chap. Awa' from his wife and weans for nine months even on, and nae sport!"

"It's no' McCallum, whatever it was," said Jinnet, picking up the winter-dykes. "She tell't me yesterday he was awa' where the nutmegs comes frae, somewhere aboot Calcutta, and wouldna be hame till February."

"Then it's Willy Grant comin' up the stair, and the wrang man's in for the Curmunnock Burghs.[3] Gang to the door and see if he hasna tummelt on your bass."

Jinnet went to the door and returned to report that nobody was on the stair. "It wasna like a man comin' hame at a', for there wasna ony noise wi't," she said to Erchie; "it was mair like something happenin' at a distance; it was — "

She was interrupted by a second tremor of the house; the tea-caddie toppled over again, the Bonnie Lass of Ballochmyle fell off her tack, and the crockery clattered even more extraordinarily than before.

"We'll hae to look into this wi' a candle," said her husband, when he had recovered from his astonishment. "I'm afraid the gasalier's awa' wi't in the paurlour. Naething less than the fa' o' yon twa hunderweicht o' chains and weichts and brass bunches o' grapes, and curly-wurlies, and cut-glass globes, no to mention a gallon o' water I put into't last week, would account for ony dacent hoose behavin' like this, and me, as ye micht say, quite teetotal. And I thocht it was McCallum! McCallum couldna mak' a stramash like that, even if his wife, puir body! kept a mangle."

They lit a candle, and went apprehensively into the room.

The gasalier was still suspended from the ceiling, as magnificently ponderous as Erchie had suggested; but a what-not, the pride of Jinnet's heart since her son had made it mainly out of empty cotton-reels, had fallen forward, and its contents were scattered — fortunately little damaged — on the floor.

"Oh Erchie! Erchie!" she exclaimed; "I was shair frae the start it was Williamson's cat."

"If Williamson's cat was the size o' a dromedary, and was dancin' the Hoolachan afore your very een, it couldna shake the hoose like yon!" said her husband, with impatience, looking, with the candle, underneath the table. "It looked to me mair like as if they had started to tak' doon the Hoose o' Lords."[4]

"Do ye think it micht be that?" asked Jinnet, seriously, thinking of explosions.

"Weel, no," he admitted; "it hadna the proper dunt for that."

"Maybe it's a judgment, for them middlin' wi' the Hoose o' Lords," said Jinnet, setting up her what-not. "If I was gaun to tak' doon onything o' that kind, I would start wi' the Hoose o' Commons. Naething'll convince me it's no' that cat o' Williamson's!"

"A cat couldna stop a nock, and there's the nock stopped," said her husband, when they returned to the kitchen; but this, at least, was not to be attributed to any mysterious agency. Jinnet pointed out that the weights of the wag-at-the-wa' had naturally run down.

"If it's no' a cat, and ye huve yet to prove it's no' a cat," said Jinnet; "it's electricity! Look at a' thae 'lectric lights in the butcher's windows; and their motor-caurs, and their skoosh-caurs scourin' up and doon a' day; and their telephones and telegrams and cinematygraphs — they're usin' up the substance o' the air, so that even a tack'll no' haud up a calendar. I was readin' in the papers just this very day that the way its awfu' wet in London is because they're cuttin' doon a lot o' trees in Canada."

Erchie laughed. "Hoo could cuttin' doon trees in Canada bring on the rain in London, ye wee fuiter?" he asked.

"It's a thing they ca' the Gulf Stream," she explained; "and I'm no' a'fuiter! There's hot air, and there's cauld air; and every time ye cut a tree in Canada there's a blash o' moisture comes on the Gulf Stream. ... Mercy on us, whit's that?"

The door-bell had rung violently; Erchie went to the door himself, and gave admission to Duffy the coalman in a state of intense excitement.

"Did ye feel it?" he inquired, when he reached the kitchen.

"The only thing I feel is a smell o' the Mull o' Kintyre Vaults," said Erchie. "I hope you and your friends doon there are daein' the best they can to keep the country gaun till this election's settled."

"Did ye no' feel the earthquake?" asked Duffy, heedless of this irony. "Man, the hale o' Gleska's shooglin' like a calf's-feet shape."

Erchie looked at the stopped clock with some surprise; it indicated only a little after nine. "I had nae idea it was efter ten, Duffy," he remarked. "Oor clock's stopped. Was it jist an ordinar' ten-past-ten o'clock shoogle, or something extra-special for the Elections?"

The coalman sat down in a chair and recounted a

thrilling tale; which carried conviction with it. Tea-cad-
dies, calendars, and tin dish-covers had been falling all
over the city, and a man he knew had had a pint of ale
upset. Mrs Duffy had taken the weans with her, and had
left her house to take refuge in her sister's out at Maryhill,
with some idea that she could depend on the protection of
the British Army.

"Oh, Erchie!" wailed Jinnet. "I tell't ye it was a judgment. They didna need to touch the Hoose o' Lords; they
could jist let on they were gaun to tak' it doon."

"And they say, doon at the Mull o' Kintyre Vaults, that
we havena passed the worst o't yet," proceeded Duffy with
gloomy pleasure. "There's aye three shocks; the third'll
come afore twelve the nicht, if it comes at a', and then ye'll
see a pant!"

"Oh, mercy be aboot us!" cried Jinnet, wringing her
hands, "and me wi' a great big ironin' the morn!"

"Wha tell't ye that aboot the three shocks?" inquired her
husband.

"A gentleman that's an expert aboot earthquakes,"
answered Duffy. "He was yince a stoker on a boat   that
went to Demerara, and he's sellin' alarm clocks. Splendid
sonsy, wee, round, tin, white-faced yins, wi'   an awfu'
birl; he was askin' haulf-a-croon for them till   the
earthquake happened, and noo he's takin' eighteenpence
to get them aff his hands afore the toon collapses. I tell ye
there's a wheen o' wise-like clocks changed hands the nicht
doon yonder at the Mull o' Kintyre Vaults."

"And whit are ye a' wantin' wi' alarm-clocks if the
earthquake's gaun to swallow Gleska in anither oor or
twa?" asked Erchie. "Are ye frichtened that ye'll sleep in
and miss it?"

"And we havena even the richt time!" moaned Jinnet,
hauling up the clock-chains.

"Do ye railly think there's ony danger, Erchie? We
micht sleep for the nicht in Mrs Williamson's."

Erchie laughed. "I would sooner risk the earthquake
than her cat," he answered. "There's no enough o' fushion

in a Scottish earthquake to upset a barrow."

"Onyway," said Duffy, making his departure, having duly warned them; "I'm gaun to live a better life if I get ower the nicht wi't."

Twenty minutes later Jinnet was in bed, convinced that that was the safest place to be in case of an earthquake.

"Erchie," she said to her husband, who had resumed his paper; "push back that tea-pot on the hob a wee; if Gleska's gaun to be swallowed up, I would be vexed to lose my good new teapot. And me plannin' for a great big ironin' in the mornin'!"

Five minutes later she was fast asleep.

33. *Erchie and the Census*[1]

DUFFY THE coalman came round to MacPherson's house on Saturday night with his Census schedule[2] carefully wrapped in a newspaper as if it were an exquisite rare etching or a Commission of the Peace.

"Do ye understand anything aboot this?" he asked, unfolding it. "There's a chap comin' roond to lift it again on Monday mornin', and it'll tak' me all that time to read it."

"I've jist filled up my ain this efternoon," said Erchie. "A solemn occasion, Duffy! We're ten years aulder than we were when we did it last, and I sair misdoot we're no' much better men. Have ye read the instructions carefully?"

"I have not! It cam' to us yesterday, but I didna want to examine it much till I washed my hands for Sunday, and noo that I'm washed I canna find my specs. I wish ye would gie me a hand. I'm tellt that if ye mak' the least bit up in fillin' it up it's a five pound fine. Nae wonder sae mony folk's gaun awa' to Canada!"

Erchie's wife produced the ink-pot and a pen; he took off his coat, drew up his chair to the kitchen table, spread Duffy's schedule out before him, and glanced over his glasses quizzingly at the coalman.

"I see they've put ye doon here already as the heid of the family," he remarked. "Whit does Mrs Duffy say to that?"

"That's richt enough," said Duffy; "I'm the heid o' the hoose: I pay the rent o't."

"But it's her that saves it; if it wasna for her I doot ye wouldna hae a hoose to be the heid o', and would be haein' your name put doon to-morrow nicht for a lodger in a Model. Whether we pay the rent or no', Duffy, I'm afraid it's the last chance we'll hae in a Census paper to put oorsel's doon for heid's o' faimilies; the Suffragettes is gaun to parade the streets on Sunday to show that they hae no heids o' any kind."

"Number o' rooms?" proceeded Erchie, "including kitchen, wi' one or more windows occupied by the person or persons entered on the schedule."

"I never occupy a window frae wan end o' the week till the other," said Duffy. "If there's ony windows that ye could ca' occupied in oor hoose, it's by the wife, and it's the parlour yin; she's generally hingin' oot[3] o't watchin' funerals."

"Hoo mony rooms hae ye wi' windows in them no' coontin' sculleries, pantries, or bathrooms?"

"Twa rooms and kitchen, a fine big lobby,[4] and a share o' a washin' hoose."

"Washin' hooses don't coont," explained Erchie, "nor lobbies either. There's nae windows in a lobby."

"There's a window in oors," insisted Duffy "a wee yin wi' a broken pane above the ootside door."

"But ye canna live in a lobby, man," said Erchie; "it's only rooms ye can live in that they're wantin'."

"Can ye no'? When my wife starts spring cleanin' in a week or twa the lobby'll be the only pairt o' the hoose I'll can turn mysel' roond in. I think I would chance the lobby, Erchie; twa room and kitchen for a faimily o' nine looks awfu' shilpit. Forby, there's three fine presses."[5]

"Three rooms," said Erchie, emphatically.

"No' a room more, or they'll fine ye! Noo for the names and ages — 'James Duffy, heid o' faimily; aged 69 —.'"

"Haud on!" cried Duffy. "Nane o' that! I'm naething like 69; I'm nearer 59."

MacPherson put down his pen. "Tak' my tip, Duffy," he said, "and don't be an idiot tryin' to pass yoursel' aff for 59. Ye'll be wantin' an auld age pension in a year or twa, and then ye would look awfu' silly if your ain Census paper made ye oot a leear. Whit's your actual age?"

"It's 65," said Duffy, hastily. "The very day I was born in Wishaw they started the Caledonian Railway."

"Nae Gaelic?" proceeded Erchie. "'Mairried,' of course; 'Personal occupation' — coalman, own account; born in Lanarkshire, Wishaw.[6] Ony infirmities?"

"I racked my back a week ago liftin' my horse on its feet in the stable," said the coalman.

"That's no' an infirmity under the Act; it's a lesson to ye to put props under that kind o' horse whenever he's oot o' the trams. I think that's a' for you, Duffy, but of course ye must tak' care and be alive at midnicht to-morow nicht or else ye'll be in for the fine. And ye must be shair and pass Sunday nicht in yer ain hoose; if ye step over the door between the time ye get your tea to-morrow nicht and Monday morning, Lord Pentland'll[7] be awfu' angry. Noo for the mistress; whit's her full maiden name?"

"Bella Carmichael," answered Duffy, breathing heavily, and perspiring with the intellectual stress of the occasion. "Whit the deevil's the use o' botherin' aboot the like o' that? She's weel enough kent as Mrs Duffy."

"Jist that! but it's a point Lord Pentland's awfu' parteecular aboot," said Erchie. "Ye canna tell whit he may be wantin' her maiden name for, and onywye it would look gey droll if your wife hadna a maiden name. Age?"

"Fifty-three, but she mak's oot hersel' it's only fifty."

"Mairried, of course. Hoo mony years has she been mairried?"

"Fifteen."

"Puir cratur! Hoo mony children born alive and still livin'?"

"Six livin' and wan in Edinburgh," said Duffy after a moment's reflection.

"Is that Jamie, the paper mill yin?" asked MacPherson. "He's livin' too, isn't he?"

"Ye could hardly say he was," said Duffy, seriously, "him being in Edinburgh. By all accoonts, there's no much life in Edinburgh."

"All the same he'll be lingerin' on, we'll put the family doon at seven. Personal occupation — your wife hasna ony Personal Occupation."

"The busiest wee woman in Gleska!" interjected Jinnet, who had occupied herself with her knitting hitherto. "It's no' fair to let Lord Pentland think that mairried wives does naething. I saw Mrs Duffy wi' a great big washin' yesterday."

"Lord Pentland doesna want to ken aboot the washin's," said her husband. "Washin's no' an occupation'; it's jist a way o' passin' by the time. Where was the mistress born, Duffy?"

"Cambuslang, but I couldna say whit county."

"We'll leave Lord Pentland to fill the county in for himsel," said Macpherson. "In ony case it's on the Gleska tramway system 'Infirmities?' — I better tell the truth aboot that and put her doon as 'totally blind.' There's nae ither way o' acoontin' for her mairryin' you.

Having filled in all the details regarding the Duffy family, Erchie winked at his wife and proceeded to invent a variety of interrogations which Lord Pentland and the Registrar-General had omitted from the schedule.

"Ony cats, dogs, canaries, or other domestic pets?" he asked solemnly.

"Michty!" exclaimed the coalman. "I didna think they would cairry the thing as far as that. We hae a cat — a — a kind o' Tom, like."

"Cat — Thomasina," said Erchie, with a graphic pretence at writing down this interesting item.

"Whit spechie?"

"Torty-shell."

"Torty-shell, richt!, Hoo mony pianos, gramaphones, motor-caurs, or other musical instruments?"

"The only musical instrument we hae in the hoose is Maggie's mandoline, and she doesna play on't," said Duffy.

"A mandoline's no' a musical instrument within the strict meanin' o' the Act, we'll hae to put it doon under Infirmities," said Erchie scribbling away with a dry pen. "Ony live stock in the shape o' horses, cattle, goats, or sheep?"

"Jist the wan horse," said Duffy, "but whit's the sense o' them takin' ony accoont o' horses?"

"It'll be for the Airmy," explained MacPherson. "Lord Pentland'll want to ken hoo mony horses are available for military purposes if we were gaun to start a war."

"Unless he's startin' gey soon he needna lippen ower much on my horse; it's no' a chicken."

"Are ye shair it'll be livin' at twelve o'clock the morn's nicht?"

"It has a fair chance," said Duffy with some hesitation, and MacPherson apparently credited him in the Census schedule with a horse. "Next," he proceeded; "whit money hae ye in the bank?" But this was carrying the joke too far in Jinnet's opinion, and she interposed.

34. *The MacPhersons at the "Ex."*[1]

ERCHIE TOOK his wife on Saturday to the Exhibition[2] where they spent ten solid hours of the most determined gaiety, and each consumed as many cups of tea. It was only by having it with a cup of tea that they could enjoy the luxury of a seat, and though Jinnet could stand a whole day over a washing-tub without expressing weariness, the tread-mill of gaiety revealed a hitherto unsuspected weakness in her legs. Wherever they saw a restaurant they looked for its least imposing entrance, and worshipped again at the shrine of St Bohea.[3] They tried it by the cup and by the pot. "The doctors say that tea's no' a food at a'", said Erchie late in the afternoon.

"That's where they're wrang; its that extraordinar' satisfyin'. I feel I could dae withoot ony mair o't a' the days o' my life." But to his wife it was like a continuous series of banquets. Sustained and fortified by these libations, she compassed the whole show, exhausted its every feature to her own satisfaction — a feat beyond the average season ticket-holder, even though he attend each day till next October.

The philosophy of Exhibitions was imparted to her early in the day by Erchie. "It's no' the fun ye get yoursel' that's to be looked for at oor time o' life," he told her; "but ye can get a lot o' sport frae watchin' ither people screichin' themsel's hoarse on the Scenic."

"Mind I'm no' gaun on it!" she warned him as she watched the crowded cars pop in and out between the painted hills, and heard the hysterical screams of their passengers as they plunged down the precipitious places.

"I'm no' askin' ye," he retorted. "To dae the Scenic properly, ye need to be under five-and-twenty, and hae a lad to haud your hand. A sport that would suit ye better is the whirly-whirly washin'-bynes."

"Whit are they like?" she inquired with interest, and he took her to the Whirlpool.

"In a' creation' whit are they daein' in the bynes?" she exclaimed, amazed at the sight of giddily gyrating tubs with their load of frenzied occupants.

"Jist whit ye see" he answered. "They're birlin' roond and roond, first yin way, and then the ither. It's a game they got the idea for frae the sweetie-works. It must be fine to be a pan-drop![4] said the inventive sowl, and skooshed awa hame at yince and took oot a patent."

"Puir craturs," said Jinnet, under a natural misapprehension. "Look at that yin wi' her hair a' doon! And it's likely they'll no' get much in the week for daein't."

He laughed. "Instead o' bein' payed for daein' it, they pay to get daein' it. They couldna be hired to dae it for ony money. I have nae idea the way ye feel when ye come aff a thing like that, but I'm shair it would mak' my heid bizz like a seidlitz poother."[5]

"Whaur's the place they ca' the Joy Hoose?" Jinnet asked, when her interest in the Whirlpool was exhausted.

"Up here on the left; I'm shair ye can hear them laughin'."

They went up and watched a stream of convulsively amused devotees of Joy go staggering along the balcony whereby the ingenious inventor of the House of Mystery made it plain to the hesitating looker-on that fun of the most excruciating kind was to be had within.

"Whit in a' the world dae they see inside?" asked Jinnet.

"I havena the least idea," said her husband, "but I'm certain shair ye couldna get a sonsy, big, wise-like woman like that yin haudin' on to the rail to laugh like that unless it was something extra comic. I believe they must tak' aff your boots and stockin's and kittle[6] your feet to start wi'. Then, in anither room, they'll hae a chap tellin' funny bawrs. Further on again they'll hae waiters trippin' on a mat and smashin' trays o' delf — in my experience as a waiter there's naething on earth mair laughable than that."

"Mercy on us! see at them comin' skytin' oot o' yon place!" exclaimed his wife. "Dae ye think there's been an accident?"

"That's the concludin' moral; when ye reach the height o' Joy ye get the heave, and land wi' some loss o' dignity on the solid, solemn firmament. I'm tellt the star comic o' the Joy House stands at the top o' that slide and gies every customer a push-aff wi' a wooden leg in the sma' o' the back."

"A wooden leg!" said Jinnet, incredulously.

"That's his speciality," said her husband solemnly. "Engaged for the season at great expense. The last wild pang o' Joy's a pin leg in the sma' o' the back."

Jinnet protested that though so much apparent joy was ridiculously cheap at sixpence, she would not venture to indulge in it, a sentiment with which her husband quite

agreed, so they passed along and examined the Mountain
Slide and the Joy Wheel.

"A proof," said Erchie, "that ony kind o' hasty motion's
joyous so lang's it's no' walkin' to your work. Ye would
think that slidin' doon a funnel on a bass, or sittin' on a
wheel for a second or twa afore it whirled ye aff would be
sports that an athletic nation would tire o', but here they're
keepin' it up frae mornin' till nicht. I watched them the
ither day when I was here wi' Duffy for mair than a couple
o' hours, hopin' to see a Bylie or a Gilmorehill Professor on
the slide or on the wheel, but nane o' them turned up.
They seem to have awfu' nerrow views aboot an Historical
Exhibition."

"I havena seen onything historical aboot it," said Jinnet.

"Then we'll try the An Clachan," said Erchie briskly.
"It's a risk, I'll admit, for though I'm a MacPherson, I
havena a word o' the language, and I'll maybe no'
understaund a word o' whit they're daein'. Here ye are,
roond here: ye can tell it's the An Clachan by the smell o'
peats and the chap wi' the kilts and medals."

Jinnet was delighted with the Clachan. "It's jist the same
as it was rale," she said; "I've seen the like o't afore in Islay.
Whit are they lads gaun to dae on the pletform?"

"They're gaun to dance a reel," said Erchie, without
hesitation. "They're aye daein' that in the genuine An
Clachans. Whenever the weather's dry the native
Hielandman puts on his medals and goes on a pletform on
the An Clachan green and does a step o' the Hoolichan.
They're daein' it at this very meenute, the day bein' fine, a'
ower the Hielands, and here it's brung to your very door.
It's a triumph o' science, like Loch Katrine water.[7] There
ye hae their wee bit hooses; there's the smiddy, and I'll
bate ye whit ye like the blacksmith's no' in, for there's the
Inns quite handy to him."

"I don't see ony Inns," said Jinnet.

"It's the Inns richt enough, I assure ye; though they ca't
the Tigg Osta,[8] them no' haein' ony English. I see they sell
tea in't; ye havena had ony tea for nearly twenty meenutes;

we'll gang in and try a cup in Gaelic. Watch ye don't tramp on a hen."

"They're rale wise-like lassies that's waitin'," said Jinnet as they took their seats at a table. "Boots and stockin's and a' their orders."

"Of course they are! the genuine Clachnacudden. Did ye think ye would find them postin' blankets? Man, I wish I kent the language! — Whit's the kind o' signs ye mak' for twa cups o' tea and some soda scones."

But the attendants, fortunately, were bilingual; signs were quite uncalled-for, and the pair emerged, refreshed anew, to pursue their studies of the Celt at Home.

"Whit I like aboot an An Clachan," said Erchie, "is that it's fine and self-contained. The inns is handy to the smiddy, and the kirk's next door to the Inns; everything's contrived for comfort and conveniency. I don't see mony people croodin' to the kirk, either, they're a' at the picture post-caird coonter; faith, naething seems to have been overlooked. And I declare to ye here's a wee private still as nate as ninepence workin' awa' beside that burn."

"Oh, Erchie!" said Jinnet, "are they no' feared? If the polis was to catch them!"

Erchie chuckled. "Nae fears o' that!" he assured her. "The polis is Hieland themsel's, and if ye asked them if that was a still they would likely tell ye it was a soda-water works."

From An Clachan to the African Village was to Jinnet like a transit by magic carpet from Paradise to a pagan orgy. She clung close to her husband's arm as they passed the dusky sons of Shepherd's Bush and Saughton Park; regarded the dancing women with pity and dismay, and felt every domestic instinct outraged by their heathen kitchen.

"Whit are thae men yowlin' and bangin' the wee barrells for?" she asked.

"They're no' yowlin'!" said Erchie; "they're croonin' the plaintive sangs o' the dear auld Mother Land but they're kind o' croupy wi' the Scottish climate. And they're no' bangin' barrells; them's the genuine native drums; they're ca'd tom-toms."

But the native babies pleased her most. "It must tak' an awfu' black-leadin' to mak' them look like that. The wee smouts! I wonder whit'll they feed them on!"

"Monkey nuts," said Erchie, "and noo and then a banana. If ye're tired o' the shows by noo we'll hae anither cup o' tea and pass on to the rale Historical!"

But of the Historical Section, all she could recall when they got home was a case of old Church tokens. And she was grieved at old familiar features they had somehow missed. "If I havena come awa' and clean forgot to hae my name embroidered on a hankey!"

35. *Togo*[1]

"I SAW Togo[2] drivin' oot to the Exhibeetion yesterday," said Duffy. "He's a fine big strong chap; I would back yon chap to shift coals if ye put him to't. He was smokin' a substantial cigar wi' wan hand and recognisin' the folk in the street wi' the other."

"Had he on a pot hat?" asked Erchie, suspecting some mistake.

"Yon's a heid that never had a pot hat on it, MacPherson; he was wearin' a yachtin' bonnet."

"Then ye're wrang again!" said Erchie. "Yon was Lord Provost M'Innes Shaw in the Loch Katrine uniform. When the Gleska Magistrates go to a Water Trip[3] they aye put on a deep-sea kep, and the Lord Provost wore his yesterday oot o' respect for the Japanese Admirality."

"I was tell't it was Togo richt enough," said Duffy. "And the crood was cheerin'."

"Togo was the wee blate chap sittin' in the shade o' Mr Shaw, wi' a jerry hat on, broodin' on the mystery o' the East and lookin' awfu' like a man that micht hae a steady job in the Prudential. I'm tell't he asked the Lord Provost through an interpreter if the weather was aye like this in

Gleska. 'There's whiles a drap o' rain,' said Mr M'Innes
Shaw, 'but this is a time of the year that's special; we ca' it
the Fair Week, and it's aye that hot that a' the folk in Gleska
gang doon to the coast to dook[4] themsel's, Your Admirality.'

"'It minds me of Nagasaki,' said Count Togo, takin' a
hankey from his sleeve and moppin' the back o' his neck
wi't.' 'I could dae fine wi' a drink o' Lemon Kali and a
piece o' ice in't.'

"'Ye'll get that!' said His Lordship, 'Jist you hold on till
we're at the Garden Club!' Togo edged up in his seat to get
mair into the shade o' Mr Shaw and wished he had brung
his fan."

"They're makin' an awfu' palaver aboot the Japanees
nooadays," said Duffy "They werena in't at a' when I was
young; the only place ye saw ony sign o' them, was on a
tea-kist or a willow-pattern plate."

"That wasna the Japs! it was the Chinese, but there's
railly no' much difference, for the Chinese and Japs is kind
o' Hie'lan' kizzens. Japan's an island aff the coast o' China,
the same as Arran's aff the Lairgs."

"They focht the Chinese,"[5] Duffy reminded him; "there
wasna much o' the kizzen aboot that."

"I said Hie'lan' kizzens. Ye couldna expect them no' to
fight at some time or other. Ye see the Japanees were
wakenin' up, but the China yins werena wakenin' up at a',
and it's awfu' aggravatin' to hear another body snorin' and
you at your work. At first the Japanese thocht o' landin' a
cargo o' yon wee roond tin wan-and-elevenpenny alarm
clocks on the China coast, but there's 750 million China-
men, and there wasna enough o' clocks to go roond, so
there was naething for't but to send an Airmy. I tell you the
China yins got a deevil o' a start! They werena richt ready
for a war. They hadna even wise-like claes for't, to begin
wi' — naething but felt slippers and a kind o' cretonne
ulster, and they hadna done onything in the gunpoother
way since they invented it. The hardy wee Japs went in at
the wan end o' China and cam' out of the ither the same's
it was a through-gaun close.[6] My Jove!"

"Was Togo leadin' them?" inquired Duffy.

"No; he was on a different shift; if I mind richt, they were led roond China by a chap Band's Eye. They did a feaful lot o' damage to the China yins, and then went hame."

"Togo is close on bein' the Nelson o' the East; if he had an eye awantin' and an empty sleeve, he would be the very ticket! The Rooshian[7] fleet went sailin' roond by the Dogger Bank, and anchored aff Japan at a place they ca'd Yahoo.[8]

"'What's this?' says Togo when he seen them. 'Do they imagine that we're handin' a Coronation? See's my spy-glass.'

"'It's Rodjestvenski[9] richt enough!' says he. 'Fancy the neck o' him!' And he cleared his ships for action. He wiped aff the Rooshian fleet afore his tea, and then went doon the stair to the caibin o' his boat and had a sleep to himsel'. When he came up he was feelin' fine and fresh, and, puttin' his spy-gless to his e'e again, he sweeps the hale horizon 'My Jove! chaps,' says he, 'there's been an awfu' stramash here! This sort o' thing 'll spoil boat-hirin' in Yahoo for July and August.'

"The Mickado[10] — that's the heid yin o' the Japs; that goes aboot below a paper umbrella — made Togo a Count, and the British Government made oot that the Japanese were a civilised nation at last, and made an alliance wi' them as fast's they could. They're a hardy race, the Japanese. They used to feed on naething but rice and cherry blossoms up till a dozen years ago, when they started takin' tinned meat from Chicago. Immediately their manly instincts was roused; they put aff their Paisley plaids and started wearing breeks. The future o' the human race is wi' the folk that ha'e a pocket at the hip for haudin' money."

"If yon was Togo, then, he wasna my idea!" said Duffy in tones of doubt and disppointment. "Yon chap might be a U.F. Elder. He didna look half as fierce as Provost M'Innes Shaw."

"He micht look like a Christian elder, Duffy, but he couldna richt be wan since he's no' a Christian," answered

Erchie. "The Japanese believes in naething but ancestors; they're hunders o' years behind the time aboot releegion. I'll bate ye that some day they'll be sorry for't! The only thing that's to be said for their releegion is that it's chape; there's nae Sustentation Fund nor Foreign Mission in't, and a' they want when they're worshippin' is a wee wooden temple and a box o' fuzee lichts. Sunday and Setterday's the same to them: the rice and cherry-blossom's in their blood yet, and they're only heathens."

"Ye would think," said Duffy, "that him bein' an Admiral, he would put on his uniform gaun to the Exhibeetion."

"Nae ordinar' uniform would stand the strain o' a' yon Coronation banquets he's bein' haein' up in London; he would hae a uniform to start wi' richt enough when he landed."

"I would hae liked to hae seen him in't," said Duffy.

"Ye wouldna be awfu' ta'en up wi't if ye had, for a Japanese Admiral in his uniform is just like an English yin, and that's no' half as fancy as the Fire Brigade. The days when a Japanese Admiral would go into action wi' a satin quilt and a parasol is a' by wi't, and the ambeetion o' the poorest Japanee noo is to hae a pair o' trousers turned up at the foot, and a there-and-back[11] collar five inch deep."

"What were they daein' afore they woke up and started fightin'?" asked Duffy.

"The puir deluded sowls were quite content makin' draught-screens, wee ivory elephants, ash-trays, and things to put in lucky bags. Their needs were few; their tastes were simple — a handful o' rice or cherry-blossoms, four bamboo poles and some sheets o' caird-board for a hoose; a vase wi' a single orange-lily in't, and a bass to sleep on. Noo they hae splendid factories, and turn oot a jute art square at 3s 11½d that's the terror o' Dundee.[12] They cam' ower to Dubs and Fairfield to learn some engineerin', and went hame wi' the genuine Gleska accent and a heid fu' o' plans for battleships. The China yins are still doverin', as ye micht say, but the Japanese are up afore it's daylicht in the mornin' pushin' tred, and I'll warrant Togo never felt sae much at hame in ony place in England as he did in Gleska."

36. Strikes[1]

"Did ye hear a noise on the stair last night?" asked Jinnet. "I was just gaun over, when it wakened me wi' an awfu' start. I thought at first it was the Grants bringin' hame their new piano, but naebody in their sober senses would bring hame a new piano in the dark, for naebody in the land would see't."

"I never heard an article," said Erchie, tapping his breakfast egg, "but I'll guarantee it wasna Grant's piano onyway. When the Grants get their piano it'll be on a Setturday efternoon, accompanied by a grand procession. It was mair like to be Jack Macallister, the tramwayman. It spiles your step on the stair to be hangin' a' day aboot the depot peacefully persuadin' your fellow-workmen to come oot and jine the strike."[2]

"It's me that's sorry for his puir wife! Nine o' a faimily and never oot o' the habble at the best o' times; she has plenty to dae withoot Macallister himsel' thrown on her hands. Whit in a' the world will he be daein' when he's no' at work?"

"Peacefully persuadin'; have I no just tell't ye? Macallister's a man that mak's a pet o' his ain parteecular tramway-caur; it's his only hobby and it would break his hert to see ony other chap tak' chairge o't."

"Whit's peacefully persuadin'?" Jinnet asked.

The popular way in the tramways is to twist the neck o' a trolley-pole, or hit the chap ye want to reason wi' behind the ear wi' a drivin'-handle. I met Macallister yesterday gaun doon the street wi' a pocketfu' o' stones, and he was nearly greetin'. 'The champion caur in the Duke Street depot[3] Mac', says he 'and I had her trained that fine she would spark like a human bein' if a dug was in the road or she saw a woman frae Carmunnock standin' on the pavement ready to mak' a breenge in front o' her. I could drive her wi' baith hands aff the crank and my een shut — she was that dependable; and noo she's in the chairge o' a ticket-inspector! If there was onything my caur couldn't thole it was a ticket-inspector; she hated the very sicht o' the uniform, and whenever yin o' them put his foot on the step she would try to jump the trolley."'

"Whit in a' the warld'll Gleska dae if there's nae tramway caurs? asked Jinnet.

"Maist unfortunate! Couldna hae happened at a waur time, jist when horses is nearly oot o' date and airyplanes[4] is only startin'. Duffy the coalman tell't me he was gaun to Maryhill this mornin' wi' a couple o' horse and cairt on the chance o' liftin' a wheen o' businessmen no' fit to walk to their businesses efter a substantial breakfast. 'There's money in't!' says he, 'if the tramwaymen stand firm for a month or twa, for the Gleska folk hae lost the use o' their legs since the skoosh-caur started ha'penny tickets.' It's richt enough whit Duffy says; my hert was sair, in the mornin' yesterday, to see sae mony dacent, weel-put-on, weel-daein' business gentlemen toilin' in frae Hillhead on their ain feet. You could see they werena used to't; they peched maist dreadful and the sweat was drappin' aff them. I'm tell't that hunders o' them frae the south-side suburbs lost their way and landed oot near Paisley; it's sae mony years since ever they came into the toon or oot o't except wi' their een glued on a newspaper, that they didna ken the road. A couple o' year after this it wouldna maitter; if the tramway-caurs stopped then, a man in a hurry for the office would only need to birl a whistle on the roof o' the washin'-hoose and tak' his pick o' half-a-dozen airyplanes[4] that would come skytin' doon to lift him."

"But maybe the airyplane men would strike, too," suggested Jinnet shrewdly.

"Richt ye are! There's naething mair likely. It's yin o' the drawbacks to an age o' science that the mair conveniences ye invent for yoursel' the mair ye miss badly when ye get the heave back on your ain resources."

"It's mercy the strike is ended," said Jinnet, some days later in the week, comforted by the resumption of the normal tramway traffic going past her window, "I felt that eerie wi' the want o' the noise o' the caurs; at nicht it fair put me aff my sleep. I've nae patience wi' their strikes; whit way can folk no' be agreeable? Everything would be fine if everybody was agreeable."

"Ye were cut oot for a Capeetalist; that's the rale Capeetalist p'int o' view," said her husband slyly. "It's the p'int o' view that's held by thoosands o' tip-top gentlemen busy shootin' grouse and scourin' roond the country in their motor-caurs. But it looks as if the habit o' bein' agreeable was gaun oot o' date, for half the country's oot on strike, and if I was you I would buy a bag o' potatoes and lay in a stock o' eggs."

"What in a' the world for?"

"The trains'll no' be runnin' efter Setturday; a' the railway men are gaun to strike."

"It doesna' matter to me; I'm no gaun onywhere on a railway," said Jinnet.

"Maybe no', but an awfu' lot that needs a railway comes to you. Stervation stares us in the face! There'll be naebody to bring the beer frae the breweries, beef frae the markets, wheat and flour frae the docks, and coals frae the mine. Naething to drink but water! Naething to eat but hens, for they're gaitherin' the hens thegither roond the country and gaun to shoo them into Gleska[5] on their ain legs and save the need for trains or cartage. Tak' you my advice for't, Jinnet and buy potatoes. Look at London last week; I tell you the folk there got a start! They were packin' up their bits o' things and gaun to mak' tracks for the coast and country so's to be near the raw material, and only changed their minds when the cairters tied their trousers below the knee again and brocht oot their cairts once more in front o' the motor traffic. And that was only the cairters, mind ye! Up till then the cairter was always thocht to be a harmless kind o' chap, that sat on a lorry-tram and damned maist dreadful wi' nae ill-will to onybody. When he stopped work on a sudden he was found to be mair important than the Hoose o' Lords. If the Hoose o' Lords struck work for a month it wouldna hae the least effect on the price o' beef or stop the motor-omnibuses, but the cairter had only to drop his whip for a day or twa and London was in consternation. Whit'll it be when we havena ony railways?"

"I'll jist hae to set to and bake scones," said Jinnet, philosophically. "But whit in a' the world's the maitter wi' the country, gaun on strike wholesale like this?"

"The doctors say it's owin' to the heat," said Erchie, "but I think mysel' it's partly the heat and partly the rideeculous price o' stimulatin' beverages. Since ever Lloyd George put up the price o' the workin'-man's refreshment[6] there has been what they ca' in the papers a smoulderin' discontent among us. Noo he's gaun to take aff us fourpence a week to pay for oor insurance. If that becomes law he'll maybe tak' other fourpence aff us for an annual health restoring fortnight in the country; twopence for the upkeep o' a Dolly washer[7] in every home in the interest o' national cleanliness and a penny-a-week for the Popular Educator to keep us up-to-date wi' the Germans.

"I only hope the waiters'll no' strike anyway' said Jinnet, with a natural solicitude for her husband's profession.

"We'll be the last to think o't." said Erchie. "We're no' in a poseetion to come oot on strike for oor customers could bide at hame and fa' back on their wives to dae their waitin'. Its their naitural occupation."

"Aye, but whit if a' the women were to strike?" asked Jinnet. "That would be a strike wi' a vengeance!"

"The peaceful persuasion would be a' on the ither side then; awa' and buy potatoes.'"

37. *Cinematographs*[1]

"ERCHIE," SAID Jinnet, knitting with a concentrated and determined air which showed that something far away from wires and three-ply fingering was in her mind, "could a man's heid swell up the height o' a four-storey land o' hooses?"

Her husband turned from the kitchen looking-glass with his face half-lathered, and regarded her with surprise.

"Don't you try to be comic, Jinnet," he advised. "It's no' in your line. An auld married woman has nae mair use for the sense o' humour than she has for a fancy box o' chocolates."

"I'm no' trying' to be comic," she protested with a little indignation. "I'm only askin' ye if ony mortal man's heid could swell up the height o' a hoose?"

"No," said Erchie, curtly, proceeding with the preliminaries of shaving. "A phenomena like that couldna happen to an ordinar' mortal man. It might happen wi' a provost. What are ye askin' for?"

"Oh, jist for curiosity!" and the wires[2] clicked more furiously than ever.

Her husband stropped his razor on the full calf cover of a solitary volume of Gibbon's "Decline and Fall" he had bought for that purpose years ago from a barrow in Stockwell,[3] and expressed a hope that these remarks were not personal to himself.

"Did ye ever hear o' a man called Lieutenant Rose?" was the next startling inquiry addressed to him.

"Look here, Jinnet," he replied impatiently, "if this is a guessin' competition, I'm no' playin'. And if it's yin o' them catches where ye cry "Kelly!" ye're no' gaun to catch me. I never heard o' ony Lieutenant Rose. And there never was ony Lieutenant Rose."

"Oh, but there was!" she replied with great assurance. "A fine young strappin' chap in the Navy. I'm awfu' surprised we didna read aboot him in the papers at the time. The Captain o' the man-o'-war cried him ben to his cabin, and says, 'Lieutenant Rose, when the Royal pairty come aboard to-morrow they'll be in serious danger o' bein' blawn up wi' a bomb. I hae a letter here that tells me the anarchists[4] are plottin' and I'm awfu' put aboot.'

'Let me ashore in disguise for the efternoon,' says Lieutenant Rose; 'I ken a wheen o' thae gentry, and I could maybe find oot their plan.'

"So the Captain o' the man-o'-war sent the Lieutenant ashore disguised wi' a straw basher[5] and his breeks turned up at the feet, and he went to an Italian restaurant and ordered a snack. When he was waitin' for't, the hale jing-bang[6] o' the anarchists passed through the room he was sittin' in and into a room but-and-ben.[7] Ye could see at yince they were anarchists; they had the very hats.

"Lieutenant Rose lifted a bass aff the floor o' the room he was sittin' in a' by himsel' and waitin' for his snack, and there was a trap-door doon into a cellar. He went doon the trap and in below the other room where the anarchists were plottin', and he heard every word they said. They were gaun to hae a motor-boat a wee bit aff frae the man-o'-war, and a man wi' a divin'-suit. The diver was to tak' a bomb wi' him and put it in below the very middle o' the man-o'-war. When they had him hauled aboard the motor-boat again the anarchists would set the bomb aff wi' electricity, and the man-o'-war and the Royal pairty would be blawn to bits."

"Is this a "Home Chat" story or a dream ye had?" her husband interjected.

"Oh, it happened richt enough," his wife assured him. "It must hae happened just the ither day, and no' a word aboot it in the papers."

"Lieutenant Rose got another motor-boat, and a divin'-suit o' his ain, and when the anarchists were thrang pumpin' win' doon to the chap that was layin' the bomb below the man-o'-war, the Lieutenant put on his divin' suit and went doon a wee bit further aff. The anarchist was walkin' roond the bottom o' the water in the weeds to find a place to put his bomb, when Lieutenant Rose crawled up ahint and cut his wind-pipe —"

"Horrible, Jinnet! horrible!" exclaimed her husband. "I aye warned ye no' to eat afore ye go to your bed; there's naething worse for nicht-mares."

"I mean the pipe that his friends pumped doon the air to him wi'. And then Lieutenant Rose did something to the bomb to keep it frae explodin', and was hauled up on the anarchists' boat, them thinkin' a' the time it was their frien'. I tell ye they got a start when they screwed the helmit aff and found Lieutenant Rose wi' a revolver orderin' them to haud up their hands! They were a' ta'en awa' to jyle, and Lieutenant Rose, back on the man-o'-war again, was introduced to the Royal pairty, and got a title on the spot."

"Where did ye hear such haivers?" asked her husband.

"I never heard the tale frae onybody," answered Jinnet; "I saw the hale affair wi' my ain een in the Cinematygraft. That's where I went wi' Duffy's wife on Setturday, and I didna like to tell ye. Yon bates a'! I saw boats fishin' cod near Iceland; and the way that corks are made; and a man wi' leggin's and a helmit catchin' lions in the bush. If I hadna seen the man wi' a heid that swelled and swelled till it reached the top o' a tenement, I would have said such a thing was hardly possible."

Erchie laughed. "Ye never were acquainted wi' a Provost, Jinnet, nor even a first year's Bylie. What ye saw at the Cinematygraft was only pictures."

"They were movin', Erchie; and they were actual photygraphs; ye canna deny't if ever ye saw a cinematygraft. The photygraph was taken aff the genuine Royal pairty and a genuine Lieutenant Rose, and when he cut the — the air-pipe, ye could see the bubbles risin' in the watter. There was anither yin wi' a horse that belanged to a married woman, Mrs Grundy, wi' a man that was awfu' foolish and went awa' noo and then gallivantin'. Mrs Grundy had only to tell her horse to go and bring her husband hame and it would trot awa' as nate as onything and follow him to a public-hoose or a pic-nic pairty and chase him hame. The way that horse could run! Ye saw it a mile awa', and afore ye could wink it was almost doon on the tap o' ye."

"Only movin' pictures, Jinnet, movin' pictures! It's a' arranged."

"Hoo could they manage to arrange Lieutenant Rose, and the deep-sea divers, and the Royal pairty, and hoo could they arrange the lend o' an actual man-o'-war? For it was an actual man-o'-war to start wi'; and the very smoke was comin' frae its funnels."

"Science," said Erchie, finishing his shaving. "The deevils can dae onything! The man-o'-war was maybe genuine, but Lieutenant Rose and the Royal pairty would be actor-bodies dressed in uniforms."

"But I tell ye, Erchie, I saw the diver wrastlin' wi' the anarchist in the bottom o' the sea and the very partans[8] walkin' roond aboot them."

"Rale partans?" said Erchie, incredulously.

"So rale that I could almost feel them nippin' me," said Jinnet with conviction.

"I don't understand aboot the partans; it's no so easy to act a partan as a Royal pairty," confessed her husband, "but I'm certain sure the thing never happened, or ye would hae seen it in the papers."

"Would ye say the cod-fishin' was genuine?" asked his wife.

"Oh, like enough; there's nae cod aboot that; cod-fishin' and cork-cuttin' could be photygraphed at ony time."

"And Mrs Grundy's horse?"

"Oh, jist a trained horse."

"Could ye train a horse," asked Jinnet, "to go gallopin' doon a crooded street and breenge richt through a motor-caur, comin' oot at the ither side as brisk as onything, and jump frae the pavement through a three-storey window?"

"Science!" said Erchie. "Jist science. You weemen don't understand, and you shouldna bother yer heids aboot it."

"I'm certain shair, at onyrate, that what I saw was genuine," said Jinnet. "I can see how it a' micht happen, but I'm bate to understand the man wi' the heid that swelled."

"That's easy," answered Erchie; "They had jist to photygraph a provost."

38. *Duffy's Coals*[1]

ERCHIE DROPPED into Duffy's house on Saturday afternoon, and found the coalman washing himself in the kitchen jawbox but otherwise quite cheerful.

"Ye're late," said Erchie, looking at his watch. "A' the banks is shut hours ago, and ye'll no' can get your money lodged afore ten o'clock on Monday mornin'. If I was you, I would start a burglar and fireproof safe. It's temptin' Providence to hae a' that money lyin' in the shuttle o' a kist."[2]

"What money?" asked Duffy, drying himself.

"Fine ye ken what money! Ye're gettin' bald wi' haudin' up the lid o' the kist to coont it. If this coal strike was to last another month, we would see ye up at Skibo playin' gowf wi' Mr Carnegie. If ye tak' my tip, Duffy, put your money into quarries; the whin-stane quarry is the great investment o' the future. There's fortunes to be made in quarries; the India Rubber Boom[3] is naethin' to't."

"I havena the least idea what ye're talkin' aboot," said Duffy.

"I wish to Providence I had been brocht up to the coal tred," said Erchie. "Wi' a wee bit quarry, a half-a-dozen stone-knappers, and a couple o' cairts, I could retire before the Gleska Fair. What's the price o' the hunderweight the day?"

"Two-and-six — no, two-and-nine." said Duffy, hastily. "It'll be three shillin's on Monday."

Erchie held up his hands in admiration. "It's an astronomer ye should be, Duffy," he exclaimed. "What a heid for big figures! That gigantic mind o' yours is quite at hame in the higher mathematics, and ye turn half-croons and three shillings roond in your mooth withoot a bit o' harm to yoursel', like a woman bitin' hair-pins."[4]

The coalman stared at his visitor dubiously, conscious of some irony, but unable to discern exactly where it lay.

"Erchie's only takin' a rise oot ye," explained Mrs Duffy with great good humour, largely due to the fact that her husband had at last been induced to see the absolute necessity for a new sewing machine and a piano. "He's grudgin' the price o' coals."

"Not me!" exclaimed Erchie. "If coals were whit they used to be and burned awa' to ash the time ye would be lookin' at them, I micht grudge the price; but no' the price o' coal as improved by modern science in the last three or four weeks. Jinnet and me sat up the maist o' last nicht wi' a fire in a slow decline that's been lingerin' on since Wednesday. It's the first o' a couple o' bags we got frae you on Monday, Duffy. I can gie ye them back as guid' as when I got them — no' a chip the waur."

"Ye're the first customer that I've heard makin' ony complaint o' my coal," said Duffy, now on familiar ground. "Everybody else is astonished at the quality."

"I'm astonished mysel'!" said Erchie. "When we tried them first, I thocht somebody had opened a new coal seam in a cemetery; every noo and then we cam' on a heid-stane. Genuine Peterheid granite.[5] If ye send up another bag on Monday I'll be able to build mysel' a mausoleum. I couldna understand it at first, but at last I minded o' readin' somewhere a while ago aboot the Fuel o' the Future, and then I saw it was it I had at two-and-three a bag. Lasts a lifetime! A' ye have to dae is to turn it twice a day and open the window. There's no' a better thing for makin' ice-cream. Highly recommended for rale ice skatin' rinks; they're usin' it oot at Crossmyloof.[6] Whaur is it ye get it?"

"Whaur would I get it except in coal-pits?" replied Duffy. "The best coal —."

"Na, na! Duffy, ye needna tell me yon comes from coal-pits." said Erchie. "If it's no' from abandoned cemeteries, it's frae the South Pole. Thon Swedish chap that got there first[7] must be coinin' money."

"The best coal in the market!" insisted Duffy. "And I'm payin' weel mysel' for it."

"I hear," said Erchie, "that the Gleska Fire Brigade's layin' in great bings o't. It's the very thing they've been lookin' for for years."

"What for?"

"For puttin' oot fires," said Erchie.

"A' the same," said Duffy, "if ye're wantin' ony mair coals, ye should lose no time in orderin' them; there's no' saying what the price'll be this day week, for the supply's runnin' short."

"No' as lang's there's a quarry open in the country, or chuckies[8] lyin' on the shore for the gaitherin' at Rothesay or Kilcreggan. But a' the same, your price is rideeculous high, Duffy; ye'll soon be wrappin' every lump in a piece o' tissue paper wi' a motto on the ootside like New-Year short-breid, and sellin' it at threepence. A young chap coortin'll be in a swither whether to gie his lass a bag o' coal or a bracelet."

"I can assure ye I'm no makin' much aff them!" protested Duffy. "Ye should see what they cost me at the bing!"[9]

"That's the miraculous thing aboot the new fuel; naebody's makin' onything aff it, I hear. It's bein' distributed at two-and-six to three shillin's the bag jist for the sake o' the advertisement. The coalowner's losin' money on every ton; if he wasna a philanthropist he would sell it for pavin'-setts to the Corporation. The retail traders — that's you, Duffy — wi' coal-rees chock-a-block since the New Year, when the genuine old fashioned coal was fifteen shillin's a ton are breakin' their herts at havin' to throw it awa' in bags at fifty to sixty shillin's."

"A' the same, Erchie, I wish the strike was over,"[9] said Mrs Duffy. "Everybody's abusin' my man, the same's he could help it!"

"Oh, I'm no' complainin'," said Duffy, cheerfully. "I can stand it a week or two longer."

"I daursay ye could stand it for anither twelve-month if the slate-quarriers didna go on strike," said Erchie. "But I'm no' for ony mair o' your patent fuel till the weather's warm. Efter a', a fire o' ony kind's a luxury; if I'm cauld I can put on a couple o' extra waistcoats, and start an argument aboot the minimum wage;[10] there's naething brings oot a genial glow so fast."

"There's aye briquettes,"[11] suggested Mrs Duffy, not disinterestedly, since her husband did some business in them also.

"The briquette," said Erchie, "is purely ornamental. It fills up a grate as well as onything, but like everything ornamental in a hoose, it means extra work."

"I don't see that," said Mrs Duffy.

"We have a 6 by 4 yin yonder for a fortnicht back, and it's a perfect he'rtbreak, Jinnet says; she has to black-lead it every time she does the grate. If coal's bottled-up sunshine, as I saw a man writin' the ither day, the briquette's fossilised Gleska fog, and it's no' quite ripe yet."

"Does Jinnet no' try gas?" asked Mrs Duffy, this time more disinterestedly.

"She micht as weel try Vesuvians," Duffy interposed, with professional repugnance to the latest enterprise of the City's Gas Department.

"Duffy's richt," said Erchie. "I have no ill-will to gas for illumination purposes,[12] and it's a fine thing on a stair, but the very sicht o't in a grate aye gies me influenza. The Corporation's crackin' it up like onything and lendin' oot gas stoves for naething noo, I see, but I never saw a gas stove yet in the Municipal Buildin's. They're auld-fashioned enough there to be content wi' a rousin' open fire. Jinnet got the gas put in the oven a year ago, and ever since she's a victim to palpitation."

"Dear me!" said Mrs Duffy, "Is't the fumes?"

"No," said Erchie. "Fricht. Every time she lichts it, it gangs aff wi' an awfu' bang, and it spiles the hale week for her to think o' the explosion that she'll hae to face afore she can mak' ready Sunday's dinner. Where a gas fire's fine is in a picture or in a scene in a pantymime.[13] If workin'-men cam' hame on winter nichts to gas-fires in their kitchens, the public-hooses wouldna haud them later on. A gas-fire fits fine in a dentist's waitin-room or a factor's office, where a man's mind's taken up wi' other things, but it's no adapted for a Christian household where there's boots to dry."

"Was he tellin' ye himsel' we're gettin' a piano?" asked Mrs Duffy, changing the conversation.

"Of course ye are!" said Erchie, heartily. "He never tell't me, but I kent ye would be gettin' something. Good luck to ye! I'll see ye yet in your motor-car. Ye'll see me when ye're skooshin' bye[14] — I'll be walkin'. Ye'll ken me by my feet."

"And we're gaun to Lamlash on the Easter holiday aren't we, Jamie?"

"So ye say yersel," said Duffy, gloomily.

"I hope the trains is on again by that time," remarked Erchie.

"Are they aff?" asked Mrs Duffy, anxiously.

"They are!" said Erchie. "Maist deplorably! The coal tred may impose on the general domestic public wi' it's patent fuel, but it canna deceive a locomotive."

39. *The Conquest of the Air*[1]

JINNET WAS going out upon her Saturday evening shopping. "Tak your umbrella wi' ye, and keep weel in on the pavement," Erchie advised her.

"It's neither wet nor windy: at least it's no' sae bad's a' that," replied his wife. "Ye're surely getting' awfu' anxious aboot me; I'm no' that auld!"

"It's no the wind or the rain I'm thinkin' on," said he; "it's them derisible machines from Germany[2] skooshin' aboot in the air at nicht that's botherin' me; ye dinna ken the minute that they'll drop a soda-water bottle on ye."

"Surely they're no' sae bad as that?" said Jinnet, incredulously.

"Bad!" said he; "they're a fair scunner! It shouldna be put up wi' — breenging over the British Isles in droves and puttin' the fear o' daith on folk that never did them ony hairm. Nae wonder we have to light the gas that early; it couldna be otherwise, and the sky congested every nicht wi' German trips! A bonny-like thing when a puir wee laddie canna get fleein' his draigon[3] for them! That's whit Duffy told me; his boy went oot to the West-End Park the other day and cam' hame greetin' because he couldna get his kite to gang; 'There'll no' be room in a while for us to draw oor breaths,' says Duffy; 'it's time we were awa' to Canada.'"

"There's a lot aboot them in the papers," said Jinnet, "but I've never seen them. Are they big?"

"They have them a' sizes'," explained her husband, twinkling: "wee chats the size o' a washin'-boyne up to monsters bigger than a land o' hooses. But, wee or big, they're as fast as lightnin': the wan meenute they're seen in Portsmouth and the next aboot the Orkney Islands. Every thrivin' man in Germany noo has his private air-machine; whenever it comes to gloamin'[4] he puts a piece and a bottle o' laager beer in his pocket, fills his machine wi' gas at the kitchen bracket, and comes fleein' over the German Ocean[5] jist for a bit o' a pant before he goes to bed.

"Airship moonlight trips to the South o' England is the craze just now aboot Berlin; it's supposed to be a tip-top cure for sleeplessness. If ye picked up ony German paper and could read it, ye would see't full o' advertisements o' moonlight cruises to the British Isles, 'the Land o' the Settin' Sun.' 'Now is the time to see them to the Best Advantage!' says the Berlin airship advertisers.[6] 'See the White Chalk Cliffs before the gas goes oot! The Greatest Bird's-Eye View in Europe! Monster Attractions! Magnificently Illuminated Upper Decks! Band of the Emperor's Imperial Guard in the   Fore Saloon! England and Back Again in Three Hours! Tickets, 5s 6d. Infants in Arms, half-price! Meat Teas, 1s 6d! Suppers, 3s. Opera-glasses, 9d.'"

"Infants!" said Jinnet, indignantly. "It's a cryin' shame bringin' weans awa' at nicht in the cauld when they should be in their beds and no' gallivantin' through the heavens. I wonder whit mothers is comin' to! But whit could ye expect o' Germans! I hope to goodness they have proper railin's round the airships so that the puir wee smouts'll no' fa' oot."

"I'm no sae sure aboot that," said Erchie; "there's some gey funny young German waiters[7] in Gleska that must ha'e fallen over the side o' something. They may have a railin' richt enough aboot their airships, but you tak' my advice and keep up your umbrella!"

"Do ye think they'll be here the nicht!" said Jinnet, anxiously. "Surely no' on a Setturday nicht; they couldn't get hame again afore the Sabbath."

"The Sabbath's naething to them!" said her husband, solemnly; "they're puir deluded Continentals. I wouldna' be a bit surprised if they were makin' specialities o' week-end trips, 30s inclusive wi' electric baths. There's wan thing certain — they've spoiled the country-side for courtin' in; a lad and his lass'll no' can venture oot the length o' Carmunnock or Canniesburn Toll withoot the risk o' a fleein'-machine wi' a pairty on board comin' swoopin' doon and makin' a cod o' them in German wi' their search-lights. I'm awfu' gled my coortin' days is bye wi't! There was nane o' that in oor time, Jinnet."

"Whit in a' the world's the meanin' o't?" said Jinnet.

"Science!" replied her husband, putting on his waist-coat. "It's the age of progress, and you tak' my advice and keep weel in on the pavement; if it's no' an infant in arms that'll drop on ye it micht be a German waiter; whenever they see the lichts o' a toon that's likely to have an hotel they give the heave to a chap called Fritz, and he lands wi' a dunt, haudin' on to his dinner-naipkin. Ten minutes after that he's handin' roond sardines and daein' his best to let on he was born in Coupar Angus."

"It's droll I never heard a word aboot them," said Jinnet.

"If you would read the papers!" said her husband.

"Ye're far ower much ta'en up wi' the motions o' the Royal Faimily. The thing has been goin' on for weeks! The first o' the German air machines was seen by the Chief Constable o' a place in the North o' England comin' home from a Thursday prayer-meetin'. He took in a couple of holes in his belt and birled his whistle on them to stop till he brought out his diary and made a pencil note. But they didna stop – not them! The band played on, and fifteen minutes later the lights were seen distinctly in the neighbourhood o' Hull by a solicitor in a large way o' business. Exactly a minute and a half after that they were seen at Ipswich as sworn to before a J.P. and a man in the horticultural trade wi' a church connection."

"We were far better the way we were," said Jinnet, "and nane o' their cairry-on wi' their fancy flyin'! It's a wonder to me the government doesna interfere. Ye never can tell whit they'll drop! I yince let a methylated lamp fa' oot a cairrage in the train frae Greenock when I was nursin' Jimmy."

"The British Government daurna interfere," said Erchie. "They're far ower deeply implicated in the flyin' tred themsel's."

"I always thought their home was on the deep,"[8] said Jinnet, who knows a song or two.

"So it is," said Erchie, "but that needna hinder them from takin' lodgin's and the conquest o' the air's the latest battle-song o' Britain. Did ye no' notice the flight o' the aerial squadron frae Farnborough to Montrose?"[9]

"Mrs Macrae has an auntie in Montrose; she's mairried on[10] a linen-draper and he's daein' awfu' weel; they have a grand piana."

"Never mind aboot that the noo," said Erchie; "the aerial squadron from Farnborough for Montrose begood to get ready to start at the Auld New Year, and landed safe and sound on Thursday last. They call it the Royal Flyin' Corps,[11] and I tell you it's a clinker! It's no' so fast as the German derisibles, but man, it fairly cuts the air! It started off at the rate o' seventy miles an oor, and kept it up for fifteen seconds; then the Royal Corps cam' doon and landed on a flesher's park to light its cigarette because the wind was blowin'.

"Exactly at half-past two by Reuter's telegram,[12] it got in the air again, pursuin' it's way wi' grim and darin' energy to the North, and stopped for lunch at Chorlton-on-the Hill, a place wi' a bottle licence.

"'Is this, can onybody tell us, Chorlton-on-the Hill?' says Commander Becke and they tell't him he was near enough, that the place was roond the corner wi' a Black Bull signboard. The Royal Flyin' Corps dragged roond their airyplanes and had a snack, and started off again in a drizzle o' rain to Scotland marked on the chart distinctly wi' a cross."

"They put up that night at a place in the South o' England, they could see the lichts o' France across the English Channel, and they grat thegither feelin' awfu' far frae hame.

"On the Thursday week the Royal Flyin' Corps (all ither kinds no right Royal, just a kind o' imitation) got the length o' Doncaster, and their airyplanes a' wet."

"'Is this Scotland?' says Lieutenant Waldron.

"'No,' says the chap in chairge o' the railway buffet: 'first to the left, then third to the right, and ye're there when ye drop doon deid; that's Edinburgh'.

"Wi' dauntless resolution the Royal Flyin' Corps resumed its weary journey to the North; and a fortnicht later, wind and weather favourin', havin' travelled at the terrific speed o' a cushion-tyred perambulator, landed at the very door o' the Provost o' Montrose.

"'Are you the Royal Flyin' Corps frae Farnborough?' says the Provost, puttin' off his brattie.[13]

"'We are!' says Commander Becke, lookin' roond aboot him for the demonstration.

"'We've often read aboot ye since ye started,' says the Provost; 'I mind o't fine though I was jist a laddie,' and he takes them roond to the Council Hall and gies them a gless o' wine and an Abernethy biscuit!"

"Man, ye're jist an auld haver!" said Jinnet, but as she went out of the close a little later she cast an apprehensive glance at the heavens lest the Germans should throw out a bottle, and put up her umbrella.

40. *Jinnet's Visitor*[1]

Before Jinnet could quite grasp the situation, her first alarming thought being that the gentleman was from the Sanitary,[2] he had passed her with his strange machine into the lobby.

"There's nae disinfectin' needed here," she told him tremulously. "It must be some mistake; there hasna been an illness in this hoose since Wullie was a baby."

"Just a little demonstration," he said to her. "Won't take ten minutes. Can I have a little flour, or meal — a couple of handfuls, say?" He was such a stylish gentleman, Englified, and with a handkerchief stuck up his sleeve, that she couldn't think of asking what he wanted flour for, so she simply went and got a bowl from the kitchen. When she came back he was in the parlour, busily screwing on a metal hose-pipe to the strange machine, and with his coat off.

"Now we shan't be long!" he said to her gaily. "The leading merit of the Dinky[3] is simplicity. You only have to see that the dust-container's screwed up tightly; lower the footboard, so; select and fix the nozzle suitable for carpets, mouldings, or upholstery as the case may be, grasp the handle, so, work back and forward slowly, and direct the nozzle to the part required ... Excuse me, madam" and he took the bowl of flour from her.

"Has it onything to dae wi' the drains?" she asked him, anxiously: she had some slight experience of smoke-test machines.[4]

"Not at all," he said briskly. "Just dust, which is quite as deleterious to the health as drains. No doubt you think this room is thoroughly clean?" and he looked at her with the compassionate eye of a well-informed English gentleman who knows better.

"If it's no' clean," she said indignantly, "it's no' for want o' elbow-grease. Far wiser-like if ye would see aboot the ashbins at the back there — no' a lid on them; a bonny close they leave us in the mornin'! ... Lord be aboot us! what is that ye're daein'?"

He had strewn the bowl of flour upon the carpet, and was rubbing it thoroughly into the fabric with his feet.

"I will now demonstrate how effectively the Dinky removes the finest dust. There are scores of imitations in the market costing twice as much, which do not have one-half the suction power of the genuine Dinky. A child can work it — see!" and working the bellows of the vacuum cleaner he ran the nozzle of the hose across the carpet, leaving it as thoroughly clean as it was before.

Jinnet stood bewildered, now convinced the man was a lunatic; they both were so engrossed in the performance that they never heard the opening of the outside door nor a footstep in the lobby; and Jinnet's husband was looking in on them before they realised his presence.

"What's this?" he asked astonished.

"Oh, Erchie!" cried his wife, relieved to see him; "I'm glad ye're here! This gentleman is — is — is tryin' an experiment."

"I thought at first it was the Fire Brigade," said Erchie, looking at the metal hose-pipe. "But then I saw the gentleman hadna on a helmet or a hatchet. Bless me, Jinnet, ye're surely no gaun in for a vacuum cleaner?"

"A vacuum cleaner!" she exclaimed. "Is that what ye ca' a vacuum cleaner. I didna understand, I thought the gentleman was frae the Sanitary."

"Cheapest in the market — £1.10s," said the canvasser. "You have no idea of the saving —"

"Saving!" cried Jinnet. "Bonny on the savin'! I couldna keep the thing in flour!"

The canvasser unscrewed the lid of the dust receptacle, took out a little bag, and exhibited a small amount of dust in the bottom with an air of triumph.

"Fairly eats it up, you see!" he remarked as if the Dinky was a horse.

"We could dae that for oursel's," said Jinnet, "but we like it baked first; there's naething in your poke but my guid flour."

"On the instalment system of easy payments, the Dinky — " he began, but Erchie cut him short with the intimation that under no conceivable system could a Dinky be thrust upon that household.

"It's three and forty years," said he, "since I got a vacuum cleaner, and I have it yet; it's jist as good as ever, and it hasna got the wheeze. It's a faur better yin than yours, and I like the smell it leaves — it's something like saft soap and water."

"Three and forty years!" said the canvasser, dismantling his machine. "Let me tell you, sir, that the vacuum cleaner was invented only — "

"Toots!" said Erchie, cheerfully; "I'm talkin o' the wife. Cleanin' and dustin's no' a task wi' her; it's her principal recreation. It would break her he'rt to think it could be done wi' a pair o' bellows flyped."

"It's a great highjinckie age!" said Erchie, taking off his coat to have his tea when the canvasser was gone. "If yon machine had a few improvements on't; could wash a blanket, darn a sock, sew on a button, cook a meal o' meat, and nurse a wean, a body wouldna need a wife. But it's comin! I'll bate ye that chap Edison's[5] thrang thinkin' o' a combination o' the phonygraph, the kinematygraph, the sewing machine, the vacuum cleaner, the Thermos flask, and the incubator that'll relieve women o' their domestic bonds, and gie them leisure to gang roond the country lettin' aff their bits o' bombs."

"Ye needna talk!" said Jinnet, with conviction; "ye couldna dae withoot the women! Him and his dust! There's no' a morsel o' stour in the four wa's o' this hoose!"

"Nae mair than what's in the top flet, No. 29," said her husband, alluding to the next-door close. "When I went oot the day, a half-a-dozen nice bit lassies and an aulder yin in specs, every yin wi' a brattie in a parcel, were troopin' up to 29 the same's it was a waddin'."

"What on earth are they daein yonder?" asked Jinnet. "Every day in the week they're there a different gang, except the wee yin wi' the specs; she's spachial."

"Domestic science!"[6] said her husband, solemnly. "It's a' the rage in Gleska. The like o' you was just heaved oot o' school[7] when ye got the length o' Long Diveesion,[8] to nurse your mother's weans, and mak the beds and dae the best ye could at makin' porridge, but things is different noo. No. 29's a trainin' ground for Gleska's comin' house-wifes. I tell you, the stour's goin' to get a fright, even withoot the Dinky vacuum!"

"Hoots, ye're haiverin' again!" said Jinnet; "what science is there aboot keepin' a hoose? It's jist a trauchle!"

Erchie helped himself to sugar. "That's your notion," said he; "but ye're far behind the times. The School Board has twa-room-and-kitchen hooses, h. and c., here and there through a' the tenements, and every wise-like lassie has to go and learn in them the way to wash a floor, and clean a grate, and mak' a bed, and cook a shillin' dinner. Every day they're up in 29, and scrubbin' at it till I'm tell't the boards is worn as thin's a tramway ticket, and the grate's as shiny as a shillin'. They've polished at the handle o' the door so much it's worn away so bad it jags ye."

"Perfect nonsense! It would be far mair like the thing if they cam' and helped puir Widow Grant doon stairs to clean her hoose on Seturday."

"Aye, but that wouldna be Domestic Science," said Erchie.

41. *Black Friday*[1]

IT WOULD be idle to deny that an almost universal gloom prevails in Glasgow in anticipation of the new Act[2] which, on and after Friday first, will shut all public-houses from ten o'clock at night till ten o'clock next morning. The innovation is looked upon as a dastardly blow at a fine old national custom, and as certain to have the most serious effects upon the social, economic, and physical conditions of the people. To have two hours per day lopped off our period of refreshment means about 600 hours per annum; which is to say that this iniquitous Act robs us in the aggregate of 25 days of what time we have in a year for stimulus and conviviality. It will be impossible to make up for the loss of those two morning hours by dispensing with dinner and tea, or by the exercise of more agility in getting washed and out again at night; there was something in those magic morning hours[3] now stolen from us that is best indicated in the words of Mr Duffy: "If ye tak' a dram at a', tak' it in the mornin', and ye get the guid o't a' day." No wonder Scotland this week is solemnised. You see apprehension and revolt in every face. Everywhere are mutterings of rebellion. Home Rule and the Suffragettes,[4] and all the clamant national topics of the hour are quite forgotten in the sense of intimate and personal injustice.

I have interviewed Mr James Duffy, the well-known coal vendor, on the crisis, as a citizen whose views were likely to be representative of those held by the rugged sons of toil for whom peculiarly the ten o'clock opening law will be a hardship.

"It's just a fair sickener!" he said with unmistakable disgust. "Ten o'clock's far ower late for ony man's breakfast. Nae wonder folk's flockin' to Canada! Everything here's against the workin'-man."

"The theory may be that it will save you money, Mr Duffy," I suggested.

"There's no' a greater mistake," he replied, "than tryin' to save money at the expense o' your health. If a man has a hard day's work to dae he needs to start weel and keep up his strength. Eight o'clock was richt enough; seven, or even six, would hae been better, but eight did fine; it kind o' broke the back o' the day; it kep' ye cheery watchin' the clock from six till eight, and after eight a schooner and a wee hauf-gill[5] made your work nae bother to ye."

"How will the new opening hour affect your own practice?" I inquired.

"I don't see hoo it'll work at a'," he answered gloomily. "I've thocht o' turnin' oot at eight instead o' six, and gettin' the better o' them that way, but there's the risk that I'll be hungry afore I get my mornin',[6] and spoil my thirst wi' tea. Anyway ye look at it, the thing's a persecution. It's a' the harder on a man o' my tred that thas to dae a lot o' roarin' in the morning'; ye canna cry coals dacently on milk and jujube lozenges."

Behind the rather flippant confidences of Mr MacPherson, whom I next interviewed, I thought I discerned a genuine antagonism to the new measure.

"Ye mean the Daylight Saving Bill?"[7] he said. It doesna' affect me personally, for I'm no' an early riser, but it's hard on the like o' Duffy, and it's a blow at Scottish history. Everybody kens that the secret o' Scotland's greatness is the "morning". A' the finer qualities o' the race come oot at eight o'clock. It comes from the national food bein' oatmeal porridge."

"How?" I asked, surprised.

"In the olden days," said Erchie, "when the tinned salmon and the closed fish[8] werena thocht o', a Scotsman's breakfast never was anything else than porridge. It's a fine upstandin' meal, and we won the Battle o' Bannockburn on't; but when there was naething else except on Sunday, the very thocht o't cast a gloom on the mornin' hours o' the workin' man, and he honestly couldna face it without a tonic.[9] The immediate result I see o' the ten o'clock openin' is that Mrs Duffy'll have to use the mornin' money on fancy breakfasts wi' ham and eggs."

"That might be a gain all round," I suggested.

"I'm afraid ye're no' better than an Englishman!" said Erchie, shaking his head. "Where's your patriotic spirit? Hae ye no feelin's for the thoosands o' chaps like Duffy gaun hame to a breakfast, even o' ham and eggs, past the

Mull o' Kintyre Vaults, and its shutters on? It'll look like every day a funeral."

"Will it not make us a more sober people?" I inquired.

"It will not," said Erchie. "That's the way that the wine, spirit, and beer trade's against it. They wouldna open till twelve if they thocht it would make Scotland soberer, but they ken fine Duffy and his friends'll spend as much as ever on refreshments; at least, that's whit they say, so I suppose they like, themsel's, the early risin', jist for health's sake. My own idea is that it's playin' into the hands o' them Italians.[10] There's an eight-o'-clock-in-the-morning feeling in a town like Glasgow — maist depressin' Nothing gives relief to't but standin' at a coonter."

"A dairy might serve the purpose," I suggested.

"Milk!" cried Erchie in horror. "Full o' germs! Ye'll recommend Broon Robin next! Ye're surely no' teetotal. Na, na! the ice-cream shops'll get the tred, and ye'll see the riveters[11] next Friday standin' oot in raws forenent[12] the ice-cream shops at breakfast time, for their turn at the slider coonter.[13] Scotland's done! There's nae inducement left for us to get up in the mornin' or bide late up at nicht."

There has, plainly, been no more staggering blow to Scotland's custom and sentiment since the days of Forbes Mackenzie.[14] Closing at ten instead of eleven was, by comparison, a step of no importance; that only called for a little more expedition in the orders. But the abolition of the traditional "morning" is involved in the newest Act; for a time, at least, it will have bewildering effect on the working-classes who discovered long before the doctors did that alcohol was a food, stimulating and sustaining, for the morning use of men, though not at all to be recommended to their women. So Glasgow this week is gloomy, though it is lucky that the new conditions start in early summer rather than the mirk morns[15] of November.

42. *Down-Hearted Duffy*[1]

"You'll see!" said Duffy. "Just you watch! In twa or three weeks there'll no' be a single steamboat sailin' — "

"Of course there'll aye be the *Fairy Queen* on the ca-nal",[2] said Erchie, cheerfully. "As lang as she keeps runnin' Britannia rules the waves."

"I'm layin' in a lot o' onions and oranges," proceeded the coalman gloomily.

"Ye have no idea the way onions and oranges'll go up when the blockadin'[3] starts, for there'll no' be ony ships get through, and the price o' foreign eggs'll be something fancy. They'll be worth their weight in — "

"In coal," said Erchie quickly. "Man, Duffy, I doot ye're a pessimist!"

"What's a pessimist?" asked the coalman.

"A pessimist's a kind o' man ye want to gie a bat on the lug to. So far as I can see, all men in the coal tred are pessimists. I think that when they gang hame at nicht and get their teas they stick their heids for the rest o' the nicht in yin o' their ain coal-bags, and say, 'Michty! doesn't things look black!' Ye have nae mair idea o' war than my leg, Duffy. Neither have I, but I aye ken bluff whan I see it, and every time I see the Germans bluffin' whit they're gaun to dae, I aye cheer up, for I ken it's no' that way that war is won. I would be far mair anxious aboot the Germans if they kept their mooths shut."

Still Duffy shook his head; he had had a counterfeit half-crown passed on him by some miscreant customer unknown that afternoon, and this personal disaster aug-mented — if it did not even wholly account for — his sombre view of the international situation.

"Hoo lang will the war last?" he asked in one of those flashes of intelligent curiosity which come at times to so many of us.

"Man, I daurna tell ye that, Duffy," said Erchie solemnly. "I'm on my oath. But I'll venture this length if ye don't repeat it — it'll finish sooner than some folk think, and it'll last langer than others imagine. But for goodnes sake, don't let on I told ye! I had it special frae a man that has a brother in London that cuts Lord Kitchener's hair when it's needin' cuttin'."

"Ye can depend on me!" said Duffy, exceedingly greatful for this reassuring confidence. "I'll no' say a wheesht to onybody. I was railly gettin' anxious, for Macrae the polisman swears it'll last three years."

"When it comes to European wars," said Erchie, "ye canna depend on the polis for the very latest information. They're a' richt for tellin' ye when the watter's to be cut aff, or showin' ye your close at nicht if the tenement looks kind o' shifted; but for the deeper secrets o' State, it's rarely ye can trust them; they'll mislead ye if they can. My ain private opeenion is that the polis is making' a fair hash o' things at present — athegither mismanaging their ain depairtment. The Germans come over here week-ends and murder weans, and ye never hear a word o' the polis doin' onything."

"If I could only mind wha I got that half-croon fae, things wouldna look sae bad," said Duffy in a little. "I doot, Erchie, I'm a comer-and-goer."

"What's that in English?" asked his friend. "Since they began puttin' wee French dictionaries in the packets o' cigarettes, ordinary human conversation's kind o' spoiled for folk like mysel' that havena ony foreign education."

"A comer-and-goer's no French," said Duffy. "I mean that I come and go aboot the war; some days I'm whistlin' at my wark, and ithers I canna cry my coals wi' ony kind o' melodiousness, I'm that doon-hearted."

"I see!" said Erchie. "My mistake! Ye're no a genuine pessimist after a', ye're jist an auld wife."

"Ay, but jist you consider this — we havena won a naval battle for nearly twa weeks; whit's the Navy daein?"

Erchie MacPherson sighed. "Man, Duffy," he said, "ye put me awfu' in mind o' an aunty my wife had oot at Stra'ven. She had a hundred and eighty hens when the Boer War started and every time ye went oot to see her she would boil ye eggs. Every time De Wet or Cronje was mentioned in the papers, and it was aye for something dashing that didna agree wi' us at a', she sold a dozen hens in an awfu' panic, sure this country was done for, and that sooner or later she would have to leave it and tak' a wee bit hoose in Gleska. 'Whaur's the Navy wi' its hunder-ton guns?' she would ask in desperation; 'here am I wi' a' they hens!' — the puir auld body had never seen a man-o'-war in her life; she never was even the length o' Gourock. At every British reverse she sold some mair o' her hens and got very little for them, for she grat that much they were plashin' wet, and looked as if they werena ony weicht at a'. And when the Boers were smashed, and my wife and me went oot to celebrate Cronje's capture, she hadna a hen in her possession nor an egg to boil us for oor tea. 'Oh, dear me,' says she, 'wasn't I the silly woman no' to trust in God and keep my hens?'"

"What I aye like to see in the papers," said Duffy, "is a regular battle. This week or twa I'm a wee bit disappinted. I hate to see them hangin' on."

"It's a mercy you're no' in the poultry line like Jinnet's aunty; ye can greet if ye like on a bag o' coals and no' lose onything on the transaction; quite the contrary. Admiral Jellicoe,[4] wi' the best will in the world, canna indulge ye to a battle every nicht to yer tea; buy haddies if ye want to keep yer strength up."

"I'm a' richt if I don't read whit the Germans say; they're most annoyin', Erchie," said Duffy.

"Ay, that's their nature; they canna help it. And a' they German wireless stories are meant particularly for folk like you and my Aunty Bella. They want to cause a flurry among auld wifes' hens. You attend to the coal tred, Duffy, and be as honest as ye can wi' the scales, and leave Lord Kitchener[5] and French[6] and Jellicoe to dae their business."

"Ah!" said Duffy, "but a man must read the papers; I'm readin' them even-on."[7]

"I have nae thing to say against the papers in moderation," said his friend. "They're fine for linin' presses — naething better. But ye have to read them wi' discretion. I'm a busy man, mysel' just now, for I'm daen' the wark o' twa or three waiter chaps called Fritz or Hans so the most I can read o' the papers is the heid-lines. And I'm no like you, at all, when I see naething startlin' in the heid-lines I say, 'Thank God! — another battle won!' For, Duffy, every day wi' naething doin' is a battle lost for the Germans."

43. *Erchie on the Egg*[1]

"EGGS ARE doon. They're a great deal lower this week," said Jinnet, returning with her grocery order.

"No' the yin I got yesteday: it was as high as Tennant's Stalk," replied her husband.

"Oh, Erchie!" cried his wife, remorsefully: "and ye never said a word! It was the last o' my ain preservin'."

"Tuts! Whit herm's a high egg in the time o' war? There's countries where they eat them fair blue-moulded. It's just a fad the new-laid egg. Nae sensible body wants new-made cheese or a fresh saut-herrin'. The Gentry like their venison and grouse hung up till it's dangerous to go past the larder door wi' a naked licht."

Jinnet shook her head. "I don't understand their tastes: it's silly! Anyway I'm glad the egg's doon; ye'll can get a couple the morn's mornin'. They're one-and-eight the dozen, fresh frae Arran."

"The Arran egg," said Erchie, "is an egg I'm very fond o'. If ye get the genuine inland Arran egg there's nae humbug aboot it; ye can almost taste the heather. I'm no sure aboot the seaside egg, though; it aye tastes like a cross between a Dorking and a cockle. I suppose it's the diet o' dulse and sand hoppers gies them the doon-the-watter flavour."

"I aye think an egg's an egg, and that's the whole o't," said his wife. "If they're fairly fresh I'm no' much heedin' aboot their genealogy".

"Ye have a coarse uneducated palate."

"That's the kind that pays a puir-body best; sae many people educate their palates till they canna eat onything that's easy got. Half the money that's spent on meat and drink is spent just on a flavour."

Her husband looked at her with mock alarm. "Jinnet," he said, "Ye're gettin' awfu' close on bein' a philosopher, and I wouldna like that to break oot in ony wife o' mine; it's the first step to bein' an atheist or an emaciated[2] female. Tak' you my word for't, that there's eggs and eggs, and whenever ye can afford it, give your custom to the hens o' the motherland, the hens o' bonny Scotland, where the heather and the bluebells grow. The alien egg is aye suspicious, even if it's frae a neutral country like Ireland, though I'll no' deny the Irish egg is a good enough put-by for fryin' when there's nane frae Arran. I'm never sure o' the Continental egg, though, till' the heid's chipped aff; it micht be just a spy. The further awa' ye go for eggs, the less ye can depend on them. Yon guaranteed Egyptian yin I got last Sunday was a case in point; ye could see quite plain it cam' frae the tomb o' the Pharaohs, and if there's onything I hate to make a breakfast o' its ancient relics."

"I don't understand eggs nooadays," said his wife, taking off her bonnet. "They used to be sixpence a dozen in my time, and plenty o' them, … If I had just a wee hoose in the country —" she sighed. That was an old ambition with very little prospect of ever being realised.

"My dear Jinnet," said her man. "If ye had ten wee hooses in the country and a thousand weel-daein' hens thrang layin' nicht and day for ye, I'll guarantee ye would never eat an egg. Ye would send the hale jing-bang to the market and buy sausages. The folk in the country that brings up eggs by haund or by machinery never eat an egg except when they come to stay wi' a friend in Gleska, and then they canna help it; they get yin o' the yins they brocht for a present in a box wi' them — a dirty trick to play on onybody.

"Forby," continued her husband, filling his pipe, "egg production nooadays is a science, like playin' the fiddle; there's naething to be made at it by rule-o-thumb. The auld-fashioned hen of Caledonia was a simple, honest, hard-workin' creature that had na conceit o' itself', and just went on layin; day after day if ye gave it onything oot o' a bowl yer werena needin' yoursel'. It lived at the back, in ony auld box that was handy, and when the nicht was cauld would come in the hoose and jine the faimily pairty; wrought hard a' its days in scrapin' at the neebours' gairdens, and dee'd the naitural death o' a hen at last when full o' years and nae langer able to contribute to the Sustentation Fund."[3]

"Don't joke aboot the Sustentation Fund, Erchie," said Jinnet with pious reproof.

"In these days there was just the yin kind o' egg — genuine and unadultered, no different from the modern egg o' commerce till ye broke it open. Ye never needed to haud it up to the gas to see its age; it was aye in the prime o' youth. The hardy and frugal sons o' Scotland were reared on such-like eggs, at their breakfast, dinner and tea. And an extra yin on Sundays, and keepin' a wheen o' hens was a lady's occupation, like playin' the pianola.

"Some silly idiot took it in his heid that the hen could be educted and refined, and that a little extra money spent on its board and lodging would rouse its gratitude to that extent it would double its egg production. They began puttin' up fancy semi-detached hooses for the hens, wi' a southern exposure, the watter laid on, and bauks[4] it was a trate for a hen to sit on. They put in fixed grates to keep them warm in winter, spent money on buying meat for them and the hen-hoose was cleaned oot as regular as the parlour. It was before the vacuum cleaner; they'll have the vacuum cleaners in them noo, and the O-Cedar mop to gie the bauks a polish."

"Ach!, ye're just haiverin'," said Jinnet.

"Naething o' the kind! The thing developed. Whenever the hen got into its heid it was a bird o' consequence, it had to get a title — Buff Orpington, Minorca, or the like (it was just a common 'hen' before) — and had to get a course o' champed shells in its daily menu, and a' its orders. If ye let a draught blaw on it, it took the jee. A' the same there's nae doot it laid mair eggs; and this encouraged the poultry-fermers to keep on coddlin' it. I'm tellin' ye they fair spoiled the hen! Just pampered it! Ye'll no' get a hen to lay an egg for ye noo unless ye put a bass at the door for it to wipe its feet on, and a hot-watter bottle, in beside it when its clockin'."

"It must be fine to be a hen," said Jinnet.

"Not at all! Just hold you on!" said Erchie, warningly. "It was all a plant to cheat the puir things oot o' mair eggs than the Almichty meant them to provide. At first the hens thocht they were on velvet — eatin' the best o' meat withoot the trouble to scratch for't and even spared the trouble o' sittin' on their ain eggs, a thing the hens in the auld days just detested, for it's no joke sitting on a dozen o' eggs at a time and them maybe no' your ain at all, but some silly jucks."[5]

"They got fine and fat — that fat that at last they couldna put their minds into their business, and stopped layin' athegether. 'What they need,' says a poultry vet that had his eye on them, 'is exercise. The hen is like the human Bailie, unless it works for its livin; it runs to creesh, and ye micht as weel have a wally yin or a weathercock, for a' the eggs ye'll get!'

"The very next day after this discovery there wasna a hen in Scotland, except the no-weel yins, that wasna workin' for its livin'! In the best-regulated egg factories noo, the hens are never let over the door at all, but kept at business even-on. They still get the pick o' meat, but they have to scratch for't in the litter, or it's hung frae the roof and they have to jump for't. Muscle like gladiators! Ye can see't in knots on them when auld age comes to them and they're slipped in a plate in front o' ye as roasted chicken. It's called the intensive system o' poultry-fermin' because it's awfu' hard lines on the hen. If it doesna lay sae mony eggs a week for the twopence that's put oot on it, for meat, there's a blue mark put aginst it in a ledger, and if it's gaun to keep on being' a dour yin at the layin', up its number goes, and the bauk's cleaned oot for a better yin."

"Poor things!" said Jinnet, feelingly.

"That's science for ye!" said her husband. "Eggs is dearer than ever they were, and the hens, for a' their luxuries, are no' a bit the happier. They were daein' fine the way they were, and noo they're payin' dear for hygiene, sanitation, clean feet, and tooth-brush drill. I never see a hen noo but I'm someway vexed for't, as if it were a human body. There it's tied doon to layin' eggs for other folk wi' a' its micht, when it's natural inclination is to live the simple life and no' be an egg-machine."

"Still," said Jinnet, "I would like fine a wee bit hoose in the country, wi' a dozen hens."

44. *Erchie on Prohibition*[1]

"WHAT's a' this aboot shuttin' the pubs to sodgers?" Duffy asked. "What harm would the sodgers dae in a pub ony mair nor onybody else? I think at a time like this the sodgers should get a' encouragement, to cheer them on."

Erchie looked at the coalman with humorous resignation. "Man, Duffy!" he replied, "ye're aye a week behind wi' your news the way ye are in takin' tuppence aff the bag when the coals come doon. It's no' against the sodgers that they're gaun to shut the pubs; they're maybe gaun to shut then a'thegither."[2]

Duffy was staggered, but incredulous. "Nane o' your coddin', Erchie! Hoo could they refuse to serve ye if ye hae the money and nae signs o' drink aboot ye? They widna daur! They would lose their licence!"

"Duffy," said his friend, "your education's painfully neglected; ye should have stayed another quarter in the night school. Ye've heard o' an Act o' Parliament? Wi' an Act o' Parliament they can dae onything. They could stop

ye eatin' eggs or gettin' your hair cut. It used to tak' years
to pass an Act o' Parliament, and even then a smert-like
chap could march through the middle o't the same's it was
a triumphal arch. But noo an Act o' Parliament taks less
than twenty seconds; they dae't wi' a rubber stamp. If they
took a notion to stop the sale o' coals the first ye would
hear o't would be a telegram frae the Hoose o' Commons,
sayin' that coals were contraband, and ony man found wi'
a bunker in his hoose on and after Monday first would be
put in jyle."

"Somebody should write to the papers and expose
them!" said Duffy, warmly, "It shouldna be allo'ed! I'll
never vote for onybody again! What sense is there in
shuttin' pubs?"

"Oh, they're no' shut yet," said Erchie; "But a lot o'
folk's got an awfu' start. I got a wee bit shake mysel'."

The coalman gloomily stared at vacancy. "My George!
It's gettin' worse and worse!" he said despairingly at last.
"First it was Zeppelins, and then it was submarines, and
noo it's pubs blockaded! It's perfectly redeeculous! What
herm's a dacent pub if ye don't abuse it?"

"Ye don't understand," said Erchie. "It's military tac-
tics; it's to get recruits. If ye want a people to win a war, ye
must mak' them desperate. Look at the Russians and the
French! The Russians, for ordinar', like to put past the
time wi' a foreign drink called vodka because it jist tastes
like that, and the French mak' a habit o' drinkin' absinthe,
if there's ony left over when they're polishin' a chest o'
drawers or a sideboard. When the war broke oot half the
French kept on busy polishin' and the Russians moved
that slow from the vodka shops to the fightin' line they ca'd
them the steam-road-rollers.

"'If things go on like this', said the Czar to the President
o' the French Republic, 'the war'll last a lifetime. We'll
need to tak' steps to mak' them move a little slippier.'

"An Act was passed prohibitin' the sale o' vodka and
absinthe till the war was settled, and the Russians and the
French flocked to the Army determined to end the war at

the earliest possible moment. Ye couldna stopped them goin' noo that there was naething to keep them at hame."

"And what did the Germans dae?" asked Duffy.

"The Germans did the same in a different way. 'If ye want good beer,' says they to their sodgers, 'there's plenty in Belgium and France is full o' champagne cellars.' That made them breenge across the border, and they'll stay in Belgium and France as lang's there's a barrel or a bottle left.

"If they shut the pubs in Scotland, Duffy, it's because your king and country needs ye' quicker than ye come. Stayin' at hame and shirkin' must be made to lose its main attraction. When it's generally understood that the only place in Europe where ye can get a tot o' rum is in the trenches every high-spirited young man'll 'list."

"It'll be gey hard on us that's no' that young," said Duffy. "Could they no' just mak' the Act apply to chaps that's under forty?"

"Na; na! if it comes at a' it'll come a' roond. The King himsel's teetotal[3] noo; no' a drop o' onything in the hoose for him but butter-milk, or maybe a bottle or two o' raspberry cordial. 'What'll ye hae, your Majesty?' says his butler, bringin' in the tray at nicht. 'I suppose there's naething for't but butter-milk as usual,' says the King. 'Right-o!' says the butler, and slaps him doon a jugful. It's a lesson to us a', Duffy. If ye want to get royal noo ye can get the whole concomitants o' a spree at the kitchen jawbox."

"But still I canna picture the pubs a' shut in Gleska," says Duffy. "Everybody'll mak' a rush for Paisley."

"Tuts! if they're shut in Gleska they'll be shut in Paisley too. But I'm like you — I canna figure to mysel' a total prohibeetion Scotland. Whaur would millionaires like you in the coal tred spend their money. A small limejuice and soda's a nice enough beverage in moderation, but ye canna spend a nicht wi't, and if there's nae pubs, a lot o' chaps, when their day's work's done 'll no' hae any place to go to but straight hame. They'll be driven to't!"

"And then," continued Erchie, "consider the effect on a' the associated industries! The peppermint and aromatic-lozenge tred'll suffer dreadfully. The cultivation o' the clove'll stop, and the cork-screw manufacturies may just as weel shut their doors. It'll tell on the fishin' tred, for naebody'll go fishin'; ye canna keep the midges aff wi' eau-de-cologne or barley-water."

"I simply WILL NOT stand it!" protested Duffy. "I need a moderate refreshment noo and then to keep my strength up. You carry fifty hunderwechts o' coal —— "

"Fifty bags ye mean," corrected Erchie.

— "Up them tenement stairs and ye'll find it canna be done on butter-milk!"

"Oh, ye'll get used to that," said Erchie cheerfully. "Drinkin's just a habit, like wearin' boots or sittin' in your shirt sleeves to your tea. There's days and days I never think o't, and if I was in a lichthoose I would clean forget that such a thing as drink existed. ... My Jove! what would happen to Campbeltown?[4] I would be vex't for Campbeltown!"

"Ye micht be vexed for yoursel'," suggested Duffy. "There wouldna be the same demand for waiters."

"Oh, just the same!" said Erchie. "They canna stop folk eatin', except in Germany, where ye need to get a ticket before ye can cut a loaf. The only difference wi' us waiters would be that we would get hame sooner frae their public banquets; there wouldna be ony aifter-dinner oratory."

"Ach! the thing's a' nonsense!" said Duffy. "If ye met a chap ye kent at nicht, what could ye stand him"

"Oh, ye would jist slip him an oranger or a tin o' Nestle's milk, and say 'Here's to ye!'. The springs o' human kindness needna be a'thegither dry because o' pro-hibeetion. At the worst ye would aye be at liberty to tak' a crony into Craig's or Cranston's,[5] and fill him up wi' Russian tea, a drink that's fairly ragin' noo across the Blue Carpathian Mountains."

"Tea's a' richt in its ain place," admitted Duffy, "but ye couldna be aye nip, nip, nippin' awa' at tea. It's maybe fine for folk that hae the time to spend on't, but it's no' for workin'men. If this calamity is railly gaun to happen us, I'll hae to lay in something in a press till the war blaws bye."

45. *Duffy Will Buy Bonds*[1]

THERE IS every indication that Mr Duffy has been doing well in the coal trade lately. For the first time in his business career he has a horse that can lie down in its stall and get up again without the least assistance — a coal-black, long-tailed, feather-footed, haughty-looking horse with an astonishingly masculine "nicher," which, coming from between the trams of a coal-lorry, provokes much interest every time it is heard, and almost saves Duffy the trouble of crying "Coal!"

It was whinnying in the most inviting way to a passing taxi-cab on Saturday when Erchie came along the street and congratulated Duffy on his new steed.

"Man," he said, "that's a great, big, fine, lump o' a horse ye hae, Duffy! He's like his meat. Is he a genuine Clydesdale ?"

"If ye kent aboot horse, ye would see quite plain he wasna a Clydesdale," answered Duffy; "he's a Belgian refugee. I bocht him frae Meikle the undertaker. A wee bit saft, like a' them funeral stallions, but, man, he's got the style!"

"What's he nich-nich-nicherin' for?" asked Erchie.

"If ye'll no' let it ony further, I'll tell ye," whispered the coalman. "He's blin' in wan e'e, and he canna see wi' the other, and he jist gangs by the sound o' wheels. That horse would nicher to a tramway caur!"

The last raik of the day had been delivered, and Erchie went to the stable with the black Belgian and its owner. Duffy gave it corn!

"That's because it's Seturday," he explained.

"Nae wonder he nichers!" said Erchie. "Pampered like that! The coal tred must be daein' weel the noo, Duffy."

"Oh, I'm no' daein' that awfu' bad!" the coalman admitted. "But, man, ye canna keep money; the wife's never aff my face noo to buy her a pianna."

"A pianna!" exclaimed his friend. "Whit on earth does she want wi' a pianna? I'm shair a' your lassies is married and aff your hands! I would think your wife had plenty to dae to keep the grate in order. Don't you encourage her, Duffy; if she got yin she would maybe try to play't — "

"Oh, I'm no' givin' in to her," said Duffy; "but I'll go as faur as a vacuum washer." He turned to his friend with an amazing outburst of confidence. "Man, Erchie," he said, "I'm makin' money! Ye have nae idea o' the fine sensation it is. I have mair than a hunder pound this very meenute in behind the meter — "

Erchie sighed. "A hunder pound!" he said. "Nae wonder ye have a horse that nichers; it's just pride! But I wouldna keep a' that money in behind the meter; the man that comes to tak' the meter micht tak' mair. Ye should invest it, Duffy."

"I thocht o' that tae," said Duffy. "A buildin' society —"

Erchie waved the suggestion aside impatiently.

"Athegither oot o' date! Ye micht as weel put it in the Sustentation Fund or doon a stank.[2] Before ye kent where ye were ye would be landed wi' a hoose and naebody to pent and paper't for ye. Whit you should dae wi' your hunder pound, Duffy, is to put it in a Bond."[3]

"I thocht aboot that tae," said Duffy, brushing down the Belgian. "Everybody's sayin' ye should put money in a Bond, but I went doon and looked at yin below a railway arch, and I wouldna trust a penny in't. As dark as a ree,[4] and an awfu' smell o' drink."

Erchie laughed. "Man," he said, "Ye're a comic, Duffy! It's no' in a bonded store ye're advised to put your money noo, though I daresay mony a penny ye put there indirectly through the Mull o' Kintyre Vaults; the thing I mean's a War Bond. Gie your money to the country and get $4\frac{1}{2}$ per cent."

"But would it be safe!" asked Duffy, cautiously.

"Onything would be safer than havin' it in beside a city o' Gleska meter. A Bond's safer than a bank, and ye ken whit banks is; every weel-daein' man in Gleska puts his money into banks, and it's there as guid as ever when he's deid. But a bank'll only gie ye twa per cent; the Government'll gie four-and-a-half, backed up wi' the security o' the British Empire, and there's naething mair secure than that unless it's the jyle at Peterheid. You buy Bonds, Duffy! Never you heed the wife and her pianna; a vacuum washer's far mair like the thing onybody can work it and it doesna need a tuner. And mind you this that every sovereign ye lend the Government's a Sodger to fight the Germans. There's no sense keepin' sodgers in beside the meter, or locked up in a Cottage Upright Grand that aye needs polishin'."

"It's a lot o' money, mind ye, a hunder pound!" said the coalman. "It's nearly twa pounds a week for a year; a man could live first-rate on that."

"Tak my advice, and put it in a War Loan Bond! It'll gie ye the status o' a landed gentleman. 'There's Mr Duffy,' the folk'll say, and touch their keps to ye; 'he keeps the country goin'!' If I had a hunder pound to spare the noo ye wouldna see my feet for stour,[5] running to the G.P.O. or the bank to get the best investment that this country's every seen."

"I'll dae't!" said Duffy, putting on his coat. "Will they use it for buyin' shells?"

"That's jist whit they want it for," said Erchie. "And if ye buy a Bond ye're daein' your wee bit to bash the Germans. It's likely there'll be a badge for the genuine War Investors. Ye'll get a button to stick in your coat lapel to show ye're no' a shirker."

"I'll awa' this very meenute and buy a vacuum washer!" said Duffy.

46. *An Ideal Profession*[1]

JOHNNY DUFFY, the coalman's son, having reached the age of seventeen, and being now, in his father's estimation, thoroughly educated, is not going back to school again.

"Whit are ye gaun to make o' him?" Erchie asked the father on Saturday.

"That's the bit!" said Duffy. "I havena ony notion — not the least! He used to hae a fancy to be a tramway guard, but that was afore they had the petticoats;[2] he would nae mair think o' bein' a guard noo than o' bein' a milliner. His mother was thinkin' o' puttin' him in a bank."

"In a bank!" exclaimed Erchie. "There's naebody puts onything in banks noo since the War Loan started. It would just be throwin' the chap awa'."

"Ay, but banks is aye looked up to; it's no' the same as sellin' coals. A clerk in a bank can keep his mind aff anything till he gets his breakfast, and his work's a' done at three in the efternoon and twelve on Seturday. And there's money made in banks; folk just come and put it in."

"Duffy," said his friend, solemnly, "don't you be so misguided as put Johnny in a bank. It's no done nooadays at a'; it's oot o' date. This time next year, if ye're spared, ye'll see naebody workin' in banks but the directors, and a wheen o' smert wee lassies new passed wi' their Intermediate. Has Johnny no' got his health?"

"There's naething wrang wi' his health since Dr Jordan sorted him efter the measles," said Duffy. He might have been talking about a clock.

"Very well," said Erchie, "if he has the health, and a' his wits aboot him, ye couldna dae better than put him into the Wine, Spirit, and Beer Trade; it's gaun to be the popular profession o' the future. Get him started richt aff. There's bound to be a rush for't. It's gaun to be a far better tred for a smert young chap than slavin' awa' in a bank seven or eight hours a day. Put Johnny in a pub, and he'll no' need to start his work till twelve o'clock. He'll get aff from half-past two till six, and be done for the day at nine, in time for the second hoose at the music-halls. On Seturday he'll only need to work frae four till nine. Five to five and-a-half hours a day! Man, it would just be sport for the fellow! He wouldna hae mair time to himsel' if he was a stock-broker!"[3]

"Five hours!"[3] said Duffy, who rarely reads the papers. "Maclachlan o' the Mull o' Kintyre Vaults is toilin' awa' in his place from efter nine in the mornin' till efter ten at night; it's no' sport keepin' a pub."

"That's true aboot Maclachlan noo, but it'll no' be true o' him efter Monday week; he'll have time, if he likes, to attend the College and come oot a minister. Man; that would be a capital chance for Johnny! Ye see, Duffy, under the new Act, Gleska and the Clyde is an infected area; naebody'll dare sell a drap o' drink except at the hours I've mentioned."

"My Jove! I wish this war was ended." fervently said the coalman.

"If you and me survive these hardships for a year or twa," said Erchie, "we'll see an awfu' difference in Gleska and the Clyde doon as far as a line drawn between Campbeltown and the Heads o' Ayr. The "mornin'" is abolished at wan fell swoop. Efter his dinner a man may just as weel go back to his work, for the pubs 'll no' be open till six o'clock, and at nine at nicht there'll be naethin for't for even the maist determined and independent man but just to gang awa' hame."

"And they talk aboot the land o' the brave and the free!" said Duffy, bitterly.

"That's richt!" said Erchie, cheerfully.

"It's a blow at British liberty. But, of course, ye'll can get tea and coffee and kola and Broon Robin, and onything of that sort at ony reasonable hour o' the day; the pubs can keep open for the sale o' them if they like."

"I can tell you there'll be a bonny run on half-peck bottles!" said Duffy, and his friend gave a chuckle.

"Na! na!" said he; "they thocht of that tae. It's only on

twa hours and a half a day ye'll can tak' away a bottle or
have yin sent to the hoose for ye, and maybe no' at a' on
Seturday. The bottle-blowin' tred is in a state o' panic, and
every cork-cutter in the country's listin' in the Airmy."

"That's no' the worst o't," proceeded Erchie. "Ye'll no'
get staunin' your hand."

Duffy's aspect brightened; momentarily he regarded the
new regulations as being not entirely unreasonable.

"Treatin' is abolished. Every man'll have to buy his ain
drink, and ye couldna order a drink at the bar for me unless
ye gave me my dinner wi't, or at least a twopenny pie; I'm
no richt sure yet whether a twopenny pie's to be regairded
as a meal or no'."

"Who on earth can keep mind o' a' that?" asked Duffy.
"It was far simpler the way it was."

"That's just it! It was far ower simple. The idea noo is to
bamboozle ye and mak' gettin' a drink as hard a job as
gettin' the V.C. It's gaun to be a grand thing for the
watchmakers; everybody'll hae to keep a wristlet watch,
and a printed caird wi' the hours for drinkin' on it. Ye
couldna keep mind o' them ony other way. And look at the
flyness o' them — 4 pm till 9 on Saturday'. By the time 4
o'clock comes round on Saturday, a poor chap must go
hame for his dinner. His wife'll get his pay and have it a'
squandered in grocers' shops before he has his face
washed. If he's no' wide awake, he'll be hurlin' a perambulator or at a picture-palace wi' her before the pubs is open,
and that's no way to start a jolly Saturday nicht."

"I never richt understood afore what they meant by this
'policy o' frightfulness'," said Duffy.

"And forbye," said Erchie;' "there's gaun to be a change
in the strength o' whisky. The publican can sell it 35 under
proof instead of 25, the strength he sells it at noo. Perhaps
he'll sell it cheaper, but it's likely no'. The weaker it is, the
better it is for the health, the government says, and ye
daurna contradict them!"

"A' nonsense!" said Duffy. "Water's adulteration. I
wouldna put Johnny in a tred like that."

"Ay, but consider the gentlemanly leisure Johnny would have!" said Erchie. "As good as a schoolmaster. And, besides, he would be a kind o' a Civil Servant, bein' strictly under Government control. I wouldna say but by-and-bye there'll be a uniform for barmen, and superannuation pensions.

47. *Margarine for Wartime*[1]

ERCHIE MACPHERSON came home on Saturday afternoon with a pound of margarine. He had bought it away in another part of the town, where he wasn't known, by instruction of his wife. "If we must hae margarine," she said, "we needna let a' the neighbours ken. Ye can let on it's just for cookin'."

It looked all right when Erchie put in on the table — firm and clean, nutritious and faintly golden; it had actually a vague attractive odour of the fields, as if of clover; to the taste it was absolutely indistinguishable from ordinary good butter. Jinnet was astonished.

"That's no what I thocht margarine was like at a'," said she. "I thocht it would just look like a daud o' creesh and taste like monkey-nuts."

"It's the rale Muir o' Stra'ven Margarine," said Erchie. "It's made that like the genuine article that the coos in the Stra'ven district's up in arms against blackleg compiteetion. Ye should hear them mooin' roond the munition factory!"

"The munition factory!" said Jinnet.

"Ay! The Muir o' Stra'ven Margarine's a' made in a munition factory under Government control. Lloyd George[2] has nearly as much high explosive shell noo as he needs to feenish the war, and maist o' the munition factories is makin' margarine three days a week. A' female labour! It's a trate to see yon smert and sonsy Stra'ven lassies in their clean print wrappers churnin' awa' at margarine made o' the very purest ingredients. There's nae monkey-nuts in the Stra'ven stuff — the pick o' Scottish hazel-nuts left over frae Hallowe'en and a reasonable proportion o' sweet milk, and whiles when there's naebody lookin' they fling in a bit o' genuine butter for the sake o' Auld Lang Syne. It's inspected every five meenuts by a chap in brass buttons wi' a microscope in case o' hairs. Just you taste the taste!"

He spread some of it on his toast, and ate with apparent relish.

Jinnet spread it on her bread as thin as possible, and nibbled dubiously. "It's just exactly the same as butter," she remarked, "but it's someway different, and I ken I'll never like it. Oh, Erchie! Little did we think we would ever be reduced to margarine, and us wi' no ill-will to onybody. But I kent for years there was something brewin' for us; we were needin' a chastisement. Look at the way we were cairryin' on! The lust o' the flesh and the pride o' the eye! We werna' half humble. Naething in our minds but pleesure, the raiment we should wear and the worship o' the belly; gallivantin' here and there: chamberin'[3] and wantonness; tiled closes, pianos, mandolines, and fancy cookery classes. When ye bocht me yon new boa a year last January I felt there was something wrang!"

"Is it moths?" asked her husband anxiously.

"No, no! Nae fear o' that; it's aye in camphor. But it was the display o' the thing. Erchie; you were that built up on my ha'en' it. And I was that conceity wi't on Sabbaths."

"Dae ye actually think," said Erchie, "that your boa brocht on the war!"

"I don't ken, but I'm shair it helped. It was the copestone of mony indulgences in things corruptible. Ye canna' deny, Erchie, that we were a wicked and extravagant generation."

Her husband twinkled. "So we were," said he, "I'm no' denyin'. Naething would would dae me but the tramway-caur frae my work instead o' walkin' the way I used to dae. Every noo and then a shilling'y tie. My bottle o' porter every Setturday, whether I was needn't it or no'. The

History o' the Clans in forty pairts wi' a' the different tartans. A yin-and-penny-ha'penny bottle o' embrocation every time my back was the least bit sair. The money I've spent on raffles in the past ten years would come to a pound or twa, I'm shair, if it was coonted up, and there's only that model in the room o' the steamer "Bonnie Doon' to show for't. It's nae wonder I havena onything to put in the War Loan, the way I was cairryin' on!"

"Indeed," said Jinnet, bridling, "ye needna blame yoursel'; ye worked hard enough for your wee bit comforts. But when I think o' that boa —"

"If ye mention that boa again I'll tak' the heid aff ye!" cried Erchie. "There was naething I ever bocht in my life I got better value in — unless it was a waddin'-ring."

"Ye're an auld haver!"[4] said his wife, smiling, with a little flush of colour. "Dear me, that's awfu' like good saut butter! I believe I could get used to 't if it hadna the taste o' nuts; no strong, but I can feel it. And, onyway, there's naething cleaner than a nut."

"But it must be rale Scotch hazel," said Erchie, firmly. "Nane o' your foreign trash! That's the motto o' the Muir o' Stra'ven Margarine Manufactory."

"We micht weel come doon to margarine," said Jinnet, sighing, "considerin' the wastery in Scotland this past twenty years. I'm black affronted when I think on't. There was me with my brand new bonnet every second year — no' even content wi' alterin' the auld yin. The last yin I got cost 10s 6d. I used to buy the print and get a wrapper made o't for twa shillin's by Katie Broon, and naething would please me at the hinder end but a costume frae a shop at thirty shillin's, and it wouldna last me mair nor a year or twa. Oh, Erchie, we were needin' a chastisin'. ... When I think o' my boa, and Mrs Duffy's Alick deid among the Germans!. ... The pride o' the eye and the lust o' the flesh! We were faur astray."

"So I see in the papers," said her husband, "Mr M'Kenna's[5] rale disappointed wi' us. When I think o' the money I spent on tobacco — sevenpence every week!"

"That's naething!" said his wife, impatiently. "A bonny hoose it would be wi' a man that didna smoke! It's my ain extravagance that vexes me. I couldna keep money. I'm shair I could hae done fine without the sewin'-machine, and think o' a' the money it cost us every year for a week at Ro'say! We werena needin' incandescent mantles for the gas, and the wee hoose that we had in Raeberry Street was fine; I'm sorry I ever egged ye on to leave it. Whit would my mither — peace be wi' her! — think o' me gaun twice to a picture-hoose, and sendin' oot your washin' to a la'ndry! A penny a collar! It's ruination! But I canna help it Erchie;' in your tred linen needs a gloss, and, though it's me that's willin', I'll assure ye, I'm no langer fit for 't."

"If ye try to iron a shirt or collar o' mine again," said her man, "I'll leave ye."

"And here we're at the margarine!" said Jinnet, sadly. "There was never in this hoose afore but honest butter. But I'll no repine: there's mony a puir body waur aff, though I ha'e my boa, and Alick Duffy's deid. I think I'll gang roond and gie Mrs Dufy a tastin' just to show her margarine's no' sae very different frae butter efter a'. Whit did ye pay for't, Erchie'!"

"One-and-nine a pound," said her husband, chuckling. "are you sure ye feel the taste o' nuts?"

"One-and-nine!" cried Jinnet. "Man, that's the price o' butter!"

"And that's just butter that ye're eatin' — plain Danish butter; I bocht it doon the stair in Campbell's. For a' we eat o' butter we can afford it. It's no whit you and me can save in pennies that's gaun to win the war: we couldna' save enough in margarine to run the war a week!"

48. *Duffy in the Dark*[1]

AT EIGHT o'clock on Saturday night, through the darkness and the snow-soup of Garscube Road, Duffy drove his empty lorry home. The night might be filthy, but he had had a good day — a real good day. There had been a delightful public uncertainty as to the selling price of coals. It varied according to circumstances. In Raeberry Street, from desperate women who saw an Arctic Sunday in prospect and had already burned up their clothes-pins for the tea, he had got as much as two-and-three the reputed bag. For carrying bags to the upper flats of tenements he had charged a War Bonus of threepence, and in at least five grateful houses he had got a small refreshment extra.

Duffy was feeling fine.

He was whistling the war-song of the trade — "Keep the Home-fires Burning," and seeing himself in fancy half an hour from now with his face washed and dry clothes on, sitting before his excellent wife's idea of a Saturday supper. He hoped it would be sausages.

At the corner of Hopehill Road a young man jumped on him out of the dark and said. "For the love of Peter, have ye ony coals!"

"No' as much as you would heave at a cat!" said Duffy. "I'm done for the day."

The young man groaned. "Oh, Jerusalem," he exclaimed. "I've been a' over the toon for a ton at ony price, and I'm bate!"

"Whit would ye ca' ony price?" asked Duffy.

'Great thoughts, great instincts, come to men.

Like feelings unaware',

as the poet says,[2] and his commercial instincts as a coalman had instantly swamped his vision, as a human being, of an early sausage supper.

"Ony mortal thing!" impulsively said the stranger. "I'm wantin' them for the kirk in Dobbie's Loan. My faither's the beadle, and he's let himsel' run oot, and the place'll be like charity the morrow."

"Whit kirk is't?" asked Duffy.

"It's the yin at the ither end," said the stranger. "ye'll easy find it."

"I think I mind o' yince seein't," said the coalman. "It's a good bit aff my bate. Forbye, it's late on a Setterday nicht and forbye, my horse and me's clean wabbit. Ye'll mind ye coals is coals them days: it's a favour to get them. They'll cost ye £2 5s, and that's wi' a half croon aff, for kirks is a kind o' charity."

"Right-o!" said the young man. "It's stiff, but we'll pay it. Ye'll no' be lang!"

"I'll be there in half an oor," said Duffy.

He was quite mistaken.

It was only when he got into Dobbie's Loan a half hour later with the load of coals that he realised fully the drastic character of the Lighting Regulations[3] and the inconspicuousness of churches. By the merest chance he came on one at the corner of Charlotte Street, but not a living soul was to be found in charge of the edifice, which looked as if it had been shut since the Coronation.

"Wasn't I the eediot?" thought Duffy. "It was 'the ither end' he said, and the ither end o' Dobbie's Loan's awa doon somewhere near the Necropolis."

That was somewhat to exaggerate the length of Dobbie's Loan, but in truth it is a ridiculous thoroughfare, in parts the dreariest in Glasgow, and twenty minutes later found Duffy at its extremity in Parliamentary Road with the church of his search still undiscovered. The only helpful information he could get in a public house (with a little nourishment), was that though Dobbie's Loan itself was rather short of churches there was a good selection in the neighbourhood, including the Catholic Apostolic.

"That sounds like a place they would be needin' coal," said Duffy. "The silly Ned micht hae gi'en me the richt direction. I'll ha'e a chaser."

"Nine o'clock," said the barman firmly, and began to clear up his counter.

When Duffy rejoined his horse the night seemed blacker than ever. The snow was falling thickly. Only the faintest light came from the public lamps: the tramway cars went past as black as hearses. Tenements were like cliffs without a chink of light in them, and the shops that were open still appeared to be using candles.

"Oh frost!" said Duffy to himself.

Twenty minutes later Duffy cried 'Woe' to his horse, jumped off the lorry's front, and peered about for somebody to speak to. A man came round a corner, feeling his way with caution.

"Do ye ken ony Catholic church?" asked Duffy.

"There's yin in Glebe Street," was the reply; "but man, ye're far ower early for't!"

"Whaur's Glebe Street frae here?" asked Duffy.

"I could tell ye if I had a licht," said the man; "but the way things is I have nae idea. I'm lost mysel'. Sae far as I can mak' oot we're near the Blin' Asylum. Whit are ye wantin' a church at this time for? Is it Easter Sunday or onything o' that sort?"

"I'm gaun to't wi' a rake o' coals," said Duffy. "Do ye no see I have a lorry?"

"My Jove!" said the man, "is that a lorry ye're standin' in front o'? I thocht it was a pend close."

"Ye micht weel think that!" said Duffy. "I have nae mair idea o' whaur I am than my horse has. It's the first time I ever took a job on for this end o' the toon, and I'll bate ye it'll be the last. I would gang hame the way I am if I only could fin' oot Dobbie's Loan."

"Dobbie's Loan!" said the other. "Ye're richt enough for Dobbie's Loan; it's scattered a' roond here; ye canna miss it. If ye see a tramway caur go efter't. And if ye don't see onything at a' its Sichthill Cemetery."

"Gee-up!" said Duffy to his horse. "This is a bonny warnin' to me to have naething to dae wi' papists. If I had ken't I would have asked for £2.10s."

The idea of following the tramway lines appealed to him. At least they would prevent him from straying out of

Glasgow altogether. By now there was nobody on the streets; the cars that went past at intervals one way or another had hardly anybody in them, so far as he could see into their dimly lit interiors. The shops were shut. Great blocks, pitch black, were on either side of him.

"And yet they say ye canna get stuff to mak' briquettes," said Duffy.

At the end of another mile or two he came on a standing tramway car, and the driver in front of it lighting matches.

"Can ye tell me where I am?" the driver asked him, with an Irish accent. His conductor was a lady who was in tears, and she was lighting matches also.

"God knows!" said Duffy. "Where were ye bound for?"

"Sure and I was makin' for Barrachnie," said the driver. "I came from the Paisley Road way and it's my first time on the rowte. I always disbelieved there could be any place wid the name Barrachnie in Glasgow, and now I'm sure av it. I've drove this kyar since eight o'clock on both sides av the river; I've been in the Roukin Glen and the Celtic football ground and the barracks at Maryhill, and divill the ticket the girl has got in her bunch 'll fit the passengers. I should be back where I started an hour ago, but the only place I knew since I started was the Cattle Market and I've passed it half a dozen times."

They stood helplessly in the darkness till a policeman came up and shone his lamp on them.

"What's a Barrachnie car doin' here?" he asked with some astonishment.

"Do ye ken a Catholic church that's needin' coals?" asked Duffy.

"No," said the constable, "nor a U.F. neither."

"Where the divvel are we!" asked the driver.

"You're within a kick of Bishopbriggs: you're on the High Possil Road," said the constable.

"Oh frost!" said Duffy.

49. *A Bawbee on the Bobbin*[1]

"THAT'S an awfu' thing that's happened in Paisley," said Erchie, putting down his paper and removing his glasses.

"What in the world is't?" cried Janet, trembling already in anticipation of some dreadfully tragic news.

"A Mr MacGallochary," said her husband, "yin o' the largest shareholders in J. & P. Coats's[2] business, went into the works on Friday mornin' and attacked the manager."

"Isn't that awfu'!" said Janet. "What did he attack him wi'?" Her sense of the tragic always depends very largely on the nature of the weapon.

Her husband pretended to consult the paper again. "Positively monstrous!" he remarked. "Bashed him ower the heid wi' a poke o' sovereigns!"[3]

"I thought ye couldna get sovereigns the noo: there's surely no' enough o' them aboot to hurt onybody."

"I havena seen yin mysel' since the year o' the Exhibition," said Erchie: "but there must be plenty gaun aboot for onybody that's in a dacent way o' business."

"What did he attack him for?" inquired Janet.

"For makin' an awfu' mistake in his calculations. MacGallochary said he was just efter gettin' his dividends from the business, and he noticed at yince there was something wrang, they were that rideeculous for the time o' war, and his anger got the better o' him."

"It was gey hard on the puir manager," said Janet. "Ony man can mak' a mistake in coontin'; there's whiles I'm no very sure o' mysel' wi' the price o' everything different to what it used to be."

"MacGallochary didna look at it that way, though, him bein' a kind o' Christian and parteecular to a faut."

"I hope we're a' Christians, Erchie," said the wife gravely.

"Oh ay, of course we are, but MacGallochary must hae belanged to a brench high up in the Christian body that canna stand the least wee deviation frae the Ten Commandments. It doesna say his age, but I think he must hae been an auld, auld man that doesna realise there should be some come and go in' Christianity. ... What dae ye pay for your pirns o' threid?"

"Threepence a piece," said Janet. "It's mair than a year since they put them up a ha'penny. It's an awfu' money for threid! I suppose it's the war."

"That's just it! That's what vexed MacGallochary. Ye see it's like this — when the war broke oot the Coats's say 'the cost o' raw material and labour's bound to gang up like onything, and we'll hae naething left for dividends at the present price of the cotton bobbin. We must dae something.' The manager made a calculation wi' a pencil on the back o' a bit o' paper he had brung his piece to the works in and said the way things was the pirn would hae to be raised to threepence. Somebody asked if a farden[4] extra on the bobbin wouldna dae, considerin' that threid would be mair in demand in the world than at any other time in its history. But he says 'No, gentlemen, the farden advance is oot o' the question. Naebody ever has a farden except on the Greenock tramways. It's no' a coin in circulation. We couldna be handin' back the customer a packet o' preens or an Abernaithy biscuit for change for every pirn she bought. No, gentlemen, it must be a threepenny bobbin to do justice to the shareholders.'"

"There's nae doot," said Janet "that the farden's oot o' date since they stopped the missionary boxes in the Sunday schools."

"Weel, ye see, when MacGallochary found that Coats made a profit o' £3,387,395 last year, or threequarters o' a million mair than in the year afore the war began, he saw the manager's calculation was lamentably wrang, and that he was far ower smert in puttin' the bawbee on the bobbin when there wasna ony need for't. When the manager came to his senses efter the poke o' sovereigns struck him on the neck, MacGallochary tell't him he wasna gaun to tak' a bonus o' a bawbee extra on the pirns, for sewin' sodgers' shirts, and that the three-quarters o' a million must be handed back to the Government, and the price o' the bobbin reduced to what it was afore the war."

"I don't care," said Janet, "but there must have been something nice aboot Mr MacGallochary to think o' such a thing."

"When the manager heard this extraordinary proposal he swooned awa' for the second time, and it wasna' till they sent oot for a little brandy he cam' tae again."

"He must ha'e been awfu' badly hurt," said Janet, sympathetically, "Just fancy you a poke o' sovereigns on the neck!"

"And the best o't is that they werena' sovereigns efter a'," said Erchie, consulting his newspaper. "It said sovereigns right enough on the ootside o' the poke, but the polis found it was filled wi' naething but auld communion tokens.[5] He was a clever man that thought o' that!"

"What did they dae wi' Mr MacGallochary?" inquired Janet.

"They took him to Gartnavel,"[6] said her husband, solemnly. "They kens that nae shareholder in his senses would be such an awfu' idiot and act like that. On the way to Gartnavel in a taxi he kept stickin' his heid oot at the window every noo and then cryin' "Paisley pirns! Paisley pirns! Gie the women and the Army back their maik"'[7] Awfu' vulgar! Fancy him sayin' 'maik'"

"And are they gaun to bring doon the price o' pirns noo that they hae found oot they were mistaken!" asked Janet innocently.

Her husband look at her with pity. "My, Jinnet," he said, "ye're almost fit for Gartnavel yoursel' to hae ony such idea! Do ye no' ken that the nation's slogan is 'Business as usual — and a wee bit better.' They found MacGallochary was aff his heid for months back, and that he never was a shareholder in Coats's or onywhere else. He was only lettin' on — like mysel'.""

50. *Nationalised Eggs*[1]

DUFFY, THE work of the week accomplished, walked home with the essentials of a satisfactory Saturday tea for himself — a half-a-pound of ham he had bought at the corner, and two fresh eggs. On Saturday aftrnoons he always caters for himself; a wife has quite inadequate ideas of a coalman's needs.

"I'll bate ye what ye like it's a present for the mistress," said Erchie, with a finger on the parcel.

"Then ye're wrang!" retorted Duffy. "I gi'ed her a present last New Year. It's my supper. Do ye ken what country eggs is, Erchie? Four shillin's a dozen! For eggs, mind ye! — just common country eggs, no' ostriches. Four shillin's! I've seen the day 4s would cairry ye roond every licensed hoose in the Coocaddena district and leave enough for your fine on the Monday mornin'. What's the maitter wi' the hens?"

"It's no the hens," said Erchie. "The loyal and patriotic hen is willin' to dae her bit. It's the faut o' a Coalition Government.[2] The London 'Times' and the 'Daily Mail' at the very start o' the war pointed oot that the egg situation was desperate and that only firm and immediate action by a Poultry Board would save the situation. The government paid nae heed. It had nae relations in the egg trade for wan thing, and there was nae ootstandin' statesman wi' that devotion to his country and intimate knowledge o' the hen to mark him oot for Egg Minister. What's the result? The country eggs at 4d to $4\frac{1}{2}$! — a price that puts it oot o' the question for workin' men and maks it the monopoly o' shipowners and teetotallers."

"Somebody's makin' a fine thing o't anyway," said Duffy, gloomily. "I'm shair the country's fair hotchin' wi' hens."

"On the contrary," said Erchie, "there's no' near enough o' them, and them we hae are fair mismanaged. Just you think! — there's 20,000,000 acres o' Scotland under deer, and half as much set aside for growin' grouse.

Hoo much o' the land dae ye think is devoted to poultry? Man, ye could hardly play a fitba' match on't! It's silly! There's naething tae be got frae deer besides the eatin' o't except the horns, and maybe a bass for your parlour, and grouse doesna lay eggs!; at least I never saw them. But you tak' a hen! — a hen's producin' something a' the time, providin' the people's breakfasts and the coalman's tea, and whiles a surplus over for elections. Even when it's deid at the end o' a lang and busy life, it's chicken croquets, a thing ye get in restaurants. Economically, for the State, a hen's worth twenty deer and a gross o' grouse, but it gets nae support frae the Game Laws and the Government.

"If the country realised the value o' the hen, it would clear the deer and grouse frae the land they occupy, and put on a good-layin' strain o' Leghorns and Minorcas. The sportin' gentry would soon adapt themselves to stalkin' Wyandotes in the shootin' season and a' the rest o' the year the hens would be busy layin'. Nae waste! On the 18th o' August ye would read then in the papers that the Duke o' Sutherland (3 guns) shootin' over the Castle Moor bagged 30 brace o' Black Minorcas and 15 Dorkins. A' the rest o' the time the hills and moors would be full o' quite fresh eggs!

"But nobody thocht o' backin' up the natural enterprise o' the hen by givin' it this expansion. Run on large intelligent lines, hen-farmin' might have been the country's salvation. We would be independent o' the foreign egg and the egg wi' the Irish accent, and the price would never be over a shillin' a dozen. It's too late to start hen forests noo that the war is on, but a sensible Government would have done the next best thing a year ago, and put the nation's egg production on a scientific basis. The business is a' in the hands o' auld wifes wi' nae capital. A farmer's wife oot about Mearns employs thirty or forty hens; a minister's wife in the parish o' Balfron keeps a hundred gaun; thoosands o' country women wi' nae appliances but a bauk and a couple o' stucca[3] eggs tak' up the tred wi a dozen or twa auld-fashiond hens; that never had any education or technical trainin', and it's on the like o' them the supply o' a reasonable breakfast for the British workin' man depends! The thing's silly!"

"Four shillin's a dozen!" said Duffy.

"If the Government had done what the newspapers wanted, they would hae pooled a' the poultry-stock in the country'; shooed a' the hens into a big kind o' national muneetion factories, and speeded them up under expert management. Mind ye, there's a lot o' labour troubles wi' hens workin' in small concerns. They're aye gaun aff to moult or cleck, or onything that'll tak' them aff their work; put them a' into half-a-dozen big national Egg Factories wi' the right kind o' supervision, and a' that nonsense would be ended. Half the puir auld wifes that's superintendin' hens the noo hae nae idea aboot science; they fling oot the heel o' a loaf and some potato peelin's, and waste half the day lookin' through the hay or under hedges for the product. Meanwhile the country's waitin' for the National Idea — and that's the All-Round Penny Egg."

"I wish I seen it," said Duffy. "Four shillin's the dozen!"

"Ye'll no see it till the government wakes up." said Erchie. "Not till the egg production o' the country's put in the hands o' Mr Winston Churchill[4] or Mr. Bottomley.[5] They're cut oot for the job. They have the very cackle for't."

51. *A Slump in Zepps*[1]

"IT'S ME that's vexed for the poor!" said Janet. "I don't ken hoo they manage at a' in the country-places where there's naething extra comin' in frae bonuses and muneetions. Everything's gaun up."

"No' exactly everything," said her husband, looking over his spectacles "Zepps[2] is comin' doon. There's a slump in Zepps. We're baggin' them by the pair like kipper herrin'. Onybody in this country that's needin' a second-handed Zepp for gaun home wi' at the New Year, can buy yin then for the price o' a pramlater, or I'm sair mistaken. If I could stable yin in the lobby I'd have it. The airyplane chaps is gettin' fair fed up wi' them, and the country's flooded wi' aluminium souvenirs. There's nae reputation to be made noo bringin' doon a Zepp. The first man that did it got the V.C., and ony amount o' money; noo they only gi'e ye a cocoa-nut."

"There must be some contrivance for puttin' them on fire," suggested Janet.

"I'll tell ye what it is if ye'll no let bug," said Erchie, mysteriously. "To let ye understand, they're lined ootside wi' flannelette. A' the airyplane chap has got to dae is to light a cigarette afore he rises, and drop it on the Zepp when he's fair above it. Every time a cocoa-nut!"

"Oh, dear me!" sighed Janet. "Ye would wonder folks would risk their life in them."

"There's nae risk!" explained her husband. "It's a deid certainty! When a German's sent aff in a Zeppelin noo his widow at yince goes into mournin'. A' his friends go doon to the airship shed to see the last o' him, and slip him a couple o' floral wreaths, and then go back to read the Will. The heid o' the German Zeppelin service noo is no' Count Zeppelin at a'; he's away back to the toy tred and makin' a fortune oot o' penny squeakers. The whole Zepp business noo is superintended by a firm o' funeral undertakers in Berlin; they're the Wylie & Locheid[3] o' Germany, and aye had the reputation o' turnin' oot a classy job in ony line o' obsequies."

"If I was a German —'

"God forbid!" cried her husband, shocked. "Please moderate your language, Jinnet!"

"If I was a German, I wouldna put a foot in their Zeppelins."

"Ye would ha'e nae choice in the maitter." said Erchie. "The Kaiser picks the crews. They're made up o' expensive auld Army and Navy chaps he's tired o', or found oot daein' something. He gies them an iron cross apiece and puts up a prayer. The cruel thing is the cross is far far ower wee for puttin' up in cemeteries. It's just makin' a cod o' the deceased. When the Zeppelin starts for England His Majesty drives hame in the first o' the mournin' coaches and says to his wife, 'We're daein' fine! There's another thirty pensions saved!'

"What does a Zeppelin look like?" inquired Janet. "I never saw yin."

"It's the shape o' a Trades Hoose cigar, if ye understand, and the size o' a pencil when ye see't first: then there's a bang, and a bleeze o' light, and the next time ye see it, it's spread ower a field like the start o' a new Corporation gas-works."

"Puir things! There's no much sport in that," said Janet.

"Oh, there's an element o' sport wi't tae! The 'Milguy Chronicle' is offerin' £3,000 to the first o' a Zeppelin crew that can land on his feet withoot stottin'."

"What good does it dae them tryin' to come here at a'?"

"I can tell ye that!" said Erchie, promptly. "It's 'frightfulness.'[4] They want to put up the price o' potatoes and milk that high we'll no' can buy them. There's nae other reason for their droppin' bombs ower the rural districts. It frightens the coos and make an awfu' hash o' the potato pits. Nae wonder the fermer greets into the tinny when he's measurin' oot the milk, and laments that he has to charge sae much for his potatoes."

"But the Germans is aye talkin' aboot hittin' fortified places; what's a fortified place?"

"It's a place," said her husband, "where there's two or more J.P.'s: a Young Women's Guild, two good kirks, and an esplanade. If there's a Casualty Sick Poorhouse in the place, it comes under the cless o' 'heavily fortified.'"

"I don't care what ye say, I wish I saw the last o' their Zeppelins," said Janet. "I can hardly mak' oot the dairy doon the street, it's that dark. Did I no' mistake the door and gang into Maclintock's public hoose last Saturday? Fancy that! And me wi' my jug in my haun'! What would they think?"[5]

"Oh, they would just think ye maybe had lodgers. What did ye dae wi' the beer?"

"Fine ye ken I never got it!" said Janet indignantly; "I came oot whenever I saw the barrels, and who did I bang into when I was comin' oot, but Duffy!"

"I hope ye explained to Duffy!" said her husband anxiously.

"He didn't gie me the chance; he jist said 'I'll no' mention it Mrs MacPherson,' and in he went!"

Erchie chuckled. "That shows ye," said he, "that the darkenin' o' Gleska's no' withoot its compensations. It gave ye an opportunity to see what Maclintock's is like inside, and to learn the naitural kindliness and courtesy o' the coalman."

"It gave me an awfu' start!" said Janet. "It's just yin tribulation after another; I sometimes think its the end o' the world."

"Nae fear o' that!" replied her husband. "If I thocht it was the end o' the world, I would tak' the first boat for Carrick Castle."

52. *The New Pub*[1]

DUFFY THE coalman came up to Erchie on Saturday with a face like a fiddle. "They're fair puttin' the lid on't now" said he. "Did ye hear the latest?"

"Don't tell me the Scottish Command has gone awa' and commandeered your horse!" exclaimed his friend. "If they've done that I'll vote for President Wilson and Peace, for it shows this country's situation is desperate."

"It's no' that," said Duffy hastily. "It's the pubs; they're shutting them athegither!"

"They've done it on Saturday nichts for years and years ever since the time o' Forbes McKenzie." said Erchie. "But they'll be open again at twelve o'clock on Monday. If ye're wife's taken ill, or onything like that, mind I havena a drop o' beer in the hoose!"

Duffy snorted indignantly. "Ye ken fine what I mean! They're shuttin' them efter the first o' January and maybe they'll never be open again, for a' the refreshments that's in them's to be sent to France to carry on the push."

It took Erchie several minutes to recover his solemnity. "Ye're a' mixed up, Duffy!" he explained with the tears of laughter in his eyes. "It's na the pubs they're shuttin' up after the New Year's Day; it's a wheen o' railway stations[2] that naebody ever went into except when it was rainin'."

"Oh, jeepers!" exclaimed the coalman, much relieved. "I was tell't it was pubs! There's far ower mony railway stations onyway at this time o' year; they jist tempt folk to trevel, instead o' stayin' at hame and keepin' on good fires."

"Ye needna be the least feared aboot the pubs," said Erchie, "They'll no be shut for a lang while yet, but before the war's feenished you and me'll be teetotal. There's no' gaun to be Prohibition, for ye can dae ony mortal thing ye like wi' the free-born British citizen except prohibit him from takin' a drink when he wants it. Ya can tak' awa' his business and his bairns, and even tak' his life, but ye daurna tak' his beer. The Government kens that fine, so it's no gaun to mak' ony frontal attack on the public-hooses; it's gaun to flank them on the lines o' what Duggie Haig[3] would ca' the higher strategy. When there's naething left in the public-hoose to drink but Boston Cream and Broon Robin it'll shut itsel'."

"When are they gaun to start?" asked Duffy anxiously looking at his watch.

"Oh ye canna lay in onything noo till Monday after-noon," said Erchie. "They've started already. Ony whisky they're makin' noo wi' ony puff in it is a' gaun ower to France in iron barrels for presentation to the Germans: what's left for sale here's half Loch Katrine, good enough for funerals but no' for first fit purposes at Ne'erday. And look at the price o't! There's thousands o' dacent workin' men in Gleska this week switherin' whether they'll buy a wristlet watch for the wife or bring hame a bottle o' five-

year-old. There's no' half the opportunity for gettin'
cheery there was twa years ago, the oors for sale in hotels
and pubs is reduced exactly that much. But the clincher is
to come wi' State control!"[4]

"What's that?" asked Duffy, anxiously. "Put me oot o'
pain."

"When a' the wee pubs is shut up and bankrupt because
they canna get whisky or sell't any langer at a profit, and
it's the price o' champagne wine, the Government'll tak'
over a' that's left and put 'G.R.' over the doors o' pubs, the
same's they were letterboxes. They've started already at
Annan and Carlisle. When the Mull o' Kintyre Vaults is
run by a chap that had to pass a Civil Service examination
and is workin' for a pension, the place'll be that different
ye'll no' ken it. It'll be a kind o' place ye wouldna like to
gang into unless ye had your face washed and your Sunday
claes. The barmen'll be in uniforms wi' red stripes doon
their breeks, and ye'll have to sign an order form for the
least wee thing ye want to drink that's no teetotal. Dupli-
cates o' the form'll be sent to your wife and your minister,
if any; if not, to the police. The new fashioned pub under
State Control'll be a large commodious place the size o' a
skatin' rink, furnished to the last degree wi' high art and a
string band in behind some bushes playin' 'Draw the
sword, Scotland!' or 'Why left I my hame?' It'll be great on
snacks; ye'll hardly can get a ginger cordial unless ye tak' a
threepenny shepherd's pie alang wi't, and if ye tak' tea
they'll gie ye a bonus. Nae standin' up'll be allooed; ye'll
hae to sit at a wee table wi' a crochet centrepiece and a jar
o'chrysanthemums in the middle. Facilities'll be given for
readin' the papers and writin' home. Every wee while in
the winter they'll have lectures."

"A chap might as weel be in the Royal Infirmary", said
Duffy, with disgust at such a prospect.

"The great aim o' the State Pub'll be to get the women
to come. Efter the first six months nae married man'll be
served unless he brings his wife wi' him. One free cup o'
Bovril will be given to every woman that tak's her knittin'

wi' her. If she tak's the cookery clesses on the Seturday nights, she gets a coupon every Seturday, and 150 coupons'll be value for a 15s 6d war savings certificate at ony post office. The alcoholic strength o' spirits'll be gradually reduced till ye could put oot a fire wi't, and the State-brewed beer'll be officially guaranteed to quench the thirst. Of course, there'll be a great reduction in the oors o' openin'. The State Pub'll open at six in the evenin' and shut at nine, and everything'll be done to prevent panic when the rush to get oot begins. Efter it has been established for eighteen months the like o' you and me, Duffy, 'll stay at hame at nichts and carouse on Boston Cream. Then they'll shut up the public hooses on the ground that naebody wants them."

53. *Marriage a la Mode*[1]

THE CLOSE was strewn with confetti and rice when Erchie got home for tea. In the house on the right-hand side of the second landing somebody was playing a melodeon. A perfume of oranges and Florida Water pervaded all the stairs. "There's surely a waddin' in Johnny Simpson's," he remarked to his wife as he put his umbrella upside down in the kitchen jawbox.

"It's his dochter Julia," said Janet — "the typist yin. What a carry-on! Ye wouldna think there was a war!"

"Do ye tell me Julia's married!" cried Erchie with surprise. "The lassie's daft; she was makin' her thirty shillings a week. Wha is she married on!"

"He's a kind o' Sergeant in the Fusiliers," said Janet. "His name's Macrae. Ten minutes after they were married he went awa' back to the Front wi' a bit o' the bridescake in his pack and her address written doon on the batters o' a Bible he got frae her Auntie Marget. Such a carry-on! Him awa' to the trenches, and them wi' a waddin' party that's shakin' the very land! And they're only engaged since Seturday!"

"Nane the waur o' that," said her husband. "I aye believed in short engagements."

"Weel, I don't," retorted Janet. "They should be happy as long's they can."

"It's the age o' short engagements," said her husband, putting on his slippers. "Yon daft-like way we had o' daunderin' in the gloamin'; for months roond the Three Tree Well and alang the Canal is oot o' date entirely. Look at the money it cost for gloves and conversation lozenges alone!"

"Ye canna cast up that I chased ye!" exclaimed his wife warmly. "Ye had to ak me six times."

"Ye're right," said her husband, twinkling; "it was exactly six times. I got 'no' every time and then my luck changed. But nooadays a' that kind o' palaverin's over; the bright young sodger home for seven days' leave is no' richt oot o' the station wi' his goatskin coat on, than some smert young lassie tracks him by his footprints to his lodgin's or his mother's, and has him gassed afore he can mak' a' grab for his respirator. If he's an officer they're roond at ten o'clock next morning at the photographers gettin' their picures taken for the 'Bulletin', and the lassie's wearin' a di'mond and ruby ring for four-and-twenty hours afore she finds oot whether its him or his brother Alexander. Ye get awfu' mixed up wi' them in their uniforms; they look a' alike."

"I never saw such merrages!" said Jinnet. "What a carry on! They go awa' and get merried the same's it was fit-on for a costume; it would put me in the nerves!"

Her husband laughed. "Ye belang to a past age, Jinnet; but if you were five-and-twenty and makin' a muneetion wage ye would nick a sodger as quick's the best o' them. There's naething that's alarmin' nooadays aboot a merrage to ony chap that's come through the war. In the old days he would have to go roond her relatives for inspection, and haud her hand at soirees, and study for months the kind o' claes to wear that would please her, and maybe have to join the Y.M.C.A. if her faither was parteecular. There's nane o' that noo. There's no' ony time for't, wi' him to be back in France on Sunday. The whole world's speeded up, and ye pick a partner for life the same's it was for a polka. Merrage has been made attractive. What used to put fellows aff the notion was the need for rentin' a hoose and furnishin't on the instalment system; goin' awa' on a honeymoon wi' a perfect stranger; jinin' the church, and handin' ower your wages every Seturday afternoon."

"Ye never rued it, ye auld rascal!" his wife rejoined. "Men have nae sense wi' money."

"The very thocht o' the jeely-pans and cruet-stands he was sure to get frae the lassie's cousins was enough to frichten a young chap. That's a' bye wi'! The sodger lover doesna need to bother about a hoose in Gleska as lang as he has his villa in France. He's married in the claes he stands in, a gift o' the Royal Family — the very latest fashion. The engagement ring's an aluminium yin made oot o' the nose o' a German whizz-bang, and the bride-groom's present to the bride is a couple o' German helmets and a rare collection o' the different rifle cartridges as used by the Allies. The relatives canna pass onything aff on him in the way o' presents except a pair o' socks and a box o' a hundred fags, and he's up and awa' for the train afore the minister gets richt started wi' 'The Health o' the Happy Couple.' At eight o'clock next mornin' the sodger's wife's on her way to business as usual and lookin' a' the newspaper bills on the road to see if her gettin' married to a corporal had made ony difference on the war."

"What a carry on!" repeated Janet. "Whit'll happen when a' they merried men come back? there'll no' be hooses[2] for them, and lots o' them couldna keep a wife."

"That's the only thing that bothers me," confessed her husband, more seriously. "And I'm no' denying that there's risks that lots o' them in their hurry's makin' a raffle o' a serious business."

"Just that!" said Janet. "But merrage is a raffle onyway ye tak' it. Julia Simpson's sergeant looks a wise-like lad; she maybe couldna pick a better if she took a year to't, the way I did mysel'."

54. *Bad News*[1]

I FOUND my old friend Erchie very depressed on Saturday night. "What's wrong?" I asked him. "Is it the weather, or the aftermath of the festive season, the new alcohol dilution order, or the fall of Braila?"[2]

"It's far worse than that," he responded gloomily; "it's the news aboot Wanton Wee Willie.[3] His health has broke doon; he's oot o' the Airmy, and awa' wi' his wife to a hydro. I doot he'll never get over it this time; his constitution is bound to be dreadfully undermined for the want o' proper nourishment. There's no' as much fat left in Germany as would grease a saw."

"Perhaps it's not true that the Crown Prince has retired," I suggested hopefully. "You mustn't be a pessimist."

"I doot it's true," said Erchie, sadly. "It's in the papers in twa places. Nerves a' shattered. It's a gloomy start wi' the New Year for the Allies: as lang as Willie was kind o' daein' his bit they could depend on him. Next to the British Navy, Willie was the guarantee o' our security. He was the Allies' Best Battle-winner; the French sodgers thocht that much o' him they had his picture printed on their pocket naipkins. A favourite a' roond! I doot his faither was gettin jealous o' Willie's popularity among the French and British; did Haig no' send him a case o' ten-year-auld and a cake o' shortbread on Christmas?"

"We'll just have to win our our own battles in future, then," I suggested.

"That's a' richt," said Erchie, "But the best way to win battles is to have a chap like Willie in command on the other side. Muneetions is no' everything; 'tanks'[4] is no' everything; ye need somebody on the other side ye can depend on to mak' a cod o' himsel' every time, and Wee Willie's presence on any pairt o' the battle front aye kept oor chaps cheery. He was the honorary Regimental Pet o' a lot o' the French battalions ever since the Indian Contingent ate up their goats.

"'Wha's in front o' us the day!' General Joffre[5] would ask, comin' up the trenches.

"'Six diveesions o' the Prussian Guards, three Grand Dukes, an awfu' smell o gas, and Wee Willie,' the Sergeant would say, like to burst himsel' wi' laughin'.

"'Mong jew!' General Joffre would cry, at that, wavin' his kep at the artillery, 'Stop firin'! ye'll maybe hit him! I'm no much heedin' aboot the Prussian Guards and the Grand Dukes, but you're no' goin' to spile oor Willie.'

"What made Willie beloved o' a' the troops he fought against was the way he put his mind into an attack. The Grand Dukes was frichtened for him. Whenever Willie sat up for two nichts wi' a wet towel on his heid, and came roond to the tent in the mornin' wi' a fine new scheme for smashin' in the French line, the Grand Dukes made up a parcel o' a' their clocks, watches, and other nicknacks collected since the start o' the campaign, and posted them to their wives wi' a tender letter o' farewell; they kent it was domino! Him bein' the Croon Prince, of course they daurna heave him oot o' the tent and tell him to go and tak' a sleep to himsel'. But a Grand Duke — except that he's fatter — is jist like onybody else; he doesna want to risk his life keepin' up a pretence that Willie's a kind o' new and improved Napoleon, and him only a Ned.

"There was nae herm in Willie; if he had been put into the drapery tred he would have done fine at dressin' windows. His faither spiled him. Every Christmas Eve since he was oot o' petticoats, they put swords an' helmets and uniforms in his stockin' and encouraged him in the notion that he was a warrior. Oh, michty! No' wi' a chin like yon! But he suited us.

"I tell you, Willie's dismissal frae the German Airmy, if it's true, is a great blow to the Allied cause! Something should be done! what's the use o' havin' diplomatists when they canna keep a chap like Willie where he's most use? It's the worst news we had since the fall o' Warsaw. So lang as the Kaiser kept Willie in a responsible job jist because he was his son, a' the bluff o' the Germans that they're up to date wouldna deceive a polisman. Mony a time I cheered mysel' wi' the reflection the Germans is maybe super-human, but they're wantin' in common sense or Willie would be in the drapery line and his faither would be trevellin' for beer.

"I'm vexed for Willie! There he's away to a hydro in his plain clothes wi' a bowler hat on, and nae chap ever suited a bowler hat and plain clothes worse than Willie; if he cam' to your door ye would think he was comin' to tak' the gas-meter or sell ye a sewin' machine. Imagine a hydro efter Verdun!"

"All the same I question if our interesting young friend is permanently out of action," I said; "they may give him a trial yet on the German fleet; a Hohenzollern must natu-rally be of amphibious genius."

"I wish they would!" said Erchie. "There's awful little sport or recreation comes in the way o' Admiral Beatty.[6]

55. *Erchie on Allotments*[1]

"DID YE pick your wee allotment[2] yet?" asked Erchie of Duffy, and the coalman looked at him dubiously, suspect-ing it was a catch.

"Where dae ye pick them!" said he. He was at least determined to conceal his ignorance of what an allotment was. A vague impression floated through the woolly parts of his intelligence that it might have something to do with those extraordinary but probably deceptive loans of unlim-ited money the banks were offering to all and sundry who wanted to carry on the war.

"Where dae ye pick them?" repeated Erchie. "Ony-where ye like that's suitable and near a tramway line. There's a thousand picked already roond about Mount Florida, Bellahouston, Alexandra Park, Whiteinch, and Plantation. If ye don't hurry up, ye'll not get as much as would fill a floo'rpot. A' ye have to dae is to write to Sir John Lindsay, The Town Clerk, tellin' him ye're gaun in

for growin' cabbages, and he'll send a polis sergeant oot wi
ye to measure aff a bit o' land that's no encumbered wi' a
tenement or used for fitba'. It's the chance o' your life,
Duffy! There's bound to be fine-growin' ground aboot the
depot where ye get your coals at Port Dundas. A' ye need
to start wi' is a seedsman's catalogue and a wab o' wire-
nettin' to keep oot the deer and rabbit. I'll buy my potatoes
aff ye."

"Ye're no gaun in for yin yersel'?" said Duffy, who had
now a more or less hazy undertanding that amateur agriculture was Erchie's topic.

"I thocht o't," said Erchie, "But Jinnet and me concluded it would be nae advantage wi' us no ha'ein' a family
to dae the delvin' and the weedin'. You're in a different
poseetion athegither, wi' a fine strong family roond ye: a'
ye would need to dae would be to put up a bit o' a summer
hoose and sit in 't watchin them workin'.''

"It takes me a' my time to sell coal," said Duffy, with
conviction.

"Ye'll be sorry for't if ye don't tak' the chance when it
comes!" declared Erchie. "Look at the price o' potatoes!
Before the summer's on ye'll only can get a half a pound o'
them in the week at the grocer's if ye buy a cheet[3] o' tea
wi't. And cabbage'll be the price o' pine-apples; a wealthy
man that gets yin 'll gie a dinner pairty. Tak' my advice,
Duffy, and you go back to the land if it's only to clean the
canisters aff' it and plant rhubarb. You would be independent! There's naething easier; try a stone o' seed potatoes, borrow a potato chip machine to slice them, bury
them no' too deep, and watch till ye see the shaws, then
grab them up like lightnin' afore they have time to change
their minds. Ye would hae potatoes to your dinner when
the best in the land was reduced to rice and savoury balls."

"What's savoury balls?" asked Duffy.

"God knows but it's no' potatoes, though we ha'e to let
on ye can hardy tell the difference. If I was you, Duffy, I
would go in for a wee allotment, and the sooner the better,
for there's gaun to be a great demand. I saw a Bylie

yesterday lookin' awfu' keen at a plot in George's Square. Ye'll see barbed wire and rabbit nettin' roon the plots in George's Square before the spring, or I'm mistaken."

"I don't see ony signs o' their new allotments," said Duffy.

"Do ye no?" said Erchie, ironically. "Ye'll maybe hear aboot them when your wife gangs oot in the mornin' some day to the washin' green and trips on a cart o' manure or tramps on a bed o' syboes. Everybody's no indifferent, like you, to the Board o' Agriculture's orders. If ye took a walk roon the ootskirts o' Glasgow ye would see the vacant land beginnin' already to blossom like the rose. There's a rush in graips⁴ that would astonish ye! Ye can hardly buy a waterin' can, and the dandelion's gaun to be that rare next summer it'll be worn at weddings instead o' the camellia. Look at the way the deer's cam a' doon frae the Hielans, that close on Gleska that the police hae to shoot them."

"Wha tell't ye that!" asked the incredulous coalman.

"Man, it's in the papers! At the first hint that Gleska was gann to be an agricultural community under powers conferred by the Government, the deer has deserted the mountains and the crofter's corn and I'm tell't that Possilpark is fair infested wi' them. If the polis didna keep them down, they would be a' ower the town at nicht like Redskin hooligans."

"I don't believe wan word of it!" cried Duffy.

"Do ye no?" said Erchie. "Have ye no' see the poulterers' shops? The best o' venison at eightpence and a shillin' a pound — a perfect glut in the market! Man, at eightpence and a shillin' a pound it wouldna pay for kilts for the gamekeepers! They're first-rate deer; there's naething wrang wi' them, and they couldna be sold at the price o' potted heid if ye had to sclim the hills for them. The way they're sold that cheap is that they're got at the door. The folk in Strathbungo canna get their sleep at night wi' listenin' to them baain'."

"I don't care!" said Duffy firmly; "Gleska's no' a place to grow potatoes in. There's far ower many rats. If land's gaun to be put under cultivation, it should be in the country."

Erchie looked at him with pity. "Man, Duffy," he remarked; "it's easily seen you haven't studied the situation. The country's the last place that ever does anything to spoil the rural peace o' the rabbit, irritate the pheasant, mar the beautiful solitude o' the parish, or adopt any reckless meaasure, even at the Government's request, that would put a penny on the Rates. Do ye see ony o' the rural County Councils, or the wee Toon Councils botherin' themsels to start and encourage allotments. Not them! A' the enthusiasm for garden allotments is roon the bigger toons where they're least needed and like to dae the least good. Maist o' the local authorities in the country have personal reasons to let things go on as they are, and they've got used to livin' in a kind o' graveyard. They'll no more think o' exercisin' intelligently and disinterestedly the powers conferred on them by the Board o' Agriculture than they would o' stalkin' deer in Possilpark. Just watch them and ye'll see! I have no great hope o' getting chape potatoes oot o' them! you start a garden, Duffy!"

56. *The Last of the Bridescakes*[1]

"IF YE gang doon the street to Maclachlan, the baker's shop," said Erchie, coming in, "ye'll see the Last o' the Bridescakes in the window. It's a topper. Near as big as the Stewart Fountain in the West-End Park.[2] Three storeys, and a couple o' angels on the garret flat blawin' trumpets. There's a crood roond the window stretchin' oot as far as the tramway lines; naething like it in the street since the pawnshop fire!"

"I seen it," said his wife. "It's Sanderson, the slater's dochter; she's merryin' a mason."

"He'll be a monumental sculptor," suggested Erchie. "Ye can see the monumental touch in it; there's bits o't awfu' like some o' the Necropolis buildin's. I never saw a bridescake that better filled the eye, and I've passed a lot through my hands."

He sat down to his tea, and first cast a depreciatory eye on the sugar-bowl, which was almost empty.

"Is that a' the sugar ye ha'e?" he asked.

"It is," said Janet, "and it's a' I'll get till Saturday.[3] They'll no gi'e me it."

Erchie sighed. "It's what I was expectin'," said he; "they must ha'e used up the maist o' the sugar in Gleska to cover Miss Sanderson's mausoleum. I'm no grudgin' it to her. It'll no be cut, that bridescake. Years efter this ye'll see't in the Kelvingrove Museum in a case wi' camphor balls and a ticket sayin' it's the only survivin' specimen o' Early British Architecture. Naebody'll tak' it for a thing that ye could eat."

"What's the crood for!" asked Janet.

"Am I no' tellin' ye? It's the Last o' the Bridescakes. The Food Controller got a piece o' bridescake sent to him last week and put it in below his pillow to see what he would dream. He was hungry through the night, and he sat up and ate a' the marzipan. A' his dreams were nichtmares, and the first thing he did in the mornin' was to pass an Act o' Parliament puttin' sugar-coated bridescakes oot o' bounds. Efter the 1st o' March ye daurna hae a cake wi' icin' on't, or the polis'll be on your track. It's an awfu' blow to the tred o' the Italian modellers and marble cutters unless they use stucca. Worse than that, it's a blow at the sacred institution o' Christian marriage. Everybody kens that yin o' the main attractions to a lassie merryin' was the joy o' seein' her bridescake in MacLachlan's window. The Post Office people's furious! It'll put the livin' expense o' the letter carriers up 25 per cent; they used to could keep their families gaun wi' bits o' bridescake cut up and posted in boxes wi' the labels kind o' torn."

"I think they were jist extravagance!" declared Janet. "Jist a show aff! The silver floo'ers were maybe kind o' nice on a parlour mantelpiece wi' a gless on them, but there's mony a hoose where they made ye kind o' melancholy — "

"Souvenirs o' a great mistake," said Erchie: I've seen them."

"It's time they were daein' something o' the sort, to gi'e us sugar for oor tea," said Janet.

"Just you stop till the 1st o' March." said her husband, "and ye'll get that much sugar ye can start the fire wi't again. Lord Devonport[4] is thinkin' o' everything, and it shows ye he's in earnest, for he's in the fancy cake line himsel'. The stoppage o' monumental bridecakes in Gleska alone'll save the country a couple o' hunderweight o' sugar every week. That in itsel' would mak' the sugar situation easy. Then there's chocolates; they're stoppin' the sale o' a' chocolates over four shillin's a pound."

"Four shillin's a pound!" cried Janet. "There's no chocolates at four shillin's a pound!"

"Oh yes!" said her husband, "lots! If you were carryin' a flag in the pantomime, or I had ships, ye wouldna look at ony chaper chocolates. It's the cocoa that's in them. And then there's the box! When you were young the fashion was motto lozenges and conversations. They're entirely oot o' date! The great mass o' people in this country noo eat chocolate at threepence an ounce and over; it's them that's makin' the sugar scarce, and the Food Controller's no' gaun to have ony mair o't."

"I don't believe in it!" said Janet oracularly. "They micht as well put a stop to valentines to help the paper tred."

"I daresay you're richt," admitted her husband, "but Lord Devonport's only feelin' his way. Him bein' English, he hasna the least idea what folk live on. He recommends the people to take no mair than 2½ lbs o' butcher meat a-heid in the week —'

"I couldna dae't!" cried Janet; "it would mak' me ill! And where could Duffy, wi' a family o' eight, get a' that meat? Wi' coals at their best he never had the money for't."

"But the Food Controller never lived in Scotland, Jinnet, and he doesna understand that maist o' us in Scotland 'll never feel the pinch o' war till they put us on an

oat meal ration and commandeer oor girdles.⁵ We've aye
lived nearer the bone than ony other folk in Europe, and
Devonport's scheme o' rations'll look to a lot o' us like a
continual Trades Hoose banquet. The only thing to bother
aboot is the sugar."

57. *How Erchie Spent the Fair*¹

THE GLOW of health was on Erchie's face when I saw him
yesterday; he had a sparkling eye and a springy gait that
seemed to betoken the utmost physical wellbeing.

"Been having your holidays?" I asked him.

"Exactly!" he responded, chuckling. "Finest Fair I've
spent in fifty years. It's done me and Jinnet a' the good in
the world. What a blessin' we had such bonny weather!"

"Where did you go?" I asked.

"Oh, just circular tours," said Erchie. "I was aff frae the
Monday to Seturday. We couldna mak' up our minds at
first where to gang to, so I bought a Murray's Diary², and
went over a' the names in't frae Aberdeen to Winchburgh,
but couldna find ony place ye could exactly ca' attractive.
'It's a droll thing,' says I to Jinnet, 'that the only place
that's no' mentioned in the Diary is Gleska.' 'It's bound to
be there!' says she. 'It's naething o' the kind,' I told her;
'It's missed oot althegither. There's ony amount o' places
like Lugton and Fintry and Markinch mentioned, but
naething at a' aboot Gleska.'

"She wouldna believe me till she put on her specs and
looked the Diary for hersel'.

"'What dae ye want to look up Gleska for?' she asked
when she couldna find it.

"'Because I think it's here we should spend oor holidays,' I tell't her, and she gave a great sigh o' relief. 'I'm
glad to hear ye say't,' says she; 'I havena slept a wink these
twa nichts thinkin' o' a box to pack and a' the habble.'

"But you said circular tours," I remarked to Erchie.

"Weel, they were circular. Oot the close and back again;

landed at your very door. Dalrymple's[3] personally conducted tours. Ye must have noticed there was a lot o'
threepenny bits in your change this few days back — they
were mine and Jinnet's, saved up for a twelvemonth to be
spent on the most luxuriant and cheapest trevellin' in the
world. I never thocht there was sae much to see in Gleska.
We took Duffy the coalman and his wife wi' us, and Duffy
said it was a fair eye-opener to him. 'If I just had a sair heid
and a hanky-fu' o' dulse,'[4] says he, 'it would be the best
Fair I ever had in a' my puff.' Do you believe me? — Duffy
never seen St. Jocelyn's crypt[5] in the Cathedral nor the
back o' the Necropolis though he's lived in Garscube Road
a' his days! 'Carrick Castle's no' in it wi' this!' says he when
we came to the Kelvingrove Art Galleries and seen the
ruins in front o't."

"Your trips seem to have been more instructive than
amusing," I suggested.

"Oh, there was ony amount o' sport, too," said Erchie.
"Every other mornin' we went doon to the Broomielaw
and watched the folk losin' the *Lord o' the Isles*."[6]

"It's just ridiculous," continued my old friend, "the way
Gleska folk neglect the advantages o' Gleska for a holiday.
They think it's only a place for workin' in. They go awa' to
Gourock, Dunoon, and Rothesay to hear pierrot bands
and see picture palaces that's no' half sae good as they
could get just roond the corner; daunder up and doon
esplanades that's no' near as crooded wi' folk as Argyle
Street or the New City Road."

"Rural sights —" I suggested.

"Ye'll no' get rural sights ony better than ye'll get in
Gleska. We went oot and watched the folk workin' their
allotments; hoein' potatoes and showin' their gallowses jist
the same's it was the wilds o' Inverness-shire. The only
thing ye missed was midges.

"The great thing aboot Gleska for holidays is that ye can
aye buy something for your tea and needna be feared ye'll
get wet if the rain comes on. It's the only place where your
lodgin's cost ye naething, and ye run nae risk o' missin' the

last boat or the last train hame. There's nae luggage to pack. When Jinnet and me used to gang doon the watter at the Fair we were in a perfect turmoil a' the time. The trains would be crooded and ye lost your hamper: there's naething o' that in Gleska. We used to let on in Arran there was something fine and fancy aboot washin' your face in a burn, and a' the same it's no' half as handy as a jaw-box."

"It is quite clear," I said, "that the perfect Guide to Glasgow as a Holiday Resort has still to be written."

"Then don't write it!" said Erchie with mock alarm. "It would spoil the fun o' the Fair in Gleska if everybody found it oot. The more folk that gang and scramble for trains to the coast and country, the better for us that bide at hame. It gie's the air a chance to become salubrious. The country was a' richt for a holiday so lang's it could depend on plenty o' breid, and eggs, and ham, and fish frae Gleska, but the war's put an end to that; ye risk landin' somewhere where's there's naething to eat but rhubarb. The country's a' richt for coortin' in when you're young, but it's spoiled even for that by the Daylight Savin' Bill,[7] and when ye're auld like me and Jinnet it's no' great catch at the best; better to stay at hame and hear the milkboy's cheery whistle."

58. *Erchie's Work in Wartime*[1]

"WHAT's best on the bill of fare today, Erchie?" I asked as I picked up the table napkin.

The old waiter blinked his eyes with a sly expression, glanced at the card, and replied in non-committal tones. "There's Paysau soup — that's lentils; herrin', sauce moutarde — the sauce moutarde's in season and it's champion; then there's devilled eggs —"

"Put it in the singular, Erchie," I said. "The devilish thing about that dish is that there's only one egg to it, and it looks so lonely on a plate!"

"Has nae appearance! I admit it! Ony gentleman in

good health would feel the same aboot a solitary egg. Fancy a doo's cleckin' o' eggs[2] for the main stand-bye to a Bylie's lunch!"

"And about the cheese, Erchie? Is the cheese still a fragrant memory o' the past?"

He sighed. "I havena seen," said he, "what ye would ca' a rale man's cheese for a year and a half. Guideness kens what's happened to the Stiltons; they must be makin' them into muneetions. At the best we can only get American cheddar, and ye ken what the Americans are — fine fighters[3] and good enough for aipples, but wi' nae richt skill o' cheeses. It's a terrible time, sir! Do ye think we'll ever get back the Gorgonzola?"

He hovered about me while I romped through a light table d'hôte menu that hasn't varied in any particular from day to day for months, and he brought in the culminating two square inches of roly poly with a comical flourish.

"There!" said he. "Don't blame me! I said roly-poly plain enough, but they must have misunderstood me, and thocht I mentioned dominoes."

"What about a coffee and cognac?" I inquired with malice prepense.

"Coffee," he repeated. "Right, sir!" and turned away. He came back without the cognac, which was just what I expected of his good sense. But I 'registered' surprise, as the cinema artists say, and asked for the liqueur.

"At twa shillin's the gless!" he whispered. "It's mair than your hale luncheon used to cost ye. Tak' my advise and instead o' liqueur hae a biscuit to augment the insufficient solids. I noticed ye didna eat your breid; nae wonder! A shave o't looks like a wee lassie's peveer,[4] and it tastes like flannel. Terrible times, sir! terrible times!"

"You seem to thrive in them, all the same." I remarked, regarding his rosy gills, his bird clear eye, and his undiminished figure.

"If I dae," said he "it's no what I can scran here. It's parridge — jist parridge! Naething better if ye have the wife to mak' it. It's the only thing in Scotland that tastes the way is used to."

"What about the band?" I asked. "It seems to me they ought to have continued it. With mixed light operatic selections we might be beguiled into the illusion that we were really lunching."

"Quite right!" said Erchie, as he moved away. "It's noo we need the music to droon the bad language o' the customers."

59. *Government Milk*[1]

"I NOTICE," said Janet, "that the Government is gaun to tak' control o' the milk supply; that'll be an awfu' blow to puir Mrs MacGlinchy, the dairy, and her wi' six o' a faimily!"

"I'm vexed for the MacGlinchys, but the day o' the wee dairy's done," said Erchie. "If they want to cairry on the business they'll hae to concentrate on the soda-scone[2] department. Before the winter's on, the mornin's milk'll be delivered to ye at the door by the letter carrier."

"Ye don't tell me!" exclaimed his wife, a little incredulous.

"Right enough! It's a moral certainty that the distribution'll be put in the hands o' the Post Office. They can dae't fine; they have the time, forbye the uniform."

"Then I'll miss the wee boys whistlin' on the stairs," said Janet, sentimentally. "Some folk didna like the clatter o' the cans[3] and the milk-boys whistlin', but I aye thought them cheery. Whit harm was the MacGlinchys daein' that the Government should tak' away their tred?"

Erchie shook his head. "I doot ye'll no' can grasp it, Jinnet," he said, "but it's part o' the great national scheme o' Industrial Reorganisation. Under private ownership the British coo has been a pampered and unprofitable animal, slackin' aff its milk supply at the very time when milk was scarcest. Under government control it'll have to fall into line wi' the riveters and hurry up. Then, again, the hale system o' milk collectin' of the country was ancient and oot o' date. When the Government taks it over, all the output o' Renfrew, Ayr, and Lanark 'll be collected in a big dam near Dalry and run in to the main distributin' centre oot aboot Dalmarnock. Dairy farmin' will be revolution-ised; instead o' risin' at the blythe hour o' 3 a.m. gantin'[4] their heids aff for the want o' sleep, the dairymaids 'll come daunderin' oot to the Governmental byres efter breakfast, press the button that starts the electric milkin', and have naething mair to dae but sort the product into the various classes o'

Warm Milk,

Skim Milk, and

Milk.

"The dazed coo'll be fed on scientific principles; her output'll be weighed every day, and whenever she drops below the gallon or twa as the case may be — it's domino for the coo! The Government'll no' stand ony hanky-panky, mind I'm tellin' ye!"

"Well I'll say this," said Janet; "I couldna get ony better milk, than I get frae Mrs MacGlinchy. And a civil, earnest, honest woman! I never had ony complaint against her."

"Ye'll hae plenty against the Post Office," said her husband. "And ony time ye're a half-cup short in the measure for your four pence worth o' milk, ye'll hae to write to the Postmaster-General. All he'll dae will be to send ye a wee blue printed form saying "Your letter has been received; the complaint is bein' inquired into. Any further communications on this subject should be marked XC40295, M. Department!"

"I never heard such nonsense," exclaimed his wife. "We were daein' fine wi' Mrs MacGlinchy!"

60. *Coal Rations*[1]

DUFFY, WITH a heave of the shoulder, emptied the bag of coals into Mrs MacPherson's bunker, and dryly remarked, "Ye're gettin' a bargain; if it was next month, they would cost ye a bonny penny."

"They're costin' plenty the way it is," said Mrs MacPherson. "And full o' sclate stanes!"

"If there's any stanes in that lot," retorted the coalman, "lay them aside and I'll gie ye a pound a ton for them; it's the price they charge for them at the quarry."

"Ye're in a poseetion to ken the quarry price o' coal best," interposed Erchie. "When do ye start the rationin?"[2]

"Whenever I get word," said Duffy, wiping his brow. "I'm fair in the dark yet, like yoursel's. But I'm tellin' ye this'll be a cauld winter; as far as I can see, the ration o' coals for a hoose o' this size'll be a stane a week."

"I got twenty stanes oot o' the last bag ye left," said Janet. "Ye can gang doon to the ashpit an' coont them for yersel'."

"A bakie o' coal'll no' gang far in them close-and-open ranges,"[3] pursued the coalman, unheeding her suggestion whether it was ironical or in earnest. "But it's wan mercy ye havena a big family. A dozen o' weans hingin' roond a kitchen fire takes up an awfu' lot o' heat; it's the big families I'm vexed for. The ration for hooses o' this cless should be accordin' to the number o' folk in them, but I needna speak to the Government; it has nae sense. A' the same, ye'll be better aff than the English; the ration's to be 20 per cent mair here."

"We'll need it a'!" said Erchie. "There's awfu' little warmth left in the national beverage.[4] But listen, Duffy: Jinnet'll use a bag o' coal betwixt Monday and Wednesday: what'll be to cook the dinner for Sunday?"

"She'll can burn her claes-pins like mony another woman," suggested Duffy unfeelingly. "A' I ken is she canna get ony extra allowance frae me. It wouldna be allo'ed."

"I'll jist hae to borrow a bakie full frae the neebours, then," said Janet, resignedly.

"Ye daurna!" said Duffy. "There's to be nae treatin' under the Ack."

"Then I doot," said Erchie, solemnly, "that I'll hae to dae withoot my hot baths and wear two or three waistcoats."

"Hot baths is a luxury under the Statute," explained the coalman with authoritative tones. "So's mair than wan waistcoat if I'm no' mistaken. I could lay ye in anither bag or twa on Monday if ye cared; I clean forgot ye had the bath."[6]

"Nae fear o' me!" said Janet. "Ye'll not mak' a coal-bing or a quarry o' my bath! What we'll dae is this — I'll get the Corporation to put in a gas ring,[6] and save the coal."

"A gas ring!" exclaimed Duffy with contempt. "God bless my sowl, Mrs MacPherson, dae ye ken whit gas is made of. Naethin' but coal tar and analine dyes: I wouldna have it in the hoose for cookin'. Ye couldna boil a wilk wi't. You stick by the coals and I'll see what we can dae for ye."

61. *Celebrating Peace*[1]

DUFFY, THE coalman, on Saturday afternoon, had gone to the stable to feed his horse, and fell asleep on a bale of hay, as may happen to any man in the coal trade in these melancholy times when Saturday assumes no real holiday hue till 4 pm. He was wakened by a passing char-a-banc that shook the street, and had on board of it a bag-piper who was giving a sketchy performance of "The Barren Rocks of Aden."

"That's something like the thing! That's what I ca' cheery!" said Duffy to himself; combed the hay partially out of his whiskers and hurried to the pend-close mouth.

The char-a-banc was disappearing in the distance and had a flag.

"Whatna trip's that?" inquired Duffy of a woman passing with two loaves and a bundle of firewood.

"It's this Peace,"[2] she informed him without a scrap of enthusiasm, "The Germans is signed. Man, ye're a' hay!"

"Hokey!" said Duffy, "that puts the lid on it! And there's no' a flag in the hoose! It's a thing that should be celebrated."

Intent upon celebrating with the requisite patriotic spirit, he consulted his watch anxiously, and was astounded to find it close upon seven o'clock. With incredible velocity he locked up his stable and made for the Mull of Kintyre Vaults, reaching the door just as the owner was shutting it with that inhuman emphasis and gladness which all publicans manifest in the most unsocial operation of their working day.

"Haud on!" panted Duffy. "Great news! The Huns has heaved in the towel!"

"Whit towel?" asked the barkeeper suspiciously with his foot firmly against the inside of the door, which was only a few inches ajar.

"They've signed the Peace and handed the Kaiser[3] ower to a squad o' the Princess Louisa's Own Argyll and Sutherlands," said the coalman wiping his brow, and trying to clear some ticklish hayseeds out of his eyebrows. "They're bringing him up to Maryhill in a barrow. Gie us half a chance, Peter! It's not seven o'clock yet, let alone eight or nine!"

"Are ye shair they're bringing him to Maryhill?" asked the barkeeper with crafty irony.

"He'll be passin' in ten meenutes," said Duffy.

"That's a pant I should be in!" said the barman with apparent eagerness. "Haud you on a meenute till I get on my jecket," and pushing the door to, he turned the lock leaving the coalman outside.

Duffy waited five minutes, coughing up hay dust, then realised that the Glasgow Wine Spirit and Beer Trade was shamefully unwilling to rise to the occasion.

He went homeward reluctantly, looking everywhere about him for signs of those Great Rejoicings in Glasgow, which would certainly figure prominently in the papers on Monday morning.

There were none. The char-a-banc and the piper appeared to have had an absolute monopoly of any rejoicing that might be going.

Crowds were tearing their way into the already full tramcars; perhaps they were hurrying home to get on their Sunday clothes and illuminate their windows. Big Jock Mackay, the night policeman, was chasing boys out of a close; they might have been trying to start a celebrative bonfire. But, on the other hand, the populace seemed depressingly sober compared with what Duffy recalled of Mafeking night and Armistice day. Without exception they looked like men and women having one common solemnising thought — such as that hooker-doon caps were likely to be dearer yet on account of the dispute in the Gorbals hat and cap trade.

"They hiv nae sense," said Duffy to himself. "Jist clods! Micht as weel never hae been ony war. It's my belief there'll no' be a single fight this night in the hale Northern Diveesion."

It was then he saw his old friend Erchie on the other side of the street, and hurried across to him, waving his cap and giving a tentative "hurrah!"

"Ye should slip up a back street where naebody kens ye, get hame as quick's ye can and hae a good strong cup o' tea," said Erchie, looking at him with disapproval under a quite erroneous impression. "Man, Duffy, I'm rale surprised at ye! Fair makin' a Ned o' yersel! Put on your bunnet like a wise man and I'll see ye hame. The hay's comin' oot o' your very lugs; it's the stuffed animal department o' the Kelvingrove Museum ye should be in."

"There's naething wrong wi' me," retorted the coalman indignantly. "You're aye finding' faut! Hae ye no heard the news?"

"Whit news?" asked Erchie, "Is the bag o' coals gaun up."

"The Germans has signed the Peace!" cried Duffy.

"It's three or four oors since I heard o' that," said Erchie, calmly. "Allooin' they have, it's nae excuse for you makin' a cod o' yoursel' and affrontin' me in broad day-light in New City Road. It'll no' bring doon the price o' ham."

He took the coalman by the coat sleeve, brushing some of the hay off him, and accompanied him towards the street to which his own and Duffy's residence give distinction.

"Ye don't see onybody wavin' keps' and cryin' 'hurrah' except yoursel'," said Erchie. "That shows ye're under some kind o' a delusion. There's an awfu' lot o' hay in your composeetion."

"Look at the fun we had at the Armistice," retorted the coalman. "I hadna oot my lorry for a couple o' days except for carryin' joy-parties."

"That's right, but the Armistice was different; there was something aboot that to understand and cheer for. It meant for at least a dozen folk in oor ain tenement that their ain particular Jocks were oot o' danger at last and that was aye worth a flag or twa. But the Germans signing a scrap o' paper's a thing that makes nae appeal to the imagination. Ye wuldna even wave your kep if ye saw them daein't wi' your ain een at Versailles. A' that was in the ceremony this efternoon was that twa fat middle-aged German business gentleman that never saw ony o' the fightin' dipped their pens in a penny bottle o' blue-black ink and wrote their names doon wi' the usual flourish, then went oot on the balcony wi' the others and had their photographs tooken.

"There's nae occasion for hingin' up flags and gaun on the batter over that. For years we have been told that onything signed by the Hun wasna worth the paper it was written on, and there's nae guarantee that their scrap o' paper this time's ony different from the others just because twa auld chaps that signed it had their minds made up for them by the Allies."

"Still the Peace is signed," said Duffy firmly, "and that's aye something."

"Oh, it's something, right enough. It lets Lloyd George and President Wilson[4] hame to their wives and families.

They're fed up wi' Paris. But do ye ken whit I'm gaun to tell ye, Duffy? I'm nae gaun to hing oot ony flags or jine ye on a skyte even o' the very mildest till boots is doon again to 12s 6d and the price o' a topcoat's something less than three weeks' wages.

"I'm no gaun to cheer till the last British sodger's landed on this side o' the English Channel and back at his tred; till the Territorials is gaun to camp at Stobs or Gailes at the Fair wi' red coats on and a toppin' brass band for their gymkana; till butter and beef's demobilised —"

"And beer," suggested Duffy.

"Till the Gleska tramcar system is equal to its reputation, till the factors are chasin' folk up to rent their hooses; till a trip doon the watter wi' high tea included is again within the means o' a waiter; till oranges are a ha'penny, bananas a penny, eggs a shillin' a dozen, and the kipper herring again in the home o' the British workin' man."

"Ye'll maybe wait a lang while," suggested Duffy.

"I'm beginnin' to doot it," admitted Erchie. "Come up and see the wife."

Jinnet opened the door to them.

"Peace is signed," said her husband, on the threshold.

"That's nice," she said, simply. "Come awa' in the pair o' ye and I'll bile ye a couple o' eggs for your teas. Oh, Mr Duffy, ye must be celebratin'; ye're full o' hay."

62. *The Coal Famine*[1]

ERCHIE WENT round on Friday night to Duffy's ree to order coals. He wanted a couple of hundredweights at the earliest possible hour on Saturday morning.

"What kind would ye like?" asked the coalman, who seemed to be in a sardonic mood.

"The kind for heatin'," replied Erchie, blandly. "Oot o' coal pits, ye understand. The stuff we've been gettin' frae ye for some time back must hae come frae a quarry. Nae wonder they canna get buildin' material for a' the new hooses needed in this country, when the coal tred's cornered the hale o't and sellin't at 1s 11½d the bag."

"Would nuts dae ye?" inquired Duffy, putting on his muffler preparatory to shutting up and going home.

"Fine!" said Erchie; "so long's they're no' peanuts. Any mortal kind that'll boil a kettle!"

"A' the coals o' ony kind that I hae at my command the noo, I can gie ye wi' ye, if ye have a hankie," said Duffy. "And there'll be nae coals the morn's mornin'; your wife'll just hae to burn her claes-pins."

"Ye're gettin' awfu' snotty!" said Erchie, warmly.

"I've got mair impudence the day frae my customers than ony human bein' could put up wi'," said the coalman. "Ye would think I was made o' coals, or could conjure them oot o' a hat. I canna get coals for mysel', but I'll tell ye what I'll dae — I'll gie ye a bakie full if ye come roond to the hoose for them, and it'll hae to carry ye ower the Sunday."

"What we're needin'," said Erchie, walking homewards with his friend, "is Lord Leverhulme[2] in the coal tred. Look at soap! Ye can get soap onywhere if ye're willin' to pay for't. There's never ony shortage. And noo his lord-ship's takin' in hand wi' the fish tred; ye'll find no shortage o' herrin' this year at the Gleska Fair; he's sittin' up at night and plannin'."

"Is he in the fish line noo?" asked Duffy, incredulous.

"Up tae the neck!" said Erchie. "His lordship was aghast at the scarcity o' finnan haddies and the price o' real Rock Turbot in the fish and chip shops. What Britain wants, he says to himsel', is more brain production to pay aff the National Debt that's noo six hundred billions. Fish makes phosphorus, and phosphorus is the chief ingredient in brains; the need o' the nation is for fish.

"What does his lordship dae! He buys up a bunch o' islands in the Hebrides[3]; carts in the native crofter popu-lace to Stornoway; runs them through a sapple o' Sunlight Soap, cuts their nails; learns them the English language; gies them an eight-oors day, and starts them fishin' on scientific principles. Stornoway becomes the Port Sunlight o' the North; every man has a nice wee red-tiled cottage, and a picture palace at his door, and the cod-fish is fair worried oot o' its life.

"There's nae fun in catchin' fish by the ton unless ye can sell them, and the next step for Lord Leverhulme is to buy up a' the fish shops he can lay hands on in London, Edinburgh, Gleska, and Greenock. For the last three weeks his lordship, disguised in a Harris tweed ulster and a hooker-doon[4], has been buyin' fish shops right and left."

"What way do ye buy a fish shop?" inquired Duffy.

"Quite easy," said Erchie, "There's naething in a fish-shop at maist times except slabs. The hale o' the stock's sold oot each day, and ye start each mornin' wi' a hose-pipe and a bundle o' cards marked 'Fresh Loch Fyne'. There's nane o' your fancy glass-fronted cases — naething but marble slabs, a guttin' knife, a Cash Register on ball bearin's, and a sign-board. The rest's good-will."

"What's good-will?" inquired the coalman.

"The only tangible good-will I ever saw," said Erchie, reflectively, "belanged to a druggist. He had a fruit-shop next door to him; the public aye slid on the orange-peel on the pavement and sprained an ankle, and he had a great tred in lint and embrocations. On the other side o' him he had a public-hoose that didna open till half-past twelve, and he had a toppin' line in pick-me-ups.

"Mark you my words, Duffy, twa or three years efter this the Sunlight Fish Shop'll be Gleska's great feature next to her tea-rooms.

"What spoils the fish trade noo, is mainly the want o' art and imagination. Ye go into a shop and ask for a pair o' kippers or a couple o' pounds o' ling; they're clapped in front o' ye, wrapped up in a sheet o' newspaper and the bell o' the Cash Register goes 'ping'!

"The fishmonger has nae human touch aboot him; he is just a large damp man that wants to get his stuff oot o' his sight and his hands dried as fast as possible. Ye never catch him whisperin' 'That's a herrin' I don't sell every day, a genuine Tarbert. Look at the lustre! Feel the resiliency! That's a pre-war herrin', there's very few left but for an old customer —' Not him!

"The Leverhulme Fish Shops'll make fishmongin' a High Art, like the sellin' o' motor-cars or four-shillin'y chocolates. Next year ye'll no see Gleska fish shops exposin' big fat cod and mammoth salmon in their windows, and ladlin' fillets into the market basket wi' the naked hand. The silvery denizens o' the deep'll be put up in nate wee cardboard boxes o' half-a-pound, wi' a coloured picture on the ootside o' the Hebridean fisherman pursuin' his avocation oot in the stormy Minch, or a view o' Stornoway Castle in a sunset.

"A box o' Sunlight Haddies tied up wi' red silk ribbon'll be the popular gift o' the young man o' the period to the girl he wants to marry, and ready-cooked sprats'll be the favourite thing for passin' round the stalls between the acts at the pantomime, or 'Chu Chin Chow.'

"In the past, the supper o' fish and chips has been regairded wi' disdain by a' but the workin'-classes; Lord Leverhulme's gaun to mak' it a' the go wi' the aristocracy. Ye'll see his big palatial fish-supper saloons start in Sauchiehall Street and extend to ev'ry part o' Gleska. 'Hot on the plate!' is to be his motto, and he has got a new way o' cookin' the potato chip that maks it as crisp as toffee. I'm tellin' you the butchers'll get a start!

"And everything centred on Stornoway! Fast steamers and express trains. The Hebridean herrin'll hardly realise it's catched till it's flappin' its tail in the Sunlight shops. I wish to goodness his Lordship should noo tak' up the coaltred."

63. *A Turned Suit*[1]

DUFFY THE coalman at any time looked awkward and unhappy in his Sunday clothes, but to-day they appeared to fit him worse than usual, and he was as dejected and restless as a pup with a tin tied to its tail. There was nothing wrong with the texture or hue of his garments, which were of his favourite pepper and salt character, yet they seemed odd to Erchie.

"Ye're an awfu' swell the day, Duffy," he remarked. "I never saw ye in a tastier suit o' claes. They would cost ye a bonny penny."

Duffy shrugged up a shoulder to get his coat collar back on his neck again and made a fumbling, ineffectual attempt to fasten up a waistcoat button with his left hand.

"It's no' a new suit at a'," he explained, irritably. "It's my auld yin turned. The wife said she'd dae't as easy as onything, and she's made a fair hash o' the job!"

"I don't see onything wrang wi't," broke in Jinnet, putting on her glasses to make a more critical survey. "Jist like new!"

"A tip-top job!" said Erchie. "Ye couldna get better in Gunn and Collies. Wi' a suit like that and a silver-mounted umbrella ye could trevel the Continent. Whit way dae ye no button your waistcoat and gie your dickie a chance?"

"That's the cursed thing!" said the coalman, perspiring with vexation. "I canna button wan particle unless there's somebody helps me. The wife buttoned up my coat and waistcoat richt enough afore I left the hoose, but I had to tak' them aff when I was roond at the stable feedin' the horse, and noo I canna get them richt again for love nor money."

He was again, making feeble fumbling efforts to master his button holes.

Erchie gazed at the clothes intently, his lips pursed and his eyes puzzled,

"There's something oot of the ordinar' aboot that coat and waistcoat o' yours," he said. "But whit it exactly is I canna tell. It's no the cut o' them — the cut's a' richt for a coalman. The pockets is in the richt place; the sleeves is the proper length — at least yin o' them is; there's the richt amount o' slack a' roond. But there's something!"

Jinnet, with quite a professional touch, plucked at the shoulders of the coat and pulled down the lapels, to her husband's admiration.

"A' ye need to be a regular foreman cutter, Jinnet," he said, "is a moothfu' o' pins, a lump o' chalk, an inch-tape, and a few aromatic losengers."

Duffy sighed, resignedly submitting himself to this expert survey.

"I canna see a hait² wrang wi' the claes!" declared Jinnet. They're a credit to your wife, Mr Duffy. It's mair than I could dae — turn a man's claes, and I'm no easy daunted. Were they made to your measure to begin wi'? Whaur did ye get them?"

"I bocht them aff a sodger, split new," said the coalman. "They were gi'en to him by the Government when he left the Army, but he was a piper to tred, and had to wear the kilts, so he had nae need for them, he telt me. There was naething wrang wi' them then; I could button them quite easy."

"It's an awfu' affliction haein' a suit o' claes ye canna venture out o' the hoose wi' unless ye bring your wife," remarked Erchie sympathetically. "I never seen a waistcoat afore that ye needed a button-hook for unless it was a Bylie's. If I was you wi' a magic suit o' that kind, I would never go ower the door withoot a waterproof."

"Tach! the pair o' ye's just haiverin'," said Jinnet, rapidly buttoning up the recalcitrant waistcoat. "Ye're fingers is a' thumbs, Mr Duffy."

The coalman surveyed himself with incredulity and scratched his head.

"I canna for my life see hoo ye dae't!" he exclaimed. "It fair bates me to get in them buttons even if I grease them. They're either ower big or ower wee, or they're no' canny. Jist let me get anither chance."

He ripped open his waistcoat and made a serious effort to re-button himself. Not one button could he restore to its proper orifice, whichever hand he used, or even with both of them together.

"Ye would think it was a pair o' spats ye were wrestlin' wi'," said Erchie; "let me try my hand."

But he, too, found Duffy's buttons unaccountably stubborn; he couldn't fasten one. He gave it up in despair.

"If I was you, Duffy," he said solemnly, "I would gie that suit to a guid-brother or send it to a jumble sale. There's something far far wrong wi't! It's something no canny in the buttons; ye micht as weel try to fasten up your claes wi' biled gooseberries. If it hadna been your wife that turned that suit, I would say it was a drunk tyler or wan o' them Spiritualists. They're up to onything! It's a clear case for Conan Doyle. Ye havena heard ony rappin' aboot the watch-pocket, have ye?"

"I wish to goodness Bella had left the suit alane!" said Duffy, almost weeping. "It was fine the way it was, except for a beer-stain. This'll be a lesson to me!"

Jinnet again, quite easily did the buttoning

"You gang hame, Mr Duffy," she said, "and hae your tea, and tak' a bit sleep to yoursel', and ye'll find your waistcoat 'll button a' richt next Sunday. They've jist ta'en a kind o' tirravee. I've seen something o' the same kind wi' Erchie, efter comin' hame frae' a funeral."

"Efter the cheeriest funeral I was ever at, I never saw buttons like them!" protested her husband. There's something wrang! I can see't in the very look o' your coat and waistcoat, Duffy. It's a classy-lookin' suit, enough, but there's something oot o' the ordinar' in it. Ye havena, by ony chance, put it on back-side foremost?"

"I'm no' that daft," said Duffy. "If it was back side foremost, hoo could I get showin' my watch-chain?"

Erchie had another look, and held up his hands in amazement. "I see whit's wrang noo!" he cried; "Bella's put on the buttons on the wrang side!"

"They're on the richt enough side," said Duffy; "they're

opposite the button-holes. Whatever's wrang, that's no' the trouble!"

"But wise-like buttons is aye on the right and yours is on the left," said Erchie; "the thing's ridiculous! I couldna understand whit way ye were workin' awa' at them wi' your caurry haund. Am I no richt Jinnet?"

"Onybody wi' ony gumption kens," said Jinnet, "that if ye turn a man's claes, the button holes is bound to be on a different side from whit the tailor put them. They're wrang to start wi', and when a woman turns a man's claes, she's glad to put them richt, even though she canna help it. Buttons on the right-hand side o' onything's jist silly; it's a man's fad, and nae woman would put up wi't. I couldna, for my life, mak' oot whit you twa men were bogglin' over, Tak you my word for't Mr Duffy, ye have a clever wife and she has your coat and waitcoat buttons on the side God meant them for!"

64. *Erchie on Divorce*[1]

"FANCY YOU," said Duffy. "Mary Pickford[2] mairried again! It's no' a month since she divorced her man; she canna be richt oot o' mournin's for him!"

"A woman doesna gang into mournin's when she loses her man that way," said Erchie. "She buys hersel' a new sealskin coat and a Pekinese terrier, and mak's for the nearest hydropathic. If there was ony mournin' over Mary's sad bereavement, it should have been her man that wore them, for she was makin' a wage o' £4,000 a week, and a wife like that's no' to be picked up in a tearoom or a laundry."

Duffy sighed. "Jerusalem!" he exclaimed; "ye would think ony hoose would be happy wi' a' that money comin' into't! Whit did she gi'e up Mr Moore[3] for?"

"It was Moore gied Mary up. As far as I can mak' oot, the chap got fed up hingin' on at the film factory every Saturday nicht wi' a barrow to hurl hame her pay. He got nae credit in the public eye; he was jist 'Mary Pickford's man,' and got to abominate the very sicht o' her picture on the hoardin's. He dropped the barrow, shaved himsel', changed his name, and hid in the Rocky Mountains, refusin' to come hame, so Mary jist divorced him.

"As soon as the news got aboot that she was quit o' him, there was a gold rush to California from every pairt o' the United States. Thoosands o' smert young Americans that were jist dune winnin' the war and had seen Mary on the films and kent aboot her earnin's, cam pourin' into Los Angeles in Pullman trains to mairry her, but Douglas Fairbanks,[4] a fellow in the same line o' business as hersel, was on the spot and nicked her first. He chased her alang the roof o' a land o' hooses, sclims efter her doon a rhone-pipe, galloped on horseback twenty miles through a forest, shootin' aff his revolver a' the time, and made up on her jist as she was divin' into a coal pit shaft.

"Tig!" he says. "You're het! Come on and get spliced afore the crush starts."

"Richt-oh!" says Mary, pechin'. "Haud on till I get my hair up."

"By a' accoonts," said Duffy, "Douglas Fairbanks was jist divorced the ither day himsel'."

"That's richt," admitted Erchie. "Matrimony's a wan reel picture wi' the cinema star; it's only wi' the like o' you and me its a lang sensational serial runnin' on frae day to day and week to week and feenishin' wi' a close-up view of Darby and Joan in the Poorshoose, frail in health but faithful until death. A cinema star gets tired sooner than onybody else o' the humdrum business o' comin' hame at nicht and takin' his tea with the same face forenenst him. It spoils his art. If the star's no' sick o' his wife, she's sick o' him. Ye would think that onybody could put up wi' Cherlie Chaplin,[5] he's such a comic, but his wife's divorcin' him. It's likely she'll no can staund his shauchly feet."

"Whit a crew!" said Duffy. "Thank God I'm in the coal tred!"

"The only difference between you and Cherlie Chaplin or ony ither cinema star is that ye're no' a public pet. If William Duffy, the Coalman Comedian, had his picture in a' the papers, and thoosands o' people were croodin' to see him jugglin' wi' briquettes or daein' a refined song and dance turn on a lorry, there's nae sayin' whit he would be up to."

"I don't think there's ony excuse for ony wife gaun awa and leavin' her man," said Duffy with conviction.

"Man, but ye're awfu nerrow!" retorted Erchie. "Ye're still in the dark ages! Whit could be mair proper and releegious than Mary Pickford's merriage? Ye could see for yoursel in the papers that the minister that married her read Ephesians 5 vv22-32[6] frae a Bible Mr Fairbanks, the handsomest man in America, got frae his mither on her death-bed. It shows ye the cinema tred is quite respectable.

"Ye have only to read the papers," continued Erchie, "to see that Divorce is noo recognised by a' the best Authorities as a kind o' Sacrament. The time's comin' fast when the rulin' elders o' the kirks'll go roond the congregations twice a year deliverin' tokens for the Coort o' Session, and I'll bate ye that in maist o' the hooses they'll get a dram."

"Criftens! ye're no' in earnest?" exclaimed Duffy, shocked.

"Of course I am!" Erchie assured him solemnly. "This rideeculous habit o' hingin' on to the wan husband or the wan wife a' your days is jist breakin' doon. It was a' richt enough in the days when ye had to gang hame if ye wanted a meal o' meat or wanted a waistcoat linin' mended, but noo that there's ony amount o' eatin'-hooses and the Valet Services, a man needna be behauden to ony wife in parteecular. On the other hand, noo that she can get a Divorce as easy as a dug licence nae wise-like woman needs to mak a hobby of her hubby.

"There was a time when gettin' a Divorce was a luxury only for weel-aff people that were payed by the month or had a lot of property. It's now within the means o' the riveter or the railway porter, and it's catched on like wild-fire. Mony a man that used to swither whether he would strangle his wife or jine the Airmy under anither name is noo in the happy position o' bein' able to get quat o' her by rookin' her o' the money he gaithered for the rent and goin' to a lawyer wi't.

"Look at the papers on Seturday nicht or Monday mornin' — a list o' Divorces as lang's the programme for the Grand National. If ye live lang enough ye'll see folk advertisin' their Divorces the same's they were Silver Weddin's or In Memoriams: —

At Edinburgh on Saturday. Before Lord Sands, Jon Diveen M'Grory and Margaret Skelford Black — By mutual consent, 'Unpleasant and unhappy in their lives now they are divided.'

"That's the kind o' thing ye'll see whenever the housin' situation is relieved."

"What has the hoosin' situation got to dae wi't?" demanded Duffy.

"Everything!" retorted Erchie. "It's only the shortage o' hooses that prevents the wave o' divorce frae sweepin' the country. Noo that the war's over and the world's determined on peace, everybody's sick o' his wife, and every wife finds it hard to thole her man."

"I don't believe wan word o't!" exclaimed the coalman. "My wife and me gets on fine. Three months efter I married her, I couldna see for my life hoo I could put up wi' her anither twelvemonth, and for twenty years noo I couldna see whit way I could dae withoot her."

Erchie shook his head. "That's a' richt for you," he replied, "but whit aboot Mrs Duffy? And whit aboot my ain wife Jinnet? Do ye no' think, Duffy, they must whiles be awfu' fed up wi' us? There's neither o' us ony great catch and never was. Ye canna' deny but we're gettin' gey chafed and shabby — the only part o' the household furniture that canna be spring-cleaned. We are oot o' date completely, and don't go richt at a' wi' the new linoleum. It's my belief that oor wifes must often wish they could send us to a jumble sale. Keep your eye on Mrs Duffy; if ye find she's takin' a suspicious interest in the divorce cases, awa richt oot and buy her an umbrella."

65. *Our Mystery Millionaire*[1]

THE FACT, as reported in the newspapers, that a Glasgow man had bought five million pounds worth of stock in an American company, so staggered Duffy the coalman last week that he rushed off at once to consult his old friend Erchie on the subject.

"Fancy you! Five millions!" he exclaimed. "A' that money gaun oot the country, and us needn't! Whaur's the polis?"

"Whit are ye yappin aboot?" inquired Erchie.

"That chap, Sir Harry M'Gowan,"[2] explained the coalman. "Gaithers up five million pounds nate, and goes awa to America and buys a motor-caur business wi't. It's a fair do! He's feared he's gaun to be taxed for his war profits, and he's awa' wi' the lot in a kit-bag before they can get on his track. Wha is he?"

"He's the Mystery Millionaire," responded Erchie, without hesitation. "Ye'll hae to wait for six months afore ye see him on the films. When the story came oot, the newspapers were offerin' a guinea apiece roond a' the best villas in Pollokshields for photographs o' Sir Harry, after tryin' a' the photographers shops, and they couldna get yin. He has never been took. He's either the most modest man in Gleska, or he's no' pleased wi' his face for it seems he never stood in front o' a camera.

"I never heard o' the chap afore," said Duffy. "Is he in the Toon Cooncil?"

"No fears!" said Erchie. "Ye don't get that kind o' man in the Toon Cooncil; he can buy his cigars for himsel'. The Toon Cooncil's a' richt for men that has plenty o' time on their hands, but when ye're onywhere near the millionaire class ye would as soon tak' up wi' the Boys' Brigade. To tell you the truth, Duffy, I never heard o' Sir Harry mysel', and I thocht I had seen everybody in Gleska worth mentionin'. If his life story appeared onywhere in print afore this it could only be in The Gospel Trumpet, and I don't read it regular."

"The Southern Polis-office'll ken something aboot him!" suggested Duffy.

"They don't," said Erchie. "I asked a Sergeant in the Maxwell Road and he said that so far as he kent there was absolutely naething that could be brung hame to him. Sir Harry, he reports, was a quate sober chap that went to his work in the mornin' regular wi' the University car,[3] and came hame punctual at six o'clock for his tea, never steppin' out over the door efter that at nicht except whiles for a game o' bools or a visit to a cinema."

"He must have a whupper o' a bag!" suggested the coalman. "Hoo could he cairt hame a' that money?"

"He never had a bag at a'!" replied Erchie. "Just a wee attachy case they surmised he had his piece in. They followed him nicht after nicht for weeks after he got the K.B.E., thinkin' they would nail him, and they photographed his fingerprints aff the bell-handle o' his door, but there was naethin daein'. He had an alibi every time.

"It's only since this American deal o' his that his career has been revealed. Thirty five years ago he was a boy that kept the petty cash in the Nobel Explosive office[4] in West George Street. He was a tip-top boy ye could aye trust on a message to the station wi' a bag o' golf clubs, and never smoked cigarettes. He was born in Gleska withoot onybody takin' ony particular notice and passed through Allan Glen's School[5] as fast as ever he could for fear they would finish his education. Efter that he had what wan o' the daily papers ca's 'a meteotric career'. But it wasna till the country was in the throes o' war that he got a richt chance to prove the stuff he was made o'. He pushed Nobel's products wi' such success that a' the Allied nations were fair clamourin' for them, and auld Hindenburg, the comic German General and story writer, had to engage a poet to write a special Hymn o' Hate addressed to Harry M'Gowan at St. Andrew's Drive, Pollokshields.

"I see from a mornin' paper," continued Erchie, "that it has been remarked by his friends, amongst whom he is a great personal favourite, that 'Sir Harry's commercial career has not only been rapid, but of the genuine type that can only be associated with pre-eminent business qualities.' I couldna' put it better mysel'.

"It is also mentioned in the same quarter, that, 'apart from his business, he has led what might almost be termed the life of a recluse, although it could be more correctly put that he is one of those silent forces that effect great revolutions, without produing great public commotion.'

"As far as I can gather", continued Erchie, "that's richt. A recluse is a man that strictly looks after his ain business, tak's hame a lot o' work frae the office to feenish at nicht in his ain hoose, and has nae hobbies except the pianola or stamp collectin'. A silent force is a man that canna be prevailed on to contribute onything vocal to the harmony o' a smokin' concert; he gets a' the fun he needs frae watchin' other folk makin' Neds o' themsel's singin' 'Out on the Deep' wi' in-growin' tenor voices, or recitin' 'Jim the Fireman' in a suit o' evenin' cla'es."

"But Sir Harry's a keen gowfer at the Troon Club, I see frae the papers," mentioned Duffy, "and an auld member o' the Queen's Park Futba' Club, and goes to a' the games."

"That's a' a plant," patiently explained Erchie. "A strong silent force is a member o' ony number o' clubs, but he never goes near any o' them; he hasna' the leisure for't. He jines them jist to mak' folk think he's wastin' his time like themsel's, and the mair clubs he belangs to the less they keep an eye on him, so he's weel on his way to win the millionaire stakes before they jalouse he's puttin' in his Seturday efternoons wi' his correspondence.

"The polis sergeant in the Maxwell Road assures me he has never seen Sir Harry in a pair o' plus-fours nor a striped jersey, so he canna be desperate keen on either

gowf or futba'. He maybe had his name doon on the books
o' the Troon Club and the Q.P., but he had his money in
Explosives, Dunlop Rubber, and British Dyestuff Corporation. There's ony amount of millionaires like him in
Gleska noo; ye would never suspect them. They're the
only folk that doesna want their exploits put in the papers.
But my opeenion, Duffy, is that millionairism should be
among the notifiable diseases, the same as chicken-pox;
it's spreadin' like onything."

"If I was shair it's bad in Pollokshields," said Duffy, " I
would give up the coal tred and drive a Belvidere ambulance."[6]

66. *Erchie Sorts the Clock*[1]

"I'M TIRED lookin' at that clock and it no gaun for the last
three month," said Erchie. "Could ye no bring it doon to
the watchmaker and get it sorted!"

"A clock like that!" exclaimed Jinnet, "Ye micht as weel
ask me to carry doon the kitchen grate to get the gas put
in't! Are ye wantin' to get rid o' me?"

The time-piece on the parlour mantel-shelf was, un-
questionably, not to be lifted like a teapot by any lady; it
was a vast Corinthian black marble temple that would
weigh about half-a-hundredweight.

"But could ye no' get Durward to come up and see
whit's wrang wi't?" pursued her husband. "It's maybe only
needin' oilin'."

"It's mair than twa months since I asked Durward to
come and see't," said Jinnet, "but he says he canna; he has
as mony clocks and watches in his shop to mend as 'll keep
him thrang till the New Year."

"Then he'll no get the chance o' mendin' this yin," said
Erchie with impatience. "I'll dae't mysel'!" He got to his
feet with an air of firm determination, the light of conquest
in his eye, and his pocket-knife in his hand.

"For goodness sake, Erchie, don't you meddle wi' the

clock!" pleaded Jinnet. "Ye'll spile it athegither!" I'm shair
you dont understand clocks!"

He paid no heed to the protest, but lifted the Corinthian
temple into the kitchen, where he placed it on the table,
and then took off his collar. The dusk was falling.

"Licht the gas," he ordered; "or, no don't licht the gas.
I'll can see better whit's the maitter wi' the clock if ye gie
me a candle."

"I wish ye wouldna touch it, Erchie!" implored his wife.
"Ye mind the last time ye worked awa' at the kitchen clock
till ye made a mess o't. There's a bit o't still in the dresser
drawer there."

"That was a different kind o' clock althegither; it was the
weights bamboozled me. This is a clock wi' a mainspring;
onybody could sort it. Get you me the candle, a wee drap
castor oil and a feather."

"Where on earth could I get you a feather?" piteously
inquired Jinnet, lighting the candle. "There's no a hen in
this hoose."

"Then the next best thing's a hairpin," said Erchie in the
most confident businesslike manner. He was beginning
thoroughly to enjoy himself.

He prised open the brass back of the timepiece with his
knife, bent down, and looked into the interior of the
temple. "We'll ha'e to shift this pendulum to start wi'," he
decided, putting in his hand. The pendulum was
unhooked with a little difficulty, but escaped from his
fingers and fell jangling noisily against the chiming spring
with which it got entangled.

"There ye are!" exclaimed Janet. "Ye've broke the bell
already! A body would think ye were shellin' mussels wi'
your knife. Would ye no' just put it aside for the nicht, and
I'll see Mr Durward the first thing in the mornin'. Clock-
mendin's a tred, Erchie; ye need the skill for't. I'm no gaun
doo to ony watchmaker wi' a' the works in a pail."

"I wish ye would calm yersel'!" remarked her husband
with dignity. "I'll ha'e your clock gaun in twenty minutes;
there's hardly onything wrang wi't."

He took from ther hands the short piece of lighted candle and held it inside the temple, the better to see the mysterious and intricate contents. His eye, as if fascinated, swept over the brassy mechanism in search of a main-spring. With a pair of scissors he captured and extracted the pendulum.

"There!" he cried triumphantly. "I tell't ye this was different althegither frae a kitchen clock. I'll need a wee screwdriver — that yin ye hae in the sewin' machine."

She brought him the screwdriver. Humming blythely to himself — for the novelty of this delightful entertainment was entirely to his mind — he took out the screws which kept the movement of the clock in situation, and, as the glass on the dial was open, his next touch on the back of the mechanism sent it toppling over the front in a mass on the table, whence it rolled to the floor with an appalling clatter.

Jinnet held up her hands in horror. "I tell't ye!" she exclaimed. "Ye were daft to meddle wi't! Your own guid presentation clock that ye got at oor marriage! It'll never gang again, and it's a lifetime's ill-luck to let it drop like that."

Her husband picked up the movement, considerably abashed at the mishap but cheered up instantly to find it seemed to be none the worse.

"Tuts!", he said. "It's no' a hait the waur for ye to mak' a song aboot. Ye would think I was a wean. Ye think I can dae naething. Durward would take a week sortin' this clock and charge ye seven shillings. I'll feenish it the nicht. Look at that — it's tickin' awa' already! Clock mendin' wi chaps like Durward's a' a humbug, it's my belief they just drop half the clocks they get to mend frae the bench on the floor to start them."

"If ye tak' my advice, Erchie," pleaded his wife again; "ye'll put they works the way they are in a newspaper, and I'll tak' them doon to Durward in the mornin'."

"I wish to peace ye would go awa' and tak' up your knittin'!" said her husband peevishly. "You women don't understand the least wee thing aboot mechanics, it's a' Greek to ye. If I could get the mainspring I would fix it up wi' a drop o' oil."

He made Jinnet hold up the candle while he scrutinised the mechanism from the sides, prodding at the wheels tentatively with the hairpin. The complication of them astonished him. Compared with the kitchen clock, of whose anatomy he had distinct recollection, this clock appeared fantastically intricate. And nowhere could he see any sign of mainsprings.

"Of a' the clocks that ever I handled this yin bates them a' for swank!" he declared, as if he had dealt with thousands. "It's fair jammed up wi' wee brass wheels. Ye couldna' get your knife in! And there's nae mainspring that I can see."

"What mak's it gang then?" inquired Jinnet, her mechanical curiosity for the moment wakened.

"I'll soon tell ye that," replied her husband, taking off his coat, picking up the screwdriver again, and briskly proceeding to extract screws with reckless impetuosity

"Is your watch richt?" pathetically inquired Jinnet.

"What are ye askin' for?" he inqured without a pause in the fascinating task of loosening screws.

"Because we'll hae to depend on't for the time for the rest o' oor days," said Jinnet seriously. "I can see this clock's a waster. Ye're awfu' heidstrang, Erchie! It's my belief ye would try and mend a pianola if we had yin!"

The last of the accessible screws was extracted, he lifted the brass plate they had passed through; the majority of the mysterious little brass wheels collapsed, and he held in his hands a hopeless mass of disintegrated machinery from which screws fell pattering like hail on the kitchen waxcloth.

Jinnet was dipping a hairpin in a phial of castor oil.

"Are ye ready for the oil?" she asked, not quite realising the tragedy of the moment.

"What oil?" inquired Erchie irritably.

"For the mainspring," replied Jinnet meekly, but with deep ironic meaning.

"Mainspring!" cried her husband. "There's nae springs o' ony kind in this clock. Ye can see for yoursel'. Nae wonder it wouldna go! They left oot the mainspring athegither an' filled it up wi' wee brass wheels for fair swank. Haud oot your brattie."

Jinnet obediently held out her apron and he poured into it all the internal fragments of a once satisfactory presentation marble clock which still dripped screw nails on the waxcloth.

"Ye would hae been faur quicker to hae ta'en a hatchet and gien it a good clourin'," she sobbed. "There's naething for't noo but the ashpit. I wonder when ye'll get sense!"

Erchie put on his coat and collar and made for the door.

"We've made a fair hash o' that clock between us!" he remarked coolly. "This wouldna hae happened if you had a wise-like feather. But, I couldna bide the look o' that marble clock since ever I got it, it aye put me in mind o' the Necropolis. I'm gaun awa oot to buy ye a fine wee tin yin wi' an alarm."

67. *The Soda-Fountain Future*[1]

DUFFY NEVER heard of the Soda Fountain till last Saturday night. That glad new American institution had crept into Glagow without his observing it, and it was a startling revelation to him to find that in many parts of the city there are frightful evening orgies over Walnut Sundaes and Manhattan High-Balls sucked through two straws to the strains of a jazz band.

He had been talking gloomily to Erchie about the prospects of Prohibition.[2]

"If they shut the pubs," he said, "whaur's a chap to go when the kitchen's full o' his wife's washin' drying'!"

"There'll aye be the Parks," suggested his friend, "and

the Kelvingrove Museum. In the winter there'll be lectures. You'll see the time'll pass fine."

"And do ye mean to say we'll no' get onything to drink
at a'?" pursued the coalman, still somewhat vague as to the
devastating influence of Pussyfoot.

"Oh, that'll be a' richt," Erchie assured him genially.
"A' ower the toon they're openin' Soda Fountains. The
naitural human fondness for a tumbler'll get every consideration."

"Whit's a Soda Fountain?" inquired Duffy.

"It's a branch o' the Fire Brigade depairtment," Erchie
informed him. "It's principal stock-in-tred is genuine Loch
Katrine watter, but they don't use a hose. Ye go in wi' a
ragin' conflagration o' thirst, and come oot wi' hoar-frost
on your whiskers. Awa' you hame, Duffy, and put on a
collar and I'll tak' ye to a Soda Fountain."

Half an hour later, Duffy was walking downstairs to a
Soda Fountain, stepping softly, with his cap in his hand,
for the band below, at the moment, was playing almost
classic music, and, so far, his entrance had been through
scenes of grandeur.

"Are ye sure we're a' richt here, Erchie?" he whispered
anxiously. "It looks awfu' cless."

"As lang's you don't start singin' Dark Lochnagar or
interfere wi' the orchestra ye're as richt's rain." Erchie
assured him. "Put on your bunnet! It's no St. Jocelyn's
crypt ye're in; ye're oot for fun. Whit'll you hae?"

They had seated themselves at a little round table in a
hall filled with little round tables, practically everyone of
them occupied by young folk, male and female, who bliss-
fully supped ices or sucked at an infinite variety of fla-
voured soda water through straws.

Duffy perspired at the very sight of this extraordinary
spectacle.

"Whit in the name o' Peter are they chewin' at them
sticks for?" he inquired, as his friend consulted a long list
of quaintly-christened beverages.

"Them's no sticks," Erchie informed him. "They're

straws to sook through. Everything to drink here's new aff the ice and if ye didna use a straw to't it would jar the teeth oot o' your heid. ... Ye'll hae a Mint Julip."

"I will not!" said Duffy firmly. "Whatever it is, I don't like the name o't."

But under pressure he consented to experiment with a Mint Julip, a green concoction in a bell-mouthed wine-glass, whose restricted size and unusual shape prejudiced him from the outset. Fortunately no straws were necessary with a Mint Julip. Erchie watched him narrowly as he sipped.

A spasm went over his visage; his eyes rolled; his mouth puckered.

"Somebody's drapped a' peppermint lozenger in this," he stuttered. "I was dubious o' the colour o't; green's no lucky. I would raither ha'e Broon Robin."

"Ye'll jist hae to tak whit ye hae," retorted his host. "There's nae local veto here. That green taste's mint. It maks a' the difference on Loch Katrine watter. To enjoy a Soda Fountain ye must concentrate your attention on the band, and then ye think ye're drinkin' champagne wine. Listen! They're playin 'Till We Meet Again'; does it no' put ye in mind o' a fine Fair Seturday afore the War?"

"It doesna' put me in mind o' onything the way a dacent drink would dae," declared the coalman. "And this green drink just puts me in mind o' the Sunday School. Could we no' get something at yon bar wi' the fancy bottles in't."

The bar, which was the most prominent feature of the Soda Fountain, had certainly a delusive air of unlimited and variegated wassail with an arrangement of entrancing taps, which, to the casual eye, recalled the beer-pulls of the Mull of Kintyre Vaults. Two ministering angels busily kept filling up glasses with water charged to the highest degree with carbonic acid gas, having first put a teaspoonful into them of some flavouring syrup; or they dexterously slapped down on saucers an exact shilling's worth of sundae —sundae being ice-cream just a little more sophisticated than Duffy had known it in the days of his youth.

Loudly the band played 'Indianola'; but it hardly drowned the animated cackle of the assembly, or the protests of an infant-in-arms whose fond parent was initiating it into the delights of a sundae supped from a teaspoon.

"There's naething in that bar ye would fancy, Duffy." Erchie said. "Ye're too late o' startin' the Soda-Fountain habit, and that's bad luck for you, for the age o' the Hole-in-the Wa' wi' the sawdust floor and the tuppeny schooner's by."

"Ye're no' in earnest, Erchie!" said the coalman, genuinely alarmed.

"Of course I'm in earnest!" retorted Erchie, as they departed from the scene of revelry. "This time next year the Mull o' Kintyre Vaults'll hae a soda fountain and a fish and chips depairtment, and Big MacGlashan, instead o' ladlin' oot halfs and schooners o' beer in his shirt sleeves on a Saturday nicht'll be gaun roond his saloon in a claw-hammer coat recommendin' some new ice-cream o' his ain invention. It's me that's vexed for the Italians! The competeetion o' MacGlashan's gaun to ruin them."

"Ye couldna dae in this climate withoot pubs," protested Duffy. "Look at the weather!"

"Ye can dae without onything except graveyairds!" retorted Erchie. "Ye're daein' noo without a half in the mornin' afore your breakfast, and a few years ago that would spoil the day for ye. But I doot ye're ower auld for the Soda Fountain; for that ye need to start in your teens, wi' an inside like a Thermos Flask. There'll be naething for it, for the like o' you and me, Duffy, but to go hame at nicht and stay there, fillin' in the time wi' the wife wi' a cup o' cocoa."

"I couldna' dae my work on cocoa!" said Duffy, emphatically.

"Tuts, man!" said Erchie, in a more reassuring mood. "By the time that comes ye'll no' be needin' to work. Ye'll hae made your fortune aff the coals."

68. *Reminiscences*[1]

"WHIT IN the name o' fortune are ye writin' there?" asked Erchie, with a look of mock alarm at the discovery of his wife in the throes of composition, with a twopenny bottle of ink and a threepenny jotter.

"I'm just puttin' doon, as lang's I mind it, a recipe I got frae Mrs Duffy for a jumper for her dochter," replied Jinnet.

"Ye gied me an aufu' start!" said Erchie. "I thocht ye were beginnin' a book o' your Reminiscences — and me with my trunk no' packed for Canada. I warn ye that if ye ever dae onything o' the kind ye'll hae to gie me a month's full notice so's I can clear oot o' the country."

"Haivers!" exclaimed his wife. "Naething ever happend to me that was worth puttin' in a book."

"I'm no' so sure o' that!" retorted her husband, darkly. "Efter this, I'll never see ye wi' a pen in your hand but I'll think ye're clockin' on something. Look at Mrs Asquith!"[2]

"Indeed and I wish I could write a book like Mrs Asquith — look at the money she's gettin' for't!" said Jinnet. "The papers doesna gie half enough o' bits oo't it; I laughed like onything at yon aboot her gallivantin' wi' the lads afore she married Henry."

Erchie looked dreadfully shocked. "I'm surprised at you, Jinnet!" he remarked solemnly. "I wonder whit kind o' woman I married! Surely you didna cairry-on flirtin' and philanderin' the way Margot Tennant did. Ye hadna the education for't."

Jinnet laughed. "Hoots awa' wi' ye!" she cried. "There's nae education needed to be naitural and young. And do you think the lads a' passed me by before I met in wi' you? Well they didna! There was half-a-dizzen I could hae merried."

"Ye don't mean to tell me they tried to kiss ye?" exclaimed her husband with a look heroically fierce. "Wha were they?"

"Na, na!" said Jinnet blithely. "I'll no tell ye that — except that the last o' the batch was a ne'er-dae-weel ca'd

Erchie MacPherson. The only fau't I hae wi' Margot is that she clypes the names o' the honest lads that liked her. That's no fair horney."[3]

"She's was a besom!" protested Erchie.

"She was naething o' the kind!" insisted Jinnet. "She was jist a licht-he'rted hullockit[4] lass that liked a ploy and could laugh at a boy, and was as brave as a wee bantam."

"But look at the lot o' gentry she has made to look redeeculous!" said Erchie. "And them no' deid!"

"A' the better for them! There's still time for them to get ower bein' rideeculous, noo that Margot's shown they had that failin'. Let me tell you, Erchie MacPherson, every man's redeeculous to a clever woman — except perhaps the man she means to mairry. I laughed like onything at the way she took the measure o' a' they namely men and showed they had jist the ordinar' human frailties. The bigger the man in the eyes o' the world the mair he's inclined to posturin', and its fine, for ance in a while, to see them scuddin' like hares in front o' a smert wee whitterick o' a wife that's feart for naebody."

"A randy!" said Erchie with emphasis. "Naething in her book but clatters!"

"Naething o' the kind! A rompin' lass; she's jist that yet, though she micht be a granny. I would like her fine for a neibour on the stair; she would get plenty o' cheery clash[5] in this close to put in another book."

"Thank goodness, there's nae material for a book o' that kind to be found in Braid Street," said Erchie with pious fervour. "Fancy her ridin' a horse into a hoose in London and pullin' down the lustre chandelier!"

"There's whiles I would like to pull doon a lustre chandelier mysel' if we had yin," said Jinnet. "But I never had Margot's chances," she added regretfully.

Erchie, somewhat shaken in his usual mood of irony, was now regarding his wife with genuine surprise.

"Ye're a most amazin' woman!" he exclaimed. "At your time o' life I thocht ye micht hae sense. Would you be seen smokin' a cigar?"

"I ance smoked a pipe — when I had the toothache," replied Jinnet brazenly. "And I felt I was awfu' gallant. That's the way Mrs Asquith would feel aboot her cigar; ye can see it wisna a habit. And that's true aboot half the escapades she was up to; they astonished hersel', and mak' her laugh at herself noo when she minds o' them."

"It's a' wi' hersel' she's ta'en up in her writin' as far's I can see," said Erchie. "There's naething aboot serious affairs in life — and — and politics. There's nae moral uplift."

"There's nae pretence at it," admitted Jinnet. "If there's ony upliftin' to be done in the Asquith family, Henry'll[6] see to't; that's his business. Wha could she be better ta'en up wi' than wi' hersel' in writin' her book? There's naebody she kens better. If she wasna' a plucky yin, she wouldna' say sae much aboot hersel' that ither folk keep secret. If her man was to write his life he would come oot like yin o' the Apostles, as glossy as a figure in a waxwork."

"It's no' a book for the youth o' the country; it'll mak' them think the highest society in the land is awfu' frivolous and peery-heided,[7] pleaded Erchie. "That's whit the papers say."

Jinnet chuckled, as she put aside her jotter.

"Noo ye're jist making fun o' me, Erchie!" she retorted. "The newspapers wouldna' daur say that, for they're a' competin' wha'll give maist aboot the frivolity and peery-heidedness o' Society. Do ye think ye could get a lend o' the book frae the minister? He's sure to hae't frae the library. I would like fine to read it if it's big print."

69. *Glad News*[1]

ERCHIE CAME home in the evening, radiant, whistling an old air of the 'Seventies as he hung up his coat in the lobby and grinned at his wife with a sly congratulatory air as he took off his boots.

"Ye're awfu' cheery the night" said Janet. "Did they raise your pay on ye?"

"I don't want my pay raised," he informed her. "Another shillin' or twa and I would be into the Income-tax. That would be the last straw!"

"Indeed and I wish we had the Income tax," said Janet. "If ye're on the Income tax ye get an allowance o' £225 for yoursel' and your wife."

"Who the mischief gied ye that information?" inquired her husband, with surprise.

"Duffy's wife. She says her man's in for't and she's getting a new room grate on the strength o't. She's expectin' a lot o' money, too, for the weans."

Erchie chuckled. "Faith, that would mak' it a land fit for heroes to live in![2] If Duffy and his wife think the Income-tax is as lavish as that they're goin' to get an awfu' start when the thing's explained to them. You tell Mrs Duffy no to go in for a room grate in the meantime, but to get a good gas ring for the kitchen and stop coals. As far as I can hear from the chaps that's sufferin' it, the Income-tax is the worst o' human afflictions. It puts ye aff your sleep."

"But whit are ye whistlin for?" pursued Janet.

"Great news!" said Erchie. "I ran a' the way hame to tell ye. THERE'S TWOPENCE AFF THE BOBBIN O' THREAD! Whit de ye think o' that?"

"It'll be bastin' thread," suggested Janet dubiously.

"No, it's no' bastin' thread; it's twopence aff the best bobbin o' thread ye ever put your teeth to. There's a chance noo I'll can get that button on my waistcoat I've been speakin' aboot for the last twelvemonth."

"Ye auld haiver! It only come aff yesterday, and it would be on afore this if ye had put on anither waistcoat in the mornin'. Wha's takin' the twopence aff."

"Coats,[3] of course! Wha else could dae't? I havena heard the parteeculars, but it's rumoured there was a mass indignation meetin' o' the Coats shareholders in the St. Andrew's Halls, where they demanded that the English pirn[4] should be eightpence instead o' tenpence, so as to bring doon the cost o' livin' in the tylerin' tred. They said they were fair affronted wi' their dividends. It gied them a bad name."

"Whit's the difference between an English pirn and a Gleska yin?" asked Janet.

"The English pirn, bobbin or reel," blithely intimated her husband, who had learned of it only an hour ago, "contains 400 yards. The Scotch pirn, bein' mainly used for kilts, is only 300 yards, wi' a choice o' a 200 yard pirn that contains only 200 yards suitable for chaps in lodgings that does their ain repairs. The English bobbin is reduced from 10d to 8d, the Scotch 300 yard pirn from $8\frac{1}{2}$d to $6\frac{1}{2}$d and the 200 yard chat to $4\frac{1}{2}$d. There's goin' to be a torchlight procession among the young students at Gilmorehill; the $4\frac{1}{2}$d pirn means a lot to them."

"It's the first time ever I heard there was ony difference between an English and a Scotch pirn," said Janet. "I never kent hoo many yards o' thread was on a pirn; I must look."

She pulled out the drawer of her sewing machine and produced a new bobbin.

"Yere richt enough," she agreed. "It's 300 yards. That's a big lump! It'll be as far as frae here to Maitland Street."

Erchie, took the bobbin into his hand and regarded it critically.

"Did ye ever measure a pirn to see if ye were gettin' the richt length?" he inquired.

"Not me!" replied Janet. "I couldna be bothered."

"Nae wonder we're poor!" exclaimed Erchie. "I'll bate ye English wifes measures their pirns! I wouldna tak' a 300-yard pirn withoot measurin' it for mysel' ony mair than I would buy a dozen o' eggs withoot countin' them. Get me your inch tape."

"Oh, Erchie!" exclaimed his wife apprehensively "ye're shairly no' gaun to waste a pirn o' thread measurin't wi' a tape. It'll be a' richt. Mr Coats wouldna lower himsel' to gie short measure. I never in a' my life heard o' onybody measurin' thread."

"Get you me the tape!" imperatively said her husband. "We'll hae to go into this. I'm dubious aboot the twopence aff the bobbin."

The tape being produced with tearful protestations, he began to unwind the thread and measure successive lengths of it with all the cheerful flourish of a ribbon counter.

"One yard, twa yards, three yards — you get a pencil and put doon the yards as I measure them. If ye don't I'll never can mind them efter the first fifty."

"I think ye're daft!" cried Janet. "Mind the way ye spoiled the clock. Ye would be far better to let things alane."

"They're no gaun to diddle me oot o' a single yard if I can help it!" declared her husband firmly. "Whaur did the Coats get their yachts?"[5]

Already the thread unwound was beginning to curl about his feet; he kicked impatiently. Thread caught on his buttons; the bobbin slipped from his fingers, and when he picked it up from the floor he was already knee-deep in a spider-web of cotton.

"Fifty yards, fifty-wan, fifty-two, fifty — did I say fifty-seven — "

"I'm gaun oot o' the hoose!" wailed Janet. "I would be better wi' a man that took drink. That thread'll never be ony use to me noo, the way it's fankled."

Indeed, it was very unlikely to be of any use to anybody, for her husband was now wrapped round with it as if he was making himself a cocoon.

"Oh, to the mischief!" he exclaimed at last; "are ye shair it says 300 yards? If I'm no' mistaken, I've measured miles. The Coats's is just palmin' aff the stuff on us! There's as much thread here as would reach to Mars; this must hae been a bobbin specially made for astronomers."

By the time the thread was all off the bobbin, he was wrapped in it up to the eyebrows, and his spectacles were lost somwhere in the mass.

"My good bobbin!" wailed Janet. "I tell't ye to leave it

alane. Cost me 8½d! I couldn't get enough oot o't noo to
put on your waistcoat button."

"I'm no botherin' aboot my waistcoat button!" warmly
declared Erchie. "A' this cairry-on for the sake o' a waistcoat button! I wish ye had left me alane and no nag-nagged
on at me to measure thread when I'm wantin' my tea. Hoo
am I to get oot o' this fankle o' thread? Paisley was aye a
place I fair abominated. See if ye can find my specs."

"Men's a' the same; they're a' silly!" declared Janet, as
she started snipping him into freedom again with a pair of
scissors.

70. *The Footballer's Life*[1]

"DID YOU notice this week," asked Duffy, "that a fitba'
player by the name o' Tom Hamilton[2] at Kilmarnock, has
been bocht by the Preston North End for £4,500?"

"I didna notice." replied Erchie. "That's a terrible lot o'
money for a human bein'! I've seen the day ye could get
tip-top fitba' players in the prime of life for five pounds
apiece, delivered at the door for ye. I've seen half-backs,
and goalkeepers that had twenty years' experience, ye
could get for a schooner o' beer."

"They're surely gettin' scarce," suggested Duffy.
"Criftens! £4,500 would buy a champion entire horse like
the Baron o' Buchlyvie.[3] Ye could buy a tenement land wi'
that money! Whit'll they dae wi' him?"

"The first thing they'll dae 'll be to insure his life, tak' his
measure for an evenin' dress suit o' clothes, and show him
aff at a conversazione and soiree at Preston North End.
That's the usual procedure. It's done like an induction
dinner to a new minister. The wifes and dochters o' the
Preston North End Club'll present him wi' a new silk
jersey and a revolvin' bookcase. I'll bate ye Hamilton's
sittin' up at nicht trainin' for his speech."

"I wisht I had gone in for fitba instead o' the coal tred,"
said Duffy. "I had nae idea there was that much money in

it. I hope Hamilton has the gumption to put it in the Bank and no' play the goat wi't, backin' horses."

Erchie laughed. "Ye're under a delusion, Duffy." he remarked. "Tom Hamilton doesna' handle a' that money; it maistly gangs to the Kilmarnock club that sold him. A' he gets frae the Preston North End is his wages and expenses. Bein' a champion fitba player's no great catch; he's the last relic o' slavery left in modern times. He has nae sooner settled doon in a nice wee hoose wi' a bit o' gairden, and the ground a' delved, than somebody comes and buys him and cairts him awa to anither pairt o' the country where he doesna ken a livin' soul and has to learn the language.

"He canna ca' his life his ain; at the top o' his fame it's jist fair martyrdom. You and me, Duffy, can live whaur we like, and dae whit we like; eat and drink onything that we can pay for or get on credit, but a fitba player micht as weel be a canary except for the glory o' seein' his picture in the papers.

"The life o' the famous fitba team in the season is beyond description, cruel. They havena even their Seturdays to themselves. The chap that trains them watches them like a hawk, and if he seen yin o' them eatin' a pie, or oot o' his bed efter nine o'clock at nicht, he would gie him an awfu' doin'. If their legs gets saft he goes ower them wi' a nutmeg-grater; at the slightest sign o' puffiness under the eyes he scrapes them wi' a curry comb and rubs them wi' embrocation.

"Ye canna alloo ony man ye've paid £4,500 for to spoil his health attendin' mairages or keepin' the New Year; the only dissipation that's permitted is to go to Hydros."

"Do ye tell me they tak' them to Hydros?" asked Duffy.

"They do," said Erchie.

"Well it's a bloomin' shame! I've heard aboot them Hydros. A' teetotal!!"

"That's the very reason they tak the fitba players to them every noo and then to feenish their trainin'.

"Just fancy you big strong chaps like Tom Hamilton

taken under escort to a Hydro for a week-end or a couple o' days afore a match.

"'Whit would ye like for your dinner?' asks the trainer — aye a brutal character wi' nae human feelin's.

"'Could we no' have hare-soup, steak and kidney pie and a dumplin'?' says the goalkeeper, speakin' polite.

"'Yous can not' says the trainer: 'yous'll have a small underdone beefsteak and a couple o' water biscuits.'

"'Whit aboot a spot o' beer?' says the Best Half-Back in Britain. 'Ony kind o' reasonable wee refreshment.'

"'A' the reasonable refreshment I hae wi' me in my bag is for mysel' and the committee,' says the trainer. 'Wha says lemonade, and wha says dry ginger? It's no' a Gleska Corporation Water trip ye're on, it's a trainin' session. Efter ye're done gorgin' yersels, yous'll come oot wi' me and dae a nice wee five miles across country. I seen some o' ye yesterday eatin' chocolates and ye'll hae to work it oot o' the system.'

"When the team comes back, a' glaur, efter scourin' roond the countryside, they're taken into the Hydro baths and washed and massaged till they're as glossy as onything. The trainer gi'es them a lecture on the muscles, and then they put on their Sunday clothes and go into the room where the ither Hydro guests is having a meal o' meat.

"The League champions toy at a side table for a while wi' Glaxo, chemical food and rusks, and the ither folk in the room says. 'Is that the Celtic? Oh, what a treat!' and a fine old gentleman in the sweetie tred moves up to the trainer and asks permission to hand the team a tract on Foreign Missions or Rome and the Irish Situation.

"Efter that the team would like fine to jine the dancin', but they don't ken the Hesitation Waltz, and the toppin'est girls in the Hydro go aff jazzin' wi' a lot o' young neds in the stockbrokin' business that couldna stop a hot shot for goal even if they had a bill hoardin' behind them.

"The auld Roman gladiator ye used to read aboot in the Sevenpenny was on velvet compared wi' the fitba players o' today. The crowd on the field heaved bags o' money or their jewels at him every time he got a wallop hame on the chap frae anither pairt o' the country, and every Seturday nicht he went hame wi' a bagful o' souvenirs o' that sort. When he got up in years and a wee bit groggy, he was bocht a bit o' a ferm and retired, respected and free o' care for a' the rest o' his life.

"But the fitba' player, passed aboot frae wan club to anither for the best ten years o' his life, and naething to show for't but cuttin's aboot him frae the Evenin' News, retires wi' naething but a worn-oot reputation, and a promise o' a' the influence that's needed to get him a public-hoose.

"Boxers and fitba' players, Duffy — they're the people's pride jist as lang's there's the puff left in them; efter that they're no' half as much in demand as coalmen."

71. *Celebrating the Eclipse*[1]

ERCHIE STEPPED out of the close on Friday morning with a feeling that somehow official Summertime had missed a cog, and looked at his watch to make certain he had not mistaken the hour. It was exactly 9.45. But somehow the morning had not a breakfast-hour look. There was sunshine, it was true, but a curious wan sunshine, more like a Fintry moonlight. The shadows were unnatural (as his instinct though not his consciousness at once detected); the air was too cold. At the corner where the Mull of Kintyre Vaults ought properly to have the dismal deserted pre-noon aspect, there was already a crowd.

"The General Strike's started, or else there's a change in the licensin' regulations," he said to himself. And then he observed that the crowd were looking at the sun through bits of glass with as much fascination as if it were a keyhole or a film of Charley Chaplin.

At that instant Duffy's coal cart came round the corner, the horse as usual, dejected, apparently wholly unaware of the cheering fact that the coal pits were out of business;

Duffy with a collar and a jacket on — both indicative of some unusual occasion.

"Whoa!" he said, and the docile animal stopped with a jerk as if actuated by electricity, with two feet suspended in the air.

"Whit's up that ye're in your evenin' dress for?" asked Erchie. "Are ye gaun a trip?"

"Nae trip aboot it!" replied the coalman. "The wife made oot I would need to put on a jecket to celebrate the eclipse. I don't see onything patent aboot it to celebrate. Do ye no' think there's some mistake aboot the date? It should be on by this time accordin' to the almanacks. I'll bate ye they forgot the clocks was shifted!"

Erchie chuckled. "Man ye're a character Duffy!" he exclaimed. "Ye don't see the eclipse and you're standin' richt in the middle o't. I have a canary yonder wi' far mair observation; it stopped whistlin' as soon's the demonsteration started, and the cat went oot like lichtnin' on the washin'-hoose slates and began yowlin'."

"I canna see onything different in't," said Duffy, shutting an eye and blinking with the other at the crescent orb of day. "Forby, whaur's the moon? They bragged ye would see the moon in front o't. There's a catch in't somewhere, Erchie. They're takin' a rise oot o' us."

"To see an eclipse proper," explained Erchie, "ye need a gless."

"Hoo the bleezes can ye get a gless wi' the pubs no' open till half-past twelve?" inquired Duffy indignantly. "If there's an eclipse to celebrate they should celebrate it richt and gie us a chance o' some refreshment. To-morrow there's to be thoosands o' chaps in Gleska frae England to see the fitba International,[2] and the restaurant bars is to be opened for them in the middle o' the day; but there's nae consideration for the Gleska man that pays the rates and taxes and wants to celebrate a Scotch eclipse."

"It's no' that kind o' gless I mean at a'," patiently explained Erchie. "Ye would lose yer eyesicht if ye looked at the sun through the bottom o' a tumbler; the glare o't's maist tremendous. Whit ye need's a bit gless smoked; there's a wee boy'll lend ye his; he must be tired noo lookin' for his eyes is waterin'!"

"I'll dae naethin' o' the kind," said the boy when appealed to by the coalman. "Awa' and get an eclipse o' your ain."

Duffy unhesitatingly grabbed him by the back of the neck, purloined the astronomical essential from him and turned his penetrating gaze upon the heavens.

"I see the moon a' richt," he said to Erchie. "It's a new yin but there's nae sun," and he searched at large across the heavens for the missing luminary.

"That's the sun ye're lookin' at, ye idiot!" said Erchie. "The moon's in front o't."

"Nane o' your coddin'! There's nae moon there; I'm no' that silly."

"It's the moon ye're lookin' at!"

"Ye said a meeenute ago it was the sun."

"Ay, but the black bit that ye see's the moon."

"Well, it's no' lichted, onyway," declared the coalman.

"Lichted!" retorted Erchie contemptuously, "do you think they would licht the moon in the middle o' the day?"

"They should ha'e the eclipse at nicht then," said Duffy. "It's awfu' badly managed. If ye seen the baith o' them lichted ye could believe it."

"Do ye no' believe there's an eclipse at a'?" inquired the astounded Erchie.

"I'm no' denying' it," replied the coalman, cautiously, "for I saw aboot it in the papers, but that's no' my idea o' an eclipse."

"Maybe no'," said Erchie, "but it's God's."

"I'm wantin' my eclipse! Duffy the coalman stole it!" wailed the weeping owner of the glass; but Duffy again was rapt in the higher astronomy.

"Gi'e the laddie his gless," commanded Erchie. "Ye'll see as much eclipse as ye need, reflected in the Mull o' Kintyre window."

Duffy restored the glass and pursued his studies in the

way suggested. "It's a perfect education!" he declared at last. "I wish the wife could see't. She's aye in the hoose and never sees onything. Would ye watch my horse till I go roond to Braid Street for her."

"It'll be a' past before she could get her furs on," said Erchie. "But ye can tell her a' aboot it."

"The next eclipse o' the sun like this I'll ha'e her oot in time. I'm vexed she missed this yin, fir it's an education."

"If ye can get her oot at the next eclipse like this it'll be fine," said Erchie. "It's shair to be visible frae Sighthill. It's to be in 1960 or thereaboot."

"Criftens!" exclaimed Duffy with genuine surprise, "I thocht they were gaun to hae them regular, efter this, like the Summer Time."

"That was talked about, but it canna be managed. It tak's an awfu' lot of plannin', like a Gleska Exhibition. The last eclipse o' this sort was sixty years ago, efter the Crimean War. But there's to be a topper — a total yin — in 1999. Be shair and ha'e a bit o' smoked glass ready for't."

72. *Firewood* [1]

"DID YE no' get some sticks?" inquired Janet, when her husband returned on Saturday. "I tell't ye I must hae sticks if there was to be ony dinner for ye. There hasna been a morsel o' coal in this hoose for a fortnicht, and dear knows whit I'm gaun to dae ower Sunday!"

"I couldna get as much stick as would gie ye a skelf in the finger," he said; hopelessly. "I think the Royal and Ancient Foresters[2] is jined the miners and struck work. I saw a procession o' them wi' a brass band gaun oot the Maryhill road."

"Whit am I to dae?" lamented Janet. "I couldna even mak' ye a cup o' tea."

"Whit did I get ye gas in the range for?" inquired her husband.

"Ye ken fine," she retorted, "that I daurna licht the gas

in the range when I'm my lane; I'm frichtened for't. It starts wi' a bang that shakes the hoose, and lang efter I've screwed it oot, it gie's a terrible explosion. Oh Erchie! I was dependin' on ye gettin' some sticks to mak' your dinner."

"Ye don't need sticks nor coal either, to mak' a dinner. I've seen a chap in the music-halls mak' a first-rate omelette in a tile hat, that wasna ony the worse o't."

"But ye ken fine there's no' a tile hat in this hoose," said Janet, quite seriously, as if that were really all that was wanted to secure an excellent omelette. "Ye sent it awa yoursel' a week ago to bring it up to date."

Erchie calmly opened up his parcel. "I'll licht the gas ring for ye," he said. "But what you're badly needin' is philosophy."

"It's not!" she retorted, "It's fuel."

"If you had philosophy," pursued her husband, "you would mind that food came into the world afore fuel. I have here a pound o' the best boiled beef ham."

"I wish we lived near a wud," sighed Janet, but half-resigned to the situation.

"Far better livin' near a grocer's shop in the New City Road district!" said her husband. "There's an awfu' lot o' humbug aboot cookin'. Naebody needs fires in weather like this as lang's they can get boiled ham. Life, Jinnet, is full o' merciful compensations; we're no actually dependin' on the coal tred as lang as there's pies in the bakers and boiled ham in M'Sorley's shop. When ye come to think o' it — coal's a sheer extravagance."

"But it's handy for washin's," pleaded his wife, "and I was gaun to hae a washin' on Monday."

"Haven't ye a vacuum washer?" asked Erchie. "As far as I've read aboot the vacuum washer, ye have only to give it a start, and then ye can go awa and leave it."

Janet held up her hands despairingly.

"Oh, dear! you men!" she exclaimed, "ye havena the least idea! ... Whit in a' the world am I to dae for sticks?"

"I've never in a' my life seen such a craze for sticks!"

exclaimed her husband impatiently. "You're lettin' it get the better o' ye, Jinnet. It's worse than drink or cigarettes. The first thing ye think aboot in the mornin's a fire, and it's the last thing at nicht wi' ye. I'm gaun aboot my work a' day and I never think aboot a fire. Even when coals was plentiful, I could pass a score o' coal-rees withoot the least temptation to go in an hae a half-a-hunder-wecht. But I'm begining' to be frichtened you're yin o' the secret fire-eaters that's tipplin' awa at the bunker a' day when yer man's at his business. And I don't like the way ye're aye clamourin' for sticks. Whit did ye dae wi' the clothes-pins!"

"If I hadna burned the clothes-pins last Seturday, ye couldn't hae got to the kirk on Sunday," retorted Janet, indignantly. "There was naethin' else to mak' a fire to iron your shirt and collar wi'."

Erchie was only for a moment rebuffed. "There ye are!" he said, "I tell't ye! Ony excuse for a lowe[3] in the chimney! As if I couldna be daein' fine at a time like this wi' a muffler. Ye'll be ruining your constitution. A confirmed fire-eater! Cairry on the way ye're daein', and the furniture'll gang next. Ye'll be ha'in' a fine spree wi' the what-not and the chiffonier, and takin' in other neibour women like yoursel' to finish off a' the doors and skirtin'-boards."

"I never can tell when ye're in earnest, Erchie," said his wife. "It's no' very nice o' ye to be makin' fun o' me, and me wi' no' a morsel o' coal."

The door bell rang. Erchie went to open it, and let in Duffy, who marched into the kitchen carrying some heavy object wrapped in newspapers.

"Here's Duffy," said Erchie; "wi' a couple o' quarter loafs."

"It's naething sae common. It's a good lump o' coal. The wife tell't me ye were in desperation for a fire, and feart to use the gas. Nae wonder! I never believed in gas for onything but lightin'. Tak's the flavour oot o' everything in cookin'."

He unwrapped a substantial block of fuel with an air of triumphant benevolence.

"There's the stuff for ye, Genuine Barrachnie! Pre-war, and full strength. I'll bate ye there's no' a bonnier lump o' coal in Kelvinside. I came on half-a-hunder-wecht this efternoon in the stable loft where I put it at the last big coal strike to keep it frae bein' commandeered."

"Oh, Mr Duffy, what a trate!" exclaimed Janet, with delight. "It's rale considerate o' ye. I couldna' be better pleased if ye brocht me a seal-skin jacket. But I hope ye're no' deprivin' yoursel'."

"Not me!" the coalman assured her. "But ye mustna let bug to onybody. A lot o' my customers in Braid Steet jaloused I had coal in the parcel, and there's twa score o' them at your close-mouth this meenute, followin' me with zinc pails and baskets."

"Puir things!" said Janet, sympathetically, "It's hard times."

"By jings! if I had coal, I could mak' money o't," said Duffy, wistfully.

"It would be a blessed thing if we could dae withoot coal a'thegither," suggsted Erchie. "There's sae mony people that abuse it."

"Whit would ye use instead?" asked Duffy, feelingly. "Peats! Ye couldna richt boil a potato wi' peat; it's only a smell."

"Coals is a curse," continued Erchie solemnly. "If people only kent when to tak' and when to leave it alane, there wouldna be much herm in't. But it's the ruin o' mony a hoose. There should be the Local Veto for coal, the same as drink. I hope the Pussyfoots'll start that next. If I had a' the money that's been spent in my hoose on coal I would be a rich man the day."

"Haivers!" interjected Duffy, with warmth. "Ye couldna dae withoot coal. The trouble is there's far ower little o't."

"That's what ye say aboot drink also, but I'm tellin' ye ye're wrang. I've jist proved to Jinnet here that so far as cookin' goes coals is an extravagance — as lang's ye can get bully beef, boiled ham, and tuppenny pies at threepence ha'penny. Forby, there's nuts, tinned herrin', and bananas."

"Then ye'll no' be needin' my lump o' coal," said Duffy moving towards it.

"Na, na," said Erchie, shifting it hurriedly to the bunker. "Jist leave it alane; I'm gaun to get it silver mounted for a trophy o' the Great Peace."

73. *Duffy's Flitting*[1]

DUFFY'S FLITTING was getting on all right on Friday till Archibald, the tailor, came, quite uninvited, to his assistance.

He had done two raiks with his own coal-lorry and the aid of his wife and her brother Peter. All the stuff put out first on the pavement, carefully selected by Mrs Duffy as best fitted to bear the prolonged scrutiny of the neighbours, was now in the new house, three streets away, and there remained but beds to take down the stairs, the chiffonier to negotiate round the bends, three clothes baskets full of crockery and pots, some valuable works of art, the what-not, the kitchen clothes poles, lobby linoleum, the bird cage and a couple of grates.

"We're gettin' on top!" said Duffy. "I'll be feenished afore my dinner."

"Ye're a fair champion'!" said his wife with honest admiration. "And there's no an iota broke, I never had a luckier flittin'."

It was exactly 12.25 p.m., and Archibald came round the corner.

The eye of Archibald, the reformed actor, lit up. A flitting to him was a joyous thing, like a trip to Rothesay or a Hogmanay. He had never had one of his own, but had helped at scores of them.

"I'll gie ye a hand," he volunteered agreeably, taking off his coat and throwing it on the lorry. "For shiftin' a cottage grand or a massive cabriole sofa, put your money on Baldy ev-e-ry time! There's no' a more willin' performer in the far-flung flittin' line. Could ye get me a brattie, Bella!"

"Are ye shair ye're a' richt?" inquired Mrs Dufy, dubiously. "I'm no' wantin' onythin' bashed."

The tailor drew himself up with a dignity not seriously impaired by the fact that his dickie scarcely filled the opening of an old evening-dress waistcoat, and cast on the lady a reproachful eye.

"Mrs Duffy" he said "—, or, in the words o' the vernacular, Bella — I'm as right as the far-famed trivet, the same bein' an appurtenance made in the Sun Foundry and warranted O.K. In all great congeries of thought, the British patriot, first at heaven's command, in these parlous times canna even greet the orb o' day wi' a modicum o' cheer till the efternoon. Is there, by any chance, what, when I played wi' John Clyde in his 1889 season, we called without divagation a bo'le o' beer?"

"Oh, you tylers!" exclaimed Mrs Duffy. "Ye'll get no beer here till the flittin's by."

Archibald sighed. "Most noble and worthy!" he said, bowing, "Kismet! We maun just thole! If there is no beer at least let me have the brattie. I'm wearin' a customer's trousers for what ye might call the nonce."

Mrs Duffy had no sooner disappeared upstairs in search of an apron for Archibald, than he turned to her husband, and the brother Peter.

"Gentlemen all" he said engagingly.

"Nothing under the cope and canopy[2] is more conducive to a flittin' than a little homologation of thought. Methinks I see now the Mull O' Kintyre Vaults open. If there is one thing more than another I can shift furniture on, it is a glass of the nut-brown. It ameliorates. In the words of the Vulgate,[3] Duffy, are ye on?"

Duffy scratched his chin. Flitting was certainly warm work, and he had had no breakfast.

"A' richt!" he agreed. "But jist the wan pint, mind ye! Peter's teetotal. Hing on by the horse, Peter, till we come

back. Tell the wife I'm awa to Mactaggart's for the lend o'
a bed-key."

"The bed-key," said Archibald, putting on his coat, "is
the palladium o' British liberty. Lead on, MacDuffy!"

At ten minutes past one o'clock Mrs Duffy came round
to the Mull of Kintyre Vaults, manifestly angry, with a
bird-cage in her hand.

"Listen! Is this a flittin' or a funeral?" she inquired
acidly. " I wonder ye're no' ashamed o' yirsels! Me moilin'
and toilin' wi' a linoleum and yous-yins drinkin'!"

"Just a small scintilla o' the nut-brown, Bella, and a
chaser — nothin' more, so help me, Peter!" explained
Archibald. "First the day! Can I relieve ye, madam, of the
songster?"

Mrs Duffy refused to surrender the bird-cage. "I
wouldna trust ye wi' a stuffed gold fish," she declared
indignantly. "Ye jist came here to spile a flittin'. We were
daein' fine withoot ye."

"Fair do, Bella!" pleaded her husband. "Baldy and me's
as richt as rain. Ye must aye mak' some allooance for a
flittin'."

"I'll mak' nae allooance for a big sumph that's cairried
awa' by a bletherin' auld play actor tyler," retorted Mrs
Duffy. "Come awa oot o' this and feenish my flittin'. A
bonny example, the pair o' ye for my brither Peter; he's
awa' to a public hoose o' his ain, and the horse is
stravaigin' the City Road wi' naething in the lorry but a
what-not and a jeely pan. Whit'll the neighbours think?"

Twenty minutes later Peter and the horse were collected; Archibald took off his coat again, and regardless of
the protestations of Mrs Duffy, helped to remove the
grates. Duffy and Peter and he bore them down the stairs,
his share of the burden being the dampers only, which he
absent-mindedly carted up again.

"Whit on earth are ye playin' at?" asked Mrs Duffy,
exasperated. "It's a wonder ye dinna bring up the horse."

"My mistake, indubitably, Bella," confessed Archibald
handsomely. "A lapsus lingus, which in the original Hebrew

means a bloomin' error. Now for the portrait gallery! My, that's a clinkin' picture o' Mr Duffy; we'll need to mind the gless o' that yin."

He was already in posession of this gem of the art collection.

"Keep your hands off that and cairry doon a bass if ye cairry onything!" cried the anxious housewife. "But I would raither ye went awa' to your tylerin'. We're no needin' ony help."

There was an ominous crash of wood on the landing, where her husband and Peter wrestled with the chiffonier; she rushed out, leaving Archibald, who got up on a step-ladder and took down the gasalier by the simple process of taking off its weights first. Luckily the gas had been turned off at the meter.

With three of the ancestral portraits draped round his shoulders by their cords, the gaslier in one hand and a coil of clothes-rope in the other, he got down on the landing, where Mrs Duffy was already weeping over a sadly-damaged chiffonier.

"Mercy on me! whaur did ye get that gasalier?" she cried distracted as she turned from watching nervously the further progress of the chiffonier downstairs. "A body's no' safe to turn her back on ye a meenute!"

"Never saw a nobler gasalier!" said Archibald, blythely. "Massive in the extreme, and still chaste to a degree. For cleanin' a gasalier the best authorities mention beer. It might be best to clean it now; I could run across and get a quart in MacKirdy's Home of Geniality."

"It's no' oor gasalier; it belangs to the hoose!" gasped Mrs Duffy. "Ye're far ower smert at shiftin' things."

"My mistake, Bella, indubitably," said Archibald, without any symptom of contrition. "Methought, most noble and worthy, ye had overlooked it."

"Overlooked your aunty!" exclaimed the lady; plucked it from him rudely, and broke two globes against the railing of the stair.

"Amn't I the puir harassed woman" she wailed. "Wi' a

lot o' silly men! Whit are ye daein' wi' my clothes rope? I was keepin' t up here to tie the beds."

She grabbed the cord from him; a loose coil of it had got about his feet, and he staggered. There was a clatter of the art collection, and the glass of Mr Duffy's portrait as an Ancient Forester was splintered hopelessly.

"That's a feenisher!" she cried. "Awa' hame like a wise man, Baldy, and leave this flittin'; ye're jist in the road."

Archibald, however, esteemed the duties of human friendship and aid too highly to abandon the flitting at that stage. He was now in the vein of a score of old-time flittings, when the world was care free and unperplexed. The spirit of youth restored, he whistled like a mavis up and down the stair, his every step attended with disaster.

It was he who let the handle of a basket slip to the manifest damage of its crockery contents that sounded too alarming to be investigated at the moment, and in carrying down the kitchen clothes-poles he put one of them through a staircase window.

"Ye have surely an awfu' spite at gless!" cried Mrs Duffy, wringing her hands. "It's a mercy I havena a book-case."

"At bookcases," said Archibald, "I am par excellence. Many a yin I shifted in the old Royal Princess's[4] days wi' my coajutor, John Clyde."

"It's shiftin' scenery ye should be yet!" said Mrs Duffy.

"Right! most noble and worthy," agreed Archibald. "I have shifted the Clachan o' Aberfoyle[5] in fifteen minutes — the cloud-capped towers and palaces[6] — and now; base scullion, am engaged in turnin' suits o' clothes. Crockery and the like is for women, and boys to handle; I wish ye had a bookcase or a grandpa clock."

"Thank God, there's naething noo but saft stuff," said Mrs Duffy piously. "Gie Peter a hand wi' that feather bed."

"Flittin's is no what they used to be," said Archibald. "I miss the geniality."

74. *After the Fight*[1]

ERCHIE, THE beadle, perfunctorily rang the bell of St. Kentigern's yesterday forenoon, as if for once his mind was not in his occupation; finished its pealing at least three minutes earlier than usual, and then, in the vestry heaved the minister into his gown in the shortest time on record. He had no sooner snibbed him into the pulpit than he shuffled hurriedly out to join two elders who were counting the copper contents of the plate with a worldly jingling that penetrated even to the congregation and was painfully out of harmony with the opening prayer.

"Did ye see a paper?" he anxiously inquired and MacColl, the elder, reaching into his coat-tail pocket, handed him the latest "Life and Work."[2]

"Ach, to the mischief!" said Erchie, impatiently, "It's no' that I mean; it's a paper for readin'."

"It's no' a day for papers for readin'," replied MacColl, solemnly.

"I ken that fine," said Erchie, "But wha won?"

"Mind I have nae interest in't mysel, but I did hear last night afore I went to my bed that ten minutes efter it started Carpenteer[3] was a corp in the fourth round," said the elder in a whisper.

"And that's a' the time it took to feenish the thing!" exclaimed Erchie. "Fancy you, the whole mortal universe hingin' in suspense for the last six weeks on a fight that's settled in the time ye would smoke a pipe! I thocht the battle would rage for a month, wi' a' the sang they made aboot it."

"The twa ruffians that was involved in the shameful proceedin's would make a lot o' money, onyway," commented MacColl. "It's that that vexes me! Everybody's wantin' everybody else to put aff his coat and work for the national prosperity, but they'll pay ony money to see chaps takin' aff their coats for nae mair useful purpose than to bash each other. The job could be far better done wi' machinery."

"Nae doot they would make a lot o' money," admitted Erchie, "but as far as I can see they were throwin' awa the chance o' makin' far mair if they just had a little gumption. Prize-fightin's badly mismanaged in a commercial way. Instead o' drawin' wan day's gate money they could be liftin' weeks o't if they opened the trainin' quarters o' the combatants and ran charabangs and trains."

"It's no' the fight that I would want to see; it would be Carpenteer and Dempsey[4] grindin' their teeth as described in the newspapers, and makin' speeches aboot the exact way they were gaun to knock each ither's block aff. I was backin' Dempsey mysel, for he has a toppin' set o' teeth accordin' to his photographs, and he confessed frae the first he was confident o' winnin'.'"

"But so was Carpenteer," pointed out the elder; "and he kept on grindin' his teeth till I'm sure they must be worn doon to the gums. Grindin' your teeth in the French language means a lot o' wear and tear that Dempsey escaped, bein' an American and maistly speakin' through his nose. But I'm no' sayin', mind ye, that I wouldna' like fine to see the fight if I happened to be in America — that's if there was nae bloodshed."

"Bloodshed!" exclaimed Erchie, contemptuously. "There's nae bloodshed in a prize fight nooadays, unless the pugilist bites his tongue by accident when he's dictatin' his daily message to the world's Press tellin' them he's feelin' fine and fit. Ye daurna draw claret[5] in America, it bein' a dry country.[6] I would far sooner see the preparations than the fight itsel'; better value for the money!

"A' the excitement's in the trainin'. Day efter day, for weeks afore a match, Carpenteer spends the mornin' brushin' his hair wi' Anzora cream to give it the proper polish. They talk aboot the Frenchman's deadly left, but believe you me, there's far mair in the way he sheds[7] his hair and keeps it glossy. That's whit mak's him the most popular pugilist pet o' the century wi' the female sect, and sells his photographs. Dempsey was badly handicapped wi' his hair — it's far ower tousy and nae sensitive woman would put his photo on the top o' the piano, he looks that brutal. If I was Dempsey's trainer, the first thing I would dae would be to mak' him spend a couple o' oors a day wi' a pail o' gum-arabic and a set o' stiff army hair-brushes. It would mak' a' the difference.

"Efter twa oors strenuous exercise at his hair and a smert bout wi' the tooth-brush, Carpenteer in his trainin' under Descamps takes a sleep to himsel' and then gets up and shaves twice. From eleven to twelve he reads the best French poetry, wi' an occasional glance at selections frae the letters from his wife and his fair admirers. Then a snack o' something, an omelet or a bunch o' grapes, and he's ready for the serious business o' the day.

"Half a dozen interviews wi' the novelists that's engaged by the newspapers to explain the mystery o' his fatal gift, and then an oor or twa wi' the photygraphers. That's a killin' part o' the trainin'; a' the time Carpenteer has to look like the film hero in the Western drama 'Tried and True, or The Manly Curate,' and it takes a lot o' doin', for the heat in America's that great, the Anzora cream runs into your eyes."

"I saw last nicht from the papers that Carpenteer said his morale was spendid, and that he had a perfect contentedness o' the mind that filled him wi' every hope o' victory. He mentioned, too, that shakin' hands last year wi' the Prince o' Wales and Sir Philip Sassoon[8] was wonderfully helpful to him." remarked MacColl.

"The thing that tells wi' him mair than shakin' hands wi' onybody is the hypnotic power o' Mr Descamps, his trainer," said Erchie. "Descamps puts the 'fluence on him afore the fightin' starts; he's in a kind o' trance when he enters the ring, and thinks that every wallop on the heid's a presentation bouquet o' flooers. It gives him a great advantage unless he's up against a man wi' tin ears and a solid brain pan.

"Dempsey's just a coorse hairy man that I'll wager ye never read Milton's poetry through, and canna conceal the fact that his face is quite unfit for puttin' on chocolate boxes. He hasna the Frenchman's classical education, and was sadly handicapped by the fact that he never shook hands wi' the Prince o' Wales in his life, an' couldna be put in a trance unless wi' a whack from a steam-hammer. If he asked him aboot his morale, ye would need to gie him a diagram o' what ye meant. But brutal in the extreme! That's the way he won — nae poetry in his composeetion.

"Still I would pay a shillin' or twa mysel' to see Dempsey in his trainin' quarters. The hack that he had above his eye that needed a pad on't up till the oor o' battle was, likely enough, a bit o' camouflage for his heid's a' made o' pewter, accordin' to the Frenchman's backers. Day efter day, when he wisna gettin' the muscles o' his back photygraphed as an offset to the refined and handsome dial o' Carpenteer, he would put in a while at stunnin' the strongest boxin' men they could gather together in America to face him.

"A rare speaker, too — ye could hear him dictatin' his reports for the newspapers at a distance o' half a mile. Of course they had to be translated for the European papers, but they read fine."

"Fifteen and sixpence and a couple o' trooser buttons," said MacColl, concluding the counting of the offertory. "This fight's fair spoilin' oor gate the day! I'll wager half the members o' the kirk are stayin' at hame to read the Sunday papers."

"They micht hae ken't that Carpenteer would lose! I had nae hope for him wance I saw he went and got his hair cut," said the beadle.

And Erchie and the elders filed silently into the congregation, while it rose to the opening strains of "Peace, Perfect Peace."

75. *Saturnalia*[1]

THERE WAS a great demand for coal on Saturday. Out New City Road way every second housewife wanted a couple of bags so urgently that Duffy was sold out by a little after noon.

"Coals is gettin' too chape!" said Duffy. "If they cost a sixpence mair they would be mair appreciated."

He felt genuinely aggrieved. For, usually, on Saturdays, his lorry load was not exhausted till about 3 o'clock, an ideal hour which enabled him to partake of some liquid nourishment before going home. If he went home now at the ridiculous hour of 12.30, the consequence would likely be a Saturday wholly ruined. He would have to wash himself and take his dinner, so spoiling the natural human Saturday appetite for beer. Nothing more likely, too, than that his wife would want to come out with him to a picture-house or on one of those dreary perambulations down Cowcaddens to see the shops. She might even want some extra money!

"If this is the comin' revival o' tred they're talkin' aboot," said the coalman, "I wish they had picked anither day for't than the Saturday."

He had stabled his horse, and was dolefully walking homewards, carrying the can that had boiled his breakfast tea, when turning the corner of the street, he found himself on the fringe of the students' carnival, the nature of which was beyond his comprehension.

"Criftens!" he explained. "Galoshans![2] It's either that or Hengler's."[3]

A nice old lady with spectacles and a rabbit-skin collarette slipped twopence into his can and remarked in warmly sympathetic tones, "For a good cause," and passed on.

Duffy stood and stared after her, amazed, incredulous, suspicious.

"Cocaine," he reflected. "Or jist dotty." He didn't know what to do about the twopence.

Before he could make up his mind whether to put them in his pocket or run after the lady, he felt his sleeve tugged, and turned round to find two laughing girls confronting him. "Isn't he a scream!" one of them exclaimed in an ecstasy of enjoyment, and behold another twopence was in the can!

Duffy flushed, as could be seen through the bare patches on his face.

"Hey you!" he exclaimed. "Do ye think I'm a blin' man? I'm sure ye see I havena a dug wi' me!"

"It's perfectly killin'!" giggled one of the girls; "Duffy to the life!" and already quite a crowd was gathered round the coalman. A shower of coppers rattled into his can.

"Speech! Speech! How's the coal trade, Duffy?" somebody shouted.

He was utterly bewildered. He didn't know one of these poeple, who seemed to know him well, and have some mania for throwing away good money. Could there, by any chance, have been a sudden change in the licensed hours for Saturday? A closed pub immediately in front of him firmly negatived any such inspiring idea. These people, then, were either escaped lunatics or taking a rise out of him.

"Awa hame and tak a strong cup o' tea to yersel's," he advised them, filling his pocket from the contents of the can. "And ye can whistle for yer money; it'll dae for the plate the morn."

He was swept away with his can in the tumult, between a pierrot and a policeman with white spats and an incredibly red nose. The policeman evoked much laughter from the public on the pavement, but Duffy was plainly regarded as the star performer. Everyone knew his name and occupation (the latter not difficult to guess from his appearance), and his can once more was getting heavy with contributory coin.

"I wish to goodness I had brung a pail," he said regretfully, every time he put the contents of his receptacle into his pockets, ... "Whit was I eatin' last nicht afore I went to my bed? Afore I wake up I hope they'll make it sovereigns."

"A great make-up, old chap!" said the policeman to him. "Perfect masterpiece! But you ought to have brought your horse and lorry. ... Ygorra! Ygorra! Ygorra!"[4]

"I know you; you're Charlie Dunn!" said a bold young lady from Queen Margaret College[5] with a red·gown, and a trencher, putting her arm through Duffy's.

"No," replied the coalman. "I'm the manager o' the Penny Savin's Bank. Whaur did ye get the comic bunnet? If you waken first don't mak' a noise; I never had a greater pant o' a dream since I dreamt I was Napoleon Bonaparte, an' I want to enjoy every minute o't."

"Are you a student or a real coalman?" asked the lady dubiously, suddenly removing her arm.

"Of course I'm a student" replied Duffy mockingly. "My name's Skerry.[6] I wish that brass band would clay up; it would waken a Necropolis monument … Do you think ye can flee? That's yin o' my dreams too. Ye're claes is a richt; ye have on a red flannel nichtgown; it's no' exactly the thing for Charin' Cross, but naebody's noticin'."

Sauchiehall Street was a riot of bizarre costumes, bands, strange vehicles, grotesque encounters, supplicatory collecting-boxes, shouts, shrieks, and laughter. A host of irresponsible and fantastic characters seemed to have taken possession of the city for the time being, its customary traffic was ludicrously impeded; a wild spirit of Disrule prevailed. Duffy with his can drifted like a leaf in a current of whose constitution he was ignorant; he was finding his accumulating coinage something of a burden.

"Old Bean," said the red-nosed policeman by whom, instinctively, he had stuck, "what football match are you going to after we've lunched with the Lord High Provost?"

"I'm no' gaun to ony lunch nor ony fitba match," replied Duffy, firmly. "I ken fine this is something I ate last nicht, for if we wis daein' this wide-awake in the streets o' Gleska they would gie us the jyle for't. I'm gaun to wake up in twa meenutes, and hear the clock chappin' six."

"I say, old fruit! are you by any chance a genuine coalman?" inquired the policeman anxiously.

"A' the time — when I'm no' sleepin'," Duffy informed him, again emptying his can.

"Then, by George, you'll have to hand over all the coin

you've collected," said the policeman. "This is a students' stunt, and it's for the Unemployed."

"I ken't I was only dreamin'" said Duffy sorrowfully, emptying his pockets in the policeman's helmet. "It's only in a dream that Gleska mak's a cod o' itself. But man — I enjoyed it fine!"

76. *Keep to the Left!*[1]

DUFFY SAW it first on the front of a tramway-car which was approaching him as he got half-way across the street. Mr Dalrymple's peremptory order to the citizens to "Keep to the Left" was in such emphatic large blue type that it immediately impressed him. He stopped suddenly, confused between an urgent desire to get as quickly as possibly into the Mull of Kintyre Vaults, whose door was just opening for the afternoon, and the problem what, exactly, the tramway manager's order meant.

Keep to the left of what?

And why?

The car was up on him before those two questions were solved by his slow-moving mind, and he would have been run over, but for the ferocious abruptness with which the driver put on his brakes.

"Somebody should be in chairge o' ye'," shouted the driver. "Take my tip, and never you step oot o' yer peramblator, or ye'll get hurt."

Next Duffy saw the great new slogan swinging from a wire above the pavement. "Keep to the Left!" it shouted in even bigger type than on the tramway-cars.

He stopped and looked all round to discover what particular left his attention was demanded for, quite prepared to be agreeable and acquiesce in anything reasonable.

The only possible left he could discern as practicable for him at the moment involved his going round an impressively stout lady who was looking intently into a jeweller's shop. So he passed between her and the window, brushing against her as he did so.

She gave a little scream, hauled in the slack of her vanity-bag, opened it quickly to see if her purse was still in it, and stared at Duffy with much suspicion.

"Sorry!" said Duffy. "My mistake."

"Imphm! Just that" she remarked with icy coldness.

He passed on, pondering on the mystery of this new message to the people, which he now perceived was on all the cars, and hung at intervals along the vista of the street.

A man with sandwich boards hung round his neck, boldly inscribed with the Dalrympian slogan, came towards him on the right-hand side of the pavement.

Now, Duffy understood! "Keep To The Left" was obviously the title of a film.

He stopped the sandwichman. "Where can ye see it? he inquired politely.

"See what?" retorted the sandwichman.

"That picture o' yours, 'Keep To The Left'; it seems to be a' the rage."

"Awa and bile yer can!" said the sandwichman.

"Criftens!" thought Duffy, "Everybody's aff their heid the day. It must be the Rangers and the He'rt o' Midlothian."[2]

He was now being swept on in a stream of pedestrians who faithfully kept to the right-hand side of the pavement as their ancestors had done, simply because it was the side next the shop windows, and the pubs and the closes they might at any moment feel like entering.

There was only one man on the outer side of the pavement, and he was, apparently, under a misapprehension as to where he was, for he was led by a dog on a string, and tapped with a stick on the flagstones as he walked.

"If that blinny doesna look oot he'll fa' aff the kerb in the gutter and hurt himsel'," thought Duffy, who has a kindly heart.

He had turned round to look after this touching spectacle and failed to perceive the approach of a painter who emerged from a pend close[3] carrying a twelve-foot ladder ingeniously balanced on his shoulders in such a way as permitted him to keep his hands in his pockets. His head was through the rungs, and a nice equilibrium was maintained by means of a pail of whitewash stuck between two other rungs in front of him.

The man turned round as the rear end of the ladder cleared the close-mouth, the fore part of it caught Duffy on the shins, the pail fell off, and the whitewash splashed over Duffy's boots.

"Whaur the bleezes are ye gaun?" angrily demanded the victim of this mishap. "Can ye no' watch yer bloomin' lether?"

"Watch yer aunty!" said the painter indignantly, 'It's you that's aff-side. Ye should keep to the left."

"Hoo the mischief do ye ken whether I should keep to the left or no' when ye don't ken whaur I'm gaun?" demanded Duffy.

"It doesna matter! If ye keep to the right ye go wrang, I'm on the right side o' the pavement."

"Then ye must be wrang!" said Duffy.

"Awa' an' bile your can!" concluded the painter. It is the one unanswerable retort in Glasgow.

"It's time I was awa' hame," thought Duffy. "This is yin o' they days I'm bound to get into trouble unless the wife's wi'me," and at that moment he was overtaken by his old friend Erchie, going in the same direction.

"Ye're aff-side!" said Erchie, elbowing him over to the left. "What's the use o' Mr Dalrymple takin' in hand wi' your education when ye'll no' tak' a tellin'?"

"What's a' this aboot keepin' to the left?" asked Duffy. "Are they expectin' a procession?"

"No," said Erchie; "Mr Dalrymple's cairryin' on the noble work o' trainin' Gleska to keep oot o' the road o' his tramway cars. Ye have nae idea the trouble he has wi' folk crossin' the street. They'll cross the street in spite o' him, come bangin' against his cars, and scrapin' a' the paint aff them; he's fair demented! Lots o' folk used to spit, too — a habit that's fair ruination to the tramway rails; noo that he's put a stop to spittin' in ony shape or form, he's determined they'll no keep on gettin' fankled up wi' the wheels o' the finest tramway system in the universe. If we keep to the left, we can see when a car's comin' and keep oot o' the road o't."

"Half the pubs o' Gleska's on the righthand side," Duffy pointed out. "Hoo could ye get near them if ye kept gaun left?"

"They're gaun to be shifted," said Erchie, cheerfully, "Efter the May term[4] a' the pubs are to be on the left-hand side o' the pavement for convenience."

"Hoo could they dae that?" asked Duffy, considerably bewildered. "The left-hand side micht be the ootside o' the pavement — it depends on the way ye're gaun — and ye canna build pubs there."

"Can ye no!" retorted Erchie. "Jist you wait and ye'll see! Dalrymple can dae onything. He'll have a' the pubs on yin side o' the street and a' the soda fountains and ice-cream bars on the other. Naebody ever fa's oot o' an ice-cream shop in front o' a tramway car."

"Come on in to M'Gashan's shop and hae a wee refreshment," suggested Duffy, feeling depressed at the very prospect of new obstacles to geniality in Glasgow.

"We canna," said Erchie. "Ye see yoursel' already it's on the wrang side. But I'll tell ye whit we'll dae; I ken a soda fountain on the left side, roond the corner; we'll go and hae a raspberry vinegar."

77. *Glasgow in 1942*[1]

"THE ONLY consolation I ha'e in gettin' auld," said Erchie, "is that wherever I am in twenty years it'll no' be in Gleska."

"Ye'll may be in a far waur place," suggested Duffy, drily.

"I couldna be. Conan Doyle[2] has nae intelligence o'

trams and motor-cars on the Ither Side; ye jist skliff aboot on your feet or whiles tak' a flee to yoursel'. There's nae vehicular traffic. Mr Dalrymple'll get an awfu' start when they hand him a trumpet and gie him a job in the orchestra. There'll be naething in his ain line for him to dae."

"What'll we get to dae oorsels?" inquired the coalman, entering into the spirit of these speculations.

"I'm a' richt!" said Erchie blythly. "There's bound to be some jobs suitable for a chap accustomed to handin' round a tray. You bein' in the fuel tred of course ye'll be in the ither department. ... Did ye ever in your life see such a habble?"

They stood at the upper end of Jamaica Street, held up by a maelstrom of traffic that made any attempt to cross look suicidal. North and South, as far as the eye could see was an unbroken line of inanimate tramcars. On the narrow margins on either side, automobiles, waggons, lorries followed each other closely.

"When I mind first o' Gleska," said Erchie, "there was some kind o' pleesure in gaun aboot in't; ye didna take your life in your hand if ye stepped aff the pavement. The folk that came in frae the country then — ye would see them daunderin' up the middle o' Jamaica Street the same's it was the Crow Road oot to Fintry. As late as the early '80's I've seen the point polisman oot in the middle o' the crossin' there talkin' Gaelic for half an oor at a time wi' a wheen o' his kizzens new aff a trip frae Campbeltown. Just every noo and then he would birl his whistle and let a hearse or a beer lorry past. Some o' the polismen had their books wi' them and carried on their studies for the college. They were fed up with the loneliness o' their job at Jamaica Street, and the craze wi' some o' them was to get a nice wee manse in some brisk place like Invergordon.

"It's gettin worse and worse every year; a man's no safe to tak' drink noo on a Setterday if he's gaun to venture nearer the centre o' the toon than Possilpark or the Half-way Hoose. He'll get nailed as sure as fate unless he tak's a tramway car.

"That's maybe Mr Dalrymple's notion — to abolish walkin' althegither. But the problem will aye be hoo to cross the street."

"Aboot 1942, if I'm no' mistaken, everybody in Gleska 'll have his jeckets made wi' a ring in the middle o' the back."

"What for?" asked Duffy.

"To cross the streets wi'. They'll sling him across on overhead wires, and the ring's 'll be needed to hook him on wi' 'The Dalrymple Patent Safety-First Slinger. Ball bearin's. No jerk at the start and no jar on landin'.' There'll be cross-traffic underground escalators too; ye'll go doon a hole at Simpson's corner; slide under the main drain-pipes and come up at Chrystal Bell's Soda Fountain."

"This is a fair beezer!" said Duffy, surveying the congested thoroughfare. "Maybe we should go doon to the Boomielaw and work oor way roond by Finnieston."

"Whit ye're seein' there, Duffy," said Erchie, gravely, "is the Triumph o' Civilization, and the Age o' Progress. It's maybe a bit awkward for the like o' you and me no' to get the safe and rational use o' the Gleska highway, but consider the swellin' revenue o' the Tramway Department and the praise that Gleska gets in the foreign newspapers for tramways that mair than pay their way!

"Do you know that 10,000 tramway cars and other vehicles no' coontin' bassinettes pass this corner every day? There's gaun to be mair, too. They're gaun to chip aff the corners o' the crossin' here, and mak' a kind o' circus."[4]

"It'll take the place o' Hengler's," suggested Duffy seriously. "We'll can see Doodles again."

"It's no' that kind o' circus exactly," explained Erchie. "You and me 'll be the Doodles. It'll look fine on the map, the circus, but it'll no mak' the least wee difference on the problem o' congested traffic in Argyle Street, Jamaica Street, and Union Street; there'll no' be ony mair room for jazzing between the cars."

"I see," said Duffy, "they're gaun to ha'e a 'No-Accident Week' in Gleska soon; it should bring a lot o' folk in frae the Mearns[5] that's frichtened to venture in at ordinar' times. Whit'll be the safety tips, I wonder?"

"I hear a rumour that, over the city generally, pedestrians is only to get movin' aboot on the convoy system-twelve at a time, in the chairge o' a policeman carryin' a red flag. For the No-Accident Week every car 'll ha'e a cow-catcher on the front and a steamboat bell. Naebody allo'ed to walk in the main thoroughfares except athletes; women and children that'll no tak' the trams 'll be conveyed in tanks kindly lent for the occasion by the War Office. Motor car and locomotive boiler traffic confined to the West-End Park. First Aid Hospital at the corner of Gordon Street and Hope street and a bulletin board in George's Square givin' the casualties from hour to hour.

"Any bloomin' thing, Duffy, that'll mak you and me believe that life and limb's as safe in the streets o' Gleska as in Balmoral Castle. Of course they're no', and never will be in oor time.

"The streets in the middle o' Gleska were laid oot for a population no' the size o' Greenock. The great mistake was that they werena made o' kahouchy."[6] As lang as Menzies' 'busses and the horse had the cairryin' traffic there was nae great inconvenience to the foot passenger; he could stop in the middle o' the street and tie his laces, and there wasna ony need for an ambulance.

"But any kahouchy quality the streets had vanished when the tram-rail and the motor came in vogue. Nae human ingenuity noo can widen them to accommodate safely what's expected o' them. In the past ten years the population's risen a quarter o' a million; the traffic's speeded up at least four times what it used to be when the horse was bloomin'; and twenty years from noo, when everybody has a motor-car; ye'll see some fun! The Tramway Department in 1942 'll need to hae break-doon gangs continually on the move, wi' derricks to deal wi' the street fatalities."

"But maybe there'll be nae tramway cars," suggested the coalman hopefully.

78. *No Accident Week*[1]

ERCHIE WAS astonished this morning to meet Duffy, the coalman, walking towards his stable with what looked like a red burgee in his hand.

"I knew the coal tred was daein' no' that bad," he remarked, "but I never thought it was payin' that weel that ye could start the yachtin'. Ye have the wrang kind o' bunnet for it, Duffy; ye should have wan o' they deep-sea keps wi' brass braid on't. Whaur's the regatta the day?"

"Ye're awfu' comic," retorted the coalman. "At least ye think ye are."

"I'm no' bein' comic at all," said Erchie. "I'm ower anxious for ye' gaun awa' yachtin' at this time o' the year. Ye'll get your death o' cold, or maybe ye'll droon yersel'. Whitever ye dae, hang on by the spinnaker. Wha gie'd ye the flag?"

"Big Macrae, the polisman. It's for No Accident Week. He said I was to wear it on my horse, cart, lorry, or other vehicle."

"As sure as daith," said Erchie, " I thocht it was the Royal Mudhook Yacht Club flag, or maybe the Corinthians! I clean forgot aboot the Accident Week, an' me wi' a safety button for it in my pocket! It was handed to me yesterday comin' frae the kirk."

He took the button out of his pocket as he spoke, and passed it through the hole in the lapel of his coat.

"There!" he said; "I'm a' richt noo; it's as good as a life insurance. All the same, I'm gaun oot for the week wi' the wife to Eaglesham[2] till this No Accident ploy blaws by. It'll no' be safe, I'm tellin' ye, in the streets o' Gleska! They're bad enough at ony time, and haein' six or seven days of a kind o' Cairter's Trip gaun through them a' the time is no gaun to help them ony. Whit did they gi'e you a flag for,

Duffy. Are ye on the committee?'

"I tell't ye," said Duffy, "I got it frae Big Macrae to put on my horse and lorry."

"Whit fur?' asked Erchie.

"So that I'll no' rin doon onybody," replied the coal-man.

Erchie laughed. "Rin doon onybody! There's no' a safer coalman's horse and lorry gaun through the streets o' Gleska. They micht as weel gi'e flags to Wylie & Lochheid or a book-barrow. I doot Macrae was pullin' your leg. Take my advice, and keep you oot o' the commotion althegither. Them No Accident Weeks is no' for a horse like yours that couldna' raise enough wind to mak' a flag fly unless ye helped it with a pair of bellowses. Stick by the back streets a' this week, or, better still, come out wi' the wife and me to Eaglesham. It's gaun to be a rale No Accident Week in Eaglesham, unless, maybe, a hen run over by an ice-cream barrow."

"Macrae said Mr Dalrymple would be awfu' angry wi' me if I didn't put on the flag," said Duffy, somewhat shaken in his first intention.

"Never you mind Mr Dalrymple! He's the cheeriest chap in Gleska — always thinkin' o' some new dydo to speed up his tramway-cars and mak' the walkin' popula-tion skliff along a wee bit quicker. It'll be wan o' the busiest, brightest weeks in the year — every other man, woman, and child wi' a Mind The Step button and every-thing on wheels, except the hearses, with the red burgee. There were Safety First sermons in the kirks yesterday, with special intercession for pedestrians weel up in years. There's a whole lot o' them no' deid or disabled yet. A special service for members o' the Scottish Automobile Club, the Motor Trade, professional chauffeurs and owner-drivers was arranged to be in the Cathedral, but was put off at the last meenute.

"There's gaun to be cinema shows at the Tramway Office, decorated cars, and the Tramway Pipe Band. The polis 'll wear white gloves and every constable 'll carry a flag wi' the motto 'Keep to the Left' in the Gaelic language.[3] The ambulance is to get a holiday, and the Infirmaries to be put on half-time."

"We were needin' something to brighten us up," said Duffy. "There has been naethin daein' in Gleska since the 1911 Exhibeetion. Will there be fireworks?"

"I havena heard o' ony fireworks yet," replied Erchie, "but I wouldna wonder if Mr Dalrymple's keepin' them up his sleeve for a grand surprise. There'll be illuminated cars. The Orpheus Choir[4] is engaged for the week to sing 'God Save the King' every half oor at the corner o' Jamaica Street, and a couple o' hardy auld chaps that's been walkin' conscientiously on the left-hand side of the pavement for the last six months are to be exhibited at Kelvingrove and gi'e lectures every afternoon on the way it feels. It's understood they're gaun to get the Freedom o' the City.

"Cheap excursions 'll be run from a' the country districts within 20 mile radius o' the city and a bumper week's expected for the tramway cars."

"There's bound to be accidents," said Duffy. "Ye canna help them, whiles."

"The idea is that there's gaun to be nane. The magic wee button's gaun to impart a cautious sense o' Safety First on everybody that wears it. That's the reason I'm gaun to Eaglesham."

79. *The Grand Old Man Comes Down*[1]

WITH REMARKABLE expedition, and unaccustomed cheerfulness, as if for once they were thoroughly enjoying their job, a gang of workmen had hoisted Gladstone[2] from his pedestal. Suspended by the neck in a most sinister manner, the grand old statesman swung at the end of the winch-chains, oscillating slowly. A fine, crisp, clear day, with the touch of Spring in it.

"Criftens!" exclaimed Duffy. "Whit are they daein' here?"

"Fifteen feet o' a drap," replied Erchie, solemnly. "Ate a good breakfast o' bacon and eggs, and asked for a cigarette. Ellis[3] was assisted by William Johnson, a young shoemaker from Northampton, and before hurryin' back to England visited the Cathedral, havin' a keen interest in Gothic architecture and stained gless."

"Awa and tak a runnin' jump at yersel!" said Duffy impatiently. "Nane o' your cod, Erchie; whit are they ca'in' the Grand Auld Man aff his feet for?"

"They have every richt to dae't," said Erchie; "he's five-and-twenty years deid."

"It's a statue that was daein' nae herm to onybody," remarked the coalman with feeling. "It's a hanged shame shiftin' it! I suppose it's Mr Dalrymple; he'll be gaun to bring his cars roond here. He has nae respect for onything."

"It's no Mr Dalrymple this time, Duffy," said Erchie, chuckling. "It's the general consensus o' public opeenion that the time's come when public statuary and triumphal arches should be annually revised, and scrapped when necessary. In an electric age, wi' wireless and a' that, ye canna be bothered wi' them when they're the least oot o' date. To you and me, Gladstone was the greatest man o' his time; but by the growin' generation all that's kent aboot him is that he wrote 'The Land o' the Leal'[4] and invented a portmanteau."

"If it wasna' for him Ireland would never ha'e had Home Rule!" said Duffy with loyal admiration.

"Whisht!" warned Erchie, "say naething aboot that. He meant it for the best."

"There's far aulder monuments than Gladstone's here," said Duffy; "they should start wi' the auldest; it's only the other day they put up the Gladstone; I mind o't fine; there was a great furore and brass bands."

"Just you wait and ye'll see the others shifted, too. Gladstone came first because, standin' aye there lookin' in at the front door o' the Municipal Buildin's he fair got on the nerves o' the Labour members. It spiled their Corona cigars for them. That's the way sae mony o' them went to London,[5] where a bronze Presbyterian conscience is no' aye glowerin' at ye. A' the time auld Willie has been standin' there he's seen a lot o' life."

"But what are they flittin' him for?" asked Duffy, who never keeps abreast of local movements by reading newspapers.

"I've told ye already," replied Erchie patiently. "Statues nooadays are like comic songs; they go awfu' quick oot o' fashion. Naebody looks at them efter they're mair than a twelve-month in position. The only yin in George Square that attracts attention noo is Mr Oswald[6] wi' the lum hat, for it has never occurred to onybody to put a lid on the hat to keep the boys frae pappin' stones in't.

"It's like this, Duffy — ye've seen yersel' wi' a grocer's calendar in the kitchen showin' The Genius of Scotland Findin' Burns at the Plough. For the first three months your eye was never aff it; a' the rest o' the year ye would never look at it unless the wife put it on the table in front o' ye on a plate. It's the same wi' statues — there's auld General Peel[7] at the other side o' the Square, naebody looks at him unless it's a polisman to see that there's naething chalked on the pedestal.

"Under the new movement for brightenin' up Gleska the authorities is gaun to put a' the statues on wheels and hurl them to different sites in the city twice a year. The priceless gift o' Art is to be brung hame to the toilers o' Brigton Cross and Maryhill. I wouldna say but ye'll have Watty Scott's monument sometime next winter clapped at the end o' Raeberry Street. Walk you roond it, Duffy, if ye're coming hame at nicht; mak' nae attempt to sclim' it."

"Ye're aye tryin' to pull my leg." said Duffy, impatiently. "I wish you would talk sense."

"I'm talkin' naething else. The perambulatin' statue is going to solve a lot o' civic problems: it's surprisin' they never went in for it wholesale sooner, seein' they had some experience wi' King William[8] at the Cross. They're goin' to shift him again. There's no' an equestrian statue in

Europe that's done mair gallopin'. It's the only way to keep up wi' the urgent needs o' the greatest Corporation tramway system in modern times.

"Whit can be done wi' King William can be done wi' every monument in sicht as occasion requires; the only site for a memorial regarded as perpetual should be the Necropolis.

"Put them a' on wheels from the start, and hurl them where they're maist required from year to year. I wouldna destroy them althegither as lang's the memory o' the departed's green, but as soon as it's only folk frae the country on a trip that looks at them, I would send them to the stone-knappers and introduce a brand-new lot."

80. *The Doctors' Strike*[1]

JINNET PUT down her newspaper on her lap, and, looking over her spectacles, threw one of those quite unexpected queries at her husband Erchie, when he came home late in the evening.

"Did ye mind yon bottle o' fruit salines I asked ye to get me?"

It rather staggered him; he had quite forgotten all about the fruit saline. In these circumstances, the tactical way of averting unpleasant recriminations was obviously to raise some other controversial issue.

"There's naething worse for ye than fruit salines," he remarked with emphasis. "Ruins the constitution! They start a crave, like drink, and afore ye ken where ye are, ye're nip-nippin' awa at them. The secret drinkin' o' fruit salines is the ruination o' thousands o' homes. Whit on earth do ye want them for?"

"Ye'll find that oot soon enough," she retorted. "Did ye' no see aboot the doctors' strike?[2] It's fair ragin'. They're leavin' their work in droves. If you or me was taken ill we would be in a bonny habble withoot some medicine in the hoose. Every panel doctor in the country's liftin' his graith."[3]

"But that'll no shut the chemists' shops," said her husband; "ye can aye get a bottle. That's where the doctors is at a disadvantage; they're no' in the strong position o' the bakers or the colliers."

"Ay, but just you wait and ye'll see the chemists 'll come oot too. They a' hang thegither."

This naive assumption of his wife's provided Erchie with what he had been looking for — a really plausible excuse for his failure to bring her fruit saline.

"By Jove!" he said, "ye're right! I doot the druggists is oot already; they were a' shut when I came by" — a statement strictly true though false in its implication. "Have ye nae medicine o' ony kind in the hoose."

"Not an article!" said Jinnet.

"Tut! tut! That's maist annoyin'! If a miners' strike was threatenin' ye would hae your bunker full o' coals. I'm awfu' surprised at ye, Jinnet! I'm a busy man; I canna think o' everything. When you learned the doctors were goin' to strike, ye should have taken steps to lay in something — a bottle or twa o' mixture and some peels. Here we are noo at the mercy o' Providence."

"I saw in the papers a week ago the doctors were goin' to strike, but I didna tak' it awfu' seriously." said Jinnet, contritely, and apparently blind to the strategy that transferred the blame to her. "I never in my life before heard o' doctors strikin' and they're no' in ony trade union."

Her husband gave a sardonic laugh. "Are they no'?" said he. "They're in the auldest and the strongest union in the country. They pay pretty sweet to get into it; it involves a lot o' money. They have funds that'll afford them strike pay for a couple o' years if need be. God pity the man that canna keep his health till this thing's settled."

"Isn't that just deplorable!" exclaimed Jinnet. "Whit's the world comin' to? I thought naebody ever went on strike except puir chaps wi' cloth bunnets. Are the strikers makin' ony trouble doon the toon?"

"Naething serious yet," replied Erchie, airily; "just the usual processions. Eight or nine hundred o' them gaithered in front o' the Municipal Buildin's, every man wi' a tile-hat and a wee black bag, and wanted a deputation into the Lord Provost. He wouldna' see them. There was a bit of a commotion, and somebody flung a mustard poultice at a Bylie, but efter a while the strikers formed four-deep and merched doon Buchanan Street and along Argyle Street to the Green, where they made the usual speeches. They had twa or three tasty banners, a pipe-band and an awfu' smell o' iodoform; but I must say they were very orderly. I think they must have got a lot o' money in their collection cans; there's a good deal o' popular sympathy wi' the doctors."

"Whit are they strikin' for? asked Jinnet. "I canna' mak' it oot. It's something aboot 8s 6d for five years; is that a' they get for their panel work?"

"Off and on," said her husband, now thoroughly enjoying himself. "It's no' enough to keep a doctor in carbolic soap. It's a' very weel for the auld chaps in the tred that get fancy prices for appendix jobs and neurasthenia, but the young panel doctor new oot o' his time must have an awfu' struggle to mak' ends meet. He's up against the most cruel competition from the multiple chemists shop and the grocer. Ye can get noo, in the shops, patent medicines that'll cure onything, and there's every inducement to buy them, for when you're cured ye get your picture in the papers.

"Forbye," continued Erchie, warming to his theme, "folk play the dirtiest tricks on the doctor; a chap'll get a prescription for a hack on his heel and pass it round the whole tenement so that it does for palpitation, gastric catarrh, blotches, scarlet fever, spine o' the back, and general paralysis, and not a penny does the puir doctor make oot o' the bunch o' them; the only man that benefits is the undertaker.

"And that's no' the only competition the doctor's up against; there's a lot o' bloomin' blacklegs breengin' in wi' patent tips for curin' yoursel' o' onything by the simple power o' the will. Christian Science struck a heavy blow at the tred, and noo there's a chap called Coue that started

everybody sayin', 'I'm better and better every day,' an'
they keep on sayin' it withoot a doctor bein' called in till
the relatives send for one to give the death certificate."

"I hope to goodness they'll no' stay oot twa years," said
Jinnet. "It's an awfu' prospect! It's no' that I ever had ony
need for doctors, but it's aye a kind o' comfort jist to ken
they're handy if ye need them."

"If the worst comes to the worst, we can aye mak' a shift
wi' Mrs Duffy; she's an awfu' skilly woman," said Erchie
consolingly. "Wi' her Aunt Kate's Domestic Medicine,
she's fit to tackle ony complaint that ever baffled science,
short o' what the doctors call 'rigor mortis,' and that's a
corker o' a trouble, terrible lingerin'.'"

'Mrs Duffy!" exclaimed Jinnet, with disdain. "I wouldna
be behauden to her for a cloth on a cut finger."

She smiled slyly, put down her paper, went to the
dresser drawer, and produced a tin of fruit-salts not yet
opened.

"I kent fine ye would forget it, Erchie," she remarked.
"Ye're that througither and puttin'-aff. I jist went doon to
the grocer mysel' an 'oor ago and got it."

"And what's a' the row aboot?" asked her husband
indignantly. "Botherin' me wi' your doctors' strike! Ye
have nae consideration. Whit way do ye drag me into it?"

"Jist to hear ye bletherin', Erchie; ye have the grandest
imagination. Tell me again aboot the procession."

He looked at her with admiration. "By jings!" he exclaimed, "ye're gettin' awfu' fly. There's nae pullin' o' your
leg at a' noo."

81. *The Coal Crisis – Duffy Explains*[1]

"IT WAS high time the folk o' this country got a lesson in the
value o' coal; they treated it like dirt," said Duffy.

"There's no other word for the last bag I got from
yoursel'," remarked Erchie, agreeably. "But, mind, I'm
no' blamin' onybody! Accidents will happen! All my wife,

Jinnet, said when she looked in the bunker this mornin'
was 'Somebody's smashed a guid marble clock near
Duffy's ree! I wonder what happened to the works?"

"Ye couldna get better coal in the city o' Gleska at the
money!" protested Duffy warmly. "I picked it special for ye."

"I'll no deny it was good enough coal o' the kind," said
Erchie. "A capital coal for Sundays, when the breakfast's
never in a hurry. The last word in smokeless fuel! The
black smoke problem solved at last! But it's too rare and
too dear at 3s 6d a bag for puttin' in grates. It should be
kept for rockeries and crazy pavements. If it's a fair question, do ye get it direct frae the quarry, or did it come frae
the demolition o' St. Enoch's Kirk?"[2]

"Away you!" retorted the coalman, impatiently. "Ye
haven't the least idea the way I'm badgered wi' people like
you that think I mak' the coal mysel'. I sell it just the way I
get it."

"That's the mistake you make," said Erchie, solemnly.
"Ye're losin' money on it that way. Ye should take it to the
lapidaries and get it cut into Scotch pebble brooches ... Ye
havena, by any chance, a bag o' pre-war full-strength coal
aboot ye? I could come roond in the dark wi' a basket and
slip it awa' in instalments."

"As shair as daith," said Duffy. "I have naething but
whit ye see! If I had a single bag o' the auld inflammable
stuff, I doot I would keep it for myself. It's no' to be got! I
never kent I had so many frien's in the world as turned up
in the last week to ask aboot the health o' my wife and
family. Men that has motor-caurs noo call me 'Mr Duffy'
and hands me a cigar. A cousin o' the wife's that we hadna
heard o' for fourteen years comes in yesterday frae aboot
Milguy[3] to call on us wi' a print of butter[4] and a dozen o'
eggs. She had them in a bag that would hold a
hunderweight. Of course I had to gie her a trate, and coal
was what she was efter, so I took oot the bag and nearly
filled it. She'll get an awfu' start when she coups it; it was a'
half-bricks at the bottom; I'm no' gaun to perjure my soul
and break the law for onybody in Milguy!"

"Ye're quite right there," said Erchie; "ye have your regular customers to consider! I'm no' that awfu' put-aboot mysel' for the want o' coal; I could dae withoot it at this time o' year so long as the gas-ring's gaun and there's cooked ham at the grocer's. What surprises me is to see them sellin' ice-cream bricks off barrows at a time like this when the best folk in Pollokshaws and Kelvinside is desperate for ready-made hot boiled eggs."

"The only folk that puts on side wi' me is the chaps that has a ton o' coal in their cellars," said Duffy. "It shouldn't be allowed! And they lift their weekly ration jist like onybody else."

"A ton doesna' go far if ye have a conservatory. If this coal Prohibition movement lasts, ye'll see all the coals in Gleska put in a central depot run by the Magistrates. A couple o' pounds a week, includin' coke, for every household. Ladies' wear next winter'll be maistly a string bag or a perambulator, and ye'll see them standin' in queues at the City Hall. Already, a well-filled bunker in the home is better than a book-case. … Ye'll no have ony dross ye could spare?"

"No' as much as would fill your pipe," said Duffy, hopelessly. "The rale old genuine dross, if I had it, would sell at the price o' the best loaf sugar."

"I dare say that!" said Erchie. "It must be an awfu' job just now in the coal ree and lorry trade to decide what the price is; there's nae agreement among ye on the question; do ye jist mak' a guess at hoo much is in the customer's pocket?"

"There ye go!" said Duffy, bitterly. "I'm fair sick o' hearin' aboot prices! There's no human gratitude. What ye don't understand is that there's different qualities o' coal, and different prices for it at the bing. There's coal ye couldna boil a kettle wi' at the best o' times — "

"I know," said Erchie. "It's greatly in demand for heatin' churches. Ye have to light it the week before."

" — and there's coal that's only safe for use in the hands o' the fire brigade, and the salvage corps, and costs a lot more money at the pit."

"Don't vex me!" pleaded Erchie. "All I'm wantin's just a plain medium coal at a medium price for democratic purposes. Ye must be makin' your fortune, Duffy."

"Fortune," exclaimed the coalman, "I'm sick o' the whole business and wish I could start a wee green-grocery. I'm only keepin' on this business for the sake o' my horse. What would he do if I was shuttin' up the ree?"

Jimmy Swan, the Joy Traveller

1. Stars to Push

MR SWAN, the work of the day accomplished, stood smoking at the Buck's Head door, and the sky was all a-glee with twinkling stars which are quite irrelevant to the story, and are merely mentioned here to indicate that it was evening. And yet, when I come to think of it, the stars deserve this mention, for their shining, so serene, and cool, and joyous, had some influence both on Jimmy and the story. They set him wondering on the mystery of things and on the purpose of his being and his life.

Behind him, in the hall of the hotel, the Boots, old Willie, piled his sample-cases ready for the boat at six o'clock next morning. The billiard-room seemed full of villagers; the sound of chaff and laughter and the clink of tumblers came from it occasionally. But Jimmy scarcely heard it — wrapt in contemplation of the stars.

From out the billiard-room, at last, there came a man who seemed to have decided, not a moment too soon — indeed, unfortunately, too late — that it was time for home. He fumbled for his top-coat, hanging with a dozen others on a stand, and he was forced to stretch himself a little over Jimmy's cases, piled up very high about the stand by Willie.

"A fine night, Mr Sloan," said Jimmy, who knew even recent incomers to Birrelton;[1] and he helped him to put on his coat.

"There's naething wrang wi' the night," said Mr Sloan, "except for thae damn bags o' yours …Perf'ly rideec'lous! A body might as weel be on a steamer … Shouldn' be allowed!" He was at that particular stage of fermentation where the scum of personal temperament come bubbling to the top.

"Sorry they should be in your road," said Jimmy, affably. "They're often in my own. It's yin o' the chief drawbacks to bein' what the papers ca' an ambassador o' commerce."[2]

"Ambass'or o' commerce!" hiccoughed Mr Sloan.

"Nonsense! Jus' a common bagman!"[3] And two younger men who had joined him laughed at this brilliant sally.

"Right ye are!" said Jimmy. "Just a common bagman! That's what I was thinkin', standin' here and takin' my bit smoke, and lookin' at the stars. Just a plain auld bagman sellin' silks and ribbons! I wish my line was traivellin' for stars. My jove! if I had stars to push, I could get orders! A line like that would gie me scope; I'm sometimes sick o' wastin' words on Shantungs[4] and on down-quilt patterns."

Mr Sloan was feeling nasty — distinctly nasty, having barked his shin on a sample case, and having an uneasy sense that he had forgotten something, and that he should have been home to his wife a good deal earlier. He wished to work himself into the proper spirit for a lively domestic altercation.

"What hae ye got in a' thae cases?" said he.

"Joy," said Jimmy, rappin' out his pipe upon his palm, and pursing up his mouth.

"Oh to bleezes!" said the man, "you're drunk."

"Just touched a wee, perhaps, wi' drinkin' starlight," said Jimmy. "But still I'm tellin' ye, I'm a traiveller for joy, and there's my samples. If I was openin' up my bags to ye, it's likely ye would only see dry-goods. I saw them, last, mysel' as dry-goods when I packed them, but it just came on me here in lookin' at the stars I was mistaken; there's naething in my bags but human joy."

The young men roared with laughter.

"'Scuse me, Mr Swan," said Mr Sloan, a little more agreeably, "I've often seen ye gaun aboot, and thought ye were in the drapery line; how was I to ken ye were traivellin' for beer?"

"No," said Jimmy, solemnly, "not beer! Wholesome human joy. Glowerin' at the stars there, I was tryin' to find some excuse for my paltry and insignificant existence, and then I minded I was an essential bit o' the mechanism for providin' dresses for the lassies o' Birrelton for next month's Territorial ball. Do ye think ye grasp me, Mr Sloan?"

"But what aboot the joy?" said Mr Sloan.

"That's joy," said Jimmy. "Youth, and a new frock! I ran over a'my samples in my mind, and there's no' a one that's no' a swatch o' something meant for comfort, consolation, the pleasure o' the eye, or the pride o' life. What would life in Birrelton be withoot me, or the like o' me? Man! that's one o' my ties ye're wearin', Mr Sloan! I wish ye would learn to put a better knot on't and gie the stuff a chance."

"Wha's tha' got to do wi' stars?" asked Mr Sloan, vaguely. "You said ye were sellin' stars. Or was it beer? I forget which."

"No," said Jimmy. "I'm not at present sellin' stars, though maybe that's in store for me if I could be a better man. I only mentioned stars because they set me wonderin' if an auld bagman was ony use at a' in that big scheme that put them twinklin' yonder … Good night, gentlemen! I'm aff to bed."

When they were gone, he watched the stars a little longer, finishing his pipe, and then went to the stand to take his coat upstairs with him. Instead of it he found the errant Sloan's.

"By George, I must get my coat," he said to Willie. "I have a pair o' gloves and a box o' chocolates for the wife in't."

Mr Sloan meandered home with that uneasy sense of something overlooked, forgotten, and only recollected what it was when his anxiously awaiting wife asked him if he had the mutton.

"Mutton!" he exclaimed with a sudden sinking of the heart. "What mutton?"

"Oh, John!" she said, "didn't you promise me to be sure and get a gigot for to-morrow? You know that it's the holiday, and all the shops 'll be shut. What am I to do for dinner?"

"As sure as death I clean forgot it, talkin' with a chap aboot the stars," said Mr Sloan, contritely, as she helped him to take off his coat.

She put a hand into its pockets and produced a pair of reindeer gloves and a box of chocolates. "What in all the world is this?" she asked him, and he stared, himself, confounded.

"I don't have ony mind o' buying them,"said he; "but that's a' right: I likely meant them for a peace offerin'."

"You're just a dear! "she cried, delightedly; "although you did forget the mutton," and she put the gloves on, finding them a perfect size.

There was a ringing at the door.

"I'm very sorry to disturb you at this hour," said Mr Swan, "but there's been a slight mistake. I have a coat the very neighbour of your husband's, and we got them mixed between us at the hotel. This, I think, is his; I wouldn't trouble you, so late, but I have to leave by the early boat."

"Oh!" she said, despairingly, "I might have known!" and started pulling off the gloves. "Then these are yours, and the box of chocolates?" The tears were in her eyes.

"No,"said Jimmy firmly. "There was nothing in my pockets, Mrs Sloan: your husband must have bought them,"and got his coat restored to him by a delighted wife.

"Who is he that?" she asked, when he was gone.

"Old Swan,"said Mr Sloan, half sleeping.

"What is he?" she asked. "I liked the look of him."

"Travels for stars," said Mr Sloan, vaguely; "bags full of joy! Old Jimmy Swan! He's drunk!"

2. *On the Road*

JIMMY WALKED briskly up No. 3 Platform, glanced in at the door of the luggage-van and counted his cases, gave twopence to the boy who had carried round his rug and hand-bag, passed off the latest pantomime wheeze on the guard, whom he addressed as "Alick,"and sank into his seat in the corner of the smoker just as the train, with a jolt, awoke to the necessity of doing something for its living. It was barely across the river when some one had produced a pack of cards, and Jimmy's rug was stretched between the knees of half a dozen men who played at Nap.[1]

"Come up to Brady's!" said Jimmy time and again, as he slammed an ace down in the centre of the rug and scooped in another shilling's-worth of coppers. On three occasions he went double Nap and got it.

"You've got all the luck the day, Mr Swan," said one of the players, an ambassador in the interest of Dray Gunn's biscuits,[2] who looked anxiously out at every stoppage of the train.

"Wrong, my son," said Jimmy. "Cards are like commercial travelling — one-fourth luck, half pluck, and the balance don't-give-a-damness."

"Bluff, you mean," suggested Dray Gunn.

"Bluff's no use unless you have the stuff," said Jimmy, shuffling. "That's the Golden Text for to-day in cards or commercial travelling ... I don't care to mention it, Maguire, but what about that twopence? ... Thanks."

"Where's this we're at?" asked the biscuit man at another station. "Stewarton. By Jinks! I should get out at Stewarton,[3] but I'll take it on the way coming back. I'm not going to break up the company."

There was a young fellow in a corner seat who didn't play, but sat embattlemented round by a pile of magazines having snappy names, like "System," "Success," and the "World's Work." He read them with the fervour of a budding sawbones studying for his First Professional. Sometimes he made notes on the back leaves of a traveller's order-book. Once he ate an apple, having pared it carefully first with an ivory paper-cutter, and Jimmy looked at him with paternal pity. It made him sad to see a fellow-creature recklessly spoil his appetite for dinner with such childish things as apples.

"Now that's a thing I never could do since I was a boy," said Jimmy — "eat apples in the middle of the day. It's a habit that grows on you till you become its slave. I don't say anything against the proper debauch of apples after business hours now and then — say at a Hallowe'en; but get into the habit of nibbling, nibbling, nibbling away at apples at all hours of the day, and before you know where you are your relatives begin to say there really ought to be Some Place of Confinement for unfortunate people with such a weakness."

"It's much more natural to eat apples than half-raw beef-steaks,"said the stranger.

"It's much more natural being dead than living,"retorted Jimmy, cheerfully; "for there's many more doing it, but hang it! look at the fun there is in being quite alive! I'm not blaming you, old man; I have some bad habits myself, but they're all in the interest of the firm. When I retire from business I'm going to take a house beside a water-fall."

"Man is really not a carnivorous animal,"said the apple-eater; "he's frugiverous."

"I don't say that he's quite so bad as all that,"said Jimmy, putting up the cards and handing them to their owner; "but he's a serious problem any way you look at him."

The young fellow got out at the same station as Jimmy, who was three-and-sixpence up on the forenoon's gambling, and as cheerful as if he had won a horse and trap in a sixpenny raffle.

"On the road?" asked Jimmy, mildly, as the porters trundled out cases for both of them from the van.

"Macdougall & Grant,"[4] said the other, handing him his card, and with the tone assumed by a visitor to Hamburg who says he is in the British Navy.

"A jolly good house!" said Jimmy, genially, though it was a formidable rival of his own. "Good luck to you! I'm Campbell & Macdonald;[5] name of Swan. So you're successor to old Kilpatrick? Good old Kil.! He and I began together on the road in the 'Seventies. Had it all our own way in these days. And a good man, too! Kil. and I would come out of any town you like to name in Ayrshire, neck and neck, and we had the whole North journey in the hollow of our hands. But Kil. had to pay pretty sweet for it . . . Kidneys, they tell me. Wonder how's his widow."

"That sort of way of making business is done,"said the young man, replete with all the philosophy of "System" and "Success." "A man, to make his own way on the road now, has got to have some knowledge of psychology."

"Oh, blazes!" said Jimmy, as they walked to the same hotel together. "What's that? Don't tell me it's nuts, or lentil soup, or anything like that. Or do you mean bumps?"

"It's the knowledge of human nature,"said the young fellow, fervently. "You've got to study your customer. Don't waste his time. Come to the point. Tickle him with some novel lines. A customer is like a trout; you mustn't throw the fly in with a splash. You must give him the idea that it's there by pure accident, and that if he doesn't hurry up and grab it some one else will have it before him. Once he takes it, you must play him gently; no jerk, no tug; and when you have his order in your basket, get out as quick as possible before he has time to meditate and make it a couple of dozen assorted instead of the level gross. The thing is to watch your customer's eye."

Jimmy chuckled — one of those deep, rich, liquid chuckles that add twenty per cent to his value for his salary. Across the flush of his countenance went a hundred wrinkled lines — the furrows of fun, irony, care, calculation, years, weather, and a little droop at the corners of the mouth begot of that sentiment known as tenderness which may be the greatest of commercial assets. His deep eyes twinkled.

"Man, Watson," he remarked, falling into the vernacular he has always made great play with in the villages: "Man, Watson! I fear you're far gone on aipples! A chap canna go about all day munchin' here and there all by himsel' at aipples without doin' himsel' harm. If old Kil. heard ye, he would turn in his grave. Ye'll no' get mony fish in your basket that way, either in Galloway or Ayr. Do ye think your customers are a' born idiots? Take my advice,

Mr Watson; I'm auld enough to be your faither: stop your
solitary aipple habit and burn a' your Yankee magazines.
There's only one way to catch and keep a customer — have
an honest liking for him as a human bein' just as clever in
his own way as yoursel', and see that your stuff's as good as
your warranty."

They dined together at the Buck's Head, where Jimmy
was *persona grata*. It couldn't very well be otherwise with a
guest who had been coming for twenty years; who had a
new cure for the rheumatism of Willie the Boots ("mix the
two and take a half-a-teaspoonful every morning in a little
tepid water, Willie. None of your hunker-slidin', now:
don't put ony spirits into the water"); who was deeply
interested in the landlady's Orpington hens, and had heard
in Glasgow a week ago with joy of her being a grand-
mother; who called the landlord Bob, and had a rattling
good cigar for him; and who asked the tablemaid when it
was coming off with her and John Mackenzie. Jimmy, to
the superficial vision, might seem an ordinary being surrounded by a rather shabby suit of Harris tweed, but as a
matter of fact he bore, for twenty yards all round him, an
aura, a personal atmosphere which took the chill from the
coldest rooms, and someway gladdened every creature
coming within its bounds.

He asked young Watson to join him in a drink; not that
he wanted one himself, but just because it is a symbol of
liberty, equality, and fraternity. And because he was
Jimmy. But Watson wouldn't; he alone was impervious to
the influence of auras.

"Good lad!" said Jimmy heartily. "Then have a small
limejuice and soda. Nothing better for brightening up the
— what-d'ye-call-it? — psychologic eye."

A little later Jimmy went toddling round to Gardener's,
the biggest draper in the place, in more respects than one,
and found young Watson there before him, practising all
he knew of the psychological on Mr Gardener, who maintained a great aloofness behind a desk from which it looked
as if all the psychology in the world and a hundred steam-

derricks could not for a moment budge him.

"Here I'm again, Bylie!"[6] Jimmy cried in at the door. "How's the wife? But I observe you're engaged; I'll see you later. See and be good to my friend Mr Watson — one of the best, and a good first journey means a lot for a young chap."

The aura appeared immediately to influence Bailie Gardener; he ponderously raised himself from off his stool, and with a perfunctory gance at drawers and shelves discovered a few items in which his stock was short, though far from being so short as it might have been had Watson been the late Kilpatrick. The science of psychology otherwise had no more effect on him than a glass of buttermilk.

Half an hour later Jimmy came sailing in to Gardener's.

"They put some queer chaps on the road now, Mr Swan," said the Bailie. "I doot yon yin's no' the weigh o' auld Kilpatrick."

"It's aipples,"said Jimmy, roguishly. "Aipples, and low-browed underground smoking-rooms in Gleska, and black coffee in the forenoon, and Yankee magazines called 'Success.' I'm sorry for the chap; a clever enough chap, mind ye, but spoiled wi' aipples. There's naething worse for wind. All the same, Bylie, we'll give the lad a chance; he'll learn. There wasna a greater idiot than mysel' when I first set out for C. & M ... I have a clinkin' story for ye for your next night's lodge harmony."[7]

Jimmy told the story as he walked behind the counter, pulled out drawers himself, and rapidly estimated how much of an order would bring the quantity of their contents to par. Bailie Gardener, sitting at the desk, complacently watched him turning over webs upon the shelving, running through the shirts, and totting up the blouses.

"Ye ken my stock better than mysel', I'm thinkin' sometimes, Mr Swan,"said he, as Jimmy blandly booked what he reckoned should be the order.

"It's what ye call the psychologic eye,"said Jimmy. "There's a whole lot o' books aboot it."

At high tea in the Buck's Head, Mr Watson seemed

unhappy; he had found the town a little unresponsive to the system of "Success" and the other snappy magazines, and in the aura of Jimmy he confessed it. Psychology itself could not have suggested a policy more likely to engage the sympathy of Jimmy Swan.

"I know, old man!" said he. "Dour! I've been there myself. You'll find it'll be all right when they know you, if you treat them like men and not like bloomin' dominoes. Get it out of your head that you're out to sell and then to hook it; you're out to make friends for yourself and the firm. You can't make friends by any process of philosophy, though you may get casual customers."

"And how can I make friends?"asked Watson humbly.

"By being sure that you need them more than they need you," said Jimmy. "That's the start of it. Another way is to live, like me, to the age of five and fifty. And then your friends are apt to be far too many."

3. *The Fatal Clock*

DAN SCOULAR, the third man in the Mantles, was to be married on Hogmanay, and the warehouse expressed its consolation in the customary way by means of a smoker and testimonial — James Swan, Esq., in the chair. For nearly twenty years there has been no presentation to an employee of C. & M. at which James Swan, Esq., has not firmly rapped on the table with the chairman's mallet, looked round the company with a pawky smile of the utmost self-possession, and said, "Gentlemen all!" preparatory to a speech which invested the occasion with almost national importance, and made the presentee determined that henceforth he should be worthy of the high encomiums passed upon his amiability, his genius, his industry, and general indispensability in the soft goods trade of Glasgow and the West of Scotland. Hundreds of brave and bright young gentlemen bound for matrimonial havens, or new drapery businesses of their own; for Leeds,

Bradford, London, Canada, or New South Wales, have gone out of Mancell's Restaurant[1] with Gladstone bags, gold watches, writing desks, silver salvers, eight-day clocks, or gorgeously illuminated addresses, whose intrinsic values were merely trivial as compared with that superimposed on them by the eloquence of Jimmy Swan. They might lose the illuminated addresses or salvers before they got home, but the memory of his speech was always a fragrant possession. For Dan Scoular's presentation, however, Mr Swan took up an unexpected attitude; he would not consent to preside as usual, unless the testimonial took some other form than a marble timepiece, and Scoular's preference was fondly set, as he told the committee, on this essential domestic feature.

"Mr Swan's determined on something else," he was told.

"What does he think it should be?" asked Scoular. "I'm sure there's nothing wrong wi' a good-goin' clock."

"He doesn't care what it is, but he bars a timepiece, and if we want him in the chair we'll have to meet his wishes."

"All right!"said Scoular. "Make it a case o' cutlery. It wouldn't be a testimonial at all unless we had him in the chair."

So a case of cutlery it was, and Mr Swan agreeably presided. When the moment came for the presentation rites, the cutlery case in tissue paper was suddenly produced in due and ancient form, as if by sleight-of-hand, from underneath the table, and Mr Scoular assumed the appropriate aspect of modest protestation and astonishment. As he said in his reply, he had not for a moment expected his friends to do anything so handsome.

Mr Swan sent the cutlery on a tour of the room that the subscribers might have the pleasure of reading the inscription on the case, and took the opportunity of expressing his gratification that the committee had selected this particular form of gift.

"For a young man startin' a house of his own," he said, "there are few things more appropriate than a case o' cutlery.

You have only got to lock it up and lose the key, and all risk of early bankruptcy due to the good-wife's social ambitions is averted. If I thought for a moment that the future Mrs Scoular was likely to use all that Sheffield steel and electroplate right off, I would advise Dan to swap it at the earliest opportunity for a sewin'-machine. But what she's sure to do, bein' a wise-like girl, as all of you know, since she has been five years in the silk department, is to place it carefully on the chiffonier,[2] with a biscuit-barrel on the top of it, till Dan becomes a partner. Meanwhile — except perhaps at a christenin' — she'll use the cutlery that's kept in the kitchen drawer. From scenes like these, gentlemen, auld Scotia's grandeur springs!"

"What about the clock?" cried some one in the background, and Jimmy twinkled.

"I was just comin' to the clock," he retorted, dropping into the vernacular his warmer moods demanded.

"Let me hasten to say, Mr Scoular, in case that remark has roused fond anticipations that are bound to be shattered, that there's naething mair for ye. There's no clock. And ye may thank me for there bein' no clock; if some o' the committee had their way o't, it's no' a dacent case o' cutlery ye would hae been gaun hame wi' on the Subway[3] the nicht, but a ton or twa o' the monumental sculptor's art on a lorry.

"Gentlemen," he proceeded, "I've seen far ower mony o' the stately tenement homes o' Scotland brought to ruin under the weddin' gift o' a massive marble timepiece, sometimes complicated wi' a couple o' objects reputed to be made o' bronze, and generously alluded to as 'ornaments.' It's a mean advantage to tak' o' ony young woman goin' to stay wi' a total stranger. For, remember, she has got to live wi' that timepiece a' day, and a' her days. Her man goes out to his work in the mornin' and comes back at night after a busy and cheerful day at the counter, and he never thinks o' her bein' shut up a' the time wi' an Italian monument that is for ever recallin' to her the shortness o' life and the solemnity o' the Necropolis.[4] There's no escape from it for her, poor soul! She canna lift it aff the mantelpiece and put it under a bed; it's as permanent in its place as a gasalier.

"The increasin' tyranny o' the marble timepiece has been obvious to some o' us for many years, but it is only within the last twa or three years I got a lesson in what it may lead to that has made me determined to discourage the marble clock as a presentation gift at ony function I may have the honour to be connected wi'.

"A customer o' mine in Mauchline went and got married three years ago. He was in the U.F. choir[5] and in the Rechabites[6] — a thing that micht happen to onybody — and the choir and the Rechabites agreed on a conjoint testimonial. They gathered £12, 10s., and when they broke the news to him that he was in for a presentation, he said he would have a marble clock, and would like to get pickin' one for himsel' in Gleska.

"Up he came to Gleska, which is the peculiar home and haunt o' the marble clock in the most deleterious forms, and drags me awa' from the warehouse to help him at the buyin'. I did my best to put him aff the notion by tellin' him o' happy homes I had seen broken up through the habit o' having aye a tombstone in the parlour; and I strongly urged a chiffonier and bookcase, or sewin'-machine, or a bedroom suite o' furniture. But no! MacLeerie had set his he'rt on a polished black sarcophagus, and would have me, richt or wrang, to a shop where they sell them in broad daylicht without the police interferin'. From scenes like these!

"I never thought there were sae mony ways o' bein' solemnly and distressingly ingenious in the cuttin' up o' black marble! The miscreants that do that kind o' work appear to have attempted everything! It was a pretty big shop, and it was full o' black monumental tombs that were made to look like Grecian temples, Roman altars, Rothesay villas, lighthouses, front elevations for Picture Palaces, tea-urns — ony mortal thing but clocks! Yonder they were, tickin' awa' like onything, and we walked up and down between the plots o' them, quite low-spirited, the same as it was a cemetery.

"MacLeerie had but the one idea about a clock — that it should be big, and black, and heavy. He picked the very biggest he could get for the money, and I tell you it was a whupper! It was three feet long and two feet high if it was an inch; had the weight of a fireproof safe, and was guaranteed a genuine reproduction o' the Madeleine Church in Paris. MacLeerie said he liked, particularly, the Madeleine touch.

"I protested to the last. I implored him, if he must have a clock, to take a small inlaid mahogany one wi' a sonsy, honest face, and buy a bangle for the mistress with the balance o' the money, but he was on for the mausoleum, and he got it! From scenes like these!

"The first time I was back in Mauchline after his marriage, he took me up to his house, and showed me the Madeleine in poseetion. I couldna have believed that ony earthly mantelpiece would stand the strain, but he showed me how it was done wi' brackets o' angle-iron.

"'How in the world did ye get it up the stairs?' I asked, and he explained that it was hoisted through the window wi' a block-and-tackle.

"That clock was in supreme possession o' the parlour! It brooked no rivals! It dwarfed the piano, the what-not, the saddle-bag suite, and the ancestral portraits. It took your eye away from the carpet, I was twenty minutes in the room before I noticed the tantalus spirit-stand. A more commandin' article o' British furniture I never saw than George MacLeerie's clock!

"But it wasna goin'!

"It hadna gone since it was erected! You see the pendulum could only be started from the back, or by givin' the whole edifice a shake, and gettin' into the back or givin' it a shake was out o' the question; ye might as well try to shift or shake the Pyramids o' Egypt.

"I ate brides-cake and drank the health o' the couple in front o' that amazin' clock, and I declare it was like layin' the memorial-stone o' a new Post Office! From scenes like these!

"Well, gentlemen, what was the natural and inevitable outcome o' MacLeerie's vanity? For a while it looked as if the couple was gettin' on quite satisfactory. By and by I found MacLeerie a little dreich in settlin' his bills, and heard that his wife was launchin' oot in the social line wi' regular days-at-home, progressive whist, and a vacuum-cleaner.[7] She was celebrated, ye understand, for having the biggest, heaviest, marble clock in Ayrshire, and she felt she had to live up to this distinction.

"She found, in a while, that her parlour furniture didna properly match the grand old Madeleine, and she had to get in a lot o' new things on the instalment system, includin' a pianolo and a fine new gramophone. The other ladies in the terrace would drop in on an efternoon and sit in front of the Madeleine listenin' to the music and thinkin' they were in Paris, and because the clock never went, they never knew the richt time, so that George's tea was seldom ready when he cam' hame. At last he didna come hame for his tea at a', but took onything that was handy at a public-house behind his shop; he couldna bear the sight o' his mausoleum. When grocers' accounts and the like o' that came to the hoose, Mrs MacLeerie aye stuck them behind the Madeleine for safety; and of course they never could be got oot again.

"The lang and the short o' it was that she, puir body, died one day in an effort to get below the clock and dust the mantelpiece, and her man, between her loss and his sequestration,[8] was so put aboot that he only survived a few weeks after her.

"It was only then the marble clock was put to its appro-priate purpose; the works were taken out of it; and it was re-erected on her final resting-place, where it mak's the brawest marble mausoleum in Mauchline. From scenes like these, gentlemen, auld Scotia's grandeur springs."

4. *A Spree*

HAVING FINISHED high tea at the George Hotel, Jimmy Swan, a little wearied after a cross-country journey of five-and-twenty miles in a badly-sprung waggonette,[1] sought out his usual bedroom, and searched his bag for slippers.

They weren't there!

The ready-flyped[2] extra socks were there; the shirts with the studs in them; the Cardigan waistcoat; the chest-protector he had never used in all his life; the little "house-wife" or bachelor's companion, with needles, thread, and buttons in it; the sticking-plaster; the bottle of fruit saline; the pocket Bible and the Poems of Burns; but not a hint of carpet slippers.

"I doubt Bella's gettin' a bit auld, like mysel'," he meditated. "It's the first time she forgot my slippers since we married. I'll hae to be awfu' angry wi' her when I get hame — if I can keep mind o't."

He went down to the Commercial Room and rang the bell for the Boots.

"Have ye a pair o' slippers, Willie?" he inquired.

"There's no' such an article in the hoose, Mr Swan,"said the Boots, "unless I got ye the lend o' the boss's."

"Oh, don't bother!" said the traveller. "I'll can dae withoot."

"We used to hae a couple o' dozen pair for the use o' you commercial gentlemen," said Willie, "but nooadays naebody asks for them; I suppose it's this new sanitary and high-jinkic education."

"The innkeepers made a great mistake when they stopped providin' slippers," said Mr Swan. "There was naething better for keepin' a customer in the hoose and no' stravaigin'[3] roon the toon wastin' his money in other premises. If ever I start an inn, I'll hae a pair o' slippers, a rockin'-chair, and a copious free supply o' cake and speldrins[4] for every customer. What's the result o' me no' hae'in' slippers? I'm just goin' awa' ootbye for a walk to mysel', and there's no sayin' where I may forgaither wi' a frien' or twa. No man's hame for the nicht until he has aff his boots."

He lit his pipe, and walked through the little town at the hour when the cows, that had been milked for the evening, were released from their byres and driven back to their common pasture. The Free Church bell was ringing for the Thursday prayer-meeting. The shops were shuttered. An odour of burning oak from the bakehouse, commingled with the curious redolence from the hot oven-sole, impregnated the atmosphere until he got so far as the smithy, where a little earlier sheep's heads had apparently been singeing. From what had once been the U.P. chapel,[5] and was now a hall for the Parish kirk, came the sound of choral voices.

Jimmy stood in front of the hall and listened. The combined Established and U.F. choirs were practising for the Ancient Shepherds'[6] annual church parade, and at the moment singing Sullivan's "Carrow"—

"My God, I thank Thee, who has made
    The earth so bright,
So full of splendour and of joy,
    Beauty and light;
So many glorious things are here,
    Noble and right."

Outside, on the pavement, he put in a restrained, but rich, resonant, and harmonious bass. A lifetime of encounter with bleak weather had not impaired his naturally mellifluent organ, and he counted no artistic joy so exquisite as the hearing of his own voice giving depth and body to the parts of a well-sung church tune. He knew all the words and harmonies of hundreds of hymns and psalms; they were ineradicable from his memory, which could never retain the words or air of a pantomime song for more than a week.

"That's Bob Fulton, my customer. puttin' them through their facin's for the Sabbath,"reflected Mr Swan. "Good soprano, capital alto, bass no' sae bad, but tenor, as usual, no' worth a docken. Ye'll no' get a dacent tenor in Scotland out o' Gleska; it must be something emollient and demulcent in Italian ice-cream.[7]

"A moment later, in a cessation of the singing, he put his head diffidently in at the hall door.

"Come awa' in, Mr Swan!" cheerfully invited the choir conductor. "We'll be nane the waur o' an extra bass."

"Oh, ye are daein' splendid, Mr Fulton!" said Jimmy, joining the musicians, with many of whom he was well acquainted. "Good attack; fine balance; tempo tip-top! Wi' an organ ye would just be as good as oor ain Cathedral."

But to his vexation, the practice was at an end. And he had just administered a peppermint lozenge to himself before entering, to get the proper atmosphere, and tone up the larynx!

"Hang it a'!" he said, "the night's but young yet, and I was fair in the key for a spree o' Psalmondy."

"The minister's for naething but the newer hymns on Sunday — except the Old Hundred[8] to begin wi'," said Mr Fulton, and the commercial traveller made a grimace.

"New hymns!" said he. "New fiddlesticks! He'll be takin' to Anthems next, and a solo soprano cocked up in the gallery cravin' the Wings o' a Dove wi' her mind on a new pair o' wings for her bonnet. There hasna been half a dozen new hymn tunes made in my time I would tolerate at my funeral; there's only 'Peace, Perfect Peace!' 'St Margaret,' 'Lead, Kindly Light,' 'St Agnes,' 'Pax Dei,' and 'Carrow' — there's no' much more in their novelties to boast o'. I wouldna gie St George's, Edinburgh, for a' the rag-time stuff in Sankey."[9]

"Let us have a try at St George's," said the conductor; "No. 141 in Carnie's Psalter — 'Ye Gates Lift Up.' and the choir, to show Mr Swan the traveller what it was equal to, proceeded to sing with astonishing vigour and address. The summer shades in zephyrs and in hosiery; new stripe and twill designs; the Mona Lisa (specialty of C. & M.), the slump in Bulloch's order, and the rumour of sequestration for Macbain might never have been in the mind of Jimmy Swan; he sang his bass like a soul transported high above the gross affairs of earth, and emulous of the cherubim. In the second part, where the voices of the males asked Who of Glory, no other bass infused the phrase with so emotional a sense of wonder, inquiry, and reverence; he might have been the warder Peter.

"Excellent!" he exclaimed, when they were finished. "I liked particularly the lah-soh-fah-me o' the tenors; it's the only bit we can aye depend on tenors gettin' a proper grip o', but a' your tenor, Mr Fulton, 's capital — what there is of it. If I might suggest another Psalm, it would be the Old 124th — 'Now Israel may say and that truly.'"

And the Old 124th it was. The inspiring bass of the visitor was enjoyed as much by the choir as by himself, and when he took his upper B's with a clarity no less assured than the sonorousness of his lower G's, there was an ecstasy in Jimmy's soul he would not barter for a fortune. He got his choice of an hour of Psalmody — Selma and Kilmarnock, Coleshill and Torwood, and Dundee, "Oh, Send Thy Light Forth" and "By Babel's Streams"; and Robin Brant, the joiner, leading bass was put upon his metal. Himself a man in his prime, of six-feet-three, he was determined no grey-headed traveller from Glasgow, rather small in stature and slightly paunchy, should beat a voice that had been brought to its perfection by daily warblings, pitched in tone to the constant bizz of a circular saw. But Jimmy Swan was envious or emulous of no one, utterly delivered over to the art of harmony and the meaning of the lines. It would there and then have seemed but reasonable to him that the portion of the blest should be to sing eternal Psalms. The weariness of his journey was dispelled; sharing a Psalm-book with another chorister, he rarely needed to glance upon its pages, he was doing what had been familiar and inspiring for him to do ever since the day the crackle left his adolescent voice, and he found he was a singer.

The rosy face was lit with animation; the shrewd grey

head just faintly moved in time to the wave of Fulton's pitchfork; when at "Invocation" he said "my harp, my harp, my harp I will employ," there was an absolutely luscious "dying fall" in the opening notes for tenor and bass which gave the flexibility and colour of his voice magnificent exposition, and he knew it, for he glanced across at Fulton with the mute inquiry in his eye — "Did ye hear me that time?"

"Ye're no' oot o' practice onyway, Mr Swan!" said Fulton. "Where in a' the world do ye keep it up?"

"Maistly on slow trains, when I ha'e a carriage to mysel',"said Jimmy. "Ye have no conception o' my compass on the N.B. Railway oot aboot Slamannan.[10] But to tell the truth, I'm no' much use at solos; I think I'm at my best when I swell the volume."

He went home to his inn with a pleasing sense of having spent a profitable evening. He had not only helped the harmony, but from a copious lore about psalm-tunes and their history he had entertained the choir to an instructive, though unpremeditated lecturette; and pledged himself to Mr Fulton to give the same at greater length with the choir as illustrators at a public gathering when he next came round.

At the door of the George the innkeeper was standing speaking to Miss Bryce, the mantua-maker, one of Jimmy's customers.

"There you are, Mr Swan," he said, "I've been asking high and low for you; I found you a pair of slippers."

"I've been employing my harp,"said Mr Swan, serenely blissful, "and I've had a glorious night o't, Robert.

'So many glorious things are here,
    Joyous and bright!'

Man! it's a blessin' we're no' born dummies! Good evening, Miss Bryce; I'm just lookin' forward to seein' ye in the mornin'."

"I hear from Mrs Clark you're going to favour us some day with a lecture on Psalmody. I hope ye'll tell us some o' your funny stories!" said the mantua-maker, who had the greatest admiration for his gifts as a raconteur, and the traveller looked ruefully at his host.

"She's a worthy body, Robert, but she doesna understand the grandeur o' solemnity, and the joy o' sacred song — if ye happen to be bass,"said Jimmy.

5. *His "Bête Noir"*

ALWAYS, WHEN Jimmy Swan is doing Birrelton, he puts off his visit to Joseph Jago's shop till the very last. The fact that there is a Joseph Jago mars, in some respects, the perfect bliss of his western journey, for of all his customers for a quarter of a century, Mr Jago is the only one to whose intelligence his peculiar humour has not penetrated. It is not because Mr Jago is old, for there are nonagenarians on the western journey who, for Jimmy Swan, are far more interesting than youngsters. Nor is it because Mr Jago is a dry old stick; Jimmy Swan makes a specialty of dry old sticks, and loves to hear them crackling when he puts, as it were, a match to them — the latest wheeze from the Merchants' Club, or a joke from "Punch," which does not circulate to any great extent in towns like Birrelton. To waste no unnecessary words on him, Mr Jago is old, and dull, and dismal, and deaf. Any one of these disabilities would seem a trifle to Jimmy Swan, but all of them combined in a single individual is more than even he can swallow.

Most distressing of all is Mr Jago's rooted conviction that C. & M.'s traveller is a wicked man of the world. He disapproves the knowing rake of Jimmy's business hat, his own idea of a tile being something much more solemn, straighter in its lines, and worn strictly perpendicular, only on Sundays and at funerals. Jimmy's patterned waistcoats, too, inspire distrust; for some unfathomable reason, fancy waistcoats are associated in Mr Jago's mind with horse-racing. And, finally, there is that unquenchable twinkle in Jimmy's eye. That twinkle, for Mr Jago, betokens many things — frivolity, foolish preoccupation with the things of time, theatres, public-houses, catch-the-ten, novelles, curling clubs, and Masons' meetings. When Jimmy Swan comes into Jago's shop, the owner always looks at him askance and troubled, feeling as he felt in 1876, when he was last away from Birrelton, and saw the frightful saturnalia of a Carters' Trip in Glasgow. It cannot be denied that Mr Swan is a first-rate traveller, and in that rôle indispensable to a country draper bound to keep abreast with the city's silly changes of fashions, but Mr Jago would have liked a man more grave; he cannot rid himself of the belief that Jimmy laughs at him, and sometimes tries to pull his leg.

Jimmy, having swept up all the other soft-goods orders of the town, went into Joseph Jago's shop the other day with a stifled sigh, prepared for a depressing hour and the usual misunderstandings.

Old Jago gave him a flaccid hand as cold and unresponsive as a flounder, and groaned some unintelligible salutation with a hanging lip and a rheumy glance of disapproval on the tilted hat.

"I would have been round sooner, but I was having a bite at the inn,"said Jimmy cheerfully.

"Better without it! better without it!" said old Jago, shaking his head. "It's a perfect ruination, morally and physically."

"Which do ye think the more deleterious?" asked Jimmy smiling: "the tea or the ham and eggs?"

"Oh, I thocht ye said drink," said Jago, taken aback.

"Not at all!" said Jimmy. "Just a solemn, single-handed affair o' stoking boilers. That's no' cloves ye smell; it's the camphor balls my wife persists in usin' to keep aff the moths. If you were a modern Gleska warehouse,[1] Mr Jago, I wouldna need to go to the inn for tea; I could have it in your room de luxe."

"My what?" said Mr Jago, with a hand behind his ear.

"Room de luxe," said Jimmy patiently. "'De luxe' is French for a penny extra on the cup and a d'oyley naipken.

All the big Gleska warehouses now, ye ken, have tea-rooms in them. The latest tip-top style o' decoration — Louis the Quatorze furniture and Adams friezes on the walls, Festoons. . . ."

"Balloons,"said Mr Jago, with a crafty look of incredulity.

"Ay!" said Jimmy, to save the time of explanation. "A band plays even-on behind a couple o' aspidestra palms, and ye can hear them quite plain daein' Maritana[2] or the Count of Luxembourg[3] quadrilles just the same as if it was in the West-End Park at the Exhibition."[4]

"It's droll I never heard of it!" said Mr Jago ironically.

"It's right, I'm tellin' ye,"said Jimmy. "It's not only tea and buns they give you; if ye want a fish and chips or a luncheon *table d'hote* at eighteenpence, it's there."

"I suppose ye'll have a place like that in C. & M.'s now?" said Mr Jago, marvelling at the traveller's imagination.

"Not at all!" said Jimmy. "We havenae any o' these facilities in the wholesale houses, and we just step out and round the corner wi' a customer the way we did a '76 when ye were there."

"Ye're a terrible man, Mr Swan!" said Mr Jago, shaking his head. "I think ye'll never be wise."

"I hope not," said Jimmy affably. "It doesna dae to be ower wise in this business."

Jimmy booked his orders as expeditiously as possible, but yearned to inform this obviously mistrustful mind of what it missed by vegetating in a shop in Birrelton. He got an unexpected opportunity. Old Jago turned again to the subject of Glasgow warehouse restaurants just to see how far the traveller's imagination would carry him.

"I suppose," said he, "they'll have the licence, Mr Swan? Ye'll can get a dram?"

"No fears o' ye!" said Jimmy. "They havena got that length yet. But there's no sayin' they're aye gettin' on. some o' them have rooms where ye can get writin' and rest-rooms."

"What dae they charge for the best rooms?" asked Mr Jago.

"There's no charge at all; ye just go into them and sit down, and tak' your crotchet wi' ye if ye like. There's naething more exhaustin' to the female frame than walkiin' for hours up and dow a warehouse looking for the hairpin department, or for some particular pattern o' taffeta not yet invented, worth a half a crown a yard but sold at eighteen pence."

"Man, ye're a great wag, Mr Swan," said old Jago with a cynical dry cough. "I wonder ye're no' frighted! I suppose the customers 'll come sailin' in in their balloons?"

"Balloons? "said Jimmy, amazed to find Mr Jago attempting a joke.

"Yes, ye said there were balloons."

"I never mentioned such a thing, Mr Jago," said the traveller, and Mr Jago groaned in tribulation for this errant soul.

"Ye did, indeed!" said he emphatically. "And may I ask if there's much advantage ta'en o' the fightin' rooms?"

Mr Swan put off his hat and wiped his forehead. His customer was decidedly more distressing than usual.

"It's no' the National Sportin' Club[5] I was talking about," he remarked, "nor the Suffrage Movement.[6] I was speakin' o' Gleska warehouses, Mr Jago. There's nane o' them hae fightin' rooms that I ken o'. When I think o't, it's may be an overlook."

"Do you know, Mr Swan, I canna believe a single word ye tell me!" said the righteous draper, fixing a remonstrant gaze on the crimson dots on Jimmy's waistcoat. "Business is business, and it might occur to you that I'm no' so daft as to credit the shrewd drapery firms o' Gleska wi' fritterin' awa' their shop room, their time, tea, potato chips, and fancy luncheons, on customers comin' in aff the street for a bolt o' tape or a cut o' worsted. We're no' that far behind in Birrelton; just last week there was a lassie frae a cocoa firm in England three days in the Store presenting cups of boilin' cocoa and Abernaithy biscuits to all and sundry. I'm perfectly certain it was for naething but the advertisement. But that's a very different thing from settin' up a restaurant and givin' awa' fish teas and fancy dinners and — "

"I didn't say you got the tea and the dinners for nothing," bawled Jimmy Swan.

"Ye needna speak so loud; I'm no' so deaf as a' that," said Mr Jago. "And ye certainly declared there was no charge at all."

The traveller pocketed his order-book and packed his samples, incapable for a while of further disputation with this perverse and afflicted customer. But he was not done with him.

"It's a lang time since ye were in Gleska, Mr Jago," he remarked. "I'm no' surprised ye're dubious."

"I'm no' dubious at all; I'm just astonished at ye, Mr Swan," said Jago.

Jimmy chuckled. "And yet," said he, "it's naething to what ye'll see in some o' the shops in London. There ye'll can play a game o' cairds or billiards while your wife's at the bargain counter fightin' for her life; and the warehouse has a creche where the careful and devoted mother leaves her baby till she gets her pattern matched."

"Just that!" said Mr Jago dryly. "Keep at it, Mr Swan, while you're warm. Do they haud your dog for ye?"

"Upon my word they do!" said Jimmy. "They'll keep your dog or stable your horse for ye, or garage your motorcar. They would do ony mortal thing to keep you on the spot; I believe they would embalm ye if they thought your widow would come in at times to see ye."

"Oh, ye're an awfu' man!" said Joseph Jago. "Do ye no' think, Mr Swan, ye've come to a time o' life when ye should be settlin' doon to think soberly o' things? It's no' richt to be makin' a mock o' everything"; and his voice was full of a quaver of pious grief.

"Ach! to the mischief!" said the traveller in a discreet undertone, as he tightened a strap on a sample case. "I might as well try to talk to a skim-milk cheese!"

6. *From Fort William*

WHEN JIMMY Swan is travelling in the North, sufficiently remote from the Second City of the Empire to run any risk of being taken immediately at his word, he proffers his customers a Glasgow hospitality which would ruin C. & M. if it were exercised at their expense. But C. & M. have nothing to do with it; the only person who has cause for apprehension, if she knew the facts, is Mrs Swan. Her little house in Ibrox couldn't hold a fiftieth part of the people Jimmy invites to come and stay there. For the last week-end on which there was an International Football Match at Hampden,[1] he had five-and-thirty customers urgently engaged to come to Glasgow and sample the cosiest flat in Gower Street.[2] They were all to come from somewhere north of the Caledonian Canal; customers south of that got a genuine Mazeppa cigar.

Nemesis waits on such commercial strategists. Jimmy forgot, some weeks ago, that Fort William is on the wrong side of the Caledonian Canal, and instead of simply giving Peter Macaskill a Mazeppa cigar, he invited him to come to Glasgow soon and see the Kinemacolor[3] pictures.

"I would like fine!" said the draper eagerly, after hearing all about them, and the Gower Street flat, and Bella's fairy touch on pastry. "Would next week-end do?"

"Capital!" said Jimmy, beaming with delight, and taking out his diary. "I see there's a fine train at ten o'clock, and the fare's only 15s. 9d. return."

"Ay; that's the fare for ordinar'," said Mr Macaskill; "but there's a special week-end trip next Saturday at 9s. 6d. Depend on me bein' there."

"Good man!" said Jimmy heartily. "If you don't come, I'll be awfully disappointed. Mind and bring a waterproof, and leave your presentation watch at hame."

A week later, at the breakfast table, he got a wire from his customer — "Arriving Queen Street 2.16." He scrutinised it through his spectacles with mock dismay.

"What's the matter, Jimmy?" asked his wife anxiously. "Is Aunty Mary deid? Or anything wrong wi' James?"

"It's naething o' that sort at a'," he answered her. "It's the world that's gettin' ower wee. When I started on the road first, Fort William was aboot the length o' Malta; men were born, and grew up, and mairried, and were made deacons o' the kirk, and died in Fort William withoot ever clappin' eyes on a railway train.[4] Nooadays the great Scottish cigar belt is steadily pushin' north till a chap's hardly safe to hand oot onything but Mazeppas nearer hand than Ullapool and Lairg. The lang and the short o't is that Peter Macaskill's comin' this afternoon, and we'll have to put him up till Monday."

"Is he a good customer?" asked Mrs Swan, no way perturbed.

"The best," said her husband.

"Then I'll have to ha'e a hen!" said Mrs Swan emphatically, and Jimmy gently nipped her.

In England, I believe, it takes the form of a caress.

Mr Macaskill came with a reassuring hand-bag little bigger than a gynaecologist's, and under Jimmy's guidance steadily worked his way through all the picture places within a radius of a mile from Sauchiehall Street. He had never seen the cinematograph before; it fulfilled every demand of a truly artistic soul hitherto starved upon pictures in the "People's Journal"[5] and monotonous scenic effects on Ben Nevis. The latest picture houses, where you could sit at a table earnestly drinking tea and eating penny sweet-cakes without the necessity for withdrawing your eyes for a single moment from the thrilling episodes of "The Bandit's Daughter," specially appealed to him; he grudged every moment that they spent in the streets going from one show to another.

"He's like a new message-boy the first day in a sweetie shop," said Jimmy to his wife that night when their guest had gone to bed. "Another day o't would scunner him. I was never so tired mysel' o' cinemas in a' my days; I've seen as mony o' them, Bella, as'll dae me for a twelvemonth. I'll dream a' nicht o' horses gallopin. and tenements on fire. I almost wish the West Hielan' Railway wouldna pander to the rural districts wi gi'en them week-end tickets at rideeculous rates; the railway fares in Scotland's far too chape."

"Tuts! he's a nice cheery chap, Mr Macaskill," said Mrs Swan. "I'm awfu' glad to see him," and Jimmy gently nipped her.

"So am I," said he. "The only thing to worry me would be that he might be a bother to yoursel'." And again he nipped her, this time on the ear.

On Sunday evening, still replete with hen, Mr Macaskill, whose salient characteristic was shrinking diffidence, became deeply and nervously engrossed in the contemplation of a penny time-table. Having cleared his throat noisily several times, he ventured the stammering remark that five in the morning was an early start.

"It depends on what ye're startin' for," said Mr Swan. "If ye're in a club, for instance, five o'clock in the mornin's no' a bit too early to go hame to supper."

"I was thinkin' o' the train to-morrow mornin' for Fort William," said the guest, embarrassed. "It leaves Queen Street Station at ten minutes to six. I'm vexed to think o' puttin' ye up for such an hour, Mrs Swan."

"Hoots!" said she, "there's surely a more wise-like train than that, Mr Macaskill?"

"Unless ye think the polis have a clue to your identity," said Jimmy. "Is the afternoon train no' good enough?"

"It would do me fine, but I'm an awful bother to ye," said Macaskill. "I'm takin' ye off your work."

"Not you!" said Jimmy, with genuine warmth. "It's a privilege. Stay till the 5.12 train in the afternoon, and see some more o' the picture-houses; there's dozens ye havena seen yet. Ye'll can easy find them yoursel' if ye follow the croods, and I'll meet ye at one o'clock for a bite o' lunch."

So Macaskill spent the forenoon writing home to his wife that he would be home to-morrow, and by four o'clock he had covered several quite fresh picture palaces and lunched with Mr Swan. At five minutes past four he looked at his watch, and stammered an allusion to the fact that there was a place called Fort William.

"There's no use o' ye goin' awa' there the day," said Jimmy, politely. "The shop would be shut before ye got hame, onyway; wait till to-morrow and go back in style."

Mr Macaskill gulped an unuttered explanation that no matter what day he went back he could not get from Glasgow to Fort William in time to find the shop open unless he started at 5.50 in the morning, and that night Mrs Swan had a splendid pie for supper.

"Ye're just a perfect wee wonder!" said Jimmy, and he nipped her.

On Tuesday, at breakfast, Mr Macaskill said, with something almost approaching firmness, that he must certainly make tracks for home in the afternoon.

"Dear me!" said Mrs Swan, "ye're surely awfu' tired o' us goin' awa' already! I'm sure to-morrow would be time enough."

It shook him. He looked at the plump and rosy little partner of James Swan the traveller; marked the dimples and the genial smile of her, and felt that nothing he could do to please her must be left undone.

"Well," he said, "I maybe might could stay till tomorrow, but I must be there to open the shop on Wednesday mornin'."

"Good man!" said Jimmy Swan, effusively; "I was just hopin' ye would change your mind. Man! ye havena seen the half o' the picture-palaces!"

Mr Macaskill wrote a letter home to say he was unfortunately detained till Wednesday, and with now unerring instinct for the real good stuff in Glasgow, found several picture-palaces on the south side of the river, where he spent the best part of the day, though by this time most of the films were become familiar.

He lost his way, and got back to Gower Street at night a little tired, but adamant in his determination to leave by the early morning train, if Mrs Swan would waken him at half-past four. That night there was for supper the finest brandered haddocks he had ever tasted.

"Look here, Bella!" said Jimmy Swan, when the guest had gone to bed; "is this a domestic house or sanatorium?"

"Don't be silly, Jimmy," said she. "I'm sure he's welcome; and him a valuable customer o' yours."

"But, my goodness!" said her husband, "if we keep him much langer awa' frae his shop he'll no' be a customer at all! It'll no' be there! Naething for me, after this, but the Mazeppa cigar, even, by heavens, if it was in Thurso!" But all the same he nipped her.

Of course, Mr Macaskill was not wakened in time for the early train; it was impossible, with all that brandered haddock. Mr Macaskill manfully concealed his chagrin at breakfast-time. He stammered and stuttered, and agreed that, after all, the afternoon train would suit him better. There are only two trains in the day from Queen Street to Fort-William. He found he had overlooked some really creditable picture-palaces in the east end of the city, and renewed acquaintance with "The Bandit's Daughter."

That night, Mrs Swan had in a couple of friends who sang divinely, and some exquisite devilled kidneys. When their visitor talked of going on the morrow, she seemed to bridle up, and said she knew he was sorry he had come to Glasgow.

"Not at all!" he eagerly declared. "I've had a tip-top time! Ye've been awfu' good to me."

"Jimmy's oldest friend!" she said (it wasn't, strictly speaking, true), "you'll vex me greatly if ye dinna bide till Thursday."

"I should think so!" said Jimmy.

So Mr Macaskill waited till Thursday, when Jimmy casually suggested Friday as a better day for setting out to Fort William. Mrs Swan continued to have the most engaging suppers, and said that Friday was unlucky.

So Mr Macaskill did not leave till Saturday, having by that time discovered all the picture-palaces in the suburbs.

When Mr Macaskill got home to Fort William after a

week of absence, his wife was at the station in a condition of nervous prostration.

"What in all the world do ye mean by this carry on?" she asked him, tearfully. "I was just makin' up my mind I was a widow woman. Just three clean collars and one pocket-naipken wi' ye, and ye stayed a whole week! I'm black affronted!"

"As sure as anything I couldna get away a minute sooner!" said Macaskill, penitently. "Mr and Mrs Swan wouldna let me."

"Ye said ye would be back on Monday," said his wife.

"And every day since then ye wrote me saying ye would be sure to be to-morrow."

"And every time I wrote I meant it," said Macaskill. "But ye don't understand the Swans, Margaret; they're that hospitable; every move I made to go, they raised some opposition. I believe they would keep me a' my days in Ibrox if I didna summon up my nerve at last, and pick up my bag and make a bolt for it."

"And what in the name o' Providence did ye find to do for a week in Gleska?"

"Ye may well ask, Margaret!" said her contrite husband. "There's nothing yonder to be seen but picture-palaces. I went to them even on, day after day, and I can tell you I was sick o' them! I would sit in them for hours on end plottin' what way I could get away home from Gleska without hurtin' the feelin's o' Mr and Mrs Swan. Nothing could exceed their kindness, but they might have considered the possibility that I had my shop waitin' on me in Fort William. I'm tellin' you, it's me that's the happy man to be home again, Margaret."

7. *Jimmy's Silver Wedding*

"Do you know what Wednesday week is?" asked Mrs Swan, with a surprising attempt at archness for a woman who had brought up a fairly large family.

"Wednesday week's a lot o' things, Bella," said Jimmy, brushing his hair in a pensive humour induced by the reflection that it was not getting any thicker on the top. "It's the day I have to get up and work, for one thing. It's the day I'm nearly goin' to lose the train. It's the day C. & M.'s no' goin' to raise my salary. It's the day I'm no'·goin' to get nearly as many orders as I think I deserve. It's the day I'm goin' to sell ls. 4¹/₂d. Cotton Shantung at ls., and muslin one-piece robes worth a guinea at 12s. 6d. It's the day I'm no' goin' to buy a motor-car or a steam yacht for ye. It's the day that's likely to be wet, for I'll be in Inverness. It's the day I'm goin' to wish to the Lord I had gone in for some other job than commercial travellin'. It's the day nobody's goin' to die and leave me anything. It's the day that's goin' to pass like any other day, and me a gey tired man at the end o't. Just the ordinary kind o' day, and when it's past it'll be bye!"

"Tuts!" said Mrs Swan, impatiently. "Do ye not mind what happened five-and-twenty years ago come Wednesday week?"

Mr Swan put on his coat reflectively. "Five-and twenty years ago? Let me see, now. Was that the day I was teetotal. Or was I hame at exactly the hour I said for my tea?"

"Never in your life," said Mrs Swan, with emphasis. "But the 13th o' July's an important date you might well keep mind o'. It's the day that we were married. It's our silver wedding."

Mr Swan gasped, "Silver weddin'!" he exclaimed. "Man, I'm astonished at ye, Bella! Ye're a' wrang wi' your calculations. It's no' a dozen years since we were married; I mind fine, for I was there!"

"And where did a' the weans come from, James Swan?" asked his wife.

"Oh, well! if you put it that way!" said Jimmy.

"Well, say fifteen years."

"John's twenty-one, and if Annie had been spared she'd have been twenty-three on Saturday."

"Silver weddin'! my jove, Bella, but that's a start! I aye thocht silver weddin's was for auld totterin' bodies wi' wan leg in the grave and the other on the road to the poorhouse. And look at us!" He surveyed himself in the looking-glass. "A fine, upstandin', fresh-complexioned, athletic young fellow, lacin' his ain boots every day he's awa' frae hame. And there's yoursel' — Bella Maclean or Swan; first in the Grand March, wearin' sky-blue dress with polka dots; the real and only belle of the ball; good for Wilton Drive![1] By jings, Bella, do ye mind the time I advertised ye? And there ye are yet, getting chubby a wee, but what an eye! and what a step runnin' up the stair! They're no' turnin' oot the same stuff nowadays at all. If only you could play the piano!"

Mr Swan did not go to Inverness on Wednesday week. Instead he took a silver wedding honeymoon holiday with his wife, and they went to Kirkfinn, chosen, first, because Mrs Swan had never been there; and, second, because there was never enough trade in the two or three drapers' shops of that sleepy village to tempt the commercial traveller to take his samples with him and combine sordid business with the poetic joys of a silver wedding celebration.

"Your cases 'll be in the van, Mr Swan?" said Charlie, the Black Bull boots, at the station.

"Not this time, Cherlie," said Jimmy. "Here's a bag; that's all. This is a special run; I'm here with a sample wife — ah! ye needna glower, ye rascal; it's ma ain. Ye'll no forget the extra pair o' boots in the mornin', and ye needna knock me up till nearly nine; nae hurl to Kirkmichael for me to-morrow."

"And this is Kirkfinn,"[2] said Mrs Swan. "It's no that big, and still many a pair o' sox you lost in it."

"It's no' the size that coonts wi' toons on the northern circuit," said her husband, cheerfully; "it's the genial atmosphere, and there's whiles when Kirkfinn is awfu' hard on sox."

She was surprised that everybody seemed to know him as they went along the street.

"Of course they do!" said he. "What would hinder them? I've been comin' here since the year o' the Tay Bridge storm,[3] and they look on me as a kind o' institution like Ord-Pinder's Circus. Ord-Pinder's clown and me's celebrities."

"It must be an awfu' dreich place in the winter," said Mrs Swan, though gratified by the public interest manifest in the lady accompanying a visitor who for more than a quarter of a century had seemed wedded only to a barrowload of sample-cases.

"Dreich!" he exclaimed, derisively. "Nae fears o't! When things get slack they start a cookery-cless or a sale o' work for a new flag for the Rechabites. There's nae dreichness about Kirkfinn, I'm tellin' ye!"

"At any rate, it must be a healthy place; everybody looks well up in years," said Mrs Swan. "They'll no' take many troubles in a bracin' place like this."

"Troubles!" retorted Jimmy. "They take every trouble that's goin' except the tattie disease, and whiles I think they don't miss even that. But that's because they're in the Rechabite Tent, and get the benefit."

"If they're all in the Rechabites," said Mrs Swan, "it must be a very sober place."

"A Tent's no' a tenement hoose," said Jimmy; "it's easier to get oot and in to."

Though he protested business was the very last thing he would permit to intrude upon their honeymoon, their dinner at the Black Bull Inn was scarcely over when the habits of thirty years possessed him, and the first place he must take his wife was to one of his customers. They started out ostensibly to walk beside the river, but for half an hour they never got farther than Abraham Buntain's shop.

"Here I am again, Mr Buntain," said Jimmy, bursting in on the drapery counter. "You wouldna get the usual card notifyin' ye o' my comin', but it's all right. A special line in quiet grey summer-weight fancy tweeds, for immediate holiday wear," and he brought his wife forward with an arm about her waist.

"None of your nonsense, Jimmy," said Mrs Swan, blushing becomingly.

"If the wearer goes with the tweeds," said Abraham Buntain, gallantly, "you can put me down for an immediate delivery. Glad to see you in Kirkfinn, Mrs Swan. We all know Mr Swan in Kirkfinn, but it's the first time he has given us the chance to see who turns him out so creditably."

"Well, there she is," said Mr Swan in his professional manner. "Unique. Chaste pattern. None of your French models; British throughout. Durable. Unshrinkable — quite the contrary. A little dearer to begin with than flashier-looking stuff, but pays itself a thousandfold in.the long run. The colours don't run."

"You're making them run pretty badly all the same," said Mrs Swan, with a smile, and blushing more than ever.

"I must say I like the style," said Mr Buntain, entering into the spirit of the thing.

"I should think you do!" said Jimmy, buoyantly. "With any eyes in your head. It's a style that caught my fancy five-and-twenty years ago, and I've never tired of it. This season it's the tip-top of fashion — one of those Victorian revivals, you understand; nothing like the old patterns! Sometimes my eye's been caught — when I was younger, I mean — by a bit of Marquisite fancy voile or French foulard, but, bless your heart! there's no wear in them, and no warmth. I don't conceal from you, Mr Buntain, that I consider mysel' pretty lucky."

Mr Buntain was prepared to make the silver wedding Jaunt to Kirkfinn a satisfactory commercial proposition by giving a handsome order there and then for autumn lines, but Jimmy resolutely refused to book it now. "I'm not with C. & M. this week," he declared; "I'm with Mrs Swan, and we're on our honeymoon — and oh, by the way, I want to buy her a costume-length of your homespun tweed." And he did it, too, at strictly local retail prices, refusing to avail himself of any trade discount.

"Before we go along the river, Bella," said Mr Swan

when they came out of Buntain's, "I want to run in and say how-d'ye-do to Miss Cleghorn. Here's her shop — a good old customer of mine."

"Good gracious!" said Miss Cleghorn. "Your silver wedding! I would never have thought it, Mr Swan, and I'm sure I wouldn't think it of you, Mrs Swan."

"She doesn't look a bit chafed, does she, Miss Cleghorn?" asked Jimmy.

"She looks a good deal too good for you," replied the roguish shopkeeper.

"Don't spoil her by giving that away," said Jimmy. "It's the truth, but I've aye kept dark about it."

"Five-and-twenty years is a long time," pensively said Miss Cleghorn, who had lived that period at least in a state of virgin expectancy, and at times was apt to become impatient with the deliberation of the local matrimonial market. "Did ye never tire of him?"

"I tired of him the very first week I married him," laughed Mrs Swan, "and I think he tired of me in less."

"I did," said Jimmy, frankly. "And now I'm sure I wouldn't tire of her in fifty years. H'm! Inscrutable are the ways o' nature! I want to buy her one o' these Vienna sun-or-shower umbrellas we sent down to you last month, Miss Cleghorn."

"You're the happy pair!" said Miss Cleghorn, when this second wedding gift had been presented. She, too, had an autumn order for C. & M. in readiness, but the traveller would have none of it this visit, saying he had not his order-book.

As they were leaving the shop she laughingly cried them back. "I wonder," said she, "if Mr Swan wouldn't book me an order for a husband?"

"What kind?" said Jimmy, whipping out the orderbook whose possession he had just a moment before denied.

"Just one like yourself," replied Miss Cleghorn gaily, and still half meaning it. "I fancy I could not do better."

"Very good!" said Jimmy, gravely, and he wrote down: "Husband; middle-aged, but feeling fine; not righteous overmuch, a fair to middling quality. Must sing bass, and be a good deal away from home."

"I'll get him for you!" he declared as he pocketed the book.

8. *A Matrimonial Order*

MISS CLEGHORN was a jocular body, or conscious that she had reached the desperate stage of spinsterdom, or was, more probably both, for a month having elapsed without James Swan implementing her order for a husband, she sent him a postcard with the expressive intimation, "Special order not yet invoiced." Jimmy took it home to his wife for her opinion as to whether his Kirkfinn correspondent was really in the market or only taking a rise out of him.

"I booked the order right enough," said he, "but I thought she was in fun."

"A maiden lady of Miss Cleghorn's age is never in fun about a thing like that, though she may think herself she is," said Mrs Swan. "Yon Kirkfinn's a very lonely place, nothing but the birds whistling, and even they get tired of it. You better hurry up and send the body what she wants before the season's over."

"It's no' in our line at all," said Jimmy; "she ought to apply to a Matrimonial Agency. They would send her down some samples or a likely fellow on appro."

"Ye were the sample yoursel', James," his wife retorted, "and she told ye she wanted something as near the pattern as possible."

"Bless your heart! I canna guarantee an absolute duplicate. There's no' mony o' my kind left, or we're aye picked up as soon as we're in the window. I have no idea where to look for the article she wants. All the bachelor chaps I ken are a bit shop-soiled and oot o' fashion."

"Ye were a bit shop-soiled yoursel', James Swan, when I got ye," said his wife. "But whit's a little Glasgow smoke? Ye were guaranteed to wash. Except that ye're a trifle frayed aboot the edges and wearin' thin on the top, ye're no discredit to your wife and family."

"She may be in fun," said Mr Swan, sitting down to tea, "but the honest truth is that Miss Cleghorn would be nane the waur o' a man. Yon shop o' hers would double its trade in a twelve-month if there was a man in it to give the genuine Gleska touch. Did ye ever see such windows? Tea-cosies and combinations, delaines[1] and Turkey reds,[2] sand-shoes and sun-bonnets; and every noo and then a bill to notify the public o' Kirkfinn that somebody's lost an umbrella. To the mischief wi' their lost umbrellas! It's no' her business to be advertisin' for lost umbrellas; let them come to her and buy a new yin! It's my opinion that when a case o' goods from C. & M. comes to Miss Cleghorn she just coups[3] as much as she can o't into her windows, wi' her eyes shut, and puts what's left in some cunning place below the counter where she canna find it again. The art o' shop-dressin', Bella, is for men. Miss Cleghorn, they tell me, is a tipper at trimmin' hats, the thing she was brought up to, but she has no more notion o' a well-trimmed shop than she has o' operatic music."

"I saw that," said Mrs Swan.

"Then she wants nerve — "

"Considering everything, I wouldn't say that was where she was deficient," said Mrs Swan.

"I mean business nerve. She's timid; wi' the dozen assorted type o' mind. If I sent her a gross o' anything — and she could easy sell it — she would take a fit. So she can never buy so cheap as Abraham Buntain can. Her selection is fair ridiculous; if I didn't keep her right she would still be tryin' to tempt Kirkfinn wi' tartan blouses and silk mitts. But where she fails most lamentably is in credit to the wrong customers. Any kind o' fairy story 'll get roond Miss Cleghorn, and her ledger's mostly a' bad debts. ' Perhaps they havna got it, puir things!' she says. Maybe no', but they've got her! And still she makes no' badly aff her business."

"Enough to keep a man?" asked Mrs Swan.

"I'm tellin' ye the right sort o' man would double it. What that shop wants is b-i-f-f — biff!"

"What the shop seems to want, and what would suit Miss Cleghorn otherwise, I think," said Mrs Swan, "is Will Allan o' the Mantles."

Her husband stared at her with admiration.

"Ye're a most astonishin' woman, Bella!" said he.

"I never thought o' Allan, and he's the very man. What made ye think o' him?"

"Oh, he comes from her quarter o' the country, and he's like hersel' — ye mind he had a disappointment in his youth."

"Had she?" asked Mr Swan, amazed at his partner's knowledge.

"Of course she had!" said Mrs Swan, emphatically.

"Can ye think o' any other reason for a wyse-like woman like yon lookin' after a shop in Kirkfinn? Forbye, she told me — when I met her on the Sunday."

That very night a letter from Mrs Swan was sent inviting Miss Cleghorn to spend some days with her in Glasgow.

Mr Swan took the earliest opportunity of having a little private conversation with Mr William Allan of the Mantle Department, and asked him casually to supper for the following Friday night. "I'll likely have one or two friends from the country," said he offhand. "There's one at least — a lady friend o' Bella's who hasna been in Gleska since the time the Haverley Minstrels[4] were in Hengler's Circus."[5]

"Lucky girl!" said Mr Allan, cynically. "There's been nothing really doing in Glasgow since about that time. I mind of taking a lady friend to see the Haverleys." It seemed a pious and moving recollection.

"Was her name, by any chance, Dunlop?" asked Mr Swan, with romantic interest.

"I don't know what it is now," said Mr Allan, pensively; "but it was certainly not Dunlop at that time. Painful subject, Jimmy; your wife knows all about it."

"She's gey close, the wife," said Mr Swan, craftily. "Anyway, this is a Miss Dunlop. Keeps a shop. No' far off fifty — "

"Prime o' life!" muttered Will Allan of the Mantles, with sober conviction; it was about his own age.

" — Plump. Fair-complexioned. As cheery as another chap's weddin'! It's a wonder to me, Will, that sort o' woman doesna marry, hersel'. Ye know Kirkfinn?"

"Fine!" said Mr Allan, emphatically. "I served my time there, but I haven't been near the place for twenty years. Painful subject, Jimmy; your wife knows all about it."

"It's no great catch havin' a bit shop wi' a lot o' bad debts in Kirkfinn. It's the sort o' place where the most attractive kind of girl might sit on a sofa till it was a' sagged down waitin' for a lad to sit beside her, and die o' auld age before the springs recovered their elasticity. It's the sort of place where it's aye so long to the Cattle Show, or so long after it. When I'm in Kirkfinn, the Boots at the Inn has to pry open my door wi' an iron pinch to waken me — sound sleep's the one thing that Kirkfinn is famous for. That and hens! Ye canna venture to walk through Kirkfinn without skliffin' your feet in case ye come on eggs."

"I aye liked poultry," confessed Mr William Allan. "And there's nothing wrong with Kirkfinn; I sometimes wish I had never left it."

Miss Cleghorn promptly accepted the Glasgow invitation, with a quite unconvincing story of being seized for the first time in many years with a desire to see the autumn shows.

"Glad to say I've managed to fill that line for you," said Mr Swan, turning up his order-book. "'Middle-aged, but feeling fine; a fair to middling quality; not righteous overmuch; sings a kind of bass, and is a good deal away from home.' I can send it off to you at any time."

"None o' your nonsense, Jimmy!" said his wife.

"I wouldn't insist on his being much away from home," said Miss Cleghorn, quite in the spirit of the thing. "You see it's pretty lonely in Kirkfinn. Is he on appro.?"

"Not in these goods, Miss Cleghorn," said Mr Swan. "They get so easily chafed. And we don't keep a big stock. You see the whole demand nowadays is for thin fancy stuff that gratifies the eye for a season at the most, but has no wearin' quality, no body. But I'm no' askin' ye to buy a pig in a poke; it's a Mr Johnson, and he's comin' here the night to supper."

Miss Cleghorn crimsoned. "Of course you understand I'm only joking, Mr Swan," she said, in nervous apprehension.

"So am I," said Mr Swan. "I'm the jokingest wee chap! Amn't I, Bella?"

When Mr and Mrs Swan retired to their bedroom that night, they sat down and laughed as heartily as consideration for the feelings of their guest next door would allow.

"My! didn't she get a start when she saw it was Will Allan?" said Mrs Swan.

"But did ye notice Will?" asked Jimmy, almost suffocated with suppressed amusement. "'I understood it was a Miss Dunlop,' says he, gaspin'. 'My mistake!' says I, 'the right name slipped my memory! Miss Cleghorn's up for autumn bargains; I had no idea that ye kent her.'

"And they quarrelled twenty years ago!" said Mrs Swan, tremulous with the thought of the still romantic possibilities of life. "She told me all about it in Kirkfinn."

"Have ye any idea what about?" her husband asked.

"She told me," replied Mrs Swan in a paroxysm of restrained merriment. "You could never guess! It was because he would insist on partin' his hair in the middle! She considered it looked frivolous. And now — oh, Jimmy, I'm sore with laughing! — now he hasn't enough to part one way or another any more than yourself!"

"Tuts!" said Jimmy, rubbing his head. "A trifle like that! No wonder they made it up again so easily! I'm sort of vexed for C. & M.; they look like losin' a first-rate man in the Mantles."

9. *A Great Night*

THERE ARE villages to which Jimmy Swan goes, burdened
with all his sample-cases, as conscientiously as if he were
visiting a metropolis, though it might appear that the
profits on the orders he secures will hardly pay for the post-
hiring. Among them is Birrelton,[1] which is so unimportant
that it isn't even given on the maps. When C. & M.'s
ambassador of commerce puts his cases down in front of
the only draper's shop in Birrelton, as he does twice a year,
the whole vehicular traffic of the Main (and only) Street is
diverted up the lane behind the smithy, and the populace
realise that the long-familiar range of tweeds, prints,
winceys, voils, and underskirts in Dawson's window will
be completely changed in a week or two in harmony with
prevailing modes in Glasgow, London, Paris. Though
their husbands don't suspect it, it is Jimmy Swan who
dictates what the Birrelton women wear — at all events,
the fabric and the pattern of it; Mr Dawson meekly leaves
all the questions of æsthetics to the traveller, who postponed the era of crêpe de chine and ninon in Birrelton (it is
said) for several years.

"About them foulards?" Mr Dawson asks with diffidence, lest their suggestion might appear presumptuous.

"Foulards are no' use for Birrelton; that's the stuff for
you!" says Jimmy; and so it is.

Jimmy "takes in" Birrelton, not for any great profit in
the place itself, but because it is on the road to several
other important places. An hour of exposition and advice
for Mr Dawson; another hour to rest the horses and refresh
himself, and Jimmy is on the road again, in the heavily-
laden deep-sea wagonette himself and his cases call for.

Last week, however, a foundered horse broke down entirely under the stress of snowy weather, and the traveller
found himself for the first time in his life compelled to stay a
night in Birrelton. Its sleepiness lay heavy on his urban soul,
and early in the afternoon he suggested to Mr Dawson that
the village badly wanted cheering up in some way.

"It's aye a quiet time o' the year here," said Dawson apologetically. "And there's naething on till Friday week, when we hae a Parish Council meetin'.'"

"I'm no' goin' to wait for that," said Jimmy. "Could ye no' get up a concert in the aid o' something?"

"A concert!" exclaimed the draper. "There hasna been a concert here since Watty Sharp brought hame his gramophone."

"Has he got it yet?" asked Jimmy. "We could hae a tip-top concert, wi' a gramophone for the nucleus."

As a result of active and immediate steps on the part of Mr Dawson and the traveller, the village bellman announced a Grand Concert in the Schoolroom at Eight o'clock that evening, James Swan, Esq., in the Chair. Collection in Silver in aid of Poor Coal Fund. The school was crowded.

"Ladies and gentlemen," said the Chairman, standing up at a table furnished with a gramophone, a jug of water, and a tumbler, "the town of Birrelton has long been celebrated for its local talent in the music line. A bush is about the very worst place on earth you could keep a talent under; the Bible says you should keep it on the house-tops. Look at Paderewski![2] Look at Madame Melba![3] But, passing on, I would ask your kind attention for a programme more than usually rich and varied in its items, a programme second to none, as I might say. Our object, I may say without the fear of contradiction, is a worthy one — to do a little for the Poor Coal Fund of Birrelton. The poor, as we know, we have always with us, and coals were never dearer.

I will now ask Mr Duncan Tod to favour us with 'Scotland Yet!'

The audience sat in petrified ecstasy while Mr Tod, the shoemaker, sang "Scotland Yet!" in a high falsetto voice, impaired to a sad degree by difficulties of respiration and a nervousness which brought the perspiration to his brow, and compelled him constantly to dry the palms of his hands on a handkerchief whose more legitimate purpose was gently to wave in time with the refrain, in which the audience joined with the encouragement and example of Mr Swan. Mr Tod was apparently a sufferer from asthma; at every bar there was a distinct interval in which, with pursed lips, he noisily recovered all his wind, which had apparently receded into the profoundest depths of his anatomy; his efforts seemed to be attended with the utmost physical and mental agony.

"Thank heaven, that's bye!" he audibly remarked when he was done, and resolutely refused to grant an encore, a desire for which is manifested by a Birrelton audience by whistling.

"We have a long programme," announced the Chairman, "and recalls must be strictly discouraged, but if time permits we may have a chance later on to hear Mr Tod, whose rendition of that fine old song shows us the stuff he is made of. Now we will be favoured by Mr George Steele of the Driepps — 'Aft, aft hae I Pondered,' or ' Memories Dear.'

Mr Steele, wearing an extraordinary suit of checks, which made him distinctly perceptible to the naked eye, dragged himself reluctantly to his feet at the very rear of the audience, came slowly forward, encouraged by exclamations of "Good old Geordie!" by the younger members of the company; cleared his throat loudly and carefully in a manner that almost amounted to ostentation; fixed a baleful glance upon a high and distant corner of the room, and kept it immovably directed there while he sang —

"Aft, aft, as I ponder on the days o' my childhood,
The days yince so happy — Oh come back again!
When I pu'd the wild brambles that grew in the
    greenwood,
And gied them awa' to my wee lovers then."

There were none of the studied and meretricious effects secured by so-called voice production in Mr Steele's performance; his voice was the gift of nature, and suffused with such deep pathetic feeling that he wept himself to hear it. The tears, by the end of the second verse, were streaming down his cheeks; in the middle of the third verse he broke down completely, overcome by his emotions, and abruptly sought his seat again with the remark, "As shair as daith, chaps, I canna come 'Memories Dear' the nicht."

"Go on, Geordie!" cried the audience, "'The Auld Quarry Knowe.'"

In the circumstances the Chairman's veto on recalls was suspended while Mr Steele, bashfully coming forward again, attempted to repress emotions which did credit to his heart in singing the ditty mentioned.

But it was too much for him: he stopped at daffing wi' his Jessie on the Auld Quarry Knowe, and bolted ignominiously for the door.

"There's nothing like the old melodies," said the Chairman, ambiguously, "and I'm sure we all owe a deep debt of gratitude to Mr Steele. But, passing on I have the pleasure to announce that the next item is of the comic gender — 'Tobermory,' by Mr William Gilkison. I would respectfully ask for strict silence at the back while we are listening to our good friend Mr Gilkison."

Mr Gilkison, with a look of ineffable sadness on his face, came forward, assumed a large red-topped Tam o' Shanter, and stared fixedly at a young lady in front, who blushed violently as she rose and took her seat at the piano, which had not hitherto been called into use. There was no music.

"It goes something like this," whispered the vocalist, and he hummed a few bars in her ear.

"What key?" she asked.

"Any key ye like," said he agreeably, "but I prefer the black yins."

After a few false starts, due to an absence of agreement between the singer and the accompanist, Mr Gilkison got fairly embarked on "Tobermory" and the youthful males of the audience signified their high appreciation of its quality by beating time on the floor with their feet and joining in the chorus.

Not even James Swan, Esq., could oppose successfully

the vociferous demand for an encore, and Mr Gilkison, with modest diffidence, not too well assumed, stood where he was at the side of the piano and plunged into "That's the reason why I wear the Kilt."

"I rise to a pint of order," said an excited little gentleman at the end of the first verse, and the audience cheered.

"What is your point of order, sir?" asked Mr Swan, in the manner, self-possessed and firm, of the best Town Councils.

"Mr Gilkison's singin' a couple o' sangs I hae among the records for my grammyphone," said the interrupter.

"Far better than he can dae them. By the man himsel' — Harry Lauder."[4]

"I am sure," said the Chairman suavely, "that the audience will be only too delighted to have an opportunity of judging whether Mr Gilkison or Mr Harry Lauder is the best exponent, as I might venture to say, of the songs in question. It will be an added pleasure, Mr Sharp, to hear the songs twice, once by the 'vox humana,' and once by — by the gramophone."

But Mr Sharp, considerably incensed that his repertoire should have been forestalled, withdrew from the room in dudgeon, fortunately, as it seemed, forgetting to take his gramophone with him, and Mr Gilkison was permitted to finish his song without any further interruption.

"We now pass on with the programme," said the Chairman, "and as a change we will have the well-known song, 'Imitations,' by Mr Peter Gourlay."

The audience laughed.

"Not a song!" whispered Mr Dawson, sitting beside the Chairman. "Imitations. Ventriloquial. Saws wud."

"I beg your pardon, ladies and gentlemen," said Mr Swan. "I find our friend Mr Gourlay's item is ventriloquial. Mr Gourlay will give imitations."

The artist came forward, singularly burdened with a draught-screen which he placed beside the table. Having secreted himself behind the screen, he produced sounds which were unmistakably suggestive of somebody sawing wood. From the same seclusion there followed what was understood to be an imitation of a joiner planing, and the audience cheered.

Mr Gourlay followed with an imitation, frankly in the open, without the aid of any draught-screen, of an infuriated wasp. He chased it over the table, up the wall, and round the back of his neck, and finally suggested its destruction by an abruptly terminated buzzing.

"I have heard all the best ventriloquial entertainers of the day," said Mr Swan, "but none of them had what I might boldly venture to call the realism of Mr Gourlay's great sawing and bumbee act. We will now pass on to the gramophone, the next time on our programme. Mr Sharp has unfortunately been called away by pressing engagements elsewhere, but perhaps there is some one present who understands the mechanism. It will form the second and concluding part of our evening's entertainment."

"Bob Crawford! Bob Crawford!" shouted the youths behind, and the young man alluded to, stuffing his cap in his trousers pocket, lurched diffidently forward, apparently with the reputation of being a skilled executant.

He selected a record, wound up the clockwork, looked anxiously about the table, and said, "Pins."

"Anything missing?" asked the Chairman.

"Pins," said Mr Crawford. "Ye canna play a grammyphone without the pins, and I think that Sharp's awa' wi' them."

It proved to be the case; the irate Sharp had successfully prevented any chance of Harry Lauder being placed in competition with Mr Gilkison, and, as nobody else would sing, the concert terminated with a speech, in which the Chairman said that the evening's entertainment had been of the most delightful character, far transcending the best that he had expected.

"Did ye hear what the collection in silver cam' to?" he asked Mr Dawson, as they wandered up to the little inn.

"Eight-and-six," said Mr Dawson. "No' sae bad for Birrelton!"

"Five shillin's for me, and the balance for the population," said Jimmy. "They have a better estimate o' whit a
Birrelton concert's worth than me."

10. *Rankine's Rookery*

THE TRAIN for Fort William stopped for a reputed five
minutes at Crianlarich,[1] and Jimmy Swan dropped off with
another Knight of the Road for some refreshment.

They entered a place in the station where the same was
indicated, and found themselves before a counter covered
with teacups and bell-shaped glasses, under which the
management seemed to be experimenting in the intensive
culture of the common Alpine or Edible Sandwich.

"They're thrivin' fine!" said Jimmy, peering through the
"cloches." "Put them out in a bed wi' a nice warm southern exposure as soon as the rain comes on, and they'll take
a prize at the autumn show."

"Tea?" said the lady behind the bar, already with a cup
below the tap of a steaming urn.

"No tea," said Jimmy firmly; "I had a cup on Sunday,
and it doesn't do to make it into a habit. Say two bottles of
lager beer, and — and a bunch of sandwiches."

"Licensed drinks in the refreshment room farther
along the platform," said the lady, turning to another
customer, and Jimmy and Mr Dawson went to the other
refreshment room with great celerity, as there was no time
to lose.

"Lovely weather," said Jimmy to the lady-attendant
there. "Two lagers and a brace of sandwiches."

"We have no eatables here," said the lady, preparing to
pull the corks. "You'll get sandwiches at the other refreshment room farther along the platform."

"Great Scot! " said Jimmy, "could you not combine
both shops and have one regular Refreshment Room, the
same as they have on the Continent? It might be wicked,
but it would be handy."

"This is not the Continent; it is Crianlarich," said the lady tartly, and Jimmy smiled.

"I knew there must be something to account for it," said he. "Drink up, Dawson; there's the whistle! After all, there's nothing worse than the eating habit. That's one up in temperance reform for Crianlarich."

Back in the compartment, Mr Dawson, who had been gloomily reading a newspaper all the way from Queen Street, descanted upon this idiocy of the refreshment department at Crianlarich as one more proof that Great Britain, so-called, was precipitously going to the dogs. He represented a modest brand of East Coast whisky (patent still), which percolated through the country quite incognito as Genuine Old Matured, and which he said himself, in strict confidence to friends, was so young and robust it couldn't be put up in bottles without cracking them.

"No wonder there's all this labour unrest," he said; "every other day there's some new Act of Parliament that gets you on the neck. It's coming to 't when you can't get a bun or a biscuit at a station bar unless you take a cup o' tea to it," a manner of stating the case not strictly fair to Crianlarich.

"Keep it up! " said a stranger, who had joined the train at Gairlochhead. "Blame Lloyd George!"[2]

Mr Dawson cordially accepted the invitation, and said things about Mr Lloyd George which it would greatly vex that statesman's wife to hear. It then transpired that the stranger was a Comrade, who had his own views about the social and industrial chaos in the country, and a firm conviction that the most urgent reform demanded was the abolition of all landlords.

"Hear! hear! " said Jimmy Swan, and the Comrade beamed fraternally on him.

"Look at the land round here," the Comrade added with a sweep of the hand that comprehended the Moor of Rannoch, through which the tram was now proceeding. "Nothing but deer! Nationalise it, and you'll see a healthy, prosperous, and contented population pouring back from the cities."

"I suppose you will," said Mr Swan agreeably. "When they start pouring they'll be well advised to bring waterproof top-boots with them and a good supply o' tinned meat, for the Moor o' Rannoch's not exactly the Carse o' Gowrie.[3] I doubt they'll no' pour much at first unless they're dragged wi' ropes."

"I thocht you were a Land Nationalist," said the Comrade.

"So I am," said Jimmy. "I'm tired o' bein' a landlord."

"I didn't know you were a landed gentleman, Mr Swan," said Dawson in surprise. "All I have myself, in that line, is a couple o' flower-pots and a lair in Sighthill Cemetery."

"I'm one of the bloated miscreants," said Jimmy. "I've been one for nearly fifteen years, but lyin' low in case I would be suspected. You don't catch me goin' round wi' a nickerbocker suit and a couple o' retriever dugs. Forbye, it's no exactly land I'm laird o'; it's stone and lime; at least it was stone and lime when I saw 't the last time. If all the landlords were like me, the steamers bound for Canada would be crooded wi' them — third-class, and their beards shaved off for a disguise. ... Do ye ken Dundee?" he asked the Comrade.

"I've been there," said the Comrade, with the air of one who could say more, but refrained from motives of politeness. "I was there last autumn."

"You're a lucky man," said Jimmy. "I had to cut Dundee out o' my circuit more than a dozen years ago, and hand it over to my fellow-traveller, Maclintock. And Dundee was a place where I aye did splendid business.

"Fifteen years ago," proceeded Jimmy, "I had no more politics than a cow; at least if I had, my customers never discovered them."

"Sat on the fence?" suggested the Comrade nastily.

"Just that!" said Mr Swan. "There was so much glaur on both sides o' the fence I couldna' venture down withoot dirtyin' my boots. But I really didna give a rap for politics; I never could bring to them that personal animosity which political enthusiasm seems to demand. When it came to the elementals, I found that folk were much alike, whether Whig or Tory. But the Will o' an Uncle I had in Montrose, ca'd Geordie Rankine, that I hadna seen since I was a boy, put an end to this blissful frame of mind; he left me a land o' hooses[4] in Dundee, and I found I was a red-hot Tory.

"The day I got the lawyer's letter and a copy o' the Will, I gave a dozen chaps in the warehouse a slap-up supper round in the Royal Restaurant, and I tell you the Landed Interests got their hair damped that nicht. There wasna a sealskin jaiket in the wareroom too good for Bella; and I bought mysel' a meerschaum pipe wi' a shammy-leather waistcoat on 't to keep it from bein' scratched. Next mornin' I was up wi' the very first train, that landed in Dundee before the milk, and I got a night-polisman to show me my estate. It was the best-known property in Dundee, as famous as the Tay Bridge,[5] the Baxter Park,[6] or the Bunnet Law,[7] he said, and I saw what he meant when he took me to the most dilapidated tenement in one o' the most appallin' slums I ever set eyes on.

"'Do folk pay rent to get livin' in a place like that?' says I, dumbfoundered at the look o' my bonny property.

"'No fears o' them!' says he. 'It taks' the puir sowls a' their time to pay their fines on a Monday mornin' at the police-coort. The Corporation condemned the place to be demolished a couple o' years ago, and jist when they were gaun to dae 't themsel's at the landlord's cost he went awa' and died on them!'

"'And wha's the landlord noo?' I asked.

"'Some chap in Gleska,' says the polisman; 'I'll bet ye they'll nick him fast enough.'

"'Will they, faith?' says I to mysel', and I made tracks for the 7.49 a.m. for Gleska, wi' my collar turned up in case I might be identified afore I got to the station.

"When I got hame, the first thing my wife asked was if I had brought a picture postcard o' the property. I broke the news to her as gently as I could, and sent word to the lawyer in Dundee to sell the place for onything it would bring. He wrote me back that I might as well try to sell the Scourin'-burn[8] for a mineral water works. My Uncle Geordie had given up all hope o' sellin' the place in the early 'Seventies. A man that lived in the tenement was factor[9] for the property, and for his trouble was supposed to sit rent free, but he considered he ought to get something extra, him bein' factor, seein' nane o' the tenants ever could be got to pay a penny, and in that way were as well aff as himsel', withoot haein' his responsibility.

"I wrote to the lawyer, then, that I refused to accept the property; he could give it awa' for naething if he liked. He replied that the property was mine by the law o' Scotland, whether I wanted it or no', and that naebody would tak' it in a gift. He also sent a bill o' charges and another for rates and taxes.

"I paid them, and then he wrote that the tenement must be demolished by the Corporation's orders, at a cost which he put at £150. I never answered him, and he wrote once or twice a week till I had to flit, leavin' no address. I tell you I was gey annoyed at my Uncle Geordie.

"For five years I heard no more about my property except when I was in Dundee on business, and then it seemed to be growin' more notorious every month. Luckily it was Uncle Geordie's name that stuck to it, and 'Rankine's Rookery' was never, by any chance, associated wi' the traveller for C. & M. I used to go round and look at it; it was getting mair and mair disgraceful every time, and every now and then the subject o' 'Rankine's Rookery' would be up before the Council. It seemed there was some legal difficulty about haulin' it down without due notification to the owner, and the owner wasna to be found.

"'Who is he?' the Labour gang would ask, indignantly, and the Toon Clerk would reply that he was a man in Gleska, but exactly whereaboots was undiscoverable.

"Then the Labour chaps would harangue aboot the scoundrel battenin' on the rents o' the miserable wretches livm' in his property, nae doot knockin' about in his motor-caur and smokin' ninepenny cigars. Me! I never battened on as much as a penny bap aff the property, and the only motor-caurs I travel in belang to the Gleska Corporation.

"The agitation aboot my tenement got so furious at last, a dozen years ago, that I got frichtened, and since then I've never gane near Dundee, in case I would be arrested. And that's the way I'm for nationalisin' property, and daein' awa' wi' landlords. Whether my property's standin' yet or no' I never venture to inquire; to indulge my curiosity on that score might cost me far mair than I bargained for."

"That all bears out my argument," said the Comrade. "The land must be for the people!"

11. *Dignity*

"THE SELLIN o' soap, butter, music, poetry, pictures, or soft goods, is just as great an art as making them," said Mr Swan, chipping the top off his second egg. "I was years ago in a factory where they made Balmoral bunnets. They had a big machine that just fair squirted oot Balmoral bunnets; the yarn went in at the one end by the ton, and the bunnets poured out at the other, a' complete, even to the toorie. I was spellbound lookin' at the thing, and the man that had the factory says to me, 'That's a great machine, Mr Swan. I see ye're lost in admiration.' 'That's just what I am!' says I; 'but it's no' at the machine; I think far more o' the men who can keep up wi 't at the sellin'. Noo that keps are comin' in, it takes me a' my time to sell a dozen bunnets in a year.'"

"That's quite true," said a man on the road for jams and sweetmeats. "Every year commercial travelling grows harder. I sometimes think the men that have to sell soor draps and kali sookers[1] after we're away 'll need to have a college education."

Dunbar & Baxter's new young man, on his first journey, stirred his coffee, and listened with great respect — indeed with veneration — to these veterans of the road. What roused this feeling in him was the thought that they should have kept their jobs so long; his own beginning was so unpropitious. Yesterday had been a rotten day, and he had said to himself, "Another week like this, and it's back wi' you to the counter, Willy!" It was not a pleasant feeling for a chap who was doing his best. It was all the more unpleasant because there were features of his new job that greatly pleased him — the sense of freedom, space, and personal responsibility, so different from being in the shop; the travelling by trains and steamers; the sight of new places, the living in hotels — particularly the living in hotels. To a young fellow who at home in Glasgow lodged in Raeberry Street,[2] and had no interest in any food he got except the midday meal picked up at a restaurant, this living in hotels was thoroughly and completely quite all right. Deferential Boots and waiters; fish, ham-and-eggs and kidneys for one's breakfast (all together, mind you, and no stinting!) a regular banquet called a lunch, and a high tea quite as lavish as the breakfast! It would be a deuce of a dunt to tumble back from these high altitudes of luxury to the hopeless and prosaic levels of Raeberry Street!

He nervously crumbled a breakfast roll and cleared his throat, and meekly put a question.

"What would you say was the secret of success in our business Mr Swan?"

Jimmy flushed. He could have laughed but remembered that he had one time been young on the road himself and full of strange illusions, and being a gentleman he made his best pretence at answering a question to which in the nature of things there is no answer.

"The secret of success, Mr Spens," said he, "is to be born lucky."

"But you need more than luck," said the jam man hurriedly. "You need brains, and pluck, and foresight, and habits of industry, and — "

"And what's all that but bein' born lucky?" broke in Jimmy. "There's many a one gets on dashed well without them, too; but that's another kind o' luck."

"I'm not sure that I have either kind," said Spens, "but I'll guarantee I do my best to sell Dunbar & Baxter's flour, and I'm finding it a gey dreich business. I begin to think that I'm a failure."

Jimmy puckered up his face, so red and weathered, like a winter apple; looked across the table at the lad with a twitching of his bushy eyebrows, and liked him for his unaffected innocence.

"Ye're all right, Mr Spens!" said he with peculiar gentleness. "The worst ill-luck I ken is to be born self-satisfied, and that's been spared ye."

"The great thing," said the jam man, "is dignity. Aye stand on your dignity, and make the customer respect you."

This time Jimmy laughed without compunction. "Man, Simpson," said he, "I'm astonished at ye. If ye had to depend upon your dignity ye wouldna sell a sweetie. Do you ken the way Scotch travellers are the best in the world? It's because they have nae dignity. A man wi' a sense o' dignity is like a man wi' a broken gallus; he's aye feared something's goin' to slip. The thing is to have your galluses[3] right, and then ye needna fash about your dignity. I'll tell you and Mr Spens a story. I used one time to think dignity was a great thing too; that it was a thing ye wore like a white waistcoat, and that the customer liked it. My George ! I had as much dignity in these days as would do for half a dozen o' statesmen or a couple o' point polismen. When I started with C. & M. I scared away half my customers by wearing my dignity like an ice-bag on my chest, and talking London English. But I got a lesson, and the only virtue ever I had in this life was that I never needed to get the same lesson twice. For five years I was travelling every season to Auchentee,[4] a place whose only interest for me was that it had three drapers' shops in 't. The drapers were all MacLellans; they were all related; they were a' in the same wee street. Auchentee's eight miles from the nearest railway station. For five years I drove up to Auchentee in a tip-top wagonette wi' my cases, and my hat cocked to the side the same as I was the Duke o' Sutherland. I lavished a' my art on the MacLellans: I choked the syvor[5] in front o' their shops wi' my cases; I flourished sixpenny cigars, and talked through the top o' my head like a man from Sheffield.

"But there was naething doin'! I never booked an order! They were gettin' their stuff from Edinburgh; they had aye got their stuff from Edinburgh, and a' they kent aboot Gleska was that it was on the maps. Three auld snuffy deevils, I mind, they were — the MacLellans; and when I offered them bargains I would lose money on, they just took another pinch o' snuff and said they couldna think to change their house.

"One day I landed at the station, took my dinner at the inn, and ordered the wagonette for Auchentee. It was goin' to be my final visit; if the MacLellans failed me this time, they could go to bleezes. There was nae wagonette; it was awa' at a roup, and the only thing left on wheels was a cairt. I said to mysel', 'There's no' much daein' wi' dignity in Auchentee,' and I took the cairt. It was an awfu' day o' wind and rain, and I had a fine silk hat, a cashmere mornin' coat, and a blue-sprigged waistcoat on. There I was, sittin' in the cairt wi' my cases piled behind me, far mair like an undertaker than a traveller for C. & M., and I tell you it was rainin' ! When I landed in the main street o' Auchentee, I created a sensation. My hat was into pulp; I was drookit to the skin; a' the dignity I had could be spread oot on a threepenny bit, and ye would see the printin' through it.

"The whole toon gathered oot, and laughed; I was the bonny spectacle, cocked up there on MacGillvray's cairt, and naebody laughed looder nor the MacLellans. It was the first time they had ever seen I was a human bein', subject to the immutable laws o' nature. Now, folk that get a hearty laugh at ye aye feel kindly to ye after. One o' the MacLellans took me in and dried my clothes; another o' them gave me my tea; the third one put me up for the night, for the inn of Auchentee was full o' county gentlemen. And, what's mair, I got a slashin' big order from a' the three. The moral is that dignity's no' worth a dump in travellin'."

Ten minutes later Jimmy was smoking in the hall with Simpson.

"That's a great lesson! " said Simpson seriously.

"Ay, it's a great lesson right enough," said Jimmy, cleaning out his pipe. "It's a good enough lesson for a young man startin', just to put him on the right lines, but it wouldna be ony use to you. Ye see, I didna finish the story for Spens; I didna want to spoil it."

"What way spoil it?" asked Simpson.

"Well, you see, the three MacLellans a' worked in one another's hands; they a' went into bankruptcy three months efter that, and a' we got o' their accounts was ninepence in the pound !"

12. *Universal Provider*

THERE ARE small paraffin-oil-lamp towns in many parts of the country for which Mr Swan is Fairy Godmother, Perpetual Grand Plenipotentiary, and Deputy Providence. Half of his time in Glasgow is taken up with the execution of countless petty commissions for his rural customers and their friends, the selection and purchase of goods quite out of his own drapery line. I met him recently in a music-warehouse critically inspecting pianos on which he gave a masterly one-finger exposition of "We're a' noddin'." "For a customer of mine in Aviemore," he told me. "He wants a genuine £16 extra-grand, high-strung, Chubb-check-action walnut one with the right kind of candlesticks on it. I think this is about the article for Aviemore" — and he indicated one with gorgeous candlesticks and a singularly robust tone.

"Why don't they come and buy their own pianos?" I asked innocently.

"They think they would be swindled," said Jimmy, "and

I daresay they're right. Besides, they don't know a thing about pianos, and they know that I've bought hundreds of pianos in the past five-and-twenty years. I never bought one for a customer yet that failed to give satisfaction. It's all in the touch" — he touched a sprightly bar of "We're a' noddin'" — "and I could tell the right touch with my eyes shut."

"You must get some odd country commissions," I said, as we left the warehouse together when the transaction was completed. "I shouldn't care, myself, to buy pianos for other people."

"In my line," said Mr Swan, "I can't afford to be particular. I don't make a penny off the job directly, but it helps to keep a good customer on the books of C. & M. A piano's a simple matter; I once had to buy a brass band for Larbert, and a dashed good brass band, too; you never heard a louder! A customer of mine was chairman of the committee, and he said he couldn't trust another man in Glasgow but myself to get the proper instruments. I got the dandiest set you ever set eyes on, and seven-and-a-half off for cash, that bought a tip-top banner, and they never expected the money they had would run to a banner."

It is impossible to enumerate the variety and extent of Mr Swan's private commissions for his country customers, who haven't the time to come to Glasgow or sufficient confidence in their own judgment to buy either a piano or a presentation silver albert and appendage for a young friend going away to Canada. He has taken the blushing orders of innumerable lads who felt the time had come for shaving, but were coy about purchasing their first razor in a local shop. There is no better judge of an engagement-ring in Scotland; and there is a piece of cardboard with a hole in it in his waistcoat pocket almost every time he returns to town from Perthshire. His knowledge of the cradle and perambulator trade is copious, and more than once he has executed telegraphic orders for a superior kind of oak coffin unprocurable in Mull.

"I never made a mistake but once in my life," he says,

"and it cost me one of my very best Kirkcudbright customers. She was a widow woman getting up in years, and she had been reading somewhere or other that Society ladies kept their fine complexions by putting on cosmetics. One day after giving me a good order for autumn goods, she took me into the back of the shop and slipped five shillings in my hand. 'I want you to send me that amount of good cosmetic, Mr Swan,' she whispered 'it's for a friend.' 'Right you are, Mrs Lamont,' says I, and made a note of it. The only place I ever saw cosmetic was in a barber's shop, so I went to one in Gordon Street and bought five shillings' worth, and sent it off to Mrs Lamont. She would never look at me again! You see it was what the call Hong Grease cosmetic for sticking out the moustache, and she distinctly had one. The best of it is that, so far as I can find out, there's not any other kind of cosmetic sold in the whole of Glasgow than the grease of the foresaid Hong."

The confidence of the agricultural districts in Mr Swan's good taste and commercial acumen is no greater than their faith in his ability to do any mortal thing for them that demands a knowledge of the world, and influence. When the drapers of the Western Journey want to start a son on a career in Glasgow, it is to Mr Swan they instinctively appeal for the requisite advice and aid. No boy is too hopelessly useless for Jimmy to find a job for in the city; the last decennial increase[1] in our population is mainly made up of immigrants to whom he is credited with giving their urban start in life.

"Send him up to me,"says Jimmy airily, "and I'll bet you I'll push him on to somebody."

The method of procedure in these cases is simplicity itself. "I take the young chap out to stay with me for a week," he told me; "get his hair cut to begin with, and another kind of cap for him. Then I take him out and start him at one end of West George Street after breakfast and tell him to make his way to the other end, going up every stair *en route* and asking a job at every office till he gets one. He generally gets a job before the third day, just because he

is a country-bred boy with a fine red face. Glasgow businessmen like to have an innocent country boy about the
office; it makes them think of what they might, themselves,
have been. And the best way to start a boy in life in
Glasgow is to let him understand that starting, like staying,
all depends upon himself."

The fact that Mr Swan has often bazaar tickets and
invitations to artists' exhibitions for disposal gratis to customers in from the country creates the impression that he
can get a friend in anywhere, at any time, for nothing. He
has rarely encouraged this flattering allusion at the cost of a
pair of stall tickets for the pantomime, but no customer or
customer's friend has ever failed to get a ticket for a
football match, for Mr Swan has apparently the mysterious
power of tapping inexhaustible supplies of free tickets for
football matches.

"But the nerve of some folk is unbelievable," he told me.
"Not long ago a customer from the North wrote asking me
to get him a pass by the Caledonian Railway to London."

"Did you manage it?" I asked.

"No," he answered, "I'm not exactly God. The best I
could do for him was to give him an introduction to the
guard and a list of places that he mustn't miss going to see
in the Metropolis, so-called. I carefully explained to him
that all the usual privileges in the way of free passes were
suspended on account of the coal strike, so my reputation
as The Universal Provider-to-the-North-for-nought is not
in the least impaired."

Another customer of Mr Swan's found the air of Glasgow so exhilarating as compared with that of Dingwall that
he spent an evening in a police cell, and had to send for C.
& M.'s traveller to bail him out on the following morning.
His peculiar dread was that the newspapers of the city
would give a copious and sensational account of the unfortunate affair, which would be copied into the "Northern
Star,"[2] and spoil the sober reputation of a lifetime. Mr
Swan did not tell him that trivial indiscretions of this sort
were never recorded in Glasgow newspapers.

"I'll fix it all right !" he said. "You can depend on me. I have only got to pass the word along to the editors that you're a friend of mine, and the thing is done."

There is a draper now in Dingwall who is convinced that Mr James Swan has the British press in his pocket. But the oddest commission Mr Swan ever got was to supply the parish of Birrelton with a minister. It would have staggered any other man, but Mr Swan set about its execution with as much cheerfulness as if he had been asked to send on a mouth harmonium.

Birrelton had spent some months of Sundays listening to candidates for the vacant charge. Every one was better than the other, and it was plainly impossible to get the congregation into a definite attitude of mind which would give the pulpit to any particular one. After many squabbling meetings the leading draper, who was ruling elder, said he saw no hope of their ever agreeing upon a minister, and proposed that Patronage[3] should be re-established to the extent of asking the traveller for C. & M. to pick a suitable clergyman in Glasgow.

"So I got the job," said Mr Swan. "It took me a couple of weeks. I knew exactly the kind of chap they would need in Birrelton — not too fancy, you understand, for fear some other kirk would grab at him before the Birrelton ladies' presentation Geneva gown[4] was right out of the tissue paper, and still, on the other hand, not one so dull that he would be likely to be left on their hands till he died at the age of ninety. The minister they aye want in places like Birrelton is a combination of the Apostle Paul, General Roberts,[5] and the cinematograph which never gives a word of offence to anybody, and that kind of minister is not a glut on the market. I did the best I could. I consulted all my acquaintances, and every man Jack of them had a first-rate minister he would recommend heartily for the vacancy. It was always their own minister, and their eagerness to see him doing well for himself by shifting somewhere else was most significant.

"At last I found a young assistant something like the

thing I wanted, and put the Birrelton pulpit to him as a business proposition. He jumped at it like a brave wee man, and I wired to my customer — 'Esteemed order will be dispatched per passenger train on Monday.'

"He's a great success," said Mr Swan, tapping his pipe on his boot-toe. "Everybody's delighted with him. I got a letter from the session-clerk thanking me for putting such a fine minister their road, and asking me if I could recommend the best place to buy a silver tea and coffee service."

"You're a marvel, Mr Swan," I said.

"Not at all!" said Jimmy. "I'm only a business man. You can get any mortal thing you like in Glasgow if you have the business experience and the ready money."

13. *The Commercial Room*

His *confrère* Grant being temporarily off the Road on account of a prolonged attack of influenza, Jimmy Swan last week took up the Fifeshire journey for him, and put up one night at an hotel he had not visited for over a dozen years. In those dozen years some drastic changes had been made on the old Buck's Head.[1] It had been re-created, mainly in the interest of golfers and the automobile traffic. Its geography was now unfamiliar to Jimmy, who, at one time, could have found his way through every corner of it in the dark. He had now the choice of sixteen wash-hand basins, all in a row; a prominent announcement in the hall informed him that eleven bathrooms were at his august command; a beauteous languid creature, with an amazing rick of yellow hair, put down his name and handed him a circular ticket with the number of his room.

"I hope," said he, "it's a southern exposure, and has a fire-escape and a telephone in it?"

The fair being, with a wonderful pretence at talking into empty space, mentioned that the Buck's Head's bedrooms always gave satisfaction.

"Dinner, sir?" said a German voice at his shoulder, and

turning round, Jimmy sighed. At that exact moment he had remembered how old Willie Boyd, for twenty years the waiter and boots of the Buck's Head, as it used to be, was wont to welcome him.

"No; tea," he answered curtly. "And ham and eggs; with two boiled eggs to follow."

The Teutonic minion sped upon this mission; Jimmy washed his hands in five of the sixteen basins, in order to test the plumber work, and, still without having seen any signs of a proprietor, walked into the old Commercial Room.[2] It had lost the printed designation on the door, and in some respects was fallen sadly from its old estate. He had it wholly to himself.

By-and-bye the waiter came in to intimate that tea was ready in the Coffee Room.

"Good!" said Jimmy. "But I want mine here. I suppose this is still the Commercial Room?"

"No, sir," said the waiter; "it is the Chauffeurs' Room; a Commercial Room we have not now got," and on that Jimmy said a bad word. He looked again about the room; there was the old familiar grate with a glowing fire in it; the sideboard and the chairs were as they used to be; there was no change in the steel engravings on the wall. A host of memories beset him.

"I don't care what it is," he said at last; "bring my tea in here. I suppose the Buck's Head has some sort of a landlord still; don't trouble to waken him, for I haven't got my motor-car wi' me this journey. I take it you haven't such a thing as a pair of commercial slippers? ... No; of course not! It doesn't matter; I aye carry my own, and I used to put the house ones on just to please old Willie Boyd.[3] Did ye ever hear of Willie Boyd, the Original Human Waiter?"

"Yes, sir," said the German. "He died."

Jimmy's face fell. "If I were you, Fritz, I wouldn't put it so blunt as that," he said. "News like that should be broken gently; the man had a thousand friends, God bless him! ... 'You must tak' another herrin', Mr Swan'; 'I wouldna risk the silverside the day, Mr Swan'; 'Still the rheumatics, gentlemen, but no' complainin'; 'A' to your beds, now, like gude boys!' … Aye, aye, and Willie's gone! No wonder I didna recognise the old Buck's Head!"

He took a solemn meal, and was ruminating wistfully at the fire when the landlord plunged into the room with tardy greetings. "Man, Mr Swan," said he, "the silly folk in front there hadn't the least suspicion who ye were, and never sent to the stable for me! I've been buyin' horse. And what in a' creation are ye daein' here in the Chauffeurs' Room ? — I'm black affronted !"

"The room's fine, Mr Lorimer," said Jimmy Swan. "Forbye, I clean forgot to bring my evenin' dress wi' me. And it's still yoursel', John Lorimer! I'm glad to see ye; I thought there was naething left o' the auld Buck's Head but this grate and sideboard, and a wheen chairs. I hear that Willie's gone."

"Three years ago," said the landlord, sitting down; "he was gey frail at the hinder end."

"Was he? Dear auld Willie! Slept in himsel' at last; I'll warrant ye it never happened once in twenty years wi' a customer that Willie had to waken for the early mornin' train! … Ye've made a wonderful change on the house since I was here last, Mr Lorimer; but sittin' here my lone at my tea, I was feelin' eerie."

"Tuts, man! ye should have gone to the Coffee Room," said the landlord. "It's perfectly ridiculous !"

"No," said Mr Swan; "I never could turn my back on the auld Buck's Head Commercial Room; do ye know it's the first I ever set foot in?"

"I mind!" said Mr Lorimer, chuckling. "You were a little jimper[4] at the waist then. You're gettin' fat, like mysel', Mr Swan."

"That's not fat," said Jimmy, soberly; "it's philosophy. … I mind on that occasion I asked a customer, old David Graham, to come round to the Buck's Head at night to see me, and it was wi' a gey red face I did it, I can tell ye, for he micht hae been my father. He came in at night, and in a little I asked him what he would ha'e. 'I drink naething but champagne,' says David Graham; 'I'll ha'e a bottle.' My he'rt sunk into my heels; the price o' a bottle o' champagne was mair than I would mak' o' profit on the journey! But the deed was done; I couldna back oot, and I rang the bell for Willie. 'A bottle o' good champagne and a bottle o' beer,' I said to him; he never blinked an e'e, though I was but a boy, and oot he goes and comes in wi' twa bottles o' beer.

"'I said champagne for one o' them,' says I, quite manly; and David Graham — peace be wi' him! a worthy man! — laughed in a quiet way, and says, 'Willie kens my auld trick wi' the young traiveller too weel to bring ony champagne in here. Na, na, laddie; beer's better for us, and I doubt it'll be mony a day before ye'll be able to afford a bottle o' Pomeroy for a country customer!'

"I'm sorry ye've given up the auld Commercial Room," proceeded Jimmy. "I look upon it in a kind o' way as consecrated. Auld times! auld men!"

"We had to move wi' the times, Mr Swan," said the landlord; "I had to make a place for the chauffeurs some-where, and our commercial trade is not what it used to be."

"I daresay no," said Jimmy. "Neither is commercial traivellin'. Do ye mind o' Cunningham and Stewart, Kerr, MacKay, J. P. Paterson, and MacLennan? Where's the like o' them the day? Kings o' the Road! By George! I've seen a polisman up in Brora touch his cap when a barrow passed wi' auld MacLennan's cases."

"Faith, aye! This room has seen some cheery company!" said Mr Lorimer.

"The first Sunday I took my dinner in't, I felt as if I was in the House o' Commons. Everything was done by ritual; J. P. Paterson in the chair. I was formally introduced as if it was the twenty-ninth degree in Masonry; Paterson made a canty[5] speech, and wished me well on behalf o' the com-pany, and they drank my health. And there was the usual bottle o' wine — I was jolly glad, I can tell ye; it was port, for port was the only wine at the time that hadna the taste o' ink to me. I've never seen a bottle o' port more ceremoniously disposed o' than the customary bottle on the Sunday in Commercial Rooms. It was an education in the *haute politesse!* At first it used actually to mak' me feel religious! And always 'Mr President, sir!' and 'By your leave, gentlemen!'"

"I havena sold a bottle o' port to a commercial in the past ten years, Mr Swan," said the landlord. "They've lost the taste for wines, I'm thinkin'."

"Not them! The only thing they've lost is the means o' payin' for them. There's no' mony pound-a-day men[6] left on the Road, Mr Lorimer. And, onyway port, I take it, is no' what it used to be. Do ye know what I was thinkin' to mysel' sittin' here mopin' at the fire afore ye came in? It was that naething nooadays was quite so good as it used to be. The ham's gane aff, chops are no' so thick and sappy as they were before the Tay Bridge storm, and ye've a' lost the art o' branderin'[7] them. The cut off the joint is no' what it was, and finnen-haddies[8] are completely aff, and there's no' the auld taste to potatoes. ... And — and Willie Boyd's awa' frae the Buck's Head Inn! And it hasna' a Commercial Room ony longer!"

"The port's as good as ever it was," said Mr Lorimer with a twinkle.

"Take me in a bottle, then," said Jimmy Swan, "and join me in a sentimental glass to the auld Commercial Room, the memory o' honest Willie, an' the auld Knights o' the Road!"

14. *The Changed Man*

JAMES SWAN had a friend, a traveller in the line of Fancy Goods, who came originally — of all places in the world for a seller of photo-frames and jumping jacks — from the Isle of Skye. His Christian name was Donald; Jimmy always called him "Donald-of-the Isles — the fusel-iles,"[1] and that, alas! did no injustice to his salient weakness, which was a preference for mountain dew at its very freshest, before the warmth of the still was out of it. He took it in considerable quantities for years, with no apparent ill effect upon a constitution which seemed to be impervious to the erosive influence of moisture, like the Coolin hills or the Quiraing. The parlour what-nots of countless happy homes in the West of Scotland were laden with celluloid jewel-boxes, antimony silver ash-trays, fantastic cats with nodding heads, and Goss-ware,[2] presents from Dunoon, or Campbeltown, or whatever the case might be, which owed their prevalence in country shops almost wholly to the persuasive eloquence of Donald. He had a way of showing jumping-jacks and expounding the moral value of Teddy Bears[3] that was positively irresistible anywhere ten miles out of Glasgow, his exposition of a doll that would say "Ma-ma,"and horizontally shut its eyes was acknowledged to be unique. In Donald's hands it assumed the dignity of an epoch-making laboratory experiment by the late Lord Kelvin.[4]

For Fancy Goods Jimmy Swan had the most extraordinary contempt. He looked (and not unreasonably) upon Fancy Goods as the proof that fancy itself, the cheapest and loveliest of all adornments, was, like porridge, almost obsolete in Scotland, and he never referred to Donald's stock of samples but as "dolls." "Anything fresh in the doll line, Donald?" he would say. "Are shammy-leather legs goin' to hold their own this season?" Or, "I see from the Board of Trade returns there's a slump in mouth-harmoniums; I doubt you are losing ground, Donald."

But all the same they were the warmest of friends. It has recently been discovered by Professor Spiltzbaum[5] of Heidelberg that the specific organism of alcoholism is a very minute motile coco-bacillus measuring from 1 to 2 micro-millimetres in length, with terminal spiral flagella. In the body of its host, the unfortunate victim of the alcoholic disease, this anærobe has a curious tickling effect. It tickles the sense of confidence, laughter, toleration, and human kindness, and is the inveterate foe of those pink hæmatozoa which are now identified in bacteriological research as the cause of self-righteousness. Thus we have explained the remarkable fact that unfortunate victims of alcohol, like Donald, are often so much more jolly to meet than fine healthy fellows without a single coco-bacillus about them.

Donald was a good traveller, and could sell a gross of mechanical mice with broken springs in the time another traveller would be shutting up his umbrella and fumbling for his pencil. He was generous, tolerant, amusing, fearless, frank, and simple as a child when the coco-bacillus tickled with its spiral flagella; he could be the most charming of companions, and most loyal of friends.

"I like Donald," Jimmy Swan would say. "I suppose it's because he's a bit o' an idiot like mysel', no' a'thegither given up to the main chance, nor always homeward bound. But I whiles wish he would settle doon and start the domestic and temperance virtues. I'm aye tellin' him that if he takes them up in the proper spirit they're almost as much fun as the other thing — forbye bein' money in your pocket."

Unfortunately the alcoholic bacillus in course of time by the assiduous application of its flagella in the tickling process wears them down to a stump, and deprived of its power to tickle to any great extent, it goes ramping round the whole intestinal system biting. An agonising thirst is created in the patient, only to be allayed by increased applications of mountain or other dew, with which, of course, are imbibed fresh colonies of the organism which take up the tickling, handicapped, however, by the increased difficulty of getting a dry spot to work on.

One day Donald came to his friend, Mr Swan, in a quiescent moment of the bacilli, looking very blue, and borrowed £10 upon the touching presentation of a story about a Sheriff-Court summons.

The occasion was too obviously providential to be neglected, and Jimmy talked to him like a teetotal lecturer. "All I needed to be John B. Gough[6] was a drunken past, my thumb-prints in the polis books, and a white dress muslin necktie," he said afterwards to his wife, describing the interview.

"Look here, Donald," he said; "not to put too fine a point on it, you're a d — d fool."

"It's the true word, Mr Swan!" admitted Donald, contritely.

"I'm the last man," said Jimmy, "to say a chap should begin in life by bein' a perfect model, for there's naething left for him to dae in the way o' self-improvement if he's perfect to begin wi', and the later part o' his life 'll be awfu' dreich. I started, mysel', wi' the full equipment o' a first-class idiot — worse than you, but for the last ten years I've got a wonderfu' lot o' pleesure and satisfaction tryin' to be better. I tell ye this — it's far more sport than keepin' a gairden!"

"The way ye are," continued Jimmy, "you're just a wasted man! Ye have a' the qualities o' a good yin except the will to use them. Men no' half your weight, nor wi' half your wits aboot them, are laughin' at ye; I'll no' say that they're takin' the prizes you should have, for that's a point that would appeal to neither me nor you, but they're laughin' at ye — no, no! I'll no' say that o' human nature; rather will I say they're sorry for ye. That should sting a Skyeman!"

"There's something in it, Mr Swan," said Donald.

"Of course there is!" said Jimmy. "A man at your age canna learn much more, but he can get a lot of fun in unlearnin'. But for heaven's sake, Donald! — always in the proper spirit! — not too certain o' yoursel', nor too self-satisfied, nor too bitter on the weaker brethren."

Donald went away, impressed, and became a changed man.

Everybody noticed it, first of all his firm, which experienced a lamentable and unaccountable decline in the demand for autograph albums with real leatherette covers, mechanical steam-engines (with broken springs), celluloid dromedary inch-tapes, and golliwogs, on the West Coast journey. Donald was blatantly and offensively teetotal; once generous, he was now as hard as nails; once full of fun and kindliness, he was now as dull as crape; once fearless, he was become as timid as a mouse; once disingenuous as a child, he was become as crafty and suspicious as a shilling lawyer. The coco-bacilli, realising the situation, uttered an agonised shriek, and turned on their backs and died. When he came to Jimmy Swan after a year to repay the borrowed money, Jimmy, who had not seen him much of late, looked at him with disappointed eyes.

"Do ye feel like a bottle o' cyder, Donald?" he asked him.

"Thank goodness, I'm beyond that sort o' thing! " said Donald. "Have ye a drop o' soda?"

Jimmy gave it to him, sadly.

"Thank ye for the money, Donald," said he; "it was good of ye to mind it. There's something aboot ye that puts me in mind o' the smell o' a wet leather school-bag. What way are ye gettin' on?"

"Oh, not so bad," said Donald, solemnly. "I have the approval of my conscience, though the firm is not quite satisfied."

"Just that! " said Jimmy, fingering the notes carelessly. "You're a muckle-improved man, but I'm feared I spoiled ye for a traiveller, and I ken I've lost ye for a friend. I told ye, man, to go about it in the proper spirit!"

15. *Vitalising the Gloomy Grants*

JIMMY SWAN, with his hands in his jacket pockets, his hat at just the tiniest angle, his chest thrown out, and his waist reduced by a conscious effort of the abdominal muscles — which things all betoken a determination never to grow old, walked along Shore Street humming "Onward, Christian Soldiers." He was, if you take me, feeling good. The sun shone on the sea-front like a benediction; enough and no more autumnal sting was in the air to give it bracing qualities; he had done a good day's business yesterday at Inverness; had slept like a babe, and breakfasted like a sailor; was freshly shaved to that degree that his cheek was like a lady's; he knew this journey's stuff was irresistible. It was going on in front of him — six weather-beaten cases in the wheel-barrow of Peter Melville, packed with sample lines to make the hair of any discerning draper fairly curl.

He felt as men feel who come with relief to long-beleaguered cities; there ought to have been a band before him playing "Umpa-umpa-ump!" and a few assorted banners. That was why he hummed, providing for himself a private and appropriate kind of military pomp. Other commercial travellers might sneak ingloriously into these northern towns and go cringing through the shops with self-depreciatory airs, inviting insults and rebuffs instead of orders — not so Mr Swan, ambassador of C. & M., Perpetual Grand Plenipotentiary and High Prince of the Soft Goods world, backed by a century's tradition, conscious of quality unassailable and prices strictly bed-rock, having due consideration for the quality.

In thirty years of the Road for C. & M. he had acquired a Psychic Touch with customers; not only did his stuff talk for itself — why, C. & M.'s trade-mark on a web of Bolton sheeting was portentous as a statesman's speech! — but his manner magnetised, and he would insinuate a new line of zephyr prints into the conversation like one who was quoting a fine unhackneyed passage from Shakespeare. He did not seem so much to seek to sell you goods as to give you the inestimable privilege of taking part with the great firm of C. & M. in a grand disinterested campaign to make the people of Scotland wear the real right thing. No city superiority or condescension, mind you! no bluff or airs! Jimmy Swan had a shrewd appreciation of the psychological advantage of liking your man to start with; of being absolutely disingenuous, and confident of the character of your own stuff.

No wonder he marched into R. & T. Grant's humming "Onward, Christian Soldiers" in his mellifluous bass, while Peter Melville out on the pavement took the straps from off the cases.

He was no sooner at the counter and shaking hands with Robert than he realised, intuitively, that the morning's sunshine and its bracing airs had no effect on the spirits of that struggling drapery concern. The shop looked more disheartened than it ever did before — more haphazard of arrangement, more dingy, more out-of-date. Robert's eye (the straight one) had the unmistakable lack-lustre of frustration and defeat. Thomas, the elder, totting up the greasy ledger in a corner, stopped in the middle of a column and came forward smiling automatically as to a customer, but lapsing instantly into a mask of gloom, his voice subdued to a funereal melancholy. The brothers were barely middle-aged in years, but for long they had indulged a singular illusion that solidity and success in commerce were only for men who looked mature, and they had always carefully cultivated an appearance of being twenty years older than they really were. Gladstone collars, made-up padded neck-ties, morning coats of the period of the Tay Bridge storm, and — whiskers ! And when I say whiskers, I mean actual mid-Victorian side-wings, not mutton-chops, but fluffy cheek appendages, the dire absurdity of which not even a doting mother could condone.

"How's business?" asked Mr Swan, with the cheerful air of one who is confident of learning that business was never better.

"Bad! " said Robert Grant, laconically. "I don't think you need to open up your cases, Mr Swan, this trip."

The countenance of the traveller fell for a moment; then he said airily, "Tuts ! it's only temporary. Everything's on the upward trend; ye're maybe just a season later here in the North to feel it, but it's working up the Highland Line, and I make out that in less than a week the Boom will be the length o' Kingussie or Aviemore."

Robert Grant shook his head till his whiskers almost made a draught. "It's too late of comin' for us, Mr Swan," he said lugubriously. "Tom and me's tired o't. We're

done! What trade we ever had is goin' back. It was never a
fat thing at the best, but now it's driftin' over to the Store[1]
across the street; ye see they've started a drapery department."

"Let them start it!" said Mr Swan, contemptuously.
"I'm sure ye ken the slogan o' the Grants — 'Stand fast,
Craigellachie !' The new department at the Store should
be a tonic to ye; send ye brisker about your business than
ever ye were before; I never do so well myself as when I'm
faced wi' solid opposition."

But the Grant brothers wagged their preposterous
whiskers, and sunk their chins lower in their obsolete
Gladstone collars, and assured their visitor that affairs
were hopeless. Thank God they could still pay twenty
shillings in the pound and have a little over, but there
seemed to be nothing now for it but Canada. Everybody
was going to Canada.

"What'll ye dae there?" asked Mr Swan, bluntly. They
would look around them for a while, and no doubt hit on
something, they remarked, and Robert's defective and
erratic eye went flashing round the shop in a manner which
suggested that at looking around in Canada he would be a
perfect marvel.

James Swan walked to the door and looked at his open
cases; threw out his chest and took a deep breath of the
stimulating sea-born air, then turned back to the counter,
and addressed the disconsolate brothers.

"Do ye ken what's the matter wi' this business and wi'
you?" he asked. "It's whiskers! Nothing else but whiskers!
For the love of Peter shave yoursel's clean like me, or start
a moustache, or a Captain Kettle[2] beard wi' a peak to't,
and be upsides wi' modern civilisation. Gie your cheeks a
chance; take aff these side-galleries and look like the year
o' grace 1912, no' the start o' the Franco-Prussian war."[3]

The brothers, too well acquainted with their visitor to
resent this personality, smiled ruefully. "I see from the
papers," said Robert, "that side whiskers are comin' into
vogue again. Tom and me's just a little ahead o' the times;

we'll soon be in the height o' fashion."

"The height o' nonsense!" cried Jimmy Swan. "There's no wise-like folk gaun back to whiskers ony mair than to the crinoline or the chignong. In either case the women wouldna stand it, and it's them that rule the fashions. Man, it's no' an age for whiskers; ye need a face on ye as clean as the bow o' a cutter yacht to sail into the winds o' commerce nooadays, and there's the pair o' ye beatin' to the marks wi' spinnakers. There's naebody wears whiskers now but undertakers and men on the Stock Exchange that havena ony dochters to cod them into common sense. If any employee o' C. & M.'s came into the warehouse wi' a whisker on, the partners in the business would tak fits, and the rest o' us would bray at him like cuddies. If the police o' Gleska saw a man your age wi' whiskers they would track him up a lane at night and hammer him wi' their batons. The way ye are, ye're an affront to me; ye're no' a day aulder than mysel', and yet ye might be onybody's faithers. The first thing they would dae to ye in Canada would be to lay ye on a block and clip ye — "

He broke off with a chuckle which disarmed annoyance; there were no customers of C. & M. for whom he had a greater respect — if only they would shave themselves; and he knew they knew it.

"Ah, if it was only a question o' whiskers!" said Thomas, sadly.

"It's ALL a question o' whiskers!" vehemently retorted Jimmy Swan. "There's naething criminal or immoral about whiskers, but in a drapery concern they're a Symbol. Your fine half-Dundrearies are an indication o' your state o' mind. The world is a' for youth — which I take to be onything under sixty, and there's the pair o' ye advertisin' that ye're nearly centenarians. It's no' on your face only that there's whiskers; they're in your philosophy and on your business. Twa men your age, wi' health, and twenty shillin's in the pound, and an auld-established business, should be oot in the mornin's whistlin' like mavises[4] and gambollin' round the shop like boys."

"I doubt we're not the gambollin' kind," said Robert humbly, for the first time in his life painfully conscious of his whiskers. "But nobody can say we haven't paid strict attention to business.".... "And walked in the fear of God," he added as an afterthought.

"That's it!" said Jimmy Swan. "More whiskers! It would suit ye better to walk in His glory and sing the 27th Psalm.[5] It's no' in the fear and admonition o' the Lord ye're walkin', but in mortal terror o' the Store. Bonny-like Grants ye are? Wi' a motto like 'Stand Fast!' that ought to stir ye up and stiffen ye like a trumpet! Man, the very sound o't dirls like the tune Dunfermline!"

"There's something in it!" said Thomas tremulously. "Perhaps we were a little too timid about the Store, Robert?"

"Ye couldna help it wi' thae whiskers!" said Jimmy Swan. "There's nothing worse for the nerve than fluff. Shave off your whiskers and I'll guarantee that between us we'll make the Store look silly. I never saw the sense o' Stores; they don't get their stuff from C. & M."

"Could ye suggest anything, Mr Swan?" asked Robert, also infected by this fearless spirit. "Anything to, as it were, buck us up in the business?"

"Man, amn't I tellin' ye? — Whiskers! whiskers! whiskers! Get them aff! Be as young as I am — twenty-six; I only begin to count from the day I married. It's a' nonsense about bein' douce and demure, and auld-lookin' — at least, in the drapery trade; it may suit a'right wi' undertakers. Take the whiskers aff your shop, and aff your stock, and aff the dressin' o' your windows!"

"There's maybe something in what you say," admitted Robert, "but there seem to be such chances out in Canada!"

"Of course there are!" said Jimmy Swan. "Wherever there's clean cheeks, there's chances, and every man in Canada has a safety razor. But, bless your heart, man! Canada's no' the only place! If half the folk that went to Canada had only stayed at home and shaved themsel's,

and took the side-wings aff their business, and the fluff frae
their way o' lookin' at things, there would be nae necessity
to emigrate. Are ye stupid enough to think this country's
done because the Store has added drapery? It's a sign that
it's only startin', and that better men are wanted. Good
luck to them in Canada! but let you and me stay here and
shave oursel's."

The brothers Grant looked at each other. "I think, after
all," said Thomas, "you might show us some of your
winter lines."

"Certainly," said Jimmy Swan with the utmost alacrity,
and humming "Onward, Christian Soldiers," went outside
to fetch his samples.

16. *Blate Rachel*

JIMMY SWAN, with a superb carnation in his coat-lapel, was
leaning on the counter of the widow Thorpe, recounting
all the splendours of a wedding he had been a guest at on
the previous day, when he observed a tear was in the
widow's eye. He promptly changed the subject, and went
back to the claims of Union Shantung for good hard wear
and smart appearance.

"You never can tell," he thought, "when a widow woman's too far on in years to be sentimental; the puir old
body's envious." But he misunderstood.

"Everybody has luck but me,"she said to him, indifferent, for the moment, to his Shantung samples; "there's my
lassie Rachel, and there's no' man looks near her."

"Toots!" said Jimmy blithely, "what's the matter wi'
her? Is she skelly-e'ed?"

"There's naething wrang wi' her,"replied the widow
peevishly; "she got a better chance, to start wi', in her looks
than ever I got, but she's blate.[1] Put her next a lad, and
she's so shy she might be skelly[2] in both e'es and he
wouldna get a chance to see it."

"Blate! " said Jimmy, with surprise. "That's a female

disease I thought was oot o' fashion. Are ye sure it's no' her adenoids?"

The widow positively wept as she disclosed the troubles she had had with Rachel. She had given her a first-rate education, up as far as Chemistry and Elocution; she had lavished dress upon her to the point of gold watch-wristlets, petticoats of silk and patent American pumps; she had taken her to hydros[3] "But there she is!" bewailed the mother; "goin' on eight-and-twenty, and I'll swear she never had a box o' chocolates I didna buy for her mysel'! It's rale disheartenin', Mr Swan. I'd give a lot to see her settled down. But there! — ye'll think I'm just a sly designin' woman."

The traveller smiled. "So far as I can see," he said, "the trouble is that ye're no' half sly enough nor much o' a dab at the designin', or otherwise, if Rachel's like the world, you should hae been a granny. I've never seen her."

"Come up the stair and ha'e a cup o' tea," said Mrs Thorpe; "I'm no' ashamed to let ye see her."

"I will!" said Jimmy with alacrity, and gave a little twitch to his superb carnation. If Rachel Thorpe was blate she showed no signs of it to him. He told her three quite funny stories, led the conversation on to operas, and sitting down to the piano vamped his own accompaniment (three good chords and a twiddly one) to "Star of Eve," which, he explained, was a good deal finer when sung by a tenor who could really sing. Rachel, thus encouraged, gave a palpitating rendering of "The Rosary," the widow looking all the time at Jimmy in expectant anguish as if he were an *entrepreneur* who was testing a soprano.

"Capital!" he murmured at the end of every verse. "Expression! Feeling! Temperament! Particularly that rallantando bit! For such a heavy song, she's simply wonderful!" He finally presented her with the carnation.

"Now, can you tell what's the matter wi' her?" asked the mother when she got him back into the shop. "Time's aye slippin' past, and a' the diffies[4] in the place are gettin' married, and Rachel's jist the way ye see her."

"A bonny, wise-like lass!" said he, with emphasis. "Perhaps it wasna fair to call her Rachel. Rachel, Ruth, Rebecca — ony o' them's a handicap in this dull material age, Mrs Thorpe; ye want a snappy, cheery sort o' name to give a girl a chance. 'Rachel's' solemn; it takes a lot o' pluck to put an arm about a Rachel. Ye should have ca'd her Jean. But she didna strike me as out o' the ordinar' shy; we got on together fine."

"Ah, yes," said Mrs Thorpe; "she got on a' right wi' you, for you're a married man, but if a lad comes to the house she hasna hardly got a word to say, and I've to do the talkin'."

"What do ye talk about to them?" asked Jimmy.

"Oh, anything at all." she answered, rather puzzled at the question. "Thank God, I never was at a loss for conversation! And Rachel, she sits fidgin'!"

"Yon's an interestin' photo album," said Jimmy, who had been personally conducted through it. "I suppose ye'll show them that?"

"Ye had to entertain them some way," said the widow sadly. "Expecially if your daughter is a dummy."

"H'm!" said Jimmy, and rubbed his chin. "It's hardly fair to Rachel! There's half a dozen photos o' her yonder that amount to a complete exposure o' her past. 'Rachel as a baby' — nice, and wee, and fat; 'Rachel at the period o' the fringe,' 'Rachel when she won the ping-pong prize' — wi' a bolero jacketee, accordion pleats, and a motor kep. Ye shouldna rake up her past like that in front o' any chap ye're wantin' to encourage. It mak's her look like the History o' Scotland in monthly parts."

"I never thought o' that! " said Mrs Thorpe.

"Besides, the album, as a whole, is obsolete as a social and domestic cheerer-up. It's done! Ye might as well attempt to rouse enthusiasm wi' a game o' dominoes or a spellin'-bee. Any young man that you show through yon album is bound to get a fright when he sees three generations o' the Thorpes and a' their ramifications down to sixty-second cousins. It reduces Rachel to a mere incident.

He's apt to say to himsel', 'Great Scot! she's no unique at all: there have been hundreds o' her!' And it's so unlucky there's so mony o' them deid! Brief life is here our portion, as the hymn says, but we needna rub it in to Rachel's friends that even the Thorpes get old and disappear; they want to think of her as in eternal youth, for ever gaily skippin' across the sands o' time in a hobble skirt and clocked silk stockin's."

"Ye're a droll man! " said Mrs Thorpe laughing.

"And then there's another thing," said Jimmy twinkling. "I'll wager ye're far too anxious to be nice to any young man ye see in Rachel's company. That's no the way to take the situation at all ! My mother-in-law knew better than that when I was after Bella — that's the mistress. She forbade me to come near the house after her lassie, and used to look on me like dirt. She said the Swans were a' geese, and warned Bella to have naething to dae wi' me. Up till then Bella, wi' me, was just a lass for walkin' hame from the dancin' wi'; but when my pride was roused I up and married her ! And the auld yin laughed !"

"That might do wi' others," said the widow, "but no wi' Rachel; she's so blate."

"Blate!" said Jimmy. "That'll be her salvation; there's far mair chance for a blate yin than the other kind. If she's really blate, and we had her down in Gleska she would be a novelty. Onything out o' the ordinar' takes in Gleska. Send her down for a week to Mrs Swan, to see the shops; there's nothing beats a change o' air for blateness."

"It's very kind of ye," said Mrs Thorpe. "She wouldna be the worse for't, maybe. But ye'll think I'm an awfu' designin' woman !"

"Good!" said Jimmy heartily. "Bella will be glad to see her. And as for the designin', Mrs Thorpe, God meant it.

17. *Rachel Comes to Town*

JAMES SWAN had mischievously described the girl from Banchory[1] to his wife as "a spindly one wi' ruby hair, a voice like the start o' a gramophone, and clothes picked up in the dark at a jumble sale," and when the visitor jumped out of a taxi-cab, which also bore a substantial trunk, a leather hat-box, a neat morocco dressing-case, and a bag of golf-clubs, from the railway station, Mrs Swan immediately realised that she had been badly done.

"I can't believe a word you say to me, sometimes, Jimmy!"she exclaimed with agitation, as the door bell rang.

There was nothing spindly about Rachel; her hair was a glorious golden; her voice was sweet and mellow as a mavis' song, and her dress alone was summed up in two seconds by Mrs Swan as costing anything over £6, 10s.

"And where's the blateness of her?" Jimmy was asked at the earliest opportunity. "I thought from your description that you couldn't drag a word from her except in the dummy alphabet."

Jimmy chuckled. "I only told ye what her mother said," he answered. "The case is desperate. She's goin' on eight and twenty — "

"Just a child!" said his wife from the point of view of forty.

"Everybody in Banchory's gettin' married but hersel'; take her round the town before we go to Kirn,[2] and give her wrinkles."

"The only kind of wrinkles I have nowadays are the sort a woman gets from being married," said Mrs Swan with a look at herself in the overmantel mirror.

But really Rachel Thorpe required no wrinkles. Jimmy was off the road for a week and busy at the warehouse; for three nights in succession, when he came home at tea-time, he found a vacant house and the fire out; a hitherto conscientious wife was being dragged around the town at the heels of the blate young thing from Banchory, and wasn't even ashamed of herself.

"I never go anywhere, James," she said; "you never take me over the door. I've seen more of Glasgow in the past three days with Rachel than I've done in twenty years with you."

The ladies together went to picture-palaces, tearooms, parks; they paraded Buchanan Street and Sauchiehall Street by the hour, fascinated by windows; they rode on the outside of tramway cars as far as cars would take them; one night they were not home till ten; Rachel had insisted on a music-hall.

"Oh, it's all right!" said Jimmy, meekly. "I'm vexed I never thought o' makin' ye a hot supper. I'll leave the door on the Chubb after this, and ye can jist slip in when ye like. There'll be something cold on the sideboard. But for goodness' sake don't start singin' and pullin' beer and make a row and wake me; mind, I'm gettin' up in years."

"You should come out with us," seriously suggested the girl from Banchory. "What's the sense of sitting in here moping all alone when you might be enjoying yourself? Mrs Swan and I are going to see "Way Back in Darkeyland" tomorrow night. I've just been telling her I hear it's fine."

"No," said he, ironically; "I canna be bothered goin' anywhere unless I can get dancin'; I'm vexed it's no' the social season; you and Bella would like a ball."

On his wife had come the most extraordinary transformation. The fashion in which she put up her hair was preposterously antiquated, according to Rachel, who dressed it to look three times as thick as it was before, with glints of sunshine in its bronze that no one had hitherto suspected. Rachel also in an hour or two devised a hat for Mrs Swan, so chic and saucy that of itself it immediately knocked ten years off her age, and induced in the wearer a corresponding spirit of youthful gaiety. She took about a breadth from the width of her Sunday gown, reduced its length amazingly, bought the nattiest kind of shiny shoes, and displayed in the frankest manner a beautiful pair of shot-silk stockings. Her husband saw her one day jump on a car with Rachel, and they looked like a couple of soubrettes in "The Girl in the Film."

"Ye seem to have picked me up a' wrang, Bella," he said to his wife when they were alone that evening.

"The idea was that Rachel Thorpe was to have her shyness polished off wi' a week in Gleska, and maybe learn a tip or twa on the way to get a sweetheart. There's no' that mony sweethearts disengaged in Gleska that ye can look for one a-piece. Besides, as lang as I hing on, it wouldna be respectable."

"Pooh!" said Bella, radiantly; "you want to see me going out a perfect fright. I never had a fling to myself since I was married, and now that Rachel's here I'm going to have it. Your idea of what is fit and proper in a married woman's fifty years behind the times. Rachel was quite astonished at the life I lead."

"And that's the girl her mither thinks is blate!" said Mr Swan, derisively.

The Swans had taken three weeks of a house at Kirn; they removed to the coast on Monday, and the girl from Banchory went with them. In two days she had taught Mrs Swan the game of golf, how to swing most effectively in a hammock, the two-step, "Hitchy-Koo"[3] and divers other pleasing ditties, the right deportment for a walking-stick, and the way to clear the bows of a steamer by ten yards in a rowing-boat so as to get the rocking of the waves and a good view of the captain dancing with rage on the bridge.

Jimmy came down from town one afternoon, and saw them waiting for him on the pier. At first he had looked at them with amiable and even approving interest, for he did not, at a distance, recognise them. They had white serge skirts, white shoes and stockings, knitted sports-coats of a vivid mustard colour, knitted caps conform thereto in hue, and walking-sticks. They were distinctly making gallant play at coquetry with two young gentlemen he did not know, and to whom he was introduced with some embarrassment on the part of all concerned.

"There's just one thing ye have overlooked," he told his wife, who had dropped behind with him while the blate girl from Banchory went up the pier between the two young gentlemen, putting down her feet with splendid artfulness so that nobody could help looking at them. Next to Mrs Swan's they were the neatest feet on the Cowal side of the coast that day.

"What do you mean? What did I overlook?" asked Mrs Swan, who seemed deliriously happy.

"The dug," said Jimmy, seriously. "Ye need a wee bit toy terrier under your oxter,[4] and instead o' the walking-stick I would hae a tennis-racket. If I may ask, where did ye pick up thae twa misguided gentlemen?"

"Oh, just on the quay," said Mrs Swan. "They're very nice. They came off a boat from Rothesay."

"Did they just wink at ye, or did you see them first and say, 'Ha, Berty!'?"

"Nothing so common!" said Mrs Swan, with dignity. "We pretended we didn't see them, but they would insist on speaking to Rachel."

"Just that!" said Jimmy. "I'm goin' to write to Rachel's mother the night and tell her to get Rachel shifted back to Banchory as quick as possible, before my happy home is broken up."

His wife laughed. "Do you know who they are?" she said. "They're just two Banchory friends of Rachel's, and the one with the fancy waistcoat wants to marry her. He came here specially to ask her, and she says she will."

"Could he no' ask her up in Banchory?" asked Jimmy with surprise.

"No," said Mrs Swan; "not without her mother over-hearing. She was always there, and kept cracking Rachel up so much that the poor lad never got a chance to shove a word in telling his intentions."

"That's exactly what I thought!" said Mr Swan. "But what are you, at the age of over forty, comin' out so strong in the nutette[5] line for?"

"Just to cheer up and encourage Rachel; just to make her think that married life's no' so dull as she would think if she saw me at my ordinary," said the amazing Mrs Swan.

18. *A Poor Programme*

"YOU'RE the last landlord on this side of the Clyde to keep slippers for your guests," said Mr Swan. "It's not that I'm needin' them myself, but I like to see them; they're one of the few surviving relics of the age *de luxe* in the history of commercial travellin'."

"Do you know the way I manage to keep them, Mr Swan?" said the landlord of the Queen's. "I got them big! There's not a coffee-room pair of slippers here that's under easy number tens. It was a waiter, Alick Russell, put me up to 't. I lost about a gross of slippers every year through gentlemen finding them so good a fit they thought they were their own. 'Whit ye want,' says Alick, 'is big and roomy yins they canna walk upstairs to their bedrooms wi'.' I went away at once and bought three dozen pair of number tens. The only man they ever fitted was a cattleman from Perth. The rest just leave them."

Mr Swan put on his own slippers.

"You're surely not in for the night?" said Mr Grant; "there's a Territorial concert[1] on."

Just for a moment Jimmy hesitated. "No," he said; "I'm bye wi' country concerts; they're too heatin' for my blood. If it was a swarry and a ball, or a Council meetin', I might risk it. That's the worst of bein' highly cultivated — I canna put up wi' ' Hitchy-Koo,' and they're bound to have ' Hitchy-Koo ' in Fochabers, especially wi' a Territorial concert. It's a hundred chances to one a Colour-Sergeant wi' a nearly tenor voice 'll stand up and give 'The Phantom Army,' and as sure as daith I cannot stand 'The Phantom Army.' It was maybe good enough till the hundred thousandth time I heard it, but then it began to spoil my sleep.

Forbye, 'The Phantom Army' 's no' a song for Territorials; it's far too personal."

"They have a lot of talent," said the landlord coaxingly.

"I know they'll have," said Mr Swan agreeably. "I notice in the country papers that they're always super-excellent. Did it ever occur to you, Mr Grant, that music's done in Scotland? I mean vocal music; of course there's aye the pianola. There are only two kinds o' singers now in Scotland — the real professional that needs an evening suit for't, and the young and healthy amateur who does 'Phil the Fluter's Ball' or 'No, John, No!' as if his life depended on it."

"The gramophone — " said Mr Grant.

"Of course! Quite right! The gramophone's the music master now; whenever 'Everybody's Doing It' comes out in a Glasgow Pantomime, they wire at once from Fochabers to send a dozen records. No time is lost! The latest rag-time tune is up at Thurso wi' the mornin' post, and everybody's whistlin't by tea-time.

"Half the folk in the country's sick-tired o' music, and the other half's tryin' to be Clara Butts[2] and Harry Lauders — a thing that sounds quite easy when you hear it in a canister. Half the nice wee lassies that could sing like laverocks if they were content to sing the way that God intended them, fair sicken ye wi' tryin' to get cadenzas like the banker's Tetrazzini,[3] ten-and-six the double-breasted disc. The other half realise they could never do anything within a mile of it, and they never try; they just put up their hair another way, and tell the chap they're fond of cookin'."

"But still it's a very decent programme," said the landlord producing it.

Mr Swan put on his glasses. "That's it! I knew it at once!" he said. "'The Prologue from Pagliacci, by Mr G. R. Williamson.' I don't ken Mr Williamson, but I'll bet ye he's a tall, thin, fair-haired chap in the Union Bank, and has a lisp. He'll be at least a light and easy baritone: he couldn't do't unless. Then there's ' A Wee Deoch an'

Doruis' — I ken that, too! He'll likely be a gas collector, a smart wee blackavised chap wi' a comic kind o' face and a crackle up aboot the F. Comic singing is sappin' the manhood o' the nation; it's worse than cigarettes. 'Angus Macdonald,' by Miss — Oh! take it away and put it in the larder! The only thing I see on the programme worth a rap is 'God save the King'; that's about the only chance that folk get now for singing.

"The place where people sing is Wales, and emulation o' the gramophone hasna spoiled them," said Mr Swan, warming to his subject. "Not being a solo vocalist myself, I always thought harmonic music was the best, and that's the notion o' the Welshmen. You see it gives a modest kind o' chap like me a chance. Thirty years ago there was some sense o' vocal music left in Scotland; there were choirs; now they think a choir is jist a special place for sittin' in the kirk. So long as there were choirs and glee parties there was some hope for us, though we maybe werena just exactly Covent Garden opera. We sang for singing's sake, and we didna try to beat the gramophone.

"There's two things worth while in this world — gettin' a Saturday to yoursel' and singin' bass in a choir that has a decent tenor. I never was happier! And music — genuine music — never got a better chance. So far as I'm aware there was never anything positively rotten put in harmony; quartet, glee, and catch were always decent. Three-fourths of the agony of life today is due to that ridiculous prefer-ence for the solo. When the average amateur soloist comes in leanin' heavily on himself wi' a couple o' music sheets — one for the poor soul at the instrument and the other for himself to hide his presentation watch-chain — I'm sorry for him.

"I'm all for choirs and a good bass part for willing gentlemen! It's only wi' part-singing that ye'll stem the tide of British musical decadence — what do you think of that for rhetoric at this early hour o' evening, Mr Grant?"

"I like 'O, Who Will o'er the Downs?' and 'Kate Dalrymple,'" said Mr Grant with modesty.

"Right you are!" said Mr Swan emphatically. "Your tastes are sound! They werena tripe — these songs — at any rate!"

"All these remarks o' mine," continued Mr Swan, "are due to the fact that at a Glasgow public dinner the other night there was a choir. I havena heard a choir at a Glasgow public dinner for twenty years, and I'm thinkin' neither did the company. The usual idea o' a Glasgow dinner now is that a dozen men spoil a' the fun wi' makin' speeches. You'll never convince the poor deluded creatures that they have not something really new to say, and that folk don't want to hear them. Nobody ever does. It just fair spoils the coffee and cigars.

"At this dinner some daring innovator introduced a choir, the speakin' was cut down to the assurance that the Navy was right and trade was boomin', and the choir took up the rest o' the evening makin' us really happy. If dinners were a' like that one, they would be my hobby."

"Then you're not coming?" said Mr Grant.

"Not me!" said Jimmy, lighting his pipe; "be sure and lock the door when ye come back. And tell the Pagliacci gentleman he hasna 't in him! Tell him to start a decent choir."

19. *Broderick's Shop*

JAMES SWAN went into an Argyle Street shop on Saturday to buy a knife. It is one of the oldest ironmongery shops[1] in town, but that was not the reason Jimmy went to it; antiquity of itself makes no appeal to him; he went to this particular shop because he knew the owner, who had for years been on the verge of losing money on it.

Elsewhere in Argyle Street[2] it was the busiest hour of the day. All the world seemed out for buying. Drapery warehouses were crowded to the doors, the grocery shops, which also advertise, appeared too small for the folk who wanted into them; the lust for giving money in exchange for something crowded the street itself with gutter merchants feverishly dispensing fruit, and flowers, and penny toys that last (with care) till Monday. Argyle Street blazed with light and roared with commerce; electric moons, refulgent, made it bright as day; a thousand windows gorgeously displayed their best; the pavements streamed with life, and every other person had a parcel.

"Beautiful!" said Jimmy to himself. "Tip-top! Lovely! And just to think that this was once a country lane!"

He felt a genuine pride in Glasgow, and a personal pride that he was an essential part in its commercial activities. It was with almost a paternal eye he stopped to look at a window with a dummy figure wearing one of C. & M.'s "Incomparable" Long-Busk Corsets, there because himself had thrown no little poetry into its recommendation.

To step from the street into Broderick's ironmongery shop, however, was to leave the roar of battle and get into a mausoleum. A solemn hush prevailed there. A customer was standing at the counter, plunged in the patient contemplation of long rows of rather dusty shelves with nothing more attractive to the eye on them than screw-nail packages. In parts behind two shopmen blew or flicked the dust from other packages; Broderick himself was on the ladder.

He came down at last, deliberately; gave a friendly nod to Jimmy; opened the parcel he had brought down with him, and found it was the wrong one. So he went up the ladder again, and in the course of time disposed of a key-ring to the customer for a penny. The customer gave sixpence for its payment. Mr Broderick picked the sixpence up and walked with dignity to some place far away in the back of his shop where he kept his cash-desk.

Jimmy took out his watch and held it in his hand.

The hum of the clamant, buying street came in, like some far murmur of a sea; below the wan, old-fashioned gas-light over Broderick's door ("Established 1812"), the multitude went skliffing past along the pavement, deigning not so much as a glance within. He hummed the funeral march from "Saul" to himself, and felt exceedingly sorry for Alick Broderick.

When Broderick had got the change for sixpence and dismissed his customer, he turned with a pathetic expansiveness to Jimmy.

"There's no' much profit aff a penny split ring, Jimmy," said he.

"I daresay no," said Jimmy, snapping up his hunter watch with a last glance at the dial. "Show me a shilling knife, and then shut up this shop o' yours, and come out and ha'e a dram."

"Indeed," said Broderick, "I might well shut it up for a' that's daein'. I never saw things worse"; and he took out a case of knives with great solemnity.

"Alick," said Mr Swan, "do ye mind the day ye blooded my nose in old Maclean's Academy?"

"Ay, fine!" said Mr Broderick. "Ye stole my jawry-bool."[3]

"Weel, I'm gaun to blood your nose the night," said Jimmy, smiling. "Ye better get oot your hanky. ... Ye say that things were never worse. Where are your ears and e'en? Take a daunder[4] alang the street and hear things humming. I could hardly get alang the pavement for folk fair daft to spend their money, and here are you sclimbin'[5] ladders and wearin' oot your shoon to get change for a customer that wants a penny ring. It took ye exactly one minute and forty-five seconds to go away back there to your cash-desk."

"For a' that's daein' —" started Mr Broderick.

"For a' that's daein' — fiddlesticks!" said Jimmy. "There's only six hundred minutes in a workin' day, and you have only the one pair o' legs on ye, and ye waste good minutes and good legs on the heid o' a penny ring. What ails ye at a cash railway, man? Or if ye canna hae a railway, can ye no' keep your cash beside your coonter? Naebody's gaun to pich it on ye! When a customer sees ye makin' a North Pole expedition awa' back there wi' his penny, he thinks he has paid too much for the ring, and ye're away behind to dance the hoolichan."[6]

"There's naething to be done in business nooadays unless ye advertise," said Mr Broderick sadly; "and I never was in wi' advertisin'."

"Were ye no'?" said Jimmy, sharply. "What's your window for but advertisin'?"

"The cost's enormous," said Mr Broderick.

"Have ye ony money bye ye?" asked Jimmy, boldly.

"Thank God I have a little," said Mr Broderick.

"It would need to be a lot," said Jimmy, "for it's you that pays for other ironmongers' advertising, and nae thanks for it."

"I don't understand ye, Jimmy," said his friend. "How do I pay for other folks' advertisin'?"

"Who in heaven's name do ye think pays for't?" said Jimmy.

"The man that advertises."

"Not him! He doesna pay a penny. All he does is to lend a little capital in advertising, that comes back a hundredfold. The more he advertises, the bigger his profits at the end of the year. When did ye ever hear o' a big advertiser failin'? The thing's unknown, and advertisin's only in its infancy."

"Ay, but in the long-run it's the customer that pays for advertisin'," said Mr Broderick.

"There, ye're wrang again!" said Jimmy. "What dae ye charge for this shilling knife?" and he picked up one that met his fancy.

"Just a shillin'," said Mr Broderick.

"Well, I can go to any ironmonger's shop in Gleska that advertises, and I'll get the same knife for a shillin'. Things are never ony dearer in a shop that advertises. So ye see it's neither the advertiser nor the customer that pays the newspapers."

"If it's no', wha is it, then?" asked Mr Broderick, with genuine interest. He had never studied the point before.

"It's you, and the like o' you!" said Jimmy. "Every customer you lose through no' advertisin', and every shop that goes doon through no' advertisin', swells the volume o' business in the shops that advertise, and indirectly pays for other folks' advertising. I never see your name in the papers, but when I read a splash o' Grant & Richards, I say to mysel', 'There's some more o' Alick Broderick's money!' ... Take you my tip, Alick, blaw the stour aff them shelves, and get a nice wee cash railway and a ladder that runs on wheels, and hing oot some dacent lights, and advertise, and ye'll no' complain o' naething daein'."

He paid for his knife and gave a genial chuckle. "Now take out your hanky, lad!" he cried as he left the shop.

A hundred yards along the street he looked at a window of Grant & Richards, in whose shop a roaring trade was doing, and he saw a knife there priced at ninepence in every respect the counterpart of the one he had bought from Broderick.

"Stung!" he said to himself, with a humorous grin. "Alick's got the best o' me again, and it's me that needs the hanky."

20. *Gent's Attire*

THE UTMOST surprise was created last Friday in Campbell & Macdonald's warehouse when Mr Swan appeared in a familiar overcoat. In the memory of the oldest employee he had never previously been known to inaugurate the winter season in any other coat than one quite unmistakably fresh from the tailor's hands. Nothing less would have seemed becoming and appropriate to the oldest traveller for the oldest soft goods firm in Glasgow. The tradition, long prevalent among the warehouse staff of C. & M., was that Jimmy Swan owed much of his renown and success as a traveller to the cut and fashion of his garments, always meticulously fresh and trim, and worn with a certain distinction which was the envy and despair of the younger travellers. They also tried to dress like gentlemen, but only partially succeeded, and always stuck at the halfway stage, where the best that can be said of a wearer of clothes is that he is a knut. They knew it themselves, when Jimmy's eyebrows would lift at the sight of their heliotrope wood-fibre sox or what they had fondly thought a stunning effect in waistcoats.

Yet here was Jimmy Swan in a last winter's greatcoat, ready to start on the northern journey through towns and villages to which, for years, he had been "the glass of fashion and the mould of form"[1] — the seasonal inspiration and example of gent's styles as approved and passed in the Metropolis!

A lapse! A decided and disquieting lapse! It was inconceivable that the best shops in, say, Aberdeen, would give such orders as they used to do, to Jimmy Swan in a last year's topcoat, however cunningly cleaned and pressed to look like new.

"Excuse the liberty, Jimmy," said Carmichael the mantle-buyer, "but what's the matter wi' your tailor? Has your credit stopped?"

Mr Swan, puffing a little, rose from the case he was bent over, packing samples, and shrugged his shoulders

"No," he answered. "If it's my coat you mean, it's just economy. Quite a good coat!"

"Ah! well," conceded Carmichael, "we have all to exercise some thrift or other these days."

"No' in the buyin' branch o' this establishment!" said Mr Swan; "Mr Macdonald's notions o' economy are concentrated in the meantime on the expenses o' the man who books the biggest orders for his firm, and — not to put too fine a point on it — that's me!"

"Good heavens! they're no' surely beginnin' to scrimp YOU, Jimmy?" ejaculated Carmichael, genuinely shocked; it was understood in the shop that up to a pound a-day, Mr Swan's bill for expenses passed the cashier unquestioned; that it was an historical right, like Magna Carta.

Mr Swan only smiled sadly. "Economy's a droll thing, Alick," he remarked, "it's like them Zeppelin bombs,[2] ye never ken where it'll licht, these days. Mr Macdonald has all of a sudden found oot that my buyin' a topcoat or a suit o' clothes noo and then from our country customers, involves us, someway, in the Corrupt Practices Act.³ At least, it's the best excuse he could think o' for knocking a bit aff my expenses."

Carmichael looked surprised. "What does it matter to him where ye buy your clothes?" he asked. "But I never dreamt ye bought any in the country."

"Many and many a time!" said Jimmy. "But nobody can cast up to me that I ever wore them!"

He shut down the lid of his case, and strapped it tightly.

"If ever you had been on the road sellin'," he said, when that was done, "you would understand yoursel' what's meant by my auld topcoat, and Macdonald's new economy. Some o' you chaps get into the buyin' branch wi' little or nae education to speak o' in human nature. A buyer's cock-o'-the-walk; he doesna even need to study to be civil to the folk he deals wi'; it's very different wi' the bagman. I've seen me buy a Hielan' cape I wouldna be dragged oot o' the Clyde by Geordie Geddes⁴ in, and wear it a couple o' days in Dornoch just to please a draper and tailor there I expected a thumpin' order frae."

"Great Scot!" said Carmichael, horrified at the very idea of Mr Swan in a Dornoch cape. "But do ye mean to say they passed the price o' a cape in your expenses?"

"No quite!" said Jimmy. "I sold it at a loss o' a pound when I got to Glasgow, and put the pound doon in my bill. This time last year old Macdonald himself would be the first to agree that it was a pound well spent on the Dornoch orders for fishermen's trousers I used to bring him. Do you know this, Carmichael? I one time went the length o' a suit o' kilts, complete even to the sporran! It was in Inverness, frae a customer that was awfu' namely for his kilts. But Mr Macdonald kicked at kilts; it cost me £2, 10s. to get rid o' them to a Hielandman that had a wee pub doon on the Broomielaw.

"It is the firmly rooted conviction o' the drapery trade in the rural districts o' Scotland that it's fit to tackle gent's attire," continued Mr Swan. "They get the designs and plans for spring lounge suits frae last year's 'Tailor and Cutter' newspaper; heave a web o' tweed at their cutter the first fine day he's aff the spree, tell him the only change this season's in lapels, remind him that cotton lining's nae langer bein' put in breeks, then press a lump o' chalk and a fret-saw into his tremblin' hands, and order him to proceed.

"I've passed through the hands o' mair country cutters than any other man in Scotland. Ye never catch me wearin' onything but a genuine Glasgow suit, but for the sake o' business I've had to order suits in lots o' places no' the size o' Fochabers, where they put rabbit-pouches in your jacket whether ye poach or no', and would palm off a waistcoat wi' sleeves on ye if ye werena watchin'. There's at least a score o' country clothiers in Scotland that expect me to buy a suit or a topcoat frae them every year; the goods is sometimes waitin' ready for me when I land; if there's any difference in the length o' my sleeve since last year, they're ready to tak' in a hem.

"What do I dae wi' the clothes? I sometimes put them into my sample case and sell them in the next wee toon I come to as a model garment fresh from London, goin' at a dead-snip bargain. Some o' them I get rid o' in the packin'-shop at fifteen shlllin's or a pound less than I paid for them; many a time I'm left wi' a Harris tweed the wife can only use for cuttin' up to go under a runner carpet. But up till now the firm has played fair horney,[5] and seen I didna lose on my diplomatic stimulation o' the tailor trade in the turnip districts."

"It's not fair!" said Carmichael emphatically.

"It is not!" agreed the traveller. "Macdonald's kickin' aboot 30s. I honestly spent in pushin' business in Clachnacudden last October. I had aye to tak' a suit in Clachnacudden; Elshiner the draper seen to that. He had aye a range o' home-dyed, homespun tweeds for the local cattle show, and a cutter that took your measure a' wrang in Gaelic wi' a piece o' string. I've got suits frae Elshiner I could never sell onywhere at a third o' what they cost me; they were that roary, and that defiant o' every law o' the male anatomy.

"Last October, when Elshiner's cutter was passin' the string all over my manly form, and stoppin' to tak' a snuff each time that Elshiner put doon the Gaelic figures in a pass-book, I says, 'Whit profit do ye expect to mak' aff this suit, Mr Elshiner?'

"'Thirty shillin's or thereabouts,' says he.

"'Ah, well!' says I; 'don't bother makin' it; I'll pay the 30s. and we'll be a' square.'

"He took the thirty shillin's right enough, but his pride was touched, for he someway jaloused I didna appreciate his suits. And, if ye believe me, he has never given me an order since! That's the way Macdonald's kickin'."

21. *Keeping up with Cochrane*

IT IS a stimulating thing to see a fellow-creature socially climbing, and up to a certain point Mr James Swan was quite delighted with the progress of his customer Watty Cochrane. He had in a sense been the making of Watty. It was he, nine years ago, who put Watty on to the excellent opening there was for an up-to-date drapery shop in Lairg.[1] He selected his first stock for him; got him a good credit from C. & M.; put him up to the art of window-dressing; and got him a wife with some sensible Glasgow notions of a mantua department.

"She's doin' fine," said Mr Cochrane, after eighteen months of married felicity. "She brought in last year £150 o' profit to the business, all out o' that bit room behind there, where I used to keep my lumber. She calls it an atelier, whatever that is; so far as I'm concerned she might call it a fusilier, so long's she draws in business the way she does in homespun costumes."

"The main thing is she's up to guarantee," said Jimmy Swan. "I knew Kate Jardine was the sort to make a 'happy

fireside clime,'[2] and ' that's the true pathos and sublime o'
human life,' as Burns says."

"There's nothing pathetic about £150," said Cochrane;
"it's nearly £3 a week. But when ye speak about a fireside
climb, ye've hit the mark; Kate and me's started climbin',
and I lie awake at nichts sometimes wondering what I'll
reach to if I keep my health. What would ye say to Provost
Walter Cochrane, eh?" And the draper rubbed his palms
together.

The traveller looked at him with a critical eye.

"'Well done!' I should say. 'Ye have fine shouthers for a
chain, and the right sort o' chest for a door-knocker. But
see and no' let your heid swell, Walter, or I'll be vexed I
went and wasted Kate on ye!'"

After that, on every journey to the North he could see
the climbing of Watty Cochrane. Mr Cochrane was made
the Captain of the Golf Club, and immediately burst forth
in knickerbocker suits. At the urgent solicitation of the
citizens — at all events at the urgent solicitation of two of
them, who were on his books — he went into the Town
Council[3] and became assured of undying local fame as the
introducer of the ash-bin cleansing system. He talked more
about ash-bins and destructors to Jimmy Swan on his visits
than about the drapery business.

"How's the mistress?" Jimmy asked him sometimes; she
was never to be seen.

"Up to the ears in the atelier," would Walter say with
pride; "she's thrang[4] on a weddin' job for Invershin."

"I hope," said Jimmy, "she's on the climb, too. There
canna be much fun in sclimbin' if your wife's to stand at
the foot a' the time and steady the ladder."

"I don't quite catch ye?" said Councillor Walter
Cochrane, convener of the Sanitary Committee.

"What I mean," said Jimmy, "is that if you're goin' to
climb awa' up to the giddy heights o' social and civic
eminence ye seem to have your mind set on, and leave her
up to the ears in the atelier, which is just the French for
workshop, I'll consider I did an ill turn by Kate Jardine

when I put her in your road. So far as I can see, this climbin's a' in the interest o' Walter Cochrane. If ye go on the way ye're doing, she'll soon no' be able to look at ye except through a bit o' smoked gless, the same's ye were an eclipse. I thought it was a wife I got for ye, and no' a heid mantle-maker."

"Do you know what she made last year in the dressmakin'?" asked Councillor Cochrane.

"I don't know, and I don't care," said Jimmy bluntly. "I could get ye scores o' dressmakers just as good from Gleska, but no' another wife like Kate Jardine, and I'm feared ye're tryin' to smother her in selvedges."[5]

On Mr Swan's next journey to Lairg he was just in time to participate in a chippy little dinner given to a select stag company at the Inn to celebrate Councillor Cochrane's elevation to the bench of Justices of the Peace. The dinner was the new J.P.'s. Councillor Cochrane was obviously becoming very fond of himself. He made three separate speeches in a newly acquired throaty kind of voice, which he seemed to consider incumbent on a J.P. Several times he took occasion to allude to his last interview with the Lord Lieutenant of the County.

"Who's he?" Jimmy took an opportunity of asking.

"The Duke, of course," said Councillor Cochrane.

"Which o' them?" asked Jimmy innocently. "I never can mind the names o' them unless I look up Orr's Penny Almanac."

"Sutherland," said the new J.P. "He's the Lord Lieutenant o' the County, and makes all the J.P.'s. At least, the names are put before him, and he signs the Commissions."

"Plucky chap!" said Jimmy. "Some men would bolt at the desperate responsibility. Listening to ye, there, Walter, I couldna help bein' sorry there's no' a uniform for J.P.'s the same as for Lord-Lieutenants. That heid o' yours'll never get a chance until ye get a helmet."

The new J.P. considered the occasion incomplete without having his portrait done in oils, and he imported from Aberdeen a fearless young artist, who in five or six days achieved a masterpiece six feet high, wherein Councillor Cochrane was brilliantly revealed as the sort of man who is in the habit of sitting in a frock-coat suit, irrelevantly but firmly grasping a roll of vellum.

The consequence was that when Mr Swan returned to Lairg in autumn in the commercial interest of C. & M., he found his customer had flitted to a grand new villa. The fact was intimated casually over a counter piled with Jimmy's samples.

"Keep it up!" said Jimmy with an air of resignation.

"Lairg's gettin' ower small for ye. And how is she gettin' on, hersel', in the atelier?"

"Thronger than ever!" said Councillor Cochrane triumphantly. "Workin' till all hours since the shootin' started."

"Puir Kate!" said Jimmy. "She used to be the cheery yin when I kent her in Gleska. She used to hae her evenin's to hersel', and nae bother aboot a villa. What put the villa in your heid, Walter?"

"It was," said Councillor Cochrane, "the portrait to begin wi'. You see, in the old house the portrait was so big in the wee parlour it fair drowned everything else. Besides, in my position — " and he closed abruptly with a gesture which plainly indicated that the position of a J.P. with the prospects of further civic dignities demanded a reasonable area of domestic space to move about in. "What I want ye to do for me, now," he proceeded, "is to send me up from the Clyde a flag-pole for the front o' the house."

"What do ye want wi' a flag-pole?" said Jimmy with surprise. "Are ye goin' to start sclimbin' flagpoles next?"

"No," said Councillor Cochrane: "but a bit of a pole goes well wi' a villa. I see a lot o' them in the villas down at Inverness. Many a time a body wants to hoist a flag. A flag-pole gives a kind o' finish."

The flag-pole was duly ordered by Mr Swan, who had dreams of a greatly inflated Cochrane painfully sprawling up and sitting on the truck with Kate Jardine sitting making costumes at the foot. For months he had no communication with his soaring customer, but at last he got a letter asking him to keep his eye about for a couple of iron cannons, second-hand. The letter came to Jimmy one morning as he sat at home at breakfast, and he groaned as he perused it.

"What's the matter, Jimmy?" asked his wife.

"It's Watty Cochrane in Lairg," he told her. "He's goin' to shoot himsel', and he thinks himsel' that big it needs a couple o' cannons to do the job."

"Nonsense!" said Mrs Swan

"No, I'm wrang!" said Jimmy, hastily, proceeding further with his reading of the letter "They're for the front of the villa; he wants them four feet lang and mounted, for he's noo a Bailie I'll see him to the mischief first! I've troked[6] aboot for mony a droll thing for my customers, but I draw the line at cannons. What'll he be wantin' next if they mak' him Provost?"

Jimmy went up to Lairg on his next North journey with a plausible tale that there was a positive dearth of second-hand cannons in the West of Scotland, as they were all taken up by the Territorial artillery.

"It doesna matter," said Bailie Cochrane, looking slightly worried. "I thought they would make a kind of artistic finish to the villa, but I doubt I'll have to do without them. What I'm wantin' more's a forewoman. You would hear the news?"

"No," said Jimmy.

"The wife's given up the atelier. … It's twins," said Bailie Cochrane.

22. *The Hen Crusade*

"Do ye mind yon hen ye were good enough to send my wife for her stall at the Bazaar?" asked Boyd the draper as Mr Swan was putting back his samples in their cases.

"Fine!" said Jimmy. "I hope it was all right?"

"It was right enough," said Mr Boyd, solemnly; "but it caused a lot o' ill-will among the customers," and Jimmy, bent above his cases, indulged in a crafty wink to himself.

"There wasn't a body came to that Bazaar," went on the draper, "that didn't want to buy the hen. There was what I might call a regular furore about her. And because one hen couldna be sold to four hundred different folk, they took the pet and went away without buyin' anything. I canna understand it; the folk in this place seem to be daft for poultry ... What are ye laughing at, Mr Swan?"

"Was the Bazaar a success?" asked Jimmy.

"Indeed and it was not! They didna get half the money that they wanted, and I'm no' vexed; it wasna wi' my will that my wife gave countenance to a Bazaar to buy an organ; what we're needin's no' an organ, but a new minister; we're all fair sick o' Cameron.. ... But what in a' the earth are ye grinnin' at, Mr Swan?"

"I'll tell ye that," said Jimmy; "I'm laughing at the continued triumph o' my Hen Crusade. You see I'm utterly against Bazaars, Mr Boyd. They're the worst form o' Sweatin' that we have in this country. They're blackleg labour. They're bad for the shopkeeper's business, and they're bad for my firm, C. & M. If the craze for Bazaars went any further, I would soon be sellin' naething else but remnants, and folk would expect to get them gratis wi' a bonus ticket. Now, when a customer like yoursel' asks me for a trifle for his wife's stall, I darena well refuse, but I took a survey of the situation some time since, and I saw how I could please my customer and at the same time put a spoke in the Bazaar. The common hen, Mr Boyd, humble, unostentatious, and industrious in life, becomes, when dead, the valued friend o' British commerce."

"Yours was the only fowl in that Bazaar," said Mr Boyd, "and it fair upset it!"

"Exactly!" said Jimmy, rubbing his hands with the greatest satisfaction. "Works like a charm, every time! I'm strongly advising C. & M. to send a hen to every Bazaar that opens."

"Every person who came into that Bazaar made a dash at once for the produce stall and grabbed the hen, though it had a ticket ' Sold' on it before the door was opened."

"The wife, I suppose?" said Jimmy, innocently.

"Yes," said Mr Boyd, a little flushed. "It was a tidy hen; well worth the half-crown you put on it."

"I always fix the price as low as that," said Jimmy, "though that hen cost me exactly three-and-nine. If the price is low, the competition is the keener."

"At last my wife had to send the fowl home before it was torn to bits by exasperated customers; but all the same everybody coming into that place till the latest hour at night was asking for the hen. And because we didn't have table-loads o' half-croon hens they took the huff and went away, as I say, without buyin' anything. The funny thing is they all kent there was a hen before they came near the place."

"They always do!" said Jimmy. "The rumour of something really useful in a Bazaar goes round a town like this like a fiery cross, and that's the phenomenon I take advantage of in my Hen Crusade. You see, it has got this length wi' Bazaars that they're filled wi' fancy-work no rational mortal soul could fancy. The first thing a woman does in the way o' contributin' to a stall is to cut up something useful and turn it into something ornamental, and the poor misguided body who buys it and brings it home is chaffed a lot about it by her husband. Then, in addition, there's, at all Bazaars, a great bulk o' stuff that's never meant for either use or ornament — it's just Bazaar stuff, made for sellin'. The buyer takes it home and puts it out o' sight till the next Bazaar comes on, and makes it her contribution. It goes from Bazaar to Bazaar till it drops in pieces, or till folk canna guess what it was first intended for.

"It's some years now since the hen came to me as an inspiration. There's something about a hen wi' its heid thrawed[1] that strongly appeals to human nature. I thought to mysel' if I can introduce one fair good hen at a temptin' price to a Bazaar, the struggle for its possession will kill the interest in fancy-work that's far better bought from the retail shops that buy from C & M. It's sure to be bought at the very start by the lady who has it in her stall, and that in itself's annoyin' to the other customers. But, further than that, it's well enough known to every woman who goes about Bazaars that the only thing she can bring home from them to please her man is something he can eat. He has no use for home-made toffee, and he wouldna thank her for the minister's wife's conception o' a seed-cake. A fowl, on the other hand, will never go wrang wi' him, and that's the way ye'll notice that the rumour o' a hen for sale at a Bazaar brings up a queue o' women to the doors an hour before they're open. Half o' them have explicit orders from their husbands to buy that hen, and the other half are planning to give him a nice surprise.

"When the crowd find that the hen's awa' wi't already at half-a-crown to the lady at the stall, it goes home indignant without a glance at the table-centres, and that's another Bazaar burst! I'm tellin' you, Mr Boyd, it's aye weel worth a draper's while to make his contribution to a kirk bazaar a sonsy[2] hen marked down to a price that's temptin'. I've tried jucks, but jucks is no use; the public's dubious about jucks; ye can only rouse the spirit o' competition wi' a hen."

"You're an awfu' sly man, Mr Swan!" exclaimed the draper. "But I'm no vexed yon hen o' yours played havoc wi' the last Bazaar. I've quarrelled wi' the minister about that very organ, and now I havena any kirk to go to."

"It's surely no' for the want o' kirks," said Jimmy. "How many are there here for less than a thousand souls?"

"Five," said Mr Boyd sadly; "the Parish, the U.F., which I belong to, the Episcopalian that belongs to Mr Snodgrass of Blairmaddy, and two different kinds o' Frees, the Wee Frees and the — "

"Oh! never mind goin' into that," said Jimmy, "just say assorted. I never could tell the difference o' one Free Kirk from another, and I've studied the thing minutely, even to the way they cut their hair. A customer up in Ullapool tells me it's a' in the way ye carry your hat in your hand goin' up the aisle; if ye happen to carry it upside down you're seen to be a slider,[3] and they fence the tables[4] against ye at the next Communion, so ye have to join the other body."

"The worst of it with me," said Mr Boyd, "is that there's no' another body in the town I could take up wi' and respect myself. But I'm done wi' Cameron! He wants an organ and a lectern. It would suit him better if he stuck to the fundamentals."

"What exactly's that?" asked Jimmy gravely, fastening a strap.

Mr Boyd was content to wave his hands in the manner which indicates that words are quite inadequate to express ideas. "It's a bonny-like thing," said he, "that I have to go to Glasgow for Communion Sunday! I certainly will not go to the table under Cameron! Could you recommend a sound U.F. in Glasgow, Mr Swan? I'll take my wife and family."

"Cameron?" said Jimmy, turning something over in his mind. "The best kirk I can recommend's my ain, though ye'll have to thole the organ."

"I don't care!" said Mr Boyd, as he took a note of it. "Anything at all to get awa' from Cameron!"

Two weeks later all the family of Boyd came back from Glasgow looking rather downed. They had been to the Communion.

"What way did ye get on?" a customer asked the draper on the day that followed their return.

"I didna get on at all!" said Mr Boyd disgustedly. "A fair take-in! It cost us £2, 10s. to go the week-end to Glasgow, and we a' went to the kirk that Swan the traveller recommended. There we were sittin' expectin' a rousin' sermon from the Rev. Walter Spiers, and sure o' havin' the fundamentals. When the bell stopped ringin', I heard a skliff o' feet from the vestry that struck me as familiar, and when I looked up to see who the beadle was snibbin' in the pulpit, who was this but Cameron!"

23. *Linoleum*

Mr James Swan has lived for fifteen years in Ibrox.[1] For the first six months he thought it horrible, and ever since he has vexed himself to think how foolish he was not to have gone there sooner. That is life. Men are like pot plants. You shift a geranium into a new pot, and for weeks it wilts disconsolate, till some fine sunny day it seems to realise that other geraniums seem happy enough in the same sort of pots, and that it isn't the pot that matters really. Whereupon the geranium (which is actually a pelargonium) strikes fresh roots into the soil, spreads out a broader leaf, throws out a couple of blossoms, and delights in making the best of it. It takes the first prize at the local flower show; content is the best fertiliser. Jimmy Swan, after fifteen years at Ibrox, thinks Ibrox is the centre of the solar system. Take him to Langside or Partickhill, and he feels chilly; at Dennistoun he feels himself a foreigner, and looks at passing tramcars for the Southside as an exile from Scotland, haunting the quays of Melbourne, looks at ships from the Clyde with the names of Denny or Fairfield on their brasses. Jimmy said to me the other day, "I canna think how people can live ony where else than Ibrox. It's the best place in the world." "How?" I asked. "Well," said he, "it's-it's-it's-it's Ibrox!" A little inconclusive, but I quite understood. Nine-tenths of us have our Ibrox; the people to be sympathised with are those who haven't.

But Jimmy got an awful start the other day! He came home from the North journey on a Saturday very tired, and exceedingly glad to see the familiar streets of Ibrox again. Nothing had changed; the same ham was in the grocery window, apparently only a slice the less, and he had exactly the high tea he expected, but his wife was different. She plainly nursed some secret discontent. Quite nice, and interested in his journey, and all that, but still —

It turned out to be the linoleum. The lobby linoleum. She put it to Jimmy if a lobby linoleum seven years old could honestly be regarded as quite decent.

"Tuts! there's naething wrang wi' the linoleum," said her husband. "As nice a linoleum as anybody need ask for; I never tripped on't yet."

"The pattern's worn off half of it," said his wife; "Mrs Grant was in to-day, and I was black affronted. In her new house in Sibbald Terrace² they have Persia rugs."

"Kirkcaldy's³ good enough for us," said Jimmy; "just you wait for a year or twa and ye'll see the fine new linoleum I'll get ye."

It was then that the shock came. Mrs Swan, having brooded for a while on the remoteness of a new linoleum, intimated with a calm that was almost inhuman that she had been looking at some of the houses to let in Sibbald Terrace. Their present house had become no longer possible. It had all the vices conceivable in any house built of human hands, and several others peculiar to itself, and evidently of their nature demoniac. It was cold, it was draughty, it was damp, it was dismal. Its chimneys did not draw properly; its doors were in the wrong places; its kitchen range was a heartbreak; its presses were inadequate, — she took ten minutes to expose all its inherent defects as a dwelling, and left her astonished listener in the feeling that he had been living for fifteen years in an orange-box without knowing it.

"We'll have to flit!" she said at last, determinedly. "Sibbald Terrace is no' in Ibrox!" said her husband, astonished at her apparent overlook of this vital consideration.

"All the better o' that!" said the amazing woman. "I'm sick o' Ibrox! You can say what you like, James Swan; I'll no' stay another year in this hoose."

"Ye're fair fagged oot, Bella," said her husband, compassionately. "I doubt ye have been washin', efter all I told ye. Ye should stay in your bed the morn, and never mind the kirk. Sick o' Ibrox? Ye shouldna say things like that even in fun!"

It was at this stage, or a few days after it, I met Mr Swan. He was chuckling broadly to himself. "Did you ever flit?" he asked me.

"Once," I said.

"That's enough for a lifetime," said he. "Men would never flit any mair than they would change their sox if it wasna for their wives. The advantage o' an auld hoose is that ye aye ken where your pipe is. My wife took a great fancy to flit the other day, and I said it was a' right; that I would look oot for a new house. At the end o' three days I said I had a fair clinker — vestibule wi' cathedral glass in the doors, oriel windows in the parlour, fifteen by eight lobby, venetian blinds, bathroom h. and c., wash-hand basin electric light, tiled close, and only five stairs up.

"She says, 'Do ye think I'm daft? Five stairs! Is it in the Municipal Buildin's?'

"'No,' says I; 'it's in Dalwhinnie Street.'

"'Where in a' the earth is Dalwhinnie Street?' says she.

"'It's a new street,' I said, 'near Ruchill. Ye take the car from aboot the foot o' Mitchell street, come off at an apothecary's shop, and take the first turn to the right and ask a message-boy.'

"'I'll not go to any such street, James Swan!' she says; 'I would rather take a place!' and the dear lass was a' trimblin' wi' agitation."

"No wonder, Mr Swan," I said. "It sounded a very out-of-the-way locality. Where is Dalwhinnie Street?"

"There's no such street,"said Mr Swan: "at least if there is, I never heard o't. But ye see I wanted to put her aff the notion o' flittin'. And there was Bella, almost greetin'! I let on I was fair set on Dalwhinnie Street because it was so handy for the Northern Merchants' Social Club. But Dalwhinnie Street, right or wrong, she would not hear tell o', and I said I would take another look round."

Mr Swan cocked his head a little and looked slyly at me. "Ye're a married man, yoursel'," said he. "Ye know what wives are. They're no' such intellectual giants as we are, thank God! or else they would find us oot; but once they've set their minds on a thing, Napoleon himself couldna shift them. Some days after that I cam' hame from Renfrew-shire wi' a great scheme for takin' a house in the country. I said I had seen the very house for us — half-way between Houston and Bridge-of-Weir."

"Whereabouts is Houston?' says the mistress in frigid tones, as they say in the novels.

"'It's half-way between the Caledonian and G. and S.-W. lines,' says I, ' and if ye're in a hurry ye take a 'bus if it's there.'

"'What sort o' house is it?' she asked, turnin' the heel o' a stockin' as fast as lightning.

"'Tip-top!' I says. 'Nine rooms and a kitchen; fine flagged floor in the kitchen; spring water frae the pump in the garden; two-stall stable. Any amount o' room for hens; ye can keep hunders o' hens. The grocer's van passes the door every Thursday.'

"She began to greet. ' That's right!' she says. ' Put me awa' in the wilds among hens, so that I'll die, and ye'll can marry a young yin. But mind you this, James Swan; I'll no' shift a step oot o' Ibrox!'

"'Tuts, Bella!' I says, 'ye canna stay ony langer in this house; it's a' wrang thegither.'

"'There's naething wrang wi' the hoose,' says she, 'if I had jist some fresh linoleum.'

"'Well, well,' says I; ' ye'll get the linoleum' — and I was much relieved. 'I'll buy't to-morrow.' And I did. It cost me 4s. 6d. a yard."

"Your wife is a very clever lady, Mr Swan," I said; "she probably never thought of flitting, but badly wanted that linoleum."

"Of course!" said Jimmy Swan. "I kent that a' alang! But ye've got to compromise!"

24. *The Grauvat[1] King*

MOST PEOPLE — even in the dry-goods trade — think the Muffler that made Mildrynie Famous, and that great woollen factory which gives employment to thousands of people in Mildrynie, and has in ten years made a fortune for the Drummonds, owed their conception wholly to Peter Drummond. A great mistake! Peter Drummond, of himself, never had any imagination, initiative, or enterprise; till this day (between ourselves) he is a pretty poor fly, and his great national reputation as the Muffler King, his grand Deeside estate, his superb collection of Old Masters, his deputy-lieutenantship, and the marriage of his daughter Cissy to Lord "Tivitty" Beauchamp, are due under Providence to Mr James Swan, traveller for the Glasgow firm of Campbell & Macdonald. There is a marble timepiece of the most ponderous and depressing character in Mr Swan's parlour, with an inscription on it which marks an epoch in the history of industrial Scotland. It says —

To JAMES SWAN, Esq.,

FROM

HIS FAITHFUL FRIEND

PETER DRUMMOND.
3 JUNE 1903.

———

"Lest we forget."

The clock doesn't go; it hasn't gone for years; it is merely a domestic monument — of ingratitude.

Peter Drummond, in 1903, was a customer of Jimmy Swan's in Mildrynie. He and his brother Alick (now Alexander Lloyd Drummond, Esq. of Ballochmawn) had a tiny draper's shop in East Street, next door to a smiddy which seemed to do nothing else from one end of the year till the other but singe sheep's heads[2] for the inhabitants of Mildrynie, who at that time numbered eight hundred souls and two policemen.

One day Jimmy Swan turned up at the door with his sample cases, and found the brothers much depressed. They were doing wretched business. Their shop was off the main street; the propinquity of the smiddy and its perpetual odour of singed wool made the shopping public avoid it; things were come to such a pass that the

Drummonds were contemplating closing up and going off to Canada.

"There's naething to be done in this hole o' a place," said Peter, who spoke Scotch in these days.

"There's plenty to be done in ony place if you're the kind o' man to do it," said Jimmy. "Mildrynie's no' much size; I've seen it missed a'thegither oot o' the maps; but for a' that it's a wonderful place, for it's fair in the middle o' the world. If it's a hole, as ye say, it's a hole to be respected, for it's like a hole in the middle o' a grindstane."

"Nonsense!" said Peter Drummond. "Aff the railway line, away up here in the North; it's oot o' the world a'thegither."

"Fair in the middle!" insisted Mr Swan. "Look you at a globe or a map o' the world, and ye'll see I'm richt. Every other place in the world's grouped roond aboot Mildrynie, just the same as if God had meant it to be great."

"Maybe that's so!" conceded Mr Drummond on reflection; "but my shop's no' in the middle o' Mildrynie, and so I whiles think I micht as weel ha'e my signboard up at the North Pole. That's the middle o' the world too."

"What do ye dae to attract customers?" asked Jimmy, adjusting his carnation.

"Just what everybody else does that keeps a shop," said Peter Drummond.

"Error No. 1," said Jimmy. "The way to attract customers is to dae what naebody else is daein'. That's where the profit as well as the fun comes in. I would get sick-tired daein' the same as everybody else; the only excuse ye have for bein' alive is that ye dae some things peculiarly in your own way."

"I carry a good stock, and I show everything at a reasonable price," said Peter Drummond.

"Error No. 2," said Jimmy, blandly. "Ye should start sellin' something at a quite unreasonable price."

"What dae ye mean?" asked Mr Drummond.

"Sell it at what it costs ye. Here's a new line I have in woollen mufflers, as cosy as a fur-lined coat, and fastens wi' a snap. They'll cost ye half-a-croon each from C. & M., and that's even coontin' aff the discoont. The winter's comin' on; you make a splash wi' the Mildrynie Muffler at half-a-croon, and ye'll get the folk to your shop, for naebody else sells them for less than three shillings. Once ye have the folk buying your mufflers at cost price, it'll be gey droll if ye canna sell them other things at a reasonable profit."

"There's something in't!" said Peter Drummond.

On the next journey Mr Swan made to Mildrynie, he found that the half-crown muffler had moved the business slightly, but not enough to lift the spirits of the brothers Drummond. Their unpopular location and the smell of the smiddy were against a really popular and fashionable success.

"Do ye advertise?" asked Jimmy.

"No," said Peter; "naebody advertises here."

"My goodness! that's the very chance for you then!" exclaimed Mr Swan eagerly. "Chip in first before the others think o't. Advertise in the county paper — 'The Real and Original Mildrynie Muffler'; ye'll sell them like Forfar Rock!"

"But if naebody's wantin' mufflers?" said Peter, sadly.

"Naebody was wantin' Beecham's pills a hundred years ago, and noo they canna dae withoot them. Look at the way that soap's come into fashion, even in the country districts — a' the result o' advertisin'."

"It's the smell o' the smiddy next door that spoils this street," said Mr Drummond.

"Error No. 4642!" said Jimmy. "The smiddy 'll be a godsend if ye'll dae what I'm gaun to tell ye. Put you this advertisement in the local paper" — and he quickly drafted it out on a sheet of wrapping-paper —

THE MARVELLOUS MILDRYNIE MUFFLER,
ONLY HALF-A-CROWN.
DRUMMOND'S SHOP, 3 EAST STREET.
Follow your Nose and the Smell of Sheep's Head Singeing.

"I never saw an advertisement like that in a' my life," said Peter Drummond.

"Exactly!" said Jimmy. "That's the sort o' advertisement to advertise when ye're advertisin'."

On his next journey he found the Drummond business booming, and got an incredibly large order for Mildrynie mufflers at a price that left a reasonable profit for the retailer. But Peter was still a little depressed.

"There's money in't sure enough," said he; "but they ca' me the Grauvat King, and I don't like it."

"Nonsense!" said Jimmy. "It's just as fine to be the Grauvat King as the Oil King, or the Diamond King, or the Cattle King; it's a' the same to you so lang's ye get them on the neck. If you're the Grauvat King in Forfarshire, it's a' the easier for ye to be Muffler Monarch to the country at large. The Mildrynie Muffler's good enough to stand pushing just as far as Hielan' Whisky; you get a pickle money thegither and advertise the Rale and Original Mildrynie Half-croon Muffler in a' the papers in the country, and ye'll mak' a fortune. Tell them the Mildrynie Muffler's made aff pure hygienic wool that's grown on high-pedigree Hielan' sheep that graze on the heathery slopes o' the Grampian Mountains, the land where the eagle soars and the cataract flashes; that it's manufactured in the cottage homes o' the God-fearin', clean, and industrious native peasantry, and is recognised by the faculty as the one garment responsible for the sturdy health and universal longevity o' the Scottish race, and C. & M. 'll keep ye supplied wi' a' ye want; there's plenty o' mills in bonny wee Gleska."

It was in recognition of this valuable tip that Peter Drummond, a twelvemonth later, gave Mr Swan the timepiece — a poor solatium to Mr Swan for his loss of Drummonds' muffler trade when they opened the enormous works of their own at Mildrynie.

25. *Jimmy's Sins Find Him Out*

MR JAMES Swan picked up a bunch of violets, which he had
been refreshing in a tumbler while he wrote out his expenses for the week, and placed it in his buttonhole. From
a pocket he took a small case-comb, and, borrowing from
Pratt, the office "knut," the little mirror which Pratt kept
always in his desk to consult as often as the Ready Reckoner, he went to the window and combed his hair.

"What side are sheds worn on this season?" he asked
Pratt, whom it was the joke of the office to treat with mock
deference as arbiter of fashion, expert, and authority upon
every giddy new twirl of the world of elegance.

"To the left," said Pratt, without a moment's hesitation,
and with the utmost solemnity; the parting of his own hair
was notoriously a matter of prayerful consideration. He
was a lank lad with a long neck; it looked as if his Adam's
apple was a green one and was shining through — a
verdant phenomenon due to the fact that he had used the
same brass stud for three years.

"Can't be done on the left," said Mr Swan. "That's the
side I do my thinkin' on, and it's worn quite thin. I envy ye
your head o' hair, Pratt; it'll last ye a life-time, no' like mine."

Pratt, with the mirror restored to him, put it back in his
desk with a final glance at it to see that his necktie was as
perfectly knotted as it was three minutes ago; put on his
hat and bolted from the office.

"They're a' in a great hurry to be off the day," said Mr
Swan to himself. "I wonder what they're up to?"

He was to find out in two minutes, to his own discomfi-
ture.

At the foot of the stair which led to the upper warehouse
he ran against Peter Grant of Aberdeen, who was in search
of him.

"My jove!" said Grant, panting; "I'm in luck! I was sure
ye would be awa' to't, and I ran doon the street like to
break my legs."

"De-lighted to see ye, Mr Grant!" said Jimmy with a radiant visage. "This is indeed a pleasant surprise! But ye don't mean to tell me ye came from Aberdeen this mornin'?"

"Left at a quarter to seven," said Grant. "I made up my mind last night to come and see it. And I says to mysel', ' If I can just catch Mr Swan before he goes to the field, the thing's velvet!'"

"De-lighted!" said Jimmy, and shook his hand again. But the feeling of icy despair in his breast was enough to wilt his violets.

His sin had found him out! There was only one inference to be drawn from Peter Grant's excited appearance; he had carried out the threat of a dozen years to come and see a Glasgow football match, and expected the expert company and guidance of C. & M.'s commercial traveller.

And Jimmy Swan had, so far as Grant was concerned, a reputation for football knowledge and enthusiasm it was impossible to justify in Glasgow, however plausible they seemed in a shop in Aberdeen. Grant, who had never seen a football match in his life, was a fanatic in his devotion to a game which for twenty years he followed in the newspapers. Jimmy in his first journeys to Aberdeen had discovered this fancy of his customer, and played up to it craftily with the aid of the "Scottish Referee,"[1] which he bought on each journey North for no other purpose, since he himself had never seen a football match since the last cap of Harry M'Neill[2] of the "Queen's,"[3] in 1881.

The appalling ignorance of Jimmy regarding modern football, and his blank indifference to the same, were never suspected by his customer, who from the traveller's breezy and familiar comments upon matches scrappily read about an hour before, credited him with knowing all there was to know about the national pastime.

When Jimmy was in doubt about the next move in a conversation with Grant, he always mentioned Quinn, and called him "good old Jimmy." He let it be understood that the Saturday afternoons when he couldn't get to Ibrox

were unhappy — which was perfectly true, since he lived in
Ibrox, though the Rangers' park was a place he never went
near.

"I'll go and see a match some day!" Grant always said;
he had said it for many years, and Jimmy always said,
"Mind and let me know when ye're comin', and I'll show
ye fitba'."

And now he was taken at his word!

What particular match could Grant have come for?
Jimmy had lost sight of football, even in the papers, for the
past three months.

With an inward sigh for a dinner spoiled at home, he
took his customer to a restaurant for lunch.

"I want to see M'Menemy,"[4] said Grant; "it was that
that brought me; he's a clinker!"

"And he never was in better form," said Jimmy. "Playin'
like a book! He says to me last Monday, 'We'll walk over
them the same's we had a brass band in front of us, Mr
Swan!'"

"Will they win, do ye think?" Grant asked with great
anxiety; he was so keen, the lunch was thrown away on him.

"Win!" said Jimmy. "Hands down! The — the — the
other chaps is shakin' in their shoes."

So far he moved in darkness. Who M'Menemy was,
and what match he was playing in that day, he had not
the faintest idea, and he played for safety. It was probably some important match. The state of the streets as they
had walked along to the restaurant suggested a great influx
of young men visitors; it might be something at Celtic
Park.

He looked at Grant's square-topped hat and had an
inspiration.

"If ye'll take my advice, Mr Grant," said he, "ye'll go
and buy a kep. A hat like that's no use at a Gleska fitba'
match; ye need a hooker. If ye wear a square-topped hat it
jist provokes them. I'm gaun round to the warehouse to
change my ain hat for a bunnet; I'll leave ye in a hat shop
on the road and then I'll jine ye."

"What fitba' match is on the day?" Jimmy asked a porter in the warehouse.

"Good Goad!" said the porter with amazement at him. "It's the International[5] against England."

"Where is it played?" asked Jimmy.

"Hampden, of course!"

"What way do ye get to't, and when does it start?"

"Red car to Mount Florida;[6] game starts at three; I wish to goodness I could get to't," said the porter.

Jimmy looked his watch. It was half-past one.

He found Grant with a headgear appropriate to the occasion, and wasted twenty minutes in depositing his hat at Buchanan Street left-luggage office. Another twenty minutes passed at the station bar, where Jimmy now discoursed with confidence on Scotland's chances, having bought an evening paper.

"Will ye no' need to hurry oot to the park?" Grant asked with some anxiety.[7]"There'l be an awfu' crood; twenty chaps wi' bunnets came on at Steenhive."[7]

"Lot's of time!" said Jimmy with assurance. "We'll tak' a car. Come awa', and I'll show ye a picture-palace."

It was fifteen minutes to three when they got to Hampden. A boiling mass of frantic people clamoured round the gates, which were shut against all further entrance, to the inner joy of Mr Swan, who lost his friend in the crowd and failed to find him.

"Where on earth were you till this time?" asked his wife when he got home to Ibrox two hours later.

"Out in the Queen's Park," said Jimmy truthfully.

"Wi' luck I lost a man outside a fitba' match, and spent an hour in Camphill — no' a soul in't but mysel' — listenin' to the birds whistlin'."

26. *A Wave of Temperance*

ONE DAY last week an hotel in Falkirk had six commercial travellers from Glasgow in its commercial room at dinner,

the president and *doyen* of them Jimmy Swan, who unfeelingly depressed the company by drinking ginger ale. It was
not so much his choice of this unorthodox beverage that
saddened them as his evident enjoyment of it; he lingered
over it, and smacked his lips upon it, and cocked his eye to
look through the bubbling glass as if it were Clicquot,
1904. The others suddenly realised that this ostentatious
gusto carried some reproach on their preference for bitter
beer — so they defiantly ordered in another pewter each.

"You should try sour milk, Mr Swan," said that hard-
ened satirist, Joe M'Guire, the boot man; "it's said to be
full o' the finest germs. If you drink sour dook you'll live to
the age o' a hundred and fifty, and you'll well deserve it."

"Ginger," said flour man, Wallace, "is all right in its
own place. One time, I mind, I tried it — at the funeral o'
an uncle o' mine who was a Rechabite; and I can tell you
that so far as I was concerned that day he was sincerely
mourned."

Jimmy Swan smiled blandly, and squinted again
through his tumbler.

"Clean, wholesome, morally stimulatin', warmth-
provokin', thirst-assuagin' — the nectar o' the gods!" he
said with the eloquence of an advertisement. "What's good
enough for the King and Kitchener[1] is good enough for
me. You chaps should give it a trial; it would save ye a lot
o' money in aromatic lozengers."

Five minutes after the Crown Hotel commercial room
was a debating club, with temperance and prohibition for
its subjects. Mr Swan had by far the best of the argument,
since none of the rest could agree upon what constituted
the particular virtues or charm of alcohol, though they
were unanimous in declaring their line of business made a
judicious use of it absolutely indispensable.

"I've taken up that line mysel' in my unregenerate days
— and that was up to a week ago," said Jimmy; "but to tell
the truth, I took a dram because I liked it; my other reasons
were a' palaver."

"But human geniality," said Peter Garvie (lubricating

oils), who was reputed on the road to have as little geniality as a haddock — "it wants a glass o' something stronger than ginger ale to bring men together. You couldna show your friendliness to a man unless you bought him a glass o' something."

"Ye could buy him a pair o' gallowses," suggested Jimmy, and saying so, he finished the last of his ginger ale hurriedly, and put down the glass with a bang. He had an inspiration.

A little later six quite rational representatives of well-known wholesale Glasgow houses were, incredible though it may seem, in a solemn pact to suspend the ancient treating customs of their country for a week; eschew all the alcoholic beverages, and maintain "the genial flow," as Jimmy called it, on a system more likely to benefit the sale of the goods they travelled in than standing rounds of beer or whisky-and-soda.

Two hours later M'Guire met Jimmy in the High Street, beaming with satisfaction at a well-filled book of orders; his own success that day left no excuse for grumbling.

"It's a raw, cold day," said Jimmy, rubbing his hands. "Have ye any good in your mind?"

"I don't mind if I do," said M'Guire, and absent-mindedly was making for the Blue Bell hostelry.

"Na! na!" said Jimmy. "Mind the pledge; there's naething 'll cross my lips but a threepenny cheroot."

They went into a tobacconist's, and their cheroots were hardly lighted when Jimmy said, 'Hurry up and we'll hae another."

"No fears!" said the boot man firmly. "I never smoked two cigars a day in my life except on Sunday and I wouldna smoke this one noo if it hadna cost me threepence."

"Do ye feel the genial flow yet?" asked Jimmy, as they walked along the street.

"Not a bit!?" said M'Guire. "It's more like burned broon paper."

Jimmy chucked away his cigar and led him into a baker's shop.

"Two London buns, miss," said he. "The best. On draught"; leaned one arm elegantly on the counter; said, "Well, here's to us!" and ate his bun with a fair pretence at relish. M'Guire, who was renowned for being able to eat anything at any time, was finished before him.

"Hurry up, Jimmy!" he said. "We'll jist have another one, for the good o' the house."

"All right!" said Jimmy. "Make it a small one this time, miss. No! I'll tell ye what — I'll split a parley[2] this time, Joe; I feel that bun in my heid already."

Wallace came round the corner just as they were leaving the baker's shop.

"Ye're just in time!" said Jimmy. "An hour till the train goes and we're on the batter." He was munching the last of the parley he had shared with M'Guire, and Wallace dropped to the situation.

"What's it goin' to be?" he asked with something less than the usual convivial abandon expected with the question.

"They're no' half fly wi' their drapery shops in Fa'kirk," said Jimmy, twinkling. "They should ha'e a back-door to them. Slip in to this yin," and he led them into the premises of one of his oldest customers.

"Back again, ye see, Mr Ross," he said to the draper. "It's somebody's birthday, and we're on the fair ran-dan. What are ye goin' to have, gentlemen?"

"My shout!" said Wallace. "Give it a name."

"I think I'll just have a small pocket-hankey this time," said M'Guire, and Jimmy Swan agreed that a pocket-hankey was the very thing he was thinking of having himself.

"We'll just have another!" he said when they had got them. "Just one more hankey 'll no' do ye a bit o' harm. I'm feelin' fine! A nasty raw cold day — ye need a hankey to cheer ye up."

M'Guire, who pretended to be looking all round the floor for a spittoon, declared he couldn't find room for another handkerchief, but could be doing with a 16 collar.

"Collars all round let it be," said Jimmy, "We'll just make a night of it. But mind ye, M'Guire, you're no' to start the singin'! When it comes to collars, I'm aye prood to say I can either take them or leave them. I'm no' one o' these chaps that's nip-nip-nippin awa' at collars a' day — the ruination o' the constitution and the breakin'-up o' mony a happy home. Three White Horse collars, Mr Ross, and what'll ye tak yoursel'?"

Mr Ross was a pawky gentleman himself, and had heard of the commercials' compact from the traveller earlier in the day. He turned his back on them, having put forth the collars, and scrutinised the shelves behind him with profound shrewdness.

"At this time o' day I never touch a collar," he remarked. "It doesna agree wi' me before my tea. I think, if you'll allow me, seeing it's so cold a day, I'll just have a Cardigan waistcoat, Mr Swan," and he pulled down a box of those garments.

27. *Country Journeys*

As THE train pulled out of Buchanan Street Station, Slymon, the tea man, drew off a fur-lined glove and put his hand inquiringly upon the foot-warmer.

"Feel that, Mr Swan!" he remarked, indignantly, and Jimmy did so.

"It's aff the bile, at any rate," he intimated cheerfully. "Or perhaps it's a new patent kind, like one of those Thermos flasks[1] my wife got a present of at Christmas, guaranteed to keep the heat for four-and-twenty hours. She wrapped it up in flannel, put it in the bed, and was awfully disappointed. 'Is that your feet?' she asked me at two o'clock in the morning. 'It is not,' says I.' Then the shop that sold John Grant that bottle swindled him; it's an ice-cream freezer,' says the mistress."

"A railway foot-warmer filled with liquid gas is no use to me," proceeded the indignant Slymon, and for the next ten minutes he said things about The True Line[2] which would have much distressed the directors of the Caledonian Railway had they been there to hear them.

Jimmy merely buttoned his coat a little tighter, tucked his rug more carefully round his legs, and looked compassionately upon his fellow-traveller.

"Man, Slymon," he remarked at last, "if you get so warm as that about the shortcomings of the Caley and every other system you'll work yourself into a perspiration that'll open all your pores, and get your death of cold when you go out at Larbert. It's your feet that's wrong to start with. Either your boots are tight or you're wearing the wrong kind of sox, or there's something up with your circulation. Thirty years ago the railways wouldn't even pretend to give us hot-water pans, and nobody in our line died of cold feet yet that I ever heard of."

"Travelling becomes more uncomfortable every year," said Slymon, irritably, and Jimmy snorted.

"Look here, Slymon!" he said. "You're making me feel old, and I don't like it. If you say travelling becomes more uncomfortable every year, I must be getting blind, or you must be thirty years younger than me, and I don't believe it. Here you are in a padded carriage — Third Class — fifty per cent. better than the First we used to use in the days before the Firm took on Macauslane for a managing director. There's an electric light you can read your paper by without losing the sight of an eye, a thing you always risked when even Firsts were lit by oil. Here's an air-tight window that doesn't rattle, and a ventilator that works; here's a bogey carriage running so smoothly that you could drink a cup o' tea — if you thought of it — without spilling a drop, and in the old days you couldn't take a tot from the bottom of a flask, but had to bite on the neck of it, and drink between the dunts."

"Oh, I daresay things have a bit improved in your time," said Slymon, cooling down; "but even now they might be better."

"We might be better ourselves," said Jimmy Swan. "It's

a conviction of that kind that keeps me from kicking a lot of folk I meet.

"If you ask me," continued Jimmy, lighting his pipe "there was far more fun on the road before cold feet came into fashion, and when the only kind of draught that did any harm was the kind you got in tumblers."

"Youth," suggested Mr Slymon, and Jimmy for a moment meditated.

"Ay, perhaps you're right," he said. "I sometimes envy the chaps that have it, and then again I'm vexed for them, knowing they'll never understand till it's bye what a jolly good thing it was. And whiles, again, I wonder if Youth in itself is ever half so fine as it's cracked up to be; it's maybe only nice to an old man's eye because it's out of reach. The young that have it, anyway, make an awful hash wi't. I did, myself. ... But all that has nothing to do with what we started out on — travelling.

"I've been on the road since the year the women wore the Dolly Vardens — d'ye mind the song? —

'Come, dear, don't fear, let your ringlets curl
If you're out of fashion, you better leave the world,
Your sweet and pretty face will wear a winning smile,
If you buy a hat and feather in the Dolly Varden style.'

"Half my journeys then were made on gigs and wagonettes; none of your hot-water bottles and hairstuffed seats! and I tell you, my feet never got time to get cold. If it wasn't gigs, and taking the reins myself for half the journey because the postboy had been out all night at a kirn[3] or a coffining; it was cargo boats that started at six o'clock in the morning, and the first bell would be ringing before the Boots chapped at my door.

"I see chaps noo gaun aboot on bicycles wi' a sample box o' biscuits strapped behind," continued Jimmy, lapsing into the vernacular as his feelings warmed.

"They call themsel's Commercials, just like the rest o' us. I'm vexed for the chaps, do ye know; I never can see ony hope for them bein' comfortably married. It's the same wi' tea."

"Tea's done!" confessed Mr Slymon, lugubriously. "Between you and me. Everybody's selling it. I know ironmongers handling Cooper's packages. There's whole-sale people going among the farmers selling 20 lb. tins at what they call a wholesale rate, and never going near a grocer. I would sooner be on the road for specs or railway tunnels. Blended tea! — that's the wheeze! 'Fine silky liquor. ... Good body. ... Rich Darjeeling flavour. ... Soupcon of Pekoe gives it character.' ... "

"I know," said Jimmy, sympathetically. "Worse than horse-cowpin'! The ordinary man kens nae mair aboot tea than I ken aboot shortbreid. And ye canna wonder at it; tea at the best's a skiddlin' thing ye tak' to wash doon breid and butter. The honestest thing ever I saw said aboot tea was in a grocer's window in Inverness — 'Our Unap-proachable; 2s. 6d.'"

"Sooner be in specs, or railway tunnels," repeated Slymon, sadly.

"I see you're no' very keen on a line wi' a lot o' heavy cases, onyway," said Jimmy. "Noo, I wadna care to be without my cases. It's the stuff that talks! Stick it in their e'e! When I put oot my stuff in a wee bit shop in Grantown it makes it look like a bargain day in Sauchiehall Street, and the shopkeeper feels awfu' lonely and sees his place infernal bare when I pack up the traps again. So doon he claps his bonny wee order! ... The only thing that would gie me cauld feet would be travellin' withoot my cases. There's a moral weight in them as weel as avoirdupois. Man, on the quays and at the railway stations the porters ken them. 'That's C. & M.'s,' they say — 'Auld Swan.' And when they're oot in the straun in front of a country shop, it's jist like a swatch o' Buchanan Street.

"I'll admit there's whiles when they're a nuisance, and that puts me in mind o' a time in the North when I got cauld feet richt enough.

"I had just got ower three weeks' rest at Christmas and New Year, a time I always used for packin' and postin' kind reminders to my customers. There was nae Secret

Commission Act then, and I tell ye I was a connoisseur at geese and turkeys, and the genuine F. & F. currant bun. I sent them by the score. I sent a hundred and twenty 'Chatterboxes'[4] every year to the children o' the drapery trade in the West o' Scotland. All I needed to be Santa Claus was a reindeer. Macauslane put an end to that; he found oot that the maist o' the weans that got the books belanged to customers a bit behind in the ledger.

"I got up to Golspie on a Hansel Monday,[5] did my business there in an oor or twa, and then ordered a machine for Brora. I couldna even get a barrow! Some minister was being inducted down at Dornoch, and every dacent trap in the place was aff to Dornoch wi' an elder.

"'We could run ye up wi' a shandry-dan,'[6] says the innkeeper, 'but then it wouldna haud your cases.'

"'I needna go to Brora wantin' cases,' says I. 'Shairly ye can dae something, Peter?'

"'There's naething in the yaird that would haud your cases except the hearse,' says Peter.

"'Well, oot wi' the hearse!' says I, and less than twenty meenutes efter I was on the road to Dornoch, sittin' beside the driver on a hearse, and the latest lines in C. & M.'s Spring goods inside it. My jove, but it was cauld! We drove richt up to the shop o' auld Mr Sutherland. Doon I draps frae the dickey o' the hearse, and in I goes wi' a face like a fiddler, and asks for a yaird o' crape.

"'Dear me! Mr Swan, wha are ye buryin' the day?' says Mr Sutherland.

"'We're buryin' Annie,' says I.

"'Whatna Annie?' says Mr Sutherland.

"'Animosity,' says I — ony auld baur'll pass in Brora — and he laughed like a young yin, though I must alloo he yoked on me later for what he ca'd my sacrilege.

"It was the first and only time, sae far, I traivelled on a hearse, and I tell ye my feet were cauld!"

28. *Raising the Wind*

MR SWAN had the counter of Cameron's shop piled high with the new season's samples of corsets, lingerie, hose, lace, ribbons, and dress material. He handled them, himself, as if they had been flowers — delicately, lovingly, caressingly, and called attention to their qualities in the ecstatic tones a dealer in pictorial art would use with a customer for Raphaels. Cameron, on the other hand — a rough, bluff, quite undraperish-looking man, who had been a baker until he came to Perth from Glasgow twenty years ago and married his cousin and her shop, had plainly no artistic pleasure in the stuff displayed by the commercial traveller; he flung it about on the counter as if it had been dough. It made the traveller squirm to see him.

"Bright colours, rich effects," said Jimmy; "that's the season's note. Look at this cerise and tango — it makes ye think o' a fine spring day and the birds whistling. It'll make up beautiful!" He tossed it tenderly into billowy folds, which showed in it the most entrancing shadows, auriferous glints, and the flush of cherries. "This stuff in stripes (we call it 'peau-depeche' from the man that thought o't first; he was a Frenchman) — it's the finest tailorin' stuff I've ever handled, goin' to be a' the go when the King comes to the Clyde."[1]

"Is he comin'?" Cameron asked with sudden interest.

"In July," said Jimmy. "There's a rush on flags already oot at Coatbridge. It's goin' to be a drapery summer, I can tell ye! Ye'll feel it even up in Perth."

And Cameron sighed.

"Na," said he; "we'll no' feel't in Perth. We never feel onything here but cattle shows. We just kind o' driddle on frae yin year's end to the ither, and read about splendid things in the papers. I never see ye strappin' up your boxes, Mr Swan, but I wish ye would strap me up wi' them and take me back wi' ye to Gleska."

Cameron, in twenty years, since he had left St Mungo,[2] had never returned to it even on the shortest visit. He

spoke of it now with a sentimental air, and expressed a firm
intention to go down and see the gaieties of July.

"I'll see a lot o' changes on Gleska," he said. "Twenty
years! It looks like a lifetime ! What would ye say yoursel',
Mr Swan, was changed the most in Gleska in twenty
years?"

Jimmy puckered up his brows and chewed a pencil, lost
in thought.

"Well," said he, "there's the picture-palaces, where ye
can get everything now except a dram and a bed for the
night — they'll be new to ye. And then there's the Central
Station;[3] ye've never seen the Central since they altered it,
have ye?"

"No," said Cameron sadly. "What's it like, noo?"

"Oh, it's beyond words!" said Jimmy, rolling ribbons
up. "Ye could put the whole o' the folk in Perth between
the bookstalls, and they would just look like a fitba' team.
It's got the biggest, brawest, nameliest lavatory in Europe,
doon a stair, where ye can get your hair cut, and a bath for
sixpence. Lots o' men go down for baths and barberin',
stayin' down for hours if they think their wives are lookin'
for them."

Cameron laughed. "What do ye want wi' a bath in a
station?" said he.

"I've kent o't bein' used for a bank," said Jimmy; "at
least it served the purpose o' a bank in a way, for it got twa
chaps I ken some money when they couldna get it otherwise."

"How that?" asked Cameron.

"It happened this way. Twa packers in our warehouse
— Dan MacGhie and Willie Lovatt — got on the scatter a
year ago at the Gleska Fair. They spent the half o' the day
goin' round the town in search of the perfect schooner that
was goin' to be the last, and they found their joint resources down to a single shilling. A shilling's a lot o' money
in Gleska if it's tramway rides you're buying, but it doesna
go far in the purchase o' liquid joy, and they were sore
distressed. A' the banks were shut, but that didna matter;

they hadna ony money in the banks onyway. And the notion o' goin' hame at three o'clock was naturally horrible.

"Dan MacGhie's such a fool in the packin' business, ye would fancy the only way he could think o' keepin' his socks up would be to stand on his heid, but on this occasion he was pretty 'cute. 'I'll tell ye what, Willie,' said he. 'You'll hae a nice hot bath at the Central Station.'

"'What dae I want wi' a bath?' says Willie. 'I had yin a while ago.'

"'That's all right!' says Dan. 'You'll go down and have a nice wee bath to yoursel'. It'll cost ye sixpence, and ye'll take your time. Ye'll slip your coat and waistcoat oot to me. I'll go, like lightning, and put them in a fine wee pawn for a pound, and buy ye an alpaca jacket for three-and-six, and we'll have a' the odds. See? Phizz!'

"'But ye'll be sure to come back?' says Willie. 'I have no notion o' goin' out the New City Road in my galluses.'

"'Right oh!' says Dan, and Willie went down wi' him and trysted[4] a bath, and slips his coat and waistcoat oot to Dan.

"Dan takes the coat and waistcoat in an awfu' hurry down to Oswald Street, and into a nice wee pawn, and asks a pound on them. The man in the pawn ripes the pouches,[5] and says he couldna gie more than seven-and-six.

"'Seven-and-six!' says Dan. 'They belang to a landed gentleman!'

"'I don't care if they belanged to Lloyd George,' says the man in the pawn, 'seven-and-six is the value, and that's no' includin' the price o' the ticket.'

"Dan took the seven-and-odd-pence-ha'penny, after switherin' a wee, and went awa' doon the stair and along Argyle Street. He was disappointed. If he bought a lustre jacket[6] for Willie, there wasna goin' to be much left for fun. A dishonest man would have just spent the money and gone awa' hame withoot botherin' aboot Willie, but Dan MacGhie wasna a chap o' that sort; he had the true British spirit.

"He goes alang the street till he comes to a shop window where there were clocks on the instalment system. If ye paid the first instalment o' half-a-crown, ye got the nock wi' ye, the notion bein' that ye paid the other seventeen-and-six in monthly instalments. Dan goes in as bold as brass and asks to see a nock. The man produced a fair clinker, fitted up wi' an alarm that would waken ye even on a Sunday. Dan tried the alarm, and made it birl, and said he thought it would dae, although he would have preferred yin a little quicker and louder in the action. He paid down half-a-crown and signed his name and address for the rest o' the instalments, and awa' oot, like the mischief, to the Trongate.

"He went into a pawn in the Trongate and pledged the nock. 'I want fifteen shillin's on that,' says he. 'It's a Kew-tested, genuine, repeater nock, jewelled in every hole.' The pawnbroker opened it wi' a knife the same's it was an oyster, and looked inside it. 'I'll gie ten shillin's on't!' says he.

"'My mither's nock!' says Dan, and him near greetin'. 'It cost five-pound-ten the year o' the *Daphne* disaster.'[7]

"'Half-a-quid !' says the pawnbroker. 'Take it or leave it!'

"Dan took the ten shillin's; looked at the time on the pawnshop clock, and ran like a lamplighter awa' back to Oswald Street. He kent fine that Willie would be vexed waitin' in the bath a' wet.

"He goes back to the first pawn and lifted Willie's coat and waiscoat, payin' back the seven-and-six and interest.

"'Ye havena been lang!' says the pawnbroker, surprised to see him.

"'No,' says Dan; 'I forgot about a funeral I'm booked for this afternoon, and I need my coat.'

"He got Willie's coat and waistcoat, and bunks awa' up to the Central Station and doon the stairs to the lavatory, and chaps at the door.

"'Is that you, Dan?' says Willie.

"'It is,' says Dan, and slips him in his clothes.

"'My goodness!' says Willie, 'and I was gettin' cauld! I was sure ye had forgotten all aboot me! What speed did ye come?'

"'Tip-top!' says Dan. 'I started wi' sixpence, and I've three shillin's. Come on oot and we'll have a pint!'

"That's Gleska!" said Jimmy Swan. "Oh, it's changed a lot since you were there last, Mr Cameron! And now, this shell-pink moire velours, just look at the style that's in it — "

"Ye're a terrible man," said Cameron.

29. *Roses, Roses, All the Way*

FROM THE 1st of May till well on in October no one for years has seen James Swan in business hours without a flower in his coat lapel. Any old kind of cigar is good enough for him, though his preference runs to black Burmese cheroots that look like bits of walking-stick; but when it comes to button-holes, he is a fastidious connoisseur. If the Karl Droschki rose is ever to have a perfume, you will find that Jimmy will anticipate the florists' shops by a week or two; he likes his buttonholes large and redolent, and a scented Karl Droschki the size of a rhododendron is a joy he sometimes dreams of. In town he gets his daily flower by some arrangement with commercial friends in the neighbourhood of the Bazaar; on his business journeys he is rather unhappy anywhere out of the reach of fresh carnations, sweet peas, roses, or camelias; but even there he can make shift with a spray of lilac or of wallflower culled from vases in the coffee-rooms of the hotels.

"The button-hole is getting a bit out o' fashion," he told me recently; "but I don't mind; it will aye go very well in the coat of a middle-aged commercial gentleman with the right breadth in the chest for it. Give me a clean shave and a carnation, and I feel as cheery as a chap that earns his bread by singing. A flower in the coat goes a long way to conceal yon tired feeling in the morning; it's a kind o' moral pick-me-up."

"I fancy," said I, "that it's also not without some beneficial effect on business"; and Jimmy slyly chuckled.

"You may be sure o' that!" said he. "Make your buttonhole big enough, and the business man behind it's almost lost to sight; there's wee shops yonder in the East End where they look on me and my carnations like a kind o' glimpse o' the country, where the mavie whistles and the milk comes from. They sniff as if it was the sea-breeze down at Millport — I tell you it puts a lot o' them in mind o' their mothers' gardens! Give me that kind o' country sentiment, and I'll be busy wi' my wee bit book!"

But Jimmy was not always a wearer of *boutonnières* and a connoisseur in cut flowers. Fifteen years ago, as he told me once, he would as soon have worn a wedding-ring or a Glengarry bonnet, and the only thing he knew about flowers was that certain ones were roses and the others weren't. His wife's pathetic struggles for bloom in a tiny front plot near the Paisley Road never, in these days, roused his slightest interest in horticulture. He is still inclined to regard flowers as a product best procured in shops, but his knowledge of them at the marketable age is now extensive. It began with an experience he had in Kirkcaldy.

For two years he had made the most valiant but unsuccessful efforts to get an order from a Kirkcaldy draper, who appeared to cherish the distressing delusion that he was well enough served by other wholesale firms than C. & M. Mr Dimister was the hardest nut Jimmy had ever tried to crack. At any hour of the day he was called on he was always too desperately busy to look at anything, and never by any luck was he to be got with a vacancy in his stock that Mr Swan could replenish.

"Man, he was a dour yin!" Jimmy said to me, narrating the circumstances. "I don't object to a dour yin in reason, for once ye nab a dour yin he's as dour to stop ye as he was to start ye; forbye it's aye a feather in your bonnet. But Dimister was a perfect he'rt-break; he had nae mair come-and-go in him than Nelson's Monument — my jove! the baurs I wasted on that man! I got the length o' jottin' the

heids o' my newest stories doon in a penny diary just to be
sure o' ticklin' him wi' something fresh, but devil the haet[1]
would tickle Dimister; he had nae mair sense o' humour
than a jyle door. There's folk like that.

"Ye have nae idea o' the patience I showed wi' the body!
I tried him on the majestic line, the same's I was sellin'
peerages, and I tried him on the meek or at least as near on
the meek as I could manage wi' half a ton o' cases from C.
& M. in a couple o' barrows at the door. It was a' the same
to Dimister — he had nae mair interest in me than if I was
selling sheep-dip or railway sleepers. I tried him wi' kirk
affairs, put oot a feeler now and then on politics, and gave
him a' the grips in Masonry; but it was nae use: he just
hotched on his stool, glowered ower his specs at me, and
let me ken there was naething doin'. For a' that was in the
cratur's business at the time, it wasna worth my while to
bother wi' him; but my pride was up, and I swore I would
have him, even if I had to take a gun to't.

"One day I asked the landlord o' the hotel I was puttin'
up at where Dimister stayed, and went oot to look at the
ootside o' his hoose. It was a nice enough bit villa, wi' a
gairden fu' o' floo'ers and a great big greenhoose. A letter-
carrier passin' told me Dimister was the champion rose-
grower and tomato hand in Fife.

"'I have ye noo!' says I to mysel', and wired to my friend
in the Bazaar to send me oot three o' the finest roses in
Gleska by the first train, even if they cost a pound. They
came in the aifternoon — fair champions! — I stuck them
in my coat and went to call on Dimister.

"'Very sorry,' he says as usual; 'I'm not needin' ' — and
then his eyes fell on my button-hole. It was the first time I
ever saw a gleam o' human interest in the body's face. His
eyes fair goggled.

"'That's a good rose,' he says, and came forward and
looked at them closer. 'A Margaret Dickson; splendid
form!'

"'No' a bad rose!' I says, aff-hand. 'It's aye worth the
trouble growin' a good one when ye're at it,' and I passed

them over to him wi' my compliments. Ye would hardly believe it, but he was mair pleased than many a man would be wi' a box o' cigars.

"'I didna know ye were a fancier,' says he. 'That's a first-rate hybrid perpetual.'

"'The craze o' my life !' says I, quite smart. 'What's better than a bit o' gairden and an intelligent interest in the works o' Nature?'"

"'Nature!' says he, wi' a girn. 'If Nature had her will o' roses, they would a' be back at the briar or killed wi' mildew and green-fly. But I needna tell you the fecht we hae wi' the randy[2] — you that can sport a bloom like that!'

"The lang and the short o't was that I got a first-rate order there and then frae Dimister, and promised to go to his gairden next time I was roond and give him the benefit o' my experience wi' hybrid perpetuals. Me! I didna ken a hybrid perpetual frae a horseradish! But I had my man! And I have him yet, there's no' a draper in the East o' Scotland that's mair glad to see me. When I had a day to mysel' in Gleska I went to my friend at the Bazaar, and learned as much aboot the rose trade in a couple o' hours as would keep me gaun in talk wi' Dimister for days. I bought a shillin' book on gairdenin', laid in a stock o' seedsmen's catalogues, and noo I ken far mair aboot the rose as a commercial plant than Dimister, though I never grew yin a' my days. What's the use? What's shops for? But every time I went to Dimister's, I aye had a button-hole that dazzled him. The droll thing is that havin' a button-hole grew into a habit; I started it to get roon' auld Sandy Dimister, and noo I'd sooner go without my watch."

30. *Citizen Soldier*

MR JAMES SWAN sat at his Saturday dinner-table, and was about to draw his customary bottle of beer, when, on reflection, he put down the corkscrew and filled up his glass with water.

"Bilious, Jimmy?" said his wife.

"No," he answered. "I'll wager there's no' a bilious man this day in the Citizen Corps.[1] Two hours' route-merchin' on the Fenwick Road is the best anti-bilious pill I ken; if it could be put up in boxes and sold in the apothecary shops, it would fetch a guinea a dozen. But ye couldna put Sergeant Watson in a box, and he's the main ingredient o' the route-merch pill. Watson's a fine, big, upstandin' chap, and it's a treat to see him handle his legs and arms the same's they were kahouchy, and double up a hill without a pech from him, but I wish he would mind at times our corps's no' made up o' gladiators or Græco-Roman wrestlers, that we're just plain business men, off and on about five-and-forty in the shade, wi' twenty years o' tramway travellin' and elevator lifts, and easy-chairs, bad air and beer in our constitution. It's no' to be expected we can pelt up braes on the Fenwick Road like a lot o' laddies."

"I hope you'll not hurt yoursel'," said Mrs Swan anxiously.

"Hurt mysel'! I'm sore all over! Sergeant Watson sees to that! It's no' the Madame Pomeroy treatment for the skin he's givin' us, nor learnin' us the dummy alphabet; he wouldna get a wink o' sleep this night if he thought we werena sore all over. 'The sorer ye feel,' says he, 'the sooner ye'll be fit.' I tell you he's a daisy! I never knew I had calves to my legs nor muscles to my back before I joined this army. ... My goodness, Bell, is that all the meat ye have the day? That's no' a sodger's dinner."

"At any rate," said Mrs Swan, "I never saw you looking better or eating more."

"I don't know about my looks," said Mr Swan, "and that bit doesna matter, for I suppose the Germans are no great Adonises themselves, but I wish to Peter they had my legs!" and he bent to rub them tenderly. "I've learned something in the last month, Bell — that a body's body's no' just a thing for hangin' shirts and stockings on — the same's it was a pair o' winter-dykes.[2] For twenty years I have been that intent on cultivatin' my intellect and the West Coast trade of C. & M., and dodgin' any kind o' physical effort that would spoil my touch wi' the country drapers, that I was turnin' into a daud o' creash,[3] and slitherin' down this vale o' tears as if the seat o' my breeks were soaped. Do ye ken what Watson said to me one day, just the week I joined? He saw me pechin', and had the decency to call a halt. 'Are ye all right?' says he; and I told him I had the doctor's word for it that all my internal organs were in first-rate order, and as strong as a lion's. 'Since that's the case,' says he, 'it's a pity we canna flype ye, for the ootside's been deplorably neglected.'"

"The idea!" said Mrs Swan, bridling.

"Oh, the man was right enough; a bonny job I could have made last month o' any German that came down the Drive wi' his bayonet fixed to look for beer! I wouldna have the strength to hand him out a bottle. But let him try't now! — Oh, michty, but I'm sore across the back!"

"I hope you haven't racked yourself?" his wife said, anxious again.

"The only thing I've racked's my braces. Just lie you down on your hands and toes, face down, wi' your body stiff, and see how often ye can touch the floor wi' your chin."

"Indeed and I'll do nothing of the kind!" said Mrs Swan. "I don't see what good that sort of thing's going to do if you have to fight the Germans. It's surely not on your hands and toes you're going to tackle them, James Swan?"

Her husband laughed. "No," said he; "and I'm no' expectin' to have to fight them even standing on the soles o' my feet, for the only Germans ye'll see in Scotland after this 'll come when their trouble's bye, wi' a pack, selling Christmas toys; their whiskers 'll be dyed for a disguise, and they'll call themselves Maclachlans."

"And what on earth are you drilling for?" said his wife. "I'm sure I wish you were on the road again. Since ever you were back in the shop six weeks ago, it's been nothing but darning socks for me, with your marching and parades."

Mr James Swan sighed, as he was helped to a man's size portion of the pie, which, to an appetite sharpened by his military duties, seemed quite inadequate.

"If ye want to know," said he, "I'm drilling mainly to make up the average for myself and for the country. The idea that the Black Watch and the Gordon Highlanders at a shilling or two a day per man were enough to keep us safe and let us carry on fine soft-goods businesses, allowing reasonable time for golf and football, was a slight mistake. It would have worked all right if the other chaps across the North Sea did the same, but you see they dinna. Instead of goin' in, like us, for a rare good time wi' athletic sports at half-a-crown for the grandstand seats, for tango dancin' and ke-hoi, the silly nyafs went, for a penny a day, into the army. So far as I can make out from the papers, they're all as tough as nails, and they cornered the toy trade too, and a lot o' other lines that's the inalienable right of the British business man. 'Our mistake, Maria!' said the Countess. All Britain is divided into two parts — the flabby-bellied and the fit; I don't expect to have the luck to shoot a German, but at least I'm no' goin' to be flabby."

"Then it's just for your health you're away parading?" said Mrs Swan.

"No," said her husband. "For self-respect. Sergeant Watson's system's gey sore on the muscles for a week or two, but it's most morally elevatin'. Four weeks ago if I had attempted to lean on mysel' wi' any weight I would have crumpled up like a taper; I'm sore all over just at present, but I feel that I could take a cow by the tail and swing it round my head. ... What you want in this house, Bella, is more beef, and a more generous sense of what is meant by dinner. Are ye not aware, my dear, that a sodger gets a pound a day of beef without bone? So far as I can judge, he needs it — every ounce!"

"Man, ye're just a great big laddie!" said Mrs Swan, with a shake of her husband's shoulder.

He shook his head. "That's just the worst of it, Bella," said he; "I'm no'! The greatest luck in the world just now is to be a lad of twenty. When I was young there was hanged-all happened in the world to waken me in the morning sure that I was needed to do something: it was just, every day, a trivial wee world of business, and feeding, and playing, and sleeping; no drums nor bugles in't, and nothing big enough to bother to roll my sleeves up for a blow at ... James Swan, Commercial Traveller. ... Sold stays! ... There was a destiny for ye! And I go along the streets just now and I see a hundred thousand men in the prime o' life who haven't the slightest notion of their luck and the chance they're missing."

"What chance?" asked Mrs Swan.

"To make a better, cleaner world of it; to help to save a nation; make themselves a name that, even if they perished, would be honoured by their people generations after. ... Pass the water, Bella, please."

"Are you not going to take your beer?" asked Mrs Swan.

"No," said Jimmy firmly.

"Why that?" she asked.

"Because I want to," he answered. "When we were doubling along the Fenwick Road I thought of that beer all the time. I could feel the very taste o't! But the oddest thing about Sergeant Watson's system is that it's learned me this — that the thing you're not particularly keen to do is the thing to do, and pays in the long-run best. So I'll just take water."

31. *The Adventures of a Country Customer*[1]

NOW THAT the Exhibition has the gravel nicely spread, and the voice of the cuckoo is adding to the monotony of a rural life, there is going to be a large and immediate influx of soft-goods men from places like Borgue in Kincardineshire and Lochinver in the North. They will come into town on the Friday trains at Exhibition excursion rates; leave their leatherette Gladstone bags at Carmichael's Temperance Hotel or the Y.M.C.A. Club, have a wash-up for the sake of our fine soft Glasgow water; take a bite,

perhaps, and sally forth to the Wholesale House of Campbell
& MacDonald (Ltd.) ostensibly to see what can be done in
cashmere hose, summer-weight underwear, and a large
discount on the winter bill. Strictly speaking they know
nothing about Campbell & MacDonald, having never seen
them, even if they have any existence, which is doubtful;
the party they are going to lean on is Mr Swan the traveller,
who covers Lochinver and Borgue two or three times a
year, and is all the Campbell & MacDonald that the rural
merchants know.

Mr Swan came through our two former Exhibitions[2]
with no apparent casualties beyond a slight chronic glow in
the countenance and a chubby tendency in the space
between the waistcoat pockets where he keeps his aromatic
lozenges and little liver pills respectively. For an hour's
convivial sprint through the various Scottish blends with a
hurried customer in from Paisley, or a real sustained effort
of four-and-twenty hours with a Perthshire man who is
good for a £250 order, Mr Swan is still the most reliable
man in Campbell & MacDonald's. He can hold his own
even with big strong drapers from the distillery districts of
the Spey; help them to take off their boots and wind their
watches for them and yet turn up at the warehouse in the
morning fresh as the ocean breeze, with an expenses bill of
£3 10s 4¹/₂d which the manger will pass without the blink
of an eye-lash. The City of Glasgow, for the heads of the
retail soft goods trade in Kirkudbrightshire and the North,
is practically Jimmy Swan and a number of delightfully
interesting streets radiating round him. In Borgue and
Lochinver he has been recognised affectionately since the
"Groveries"[3] year as a Regular Corker and Only Official
Guide to Glasgow, and no one knew better than himself
when the turf was turned up again in Kelvingrove, just
when the grass was taking root, that 1911 was going to be a
strenuous year.

"I feel I'm getting a little too old for the game," he said
to his wife with a sigh.

"You ought to have got out of the rut long ago, Jimmy,"

said Mrs Swan. "It isn't good for your health."

"A rut that's thirty years deep isn't a tramway rail, Bella," he rejoined, "and anyhow, I'm not in it for the fun of the thing, but mainly because I like to see you in a sealskin coat. But mark my words! this is going to be a naughty summer for your little Jimmy; every customer I have from Gretna to Thurso is going to have some excuse to be in Glasgow sometime when the Fairy Fountain's[4] on."

The first of the important country customers turned up on Friday afternoon. He came from Galloway, and ran all the way from the station to the warehouse so as not to lose any time in seeing Mr Swan, who was just going out for a cup of tea. "Why! Mr MacWatters! Delighted to see you!" said Jimmy, with a radiant smile kneading the customer's left arm all over as if he were feeling for a fracture. "Come right in and see our manager! He was just saying yesterday, 'We never see Mr MacWatters' own self,' and I said: 'No, Mr Simpson, but I'll bet you see his cheques as prompt as the cheques of any man in Campbell & MacDonald's books!' I had him there, Mac, had him there!"

The manager was exceedingly affable to Mr MacWatters, but vexed that he had not sent a post-card to say he was coming. "I should have liked," he said, "to take you out to the Exhibition, but unfortunately I have a Board meeting at three o'clock — of course I could have the meeting postponed."

"Not at all! not on my account!" said the Galloway customer with genuine alarm and a wistful glance at Jimmy. "I just want to look over some lines and leave an order, and then —"

"But my dear Mr MacWatters, you must see the Exhibition, and you must have a bit of dinner, and — Perhaps Mr Swan would take my place?"

"Delighted!" said Jimmy, heartily.

Mr MacWatters was introduced to some attractive lines in foulards, Ceylons, blouses, and the like, and said he would think it over and give Mr Swan his order at his leisure.

"Very good!" said the manager, shaking him by the hand at leaving. "I'm sure you'll have a pleasant evening and enjoy the Exhibition. You will be immensely struck by the Historical section: it will show you what an intensely interesting past we have had; and I'll wager you'll be delighted with the picture gallery. Then there's Sir Henry Wood's[5] Orchestra — I wish I could be with you. But Mr Swan will show you everything; you can depend on Mr Swan."

Five minutes later Jimmy and his country customer sat on tall stools in a lovely mahogany salon, and Jimmy was calling the country customer Bob, an affability which greatly pleased any man from Galloway. It was Bob's first experience of the mahogany salon; his business relations with the firm of Campbell & MacDonald didn't go back to the "Groceries", and he had so far only the assurance of the soft-goods trade in Galloway that in Glasgow Jimmy was decidedly a good man to know.

In Galloway it is drunk out of a plain thick glass, with a little water, and it is always the same old stuff. In this mahogany salon, Jimmy appeared to control magical artesian wells from which the most beautiful ladies, with incredibly abundant hair, drew variegated and aromatic beverages into long thin glasses that tinkled melodiously when you brought them against your teeth. Jimmy gave his assurance that they were quite safe, and the very thing for an appetiser, and the man from Galloway said he never dreamt you could get the like of that anywhere except on the Continent. He added, reflectively, that he really must take home a small bottle. Pleased with his approval, Jimmy prescribed another kind called a Manhattan Cocktail[6], and the country customer enjoyed it so much that he started feeling his hip-pocket for his purse that he might buy another. But Jimmy said, "On no account, old man! Leave this to me, it happens to be the centenary of the firm." So the country customer carefully buttoned up his hoppocket again, and consented to have another cocktail solely out of respect for the firm.

It was now decided by Jimmy that they could safely have a snack upstairs where the band was, and the country customer, being a corporal in the Territorials, walked upstairs carefully keeping time to the music, but somewhat chagrined that he had not divested himself, somewhere, of his yellow leggings.

They began with "Hors d'oeuvres", which tasted exactly like sardines, then they had soup, of which the country customer had a second helping after which he looked round for his cap and was preparing to go. But Jimmy laughingly said the thing was just starting, and a banquet followed which reminded the country customer of the one they had had at the Solway Arms Hotel in 1903 when the Grand Lodge deputation visited the local brethren.[7]

When the fish had passed, Jimmy picked up a List Price card or catalogue affair and said something about a bottle of "buzz-water." Concealing his disappointment, the country customer, who never had cared for lemonade, said he didn't mind. It turned out to be quite a large bottle with a gilt neck, and except for a singular tendency to go up the nose, it was the most pleasant kind of lemonade he had ever tasted. He was surprised that Jimmy hadn't ordered two bottles and said so, and Jimmy, begging his pardon, promptly did so.

This stage of the proceedings terminated with cups of black coffee and two absurdly minute glasses of a most soothing green syrup strongly recommended by Jimmy as an aid to digestion. There was also a large cigar.

"I think," said Jimmy, in dulcet tones, with the flush of health upon his countenance, and a roguish eye, "I think we will be getting a move on, and as one might say, divagating towards the Grove of Gladness."

They had just one more, seeing it really was the centenary of the firm, and the country customer, as he walked downstairs, was struck by the beautiful convoluted design of the marble balustrade.

In the very next moment the country customer asked "What is this?" and Jimmy responded, "It is the Scenic

Railway. Feel the refreshing breeze upon your brow!"[8]
They were dashing with considerable celerity past a mountain tarn, and the country customer expressed a desire to
stop for a moment that he might have his fevered temples
in the water. Far off a band was playing a dreamy waltz. A
myriad lamps were shining in the night, and restlessly
flitting from place to place. The air had a curious balmi-
ness that is not felt in Galloway. It was borne home to the
country customer that he must there and then tell Mr
Swan — good old Jimmy Swan! — about Jean Dykes in
Girvan, and how he loved her and meant to marry her if he
could get another extension of the lease of his shop at
present terms, but before he could lead up to this subject
with the necessary delicacy, he found himself on a balcony
looking down on an enormous crescent of humanity, con-
fronted by a bandstand and a tumbler.

"The firm," Jimmy was saying solemnly, "has always
appreciated your custom. Our Mr Simpson says over and
over again 'Give me the Galloway men; they know what
they want, and they always see that they get it!' he says,
'Whatever you do, Mr Swan, pay particular attention to
Mr MacWatters, and put him on bedrock prices.' I have
always done so, Galloway has been, as you might say, the
guiding-star of my business life."

The country customer, profoundly moved, shook
Jimmy by the hand.

"Where are we now?" he asked and the balcony began to
revolve rapidly. He steadied it with one hand, and tried to
count the myriad lights with the other. They, too, were
swinging round terrifically, and he realised that they must
be stopped. He became cunning. He would pretend indifference to them as they swung round him, and then spring
on them when they were off their guard. "Where are we
now?" he repeated.

"The Garden Club,"said the voice of Jimmy, coming out
of the distance. "Try and sit up and have this soda-water."

Next morning, sharp at nine, Mr Swan came into the
warehouse with a sparkling eye, a jaunty step, a voice as

mellifluous as a silver bell and a camelia in his button-hole.

"Morning! Morning!" he cheerily said to the Ribbons Department, as he passed to the manager's room.

"Old Swan's looking pretty chirpy," said the Ribbons enviously. "He's been having a day at Turnberry[9] or the Coast."

Jimmy laid a substantial order for Autumn goods for Galloway and a bill of expenses for £3 9s before the manager.

"Ah! just so!" said the manager. "And how did Mr MacWatters like the Exhibition?"

"Immensely impressed!" said Jimmy.

"It is bound to have a great educative influence. Great! And such a noble object — Chair of History![10] What did Mr MacWatters think of the Art and Historical sections?"

"He was greatly pleased with them particularly," said Jimmy. "I have just seen him off in the train, and he said he would never forget it."

The manager placed his initials at the foot of the expenses bill and handed it back to Jimmy who proceeded at once to the cashier's department.

"£3 9s," said the manager to himself. "Art and History in Kelvingrove appear to come a little high, but it's a good order. And there's only one Jimmy Swan."

32. *The Radiant James Swan*[1]

MR SWAN, with a white pique waistcoat, a one-button morning coat, an absolutely perfect crease down his discreet grey cambric trousers, the sauciest of silk hats just faintly tilted to the right (a weakness he could never get out of) and an orchid in his button-hole, went round his own samples-cases, piled up in the hall of the hotel, as if he had never seen them in his life before. He shook hands ceremoniously with the lady clerk in the office, put down his name in the flourish of his signature, and mentioned to the clerkess in a tone that was almost a caress that he had never seen her looking better.

"It's this salubrious air you have here, I suppose," he added. "I really must send my wife down for a holiday ... How is the fishing doing?"

Several obvious anglers were lounging in the hall, their presence accounted for Mr Swan's failure to recognise his own sample-cases.

"Some good catches were got yesterday," said the clerkess, paling down again to her natural colour.

"Ah!" said Mr Swan, delightedly, rubbing his hands. "That's good! I hope we have a little rain tonight; then we must see about the river tomorrow." The ecstasy of the ardent angler was in his eye, though, to tell the truth, his honest conviction always was that the noblest of the fish species, and the only one worth getting up early for, was the brandered finnan haddock.

He moved in a stately way round the corner, tapped at the landlord's private door; opened it on a cry from within, put in his head, and said, "Scene Two — Mountain Glade. Cave of the Mountain Robbers. In centre Chief of the Mountain Robbers lying in wait for the defenceless traveller. Sound of Muffled Cocoa-Nuts in the distance ... How's a' wi' ye, Mr Coats?"

"Good heavens, Mr Swan!" said the landlord. "Is that really you? You're the greatest nut yourself I've seen this season. Where's your wee pea-jacket?"

"From scenes like these, Auld Scotia's grandeur springs!" said Mr Swan, posing majestically in the middle of the sanctum. "Cast your eye on this coat — fits like the peeling o' a plum! In waistcoats, now, have you ever seen anything so judiciously evading vulgar ostentation while yet arresting to the eye of taste? Genuine orchid — cypripedium, something-or-other, secured at great expense from Watty Grant in the Bazaar this morning; silk hat the latest touch; look at the brim of it! You haven't a hat like that in Banchory. Solomon, sir, at his best, would look like a remnant sale if brought in here for comparison[2] ... I'm tired, Mr Coats; I've been on the road since six o'clock this morning," and he sat down wearily on a chair.

"I'm gettin' too old, Robert, for any protracted performance in the role of tailor's dummy, but if you ask me, that's
a jolly smart hat!" and he surveyed it at arm's length with
approval.

"You're going to Rachel Thorpe's[3] wedding to-morrow,
I suppose?" said the landlord, juggling with some bottles
behind and putting out two glasses containing an amber
fluid.

"You'll mak' a mistake wi' these bottles some day, and
gie me the cauld tea yin," said Jimmy. "However, here's
tae ye! And ye're right about Rachel; her mother fixed the
wedding to suit my journey; she says I found the man for
Rachel — a' nonsense! Rachel had the chap picked and
settled on before he jaloused anything himself. But this is
my last weddin' in the way o' business; after this I'm only
goin' to the weddin's o' folk I have a spite to."

"You've launched a lot in your time," said the landlord.

"For twenty years," said Jimmy "I was the champion
thrower of the rice in the West of Scotland, and held the
record for heaving bowl-money[4] in the rural districts till
the sport went oot o' fashion. I've put in a luscious bass to
'The Voice that Breathed O'er Eden,' and proposed 'The
Ladies' oftener than any other man in Britain. But I'm no'
goin' to dae it ony mair; I don't need! I doubt, indeed, if
my bein' the ever-joyous Aye-Ready paid me or my firm in
the long run. Now I'm goin' to settle down and enjoy
mysel', and tell all kind inquirin' friends more or less
connected wi' the drapery trade that I've the doctor's
orders no' to go oot at night, or excite mysel' at public
functions. The heart, Mr Coats! The heart!" — and Jimmy
slightly tragically rose and tapped himself on the place
where he keeps his pocket-book.

"You're not giving up bowling!" said the landlord with
genuine distress. "We expected to have you out at the
green to-night."

"Bowls is off!" said Jimmy firmly, "I aye hated bowlin',
but kept it up to please my customers. Same wi' curlin';
since they stopped lang kale soup there's nothin' in the

rorarin' game for me. But the lang and the short o't is that
I've learned my trade, paid my 'prentice fees, and can now
afford to dae what I like."

"Lucky man!" said the landlord. "They're making me a
Baillie!"

"Do you know?" said Mr Swan, "twenty to thirty years
o' my bright young life was wasted o' the cultivation o' the
social side o' business? When I came first on the road for C
& M, the man that took me roond and introduced me said
that nine-tenths o' the customers would be no use to me
unless they got the length o' callin' me 'Jimmy' and saw me
wi' their own een ride a goat.[5] It was Big Campbell — ye
mind o' him? — The Prince? He was somethin' devilish
fancy in the Royal Arch[6] and he got me made a Mason in
Inverness to please a customer that was R.W.M.[7] Next
year at Aberdeen, I got the Mark, to please a tailor and
clothier chap who took some tweed from me and took my
measure for a knickerbocker suit the time he was puttin'
me through the grips and passwords!

"I laid mysel' oot to be the most widely-kent and popular man in the wholesale dry-goods trade. I was an Ancient
Shepherd in Kirkcudbright, wi' a six-foot crook and a
bunnet the width o' a barrel, and I wouldna ken a yowe
from a ram if I saw them in a park. I was a Royal Forester
in Alloway — me that never planted a tree in my life! I was
affiliated to six Gardeners' Lodges[8] north o' the Forth. If
there had been an Ancient and Royal Order o' Sanitary
Engineers, I would have been one like winkin'.

"Every time I struck a town in the way o' business, they
skirmished roond and got some poor sowl to put through
the First, and Brother Swan was the life and soul of the
succeeding harmony. My boxes were no sooner clapped aff
the train than a bill was up in the baker's window callin' an
emergency meetin' o' the Gardeners, or the Shepherds, or
the Foresters, or the Oddfellows. If they had nae other
excuse for the meetin', they had some doleful cause o' an
afflicted brother, lyin' ill in the infirmary, and I was aye at
the top o' the subscription sheet.

"There's ony number o' football clubs goin' to stop this summer because James Swan, Esq. is no longer goin' to be a Patron — ."

"But you were a great football enthusiast!" said Mr Coats, with surprise.

"Me! I'm just as keen on the game o'moshy![9] I got mixed up wi' football in the country because I sometimes do a line in strippit jerseys. Oh! I tell you, Robert, my reputation for affability and high spirits cost me some trouble and a lot o' sundries that werena covered by C & M's pound a day.

"I drank when I didna want to drink; I took tickets for balls and concerts and subscription o' sales that were nae mair interest to me than the Balkan Imbroglio or the Pan-Germanic Conference. I drove to weddin's or walked to funerals o' folk I never kent; I took the chair or sung at concerts when I should be in my bed. Never again, Robert, never again!"

"How's that, Jimmy?"

"Doctor's orders!" said Mr Swan. "A quiet life. No undue exertion. Forbye, it doesn't pay. I doubt if in the last twelve years it got me a single order; this is no' an age for the cultivation o' the social side in business; it's the stuff ye sell, and the terms, that talk, and the right sort o' crack across a counter goes far further than the Mark Degree and 'Out on the Deep when the Sun is Low' at the local smokin'-concert. ... Is it No. 20, Mr Coats?"

33. *Jimmy Swan's German Spy*[1]

THE LANDLORD of the Cross-Keys Inn filled up his evening schedule[2] for the Sergeant of Police — the names and addresses of his guests; when they had arrived, and when they meant to go away; their nationality, and their business. There were only three or four, and the last entry was "James Swan, Commercial Traveller, Glasgow."

Mr Swan himself, with his slippers on, and his pipe going, looked over the landlord's shoulder.

"There's no a German spy in that bunch, anyway, Mr Grant," he said. "Two Macs and a Fisher; and as for the name o' Swan it's so reassurin' to the police that whenever they see't on a hotel list now they gang hame to their beds for the nicht."

The landlord of the Cross-Key Inn apparently had no comment to make. He completed his filling-in of the daily report with his signed testimony on soul and conscience that it was correct so far as he knew. He looked at Mr Swan a little curiously, and then without a word went out on the verandah. It was a perfect night, of mildly frosty moonshine; a flock of sheep was bleating on the golf-course, and someone with a winking light was moving about the first hole.

Mr Grant, having watched the light a while, came in and took up his schedule again.

"You don't happen to know any Samuel Fisher in Strathbungo³, Mr Swan?" he asked. "In the ship chandler business."

"No," said Jimmy on reflection. "Whoever he is, he's been done in the eye, for there's no river Bungo, and there's no fish and no ship-chandlin' there either. Is Fisher the sandy-haired wee bald young yin wi' the crimson cardigan waistcoat?"

"Yes," said Mr Grant, who appeared to be a little nervous. "I never saw him before. He drove in just at the gloamin', with a droll kind of box, and when I asked him all about himself, as we have to do now, and what his business was, he looked quite startled."

"It would startle onybody that had no experience before o' wartime conditions in Hielan' hotels, Mr Grant. Very few o' us could come through the test without a sudden sinkin' at the he'rt, for fear we were discovered at last. What's the worst that ye suspect him of?"

"There is something in his look," said Mr Grant.

"I know!" said Jimmy; "I noticed it — A kind o' vacancy. It's a kind o' look that aye goes wi' the higher branches o' ship-chandlin".

"And there's something in his manner o' speech," continued the landlord. "His accent's no English, and it's no' Scotch, and it's no' Irish."

"I have it!" said Jimmy, snapping his fingers. "It'll be Hydropathic."

"And he's been out there for the last half-hour wi' a light on the golf course, signallin'," proceeded Mr Grant's indictment.

At the suggestion of Mr Swan they went into the hall and had a look at the mysterious Fisher's box.

"H'm!" said Jimmy, pursing his mouth and rubbing his chin. "Damnin' fact to start wi', it's a wooden-box! It's painted broon, and it's locked — that shows the owner has something to conceal. There's no doot, Mr Grant, that we're on the track o' a big thing here. 'S.L.F.' is painted on the lid — a pure blind!"

It was a long, narrow box, apparently quite new; Mr Grant took hold of it by handle which was on the top for convenience of carriage, and shook it. There was no sound.

"Thirty years in the trade," said the hotel-keeper, significantly; "I never saw a box in this house exactly like that before."

"What do you think it'll be?" asked Jimmy, solemnly. "Airoplanes?"

"Oh, no," said Mr Grant, a little surprised at Jimmy's innocence, "It couldn't be airoplanes — not in that space. The engines alone — "

"True!" said Jimmy, hurriedly.

"True! It might be bombs, if we could think o' onything that could be done aboot here wi' bombs except blaw up the gas-works, and considerin' the quality o' your gas, Mr Grant, I think that could be considered no unfriendly action … Again, it might be wireless telegraphy."

"That would mean big masts," suggested the innkeeper who knew science.

"Not the latest," said Jimmy. "Rhones. Ye can get the effect wi' rhones."

"When I think," said Mr Grant, piteously, "of the hundreds o' German waiters I've had here, payin' them the best wages, I must say I consider I should be the last man to be harassed … "

"Harassed!" said Jimmy. "They wouldna hesitate to harass onybody; it's a fair delight to them."

Mr Grant was getting more nervous and agitated every minute. He went out to the verandah and looked towards the golf course again; no light was to be seen. "I will not put up with it!" he came back crying. "I'll have no filthy German spies about my place; out he goes this very evening, box and baggage."

Mr Swan, however, pointed out that this would be a great mistake; if Mr Fisher was able to prove his innocence, he could claim substantial damages for being thrown out of his hotel at night. On the other hand, if he were a spy, the crafty thing for them to do was to pretend he was not suspected, and keep an eye on him till he could be discovered in the act.

When Mr Fisher came in from his belated ramblings round a golf course which had not seen a player for five months, he got quite an affable "good night" from the landlord and Mr Swan as he passed upstairs to his bedroom.

Next morning, when Mr Grant came down to breakfast, he found Mr Swan in the hall before him contemplating the mysterious box, which was now unlocked and empty.

"He's gone!" said Jimmy, gravely.

"Gone!" said the landlord; "when?"

"More than an hour ago," said Jimmy, "whenever it was light. I heard the front door bang, and I looked out at my bedroom window, and there was the bold Fisher sneaking up the road, hiding something under his topcoat. Guilt was in every step o' him; the sparks were fleein' from the very tackets in his boots. Whenever I understood what he was up to I opened my window, and cries — 'Ah, Mr

Fisher! Mr Fisher! Ye think ye're not observed, but God sees ye!"'

"The ruffian!" exclaimed Mr Grant, all trembling; "I wish you had warned me, and we could have had him stopped."

"Oh, he'll be back for breakfast," said Mr Swan. "Then ye can have it oot wi' him."

"Back for breakfast," said Mr Grant, bewildered. "If he's a spy ... "

"Tuts!" said Jimmy, chuckling. "He's no a spy; he's the last that's left o' the young Glasgow golfers, and he's here incognito as a chandileer. You see he daurna, at his age[4] be seen near Glasgow wi' a golf bag, so he puts it in a box and hies him as far as he can into the country where he thinks he'll no be noticed."

34. *Jimmy Swan in Warm Weather*[1]

As A classy dresser, James Swan, the traveller for Macdonald and Campbell[2], leaves nothing to be desired. You cannot be two minutes in his company without an uneasy feeling that you ought really to have shaved this morning, and that the right sort of hat or necktie actually does contribute to an impressive human personality. Mr Swan always looks like my idea of a thoroughly well-dressed man — a retired Colonel with a smart little place in the country, two setter dogs, and a whole row of boot-trees. The sort of man whose trousers for the day are dictated by the barograph, and who would not be found dead in a bow-tie with a turn-over collar.

He looked exceptionally smart on Friday coming home from his Aberdeen journey, not a superfluous crease in his garments. The dove-grey spats, the ash-grey bowler hat, the unsoiled creamy gloves, the lustrous footwear of the same leather as the best dukes' cigar-cases are made of, the ebony walking-cane, the faintly-spotted foulard necktie, and the handkerchief en suite would have gained him an entrance to the Royal enclosure at Ascot without a ticket.

The rest of us were sweltering with the heat, feeling sticky underneath, horribly baggy at the knees, caught in a tropic atmosphere with semi-winter clothes on.[3] He looked as cool and clean as the Sound of Kerrara.

"How do you manage it, Jimmy?" I asked, indicating the perfect sartorial ensemble and the air of 45 Fahrenheit.

"Thought," he answered, lighting a cigar. "Profound and unremitting thought. Considering that I put on my clothes only once a day except on Sundays I feel justified in putting my mind into the job. Most people in this town have souls far above trivial considerations of that sort; they're so taken up with the Ruhr situation,[4] poetry, the rising Bank rate or the tennis tournament that they would go to their work without a waistcoat if their wives didn't watch them. But I'm a humble, low-browed sort of chap, and I feel that I'm not depriving my fellow-creatures of any priceless contribution to human thought if I concentrate my attention for a wee while every morning on my personal appearance."

"Yet I fancy some crafty consideration of the effect of clothes on business comes into the question too," I suggested.

He chuckled. "Ye may be sure o' that!" he admitted, a little relinquishing the fastidious English that usually goes with a flower in his coat. "When I went first on the road I thought it didn't matter a hang what I wore or the way I wore it so long as my samples were attractive and the prices right. If plus fours[5] had been invented then I would have had them. Yes I'd have had the neck to try to sell two-piece tennis suits, fancy Shetland wool hip panels in contrastin' colours on a day as hot as this with me in Harris tweeds! I had no sense! Not an iota of sense.

"Now if here's one thing a traveller in the dry goods line should study it's the human mind as often seen in drapers. Ye may tell them the funniest Gleska bawrs[6] and show them Jap schappes and silk marocains there's no the like o' offered north o' Perth, at prices fair ridiculous, but if the suit ye're wearin' yoursel' is scuffed and your hat's the least bit chafed its domino for big orders.

"Ye have no idea o' the effect o' a good silk hat and nae dandruff on the retail trade. It fair dazzles shopkeepers in the rural belt that never themselves wear anything but a hooker-doon[7], and aye look as if they shed their hair wi' a curry-comb.

"It was our late Mr Williams who put me up to it first, after I had been six months goin' round the country tryin' to sell the daintiest ladies' wear in a D.B. navy blue suit that gathered a' the dust and one of' yon 1880 waterproof coats made oot o' the same kind o' rubber as hose-pipes and hot-water bottles.

"'Mr Swan,' he says one day, 'did it ever occur to you ye should look like the stuff you're sellin'. It's no a sheep dip firm ye represent' for one thing, ye havena the whiskers for't, and ye have no great head for drink. Ye may think these people in Dornoch don't care a rap even if ye came to them in a kilt and a suit o' oilskins, but ye're wrong. Dornoch's a long way from Buchanan Street, but even in Dornoch they don't like a glass o' champagne offered to them on a porridge plate; they have an intuition that it should be a silver salver. Dress like the season, dress like your samples, dress like a pound a day expenses, and for God's sake don't wear cuffs that need clippin' wi' a pair o' shears.'

"He was a great man, William Campbell — by George, he knew his business! I never forgot what he said — 'Look like the stuff you're sellin', look like the season.'"

"There's no' one man in a hundred in Glasgow dresses like the weather. Even men in a good way o' business go through the year in winter-weight underwear and havena a thin flannel suit in their repertoire. Look a yoursel', for instance, wearin' on a day like this a thick tweed suit adapted for the January fishin' on Loch Tay. No wonder you're so glossy about the face and pechin' aboot sultry weather and relaxin' climates. Ye would be far better wi' an alpaca jacket. If I went into a customer's shop perspirin' that way, I doubt he would let me open up a single case. Half my care in life is keepin' cool when other folks are moppin' their silly heids wi' naipkins and in lookin' snug and cosy when it's frost.

"In dull grey weather I'm the little ray of sunshine. If I'm doin' Oban in November, they put the time I spend in the town in their statistics, and report "Sunshine 6 hours' to be upsides wi' Bournemouth or Torquay. All this week, in the North, my aim was to be like an evenin' breeze from the sea blowin' through a tailor's workshop.

"A draper in Dingwall on Monday says to me, 'Man, Mr Swan, ye put me in mind o' a plate o' ice-cream at a night's dancin'.' He had the humid hand o' a herrin'-curer, and generally looked parboiled, wi' a big bottle o' lime juice and a carafe o' water constant on his desk. Just to keep me by him for the coolness I brought into his wee bit shop he gave me the biggest order ever I had from him."

"It's all very well, Jimmy," I said, "but in a variable climate like this your psychology must sometimes get you into trouble."

He laughed. "Quite right! But I have to risk it. I once went up to Elgin in the month o' June in swelterin' weather, wi' not so much as an umbrella' wi' a panama hat, a white pique waistcoat, patent-leather shoes, and a bottle o' midge lotion. The very day I landed it started to snow! "James Swan," I says to mysel', "ye're in the soup!" If I had tried to go through my customers in my Isle o' Man turn-out, in weather like thon, heaven pity Macdonald and Campbell! What I did was this — I got fearful ill in the hotel wi' threatened peritonitis, whatever that is; went to my bed in a sample pair of Jap silk pyjamas, broad stripe effect, and sent word round to my customers that I was poorly.

"They came in droves to my bedroom; I ordered in a drop o' spirits, sat up in bed in the tastiest gentleman's night attire that was ever seen in Elgin, no countin' the shootin' tenants, and I booked bumper orders."

35. *The Tall Hat*[1]

FOR A dozen years at least I have not seen Jimmy Swan wear a tall silk hat. When he started a bowler, even on his Northern journeys, I recognised it was a portent, and that 'lums' were doomed. For at least quarter of a century before that, his silk hats, in sauciness and gloss, made him conspicuous among all the commercial travellers who do business for Glasgow firms in these country towns where they still ring curfew bells and have shutters on shop windows.

"I was getting into a rut with my topper hat," he explained to me when he made the change to bowlers, "and for any man on the road in the soft goods line that's fatal. Wearing a top hat all the time left me with no latitude for rising to what you might call a supreme occasion. A top hat is the acme, the ne plus ultra of ceremonial garb for gents; you can put on nothing more respectful to the departed or more consoling to the victims of a weddin'. But wearing a topper always, as I did in the way of business, I felt no special moral uplift or elation at a wedding or a funeral; it was just like being there in my working clothes. The commonest country stone-mason on these occasions, with a mid-Victorian 'lum' and crape on it experienced a satisfaction with himself that was denied to me.

"Forbye," he added, more colloquially, "the top hat, as a regular head-dress, dates a commercial man and puts him in the septuagenarian class. You might as well go about wi' a brocaded waistcoat and carry a snuff-box. It's held in a certain respect, I admit, but it's apt to be the same respect as folk have for the ruins o' Tillietudlem Castle."[2]

Mr Swan, when I met him the other day, had the jauntiest of bowler hats — a perfectly priceless shade of Cuban brown.

"Then the topper's gone for good?" I remarked to him.

"Completely!" he replied, with emphasis. "I'd as soon wear a fireman's helmet — except it was for a Royal garden party. I flatter mysel' I was one o' the first in the national movement for its abolition. It was a species o' hat never

right adapted for Gleska heids. It cast a gloom o' its own
on the Scottish Sabbath, for ye daurna cock it, and im-
posed the most cruel physical restraint on the right enjoyment o' a weddin'.'

"When I went in to business first, tile hats were at their
zenith. They were held as heirlooms in a family, and
descended from father to son. It took the wearer years to
get used to them; ye had to learn them like the fiddle. But,
all the same, they had an air o' money in the bank and
strict sobriety. On the strength o' a well-brushed topper
hat, wi' nothing inside but hair, many a Gleska business
was built up, that's now been' ruined by sons that go in for
velours and Homburgs."

"You have never gone in for the velour or Homburg
yourself," I remarked.

"I have more gumption that that," replied Jimmy. "As
head-gears they are far too flippant and don't give-a-dam,
if ye follow me. A soft hat's all right for the Fair at
Rothesay, for a man in the rural districts wi' a bit o'
shooting, or for a chap like yoursel' that's steeped to the
neck in the newspaper business; but a man in commerce
wi' a soft hat on in his business moments always raises
doubts about his strict integrity. When one o' my customers starts the soft hat habit in the streets o' Gleska I keep
my eye on Stubbs[3] for the earliest mention o' his name.

"No, the bowler's the thing! Ye'll still see a lot o' reckless young men that came out o' the Army carryin' on wi'
more-or-less velours that they have down on their ears like
a jelly-bag, but they're far astray. The head o' the firm says
nothing to them about it, but in his mind he says 'billiards
or the palais de danse,' and goes sniffin' about the warehouse lookin' for surreptitious golf-bags. To any young
chap comin' from the country to start his career in Gleska,
unless it's in the police force or tramways, I would say
"learn Double Entry and aye wear a bowler hat."

"Unless ye stick it on the back o' your head and have
cobwebs on it, the bowler hat never gives ye away. It's
equally good for a Temperance festival or a football match;

a Corporation banquet or a rally in the Stock Exchange. If you're anyway over fifty, your bowler hat should be just a trifle square on the top; there's no' a surer sign of solvency and earnest endeavour.

"Look at the photographic group o' the Hammermen[4] or any other prosperous group o' incorporated merchant princes — all square-topped bowler hats. I aye put on a square one when I go to Aberdeen."

"But one sees an occasional topper still in Glasgow," I pointed out.

"I admit ye do," said Jimmy, "but it's at its last kick. A business man is apt still to keep one in the office for goin' to a funeral or to see about an overdraft, but he daurna take it home for fear o' his wife and family if they're anyway free and easy wi' him. The man who keeps a top-hat in the office may escape the frightful ordeal o' wearin' it in the train or on a tram-car, but yet can tell by his look when it's on his mind that he has to go through the office wi' it. The very thought of it makes him haggard.

"I can tell when our senior — old Macdonald — has a funeral engagement. He rampages all forenoon round the office, findin' fault wi' everything, and when it's gettin' near time for the obsequies he keeps talkin' wi' me just to secure my company as far as St. George's Church[5], where the mournin' cars are. Ye'll never see a Gleska man walkin' his lone through the streets wi' a topper on; he must always have somebody wi' him to share the blame wi'.

"Everybody looks at him and wonders who's deid. It's universally recognised as a thing he wouldna be wearin' if he could help it, and so there's a certain amount o' popular sympathy that keeps even boys from throwin' snowballs at him. He knows himself that it doesna fit him; he is harrowed by the thought that bein' twelve years old it's likely out o' date; he canna keep his mind off it, and it spoils his day. As a matter of fact, the art of wearin' a tile-hat as unconsciously as a watch-chain is practically forgotten in Scotland except in places like Milngavie[6] where ye can smoke a pipe wi't and forget your trouble."

36. *The Groveries in Retrospect*[1]

JIMMY SWAN put down his evening paper with an air of finality, took off his spectacles and wiped them carefully. "It looks to me," he remarked "as if it might be a toss-up between a new Municipal Buildings altogether or an International Exhibition. It's ominous that they've started on already on the Municipal Buildings; at least they have the plans prepared for another big extension. I doubt that means postponing the Exhibition till I'm too frail for diversion on the switchback railway. We're due an Exhibition![2] There's hundreds of young chaps in Glasgow wi' their education incomplete; they never saw the fairy fountain going at Kelvingrove, nor heard the joyous squeals of the summer flapper skooshing down the water chute. They've got to the age of manhood oblivious of what can be done with stucco, bands, bright lights and balloon ascents to make Glasgow really jolly. Lots of them think, no doubt, that the West End Park[3] is fine the way it is, with snowdrops in it, a rockery, a duck pond, seats for the aged and bowling greens. They have no conception what we used to do with it when they were babies. Mighty! when I mind o' the gondolas, the Clanneries[4], the Royal visits[5], the athletic competitions, the fireworks, the fairy lamps, the Russians[6], and the champion cornet player of the world that played 'The Lost Chord' every night to a populace that sat round holding each other's hands, full of pathos to the last degree, I am vexed for the present generation."

"There was also the educational effect," I said — "the Art Sections, if you remember, and the Palaces of Industry and Engineering."

"Quite right!" said Jimmy Swan. "I mind that fine — the machinery for making sweeties and the pictures — miles of them! But I was thinking more of the general uplifting effect of the Exhibitions, their social hilarity. A season-ticket for the Groveries was a good as a year of foreign travel; you saw life.

"I don't suppose we'll ever have another Exhibition at

Kelvingrove;' there's not the room for it now, but I can hardly imagine an Exhibition in Glasgow anywhere else.[7] Do you mind the first one — 1888? Wasn't it a corker? It changed the habits of the whole community. Folk began to put on their Sunday clothes every other day in the week, and the joys of daundering down the Kelvin-side were rediscovered for the first time in a hundred years. It was found that it didn't hurt in the least to have the band of the Grenadier Guards playing 'The Departure of a Troopship' outside the place where you took your tea. Great times! Everybody was young then. I don't think it ever rained that Summer, and there was no Income-tax — at least I never had to pay it. The Chesterfield covert coat was the vogue for all smart young gentlemen, and the smart young women carried themselves well in front to make up the loss of the bustle that had just gone out of fashion.

"You could take your lunch at the Clanneries any day with all the stars of the Italian Opera Company at the next table to you, and if you wanted Science to the utmost limit you had only to go out to Hamilton Park and see Baldwin[8] drop in a parachute from his balloon. The idea was that in a few months afterwards we would all have parachutes and the bicycle would be extinct. When the last night of the Groveries of 1888 came on November 11th with the summer still going strong the turnstiles clicked for an attendance of 117,904, and there wasn't a tumbler left on the place that wasn't pinched for a souvenir.

"Everybody was bit older when the next Exhibition came in 1901, but, thanks to that indomitable Scottish thrift that makes us the people we are, we had all saved a little money, and Gray Street was jammed every night with season-ticket holders. The whangee cane of 1888 was out of fashion, and the bowler hat was giving way to the Homburg or the straw basher, but the lads o' the old brigade were still the same stout fellows who wrecked the Clanneries on the last night thirteen years before. And we beat all the 1888 records in attendance, mirth, vivacity.

"There was the Dome, and in below it the piazza — I

tell you strolling the piazza was worth the money itself! The Grosvenor and the Royal Bungalow and the Princes Restaurant — the Russian pavilions, the Indian Theatre, the Japanese, the fireworks and the searchlights, the — "

"The new Art Galleries," I suggested. "They were, I think, what we called the "clou' of that Exhibition. I remember the Rodin sculptures."

"Quite!" said Jimmy, cheerfully. "Most artistic! We must always keep Art going but do you mind the gondolas on the river? Genuine Venetian! there was another marine delight, outside the Exhibition,where the Mitchell Library is now[9], called the 'Hidden Rivers'. You sat in a boat singing 'Funiculi Funicula,'[10] and sailed through tunnels opening up every now and then on foreign scenery as in Hamilton's Diorama. Great!

"But some of the survivors of 1888 never right caught the old abandon — especially if they were married, and I mind an old maid's poem of the time that went:

'There's no such music now as that the Blue
      Hungarians[11] played
When fiddles thrilled to fingers skilled in Kelvin's
      greenwood shade
No eager swain will wait for me an hour beneath
      the Dome.
And now sit and watch the game and cannot feel elate
The girls in socks and baby frocks in 1888
Are having all the innings now, and getting all the fun —
I've only got the memory of Groveries No. 1'

"The 1911 Exhibition at Kelvingrove still found the natural appetite of Glasgow for art, education, and a high old time unabated; but I had to miss a lot of the attractions for the sake of my commercial reputation. Would you believe me? — I never went on the Aeriel Railway or the Joy Wheel; I thought they didn't comport wi' my dignity and now I'm vexed for it. The Mountain Scenic Railway was my favourite touch. But everything else was educative to a degree — the Historical collection, the Africa and Esquimaux villages, the Laplanders with their reindeer, the 'Auld Toon[12]' and 'The Clachan'[13].

"And then there was the music! the Blue Hungarian Band again; the Berlin Philharmonic, the Italian Carabinieri; the Roumanian Orchestra, the Scottish Orchestra with Mlynarksi; Pachman, Kubelik, Backhaus, Marchesi; the Queen's Hall Orchestra under Sir Henry Wood, and all the best bands in the British Army! ... It's certainly time we had another Exhibition!"

37. Selling Shoes[1]

THE LATEST device of the retail boot trade to ensure a perfect fit for the customer and eliminate all risk of corns, bunions, fallen arch, hammer-toe and ingrowing nails, is an adaptation of the Rontgen[2] rays. A shadow image of the feet, inside the boot, is thrown on a fluorescent screen, revealing all points of pressure or distortion. The customer may go away with a strong conviction that his new boots pinch him across the instep, but it is impossible to argue with an X-ray instrument.

I was speaking about this beneficent new appliance on Saturday to Mr James Swan the doyen of commercial travellers in the West of Scotland soft goods world, and found him unusually sardonic.

"We'll have a Chair of Bootmaking at Gilmorehill[3] before long," he remarked drily. "It only wants a start from Sir Daniel Stevenson.[4] We'll have a professor of Pedology; special classes in Anatomy, the French Heel, Brogues in the Middle Ages, Slippers for Sedentary Gents, and Comparative Physiology of the Hack and Chilblain.

"There's sure to be travelling scholarships; the champion student of the year will get three years tourin' abroad to inspect the lark or laverock heel of the native African races, the Chinese club-foot, and the American extra wide welt. No man'll get a responsisble job in a bootshop unless he has the B.Sc. and a Rontgen Ray diploma. He'll be called a Pedologist or a Bootician, wear horn-rim specs, and have a wee place of his own in the shop, hung round wi' charts and photographs o' the leading feet among the Crowned Heads in Europe.

"There is no trade in the country with more go in it than the shoemakers" (continued Mr Swan). "It started humbly as a cottage industry when the first roads were made, and the native tribes were gettin' their feet all cut wi' broken bottles. The man that made the first pair of shoes is supposed to have been a chap in Fintry. He killed a cow and made from the hide of it a rough kind of leather socks for himself and his family. Ye'll see a pair in the Kelvingrove Museum — no heels, the hair inside — fine for dancin' the Hoolachan!

"For centuries every man made his own shoes wi' a knife or a hatchet, and history says the human foot was then at its highest perfection. When they started heels and water-tights the job became more complicated. Men that were sick of ploughing in dirty weather took up shoemakin' as a trade and made money of it.

"When I was a lump of a lad, the ploughman-snab[5] was at his zenith. In my native place, you went into his workshop for a pair of either trysted or ready made. If you wanted them made to measure, he went over you wi' an inch-tape, chewin' away at a rossety-end[6] and your shoes were ready for you by the next Fast Day. But if ye had only the money for ready-mades, he took the first pair he laid hands on from a boxful made in Glasgow, squeezed them on to you, fastened them up in a hurry wi' porpoise laces; tied a knot on them you could hardly loosen in a fortnight, and sent ye off hirplin'.

"No tact, you notice! No Salesmanship! The word 'psychology' was unknown. A man had no inducement to buy boots unless he was absolutely needin' them.

"For generations, the public bought its boots wi' as little concern about fittin' as if they were buyin' coffins. There were only two species of them — them with sparrables or tackets, and Sunday boots wi' a squeak in them, usually 'lastic-sided. The boot-seller was no help to you at all; he just flung them at ye, and you could take them or leave them.

"Look at the art that's put into the sale of boots and shoes to-day! A shoe-shop window's a perfect treat; when you look at it you're black affronted wi' yon shabby old bauchles, and make up your mind to have the perfect shoe at last and be a gentleman.

"You go in wi' your heart in your mouth to a grand saloon wi' Persian carpets and no' a shoe in sight, but the walls all piled round wi' cardboard boxes.

"There is a solemn hush in the place, and a faint, religious aroma of Nugget Polish. It might be a Savings Bank. A fine up-standin', nicespoken young gentleman comes up to you and puts you in a seat. With some chatty discourse about the weather, he takes off one of your shoes and looks closely at it. You can see at once he does not think much of it, unless it was bought in his own shop. You're just as much ashamed of your shoes as of the hole in your sock.

"Wi' the practised hand of the expert, he takes the length of your foot wi' a calliper foot-rule; says 'nine and five-eighths,' but that's not, seemingly, close enough, so he uses a micrometer. Havin' looked at your foot from every angle, and grasped, as you feel sure, its every short-comin', he glides up a ladder and takes down a box. Reverently openin' it, he produces the shoe of your dreams!

"Such elegance! Such smooth unwrinkled leather! Such lustre! Such a delightful nut-brown tone! And what a pleasant leathery smell! Such shoes, you feel, would make you a really good man, and distract attention from your hat or the baggin' at your knees.

"He coaxes your foot into one, almost without your knowin' it, as if it was a New Year's Honour, laces it up deftly with a 'love-knot'; stands back wi' his head to the side like a landscape painter and says 'Now that's a sound shoe!'

"It doesn't seem to you extravagant praise for a shoe that not only looks delightful, but feels as easy-fittin' as a slipper, and you make up your mind immediately that it will do. But the art of salesmanship in the shoe trade calls for more subtlety than letting you away wi' a first pair you try on.

"The young scientist discerns a small degree of tightness oer the instep, or a narrowness at the toe. He fondles your foot all over again, applies another pair of callipers; feels every joint, like a bonesetter; then up the ladder again like a whitterick and down wi' another pair that looks the identical.

"He may try on you half-a-dozen pair before he's pleased, but you go away wi' the first pair you tried on, convinced that for the first time in your life you have had scientific treatment. But shoes never look so splendid as in the shop where they're for sale. Perhaps the X-ray treatment will put this right."

Notes to Erchie, My Droll Friend

1 **Introductory to an Odd Character**
 1 A church officer occupied in a variety of tasks, most of them useful. St Kentigern's is of course entirely appropriate, being an alternative name for Mungo, the patron saint of Glasgow. Beadling is Erchie's "day-job"; he also acts as a waiter and thus satisfactorily serves both God and Mammon.
 2 Since 1843, when Thomas Chalmers led more than a third of the ministers and congregations of the Established Church of Scotland "along the High Street" to set up the Free Church of Scotland. The issue which led to the Disruption or sundering of the kirk was Parliament's right to intervene in its affairs. It is not totally clear which cause is espoused by St Kentigern's—we learn that it is a "genteel congregation", which may indicate the established kirk, and in "Degenerate Days" Erchie speaks disparagingly of the beadles in United Free Kirks who lack the "rale releegious glide". On the other hand St Kentigern's seems to be well-attended and the old rhyme may be relevant here:
    "The auld Kirk, the cauld Kirk,
    The Kirk that has the steeple,
    The Free Kirk, the wee Kirk,
    The Kirk wi' a' the people!"
 3 A flat foot but a warm heart.
 4 Cold, chilly.
 5 Suppose or suspect.
 6 Onomatopoeic name for a turkey.
 7 Whisky.
 8 A curling match played in the open air on a frozen pond or loch.
 9 Dress shirt front.
 10 A reference to the Russo-Japanese War of 1904-5, which ended in a humiliating defeat for Russia. Erchie's apparently neutral stance was not shared by H.M. Government, which had ended a period of "splendid isolation" by forming an alliance with the Japanese Empire in 1902.

11 In a tenement property, the communal wash-house was an essential and collective responsibility, and a possible source of unneighbourly strife.

12 Not a scholastic usage. A Term was one of the four days of the year (Candlemas, Whitsunday, Lamas and Martinmas) on which payments such as rents fell due.

13 A pie dish. The word is derived from the French *assiette*, a plate, and is probably one of the relics of the Auld Alliance between Scotland and France.

14 Fold his own socks. Evidence of his good intentions and Erchie as an early example of a "New Man".

15 Scuffing the feet carelessly.

16 Looking glass on stand.

2 Erchie's Flitting

1 Here used intransitively, in the sense of leaving one house to move into another. A flitting can also mean the act of moving household belongings, in this case on Duffy's coal cart.

2 Vases. More fragile items would be safer in the flitting if carried to the new abode by hand. The picture of William Ewart Gladstone (1809-98) the great Liberal leader and Prime Minister is an obvious clue to Erchie's political sympathies—in this respect he differs from Para Handy, who is unwilling to vouchsafe more than that he has voted for the "right man" (*Para Handy at the Poll* no. 84 in the Birlinn edition of the Complete Para Handy Stories.)

3 Because of the impression it would make on the new neighbours if the flitting needed two "rakes" or loads on the cart.

4 A superior kind of grate or fire-basket was one which had "wally" or porcelain sides and not simply cast iron throughout.

5 A valance or pelmet was needed on the mantelpiece to set off the grate nicely.

6 Extraordinary. A dram given to those helping with a removal is expected to be an extraordinarily large measure (probably a "glass" or "double double".)

7 An ornamental cabinet with shelves or drawers.

8 The residents of the same landing shared a rota for brushing, then washing out the landing and stair or, if on the ground floor, the closemouth or common entry. Finally the close would be pipe clayed to give a good appearance. A frequent cause of dispute with complex arrangements for determining "whose turn of the close" it was.

3 Degenerate Days

1 An extremely thin person, as in the children's rhyme:
   "Skinymalinky longlegs, big banana feet
   Went tae the pictures, fell through the seat!"

2 In the Gallowgate of Glasgow, built in 1754 by Robert Tennent, of "good hewen stone", taken from the ruins of the Bishops' Castle. Boswell and Johnson stayed in the Saracen's Head in 1773. Erchie explains that he began his career as a waiter there forty-five years previously, when the Gallowgate was more prosperous.

3 A half-grown fellow. In this case a country bumpkin from Strathaven in Lanarkshire.

4 Vesuvian lights—a brand of safety match.

5 A coalman was dependent on a strong pair of lungs for calling his wares, so that he could be audible in the farthest recesses of tenement buildings.

6 Erchie is reminiscing about the good old days when waiters could be so weighed down with purloined bottles or food after serving at dinners that they had a list rather like a Clyde steamer. Blythswood Square (designed by John Brash in 1823-29) had at that time been a fashionable residential area. It was originally called Garden Square after its developer Hamilton William Garden and, with its four regular ashlar terraces facing on to the central gardens, formed a fine centre piece to the patrician "Blythswood New Town". Much later, it was to be a haunt of many professions, including the oldest of all.

7 Playing hide-and-seek. Kee-hoi so-called because of the cries uttered by the participants in the game.

8 The Baillies, senior Councillors or Aldermen, of the Corporation, whom one once would have expected to have had well-rounded waistcoats, were now but poorly fed according to the dictates of culinary fashion.

9 To loose the neckties of the recumbent causalties of the groaning board. A well established Scottish custom: Henry Mackenzie (1745-1831), the author of *The Man of Feeling* tells how he collapsed under the table after a convivial evening and was alarmed to discover hands tugging at his neck; however this proved to be merely a helpful servant who identified himself as "the lad that louses the cravats."

10 Infusing tea: an essential skill for the hostess.

11 With a yawn. The Baillie in question is not enamoured of the combination of light suppers and musical accompaniment.

12 Erchie regards smoking concerts, where the organisers simply hired a room and the refreshments were mainly liquid, as an inferior social occasion for a waiter.

4 The Burial of Big Macphee

1 The Second Reform Act of 1867 had extended the vote to artisans, or working men, including lodgers, in large towns and cities. The Third Reform Act of 1884 gave the vote to all male householders and lodgers, so that about eighty per cent of the male adults in the country were now enfranchised.

2 As Chancellor of the Exchequer in Balfour's Unionist Ministry of 1902-5, Joseph Chamberlain espoused the cause of tariff reform in a time of economic depression. This introduction of Protectionism mean that imports of cheap foreign food, including grain, were taxed on entry. Whether economically correct or not this measure proved politically inept, enabling the Liberal Free Traders to take up the cause of the "poor man's bread" and led to Big Macphee and thousands like him voting the Unionists out of office at three successive General Elections.

3 High tea was a substantial meal, incorporating a "knife and fork" dish

of perhaps fish and chips, in addition to bread and butter, teabreads and cakes. The whole served with the best china and cutlery.
4 Fuss about trifles.
5 The Britannia Music Hall in the Trongate played host to most of the leading figures of the Victorian variety stage. It was later bought by the kenspeckle Glasgow eccentric A. E. Pickard and renamed the Panopticon.
6 Hired mourners paid to accompany the funeral cortege.
7 Mourning bands worn by relatives or close friends.
8 An oaf or slow-witted person.
9 A member of one of the many orders of Friendly Societies which played such an important part in Victorian and Edwardian life.

5 The Prodigal Son
1 The courtyard at the back of a tenement block. A scene of a great deal of bustle and activity; as well as its designed use as a drying green for the tenement's occupiers, it might at various times serve as a trysting place for "winching" couples, as a playground or even as an auditorium for "backcoort singers".
2 A street in north central Glasgow linking Cowcaddens with Great Western Road.
3 David Stow (1793-1864), educational reformer, had created in Dundas Vale in 1827 the first "Normal Seminary" or teacher-training institution in Britain. This was followed in 1846 by a Free Church Normal School, also used for the purposes of teacher-training, situated in the Cowcaddens, and attended by Willie Macpherson.
4 Mint sweets also known as "Imperials", famed for their long-lasting qualities.
5 Mean or stingy.
6 On a binge or drinking session.
7 Troubled, disturbed. This evocative description recalls other passages from Munro's writings, e.g.:
    "In such an hour and season we forget the cost of mercantile supremacy, and see in that wide fissure through the close-packed town a golden pathway to romance, or the highway home to our native hills and isles." (*The Clyde, River and Firth* p. 75)
8 To bring under control. The figure of speech is derived from haims or hems, the two pieces of wood forming the collar of a draught horse.

6 Mrs Duffy deserts her man
1 A topical reference to one of the celebrated divorce scandals of the day. Such references serve to remind us that divorce was, at this period, a very uncommon phenomenon with only 801 decrees absolute being recorded in Britain in 1910. The comparative figure for 1989 is 162,531.
2 A steep street or brae in central Glasgow leading northwards to Rotten Row from George Street. Now in the area occupied by the buildings of Strathclyde University.
3 A dish made from the head (or shin—potted hough) of a cow or pig, boiled, shredded and served cold in a jelly made from the stock.

4 An Irish Catholic, who would be infuriated by Duffy's singing of *Boyne Water*, a battle hymn of the Orange persuasion and Protestant Ascendancy. Like many other, this song celebrated the victory of King William of Orange ("King Billy") over the forces of James VII at the Battle of the Boyne in 1690. Those familiar with the socio-religious map of Glasgow and the West of Scotland will nevertheless be puzzled by Duffy's behaviour on this occasion and his avowed support for Glasgow Celtic Football Club (see notes to No. 13 *Erchie goes to a Bazaar*).

5 The inhabitants of the flat above the Duffy domicile would be so disturbed by the racket from downstairs that they would knock on the floor (i.e. Duffy's ceiling) with a poker, to tell them to be quiet.

6 A type of cloak with large cap-like sleeves. Dolmans had been in and out of fashion during the nineteenth century but had fallen out of popularity around 1892.

7 From the French *menage* or household. A menodge or menoj was a kind of savings club to which each member contributes a fixed sum weekly for an agreed period of time. An easily administered arrangement, hence the popular accusation that a poor organiser "couldnae run a menodge".

8 Insignificant impudent rascals. The nyafs living above Duffy are bringing down the ceiling plaster by their "rapping doon".

9 Duffy is incapable of even washing up for himself. A poorie is the milk or cream jug which he should have cleaned and taken to be filled at the travelling milk cart.

10 Rubber.

11 So affected is the hapless Duffy by fending for himself, that in his distraught condition he fills the bags with the correct weight of coal, instead of, as is the invariable practice of coal men, giving short measure.

12 Edward VII's Coronation in 1902 had had to be postponed because of an operation for appendicitis. Because of the trend-setting influence of Royalty this operation actually became fashionable for a while. Whether Duffy's G.P. has made a similar diagnosis or not is not made clear.

13 Part of the children's pursuit game of tig, meaning "You have been tagged!" An affectionate touch, signalling the end of hostilities between Duffy and his wife.

14 Similar to the above; meaning "Are you 'in the Den' with me".

7 Carnegie's Wee Lassie

1 Andrew Carnegie (1835-1918), son of a Dunfermline handloom weaver, had emigrated to the United States and, in the course of becoming a multi-millionaire, was instrumental in making that country the leader in steel production, based on Pittsburg.

2 On his return visits to Scotland Carnegie stayed at Skibo Castle in Sutherland.

3 The Bessemer Process for producing cheap steel from iron ore had revolutionised the Pennsylvanian based industry.

"It was not until the advent of Bessemer that the Americans found

how lavishly nature had endowed them…That solid mountain of iron, the greatest ore-bed known to man, the richest in metallic content, the most easily mined, the most readily transported—and at the same time practically free from phosphorus—that, in fine, is the story of the Lake Superior fields. Such a miraculous conjunction of forces a nation has seldom had laid at its feet. The result has been to give industrial leadership to the United States."
(Burton Hendrick : *Life of Andrew Carnegie*)

4 The historic first flight of a powered aircraft by the Wright Brothers at Kitty Hawk in North Carolina would not take place until December 1903 and at this time a "fleein' machine" would be a hot air balloon or one the new-fangled dirigibles such as those being developed by Zeppelin in Germany.

5 Many towns benefitted from Carnegie's generosity, a particular feature being his support for libraries (over 600 being endowed throughout the world) as an expression of his improving, philanthropic intentions. As for the kirk organs, Carnegie seems to have had little difficulty in reconciling material success with religious zeal— "The gospel of wealth but echoes Christ's words". All told he was to give away £70 million, in keeping with his doctrine that "The man who dies rich…dies disgraced."

6 "Go ahead and search my pockets."

7 Buy sweets.

8 Weasel.

8   A Son of the City

1 A reference to the annual movement of Glaswegians to Clyde Coast resorts like Rothesay and Dunoon at the Glasgow Fair holidays, in the second fortnight of July. Boarding the steamers at Bridge Wharf, the trippers had their bedding and other household goods as well as clothing packed in tin trunks, which were piled on deck.

2 Merry passengers, on disembarking, would celebrate with a "clog-wallop" or clog dance on the pier.

3 The electric powered tramcar. Tramcars were generally known as "cars" or "caurs" in Glasgow—"skoosh" refers to the speed of the vehicle (as compared to their horse-drawn predecessors), as well as, onomatopoeically, to the distinctive sound produced by the release of the brakes. Tramways had been introduced to the streets of Glasgow in 1870, a service which was taken over by the Corporation in 1894. Electrification was completed in 1902, to general satisfaction.
      "The experience of the Tramway Department has been that the working expenses for electric haulage are 2.35 pence per mile less, and the average return 2.57 pence greater than for horse haulage. Beyond question, the Corporation have deserved well of the citizens by their management of the cars."

4 Keating's Powder was a proprietary treatment used for delousing.

5 The rookeries was a popular term for any densely populated slum building.

6 A room and kitchen or two-roomed house would be regarded as an immense improvement in living conditions by most slum-dwellers;

"wally jawboxes" or sinks with running water would be an unimaginable luxury.

7 A term for no place in particular, but obviously in the Gàidhealtachd, since there is an obvious reference to the Gaelic greeting "Ciamar a tha thu?" (How are you?).

8 *Clansman* was a much used name in the shipping fleet of David MacBrayne, with no fewer than four vessels having carried the name under their flag. The vessel Erchie refers to was the second of the line, build in 1870 at Clydebank at the yard of J & G Thomson (later John Brown's). She was employed on the company's year-round Glasgow to Stornoway service. *Clansman II* was sold out of MacBrayne's service in 1910, when another steamer, the less romantically named *Ethel*, was re-christened *Clansman*, to preserve what was a familiar and popular name in the West Coast shipping trade.

9 Deid Slow is rather like Kamerhashinjoo in being no place in particular—somewhere beyond the Glasgow boundary, where ships proceeding up-river were signalled to proceed with engines at Dead Slow. An unsophisticated place—"in the sticks".

10 Spring onions.

11 When the weather was at its worst. A weather station was maintained on the summit of Ben Nevis (4406 feet) between 1883 and 1904.

12 See notes to No. 5 *The Prodigal Son*.

13 i.e. to the Britannia Music Hall. See notes to No. 4 *"The Burial of Big Macphee"*.

14 Strolling along the Cowcaddens. The Cowcaddens was once a densely populated district of central Glasgow, lying to the north of Sauchiehall Street. It is now largely given over to motorway flyovers and multi-storey car parks.

9 Erchie on the King's Cruise

1 In August 1902, shortly after his delayed Coronation (see No. 6 *Mrs Duffy deserts her man* Note 12), King Edward and Queen Alexandra sailed from Cowes up the West Coast, calling at Weymouth, Pembroke Dock, the Isle of Man (see note 3 below) and on into Scottish waters, visiting Arran, Skye and Lewis, and visiting Andrew Carnegie at Skibo Castle (see No. 7 *Carnegie's Wee Lassie*) before sailing round to Invergordon. Thereafter the Royal party proceeded by land to Balmoral for the usual Autumn visit.

2 The Royal Yacht, the third to bear this name, was a screw steamer of 4,700 tons, built in 1899 at Pembroke Dock, and served until replaced by the present Royal Yacht *Britannia*. She was broken up, after war service as an accommodation vessel, at Faslane on the Gareloch in December 1954.

3 Here Erchie accidentally or facetiously (and who would know with Erchie) has transposed the surnames of two famous writers of the day—Marie Corelli and Hall Caine. Marie Corelli, was the pseudonym of Mary Mackay (1856-1924) whose romantic melodramas, such as *The Sorrows of Satan* and *The Mighty Atom* were immensely popular among a wide range of admirers, including Gladstone. Her theories about matters ranging from morality to radioactive vibrations soon

dated, however, and her reputation was to decline sadly in later years. In fact Hall Caine (1853-1931) was the "great novelist", resident in the Isle of Man, mentioned by Erchie. Caine gave many of his stories a Manx setting and acquired a sensational reputation leading to the banning of his books by serveral circulating libraries.

4 Very great struggle.

5 Plunged away suddenly.

6 Campbeltown was noted for the distillation of its distinctively full-flavoured malt whisky. The town undoubtedly bore an industrial front (coal mining and fish curing were carried on in the neighbourhood) which contrasted with other towns on the West Coast.

7 Raking or gathering in the money. A bawbee was originally a coin worth six pence Scots—later a halfpenny sterling.

8 This was an epithet bestowed on the town of Oban by the Victorians, because of its importance as a centre of road and steamer, and later rail, communications.

> "Oban is a place of passage and not of rest. Tourists go to Oban simply for the purpose of getting to somewhere else." (F. H. Groome: *Ordnance Gazetteer of Scotland*)

10 How Jinnet saw the King

1 The "him and her" are of course King Edward VII and Queen Alexandra. The King and Queen visited Glasgow on Thursday, May 14th 1903, and the Glasgow magazine *The Baillie* noted this was the first recorded visit of a reigning King to Glasgow. Edward's mother, Queen Victoria, had of course visited the city on a number of occasions. The King and Queen carried out, as Erchie's comments will suggest, a busy programme of engagements; chief amongst which was laying the foundation stone for the new buildings, in George Street, of the Glasgow and West of Scotland Technical College, later the Royal College of Science and Technology and still later Strathclyde University.

2 Gairbraid Street is in the Maryhill district of Glasgow.

3 The "Sunny Jim" in question is probably the character invented by Edwardian advertising agents to publicise the strength-giving cereal "Force". Sadly, any thoughts that Munro is introducing the cook of the *Vital Spark* into the Erchie tales will have to be resisted on grounds of chronology, Sunny Jim not making his first voyage on the *Vital Spark* until February 1908. Erchie himself appears in the Para canon (in *The Disappointment of Erchie's Niece* No. 24 in the Birlinn edition of the Complete Para Handy Stories) and Para's shipmate, with his brio and irrepressible nature might well have served as a model for any kind of life "Force".

4 The association of the Co-operative and Labour movements was reflected in the working classes' habits and attitudes. Thus Jinnet, as a member of the "co-op" or the "store", would be expected to have left-wing and anti-establishment views.

5 *Reynolds News* was published between 1850 and 1967 and was a popular Sunday paper supporting the Labour and Co-operative movements.

6   A gloomy expression. A tontine was a club in which all the partici-
    pants contributed a sum all of which went to the last survivor, thus the
    surviving member of a tontine would be well used to mourning the
    deaths of his fellow members. The usage "a ... face on him" is
    typically Glasgow and has survived to the present day.

7   A non-alcoholic beverage.

8   The Edinburgh and Glasgow Railway Company had opened the route
    between the two cities in 1842. One major problem had been the
    Cowlairs incline (1 in 45) leading to the Glasgow terminus at Queen
    Street. This was beyond the capacity of the locomotives of the period
    and a winding engine was installed to haul trains up the hill. The
    provision continued until 1908 and from then until the end of the
    steam era banking engines were provided to assist trains leaving
    Glasgow.

9   As the King moved out of the station into George Square he would
    have seen the many statues of politicians, national heroes and writers
    arrayed there. Erchie avers that he mistook them for monuments, as it
    were in a cemetery.

10 In Victorian days the citizens of Glasgow insisted on this honorific for
    their city. "James Hamilton Muir" (Neil Munro identified, in one of
    his pieces reprinted in *The Brave Days*, the writers behind the pseudo-
    nym as Muirhead Bone, the etcher; his brother the journalist James
    Bone and Archibald Hamilton Charteris, a lawyer) writing in 1901,
    expressed some doubts:

    "Considering the situation of the town there are few traces
    anywhere of decoration or ornament adequate to its opportunities.
    Frankly, Glasgow seems a thriving city, but as little as Manchester
    or Liverpool does it look the 'Second city of the Empire'"(*Glasgow
    in 1901*).

11 The junction of Argyle, Jamaica and Hope Street was formerly known
    as the Hielan'man's Cross or "Umbrella"—A reference to the Central
    Station bridge which covered that part of Argyle Street. It was given
    this name because of the fondness exiled Highlanders had for meeting
    "Celtic compatriots" here.

12 The principal throughfares of Glasgow were well made with hard-
    wearing granite setts or paving stones, unlike many of the streets of the
    capital. Another cause for local pride.

13 Glasgow has a considerable artistic tradition which perhaps can be
    considered as beginning with the early nineteenth century topographi-
    cal painter John Knox. The late nineteenth and early twentieth
    century saw a flowering of talent which put the city at the forefront of
    British art—particularly the group of painters, many influenced by the
    French impressionists, who became known as the "Glasgow Boys",
    artists such as Hornel, Melville, Lavery, Henry, Guthrie and Walton.
    The presence of works by these living Glasgow artists, and their
    Continental contemporaries in Kelvingrove is testimony both to the
    Glasgow taste for *avant garde* art and to the enthusiasm with which
    the civic collection was built up.

14 A tall black silk hat, with a supposed resemblance to liquorice, worn at
    one time by the Glasgow constabulary or "polis".

15 The King and Queen had been visiting the Duke of Buccleuch at his magnificent residence of Dalkeith Palace, just outside Edinburgh.

16 Kinderspiels (from the German "child's play") were groups for young children supposedly run on the best educational principles of the day.

17 The student was no doubt dressing up as a black-faced minstrel. Gilmorehill was the site of Sir George Gilbert Scott's Glasgow University buildings. The university had moved west from the Old College in the High Street in 1866. Students from the "Yooni" were known for their energetic pursuit of extra-curricular activities, including the Charities Day pranks, when undergraduates would dress up in exotic costumes and spread out all over the city with collecting tins. (See also No. 75 *Saturnalia*)

11 Erchie Returns

1 An expressive exclamation meaning something like "Isn't it just like Erchie!" or "Good old Erchie!".

2 Edinburgh tenement blocks featured drying poles arrayed outside their windows, looking rather like hay rakes to the sceptical Erchie. Erchie here is indulging in the time-honoured ritual of "misca'in'" or poking fun at Scotland's capital city. Edinburgh-Glasgow rivalry really begins to emerge with the mercantile and industrial rise of the western city in the nineteenth century, a century which saw Glasgow overtake Edinburgh in population.

3 Literally dredgers scraping up the mud from the river. It was dredging and river deepening operations of course which in the nineteenth century had made the Clyde navigable to Glasgow for ocean-going ships and made her thriving shipbuilding industry and ports possible.

4 Another example of Erchie's assertion of the innate superiority of Glasgow. While the independent Leith tramway system had been electrified in 1905 the capital city itself persisted in cable cars until the first electrified route was opened in June 1922 between Pilrig, Churchhill and Liberton.

5 Milliken Park is a rural suburb of the small industrial town of Johnstone in Renfrewshire.

12 Duffy's First Family

1 Patriotic fare indeed; porridge and soor (sour) dook or buttermilk was plain wholesome food from readily available local produce, if rather unappetising for the "wean" or "wee smout".

2 Unclear. Most probably this is a reference to the left wing of the Conservative Party, known as Tory Democrats, who favoured a policy of social reform and were therefore likely to appeal to a working class entrepreneur like Duffy.

3 "From scenes like these Auld Scotia's grandeur springs". There is a school of thought which attributed the former greatness of the nation to a mixture of porridge and regular dosing with Gregory's mixture; a foul-tasting purgative blend of rhubarb, magnesia & ginger, invented by James Gregory (1753-1821), Professor of Medicine at Edinburgh University.

4 A general term for unpleasant illness in children, including inflamma-

tion of the bowels and skin eruptions—almost any ailment, but certainly not including "gymnastics".

5 One of a number of practitioners specialising in phrenology, or the study of cranial features and their relationship with character and illness. Munro seems to have, with justice, regarded them as quacks and often makes sport of them. The scene from Para Handy where Para tells how Dougie had his bumps read by a mesmeriser at Tarbert Fair comes to mind (*Queer Cargoes* No. 12 in the Birlinn edition of the Complete Para Handy Stories)

6 Bowl-money was money thrown to children at a wedding, especially by the bride or groom on leaving for the ceremony. The coins would be scattered or "bowled" along for the children to scramble after. Probably a survival of a propitiatory or sacrificial practice.

13 Erchie goes to a Bazaar

1 Glasgow at the time this story was published was very much to the fore in European contemporary art and design. The work of Charles Rennnie Mackintosh and his contemporaries was recognised internationally and commented on locally, as we will see in story 22 *Erchie in an Art Tea Room* which takes our hero into the art nouveau delights of Miss Cranston's Willow Tea Rooms.

2 A bassinette is a form of perambulator and Jinnet is assumed to be past child-bearing age.

3 Glasgow Celtic were founded in 1888 by a Marist Brother and attracted a loyal following from the East End of the city largely from the many people of Irish Catholic descent. Traditionally the rivals of Glasgow Rangers, they played in green and white; these obviously are the colours favoured by Duffy.

4 A tall silk hat or top hat, so named because of its resemblance to a "lum" or chimney.

5 St Andrew's Hall, built by James Sellars in 1873 in Berkeley Street in the West End, was the city's principal concert hall, with an international reputation. Originally commissioned by a private association of well-to-do citizens, the halls were the centre of Glasgow's musical life for generations, until burned down in the disastrous fire of 1962. The west facade of the Mitchell Library is all that remains and "there is no more masterly or powerful classical facade in the city" (*Central Glasgow—an Illustrated Architectural Guide.*)

6 The Grosvenor Restaurant formed part of the impressive Grosvenor Building in Gordon Street and for many years was frequented by the Glasgow *glitterati*; hence the comment from Erchie about "the richt kind o' claes, wi' a crease doon the front o' their breeks." Like the St Andrew's Halls, the Grosvenor has vanished from the Glasgow scene; a great loss, with its resplendent centrepiece the German baroque banqueting hall extending over both the second and third floors.

7 Erchie argued or contended persistently that the winning of the pony was all a mistake.

8 Jinnet was worried that the pony would scrape the linoleum floor with its iron "buits" or horseshoes. One of Erchie's tallest tales.

9 Dandelions.

14 Holidays

1 The Glasgow Foundry Boys Religious Society founded in 1865 was an organisation devoted to the religious, moral and physical improvement of the lot of city children. Originally concerned with, as the title suggests, boys working in the foundry trades, later the society's activities widened to other employment areas and to work with girls. They had religious classes on Sundays and educational classes, drill exercises, banking and other provident facilities, musical and social meetings during the week. An interesting Munro connection is that in 1869 the 8th Duke of Argyll became Honorary President of the Society and took a great interest in the movement and encouraged the Society to bring the boys to the grounds of Inveraray Castle for their week's camp at the Glasgow Fair. Doubtless young Neil would have been very aware of the excitement caused by the annual arrival of the "Foondry Boys" in his quiet Highland town.

2 A dish of oatmeal or rolled oats boiled in salted water and forming part of the staple diet of Scots for centuries. Still, in Erchie's time, treated as a plural noun ("taking them every mornin'").

3 The musician assaulted with an egg was presumably playing the ophicleide, a brass instrument, related to the bugle, playing in the bass register.

4 An area in the East End of Glasgow, near the Gallowgate, used by travelling circuses and the "shows" or fairs.

5 A glee party was a singing group, usually male, which favoured close harmony singing.

6 Another East End location, close to the Saracen's Head Inn.

7 A paddle-steamer, built in 1876, by T. B. Seath and Co. of Rutherglen, named after the song by Robert Burns, and appropriately enough saw service on the Glasgow-Ayr route. Due to her frequent mechanical problems, she acquired the nickname of "Bonnie Breakdoon" or "Bloody Breakdoon".

8 Gooseberries. Wee Hughie has presumably plucked them, unripe, from a kitchen garden. Erchie is ironically contrasting a rural, coastal idyll at the Fair which contrasts with city life during the rest of the year.

9 A game of marbles (also called bools or jiggies), which involves rolling marbles into hollows scooped in the soft ground.

15 The Student Lodger

1 The Calvinist doctrine of predestination, lampooned by Burns in "Holy Willie's Prayer"

> "What was I, or my generation,
> That I should get such exaltation?
> I, wha deserv'd most just damnation,
> For broken laws
> Sax thousand years ere my creation,
> Thro' Adam's cause."

2 In a densely populated tenement like Erchie's any activity or noise out of the ordinary could attract the comments or disapproval of the neighbours.

3 The Carter's Trip was a high spirited annual event when the cart drivers of the city, and there were many in an age when horse-drawn transport predominated, went off to the country for a day's merry-making.

4 A Gaudiamus, so called from the student song *Gaudiamus igitur, Iuvenes dum sumus* (Let us rejoice, for we are students), was a "smoker" or drinking party for students.

5 Divinity students were generally acknowledged to be the wildest of all undergraduates; hence Erchie's alarm.

6 Mr Tod, showing off his learning, is quoting from the ballad poem by Walter Scott *Jock o' Hazledean*

> "Why weep ye by the tide, ladye?
> Why weep ye by the tide?
> I'll wed ye to my youngest son
> And ye sall be his bride;
> And ye shall be his bride, ladye,
> Sae comely to be seen:
> But aye she loot the tears down fa'
> For Jock o' Hazledean."

7 Gibson Street is situated close to the University on Gilmorehill; the references to the Rectorial Election and Conservative Committee-rooms are reminders that university politics and national politics were closely intertwined with major political figures standing for election as Lord Rector of the University and graduates having two votes at General Elections until 1948 by virtue of the University seats. This story would seem to have been sparked off by the November 1903 Rectorial election which saw the victory of the Conservative M.P. for Dover and Chief Secretary to the Lord Lieutenant of Ireland (in effect Secretary of State for Ireland) Rt. Hon George Wyndham (1863-1913).

8 Soda syphon.

9 Gash means pale. This is a reference to an old tale from Dumbartonshire, illustrating the convivial habits of the eighteenth century gentry. Garscadden lies on the north bank of the Clyde near Yoker.

> "Some of the Kilpatrick lairds had met together and ... as the evening wore on, the whisky bottle was passed round and round until even the hardest drinker began to weaken. It was in the small hours that one said to his host, "Garscadden looks unco gash," pointing to the pale face of the Laird of Garscadden. "De'il mend him!" was the reply, "He's been wi' his Maker these last two hoors. I saw him slip awa' but I didan' like to disturb good company by saying aught aboot it." (I. M. M. MacPhail: *Short History of Dumbartonshire*)

10 He took me on in argument.

11 Mixed up or muddled—hasn't sorted himself out yet.

16 Jinnet's Tea Party

1 Duffy is swollen up and bloated with a surfeit of milk from the dairy

where his lady-love works.

2 By the early years of the century, the U.S.A., and to a certain extent Germany, had gained economic leadership from Great Britain; American production of coal, iron and steel as well as most foodstuffs outstripped Britain's and Joseph Chamberlain's proposals for protectionist tariff reforms were the result. Duffy's reference is to the Americans' ability to dump cheap coal on the British market, because of the traditional British policy of Free Trade, something which Chamberlain proposed to end.

3 Duffy comments that Jinnet is very smart, quick on the uptake and has noted that he is "chief" or especially friendly with Leezie.

4 "Dough-feet", as Erchie describes the policeman, is sulking, or in the huff, because he has correctly surmised that Leezie has bestowed her favours eleswhere.

5 Wash out or rinse. The impression given when "syning" is used is one of perfunctory or hasty washing—as here when it is only the tea-things which have been deployed by the lady of the house. Greasy dinner-dishes or pots would require "scoorin'".

17 The Natives of Clachnacudden

1 Erchie, as a Lowland Scot (despite his Highland surname), is describing the Gaels' conversing in their own language as "tearin' the tartan."

2 A door-mat, especially one made of coconut fibre.

3 Even allowing for Erchie's reporting, this is a misquotation from the "Canadian Boat Song", a popular, yearning song of exile. The stanza ought to read:

> "From the lone shieling of the misty island
> Mountains divide us, and the waste of seas-
> Yet still the blood is strong, the heart is Highland,
> And we in dreams behold the Hebrides."

The authorship of these lines, which first appeared in Blackwood's Magazine in September 1829, is disputed; the Oxford Book of Scottish Verse states authoritatively—"Anonymous", while other authorities attribute it to David Macbeth Moir ("Delta").

4 Harry Linn was a Scots music-hall entertainer of the generation before Harry Lauder specialising in the portrayal of the comic stage Highlander. Jack House in his *Music Hall Memories* (1986) describes him as "a tall, thin man with a somewhat lugubrious expression". His most characteristic piece was the comic song "The Fattest Man in the Forty-Twa". This story seems to be about the Glaswegian's stereotypical portrayal of the Gael, yet Munro, as a Highlander himself, suffuses the knock-about stuff with his customary affectionate humour. Like the Clachnacudden folk themselves—and of course Clachnacudden (though boasting a Highland League Football Team) is a generalised construct rather than a specific locality—he is given to humour "that kind o' codded themselves".

5 Bamber's superior hairdressing establishment was at the corner of Hope Streeet and Gordon Street (very close to the Grosvenor Restaurant).

18 Mary Ann

1 A maid of all work. In this, Erchie's ironic commentary on the middle class household and the "servant problem" reference is made to various categories of maids and others in service; a "general" is a maidservant with general duties, and one likely to be found in smaller establishments. The extent of domestic service in early twentieth century society should not be underestimated—many comparatively modest households would employ a "general"—thus contributing to the employment of 25,947 persons in domestic service in Glasgow in 1901—or 7.25% of the total labour force of the city.

2 A favourable reference.

3 A South African town, scene of fighting during the Boer War (1899-1902). In the early period of Boer success and several heavy British defeats, Kimberley, the wealthy centre of the diamond industry, was besieged by smaller Boer forces and not relieved until the first half of 1900, together with Ladysmith and Mafeking. Thus was Queen Victoria's defiance vindicated—"we are not interested in the possibilities of defeat: they do not exist."

4 An area in the West End of Glasgow noted for its large impressive terraced houses, establishments which would certainly require servants.

5 Glasgow had experienced as much of municipal enterprise as any town in the Kingdom with tramways, electricity, gas, telephones, bath-houses, water-supply, slum clearance, etc. being provided by the city council. Erchie, in his role as social satirist advocates taking domestic service into the public sector.

6 Perambulator, or pram.

19 Duffy's Wedding

1 The new Mrs Duffy, with undoubted social ambitions, considers that her husband's normal way of advertising his wares is beneath his (or more probably) her dignity.

2 A surtout coat, similar to a frock coat. From the French "sur tout"— "over all", and therefore a translation of "overcoat".

3 Probably the dance hall of that name in Dumbarton Road, Partick. Dance halls at this time served refreshments.

4 Literally wooden ("timmer" is timber) in the tune—i.e. tone deaf.

20 On Corporal Punishment

1 An area in the East End of Glasgow between the Gallowgate and Glasgow Green.

2 One of the city's leading enterprises was the locomotive works of Henry Dübs.

3 A tautology. "Wee;" means small and "smouts" is a generally affec-tionate appellation given to small children or other creatures.

4 The palm of the hand.

5 A leather strap used in Scottish schools; punishment was administered by striking the offender's palms. "The belt" as it was also known, had two, three or four tongues or "fingers", came in different weights and was probably manufactured by Messrs. Dick of Lochgelly in Fife, who

enjoyed a virtual monopoly. Indeed a "Lochgelly" was another eponymous term for this terror of the classroom.

6 Alick is finding his "coonts" or arithmetic difficult and is dreading the inevitable punishment on his return to school, if he doesn't get them right. The arithmetic wee Alick is wrestling with might be "mental arithmetic" or "speed and accuracy", but in this case is the dreaded "problem arithmetic"—as we learn from Erchie's comic recital of the cistern problem—a real "staggerer".

21 The Follies of Fashion

1 The fashion of a fore and aft crease in men's trousers became popular only in the 1890s and the acceptance of the new style by the Prince of Wales (later Edward VII) resulted in its widespread adoption.

2 Fussy or obsessed by detail.

3 Neat, smart.

4 Also "galluses"—trouser braces. The spelling used here more accurately conveys the idea of hanging or suspending the trousers.

5 Iron suits—or suits of armour.

6 One of the small passenger steamers operating to various piers on the Clyde between Victoria Bridge and, as here, Whiteinch, on the north bank of the river.

7 Left-handed. Also corry-handed or corry-fisted; from the Gaelic *cearr* wrong or awkward, thus imparting to left-handedness a similar pejorative quality to the Latin *sinister*.

8 This would be the book in which the weekly payments to the "penny a week man" of the Prudential Assurance Company, a noted life insurance agency, would be recorded. Erchie jokingly reacts to Jinnet's fears that he was drowned by suggesting that she would hurry home to check what she would collect from the insurance.

9 Jinnet states her intention of not being dependent on anyone.

22 Erchie in an Art Tea-Room

1 The year is 1904. Erchie and Duffy are patronising the newly opened Willow Tea Room in Sauchiehall Street—an appropriately named tea room since Sauchiehall is from *sauch* (willow tree) and *haugh* (meadow). Glasgow's tea rooms were famous and numerous, and were seen as emblems of the Temperance Movement, and increasingly as temples to good design. The Willow Tea Room was the work of Charles Rennie Mackintosh (1868-1928) and formed a fitting climax to his association with Kate Cranston (see below). It was restored in the 1980s by Geofrey Wimpenny.

> "It is not the accent of the people, nor the painted houses, nor yet the absence of Highland policemen that makes the Glasgow man in London feel that he is in a foreign town and far from home. It is a simpler matter. It is the lack of tea shops … Glasgow, in truth, is a very Tokyo for tea rooms." J. H. Muir *Glasgow in 1901*.

2 Kate Cranston, noted businesswoman and temperance advocate had set new standards in tea room service and design, since opening her Argyle Street premises in 1892, followed by others in Buchanan Street

and Ingram Street. By employing the best architects and designers like Mackintosh and George Walton and imparting her own special combination of verve and shrewdness, her establishments gained such a reputation for excellence that they became synonymous with beauty and taste. So it might be said of something well designed; "It's quite Kate Cranstonish!"

> "Miss Cranston has started large restaurants, all very elaborately simple on the new high art lines. The result is gorgeous! And a wee bit vulgar!" (Letter from Sir Edwin Lutyens, 1897).

3 Three pound notes and a ten shilling note (£3.50). The affluent Mr Duffy assumes that the impressive decor implies a hefty bill. In fact, Miss Cranston's policy was to keep prices reasonably low so as to compare favourably, if not actually compete, with public houses such as the "Mull o' Kintyre Vaults".

> "(The expatriate Scot) returns with pleasure to his town, where he may lunch on lighter fare than steak and porter for the sum of fivepence amid surroundings that remind him of a pleasant home." (J. H. Muir *Glasgow in 1901*).

4 The shafts of a coal cart.

5 The Room de Luxe was the jewel of the Willow Tea Rooms. The colours ("o' a goon Jinnet used to hae") were silver grey and pink and in fact Erchie gives a fairly good account of the decor, if more than slightly tinged with irony—"ye could easy guess they were chairs" being a reference to Mackintosh's specially designed seating.

6 Not "purple leeks" as they are called by Erchie, but the classic *art nouveau* rose of the Glasgow style. The "gasalier" was not precisely that, (illumination was by electricity) but a magnificent chandelier with a flower-like arrangement.

7 Glass balls or marbles as big as your fist. Glass and mirrored glass was very much a feature of the Willow Tea Room.

8 Erchie's joke is a play on "bead"—"to tak a bead" is to take a good drink or quantity of spirits. There are still photographs showing waitresses wearing the red beads just as Erchie describes them.

9 The Zoo referred to is Wombwell's Menagerie (see No. 31 *A Menagerie Marriage*).

10 The batters are the front and back covers of a book.

11 Pairs of matching ornamental china dogs were very popular on tasteful Edwardian mantelpieces.

12 Different coloured glass balls, representing items on the menu of the restaurant (or "solid meat department"), were sent down a tube to the kitchen. "Moshy" is a game of marbles. As to Mackintosh's idea of "Miss Cranston's" as a "total work of art", Duffy appears irredeemably Philistine, but Erchie's true opinions are not revealed.

23 The Hidden Treasure

1 Mrs Duffy is referring to the contemporary craze for pianolas or player pianos.

2 A sign of a superior neighbourhood. Note that the upwardly-mobile Mrs Duffy does not use the term "wally-close".

3 Nonsense, tricks.

24   The Valenteen

1   The Trades House (1791), designed by Robert Adam for the Trades Guild. A sign of the "increasing respectability of the Trades Rank" and erected in Stockwell Street in what is now termed the "Merchant City". Erchie's dinner would be held in the magnificent pilastered Great Hall.

2   A diminuitive of Euphemia.

3   A form of embroidery carried out on a cloth stretched over a hoop—the name comes from the frame's resemblance to a drum or tambour.

4   Diamond tiaras.

25   Among the Pictures

1   Late or sports edition of the evening newspapers—note that Munro resists the temptation to "plug" the *Evening News*.

2   Erchie and Duffy are paying a visit to the annual exhibition of the Glasgow Institute of the Fine Arts at their Sauchiehall Street gallery, now vanished beneath the mass of the Sauchiehall Centre. The Institute Galleries were designed by the young J. J. Burnett and opened in 1880.

3   After the International Exhibition of 1888 it was felt that provision should be made for an exhibition of arts, crafts and sciences in the working class area of the East End and in December 1890 the East End Exhibition was opened in the old Reformatory buildings in Duke Street by the Scottish Secretary, Lord Lothian. The exhibition ran for four months and attracted a total attendance of 747,873. The surplus of £3000 went towards the achievement of the long-held ambition to build a People's Palace in the East End. The People's Palace on Glasgow Green eventually opened in January 1898.

4   Henri-Eugène-Augustin Le Sidaner (1862-1939) was a distinguished French artist, honoured by the French Government by being made an Officer of the Legion of Honour. Sidaner exhibited two paintings at the Spring 1904 Exhibition of the Glasgow Institute of Fine Arts, of which "La Terrasse" seems the more likely than "Le Bouquet" to fit Munro's description of a "foggy impression by Sidaner". Munro's comment reminds us that one of his roles on the *Evening News* had been as art critic and his comment on Sidaner's style accords with the remark in Bénézit's *Dictionnaire critique et documentaire des Peintres, Sculpteurs, Desinateurs et Graveurs*, that Sidaner was particularly praised for his twilight effects ("on a particullièrement vanté ses effets de crespuscule").

5   Calandering is a finishing process in the textile trades and involves the smoothing and pressing of the cloth.

6   Duffy's "culture-shock" leads him to suppose that he is at the kind of entertainment where "pass-outs", i.e. tickets which entitle the holder to leave and later gain readmittance, are issued to patrons seeking alcoholic refreshment—the "something" which they might have "at the tea bar".

7   The 1904 Exhibition included a watercolour of this title (price £45) by Margaret Macdonald Mackintosh (1864-1933), the wife of Charles Rennie Mackintosh, and one of the most distinguished of the Glasgow

"weemen painters". "The Sleeper" was later exhibited in London (1911) and Chicago (1922) but when, in 1987, the Hunterian Museum in Glasgow organised an exhibition on Margaret Macdonald Mackintosh this work was listed as untraced. Margaret Mackintosh's somewhat attenuated *art nouveau* style and use of muted colours could certainly lead Erchie into his later comment that she "wasna ower lavish wi' her pent".

8 Duffy wonders how lady painters (assuming them to be of the house-painting variety) can get up and down ladders, whilst wearing skirts.

9 Since the year of this story is uncertain this particular "late edeetion" is unable to give the semi-final result. However, we can be fairly sure that the match did not involve Celtic, since it is unlikely that Duffy, as a declared supporter (see No. 13 *Erchie goes to a Bazaar*) would pass up the game to look at paintings.

26 The Probationary Ghost

1 Garnethill (originally Summerhill) is an area of fine red sandstone tenements on a steep-sided hill to the north of Sauchiehall Street. This was the second hill on which the Blythswood New Town grew up and it was called Garnethill after Professor Thomas Garnet (1766-1806), whose name is associated with the Observatory which stood there in the first half of the nineteenth century.

2 Wandering or roaming about.

3 Buccleuch Street in Garnethill subsequently gained some further celebrity from No. 145 "The Tenement House", owned by the National Trust for Scotland and, coincidentally, a splendid evocation of tenement life in Erchie's day.

4 See note 2 to No. 16 *Jinnet's Tea Party*.

5 Stairs to climb.

27 Jimmy's Christmas shopping

1 Even in the early years of the new century, Jinnet is drawing on the collective memory of the disastrous collapse of the City of Glasgow Bank in 1878.

> "Most of [the shareholders] were local people. The first call on them was for five times the amount of the investment. The majority found themselves ruined ... Depression swept over the wintry city, factories closed, buildings stood half-completed."
> (J. M. Reid *Glasgow*).

2 In receipt of poor relief—"on the parish".

3 Busy, here in the sense of full up or crowded.

4 In front of or before.

28 A Bet on Burns

1 "The chap" is quite right to challenge Duffy's ideas about the authorship of *Dark Lochnagar* and Erchie is right too in attributing it to Byron. However Byron used another form of spelling, as may be seen from these lines from the final stanza:

> "England! thy beauties are tame and domestic.
> To one who has roved o'er the mountains afar;

Oh for the crags that are wild and majestic!
The steep frowning glories of dark Loch na Garr."

Just to add to the confusion the poem is titled *Lachin Y Gair*. It may
be noted that Burns did not in fact write any of the songs on Duffy's
list.

2 Another gaffe from Duffy, Burns met Mary Campbell in Ayrshire,
where she was in service.

29 The Prodigal's Return

1 A sailor's kit bag.
2 China was a principal theatre of war for the Russo-Japanese conflict of
1904-5, in which the Japanese inflicted a decisive defeat on the forces
of the Tsar. Britain, although allied with Japan since 1902, was bound
to remain neutral in the event of a war with Russia.
3 Turning a handle. Probably in the case of the Captain a ship's
telegraph, and in Jinnet's mind's eye her son is ca'in a handle rather
like the driver's control on a tram car.
4 A beating or hammering.
5 A sore heart. This was the story chosen by Munro to end the collected
edition of Erchie stories published in 1904, and, as the story title
suggests, provided a charming and touching finale.

30 Erchie's Politics

1 This previously uncollected story first appeared in the Evening News
on 7th January 1910.
2 A reminder that the January 1910 General Election, the first of two to
be held in that year, was being fought as this story went to press.
3 Adam Smith (1723-90) the Scottish philosopher and political
economist would obviously have had very great practical difficulties in
saying anything to William Ewart Gladstone (1809-98) in 1863 or any
other year.
4 The British battleship H.M.S. *Dreadnought*, launched in 1906, gave its
name to a new generation of capital ships. The Dreadnoughts were
fast, heavily gunned and outperformed the older classes of battleship.
The German Naval Act of 1906 committed Germany to matching
British battleship production in number and quality, but even this
commitment never quite reached Erchie's level of three a month.
5 German-British rivalry was a fairly constant feature of the first years of
the century and sparked off a wide range of literature on the coming
war of which Erskine Childers *The Riddle of the Sands*, published in
1903, is perhaps the best known example.
6 Jinnet had little option, women being denied the parliamentary vote
until after the 1914-18 War.

31 A Menagerie Marriage

1 This previously uncollected story first appeared in the Evening News
on 8th April 1910.
2 Messrs Bostock & Wombwell's Menagerie, in New City Road,
convenient to Erchie's home.

32 Erchie and the Earthquake

1 This previously uncollected story first appeared in the Evening News on 19th December 1910.

2 The typical Glasgow tenement flat had a bed-recess in the living-room.

3 A constituency unknown to Hansard. However it is a reminder to us that this story appeared during the General Election campaign of December 1910.

4 One of the issues of the December 1910 election was the Liberal party's threat to reform the House of Lords by removing from it the power to oppose money bills and to restrict its delaying power in other matters.

33 Erchie and the census

1 This previously uncollected story first appeared in the Evening News on 3rd April 1911.

2 The decennial census was underway as this story appeared.

3 Duffy is referring to one of the characteristic delights of tenement life, leaning out of the window watching the world go by and exchanging news and views with neighbours (unkindly referred to as gossiping by some mean spirited critics.).

4 Entrance hall.

5 Cupboards.

6 The Lanarkshire steel town of Wishaw, a close neighbour of Mother-well (the home town of Para Handy's engineer Macphail), lay on the Caledonian Railway route. This opened in February 1848 from Carlisle to Carstairs with branches on from Carstairs to both Edin-burgh and Glasgow, however if we accept that Duffy was born at that time this would only make him 63 rather than the 65 he claimed.

7 John Sinclair (1860-1925) Liberal politician and Secretary of State for Scotland from 1905-12. Among the tasks of this office was responsi-bility for the Census. There is a pleasant appropriateness in Lord Pentland's nominal involvement with this statistical undertaking as he was of the Caithness family of Sinclairs whose 18th century forebear Sir John Sinclair of Ulbster had organised the First Statistical Account of Scotland in the 1790's.

34 The MacPhersons at the "Ex"

1 This previously uncollected story first appeared in the Evening News on 29th May 1911.

2 The Scottish Exhibition of National History, Art and Industry at Kelvingrove had been opened on 3rd May 1911 by the Duke and Duchess of Connaught. See also comments on Glasgow Exhibitions in the Introduction.

3 Bohea was a black Chinese tea, once highly favoured, whose name became almost synonymous with the beverage; for example in Alexander Pope's *Rape of the Lock* we are told of "distant northern lands ... where none e'er taste bohea".

4 A hard peppermint confectionary much favoured for surreptitious sucking during Church services. Also known as Imperials or granny sookers.

5 A Seidlitz powder was an effervescing mixture of sodium bicarbonate,
   tartaric acid and potassium tartrate once extensively used as an
   aperient.
6 Tickle.
7 The provision of an abundant supply of pure drinking water from
   Loch Katrine in the Trossachs to Glasgow by a 34 mile pipe-line was
   one of the great achievements of civic enterprise in the nineteenth
   century. The undertaking was inaugurated by Queen Victoria in
   October 1859.
8 One of the features of the 1911 Exhibition was An Clachan a recre-
   ated Highland village, which naturally enough had an Inn—in Gaelic,
   An Tigh Osda, which served such typical Highland delicacies as tea
   and non-alcoholic heather ale.

35 Togo

1 This previously uncollected story first appeared in the Evening News
   on 17th July 1911.
2 Among the features of the 1911 Exhibition was a Japanese Tea
   Garden and in July the Exhibition was visited by Admiral Count
   Heihachiro Togo (1847-1934) the victor of the battle against the
   Russian fleet at the Battle of Tsushima in 1905 and 650 sailors from
   two Japanese warships.
3 One of the convivial highlights of the civic calendar was the annual
   inspection of municipal water undertakings; a tour of reservoirs, filter
   works and pumping stations during which the quality of the water
   supply was tested and its purity and character, when appropriately
   diluted with whisky, assessed.
4 Swim, bathe.
5 Japan had fought a war against China in 1895 which resulted in
   Formosa and the strategic harbour of Port Arthur being ceded to Japan.
6 A passage-way providing access from one property to another; used
   colloquially of any busy or crowded location.
7 In the Russo-Japanese War of 1904-5 a Russian fleet sailed from the
   Baltic to the Far East. On their way they fired on some Hull trawlers
   fishing on the Dogger Bank under the somewhat strange misapprehension that they were Japanese torpedo boats. One trawler was sunk
   and two crew members killed.
8 Careful examination of the map fails to reveal a Yahoo in the Straits of
   Tsushima, between Japan and Korea. However one of the land battles
   of the Russo-Japanese War was the Battle of the Yalu River, fought in
   Korea in 1904 and Erchie may have a confused recollection of this.
9 Admiral Zinoviev Rozhestvensky was commander of the Russian
   Baltic fleet which sailed round the world to be defeated at the Battle of
   Tsushima.
10 Mikado. Clearly Erchie was not a devotee of Gilbert & Sullivan or he
   would not have so mishandled the former title of the Emperors of
   Japan. As the text indicates the British government had made an
   alliance with Japan, however this been signed in 1902, before the
   Russo-Japanese War. See also note 10 to story 1 *Introductory to an odd
   character.*

11 A high collar forming part of dress uniform.
12 Dundee had a large jute manufacturing industry which was being threatened by lower cost Japanese imports.
13 Two of Glasgow's leading industrial concerns—the Queen's Park Locomotive Works of Henry Dübs and the Fairfield Shipbuilding and Engineering Company in Govan.
14 Hesitating.

36 Strikes
1 This previously uncollected story first appeared in the Evening News on 21st August 1911.
2 1910 and 1911 saw a considerable number of industrial disputes and in July and August 1911 the entire country was affected by a transport workers strike. Troops were called out to move supplies and serious disturbances were reported from various industrial centres.
3 The Dennistoun depot of the Glasgow Corporation Tramways Department was in Paton Street, just off Duke Street in the East End of the City.
4 In 1911 aviation was the coming thing with a Round Britain air race being held.
5 Drive them.
6 Lloyd George had become Chancellor of the Exchequer in 1908 and in the so-called "People's Budget" of 1909 had funded both re-armament and the Liberal social reform programme by increased taxation. His range of measures included a capital gains tax, higher income tax, death duties as well as increased taxes on alcohol and tobacco.
7 A wash tub fitted with an agitator to stir or pound the dirty clothes.

37 Cinematographs
1 This previously uncollected story first appeared in the Evening News on 23 October 1911.
2 Knitting needles.
3 Stockwell Street between the Clyde and Argyll Street.
4 Always a popular subject in the early years of the century and not an unlikely subject for one of the early cinema films. As the story suggests the cinema had by this date become an established, if not yet totally understood, part of Glasgow life. In 1911 there were 57 premises in the city licensed to show films. For another view of the cinema craze see the Jimmy Swan story *From Fort William* in which a Highland customer comes to Glasgow and visits the "picture-palaces".
5 A straw hat.
6 All, everyone, the totality.
7 A but-and-ben was a two-roomed house, here Jinnet is using the phrase to indicate a room behind that in which Lieutenant Rose was eating.
8 Crabs.

38 Duffy's coals
1 This previously uncollected story first appeared in the Evening News on 1st April 1912.

2 A small compartment in a chest or trunk.
3 The most famous example of the India Rubber Room was probably
   the Brazilian city of Manaus, situated on the Rio Negro, some 900
   miles inland from the coast in Amazonas State. From 1890 onwards it
   experienced a remarkable prosperity due to the rubber boom and went
   through a vast and elaborate building programme, including a
   cathedral (Manaus became an episcopal see in 1892) and an opera
   house, the Teatro Amazonas, built in 1896.
4 A colourful description of the feminine habit of holding spare hair-
   pins in the mouth.
5 The Aberdeenshire seaport of Peterhead produces a red granite stone
   once much used in building.
6 The Glasgow ice-rink at Crossmyloof in the South Side of the city.
7 Roald Amundsen (1872-1928) was in fact Norwegian, not Swedish
   but had indeed got to the South Pole first; reaching there in December 1911, a month ahead of Captain Scott. The news of his triumph
   would have only just reached Europe as this story appeared, and
   obviously the tragic news of the loss of Scott's South Pole party had
   not yet emerged.
8 Stones.
9 A coal heap.
10 Minimum wage legislation enforced by Wages Councils had been
   introduced by Winston Churchill, President of the Board of Trade, in
   the 1909 Trade Boards Act. In 1992 it was announced that the last
   vestiges of this legislation were to be dismantled.
11 Blocks of fuel consisting of coal dust bound together with pitch.
12 Glasgow's gas supply had been municipalised in 1870 and despite
   Duffy's professional jealousy supplied gas for street, stair and household lighting as well as for domestic heating.
13 Possibly a reference to gas-lighting in theatres.
14 "Skooshing": an onomatopoeic term, *cf* swishing. It will be recollected
   from earlier tales that Glasgow's electric tramcars were referred to as
   "skoosh-cars".

39 The Conquest of the air

1 This previously uncollected story first appeared in the Evening News
   on 3rd March 1913.
2 The Germans, under the leadership of Count von Zepellin had been
   developing airships, or dirigibles, since the beginning of the century.
3 Flying a kite.
4 Evening.
5 The North Sea. For understandable reasons the expression "German
   Ocean" finally passed out of currency with the First World War.
6 Erchie, we feel, is letting his imagination run away with him. German
   airship development was primarily military and it might prove difficult
   to find advertisements in the German press for moonlight aerial
   cruises.
7 The number of Germans working as waiters was a subject of frequent
   comment. Jimmy Swan in *The Commercial Room*, a story published in
   February 1913, has an encounter with an unsympathetic German

waiter and in a war-time story *Jimmy Swan's German Spy* Jimmy is told by a hotelier of "the hundreds o' German waiters I've had here, payin' them the best wages...". Germans were a significant part of the resident alien population with 52,000 Germans being recorded in Great Britain in 1901—approximately 20% of the total alien population. Another high profile occupation for Germans was as musicians on Clyde steamers—Dougie & Sunny Jim's comments on this phenomenon may be consulted in *The Stowaway No 48* in the Birlinn edition of the Complete Para Handy Stories.

8 The musical Jinnet is referring to Epes Sargent's well known ballad, the opening lines of which run:
    "A life on the ocean wave
    A home on the rolling deep
    Where the scatter'd waters rave
    And the winds their revels keep..."

9 The origins of interest in military aviation in Britain had been the formation of the Royal Naval Air Service in 1908; as a result the terminology adopted, e.g. squadron, owed much to this source. It will be noted that Farnborough's long link with aviation was early established.

10 A characteristic Scottisicm replacing the English "married to".

11 The Royal Flying Corps had been formed in 1912.

12 The Reuter's News Agency had been founded in 1849, using pigeon post, and in 1858 become a world wide organisation following the development of the electric telegraph.

13 Apron.

40 Jinnet's visitor

1 This previously uncollected story first appeared in the Evening News on 12th May 1913.

2 The public health department of the City Council.

3 Vacuum cleaners, originally operated from the street, had been invented in 1901. By the time of this story smaller machines suitable for domestic use were becoming available. The manufacturers of a rival to the "Dinky", the "Hydrovakum" had as early as 1910 advertised their machines pointing out that their system involved "No noisy engines, no strange men tramping through the house. No dirt. No mess. No machinery. Your own maids do the work, and it is easier than sweeping or beating carpets, and far more thorough."

4 Used by plumbers to detect leaks.

5 Thomas Alva Edison (1841-1931) the American inventor was indeed, as Erchie hints, thrang (or busy) thinking of new inventions. With more than a 1000 patents to his credit he has some claim to be considered as the world's most prolific inventor. The incandescent light bulb and the gramophone are perhaps the best known products of his genius.

6 The presence in the city of the Glasgow & West of Scotland College of Domestic Science, founded in 1875, doubtless contributed to the subject being all the rage, even if the grandly named institution was more commonly referred to as the "Dough School".

41 Black Friday

1 This previously uncollected story first appeared in the Evening News on 25th May 1914.

2 For further comment on the effects of the Temperance (Scotland) Act of 1913 see note 2 to No. 67 *The Soda Fountain Future.*

3 The new legislation restricted the long established custom of morning opening.

4 Two of the great political issues of the day—Irish Home rule and the campaign to win the vote for women, the latter chiefly associated with the Pankhursts and the Women's Social and Political Union.

5 A schooner of beer was a glass containing 14 fluid ounces. The conventional Scottish measure of spirits in our degenerate days is a fifth of a gill though some hostelries still advertise themselves as "Quarter-gill shops"; in England the barely moist sixth of a gill measure is favoured. The "wee hauf-gill" is thus a modern English treble. Very shortly all this will have changed in the name of European standardisation and the gill or part thereof will be but a memory—"O tempora, O mores!"

6 A morning drink.

7 The idea of summer-time or Daylight Saving had been discussed pre-war but was not introduced until 1916. Erchie is being ironic and comparing the effects of the licensing hours changes in making more time available for productive purposes to a change in the clock.

8 A mystery. The obvious reading is a whole or round fish, such as a herring, as opposed to a filleted fish such as a kipper. However the context suggests an innovation, comparable to the advent of the tinned salmon, and the availability of kippers and other filleted and cured fish obviously predates tinned salmon.

9 An alcoholic stimulant, as opposed to the traditional accompaniment to gin.

10 The influx of Italians, from the 1890's, into the catering industry had a major impact on the eating and social habits of Glasgow and the West of Scotland.

11 One of the elite groups of the shipbuilding labour force, rivetters were, we may feel, unlikely to be seen queuing outside an ice-cream shop.

12 In front of.

13 The two commonest forms of ice-cream purveyed by the Italians were the slider—or rectangular block of ice-cream between two wafers and the pokey hat—a cone filled with a scoop or scoops of ice-cream. The latter could be converted into the ever-popular Macallum by the addition of raspberry syrup.

14 The Forbes Mackenzie Act—the Public Houses (Scotland) Act 1853 had introduced the novelty of an official closing time for pubs and forbidden Sunday opening except for the service of *bona fide* travellers.

15 Dark mornings.

42 Downhearted Duffy

1 This previously uncollected story first appeared in the Evening News on 8th February 1915.

2 With the coming of war many of the Clyde steamers were comman-

deered for military service. The Caledonian Steam Packet Company's *Duchess of Hamilton, Duchess of Montrose & Duchess of Argyll* were taken as transports in February 1915 and many paddle-steamers were to be used as minesweepers. However the cheerful Erchie suggests that the *Fairy Queen* on the Forth & Clyde Canal was still available to maintain Britannia's claim to rule the waves. The *Fairy Queen* was a much loved pleasure craft which ran canal excursions between Glasgow and Craigmarloch. She had been built in 1897 by J. McArthur & Coy at Paisley for James Aitken & Coy of Kirkintilloch and was a single screw steamer 65' in length. So popular was she that the route she sailed was advertised as the "Fairy Queen Route" even after 1912 when she was sold off the Canal and became a ferry on the Tyne. This news seems not to have reached Erchie, though he would have doubtless been just as happy to sail on her sister ship the *Gypsy Queen*.

3   German submarine warfare against merchant shipping commenced in February 1915.

4   Admiral Sir John R. Jellicoe (1859-1935) Commander-in-Chief of the Grand Fleet. He was to lead his forces to an expensive but strategically important victory at the Battle of Jutland (May 1916) and in December 1916 became First Sea Lord.

5   Horatio Hubert Kitchener (1850-1916), a former Commander-in-Chief in India, had been appointed as Secretary of State for War in Asquith's cabinet on the outbreak of hostilities. In 1916 he was to go on a military mission to Russia and was drowned off Orkney when the cruiser *Hampshire* struck a mine.

6   Sir John French (1852-1925) was the first Commander-in-Chief of the British Expeditionary Force, commanding what the Kaiser had referred to as "a contemptible little army" from the outbreak of war to December 1915, when he was replaced by Haig.

7   Continuously or persistently.

43   Erchie on the Egg

1   This previously uncollected story first appeared in the Evening News on 15th March 1915.

2   Some of the suffragettes and other "new women" may have been slim to the point of anorexia but we suspect Erchie is thinking of emancipation rather than emaciation.

3   The Sustentation Fund of the Free Church of Scotland provided for the maintenance of clergy and churches in parishes otherwise unable to support the costs.

4   Hen roosts.

5   Ducks, being somewhat unsatisfactory parents, were frequently reared by the clutch of duck eggs being placed under a hen to incubate.

44   Erchie on Prohibition

1   This previously uncollected story first appeared in the Evening News on 5th April 1915.

2   Such dramatic and draconian measures were avoided but nonetheless considerable official efforts went into reducing the consumption of

alcohol in the industrial areas.
3 King George V on behalf of himself and the Royal Household
   renounced the use of alcoholic beverages for the duration of hostilities.
4 The Kintyre town of Campbeltown's prosperity was founded on
   whisky distilling. A standard work on the subject lists at least 34
   distilleries operating in the town at various dates in the 19th and 20th
   centuries.
5 Two of the famous Glasgow tea rooms. It will be recollected that Miss
   Cranston's Willow Tea Rooms were visited by Erchie and Duffy in
   story no. 22 in this collection *Erchie in an Art Tea-Room.*

45 Duffy will buy bonds

1 This previously uncollected story first appeared in the Evening News
   on 28th June 1915.
2 Drain.
3 As a means of financing national defence War Bonds paying $4^1/2\%$
   interest were energetically promoted and bond purchase encouraged
   as a patriotic duty.
4 A coal dump, a coal merchant's store.
5 Dust.

46 An Ideal Profession

1 This previously uncollected story first appeared in the Evening News
   on 16th August 1915.
2 With all available men needed for the armed forces women came
   increasingly to take over what had been previously exclusively male
   occupations. This included the replacement of male tram-car conduc-
   tors with female employees.
3 The restriction of public house opening hours in areas of importance
   to munitions production was not designed to provide a gentleman's
   life for young Johnny Duffy but was part of Lloyd George's campaign
   to fight the drink menace.

47 Margarine for Wartime

1 This previously uncollected story first appeared in the Evening News
   on 6th December 1915.
2 David Lloyd George (1863-1945), Liberal politician, was Chancellor
   of the Exchequer at the outbreak of war but became Minister of
   Munitions in July 1915 and planned a major expansion of munitions
   production. On Kitchener's death (see above No. 42 note 5) he
   became Secretary of State for War and eventually in December 1916,
   Prime Minister.
3 A chaumer or chamber was a bothy used for the accommodation of
   unmarried farm workers. The moral condition of such chaumer
   dwellers was a cause for frequent concern and had attracted the
   attention of various inquiries into housing and social welfare.
   "Chambering" is here being used by Jinnet as a polite euphemism for
   sexual promiscuity.
4 To haver is to talk foolishly.

5 Reginald McKenna (1863-1943) was Lloyd George's successor as
   Chancellor of the Exchequer. In this role he advocated strict economy
   and introduced a range of new taxation measures.

48 Duffy in the Dark

1 This previously uncollected story first appeared in the Evening News
   on 27th March 1916.
2 Well not exactly; what the poet (Richard Monckton Milnes
   1809-1895) actually said in *The men of old* was:
       "Great thoughts, great feelings came to him,
       Like instincts, unawares."
3 As with so many of these stories a topical reference, this time to war
   economy measures.

49 A Bawbee on the Bobbin

1 This previously uncollected story first appeared in the Evening News
   on 13th November 1916.
2 The Paisley firm of J & P Coats was the world's largest manufacturer
   of sewing thread.
3 One of the effects of war had been the increasingly rapid replacement
   of gold sovereigns by Treasury notes.
4 A farthing, a quarter of a penny, the smallest coin.
5 Metal tokens stamped with a church's name or a Biblical text given to
   members in good standing as their proof of communicant status, thus
   admitting them to the Sacrament. As they were typically made of lead
   a bag of communion tokens would make a formidable weapon. Tokens
   were, in the twentieth century, increasingly replaced by printed
   communion cards—hence we may speculate the reason for the ready
   availability of a bag of old tokens for the irate Mr MacGallochary.
6 Gartnavel Royal Hospital, Glasgow's main psychiatric hospital.
7 A halfpenny.

50 Nationalised Eggs

1 This previously uncollected story first appeared in the Evening News
   on 20th November 1916. For another contemporary view on the egg
   crisis see *Para Handy in the Egg Trade*, number 96 in the Birlinn
   edition of the Complete Para Handy Stories, a story originally
   published in October 1916.
2 The wartime coalition government had been established by Asquith in
   May 1915.
3 China eggs used to persuade hens to continue laying.
4 Winston Churchill (1874-1965) was in fact available for the Erchie-
   inspired role of National Egg Co-ordinator. He had resigned as First
   Lord of the Admiralty in May 1915 following the failure of the
   Dardanelles expedition and did not return to Government office until
   June 1917 when he became Minister of Munitions.
5 The controversial figure of Horatio Bottomley (1860-1933), financier,
   company promoter, founder of *John Bull* and bankrupt, cropped up in
   many political contexts but not so far as is known, as Minister of Hens
   and Eggs.

51 A Slump in Zepps
1 This previously uncollected story first appeared in the Evening News
   on 4th December 1916.
2 A German Zeppelin or airship.
3 The Glasgow firm of Wylie and Lochhead were among the city's
   leading funeral undertakers.
4 German "frightfulness" and war atrocity stories were a commonplace
   of Allied propagandists from the earliest days of the war. Many of the
   stories were later proved to be ill-founded, however Erchie's reference
   to Zeppelin raids does reflect the fact that during the war 53 separate
   raids were carried out on British targets, including civilian centres,
   with the loss of 556 civilian lives. A small figure compared to the
   horrors of air raids in the Second World War but at the time a
   shocking extension of war to the home front.
5 A reminder that the public houses of the period were exclusively male
   domains where no respectable woman like Jinnet would be seen,
   except perhaps at the off-licence counter.

52 The New Pub
1 This previously uncollected story first appeared in the Evening News
   on 25th December 1916.
2 In order to release manpower for the war effort and to concentrate
   transport resources many lesser-used passenger stations were closed in
   the third year of the War.
3 General Sir Douglas Haig (1861-1928) British Commander-in-Chief
   on the Western Front from December 1915. Seven days after this
   story appeared Haig was promoted to Field Marshal.
4 As part of the government campaign to reduce the consumption of
   alcohol state control of public houses was introduced into various
   industrial areas and measures were taken to further control opening
   hours. Lloyd George, the Minister of Munitions said "Drink is doing
   us more damage than all the German submarines put together."

53 Marriage a la mode
1 This previously uncollected story first appeared in the Evening News
   on 1st January 1917.
2 A perceptive forecast of the post-war housing shortage and the
   pressure for "Homes for Heroes".

54 Bad news
1 This previously uncollected story first appeared in the Evening News
   on 8th January 1917.
2 A Danube river port captured by the Central Powers in their successful campaign against Rumania which had entered the war on the
   Allied side in August 1916.
3 A less than complimentary reference to Crown Prince Wilhelm
   (1882-1951) who had, with little evident military experience, commanded the 5th Army on the Western Front and directed the German
   offensive at Verdun in February 1916. This engagement lasted until

December and cost over 400,000 German and 540,00 French lives.

4 The world's first tank, went into action in September 1915 during the Battle of the Somme. "Tank", it will be noted, appears in quotations in this story, a usage indicative of contemporary uncertainty about the invention. The name was given to what was officially described as a "landship" in an attempt to disguise its identity for security reasons.

5 Joseph Joffre (1852-1931) was the French field commander until the end of 1916 when the losses of Verdun and the failure to achieve a breakthrough on the Somme front resulted in his promotion to Marshal of France, appointment as President of the Supreme War Council and removal from active command.

6 Sir David Beatty (1872-1936) had just succeeded Jellicoe as Commander in Chief of the Grand Fleet. He had won national fame for his dashing command of the Battle Cruiser Squadron in the early years of the War.

55 Erchie on Allotments

1 This previously uncollected story first appeared in the Evening News on 22nd January 1917.

2 As part of the nation's wartime effort to maximise food production official encouragement was given to the establishment of allotment gardens.

3 A small quantity.

4 Garden forks.

56 The Last of the Bridescakes

1 This previously uncollected story first appeared in the Evening News on 12th February 1917.

2 The West End, or Kelvingrove Park in Glasgow was a favourite place of resort as well as being the venue for the city's series of International Exhibitions. The highly ornate Stewart Memorial Fountain was designed by the distinguished Glasgow architect James Sellars and built in 1872-3 as a tribute to Robert Stewart (Lord Provost from 1851-4) the originator of the city's Loch Katrine water-supply scheme.

3 By this stage in the war, food shortages, especially of imported products such as sugar, were becoming severe. German submarines were to sink over 2600 Allied ships, a total of 11 million tons of shipping. A few weeks earlier the *News* had noted that in city tea rooms " ... each person ordering tea is visited by a waitress, who doles out the sweet stuff in sparing spoonfulls." See also note 4.

4 Hudson Ewbanke Kearley (1856-1934), 1st Baron Devonport, a businessman and Liberal politician, was created food controller in November 1916 and given the remit of regulating maximum prices for foodstuffs and achieving economies in the use of food. He developed a voluntary rationing scheme and, as this story implies, was particularly concerned with the problem of sugar supplies, chairing a Royal Commission on the issue. He resigned, due to ill-health, in May 1917.

5 Flat iron pans used for cooking oatcakes or girdle scones.

57 How Erchie Spent the Fair
1 This previously uncollected story first appeared in the Evening News on 23rd July 1917.
2 A small pocket timetable showing the times of transport connections from Glasgow, together with useful information on local holidays, weekly half-days etc.
3 James Dalrymple, C.B.E., was General Manager of the Glasgow Corporation Tramways from 1904.
4 Seaweed.
5 The south-west portion of the crypt of the Cathedral Church of St Mungo is all that remains of the Bishop Jocelyn's extension and remodelling of the first Cathedral building. Jocelyn's work was carried out in 1197, two years before the Bishop's death.
6 The *Lord of the Isles* that Erchie and Jinnet watched people missing at the Broomielaw (Glasgow Bridge Quay) was a magnificent paddle steamer built in 1891 for the Glasgow and Inveraray Steamboat Coy. by Messrs D. & W. Henderson at their Meadowside, Partick, yard. Designed to operate the daily "all the way" sailing from the centre of Glasgow to Inveraray, she was, from 1912 onwards in the ownership of Turbine Steamers Ltd. who employed her on their popular daily cruise from Glasgow down the Clyde and round the Island of Bute. During the War she remained in civilian service and was used on the route to Lochgoilhead.
7 Originally intended as a war-time measure the concept of "Summer Time" had been introduced in 1916.

58 Erchie's Work in Wartime
1 This previously uncollected story first appeared in the Evening News on 16th May 1918.
2 Literally a pigeon's clutch or hatching of eggs.
3 The United States had declared war on Germany in April 1917 and by the time of this story the troops of the American Expeditionary Force had just fought a successful major engagement at Belleau Wood and were engaged in the Second Battle of the Marne.
4 A flat stone used in the game of hopscotch.

59 Government Milk
1 This previously uncollected story first appeared in the Evening News on 2nd July 1918.
2 The Scottish delicacy of the soda-scone used buttermilk in its recipe.
3 A reminder that milk was distributed in bulk rather than in our now familiar bottles or cartons.
4 Yawning.

60 Coal Rations
1 This previously uncollected story first appeared in the Evening News on 17th August 1918.
2 Coal rationing had been announced in March 1918.
3 A kitchen fireplace fabricated in cast iron and incorporating an oven and a hotplate which was typically used for both heating and cooking

purposes in tenement flats of this period.
4 Another reflection on wartime steps to reduce the strength, and discourage the consumption, of alcoholic beverages.
5 Erchie was clearly living in a quite superior tenement flat in that it possessed a bath, a fairly unusual fitting in such properties at this period.
6 Glasgow city council, the "Corporation", ran a large scale municipal gas undertaking.

61 Celebrating Peace
1 This previously uncollected story first appeared in the Evening News on the 30th June 1919.
2 The signature of the Peace Treaty between the Allied Powers and Germany took place at Versailles on Saturday, 28th June 1919, two days before this story appeared. Fighting had of course stopped with the Armistice on 11th November 1918.
3 The German Emperor was not in fact handed over to justice or even to the Argyll & Sutherland Highlanders. He had abdicated on 9th November 1918 and had fled to the neutral Netherlands, where he lived peacefully until his death in 1941.

62 The Coal Famine
1 This previously uncollected story first appeared in the Evening News on 12th January 1920.
2 William Hesketh Lever (1851-1925) made a fortune from the manufacture of soap, founding the model industrial town of Port Sunlight on Merseyside. Involved in a wide range of philanthropic activities he received a baronetcy in 1911, became Baron Leverhulme in 1917 and was advanced to the rank of Viscount Leverhulme of the Western Isles in 1922.
3 In 1918 Leverhulme bought the Island of Lewis and in 1919 added the Harris estate to his holdings. His intention was to develop fishing and fish processing and improve the conditions of the crofting population. However the scheme was unsuccessful, in part due to problems of crofting tenure and in part to local reluctance to surrender independence in favour of a weekly wage. He ceased operations in Lewis in 1922 passing over part of his holdings to a local trust in Stornoway. Leverhulme continued to develop fisheries and fish processing in Harris, developing the port of Obbe, renamed Leverburgh. When he died in 1925 his trustees immediately halted all his Hebridean projects.
4 A deerstalker hat.

63 A Turned Suit
1 This previously uncollected story first appeared in the Evening News on 1st March 1920.
2 A dashed thing.

64 Erchie on Divorce
1 This previously uncollected story first appeared in the Evening News

on 12th April 1920.

2　Mary Pickford (1893-1979) was a Canadian born American film actress who rose to prominence in the silent movies where she won the nickname of "The World's Sweetheart". A founding partner of United Artists Film Corporation.

3　The actor Owen Moore was the first husband of Mary Pickford, marrying her in 1911 and was divorced from her in 1919.

4　Douglas Fairbanks (1883-1939) American film star, married Mary Pickford in 1920; they divorced in 1935.

5　Charlie Chaplin (1889-1977) English born film actor and director moved to Hollywood in 1914 and played a leading part in the development of the film industry. Married to Mildred Harris in 1918, she divorced him and he married Lila Grey in 1924. Chaplin later married Paulette Goddard and Oona O'Neill, contributing to Erchie's "wave o' divorce".

6　This familiar passage of instruction from the Apostle Paul begins "Wives, submit yourselves unto your own husbands, as unto the Lord."

65　Our Mystery Millionaire

1　This previously uncollected story first appeared in the Evening News on 17th May 1920.

2　Harry Duncan McGowan (1874-1961) Glasgow born businessman, started work in the Nobel Explosives Co. as an office boy and rose to prominence in business in Britain and Canada. In 1926 he was to be instrumental in bringing about the merger of British chemical firms and creating Imperial Chemical Industries; he became Chairman and Managing Director of I.C.I. in 1930. Knighted in 1918, he was created a baron in 1937.

3　The tramcar heading towards Glasgow University.

4　In 1871 Alfred Nobel, the Swedish inventor, licensed production of dynamite in the British Empire to the British Dynamite Company. This concern, with offices in Glasgow, established a factory at Ardeer in Ayrshire, and later became the Nobel Division of I.C.I.

5　Allan Glen's School was founded in 1853 and specialised in scientific and technical education.

6　A curious comment. Belvidere Hospital is in London Road, on the north bank of the Clyde, and not particularly convenient for catching millionairism in Pollokshields, which one would think would be more conveniently served by the Victoria Infirmary in Langside Road.

66　Erchie Sorts the Clock

1　This previously uncollected story first appeared in the Evening News on 13th September 1920.

67　The Soda Fountain Future

1　This previously uncollected story first appeared in the Evening News on 11th October 1920.

2　This story was first published in the year in which the Volstead Act had introduced Prohibition into the United States and in many circles in Britain similar sentiments were being expressed. It was possible for a local community, through the Veto Poll mechanism of the Temperance (Scotland) Act of 1913, to declare itself "dry" and to refuse to grant licenses. Because of the War the first such Veto Polls were not in fact held until 1920 and in that year several communities, such as Kirkintilloch, went "dry".

68 Reminiscences
1 This previously uncollected story first appeared in the Evening News on 8th November 1920.
2 Margot Asquith neé Tennant (1865-1945) was the second wife of Henry Herbert Asquith, the Liberal Prime Minister. Her popular and colourful *Autobiography* was published in 1920 and had clearly provided the cue for Munro's writing this story.
3 Fair dealing or fair play.
4 Harum-scarum.
5 Gossip.
6 H. H. Asquith (1852-1928) (see note 2 above). As Jinnet goes on to suggest, a somewhat stuffy and reserved character, in contrast to his ebullient and spirited wife. "Wait and see" was a phrase associated with him and indicative of his character. Asquith had lost his East Fife seat in the 1918 General Election in the general rout of non-Coalition Liberals. He was elected for Paisley at a by-election in 1920 and held this seat until created Earl of Oxford and Asquith in 1925.
7 Giddy, empty-headed.

69 Glad News
1 This previously uncollected story first appeared in the Evening News on 17th January 1921.
2 Erchie is paraphrasing the well known phrase of Lloyd George's "What is our task? To make Britain a fit country for heroes to live in." This phrase was used in a speech in November 1918 and became a popular slogan for post-war reconstruction.
3 The Coats family from Paisley were the dominant force in that town's important thread milling and textile industry.
4 Bobbin.
5 Where indeed? The Coats family were extremely keen yacht owners and the 1910 Lloyd's Register of Yachts lists twelve sail and steam yachts owned by the Coats clan. For another account of the Coats yacht-owning interests see the Para Handy story *Among the Yachts* No. 41 in the Birlinn edition of the Complete Para Handy Stories.

70 The Footballer's Life
1 This previously uncollected story first appeared in the Evening News on 21st March 1921.
2 The Kilmarnock player whose high transfer fee so attracted Duffy's comment was joining one of England's most successful football teams. Placed 16th in the English First Division in season 1920/21 Preston North End were also semi-finalists in the F.A. Cup. In the next season they were again 16th in the League and were the beaten finalists in the

Cup. In 1992/93 Preston are competing two divisions lower.
3 A celebrated Clydesdale stallion which in 1911 had been sold for the
   then world record price of £9500. On its death in 1914 the Baron was
   buried but was exhumed four years later and its skeleton presented to
   Glasgow's Kelvingrove Museum, where it is still a popular exhibit.

71 Celebrating the Eclipse
1 This previously uncollected story first appeared in the Evening News
   on 11th April 1921.
2 As usual Munro is highly topical with a reference not only to the
   eclipse but to the Scotland-England match played on the Saturday
   before this story appeared. The result—Scotland 3, England 0.

72 Firewood
1 This previously uncollected story first appeared in the Evening News
   on 9th May 1921.
2 The Royal Order of Foresters and the breakaway Ancient Order of
   Foresters were popular friendly societies founded in the early nineteenth century.
3 The gleam of a fire.

73 Duffy's Flitting
1 This previously uncollected story first appeared in the Evening News
   on 30th May 1921.
2 A poetic term for the heavens, used by Munro both here and in his
   Para Handy stories, e.g. *Hurricane Jack* no. 53 in the Birlinn edition of
   the Complete Para Handy Stories. *cf* "This most excellent Canopy the
   Ayre..." (Shakespeare *Hamlet* Act 2 Scene 2) or "Without any other
   cover than the cope of Heaven" (Tobias Smollett: *Humphry Clinker*)
3 As the Vulgate is the Latin translation of the Bible it is a little difficult
   to accept that "Duffy are you on" appears in it—through perhaps the
   Apocrypha...?
4 The Royal Princess Theatre in the Gorbals (built in 1978 as Her
   Majesty's) is now known to Glasgow theatre-goers as the Citizen's
   Theatre.
5 The reference is to the popular stage version of Walter Scott's *Rob Roy*
   by Isaac Pocock. This work, first produced in 1818 was for many
   years the most popular dramatic work in Scotland. It, like the novel,
   has scenes set in the Trossachs village of Aberfoyle.
6 Archibald is mis-quoting Prospero's words from *The Tempest*, Act 4,
   Scene 1:
       "Our revels now are ended. These our actors,
       As I foretold you, were all spirits and
       are melted into air, into thin air:
       And, like the baseless fabric of this vision
       The cloud-capp'd towers, the gorgeous palaces,
       The solemn temples, the great globe itself,
       Yea, all which it inherit, shall dissolve,
       And, like this insubstantial pageant faded,
       Leave not a rack behind...."

74 After the Fight

1 This previously uncollected story first appeared in the Evening News on July 4th 1921.

2 The reference is to the monthly magazine of the Church of Scotland—not generally considered to be a good source for up to date boxing results.

3 George Carpentier (1894-1975) French boxer who won the world light-heavyweight championship and unsuccessfully challenged Dempsey for the heavyweight title.

4 Jack "The Manassa Mauler" Dempsey (1895-1983) was world heavyweight champion between 1919 and 1926. His defence of the title which occasioned this story took place on 2nd July 1921 at Jersey City and was the first boxing match to produce a $1 million gate. Dempsey knocked out Carpentier in the fourth round.

5 An expression from the days of prize-fighting, meaning to produce a flow of blood.

6 The 18th amendment to the United States Constitution had come into force in January 1920 and introduced the Prohibition era.

7 Not a reference to hair loss but a Scottish term for parting hair.

8 Sir Philip Sassoon Bt. (1888-1939) Millionaire, Conservative politician and art connoisseur and a close friend of the Prince of Wales (later Edward VIII).

75 Saturnalia

1 This previously uncollected story first appeared in the Evening News on 23rd January 1922.

2 Plays performed by guisers at Hallowe'en.

3 The Hengler family were prominent in British entertainment from the 18th century. Among the family's enterprises were permanent circuses in London, Dublin, Hull and Glasgow. The Glasgow establishment was opened in Wellington Street by Charles Hengler in November 1885 and operated there until 1903. From the next year Hengler's Cirque performed in the Hippodrome building in Sauchiehall Street.

4 The title of the student's rag magazine and mystic cry of collectors—claimed to be derived from the exhortation "Ygorra hand over the money".

5 A higher education college for women associated with Glasgow University. The buildings are now incorporated into BBC Scotland's headquarters, Broadcasting House.

6 The name of a prominent Glasgow crammers and commercial college.

76 Keep to the Left

1 This previously uncollected story first appeared in the Evening News on 27th February 1922.

2 Erchie attributes the excitement to a clash between the Glasgow Rangers F.C. and their Edinburgh rivals Heart of Midlothian.

3 An opening in a tenement building providing access to the back yard.

4 May 15th. (Whitsunday) was one of the Scottish Quarter Days on which rents etc. were payable and tenancies were renewed or surrendered.

77 Glasgow in 1942

1 This previously uncollected story first appeared in the Evening News on 23rd October 1922.

2 Sir Arthur Conan Doyle (1859-1930) the historical novelist and creator of Sherlock Holmes became in later life a convert to spiritualism, writing and lecturing extensively on the subject. Another writer who looked into the future with an even larger measure of bleak pessimism than Erchie was George Orwell, author of *1984*. Attractive as it may be to draw comparisons it is unlikely that he was greatly influenced in his dystopian view of the future by Erchie's reflections. Orwell (Eric Arthur Blair) was at this time serving in Burma in the Indian Imperial Police—though in view of the significant Scottish influence in those parts it is not impossible that copies of the *Evening News* found their way to Scots engineers serving with the Irrawaddy Flotilla Company.

3 Noise or confusion.

4 The proposal to create a circus, or as we would now say, a roundabout, at the busy intersection of Argyle Street, Jamaica Street and Union Street never came to fruition and the corner is still one of Glasgow's busiest.

5 Erchie is not, we may assume, suggesting that the "No-Accident Week" initiative would bring in visitors from The Mearns, an agricultural district in Kincardineshire. A more likely source for these timid travellers is Newton Mearns, an affluent Renfrewshire suburb of Glasgow.

6 Rubber, a corruption of caoutchouc.

78 No Accident Week

1 This previously uncollected story first appeared in the Evening News on 15th January 1923.

2 A picturesque, and remarkably peaceful, village in rural Renfrewshire.

3 Many of Glasgow's policemen were traditionally recruited from the Highlands and Islands and were, in consequence, native Gaelic speakers.

4 The Glasgow Orpheus Choir was an important part of the city's cultural life for many years. Founded in 1906 by Hugh Roberton (1874-1952) it made many famous recordings. Roberton was knighted for his services to music in 1931 and continued as conductor of the Choir until 1951.

79 The Grand Old Man Comes Down

1 This previously uncollected story first appeared in the Evening News on 19th March 1923.

2 William Ewart Gladstone (1809-1898) Liberal statesman and Prime Minister; frequently referred to as the "Grand Old Man". Gladstone's statue in George Square was originally sited in front of the City Chambers, where the Cenotaph now stands, and was moved, as the story indicates, to accommodate the monument to the dead of the Great War. The Cenotaph was unveiled in May 1924 by Earl Haig.

3 John Ellis, a Rochdale barber, was appointed as the public hangman

in 1899 and retired from his position in March 1924 having officiated
at 203 executions.

4   Gladstone's name may be associated with a design of bag or portmanteau as Erchie has it; he is much less clearly identified with *The Land
o' the Leal*, a touching poem by Lady Nairne (1766-1845). The land
of the leal (loyal or true-hearted) is heaven and the poem tells of a
dying woman's words. The last verse gives the flavour of the piece:
    "Now fare ye weel, my ain John,
    This world's cares are vain, John,
    We'll meet, and we'll be fain,
    In the land o' the leal."

5   Many of the "Red Clydesiders" of the Independent Labour Party,
such as Emmanuel Shinwell, James Maxton and David Kirkwood,
elected to Parliament in 1922 had previously served on the Glasgow
City Council or other public bodies such as Education Boards.

6   James Oswald (1779-1853) was a Liberal politician and active in the
campaign for the 1832 Reform Bill. Oswald's statue has the reformer
with his top hat in his hand—an obvious target for mischief makers of
all ages. The tale is told by George Blake that Neil Munro took the
novelist Joseph Conrad across the Square to Oswald's statue after a
dinner in the North British Hotel and encouraged Conrad to throw
stones in the top hat and by so doing become an "honorary Glaswegian."

7   George Square does not lack for a statue of a General, having monu-
ments both to Sir John Moore (of Corunna fame) and Colin
Campbell (Lord Clyde) who won renown in the Crimea and the
Indian Mutiny. However Sir Robert Peel's fame was as a Tory Prime
Minister and repealer of the Corn Laws. More locally he was elected
Lord Rector of Glasgow University in 1836.

8   The point of this reference is that the equestrian statue of King
William III, which stood until 1923 at Glasgow Cross, was removed in
that year due to road alterations. It was later re-elected in Cathedral
Square.

80   The Doctor's Strike

1   This previously uncollected story first appeared in the Evening News
on 5th November 1923.

2   As is so often the case Munro is being highly topical. A major dispute
between medical practitioners and the friendly societies which
administered the National Health Insurance system had broken out
earlier in the year, the occasion being a proposal to reduce the
capitation fee from 9/6 (47p) per head to 7/- (35p). At one stage 95%
of the Glasgow doctors had withdrawn from the panel system. As may
be expected the crisis provoked the standard response of a Court of
Inquiry and a Royal Commission.

3   A "panel doctor" was one who treated patients under the health
insurance scheme. "Graith" is a term for tools, implements, machinery required for a particular job—thus the striking doctors were
picking up their tools and walking out of the quasi-state system of
health care.

81 The Coal Crisis

1 This previously uncollected story first appeared in the Evening News on 7th June 1926.

2 St Enoch's Church, at the south end of St Enoch Square had been built by the City Council in 1780 and replaced in 1827. This building was demolished in 1925, the year before this story appeared. The crisis which resulted in yet another attack on Duffy's coal quality was of course the General Strike of 4th-12th May 1926. Although the other unions returned to work after nine days the miners, a cut in whose wages was the immediate occasion for the strike, remained out until August.

3 An accurate phonetic rendering of the Dumbartonshire town of Milngavie, a noted pronunciation test for foreign visitors, English news-readers etc.

4 Butter was normally sold by the grocer or dairyman cutting a quantity off a 56lb. block and moulding it to shape with wooden handles—these frequently had a design of a thistle or other appropriate motif.

Notes to *Jimmy Swan, the Joy Traveller*

1 Stars to Push
 1 A fictitious location used for many of these tales.
 2 A somewhat pretentious term for a commercial traveller.
 3 A commercial traveller. So called because, like Jimmy Swan, they normally carried samples of their wares in bags and cases.
 4 A soft silk fabric originating from the Chinese northern coastal province of the same name.

2 On the Road
 1 A card game similar to whist in which players undertake to win a certain number of tricks.
 2 An unconvincing disguise for the well-known firm of Gray Dunn, who had a large biscuit factory at Kinning Park on the South Side of Glasgow.
 3 An Ayrshire town noted for its textile industry.
 4 The identity of this trade rival is unclear. Glasgow, however, had a great range of such firms and the reader may select from such famous names as Copland & Lye or Trerons.
 5 Jimmy Swan's employers have been tentatively identified with the major Glasgow manufacturing and wholesale warehouse firm of Stewart and MacDonald. This concern had clothing factories in Glasgow, Leeds and Strabane, with warehouses in Mitchell Street, Argyle Street and Buchanan Street in Glasgow. Seventy travellers represented the firm in territories as diverse as Sweden and Australia. In a curious case of life imitating art the company later changed its name to Campbell, Stewart & MacDonald.
 6 Baillie. A senior councillor in a Scottish town or city with a legal function as an *ex-officio* justice of the Peace.
 7 Social evening at a Masonic lodge.

3 The Fatal Clock
 1 No establishment of this name appears in the Glasgow Post Office Directory for 1913, the year of publication of this story.

2 Tall chest of drawers.

3 The Glasgow underground system was completed in 1896.

4 The Glasgow Necropolis was one of the city's most famous burying-places and from its establishment in 1833 was extensively used by Glasgow's industrial and commercial elite. The Southern Necropolis in the Hutchesontown area of the Gorbals was a later creation.

5 The United Free Church, formed by a union in 1901.

6 A popular total abstinence movement. The Rechabites, apart from their campaign against drink had an important role as a major friendly society with over 200,000 members. The movement's name comes from Jeremiah Ch. 35 vv 5 & 6—"And I set before the sons of the house of the Rechabites pots full of wine, and cups, and I said unto them, drink ye wine. But they said, we will drink no wine: for Jonadab the son of Rechab our Father commanded us, saying ye shall drink no wine, neither ye, nor your sons for ever."

7 At this time (1911) still a novelty. The first vacuum cleaner, a large machine mounted on wheels and operated from outside the house, had been invented by the Scot, Herbert Cecil Booth, in 1901.

8 Bankruptcy.

4 A Spree

1 An open, four-wheeled carriage with an inward-facing bench seat along each side.

2 Turned inside out.

3 Wandering.

4 Dried fish, such as whiting or haddock.

5 The United Presbyterian Church was formed in 1847 from a union of the Secession and Relief Churches. In 1901 the U.P. Church merged with the Free Church to form the United Free Church. As a result this building was surplus to requirements and had become the established Church of Scotland's Church Hall.

6 Not a reference to aged farmers. The Loyal Order of Ancient Shepherds was a popular friendly society. A Royal Commission in the 1870s had reported it to have 46,000 members organised in local lodges. The coming together of the Established and U.F. Church choirs for the Shepherds' Church parade is indicative of better relationships between the presbyterian denominations at this time. The United Free Church and the Church of Scotland were finally to sink their differences and unite in 1929.

7 At the end of the nineteenth century and in the early years of the twentieth century many Italians emigrated to Scotland. Large numbers of them entered the catering industry and came to dominate the two key areas of the fried fish trade and the ice cream parlour. Glasgow and the seaside resorts of the West of Scotland would have been unimaginable without the presence of these early fast-food operations.

8 The 100th Metrical Psalm "All People that on Earth do dwell". With its familiar tune "Old 100th" taken from the Franco-Genevan Psalter of 1551, it was probably second only to the 23rd Psalm in the affections of Scots worshippers.

9 The American evangelist D. L. Moody and I. D. Sankey published two collections of gospel hymns in the 1870s. These were highly popular, though obviously not with the traditionalist Jimmy Swan.

10 The North British Railway's routes included a branch line through the Stirlingshire town of Slamannan.

5 His "Bête Noir"

1 Many of the leading Glasgow drapers and outfitters such as Copland and Lye and Trerons had build magnificent stores, with, as Jimmy suggests, attractive catering facilities to restore their customer's strength. In a much later piece in his "Looker-On" column which discussed Glasgow restaurants and their innovations Munro has a Scot returning to this native city after many years in America remark

"But say! That's a nifty dodge of the Department Stores to start up restaurants and get the dames warmed up and replete with wholesome soup and sundaes before they go over the top and attack the bargain counters."

2 An opera by Vincent Wallace, first produced in 1845.

3 Franz Lehar's operetta, first produced in Vienna in 1909 as "Der Graf von Luxemburg", opened in London in English translation in May 1911. Its popularity ensured a wide and speedy circulation for the music.

4 Glasgow's unique series of Exhibitions included the 1901 International Exhibition and 1911 Scottish National Exhibition held at Kelvingrove Park in the west end of the city. Still an obviously topical reference when this story first appeared in the *Glasgow Evening News* in December 1912.

5 A London institution dedicated to the sport of boxing.

6 The women's suffrage movement, as represented by organisations such as Emmeline Pankhurst's Women's Social and Political Movement, was actively campaigning for their cause in the years before the First World War. As Jimmy's comment suggest, these campaigns became increasingly given to direct action.

6 From Fort William

1 The home ground of Queen's Park Football Club and Scotland's national football stadium.

2 Elsewhere, Gower Street is described as being in Glasgow's Ibrox District. However street maps show it situated between Bellahouston and Pollokshields, about a third of a mile south of what might normally be thought of as Ibrox.

3 This story was first published in 1912, a time when the cinema craze was a matter of regular press comment.

4 The citizens of Fort William had only gained the benefits of rail travel in 1894 when the West Highland Railway, running from Glasgow's Queen Street station to an initial terminus in Fort William was opened. The line was later extended to Mallaig in 1901, doubtless extending still further Jimmy's Mazepa cigar zone.

5 A once popular product of the great Dundonian publishing empire of D. C. Thomson.

7   Jimmy's Silver Wedding

1   A superior neighbourhood in the fashionable Kelvinside district of Glasgow's West End.

2   So sleepy is the village of Kirkfinn that it has quite escaped the attention of the Ordnance Survey.

3   The first Tay Railway Bridge was destroyed in a severe gale in December 1879 with the loss of 77 lives of crew and passengers on a train from Edinburgh to Dundee.

8   A Matrimonial Order

1   A high quality woollen fabric used for women's dresses. From the French *de laine*—of wool.

2   A dyeing process for calico. A main centre of the industry was in the Vale of Leven, Dumbartonshire, some 20 miles from Glasgow.

3   Tips, pours, cascades.

4   J. H. Haverly (Munro miss-spells the name) was the manager of "Haverly's Mastodon Minstrels" the first of the large-scale American minstrel troupes. The Haverly Minstrels were disbanded in 1896.

5   The Hengler family were prominent in British entertainment from the 18th century. Among their many enterprises were permanent circuses in London, Dublin, Hull and Glasgow. Their Glasgow circus was located in Wellington Street from 1885-1903 and re-opened in the Hippodrome Building in Sauchiehall Street in 1904.

9   A Great Night

1   While we noted in the first story that Birrelton is fictitious, it is also curiously protean. Its characteristics change in a quite alarming way. In this tale Dawson's is described as the only draper's shop in Birrelton, and Jimmy, as we will be told, spends the night there for the first time due to bad weather and a foundered horse. In "His Bete Noir", also set in Birrelton we are told that Jimmy puts off his visit to Joseph Jago's shop till the very last, having "swept up all the other soft-goods orders of the town." In "Stars to Push" he is staying overnight at the "Buck's Head" Hotel in Birrelton and is on terms of familiarity with the residents of the community—experience surely hard to come by if he only made a brief visit to Birrelton. Even more curiously in the present story we are told that Birrelton is only of significance in that it is on the road to several other places of importance. In "Stars to Push" (written a year and half after "A Great Night") Birrelton has become a sea-port from which Jimmy is to sail the next morning. Curious! Can there be two Birreltons?

2   Ignace Jan Paderewski (1860-1941) Polish violin virtuoso and advocate of Polish independence. Briefly Prime Minister of Poland in 1919.

3   Nellie Melba. Stage name of Helen Porter Mitchell (1861-1931), an Australian soprano of Scots descent who specialised in the Italian operatic repertoire. Created Dame Commander of the Order of the British Empire in 1927.

4   Scottish music hall singer and composer. Lauder (1870-1950) was an active recruiter and troop entertainer during the First World War and

was knighted for his services in 1919. Lauder and Munro were friends and Lauder attended Munro's funeral in 1930.

10 Rankine's Rookery

1 A Perthshire village situated at the junction of a number of important transport routes. In particular it was an interchange point between the West Highland Railway and the Callander and Oban Railway.

2 David Lloyd George (1853-1944), Liberal politician. In June 1912 when this story appeared he was Chancellor of the Exchequer in Asquith's administration.

3 A famously fertile stretch of land on the North bank of the Tay between Perth and Dundee. Anywhere less like Rannoch Moor, an infertile and inhospitable acid peat-bog lying at an average height of 300 metres in the West Highlands, is hard to imagine.

4 A tenement property of flats.

5 Jimmy is talking of the second Tay Rail Bridge, completed in 1887 and Europe's longest railway bridge.

6 A public park donated to the City of Dundee in 1863 by Sir David Baxter, a local jute magnate.

7 Bonnethill was a district to the North of Dundee's city centre largely settled in earlier centuries by the makers of knitted woollen bonnets.

8 The Scouring-burn is a small stream running into a creek in the centre of Dundee and which may have formed the site of the first harbour of the town.

9 A property manager responsible for collecting rents.

11 Dignity

1 Confectionery—acid drops.

2 Raeberry Street is situated off Maryhill Road, Glasgow.

3 Trouser braces.

4 Like all the best stories this one is set in the country of the imagination—Auchentee has escaped the map-makers.

5 A street-gutter, or the drain and cover in such a gutter.

12 Universal Provider

1 This story first appeared in April 1912, just as the results of the 1911 Census would have been in the news.

2 Jimmy's customer need hardly have feared exposure in the "Northern Star", a paper circulating in Wick in the 1830's. A more probable source of home-town embarrassment would have been the Golspie-based "Northern Times".

3 One of the great issue in Scottish church history was the fight to abolish patronage (the presentation to a clerical vacancy by the Crown or a local landowner) and to ensure for the local congregation the right to choose their own minister.

4 The black preaching gown worn by ministers of the reformed churches.

5 One of the great Victorian hero-figures, Field Marshal Roberts (1832-1914) first came to prominence by winning the Victoria Cross during the Indian Mutiny. In 1880 he marched through Afghanistan

to relieve Kandahar. Later Roberts was Commander-in-Chief in India. During the 2nd Boer War "Our Bobs", as he was knicknamed, was sent out to South Africa to take command and relieved Kimberley and marched on Pretoria. Created Earl Roberts of Kandahar in 1901.

13 The Commercial Room

1 This Fifeshire inn is not to be confused with the Birrelton "Buck's Head".

2 A room in a hotel set aside for the use of commercial travellers.

3 Oddly enough all the Boots in hotels patronised by Jimmy Swan appear to have been called Willie. Perhaps the name went with the position.

4 Slimmer.

5 Lively, cheerful.

6 In a later story (No. 20 "Gent's Attire") we will learn the definition of a pound-a-day man. "... it was understood in the shop that up to a pound-a-day Mr Swan's bill for expenses passed the cashier unquestioned; that it was an historical right, like Magna Charta."

7 To broil on a griddle.

8 Finnan haddock; a cured haddock. The name is usually held to derive from the Kincardineshire village of Findon, some six miles south of Aberdeen. The *Concise Scots Dictionary* suggest that the alternative form "Findram Haddie" may arise from a confusion with the Morayshire village of Findhorn.

14 The Changed Man

1 A reference to fusel-oil, an undesirable by-product of spirit distillation.

2 A popular range of souvenir china—either plates or vases with a town's coat of arms or models of famous buildings; a particularly popular example of the latter being J. M. Barrie's house in Kirriemuir "A Window in Thrums".

3 Popularised after a newspaper cartoon in 1902 showed President Theodore "Teddy" Roosevelt with a bear cub.

4 William Thomson (1824-1907) was a Scottish physicist and mathematician who was professor at Glasgow University for over 50 years; advised on the laying of the first transatlantic telegraph cable, developed the Kelvin or absolute temperature scale and carried out a wide range of pioneering work in theoretical and applied physics, electricity and hydrodynamics. Created 1st Baron Kelvin in 1892.

5 Sadly, though unsurprisingly this distinguished ornament of the Heidelberg faculty and his novel theory seem both to be fictitious.

6 John Gough (1817-1886) was an English-born temperance reformer who, having emigrated to the United States at the age of 12 and succumbing to alcohol, later became one of the leading figures in the temperance movement in both the USA and Britain.

15 Vitalising the Gloomy Grants

1 "The store" was the usual popular term for a Co-operative society shop.

2 Captain Kettle was a Welsh sea-captain with a red beard and the hero

of a successful series of novels by C. J. Cutcliffe Hynd which appeared
between 1898 and 1932.
3 The Franco-Prussian War commenced in July 1870 and ended with
the fall of Paris in January 1871.
4 Song thrush (*Turdus ericetorum*)
5 In the metrical version in the Scottish Psalter this psalm opens:
    "The Lord's my light and saving health,
    who shall make me dismayed.
    My life's strength is the Lord of whom
    then shall I be afraid?"
The tune "Dunfermline" comes from the Scottish Psalter of 1615.

16 Blate Rachel
1 Shy, backward.
2 Having a squint (strabismus) in one eye.
3 Hydropathic establishments set up as spa hotels and specialising in the
treatment of minor, or perhaps imaginary disorders by one form or
another of water treatment—sea bathing, medicinal springs etc.
4 Literally someone who is deaf or hard of hearing, but used here in a
pejorative sense to indicate someone who is generally dull or backward.

17 Rachel Comes to Town
1 Small town in Kincardineshire, 18 miles east of Aberdeen.
2 Resort on the Cowal Peninsula on the Firth of Clyde.
3 A popular dance of the period.
4 Armpit.
5 A female nut. A nut or knut was a period term for a dandy.

18 A Poor Programme
1 The Territorial Force was created in 1908 as a citizen's army to
replace the earlier Volunteers. The Territorial Army, as it was later renamed, was designed as a home service force but could, and did
during the First World War, volunteer for foreign service.
2 Clara Butt (1873-1936) was an English contralto whose chief fame
was won on the concert platform rather than in opera; a specialisation
perhaps resulting from her statuesque build and height of 6'2".
Created Dame Commander of the Order of the British Empire in
1920.
3 Louisa Tetrazzini (1871-1940); Italian soprano. She made her
London debut as Violetta in Verdi's "La Traviata" in 1902.

19 Broderick's Shop
1 Neil Munro had a continuing interest in the ironmonger's trade. As a
young man coming to Glasgow to seek his fortune he started work in
an ironmongers' shop in the Trongate—an eastward extension of
Argyle Street. In one of his articles reprinted in *Brave Days* he wrote:
"My passion was, as it still remains, the windows of toolshops and
ironmongers, and MacHaffie and Colquhoun's, next door to "Pie
Smith's" at the corner of Maxwell Street, particularly intrigued me. It

proclaimed itself the oldest ironmongers's firm, wholesale and retail, in the city, and it looked it."

He later wrote of the closure of what seems to have been the same shop, though this time using the name Macaulay and Buchanan, and this piece is preserved in another posthumous collection of his journalism, *News from the North*.

2   "We came to "Glasgow of the Steeples" from the hills, expecting from generations of Gaelic tradition to find Argyle Street the most amazing thoroughfare in Scotland, and we were not disappointed." Neil Munro *Brave Days*.

3   An earthenware ball used in the childrens' game of marbles.

4   Stroll.

5   Climbing.

6   A reel. The *Concise Scots Dictionary* points out that this word specifically relates to the "Reel of Tulloch" being a corruption of the Gaelic for Tulloch—Thulachain.

20   Gent's Attire

1   A quotation from *Hamlet* Act 3 Sc.1 Ophelia says of the apparently deranged Hamlet:

> "O, what a noble mind is here o'erthrown!
> The courtier's, soldier's, scholar's, eye, tongue, sword;
> The expectancy and rose of the fair state,
> The glass of fashion and the mould of form
> The observ'd of all observers…"

2   The German armed forces had developed airships to a considerable extent between 1900 and the outbreak of the World War. They were named after Ferdinand, Count von Zeppelin, the German soldier who had pioneered their military use. This story was published in September 1915, some months after the first Zeppelin raid on Yarmouth.

3   The Prevention of Corruption Act (6 Edward VII Ch. 32) of 1906.

4   George Geddes II was employed by the Glasgow Humane Society as their officer between 1889 and 1932 and was responsible for many rescues from the River Clyde as well as the less rewarding task of recovering corpses from the river.

5   Fair play.

21   Keeping up with Cochrane

1   Sutherlandshire village strategically situated at the intersection of the main North/South and East/West routes through the County.

2   Jimmy is quoting from Burns's poem *To Dr Blacklock*

> "To make a happy fire-side clime to weans and wife
> That's the true pathos and sublime of human life."

3   Despite Jimmy's convincing tale Lairg was never more than a village, so never had a Town Council and could never have offered a civic career to Watty Cochrane.

4   Busy.

5   The finished edges of a piece of fabric.

6   Busied one's self.

22 The Hen Crusade
1 Wrung.
2 Amply proportioned.
3 Backslider, reprobate.
4 Bar from the Sacrament of Holy Communion.

23 Linoleum
1 See No. 6 for discussion of the location of Jimmy's Gower Street
   residence.
2 So select is Sibbald Terrace that it does not appear in the Glasgow
   street atlas.
3 The Fife town of Kirkcaldy was recognised as the centre of the
   linoleum industry. Its fame, and the characteristic smell of the process
   was celebrated in the poem "The Boy in the Train" by Munro's
   contemporary M. C. Smith, with its final two lines:
     "For I ken mysel' by the queer-like smell
     That the next stop's Kirkcaddy!"

24 The Grauvat King
1 Cravat, scarf or muffler.
2 To prepare a sheep's head for the popular Scottish delicacy of sheep's
   head broth.

25 Jimmy's Sins Find Him Out
1 A popular sporting paper published between 1888 and November
   1914.
2 Harold MacNeill of Queen's Park won ten international caps between
   1874 and 1881.
3 Queen's Park Football Club.
4 Jimmy McMenemy of Celtic and Patrick Thistle amassed a total of
   503 Scottish League appearances. He also represented Scotland 12
   times between 1905 and 1920.
5 This story was published on Monday, 6th April 1914, the International match against England at Hampden having been played on
   Saturday 4th. The 3-1 victory for Scotland doubtless pleased the
   majority of the 105,000 crowd.
6 Internationals were played at Hampden Park, situated in this South-
   side suburb.
7 Stonehaven, the county town of Kincardineshire, some 12 miles south
   of Aberdeen.

26 A Wave of Temperance
1 This war-time story, first published in May 1915, reflects something
   of the austerity and temperance movements which were encouraged as
   part of the war effort. King George V had announced in April 1915
   that the Royal Household would cease to drink beer, wine or spirits
   for the duration. Horatio Hubert Kitchener (1850-1916) 1st Earl
   Kitchener of Khartoum, had been Secretary of State for War from

August 1914.

2 Ginger biscuit (from Parliamentary cake).

27 Country Journeys

1 The Thermos flask, invented by Sir James Dewar, was patented in 1904, so would still be something of a novelty when this story appeared in January 1912.

2 A slogan used by the Caledonian Railway in their advertising at this time.

3 Harvest-home.

4 A once-popular children's magazine.

5 The first Monday of the New Year–a traditional time for the exchange of gifts.

6 A type of light chaise, but often used as a term of mockery for any old or rickety coach or carriage.

28 Raising the Wind

1 The Royal visit to Scotland in July 1914 was indeed an extensive one. King George V visited Edinburgh, Glasgow, Clydebank & Dumbarton, Coatbridge & Hamilton, Dundee & Perth, Dunblane & Stirling.

2 The patron saint of Glasgow, here used metonymically for the city itself.

3 Glasgow Central Railway Station, built for the Caledonian railway and opened in 1879, was, as Jimmy suggests, greatly extended between 1899 and 1906.

4 Booked.

5 Searches the pockets.

6 A jacket of a wool, or wool and cotton mix, with a shiny finish.

7 The *Daphne* steamer was launched on 3rd July 1883 from the Clydeside yard of Alexander Stephen & Sons. On entering the water she turned turtle and sank with the loss of 124 lives. The inherent instability of *Daphne's* design, combined with loose machinery and the rapid inflow of water through a boiler access hole in the main deck contributed to this disaster.

29 Roses, Roses All The Way

1 Not an iota.

2 A generalised term of disapprobation indicative of coarseness, rowdiness, etc. and frequently used of women; not necessarily with the sense of sexual looseness.

30 Citizen Soldier

1 This war-time story (first published in December 1914) sees Jimmy enlisted in the Citizen Training Force, formed in October to provide the First World War equivalent of the Home Guard. Two drill parades a week and battalion exercise every second Saturday gave basic training to men over the age for military service or otherwise disqualified.

2 Frames for the indoor drying of clothes.

3 A piece of grease or fat.

31 The Adventures of a Country Customer

1 This previously uncollected story first appeared in the Glasgow
   Evening News of 8th May 1911.
2 Glasgow had held major Exhibitions in Kelvingrove Park in 1888 and
   1901. The 1888 International Exhibition had as one of its aims the
   funding of a new Civic Art Gallery and Museum. The 1901 Glasgow
   International Exhibition was designed, in part to inaugurate this new
   civic treasure.
3 "The Groveries" was a popular, if unofficial, name for the Kelvingrove
   Exhibitions. However Munro was unimpressed with this term and
   wrote elsewhere "On Saturday, 10th November, 1888, 'The
   Groveries' — silly name for an International Exhibition — had
   closed..." *The Brave Days* p. 64
4 A Fairy Fountain, a large central water feature illuminated by coloured electric light, was a feature of both the 1888 and 1911 Exhibitions.
5 Sir Henry Wood (1869—1944) is of course otherwise best remembered as the originator of the Promenade Concerts.
6 A Manhattan Cocktail consists of bourbon or rye whiskey, vermouth
   & bitters.
7 One of a number of references to freemasonry in these stories.
8 The mile-long Mountain Scenic Ride was one of the most popular
   features of the Exhibition.
9 A seaside resort in Ayrshire much frequented by golfers and the
   location of a luxury hotel.
10 The 1911 Scottish Exhibition of National History, Art and Industry,
   raised £15,000 to endow a Chair of Scottish History at Glasgow
   University.

32 The Radiant James Swan

1 This previously uncollected story first appeared in the Glasgow
   Evening News on 21st July 1913.
2 "Consider the lilies of the field, how they grow; they toil not, neither
   do they spin: And yet I say unto you, That even Solomon in all his
   glory was not arrayed like one of these" Matthew Ch 6 vv 28—29.
3 See no. 16 "Blate Rachel' and no. 17 "Rachel Comes to Town" for
   the earlier adventures of Jimmy Swan and Rachel Thorpe.
4 Money scattered to the crowd at a wedding to ensure good fortune
   and prosperity for the newly married couple.
5 A reference to the rituals of freemasonry.
6 The Royal Arch is a higher order of freemasonry.
7 Right Worshipful Master, the chief officer of a masonic lodge.
8 Jimmy is referring to various Friendly Societies which were active in
   the period.
9 Marbles.

33 Jimmy Swan's German Spy

1 This previously uncollected story first appeared in the Glasgow
   Evening News on January 18th 1915.
2 As part of the security precautions during the First World War,

introduced under the Defence of the Realm Act, hoteliers had to register guests and notify new arrivals to the local police.

3 Strathbungo is a select residential district on the South Side of Glasgow.

4 Mr Fisher, as a young man of military age, would not wish to be seen engaging in a frivolous pursuit like golf, lest questions be raised about his failure to volunteer for service. Compulsory conscription was not introduced until January 1916.

34 Jimmy Swan in Warm Weather

1 This previously uncollected story first appeared in the Glasgow Evening News on 9th July 1923.

2 The attentive reader will have noted that Mr Swan's employers have undergone an unaccountable change of name in the eight years since the previous Jimmy Swan story appeared. In all the other stories the company's name was Campbell & Macdonald. Readers may choose to believe in either an internal power struggle within the firm and a consequent re-naming of the company or in a fit of forgetfulness on the part of Neil Munro.

3 At the time of first publication Scotland was enjoying a remarkable heatwave.

4 In January 1923 French and Belgian troops had occupied the Ruhr following the failure of the German government to pay reparations demanded under the Treaty of Versailles.

5 Plus fours, a type of baggy trouser favoured by golfers, became fashionable around 1920.

6 A joke, tale or anecdote. An all purpose word (often spelled "baur") more often associated with Jimmy Swan's sea-going contemporary Para Handy.

35 The Tall Hat

1 This previously uncollected story first appeared in the Glasgow Evening News on August 13th 1923

2 Tillietudlem (the Evening News spells it Tullietudlem) Castle features in Walter Scott's *Old Mortality* and is identified with Craignethan Castle in the parish of Lesmahagow, Lanarkshire.

3 A publication listing bankruptcy actions.

4 The Incorporation of Hammermen is one of the fourteen trade incorporations of Glasgow. Originally a craft guild, by the time of this story the member's proficiency in the manual skills of blacksmith and engineer had become somewhat attenuated.

5 St George's Tron Church in Buchanan Street. A conspicuous city centre landmark designed by William Stark and built in 1807-9.

6 Milngavie is a small town a few miles north west of Glasgow favoured by city businessmen as a residential area. It has never been noted as a centre of the avant-garde.

36 The Groveries in Retrospect

1 This previously uncollected story first appeared in the Glasgow Evening News on February 11th 1924.

2 Despite such views Glasgow had to wait until 1938 for its next
   Exhibition.
3 Kelvingrove, or West End Park, was the site of the 1888, 1901 & 1911
   Exhibitions.
4 Dining rooms decorated in clan tartans.
5 The 1888 Exhibition was opened by the Prince & Princess of Wales
   and visited by Queen Victoria in August.
6 The Russian section in the 1901 Exhibition was the largest of the
   foreign contributions.
7 Despite the strength of Jimmy's views the 1938 Exhibition was held at
   Bellahouston Park on the South-Side of Glasgow.
8 Captain Thomas Scott Baldwin, American balloonist, parachute
   jumper and pioneer aviator. Munro, as so often the case, made
   repeated use of his memories and experiences. His other account of
   Baldwin dropping in to Hamilton Park appears in *The Brave Days* and
   gives a flavour of the excitement of these days of pioneer aviators:
   "On September 25th a performance of his [Baldwin's] at Hamilton
   Park proved a serious rival to the fascinations of Kelvingrove. Special
   trains were run to Hamilton; the curious flocked from all parts of
   midland Scotland to see a man risk his life in a dive from a balloon at
   4000 feet.
   When I got to the race-course, myself, I found Baldwin in the centre of
   a vast concourse gathered about his balloon, already inflated. His wife,
   a fragile little woman, who was said to have made the parachute, was
   standing anxiously by while the husband finally scrutinised her handi-
   work. He crawled out of sight inside the parachute to make certain that
   the rain which had fallen in the morning had not handicapped its
   chance of opening out in the air when the crucial moment came.
   Fifteen minutes later, a tinselled circus acrobat, he was swinging from a
   trapeze below the balloon and waving flags. We took his word for it,
   later, that he reached an altitude of 4000 feet before he dived with the
   parachute strapped to him. It opened after a vertiginous second or two
   and soon he was on terra firma with Mrs Baldwin kissing him. The
   balloon, ripped open by a cord control at the moment of the dive, sailed
   into a neighbouring parish. We didn't go to look for it. We had got the
   worth of our money in the gasp of apprehension before the umbrella
   opened out."
9 "The River", an aquatic panorama, invented by Captain Paul Boyton,
   and premiered in New York, was presented in Berkeley Street,
   Charing Cross. The Mitchell Library, the city's major reference
   library, was built between 1906 and 1911.
10 A popular song by the Neapolitan composer Luigi Denza (1846-1922).
11 Herr Wilhelm Morgan's Blue Hungarian Band was a leading continental ensemble and regular visitors to Glasgow exhibitions. They
   were the subject of a well-known painting by the Glasgow artist Sir
   John Lavery.
12 A recreation of Scottish urban vernacular architecture.
13 A feature of the 1911 exhibition was a reconstruction of a Highland
   village or clachan with Highlanders practising various crafts and
   domestic activities, singing in Gaelic and wearing the national dress.

37 Selling Shoes

1   This previously uncollected story first appeared in the Glasgow
    Evening News on January 4th 1926.
2   Now more commonly known as X-Rays. Named after their discoverer,
    Wilhelm Konrad von Rontgen (1845-1923), the Nobel prize-winning
    German physicist.
3   The location of the University of Glasgow.
4   Daniel Macaulay Stevenson (1851-1944) was a Glasgow merchant
    and philanthropist who was a major benefactor of Glasgow University,
    endowing the Chairs of Italian and Spanish among many other
    benefactions. He was given an Honorary Doctorate of Law by the
    University in 1934. He was Lord Provost of Glasgow from 1911-1914
    having served on the City Council since 1892.
5   Cobbler or bootmaker. Also often used in the form "snob".
6   A rosin-treated thread used in bootmaking.

Also available from

BIRLINN

PARA HANDY

Collected stories from *The Vital Spark*,
In Highland Harbours with Para Handy &
Hurricane Jack of the Vital Spark

Neil Munro

Introduced by *Brian Osborne* and *Ronald Armstrong*

This, first ever complete Para Handy, contains all the stories
from Neil Munro's previous collections, plus fifteen entirely
new stories, discovered this year. The new stories show Munro
writing at the height of his powers about Para Handy and the
Great War, Para Handy and the Naval Review of 1912, and
Para Handy and the introduction of radio in Scotland.

Brian Osborne and Ronnie Armstrong provide a full
introduction and notes to each of the stories, rendering this the
definitive 'Para Handy'.

ISBN 1 874744 02 5

WILLIAM McGONAGALL

Collected Poems

'The most startling incident in my life was the time I discovered myself to be a poet, which was in the year 1877'

Since then thousands of people the world over have enjoyed the verse of Scotland's alternative national poet - William McGonagall. This omnibus edition brings together in one volume the three famous collections *Poetic Gems*, *More Poetic Gems* and *Last Poetic Gems* and includes all the valuable autobiographical material which appeared in the original volumes. It includes all his most famous work 'The Tay Bridge Disaster', 'The Death of Lord and Lady Dalhousie', and many more.

ISBN 1 874744 01 7

TALES FROM BARRA

The Coddy

'At any rate nothing can rob Barra of its beauty or of the
memory of its splendid tradition of folk song and story; and
many of us have to thank the Coddy for an introduction to all
these. We may therefore wish that his memory be long
preserved.'   JOHN LORNE CAMPBELL

One of the inspirations for *Whisky Galore*, one of the great
story tellers and characters of the Western Isles, the tales and
stories of John MacPherson of Barra the Coddy - were an
instant success on their first publication, and have been in
constant demand ever since. For any student of folklore, for
anyone interested in the tales, traditions and history of the west,
or for anyone who simply likes a good tale well told, the
Coddy is essential reading.

The book is introduced by Compton Mackenzie
and John Lorne Campbell.

ISBN 1 874744 03 3